TALES OF THE OUTLAW MAGES SET 2

DREAMER & PERSUADER

AMY CAMPBELL

Cover design by Amy Campbell

Edited by Vicky Brewster

Map by Amy Campbell, designed in Wonderdraft

Pegasus chapter heading art © Depositphotos.com.

ISBN-13:978-1-957816-04-3, 978-1-957816-03-6 (EBOOK)

First edition: January 2024

10 9 8 7 6 5 4 3 2 1

www.amycampbell.info

v120823

DREAMER

TALES OF THE OUTLAW MAGES BOOK
THREE

Author's Note

As in reality, sometimes our beloved characters encounter circumstances that cause deep emotional wounds. I don't want any of my readers to have adverse reactions to these scenes, so please be aware that *Dreamer* includes animal injury, blood, death, drinking, forced captivity, guns, kidnapping, murder, PTSD, violence, and weapons.

Pronunciation Guide

Argor – ARR-gor
Blaise – BLAY-z
Canen – KAY-nun
Chupacabra – CHOO-puh-cah-bruh
Desina – Dess-EE-nuh
Effigest – Eff-IH-jest
Emmaline – Em-uh-LINE
Emrys – Em-RISS
Faedra – FAY-druh
Faedran – FAY-drun
Ganland – Gan-LUND
Garus – Gair-USS
Geasa – GESH-uh
Hospitalier — Hoss-pih-tal-yer
Iphyria — Ih-feer-EE-uh
Itude – Ih-TOOD
Izhadell – Iz-UH-dell
Knossan – NOSS-uhn
Knossas – NOSS-us

Kur Agur – Kur Ah-GRR
Leonora – LEE-oh-nor-uh
Leorus — LEE-oh-russ
Lucienne – Loo-SEE-ann
Marian – Mayr-EE-uhn
Marta – Mahr-tuh
Mella – Mell-UH
Mellan – Mell-UHN
Nadine – Nay-DEEN
Nera – NEER-uh
Nexarae – Nex-UH-ray
Oberidon – Oh-BEAR-uh-don (alternate: Oby – Oh-BEE)
Oscen – Oss-KIN
Petria – Pet-RIA
Phinora – Fin-OR-uh
Ravance – Ruh-VAN-s
Ravanchen – Ruh-VAN-chen
Reuben – Roo-ben
Seledora – Sel-uh-DOR-uh
Seward – SOO-urd
Tabris – Tab-RISS
Tabrisian – Tab-REE-shen
Theilia – Thee-LEE-uh
Theilian – Thee-LEE-uhn
Theurgist – THEE-ur-jest
Zepheus – Zeff-EE-us

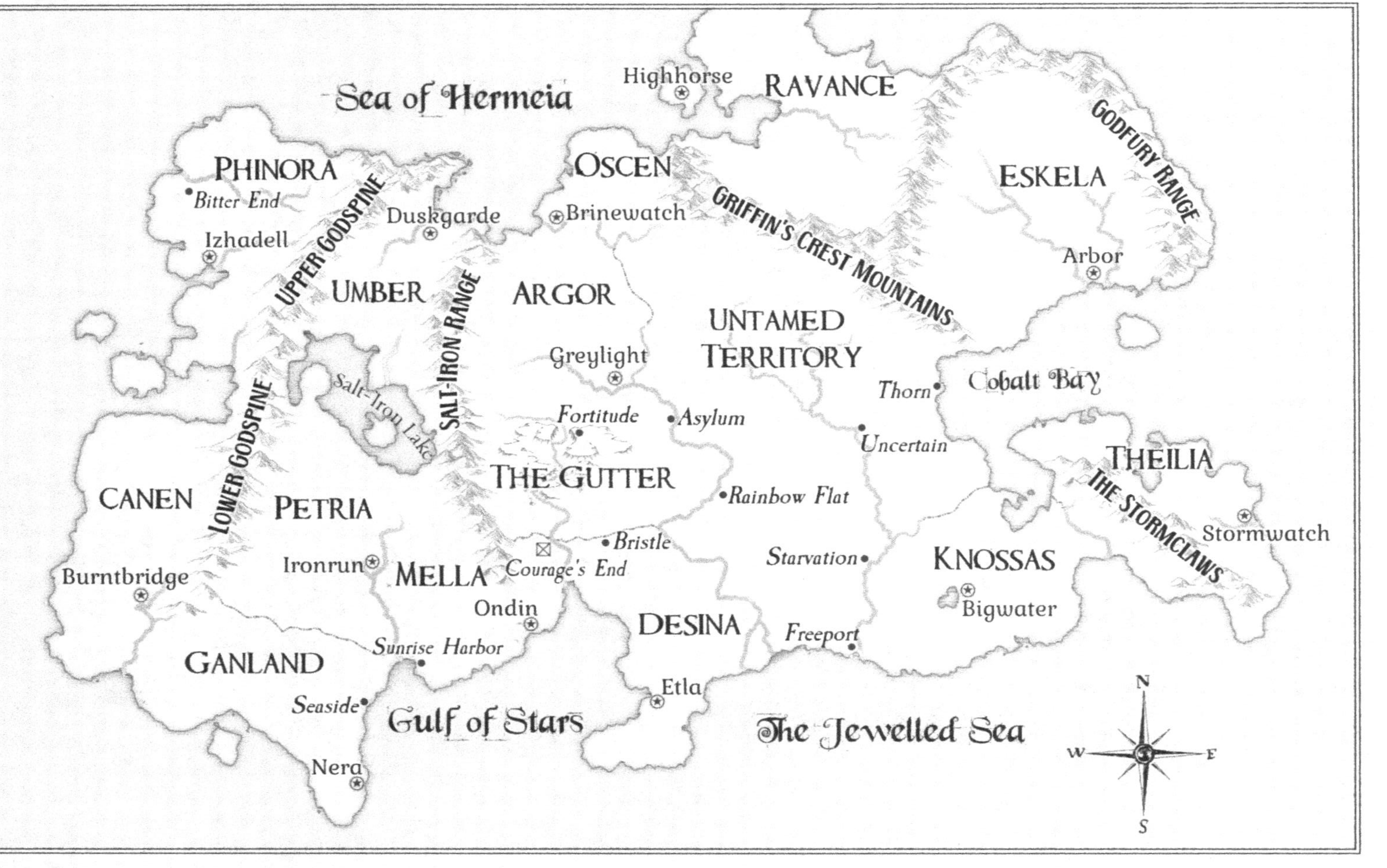

Sea of Hermeia
Highhorse
RAVANCE
GODFURY RANGE
PHINORA
Bitter End
Izhadell
UPPER GODSPINE
Duskgarde
OSCEN
Brinewatch
GRIFFIN'S CREST MOUNTAINS
ESKELA
Arbor
UMBER
SALT-IRON RANGE
ARGOR
UNTAMED TERRITORY
Greylight
Thorn
Cobalt Bay
Salt-Iron Lake
Fortitude
Asylum
Uncertain
THEILIA
LOWER GODSPINE
THE GUTTER
Rainbow Flat
THE STORMCLAWS
Stormwatch
CANEN
PETRIA
Bristle
Starvation
KNOSSAS
Burntbridge
Ironrun
MELLA
Courage's End
Bigwater
Ondin
DESINA
Freeport
GANLAND
Sunrise Harbor
Etla
Seaside
Gulf of Stars
The Jewelled Sea
Nera
N
W
E
S

CHAPTER ONE

The Herald

Gregor

Gregor had known they would come for him. It was only a matter of *when*. Trapped in an unceasing web of nightmares, he often lost track of time—a circumstance that had never happened to him before. He didn't know if it had been days, weeks, or months since Jefferson Cole had cursed him to this horrifying existence. But he knew, even in the depths of despair, that the Quiet Ones would come for him.

The mage they sent was as thin as a rail, with spidery limbs and a severe face. She said nothing as she entered his study, flowing into it through the floral wallpaper like an alligator breaking the surface of a bayou. Gregor had encountered the Herald before, and while her entrance was disconcerting, at least it wasn't as terrifying as it had been the first time he'd witnessed her foul magic.

"You are summoned," the Herald said, void of inflection. Her voice was always monotone, as if any joy she held in life had long since bled away. Idly, Gregor wondered if she'd ever had a day of free will. From what he understood, the geasa did not bind her as a true theurgist. But he knew well that control over a person could be attained in other ways.

"I don't wish to go. I'm still healing." Gregor crossed his arms as he spoke. That had been his reasoning the first time a summons had gone out for him, and it had been accurate enough. He was better now, but still not himself—no, far from it. It was difficult to concentrate on anything. Impossible to keep the terrors that were waiting behind his closed eyelids at bay.

"That was your excuse two months ago. It no longer suffices."

Two months? Had it truly been that long? Gregor sighed, shakily rising from his favorite chair. To delay the inevitable would only risk further angering the Quiet Ones, and their favor was tenuous at best.

The Herald extended her hand, as pale as a fish's belly. Gregor reached out to take it and discovered it was just as cold and clammy. He grimaced as she tightened her fingers around his hand, her nails digging crescents into his skin, and led him to the wall.

He hated this, hated this blasted Walker and her freakish ability to spirit herself from one wall to another, from building to building like a specter. She tugged him *through* the wall, and for far too long, he existed in a yawning emptiness that was a nightmare all its own. Though now, after *living* in nightmares, he knew the difference. This would end. The others might not.

There was a sensation like the shattering of ice, and then they were in an ornate room far from Gregor's plantation home. Mage-lights flanked the walls, bathing the room in their brilliance. Well-dressed men and women sat at an oval table, the cherry wood agleam with a freshly polished shine. Behind each of the seated Quiet Ones, a mage stood vigil, so still they reminded Gregor of human statuary.

So unjust. Gregor should have been seated there with a Breaker at his back. Or, barring that, that blasted Effigest outlaw. Having the Scourge of the Untamed Territory at his beck and call would have been a coup. But no, they had denied him. Everything had gone wrong, and now he was being called on it.

"Doyen Gaitwood, how kind of you to *finally* join us," a voice rang out with false cheer. The speaker sat at the far side of the room, elbows on the table with fingers steepled in front of him. The Herald parted ways with Gregor, slipping behind the man who had spoken as if she were his shadow.

Gregor did his best to compose himself, crossing the short distance to claim a seat at the table. "With all due respect, Phillip, you *are* aware I nearly lost my life in the fire that claimed Stafford Wells." He hadn't spoken to anyone about the nightmares, not yet. Part of Gregor wasn't certain that Jefferson Cole had been the one to imprison him in a never-ending world of terror. How could it even be possible? But then again, Jefferson Cole had *also* been Malcolm Wells.

A tepid smile slid onto Phillip Dillon's face. He was a classically hand-some man, though his once dark hair was more salt than pepper. His sharp eyes shifted to the only other empty chair at the table—the seat that belonged to the late Stafford Wells. The seat that Gregor desperately wanted; if only he could show them he was worthy. "You seem to be faring well enough now. And we need answers." He leaned forward, and the lithe woman at his back mimicked him, lending the movement a predatory air. "You had the Breaker in hand."

"He couldn't be bound," Gregor started, then realized that was untrue and wouldn't stand up to scrutiny. Not with all the Quiet Ones, who knew better, staring at him. Anyone with any connections had heard the tale of his failure with the Breaker. "He couldn't be bound to *me*. Doyen Wells snagged him first."

"We heard of this." A raven-haired woman, who appeared bored by the entire affair, reclined in her chair. She wore trousers like a man, which suited her. She casually slung one leg over the arm of her chair. Tara was one of the more *unusual* Quiet Ones, from what Gregor had seen. "And my darling *pet* even gave you the means to fulfill your end of our dealings." She jerked a meaningful thumb toward the man at her shoulder. Tara was the only Quiet One who hadn't laid claim to a mage. But she had nabbed something almost as good. She had seduced and married a talented alchemist, one of the best. Her handsome alchemist had the gall to flash a brilliant smile at Gregor, a taunt.

Gregor's jaw clenched, and he felt a headache swarm in the base of his skull. Headaches plagued him often. Lack of sleep, according to his physician. "We nearly got the Breaker to the council chambers, as you asked me to do. But his allies thwarted me."

"*Nearly* isn't good enough." Tara cocked her head, winking at him. "And besides, you act as if *we* were too stupid to figure out your play after it all went wrong."

Gregor went still. It should have been impossible for them to—wait. He scanned the others at the table, eyes roving over the array of mages. Not all of the magic types present were known to him. He knew of Dillon's Herald and her Wall Walking magic, of course. And Tara's alchemist, who wasn't a mage at all. But he didn't know the others. Such information was on a need-to-know basis, and he hadn't needed to know. Did they have a Scryer? Or had Stafford Wells simply sold him out, hoping to benefit from both sides of the deal?

Phillip Dillon chuckled. "You thought we wouldn't figure it out." Around the table, no one else joined in the laughter. Their gazes fell on him like hunting wolves, assessing him for weakness. "Tell us why we should not only let you walk out of here alive, Gregor, but remain a Doyen."

He swallowed, blinking. In the split second of darkness, another nightmare found him. His lips curled in momentary horror at the sensation of phantom blood running down his arm, and he panted for breath. Gregor hated this. It made him look weak and vulnerable, all because of—

wait. He might have currency for them after all. True, his gambit may lose him any chance for a seat, but he was a patient man.

"You still want the Breaker, correct? And…" His gaze skated to the empty seat. "You need a successor for Stafford Wells."

Dillon narrowed his eyes. "I hope you're not suggesting the position for yourself."

Gregor waved a hand, dismissing the notion. No, he knew that the Quiet One positions were usually hereditary. When there were no available heirs, the Quiet Ones selected someone new. Gregor knew at the moment he was a longshot until he made amends. So, why not offer them someone else?

"No. I'm suggesting Malcolm Wells."

Around the table, the Quiet Ones scoffed at his audacious words. Tara lazily slouched forward. "You know he's *dead*, right?"

"I know he's *not*. He just wants everyone to believe that."

They stared at him, silence reigning for a dozen heartbeats before Phillip dared to speak. "And how did he manage *that* little trick?"

"Magic of some sort, I assume," Gregor said with a shrug. He wondered if he should offer information about the man's magic—but no, he needed to keep some of his cards to himself. "He masquerades as Jefferson Cole."

Recognition lit the eyes of the Quiet Ones. Cole was a known commodity, and the allegation startled them. "How…?" Everett Duncan, a magnate from Phinora, shook his head like a wet dog. "Impossible. I saw them both attend the Ganland Derby ball two years ago!"

Gregor crossed his arms. "I don't know how he does it. I only know that he does. He's maintained this charade for Garus knows how many years."

Phillip frowned. "And you suggest we bring him in for his father's seat? This sounds like a foolish endeavor on our part. He made it quite clear that he doesn't condone the shadow work we do."

Gregor shook his head. "You're not looking far enough. Malcolm Wells can give you access to the Breaker. And he'll play right into your hands if you let him know you're aware of his little secret."

Tara gave him a dubious look. "Why are you interested in Malcolm Wells becoming a Quiet One? We're not stupid, no matter what you may think. We know you weren't on the best terms."

Gregor held up his hands, placating. "I'm not firing a cannonball in your plans. Quite the opposite. Malcolm wants to hide from his birthright —from the power he was born into." Gregor smiled. "He needs to own it. And you have the leverage to make it happen now."

Dillon steepled his fingers. "You believe it will be enough to make him comply?"

Gregor smiled. "Any man desperate enough to hide the truth about himself will go to great lengths to make sure it doesn't come out."

"And what do you get out of it?" Tara asked.

When Gregor blinked, renewed nightmares danced across the canvas of his mind. He shuddered, banishing them and regaining his composure. "Revenge."

CHAPTER TWO
The Thing About Salt-Iron

Blaise

Blaise licked his dry lips, staring at the tiny chunk of salt-iron resting on the silver tray before him. Nadine, the town Healer, stood across the clinic from where Blaise sat on a cot, eyeing the nefarious metal. She didn't desire to be anywhere near the salt-iron, reluctant to let it drain her magic. The only reason she allowed it in her presence was because of Blaise.

"Well?" Nadine asked, scrutinizing him. "Do you feel it leeching your magic?"

Frowning thoughtfully, Blaise gave a small nod. "A little. Not enough to be a concern, though." It was true. There was the sluggish drip of his magic wisping to the chunk, but as quickly as it ebbed away, his internal well of power refilled like a lake fed by a rain-swollen river. It was different from what he'd felt with salt-iron in the past. Like the time he had been on the deck of the salt-iron-reinforced airship, in the struggle of his life as he pitted magic against the metal. His exertion and the inexorable pull of the salt-iron had emptied him completely.

"Hmm." Nadine tapped a pen against the notebook she held, jotting down a note. "What happens if you pick it up?"

Blaise cocked his head, considering. He usually handled the chunk while wearing a pair of sturdy leather gloves. Really, they weren't supposed to even have the piece of salt-iron, but after Jefferson's loyal half-knocker confidant Flora had admitted she was attuned to the foul metal, Jefferson had made it a point to squirrel away the nub in the bakery's loft. Under normal circumstances, they kept it swaddled in a layer of cotton, locked inside a small wooden chest. Anything less, and Jefferson, the newest—and most secretive—mage in town, was prone to headaches as it leeched his magic.

"Guess we'll find out," Blaise said with a shrug. It wouldn't be the first time he'd touched salt-iron with his bare skin on purpose.

Blaise reached out and gingerly picked up the glob. Just because he *could*, didn't mean he wanted to do it. He winced, expecting the sharp bite of it lacing through his skin. The sensation differed from before—in the past, it had been like touching a hot stove. A flash fire of pain. This was… tolerable? Maybe that wasn't exactly right, but he could grasp it with only mild discomfort. More like carefully holding jagged shards of glass than anything else.

Nadine stared at him. "How does it feel?"

"Um." Blaise had never been eloquent. "It hurts, but not that bad, I guess?"

"Is it leeching your power more than before or the same?"

Blaise took a moment to consider the question. "The same." He knew it should have been worse with direct contact. Blaise set the block back down on the tray, wiggling his fingers. His skin had reddened but hadn't developed the characteristic welts associated with touching salt-iron. On the one hand, that was a relief because the welts *hurt*. Tiny scars dimpled the undersides of his wrists, courtesy of the salt-iron shackles used on him in the Golden Citadel. But this new resistance to salt-iron? It made him different from other mages—and Blaise didn't like being different. Maybe he should have been used to it by now, but it was something that would always bother him.

Nadine's eyebrows lifted high, furrowing the pocked skin on her forehead. Even with all her power, she'd never fully recovered from the assault on Itude. "When did this start?"

Blaise edged away from the salt-iron. "It bothered me less after…" He faltered, heart racing as phantom memories reared up. The sickening sensation of a wooden deck plunging beneath his feet. The helpless feeling of *falling, falling, falling* and then hitting Lamar Gaitwood's magical trap. *Darkness.*

"You're not there. Think of something happy. Go there instead." Nadine's voice was soft but insistent.

He swallowed, summoning up his happy place in his mind's eye. *My bakery, golden in the early morning sunrise. Jefferson drowsily climbing down from the loft, hair tousled. Scents of yeast and sugar riding the air currents, drawing Emrys to the open window.* Blaise nodded, opening eyes he hadn't realized he'd closed.

"Thanks." He rubbed the ridge of his jaw, scuffing his beard. He had appointments with Nadine weekly for this very reason. Physically, he had recovered. But memories of the things he had endured plagued him, giving him nightmares. Jefferson used his magic to hold them off at night, but when Blaise was awake, the Dreamer was helpless against the bouts of panic that came and went. Out of desperation, he had sought the Healer, who had known of his oldest emotional wounds but never forced him to speak about them unless he wanted to.

"Blaise?" Nadine prompted, a reminder that she still expected an answer.

Right. Blaise could do this. It was only three words. He swallowed. "After the airship."

Nadine nodded in understanding, waiting for him to expand on the topic. That hadn't been the only time, though. Salt-iron had still affected him after that. *Until...* He swallowed, concentrating on the feel of dough in his hands, companionable conversation with Emmaline and Reuben. "And after they dosed me with the potion."

Nadine didn't know the specifics of this potion. He had mentioned it in passing during a previous session while explaining the circumstances of his rescue. Blaise had left it at that since discussion of the potion could lead down a dangerous path, one littered with painful memories of betrayal, of a life that he had thought was his.

The Healer studied him with her cool eyes, unflinching as she waited to see if he would continue. Blaise shivered. He didn't want to speak more on the topic, too afraid he would stumble onward and reveal the awful secret. The information that was far more problematic than the fact that he was a Breaker. How could he tell her that alchemy had *transmuted* him into a mage? That he had been born normal? That was dangerous information, and the less people who knew, the better.

When it became clear Blaise wouldn't speak further, Nadine tapped the point of her pen against her notebook. "And you think the potion that nearly killed you had something to do with this?"

He nodded. "It's hard to explain." Blaise swallowed, aware of her keen interest once again. His resistance to salt-iron intrigued Nadine. "You ever seen a pond get dredged?"

Nadine raised her brows at the analogy. "I have."

"It's like that." Blaise looked down at the floor, wondering if he should even say that much. But it wasn't as if anyone here had easy access to such a potion. "The potion...I think it did something like that to me. It dug so deep into me. Almost hollowed me out." He shivered at the memory, taking a gasping breath as he summoned up a happy thought to chase it away. *Emrys shoving his head against Blaise, nearly knocking him over as he laughed at the stallion's exuberance.* "And I just keep filling up, almost as fast as it's drained. It doesn't matter."

The Healer watched him, lips pursed as she weighed his words. "There're a lot of mages who'd be very interested in that."

Blaise nodded, shoulders hunching. "It's *alchemy*."

"There is that," Nadine agreed. Mages had a troublesome relationship with alchemy. The Salt-Iron Confederation employed it as a tool to control the mages in their domain. She massaged her forehead. "Doesn't matter, though. I'm not telling another soul of this. Healer-patient confidentiality, as always."

He relaxed at her words. She had mentioned it before, but Blaise couldn't help but wonder what might be the tipping point. What would be the piece of information that might be too tempting to share? He rubbed his hands together, staring down at them.

"Put it away," Nadine said, jerking her chin toward the salt-iron. As Blaise pulled out his gloves, she added, "And how are you handling Jefferson's upcoming departure?"

I should have known she would ask. He tugged at the leather gloves, focusing on the task as he spoke. "I'm thinking of taking a trip of my own." She raised a single silver brow, inquisitive. "Not to Ganland, if that's what you're wondering." *Not with Jefferson.* It was ridiculous, the very thought that he didn't *want* to be apart from Jefferson. But there it was.

"Oh?" Nadine prodded as Blaise picked up the salt-iron lump and wrapped it in a layer of cotton before slipping it into a carry sack. "Where are you going?"

He tightened the drawstrings on the sack and placed it on a nearby cot. "I said I was *thinking* of taking a trip. I'm not sure where yet." That part was a lie, and he suspected she knew. But there were some things he didn't want to talk about.

Her light grey eyes narrowed. "A change of scenery might be what you need."

He wrinkled his nose. "Nadine, I know you mean well, but I've had enough changes of scenery to last me a lifetime."

The Healer scowled. "There's a difference between *that* and traveling because you can. Because you *want* to."

But I don't know if I want to. Blaise rubbed his forehead, well aware that when Nadine had an idea in her head, she would keep at it. She was a lot like Jack in that way, though both the outlaws would be mightily offended if he told them as much. He frowned, deciding in this case, he might do better to throw her a bone. "The truth is, I'm thinking of going to Rainbow Flat to see my family."

Nadine nodded at his words. Blaise hadn't told her everything, but the Healer wasn't stupid. She knew his mother was an alchemist and that something had happened in relation to her. Something that had hurt him on a deep, emotional level.

"That I can understand." She stepped closer and laid a hand on his shoulder, meeting his eyes. "I've had bad blood with my family. Sometimes it can't be helped. But if there's a chance whatever's happened can be fixed, you should try." Nadine squeezed his shoulder for a second before releasing it. "But that's up to you. Only you know how to cure what ails you in that regard."

Blaise reached up to touch his shoulder in the spot she'd gripped. It tingled for a heartbeat, as if she'd left a trace of her magic behind. "I'll think about it."

"You do that," Nadine said, stepping over to her desk to check the time as they heard the approach of hooves. "We're at the end of our session. Come see me again if you need."

"Thanks," Blaise told her, picking up the salt-iron parcel and heading for the door. When he stepped out into the late afternoon sunshine, Emrys trotted up to greet him.

The pegasus nearly knocked him over as he rammed his head into Blaise's chest, blowing out a snotty breath. <Took you long enough.>

"This shirt *was* clean," Blaise grumbled, tottering beneath the enthusiastic greeting. He braced a hand against Emrys's neck to steady himself, pulling back enough to give his shirt a critical look. Equine hair clung to the fabric, and a streak of glinting mucus shone in the sunlight. "You know Jefferson's going to make me change, right?"

<Oh no, how terrible.> Emrys didn't sound in the least contrite. In fact, his dark eyes danced with amusement.

"Did he put you up to this?" That would have been a very Jefferson thing to do. Jefferson had *opinions* about Blaise's selection of clothing. Sometimes Blaise had taken to dressing in his most mismatched or threadbare garments just to see how Jefferson would react. It had almost become a strange game between the pair.

<I imagine he does like you with your shirt off,> Emrys said.

"Now I *really* think he put you up to this. Did he offer you a slice of apple pie? Whatever he's offered, I'll double it," Blaise said as he dug into a pocket for a handkerchief. He mopped up the trail of pegasus snot.

<He didn't, but now I wish he had,> Emrys admitted, his mental tone wistful.

"I saved some for you anyway," Blaise told the stallion, tucking the handkerchief away and rubbing Emrys's broad forehead. "Let's go get you a treat."

<Those are my favorite words.> Emrys fell into step beside him as they strode up the dusty street the short distance to the bakery.

The building was dark as Blaise entered. He tapped a mage-light on, then moved to open the window at the back so Emrys could thrust his head inside. "I suppose Jefferson is still meeting with the Ringleaders and the representatives from Asylum and Rainbow Flat?"

Emrys bobbed his head with enthusiasm, nostrils distended, as Blaise uncovered a tin with the leftover remnants of the promised pie. <Yes. Seledora was still outside HQ when I went to the clinic to wait for you.>

"Gotcha." Blaise slid the pie onto the counter, though he held the tin in place so it wouldn't slide around as the pegasus dug in. In the past, Nadine would have attended the meeting, too. But as the population of Fortitude expanded with more mages and their families seeking a home out of the Confederation's clutches, she had resigned as a Ringleader to see to the demands of her profession. Mindy, the Hospitalier mage who co-owned the Jitterbug, had stepped up for the position and been voted in. Their meeting couldn't run much later, though, or it would affect the Jitterbug's dinner service. "I imagine they'll finish soon."

Emrys's velvety lips and pink tongue quested after the last dregs of sweetness in the tin. <You're stuck with me in the meantime.>

Blaise couldn't help but smile. "I'm glad to be stuck with you."

CHAPTER THREE

Impostor Syndrome

Kittie

*K*ittie felt like an impostor. There was no other way around it. Everyone else gathered in the meeting room at Ringleader HQ knew what they were about, and they seemed secure in who they were and what they were doing. Kittie was a pretender, struggling to be something she had once been, but didn't feel like she was any longer.

She hadn't realized how hard this would be, and a part of her wondered how long it would take for Jack to figure out that she wasn't the same woman he'd married so many years ago. Most days, Kittie didn't feel like the Firebrand, the notorious young woman who had once sought to rally the mages of the Confederation. She was trying to find that part of her again, those embers buried deep down, but Kittie feared it was forever doused.

Kittie blinked when Jack nudged her with his elbow. She winced, realizing he'd noticed she was busy wool-gathering and not focusing on the logistics of their delegation. They were planning to travel to Ganland to gain support to recognize the Gutter as its own country.

"—still plan to leave later this week?" The question was posed by Eileen Harker, the mayor of Asylum. Eileen was dubious about their gambit to make a nation of outlaws. She crossed her arms, the corners of her lips down-turned.

"Yes, we do," Jefferson replied. The well-dressed would-be ambassador sat beside Ringleader Vixen Valerie, which placed him across from Kittie. Jack always grumbled that Jefferson was a dandy or a peacock, but Kittie wondered if the younger man intimidated her husband. Jefferson was handsome and knew it. He wore the finest clothes and was clean-shaven, with golden-brown hair sculpted to rakish perfection. He wasn't overly large or muscular, but the power that came with self-assurance and wealth cloaked him. "And both Asylum and Rainbow Flat are welcome to send along anyone you'd like to join our delegation."

Wesley Slen, the mayor of Rainbow Flat, shook his head. "You know I'm not willing to risk my people with that, Jefferson. Nations are born from battle and blood, not diplomacy and words."

Beside Kittie, Jack made a soft grunt of agreement. Her husband had similar concerns, though, in a surprising turn, he actually thought their diplomatic mission stood a chance.

Jefferson's eyes glittered at the challenge presented by Slen. "You're welcome to your opinion. But this wouldn't be the first time I've been a player in a radical shift."

"We're seeing this through regardless," Kittie finally said, drawing the attention of the others in the room. Of the mages in attendance, she knew she was one of the most powerful as a Pyromancer. Fortitude boasted three other Pyromancers, but their magics were mere sparks compared to the inferno she could command. Her words had weight simply because of who and what she was.

"We would look better with at least one more outlaw along." This from Ringleader Raven Dawson, who leaned back in his seat, the skin around his dark eyes crinkling with concern. "I could—"

"*No.*" Vixen's voice was sharp as she scowled at her beau through the smoky lenses of her glasses. "We only..." The redhead trailed off, shaking her head. She was reluctant to finish her sentence, but Kittie knew where she was going. The Confederation had stripped Vixen and Raven's magic, and only recently had the Breaker restored it. Kittie didn't know the details beyond the fact that he'd done the same for Jack.

"I can join the delegation, if you'll have me." The assertion pulled everyone's attention away from Kittie, which was welcome. Kittie raised her brows at the newest member of the Fortitude Ringleaders, the Hospitalier Mindy Carman. The young woman didn't wilt beneath their gazes, instead straightening her spine. "You'll need more than just the pair of you."

"And Flora," Jefferson reminded them gently. Kittie noted the pucker in his brow, a sign that it bothered him when the half-knocker wasn't in attendance. "If she's back in time, anyway." He cleared his throat, smiling at Mindy. "You're welcome, of course, if you like."

"I think I'm *needed*," Mindy clarified. "I'm invested in Fortitude—in the

Gutter. I want us to succeed, and if that means I need to tag along, then so be it." Her gaze slid over to Kittie.

"Didn't know Hospitaliers were also Seers," Jack murmured so softly only Kittie could hear. But he didn't seem opposed to the idea—Kittie knew he would have objected aloud if he had strong feelings. Which meant her husband thought Mindy had value in coming along, too. *Interesting.*

They hashed out further details for their delegation's departure before adjourning for the day. Jefferson slipped over to Mindy, stepping aside with her to discuss something out of earshot. Kittie headed to the door with Jack, though Vixen ghosted over to them as soon as they made it outside.

"Mindy's a solid addition," Vixen told them, keeping her voice low. Jack cocked his head but didn't ask for specifics. "Just trust her, okay?" She lifted a finger to reposition her glasses on her nose.

Jack tensed when Vixen touched her glasses, then settled. "You know more about her than I do, Vix?"

The Persuader shrugged with one shoulder. "I know some stuff she's had to keep quiet, is all." Then she poked an index finger into Jack's chest. "And I didn't want you scaring her off by huffing and puffing that she shouldn't go."

"I wouldn't do that," Jack grumbled. Vixen and Kittie both scoffed. The Effigest grunted. "Maybe I would. But I didn't object in there. I was *reasonable.* Kept my trap shut."

"A surprise to everyone," Vixen said with a grin before sobering. "Yeah, you behaved in there. But I know how you can be, going behind someone to intimidate them." To his credit, Jack didn't deny it. Vixen nodded to Kittie. "Just wanted you to know. We're counting on this."

"Everyone is," Kittie agreed, watching as Vixen strode off. When she was gone, Kittie rubbed her forehead. Jack stepped closer, snugging an arm around her. "Can we go to the Broken Horn?"

He glanced at her, lips pursed. "You want a drink for nerves or because you can't do without?"

Both. Can't it be both? Kittie gritted her teeth. "I'm worried about this mission, is all. One little drink. Then I can stop."

"We both know that's a lie." His voice was whisper-soft, full of disapproval. And that was unfair, since Jack enjoyed a good whiskey as much as the next outlaw. But the difference was he didn't *need* it the way she did. "I thought you were going dry."

"Dry brush burns so easily," Kittie muttered. That was how she felt about all this, at any rate. She was trying to lose her dependency on alcohol—and failing miserably. Like she was burning up from the inside with all of her inadequacies and the shadow of what she had been before.

"If you won't do it for me, then at *least* do it for our daughter."

Oh, that hurt. Kittie's hackles raised as she jerked out from under his arm. "You think it's so easy? Like I can just snap my fingers and, poof, I don't *need* it anymore?" As she spoke, she snapped her fingers, and a tongue of flame appeared in her palm. Kittie curled her hand, extinguishing it into nothingness. Not even a wisp of smoke. "It's not *magic*, Jack."

His lovely eyes bored into hers, intense and full of so much passion for her it was almost painful. "I never said it was easy. But you have to *want* it." Jack tilted his head. "And I don't think you do."

It was damned annoying how right he was. She wanted to stop. But she also *wanted* a drink, which ran counter to this entire conversation. She didn't like the idea of leaving her husband and daughter. Didn't want to travel to Confederation lands, even if she was going as a diplomat. Kittie balled her fists, nails biting into the palms. "Could say the same for how well you and Emmaline get along."

Jack twitched, almost as if she'd moved to slap him. That was a sore spot, and maybe unfair that she'd gone for it. His relationship with their daughter was still on the mend, and lately, he'd been lax. He squared his shoulders, eyes glinting as if he were about to pull his ace in the hole. "Yeah? Well, I've got plans."

"Do you?" Kittie asked, surprised. "Want to tell me over a drink?"

He snorted. "I'll treat you to dinner at the Jitterbug. Deal?"

Kittie wrinkled her nose. "They're going to suggest the strawberry ginger switchel for me again, I bet."

Jack chuckled. "Can't be that bad. Blaise swears by the stuff." He cleared his throat. "I'll try some with you. How about that?"

Kittie sighed. He would not relent, and she both loved and hated him for it. "It's a date."

CHAPTER FOUR
Nightmare Fuel

Jefferson

The bell above the bakery door jingled as Jefferson opened it. Blaise glanced back, his shoulders taut with tension. *Odd. He's not usually worked up when he's baking.* Jefferson gave an appreciative sniff as he moved inside and shut the door behind him.

"Is that pork pie I smell?" Jefferson asked, his stomach rumbling at the savory scents wafting through the air.

"Yes and no," Blaise said, which wasn't an answer at all. He glanced over his shoulder, the hardness around his eyes easing. "Trying a new recipe. They're more like rolls stuffed with meat and cheese." He shifted to the side, pointing to a tray where a set of tawny brown orbs rested.

"Whatever they are, they smell amazing." Jefferson studied Blaise as he moved closer, searching for clues as to what had him on edge. *Oh. Wait. Today's the day he...yes.* "How did things go with Nadine?"

Blaise slid a pair of meat rolls onto a tin plate and handed it to Jefferson. He didn't answer until he had similarly loaded a plate for himself and moved over to the small table in the corner. "It was okay."

Jefferson bit into the savory bun to buy himself time as he waited for Blaise to expand on the topic, but the Breaker never did. Blaise's new recipe was just as delectable as it smelled—tangy bits of honey ham mixed with one of the sharp white cheeses brought in from the outlying ranches. Jefferson made an appreciative noise as he chewed. When he finished, he pressed on. "I can tell something is bothering you."

Blaise looked up from his plate, a frown creasing his face for a moment before it melted into a wince. "She thinks I should go to Rainbow Flat, too."

Ah-ha. Jefferson gave a small nod. He and Blaise had spoken about this before. Blaise was torn—he loved his family, but the recent truths revealed by his mother had cut him to the core. Jefferson had mixed thoughts on Marian Hawthorne. From what he had seen, she truly loved Blaise. But he also understood Blaise's feelings of betrayal and hurt. Oh, he understood those only too well from his own family history.

All the same, Blaise *wasn't* Jefferson. And the Hawthornes were *not* the Wellses, thank the gods. Blaise was more likely to forgive someone once he overcame the hurt—but for that, he needed to reconcile with his mother. Jefferson had suggested that he at least try. It wasn't only to make Blaise feel better—the young man needed answers, too.

"That would be a good thing for you to do while I'm away," Jefferson agreed, licking his lips. He had briefly entertained the idea of Blaise traveling to Ganland with him. Well, not just entertained. Fantasized about it, more like. He wanted to show Blaise everything, to share the world with him. But that was a flight of fancy—Blaise had too many damaging memories to overcome.

"I'm considering it," Blaise said. He rubbed his cheek. "It would keep my mind off of you."

"I'll pretend that sentence doesn't wound my pride."

"I meant it would keep me from worrying about you."

Jefferson chuckled. Oh, he'd known. "I'll be *fine.* It's my home turf."

Blaise huffed at that, and he seemed to shake off some of his nerves. His voice was more certain when he spoke. "No, it's the home turf of entrepreneur Jefferson Cole. Not *mage* Jefferson Cole."

"Same thing." Jefferson shrugged, then realized he'd misspoken by the way Blaise's eyebrows slanted. *Time for a change of topic.* "I certainly hope Flora will return from your *errand* soon."

Jefferson knew very well that Blaise was up to *something* with Flora. The Breaker wasn't practiced in getting away with intrigue. The statement disarmed Blaise's previous argument, and he stumbled over his words before he found his proverbial footing. "I...probably?" Blaise scowled at him, annoyed at the change of topic but unable to combat it.

You're so bad at being sneaky, but at least you're cute. Jefferson grinned. "Anyway, enough of that. Our time together is limited. We should do something fun."

Blaise relaxed, though he gave Jefferson a dubious look. "Define *fun.*"

Do I suggest something scandalous or mundane? Jefferson finished the last of his bun, deciding to err on the side of caution. "What do *you* think is fun?"

Blaise's expression softened. "A game. We can play a game—after you do the dishes."

My staff back home would absolutely have kittens to hear that. Jefferson chuckled. He enjoyed these simple things with Blaise. "Fine. I'll wash if you dry."

ONE STACK OF DISHES AND A CARD GAME LATER, JEFFERSON CURLED UP facing Blaise. The Breaker twitched as he dropped into slumber, his previously slack face twisting into a grimace. Jefferson's power was especially sensitive to Blaise, and he felt the nightmares rising to greet the young man. *No. Leave him be. I have someone else to feed you to.* Jefferson snared the nightmares with his magic, tugging them away from Blaise.

Jefferson's hand rested on Blaise's bicep, listening as his breath evened out in the darkness. Muscles relaxed beneath his touch. Jefferson was tempted to allow the nightmares to coalesce, so he could see for himself what was bothering Blaise. But there was no guarantee that whatever manifested was the actual problem. The subconscious, Jefferson had learned, was fickle. No, it was better to keep the nightmares away from Blaise and be done with it.

He leaned over and gave the Breaker a gentle kiss on the cheek, running a finger along his jawline, savoring his well-kempt beard. This was what Jefferson would miss most on his trip to Ganland. Blaise and everything about him. *I'm being ridiculous. I have an advantage no one else has. The dreamscape. We won't always be apart.*

"And I've delayed it too long," Jefferson murmured as a thought occurred to him. He settled alongside Blaise, fingers tracing the fading tattoo on the Breaker's arm. The geasa tattoo was dead, though for a while, it had been the bond between Jefferson as handler and Blaise as theurgist. They were neither of those now. In fact, with his magic, Jefferson was now the furthest thing from a handler. And Blaise was free of the geasa—a true outlaw mage. But there was still someone who had to *pay* for that. "I'll see you soon, Blaise. Until then, sweet dreams."

Jefferson burrowed into the mattress. The bed left much to be desired —the mattress was lumpy and not as soft as those Jefferson liked. And because of the size of the loft over the bakery, it was barely large enough to fit the pair. Well, perhaps Jefferson didn't object to *that* part too much. He enjoyed being nestled close to Blaise, and the Breaker had made it clear the feeling was mutual.

He closed his eyes, summoning up a wisp of his Dreamer magic to ease himself into the dreamscape. It was an odd thing, but for someone who commanded dreams, he was finding it harder and harder to fall asleep at night. Though he had a lot on his mind, and none of that helped.

Jefferson practiced breathing exercises to relax his body—a suggestion that had come from Vixen. It helped, and before long, he was in the grey expanse that led to the dreamscape.

He was still unclear on exactly what the dreamscape was. Jefferson didn't know if it was some sort of magical plane, an overlay of the waking world, or something beyond his comprehension. All he knew without a doubt was that it was real and that, as a Dreamer, he could exert his will on it. Mold it into a thing of *his* design.

He could pull others into it, though that was sometimes difficult. Bringing Blaise there had become second nature. Jefferson had brought others there, too. Jack. Flora.

And Gregor Gaitwood.

Gaitwood was the one he needed to attend to. Jefferson called up his magic, and before him, stone grated as a floor rose from nothing, the blocks coming together like the pieces of a puzzle. Walls reared up, lit by phantom mage-lights. Jefferson strode down the newly created corridor, his footfalls echoing.

He didn't like this place, but it was a necessity. It was a shadow of the Golden Citadel, the prison where the Confederation had held Blaise. Tormented him. Abused him. Jefferson released a resentful breath, old anger burning in his heart. He hadn't told Blaise he allowed a version of the Cit to exist in the dreamscape. The dreamscape was supposed to be a safe place, and Jefferson made certain that, for Blaise, this was always the case.

Jefferson's steps slowed as he neared his destination. Around him, the walls bore signs of strain. Spider web cracks ran from floor to ceiling, the lumber reinforcing the damaged wall doing very little. Salt-iron reinforced the wall, too, though in the dreamscape, the metal was inert. Little more than set dressing.

He frowned. Though this resembled Blaise's cell in the Cit, it wasn't supposed to be so damaged. Jefferson wondered if he had weakened the walls without intending to, merely because his subconscious knew what Blaise had done to them. Licking his lips, Jefferson sent his magic into the substance of the walls, strengthening them. The cracks receded as the stone sealed itself.

"I was wondering when you'd show your face again."

The voice put Jefferson on edge, fury boiling through him. He crossed his arms and released a tendril of power, causing the door to the cell to swing open with a creak. Gregor Gaitwood stood inches from the threshold. The enemy Doyen had learned from past visits that although the door appeared open, Jefferson wouldn't allow him to cross the invisible barrier. Jefferson had promised Gregor a life of nightmares every time his eyes closed, and he was a man of his word.

He met Gregor's gaze, staring back at him. It was like old times, when he had been Doyen Malcolm Wells, going toe-to-toe against this man. Neither of them backed down for what felt like an eternity. Gregor finally averted his gaze with a frustrated hiss.

This was how it went every time Jefferson came to reinforce the magic he used to keep Gregor ensnared—and to infuse him with more nightmares. Gregor always tried to get him to speak, to offer information that the Doyen no doubt hoped to use. Jefferson still couldn't believe that Phinora allowed the man to sit on the Council. The newspapers that had slowly made their way to Fortitude declared the Doyen had suffered a "mental collapse over the loss of fellow Doyen Malcolm Wells" and convalesced on his estate for a time.

"You can't keep me here forever, Cole!"

Jefferson raised his brows. He was tempted to reply to the challenge, but that would play into Gaitwood's hands. The trapped Doyen had slowly become more lucid in the dreamscape, and Jefferson couldn't figure out how. Was he developing a resistance to Jefferson's influence? Blaise hadn't, but then again, the Breaker *wanted* Jefferson's help. Gregor actively fought against it.

"I brought you something," Jefferson said, a self-righteous thrill shivering through him when Gregor's eyes widened in alarm. "More fuel for the fire."

"No!" Gregor howled as Jefferson pulled on the freshly culled nightmares, forcing them into the Doyen's psyche. Gaitwood collapsed to his knees with a pathetic whimper. Jefferson didn't have a shred of compassion for the man. Every terror he fed to Gregor came directly from Blaise, from the traumas of his past. Gregor had been responsible for more than his fair share of them.

"Sleep tight," Jefferson called, turning his back on the prisoner. It was time to join Blaise. He raised a hand, the cell door slamming shut with the final click of a lock falling into place. Gregor made a choked half-sob, followed by the thud of the man ramming his body against the door in frustration. In desperation. Jefferson tucked his chin. Gregor wanted him to cave, to feel sorry for him. But he wouldn't. Not after what Blaise had endured.

He headed up the stone hallway, and as he walked, it shifted into a black and white patterned floor. The same sort of design as the floorboards of Blaise's Bakery. The yellow-painted walls of the bakery swooped in around Jefferson as he appeared beside Blaise. Then he raised his brows, realizing he had spent perhaps a bit too long with Gaitwood. Blaise's slumbering mind had wandered into ridiculousness.

The bakery itself was normal, though the new sink (with running water) Jefferson had paid to have installed had...a tree in it? Leaves littered the interior of the sink, and Blaise was shaking his head as he cleared the debris into a bucket.

"Why would a tree grow in your bakery?" Jefferson asked, eyes roving up the length of the trunk that somehow pierced the ceiling without damaging it. Dreams were strange that way.

Blaise shrugged. "Because you took too long to get here, and my brain is weird."

"Your brain is *not* weird. Everyone has odd dreams," Jefferson said. "You're just spoiled because I can make your dreams whatever we'd like them to be."

Blaise scoffed, setting down the leaf-filled bucket. He poked his chest with a thumb. "*I'm* the spoiled one?"

"I bought you a very expensive sink, complete with the plumbing for running water. I stand by what I said."

Blaise chuckled, his mood much improved from earlier in the evening. "Fair enough." He gestured to the tree. "Can you make this not be here?"

Jefferson grinned. He touched a finger to a bough. The tree misted away from existence, taking the leaf remnants with it. "As you wish."

"Show off."

This banter...this was *good*. Jefferson breathed a sigh of relief, pleased that Blaise was feeling more like himself in the dreamscape. "Yes, I've been called a peacock often enough. It goes with the territory." Jack had taken to calling him that. *I suppose it's better than* dandy. Jefferson didn't mind it. Peacocks were territorial, which seemed fitting.

"Did you have trouble falling asleep?" Blaise asked, moving closer to Jefferson until they were shoulder to shoulder.

Jefferson couldn't help looping an arm around Blaise's lower back, pulling him closer. "A little. And I had to take care of something before I could join you."

Blaise glanced at him, the unasked question on his lips. Jefferson didn't want to keep secrets from him—but he didn't want to hurt him, either. He knew that eventually, he needed to tell the Breaker about Gregor. Not anytime soon, though. Not while he was still learning how to cope with his trauma.

"A few simple things related to the dreamscape," Jefferson said, resting his head against Blaise's shoulder. "I had to keep parts of it stabilized." That was the truth, at least.

Blaise nodded, accepting the answer. "Thanks for fixing the tree." He shifted beneath Jefferson. "I have a special request for tonight."

"Oh?" Blaise's idea of a special request rarely aligned with his own—as evidenced by the card game. That was also what made the younger man so *interesting*. And honestly, Jefferson savored every moment he spent with Blaise. The Breaker made him feel whole. Blaise accepted him for who he was, not caring a lick for his wealth or influence.

"You've traveled a lot more than I have. Show me some of the places you've been?"

Jefferson blinked. That was a good idea. He smiled. "I doubt I can show you *all* the places I've been in one night without expending an immense amount of magic. But we could take a tour. A different destination each night? All without the fuss of having to pack your bags and go anywhere." *Though, I hope to do that with you. Some day.*

Blaise sighed with contentment. "I'd like that a lot."

CHAPTER FIVE

I Don't Fret. I Brood.

Jack

"Jack!"

The Effigest paused mid-stride at the voice, pivoting to face the speaker. When Nadine called, he knew it was in his best interest to listen. There was an urgency in the single word that made him frown. She stood outside her clinic, framed by the bright mid-morning sunshine, glowering at him as if something was his fault. Maybe that was the case. A lot of things were Jack's fault. But this time, he honestly didn't know what he might have done to earn her ire.

"Yeah?" he asked, crossing his arms to meet her surliness with his own.

"Get over here. It's rude to have a conversation shouting across the town square."

He snorted at her hypocrisy but ambled over nonetheless. Nadine wasn't one to trifle with. Not only could she use her magic to suck the life out of someone if she so chose, but as the most skilled Healer in town, for the sake of his long-term health, it was important to be on her good side. Or at least as good as he could get. A couple of new mages with Healing power had joined their town recently, but none of them were on a par with Nadine. One of them was a Beast Healer anyhow, which would do little good for Jack.

When he was closer, Nadine retreated into the clinic, and he followed. That was curious. Whatever she wanted to discuss, it was something she sought to keep private. As Nadine shut the door, he claimed the chair she usually had her patients sit in. The Healer raised an eyebrow at him, then climbed atop her stool with a shrug.

"What's got you hollering across the town at me?" Jack asked.

She pursed her lips. "Two things. First, Blaise."

Jack cocked his head. "What's *he* got to do with me?" He almost regretted the sting in his voice, but not really. Wouldn't do to have people think he actually *liked* the Breaker.

Nadine made a soft snort. "Not that you'll ever say as much, but I think you know more about what's happened to him than he'll even tell me." Jack met her eyes at the assertion, dipping his chin in silent agreement. "His physical wounds have healed as much as they can. But he's hurt on the inside, and that's not something I can fix."

Jack shrugged. "We all have those wounds." While that was true, he knew that few outlaws in Fortitude had been hurt as deeply as their Breaker. And if Blaise had kept that from Nadine…well, it wasn't Jack's place to inform her.

Nadine scowled. "All I know is, it's something to do with his family. He's thinking of going to Rainbow Flat."

Rainbow Flat. Jack tensed at the town's name. So Blaise was thinking of confronting his mother on the bitter truth. That was his right—but Nadine's worry was justified. The young man was so emotionally wounded that Jack wasn't sure how he'd stand up to facing the issue head-on. There was only so much a person could take before they unraveled.

He met her silver eyes. "Why are you telling *me* this? You should tell the peacock."

"Don't be daft. Jefferson Cole is leaving for Ganland. I won't breathe a word of this to him because we *need* him to go with the delegation." There was a sharp desperation in her voice that drew Jack's interest. Nadine wanted this for the Gutter, and badly. "This is something Blaise needs, too, but I don't think Emrys is enough to keep him stable."

Jack crossed his arms. "Are you insinuating that I should go with him? Because we're…partners or some such?" He uttered a derisive snort. "You forgetting I punched him in the face the first time we met?"

Nadine pinned him with a knowing look. She saw through his drag-onshit. Jack made a face at her, annoyed. He had a reputation to maintain, after all. Couldn't have people thinking Wildfire Jack, Scourge of the Untamed Territory, was cuddly and lovable as a jackalope.

"Maybe I think it would be good for *you*," she said.

His brows knit at her new ploy. "What?"

The Healer crossed her arms. "You forget this place is a rumor mill? I heard you intend to spend more time with your daughter. This is the perfect chance." Then she leaned closer to him. "And your wife is about to travel to Confederation territory, and you need a worthwhile distraction. I can't imagine what it's going to do to you when your brain catches up with the fact that she's not here, and you have to wait and fret about her."

"I don't fret," Jack grumbled. "I brood."

"Fine, *brood*. When you brood, you tend to get violent."

He shrugged. "Ain't nothing wrong with that."

Nadine heaved a pained sigh. She was the one who healed him when his tendencies put him on the receiving end of a beat-down. "What I'm saying is, Blaise needs someone he can trust. Emmaline is one of his closest friends. And you? You're going to need a distraction, even if you don't think you do right now. You've worked with him before, and you know him. Blaise is comfortable around you, no matter how much of an ornery cuss you are."

"Did he tell you that?" Jack was genuinely curious.

"In not so many words," Nadine said. She licked her lips. "Consider going with him, that's all I ask. Fortitude will be fine. More mages arrive every week. We're not as soft a target as we once were."

She was right, but he would still worry about his town. He rubbed the back of his neck. "I'll think about it. You said there were two things. What's the second?"

Nadine crossed her arms, pinning him with another of her no-nonsense looks. "Your wife."

Jack went rigid. He'd approached Nadine about Kittie's problem, and the Healer had taken pains to speak to the Pyromancer. Kittie hadn't appreciated it at all. "Yeah?"

"Mindy's going along for several reasons. Kittie is one of 'em," Nadine started. Jack couldn't hide his surprise at the revelation, but the Healer didn't give him room to comment before plowing on. "She won't listen to me, but she might listen to Mindy. At any rate, a Hospitalier will have good instincts about what to shovel into her body to keep her healthy. And that ain't liquor." Nadine snorted with disdain.

Jack relaxed. That wasn't a bad idea. He liked Mindy—he'd go so far as to say he trusted her, which wasn't true of most people. Jack cocked his head. He wasn't used to people doing thoughtful things for those he cared about, not like that. "Thanks."

The Healer gave him a rare smile. "Don't mention it. And I mean that literally. Don't mention it, because I'm not sure I could heal myself if she took offense and barbecued me."

CHAPTER SIX

The One and Only Flora Strop

Blaise

*B*laise smiled, reminiscing on the previous night. Asking Jefferson to show him new places in the dreamscape had been the diversion he needed. Jefferson's enthusiasm for travel was downright infectious, and they had both awoken in a pleasant mood. Well, Blaise had, anyway. As usual, Jefferson had languished in bed for another hour while Blaise readied the bakery for the day's work. Jefferson didn't get up before the sun if he could help it.

Now Jefferson was off at another meeting, and Blaise was preparing a baker's dozen of the meat-filled buns that they had enjoyed the previous evening. He lost himself to the familiar work of kneading the dough, his mind drifting to Jefferson. And how in a few short days, Jefferson would leave him.

No, that was the wrong way to think of it. Blaise wrinkled his nose as he reconsidered. Jefferson wasn't leaving because he *wanted* to, but because it was *necessary. And he's not leaving* me—*not leaving this...whatever we have.* That was noteworthy. A small part of Blaise wanted to be selfish and keep Jefferson here for himself. If he asked Jefferson to stay, Blaise had no doubt that he would. But the thing Jefferson was going to do was bigger than the both of them. It was important, and Jefferson's political savvy and deep ties to Ganland would help their cause. Didn't mean that Blaise had to be happy he was leaving, though.

Someone poked his shoulder, and he spun, heart racing as he found

Emmaline giving him a squinty-eyed look that would have made her father proud. "What?"

"I asked you a question three times, and you're standing there gathering wool. What's going on?" Her hands were on her hips, her blonde ponytail swinging at her back.

He winced, glancing around the bakery. *His* bakery. It was one of the few places he could always stay on track—though apparently not today. Sheepishly, he turned back to the dough. "Oh, I guess this is ready to be rolled out so we can add the meat and cheese. Sorry. I was thinking."

Emmaline's face softened. She understood the traumas of his past in her own way. He still didn't know what had happened to her at Fort Courage, but he knew it wasn't good. In the time between her rescue and the gambit that had freed him from the Golden Citadel, she had changed. She'd become a little harder, like her father. Jaded. Sometimes angry. Blaise understood that, too.

"The diced ham is ready." She nodded to a nearby ceramic bowl. "Sometimes you think too much."

"I *have* to think about the people I care about." Blaise laid out a sphere of dough before taking a rolling pin to it. "I'm not about to stop doing that."

"I don't think that's what she's saying," Reuben piped up quietly from across the small bakery, where he had been decorating a tray of cookies while he waited for customers. It was late morning, and they weren't busy. "You latch onto things and worry them to shreds."

"I do *not*," Blaise muttered, feeling the back of his neck warm at the good-natured accusation. A part of him realized they were probably right. But it wasn't like he knew how to change that part of himself. Not without losing the ability to care about people. Or to just *care*.

Emmaline opened her mouth to say something, but the jingle of the bell over the door cut her off. Reuben straightened, setting down his piping bag to see to the customer, when they saw it was Jack. The outlaw swaggered into the bakery, all business, and by the way he draped an arm atop the glass display case, Blaise figured he hadn't come for a donut.

But it didn't hurt to coddle the Effigest's sweet tooth. And it would take the focus off himself, which was a bonus. Blaise set aside his rolling pin. "Morning, Jack. Want a donut? On the house."

Emmaline huffed out a breath, seeing through his plot. Amusement flickered in her father's eyes, as if he knew he had interrupted something with his entrance. "I'm not fool enough to turn down a donut."

"I got it, Reuben," Blaise called, slipping over to snag a piece of waxed paper so that he could retrieve a donut.

The outlaw watched his every move like a hawk preparing to stoop on prey. "Word is you're going to Rainbow Flat."

Blaise froze for a beat, then forced himself to finish the task. He straightened, handing the donut over to Jack. "Might be. Not sure if I want to leave the bakery, though." That was always a worthwhile excuse. And truth be told, Blaise *didn't* want to leave it. He loved every inch of the place.

That was the wrong thing to say, though. Reuben bounced on his heels, his face suddenly animated. "You can go if you need to, Blaise. We can make the basics. Did it before, and we're so much better at it now."

Blaise blinked, stymied by the teenager's words. It was true, too. Reuben and Emmaline had run the bakery when he and Jack had taken a previous ill-fated trip into Desina. And while he had been…never mind. Best not to think of that.

"Won't be a *we* thing because Emmaline won't be here," Jack said, interrupting Blaise's train of thought. Emmaline shot a look at her father that was half glare and half amazement at his audacity. "'Cause she'll be going to Rainbow Flat with me." The outlaw punctuated the statement with a bite of his donut, ignoring the motes of powdered sugar that fell to his chest.

At that, Emmaline's expression shifted yet again. This time, excitement reigned. "Wait, Rainbow Flat? We're going to Rainbow Flat?" She nearly squealed the question.

"Yep." Jack was gloating, his frosty eyes falling on Blaise in what was almost a dare.

Blaise's lower lip jutted out in consternation. He hadn't even decided that he was going, and Jack had the nerve to bluster into the bakery and all but demand it happen. "Well, I hope you have a good time."

Jack tilted his head. "I think we will. I heard that fancy musical *Breaker* is going to make its debut there next week. Bet I can finagle some tickets." He grinned.

"Go lick salt-iron," Blaise growled, earning a bark of laughter from Jack.

"C'mon, Blaise," Emmaline said. "You should go! Have a little adventure. Take your mind off your worries."

This would be the exact opposite of that. By the way Jack's gaze cut over to him, the outlaw knew. Blaise rubbed the back of his neck, glancing at Reuben. It was getting harder and harder to say no without bursting Emmaline's bubble. And the blasted outlaw knew it. "We'd have to close the bakery if I went. This place is too much for a single person to run." *Please tell them what a bad idea that is, Reuben.*

Instead, Reuben's face lit up. "I know exactly who I can ask to help!

Hannah's back in town, working at the Jitterbug. But I think she and her sister are about to have it out again. I could ask if she'd like to help here?"

Oh gods, Hannah. Blaise had so many mixed emotions over the young woman who had been one of the first to befriend him in the outlaw town. Looking back, he realized that she'd *liked* him—in ways that he would never be comfortable reciprocating. And that was complicated because she was nice and kind and...*argh. Maybe there's a cave I can crawl into until Jefferson gets back.*

Reuben was watching him, waiting for an answer. Blaise wasn't about to unleash any of his confusing thoughts on his current audience. "Um, I guess it wouldn't hurt to ask."

Reuben punched a fist into the air. "I'll ask her this afternoon!"

Emmaline clapped her hands. "This is so exciting! When do we leave?"

Jack tipped his head. "That's entirely up to Blaise."

BLAISE GLANCED AT THE SADDLEBAG DRAPED ACROSS THE FOOT OF THE BED, a neat assortment of clothing nestled beside it. Jefferson's things, ready to be slipped into the compartments for his journey. He couldn't help but grin at the cobalt blue bottle nestled amidst the garments. *Of course, he would pack cologne.*

He shifted his focus from Jefferson's luggage to himself. Blaise had put on one of the crisp, button-down shirts that Jefferson had given him, pairing it with a blue greatcoat. If it was to be their last evening together for a while, Blaise had decided to make it memorable. No games over proper attire tonight.

But I really wish he wouldn't leave until Flora was back. As much as Jefferson had evaded the discussion, Blaise worried about him traveling to Ganland. He would feel slightly better if Flora were along to accompany him from the start. The wily half-knocker would be able to catch up to Jefferson on her own, but Blaise hoped that wouldn't be necessary. Especially since it would complicate the entire reason he had sent her off on this little errand in the first place.

Blaise heard the soft pop of displaced air, freezing as he reached down to pull out his least scuffed pair of boots. "Flora? That you?"

"The one and only!" she called back. "You coming down or want me to come up? If you're not decent, I'm more than happy to come up." A raucous laugh followed her bold words.

Blaise snorted. "Sorry to disappoint you, but I'm fully clothed. You can come up."

"You're no fun at all." The thud of feet on the perilously steep stairs that led to the small loft room heralded her arrival.

"Not that kind of fun, no," Blaise agreed. He had grown accustomed to Flora's filter-free conversational style. "Did you get it?"

Flora grinned at him as she mounted the top of the stairs. In reply, she pulled a small, velvet-covered box out of a pouch at her side. "Of course I did. This was a good idea you had. Expensive, but a good idea."

Blaise winced at the reminder. Jefferson didn't know it yet, but Blaise had sunk his full inheritance from Malcolm Wells into the contents of this box. "Did the Enchanter tell you how it works?"

Flora tossed the box into the air and caught it, ignoring Blaise's moment of panic at her flippant treatment of the pricey investment. "Similar to the one he has, 'cause I went to the same Enchanter. Top of the line, that one." Then she paused, tilting her head. "There're instructions inside the box. I peeked, since I wanted to make sure we weren't getting cheated."

"How do we know it'll work?" Blaise asked, extending his hand.

Flora dropped the velvet box into his palm. "You won't know until it's on. But that's also why I went to the best. Better odds it'll do what you need it to do."

"Hmm." The box rested in Blaise's palm, small and unassuming. He unleashed a tendril of his magic, sending it into the box—careful to only quest and prod with it, not allowing it to exert its true power. He'd learned he could use his magic to assess things, to an extent. Sort of like groping for something in the dark. Blaise knew by touching a glass exactly how much magic he had to spend to shatter it; where the most vulnerable parts were. And when he encountered something magical, he gained a sense about that, too.

His magic raced along the circle of metal nestled within the box. Blaise didn't even have to open it to confirm that it was a ring. He could almost feel the cool smoothness of the metal and the tiny chasms of the sigils engraved in the band. At first, nothing about the ring felt remarkable to him, as if it were completely ordinary. Flora was right. This Enchanter was a master at their work.

"Well?" Flora asked, watching him expectantly.

"Gimme a moment," he murmured, continuing his exploration. He was tempted to open the box, but he would have to withdraw his magic and start anew. And it took a lot of effort to keep his power in line, assessing rather than destroying.

Ah. He was suddenly glad he had continued on. There it was. The Enchanter had folded whatever spell they'd used back on itself, making it almost imperceptible unless someone knew to look for it. *Jefferson's cabochon ring is probably similar. That one never felt magical to me, either.*

Blaise pulled back his power. "There's definitely a spell enhancing it. Now we'll see if it works when I give it to him."

Flora eyed him appreciatively. "Hot date tonight?"

"Something like that," Blaise agreed, slipping the velvet box into the pocket concealed beneath his greatcoat.

Blaise was certain she would needle him about it, but to his surprise, she let it go. Something like happiness sparked in her violet eyes for a moment before she yawned. "Well, have fun. Tell Jefferson I'll be ready in the morning. I'm gonna get some shut-eye since I used a lot of magic hustling back here."

"Hey, Flora?" She paused, looking back at him. "Thanks. I mean, for getting this. And for...everything."

Flora waved over her shoulder. "No thanks needed. Aside from maybe some sugar cookies for the road. And cinnamon rolls to start the day tomorrow would hit the spot. Notice I said cinnamon *rolls*. More than one. I wouldn't turn down an entire pan."

Blaise chuckled. "I can do that."

CHAPTER SEVEN

Socially Awkward

Jefferson

Jefferson hesitated, clutching the bakery's door knob. This would be the last time he'd come home to Blaise for…well, he didn't know how long. He felt a little guilty—he was excited about the prospect of going to Ganland and dabbling in politics to help the Gutter. It was a good thing he was doing, a *necessary* thing. But by the same token, he didn't want to leave Blaise.

"Howdy."

He couldn't help the grin that slid onto his face at the sight of Blaise leaning against the bakery counter, waiting for him. Blaise did that sometimes—waited downstairs until Jefferson arrived. A pair of saddlebags rested against the wall near the door, an unpleasant reminder that they would soon part ways, if only temporarily. Jefferson shoved those thoughts aside, focusing instead on the young man watching him. "What's that? Did you finish packing for me?"

"I thought you might not have enough time tonight," Blaise replied. "Though you're welcome to make sure I got everything you need. I left your grooming supplies alone, since I figured you'd want to use them in the morning."

"I'll check later," Jefferson said, touched by Blaise's gesture. Then he paused, taking in Blaise's attire. "Did someone die? Why are you dressed up?"

"Oh my *gods*," Blaise mumbled, pushing off from the counter and inadvertently displaying the amount of care he'd taken to look good. "Why is that the first place you go with that question?"

Because you're not one to dress up fancy. It's not you, *although, sweet Tabris, you look good. Wait, focus.* Jefferson cleared his throat as he cycled through a proper response. "Ahem, forgive me. You took me by surprise." Then he allowed an edge of roughness into his voice. "But very *appealing*ly, I assure you."

The apology soothed the Breaker. "I was hoping we could enjoy the evening together." His voice was soft. Wistful.

"I would like that *very* much," Jefferson said immediately. Really, he wanted nothing more than to spend the rest of the night curled up beside Blaise, memorizing the planes of his face and the rightness that accompanied just being with him. "What are you thinking?"

"Maybe we could go eat at the Jitterbug."

The suggestion gave Jefferson cause to raise his eyebrows. Most evenings, Blaise was content to whip up a simple meal for them to share or dine with Clover at the Broken Horn. They seldom ate at the Jitterbug, though Blaise still provided bread to the diner daily. "Is this a *date?*"

A smile curled Blaise's lips. Whatever he was thinking, it made him happy. Jefferson liked to see that. "You tell me."

"You're trying to play coy, so it must be." Jefferson chuckled.

"It's not working, is it?"

Jefferson stepped closer until only a hand span separated them. "No, but it's endearing and very *you*. And I mean that in all the best ways."

A shy smile returned to Blaise's face, making Jefferson glad he had offered the compliment. One day, he hoped Blaise would truly understand how much Jefferson treasured him for being exactly who he was. Something flickered in the Breaker's eyes, as if a stray thought had interrupted his plans. "Oh. Flora is back."

Jefferson blinked. "Wait, really?" He hadn't been aware—but then again, he had been in meetings all afternoon. No doubt Blaise had told her as much, and Flora knew better than to interrupt him in a meeting unless it was dire. "Where is she?"

"Resting. And getting ready to eat an entire pan of cinnamon rolls, if she's to be believed." Blaise stepped away, heading for the door. "She's still planning to go with you tomorrow."

"I certainly hope she'll save a cinnamon roll for me." Jefferson moved to follow. "She arrived just in time, then."

"I'll make you anything you want tomorrow," Blaise promised. "Now, let's get over to the Jitterbug before they get too busy."

The Jitterbug was only half-full, with most of the evening crowd over at the Broken Horn Saloon or not yet arrived. Mindy waved to them as they seated themselves at a table, swooping over. "Evening. You planning to chance the menu or leave it to me?" She grinned. Mindy's Hospitalier magic helped her to perceive the best food and drink for those around her. She was never wrong.

"The usual," Blaise said, meaning that Mindy could pick for him.

"Likewise," Jefferson echoed, nodding to her.

"Got it!" the Hospitalier replied, rubbing her hands together. "Hmm. Something special is going to be required tonight!" She sounded pleased with herself, and as she spun on her heel, she nearly glowed with excitement at the challenge they presented.

Blaise rubbed his cheek, seeming to have second thoughts. "Maybe we *should* have gone to the saloon."

Jefferson chuckled. Blaise hated being fussed over, and he felt awkward at fancy dinners. Jefferson loved both of those things. It meant a lot that Blaise was doing this. "What, you don't want a romantic dinner with me?"

Blaise shook his head. "It's not that. I don't like being reminded it's our last night together."

Jefferson reached over and placed a hand atop Blaise's, lightly, in case the Breaker would rather not be touched. He didn't shrink away, instead, relaxing beneath his hand. "It's *not* our last night together. And it will take more than distance to keep us apart." Jefferson didn't dare expand on that. Very few people knew he was a mage, and it was critical that it stayed that way—for both their sakes.

Blaise rubbed the back of his neck with his free hand. Worry reflected in his blue eyes, fears that he seemed unable or unwilling to express at the moment. He shook his head, releasing a soft sigh. "Something you said earlier stuck with me."

Jefferson raised his brows. "What was it?"

The corners of Blaise's eyes wrinkled. "When you asked why I dressed this way. If someone had died." He paused, reluctant to finish the thought, though he seemed to decide to plow onward. "You're going to Malcolm's funeral when you go to Nera."

Oh. Jefferson winced. Honestly, that was something he'd given little thought to. Seledora had acted on his behalf to put everything in motion for a proper service to bid goodbye forever to Malcolm Wells. The least he could do was attend his own funeral.

"Well, yes, but *I* haven't thought about it very much," Jefferson admitted.

"Doesn't it bother you?" Blaise asked, pulling his hand away. He made a circular gesture, as if attempting to explain and failing. "It's..." Blaise pointed an index finger at Jefferson meaningfully.

Jefferson sighed inwardly. Blaise had a very confusing relationship with Malcolm—which was odd since Jefferson and Malcolm were one and the same. It had taken time for Blaise to reconcile his dual identities, and now it clearly bothered him that Malcolm was, for all purposes, dead. Jefferson idly rubbed the scarlet-stoned cabochon ring that made his preferred visage possible.

"It would be a lie to say it doesn't bother me." Jefferson kept his voice soft, the words for Blaise alone. "But you also know how I feel about Malcolm." *And you know why I'm trying so hard to separate myself from the Wells name.*

Blaise relaxed, offering a small nod and the hint of a smile. "He wasn't such a bad guy in the end."

"I *told* you so," Jefferson said, chuckling.

"He was just a little arrogant, is all."

And now he's teasing me. Good. That means he feels a little better about things. "If that's his greatest flaw in your eyes, then I believe he would be quite happy with that." Jefferson didn't know if Blaise was being flippant or if that was truly what he saw as Malcolm's biggest flaw.

Blaise's gaze flicked toward the kitchen area, his forehead crinkling. A young woman bustled out, carrying plates in their direction. Hmm, something about her was familiar. Jefferson hadn't seen her in town recently, but…oh yes, *now* he remembered. She was the one who had asked Blaise to dance ages ago at the Feast of Flight. The pretty brunette he had shied away from in a panic when no one else had understood that he didn't want to be touched. Jefferson glanced at Blaise, expecting that her approach might alarm him, but to Jefferson's surprise, he discovered that his beau didn't seem any more tense than usual.

"Howdy, Blaise, it's been a while," she greeted him, the smile in her voice extending to the shine in her eyes. She nodded to Jefferson, but her focus was fully on Blaise.

"Howdy, Hannah," Blaise said, shifting to make room for her to slip a plate in front of him. "You remember Jefferson Cole?"

Hannah set a plate before Jefferson, too. Like Blaise's, it was loaded with wine-braised beef and mushrooms, buttered peas, and fresh rolls. "I do recall Mr. Cole. It's a pleasure to see you again." She flashed a smile at Jefferson.

"Likewise," Jefferson replied, though, in truth, he was watching for the slightest hint that Blaise was uncomfortable. Hannah seemed innocent enough, and the Breaker had come a long way from the insecure young man he had been. But he had also been through so much since then.

Hannah clasped her hands behind her back. "I appreciate the opportunity to work at your bakery."

What? That was new. Jefferson knew nothing of this, and it was either a recent development or Blaise had forgotten to tell him. Small wonder, though. Jefferson had been in so many meetings lately. He caught Blaise's eye and mouthed the words, "Work at the bakery?"

"It'll be a big help to Reuben when I'm traveling," Blaise said in response to both Hannah and Jefferson. "I appreciate it."

Ah. That makes sense. Hmm, but what about Emmaline? Though it was promising to hear Blaise was seriously considering a trip to Rainbow Flat.

Hannah beamed, tilting her head. "I tried my hand at the rolls today." She shifted her weight from one foot to the other. "Thought it was worth a shot."

The Breaker raised his eyebrows, tapping the still-warm roll. There was a soft, hollow sound. "The top is firm. Sounds good." He inhaled deeply, the corners of his lips lifting. "Smells good, too."

Hannah nearly blushed at his comments. Then she straightened, remembering her current task. "Be right back. Need to get your drinks."

Jefferson watched her go. "Where's Celeste?"

"Hannah doesn't get on well with her sister. Celeste is probably lying low." Blaise picked up the roll, breaking it open.

"And so you invited her to work at the bakery?" Jefferson asked, keeping his tone neutral.

"It was Reuben's idea, actually. He asked for permission, and I told him to go ahead. He'll need help," Blaise replied, though he didn't sound happy with the arrangement. The Breaker slathered a pat of butter on one side of the roll.

Before Jefferson could ask any further questions, Hannah returned with their drinks, no doubt suggested by Mindy. She placed a glass of wine before Jefferson—Knossan dandelion wine, one of his favorites— and something that Jefferson was willing to bet was a switchel for Blaise. "Thank you."

Hannah nodded to him, then licked her lips. "I just wanted to tell you…I'm glad you found someone, Blaise."

A momentary look of surprise flashed across Blaise's face. The Breaker stiffened as all of his anxiety about awkward social situations no doubt came to a head. Beneath the table, Jefferson nudged his foot against Blaise's, a reminder that he wasn't alone. That he had no reason to be nervous.

"Me, too," Blaise said after a moment. "Um, thanks."

Ah, she was sweet on him. Jefferson watched as Hannah drifted off to see to another table, then glanced back at Blaise. "Nothing about that was awkward in the least."

"Not at all," Blaise muttered, making a face. "But I sort of figured that conversation was going to happen, eventually. Better now than later."

They ate in companionable silence, speaking occasionally but mostly focusing on the food laid out before them. Mindy was right—it was delicious, a worthy meal for his last evening with Blaise for the foreseeable future.

Blaise sighed with contentment as he finished eating, setting his knife and fork on his plate with a clatter. His blue eyes flicked up to Jefferson, and Blaise's lips pursed as if he were uncertain about something. "Want to go for a walk with me?"

A walk? Jefferson canted his head, wondering what this was about. Blaise was definitely not the sort who took romantic walks. "I would love to."

A small smile lit Blaise's face, and together they rose from the table. Jefferson paid for the meal before stepping out to join Blaise on the porch. The Breaker was staring at the western horizon, where the clouds were afire with brilliant hues of scarlet and gold.

They headed toward the rim of the canyon overlooking the Deadwood River. Overhead, the stars slowly became visible as the sun sank lower on the horizon. Sleepy birds called in the distance, and Jefferson heard the thunder of wings as a sentry pegasus flew nearby on a round. The river rumbled in the depths below them as Blaise found a chunk of sandstone that had been formed into a rudimentary bench by one of Fortitude's new Earthshaper mages.

Jefferson sat down beside him, hazarding a glance at Blaise. He looked brilliant with the sunset making his hair gleam like copper, his face bathed in the glow. Jefferson tried to commit this moment to memory, this fleeting time when Blaise looked like the legend many said he was.

"There're no views like this in Ganland," Jefferson murmured, nudging Blaise with his shoulder.

At the mention of Ganland, Blaise's expression cooled. He licked his lips, shifting to better face Jefferson. "Speaking of that. I, ah, got you something." The Breaker fumbled in his pocket and pulled out the box, holding it lightly in his hand.

"Oh." Jefferson didn't know what else to say. Should he have gotten Blaise a present? He thought about asking, but he saw Blaise was gathering the courage to speak.

"It's...well, let me show you." The younger man's fingers fluttered against the edges of the box as he pulled it open. Something glinted in the waning light.

A ring? Jefferson inhaled a sharp breath. *Is he proposing?* His traitorous tongue almost asked, but he pulled it back at the last second, coughing instead. He knew Blaise better than that, but his enthusiasm sometimes got away from him. Jefferson laced his fingers together, resting them atop one knee as he bit his lower lip to keep any potential comments at bay.

Apparently, Blaise knew how things looked. His cheeks flamed, and he shook his head as the box flipped closed. "It's not…I mean…" The Breaker made a frustrated sound.

"Whatever it is, it's only you and I here," Jefferson reminded him. "You have no reason to be embarrassed." At least he hoped Blaise never had reason to be embarrassed with him.

Blaise rubbed the back of his neck, though his shoulders lost some of their tension. "This conversation was a lot easier in my head."

Jefferson laughed. "That, I can understand." He eyed the box, unable to help his curiosity.

Blaise opened the box again. "It's for your trip."

"Oh." Jefferson watched as Blaise pulled the silver ring out from where it nestled in the cushion. What sort of ring would Blaise get him for his trip? "Is it for good luck?"

"Better," Blaise said, holding it in his palm. He had mastered himself, regaining his lost confidence. "It's supposed to prevent your magic from being detected."

At that, Jefferson pursed his lips. "You got me an enchanted ring? Blaise…how? They're so expensive. Especially *good* ones." And even without touching it, Jefferson saw it was a quality ring, on a par with his cabochon.

"I'm not as wealthy as you, but I'm not *poor*." Blaise's brow furrowed with indignation.

Jefferson sighed. "Sorry, that came out wrong. I'm just surprised. And honored. I know how costly things like this can be."

"Try it on," Blaise said, brushing away the apology.

Jefferson accepted the proffered ring, sliding it onto his left ring finger. It fit well, which led him to believe whoever had crafted it knew his size. Flora had had a hand in this, no doubt. As the silver loop settled against his skin, he felt whatever magic was within it activate, as his cabochon ring did. Only this was different. He gasped as something seared through him. He felt as if he'd suddenly been cut off from something. *Something important…oh.*

"What's wrong?" Blaise asked, noticing his discomfort.

Jefferson swallowed. "Ah, this ring seems to *cut off* my magic."

Blaise's eyes widened, and he flipped open the lid of the velvet box, pulling out a small piece of paper. He unfolded and read it, dismay crossing his face. "Oh. That's part of how it conceals your magic."

Jefferson studied the ring. It was a thing of beauty, a line of sigils engraved along the band. Something that gleamed like a fire opal blazed in the setting—no, it wasn't quite a fire opal. It was different but somehow familiar. He swallowed when he realized what he was looking at. "This ring has *ivory* from a unicorn's horn."

"I wondered what that was. Not sure I like that they had to use part of a unicorn for this. But I guess that makes sense." Blaise sighed, disappointment lining his face. "I didn't know it would lock out your magic. I only want you to be safe."

He was so earnest that Jefferson immediately put an arm around him, leaning over to give him a gentle kiss. "This is an incredibly thoughtful gift. And if it makes you feel better, I promise to wear it when I'm traveling with the delegation."

Blaise leaned against him. "It *would* make me feel better." His voice quavered, and he rested his head against Jefferson's shoulder.

The Breaker's worry reminded Jefferson of how delicate his situation was. If anyone found out Jefferson had magic, they would no doubt want to know what kind he had. And how he'd *gotten* it. *Your secret is safe with me. I promise.* But… "It will mean I can't visit you at night."

Blaise swallowed a lump in his throat. "It won't be forever."

"No, it won't," Jefferson agreed. He slipped the ring off, relief suffusing him as he felt the connection to his power return. Blaise held out the box, and Jefferson took it, nestling the ring inside. "I'll always think of you when I look at it."

Blaise glanced at him. "Did you think I was proposing?"

Yes. No. I don't know. I wish you would, but I know you won't. Not yet, anyway. I know you need time. All of those thoughts raced through Jefferson's mind in a blur. "I know you too well."

"That's not an answer."

"It is," Jefferson insisted. Blaise puffed out a breath. "Look, I know most things between us aren't easy for you. They don't come naturally, but you try. You're cautious and want to understand what something will cost you before you commit." He chuckled at the grudging look Blaise gave him. "What? You can't be mad that I'm right."

"I'm annoyed that you're accurate," Blaise grumbled, "which is another thing entirely."

Jefferson cocked his head. "You do realize the way I've survived this long is by figuring people out, yes? That's like ninety-five percent of my life as a politician and entrepreneur."

"And here I thought more of it would have to do with knowing who to sweet talk and where to invest your money."

Jefferson grinned. He rather enjoyed it when Blaise sassed back. "Obviously, that's the other five percent."

Blaise relaxed. "I guess I'll be glad for that, then. You'll probably need that with the delegation."

"No doubt," Jefferson agreed. He turned the box over in his hands, still charmed by all the effort Blaise had gone through on his behalf. "I'd rather not speak of that now, though. Better to focus on this moment."

Blaise took Jefferson's hand and gave it a light tug as he rose from the stone. "Come on. Let's go home."

"Already? I wouldn't mind watching the stars." Jefferson was reluctant to leave. The sooner they reached the bakery, the sooner dawn would come. A soft sound of amusement from Blaise caught his attention. "What?"

In answer, the Breaker merely raised his eyebrows.

"Let me guess. You expect me to use my amazing powers to figure you out, hmm?" Jefferson asked with a laugh.

"Something like that."

Jefferson rubbed his chin, suspecting what Blaise hinted at. "Forgive me, but in this, you lead and I follow. You're too important for me to risk misunderstanding."

Blaise's eyes softened, as if Jefferson had offered him something he hadn't known he needed. "You. I want you."

The Breaker's soft words sent a jolt of anticipation through Jefferson, his breath hitching. Blaise had firm boundaries. It had taken them time to reach an agreement to satisfy both of their needs. Jefferson craved the physical closeness that Blaise had never sought in his adult life. By all rights, that should have made them incompatible, but Jefferson had learned there was more to a relationship than lust.

A victorious rush of heat flooded through Jefferson's veins. "Do you, now?"

"I do," Blaise murmured, leaning in to capture his mouth in a kiss.

Oh yes, these unexpected moments were far better than any Jefferson had experienced in the past. He enjoyed the sugar-sweet taste of Blaise on his lips before pulling away. "Home?"

Blaise released a soft breath. "Home."

CHAPTER EIGHT

Break the Cycle

Blaise

Jefferson was warm beside him. Blaise didn't want to get up, didn't want to relinquish Jefferson to his responsibilities. Didn't want what they had to end. He was quite willing to ignore the incessant ring of the expensive, new-fangled alarm clock perched on the bedside table.

"Ugh, make it stop," Jefferson mumbled beside him, rolling over.

The blasted clock was closest to Blaise. He reached out to turn it off but missed, instead knocking it to the floor, where it continued to chime aggressively. Under normal circumstances, Blaise wouldn't mind the clock. But today? He considered using his magic on it, but it wasn't the clock's fault. He slung an arm over the side of the bed, fumbling until he found it. Blaise hauled it up and turned it off, then deposited it back on the bedside table.

Jefferson stirred, grumbling something as he came to wakefulness. The bare skin of his chest nestled snug against Blaise's back. Blaise shifted to face him, placing a hand against the other man's chest, contented by the rhythmic beat of the heart within.

"Getting handsy, are we?" Jefferson murmured, amusement in his voice.

"Don't ruin this," Blaise whispered.

Jefferson chuckled. "Nothing could ruin this. You're here with me, and there's *nothing* better." He placed a hand over Blaise's. "And we're opposites this way. As much as you shy away from touch, you know I crave it. I'll miss this, so thank you."

Blaise knew. And while it was true he disliked most touch, he didn't mind Jefferson as much as others. Jefferson was safe. And complicated. And sometimes not complicated at all. "I thought about breaking the clock."

Jefferson withdrew his hand, undaunted by Blaise's odd change of topic. "Better the clock wake us than Flora."

Flora. He owed her cinnamon rolls, plus whatever Jefferson wanted. Blaise glanced at the window. It was still dark, with no sign that the sun had any intention of coming up soon.

"We could stay curled up and warm here for another hour," Jefferson suggested with a yawn.

"I would, but cinnamon rolls don't bake themselves." Blaise leaned over to kiss him. "And I need to have the oven warm before Reuben arrives."

"Mmm, the demands of a small business owner," Jefferson marveled, satisfied. "I love the sound of free enterprise in the morning."

Blaise snorted a laugh. "Wait until I tell you I have to do the inventory later."

"Just when I thought you couldn't possibly be any more attractive to me..." Jefferson propped himself up on one elbow, grinning.

Blaise's cheeks warmed with pleasure. He ducked his head and pulled away, sitting up and swinging his legs over the side of the bed. The sudden draft was a stark reminder of his lack of clothing. He rose and crossed to the trunk that contained his limited wardrobe, dragging the lid open. Blaise even picked out clothing that matched, declaring a truce in their ongoing style battle.

When he looked up, Jefferson was watching him intently, as if the other man were trying to commit him to memory. "Last night, you told me that when I got up, you needed to get ready, too," Blaise commented, nodding at the nearby selection of clothing Jefferson had laid out the previous evening.

"The Jefferson of last night has no appreciation for the fact that Present Jefferson would like to stay curled up in the blankets. Preferably with you."

Blaise snorted. "Past Jefferson told me to tell you that you can't stay in bed. If you do, you'll never be ready in time, and you don't want to be late."

"I dislike Past Jefferson." Though, despite his complaint, Jefferson sat up, raking a hand through his hair. It was unfair that even disheveled, he still looked *good.*

"Future Jefferson will like the cinnamon rolls that will be waiting for him later, though," Blaise said as he buttoned his shirt. "So, you've got that going for you."

With a yawn and a stretch, Jefferson lumbered up from the bed, collecting his clothing. "Would you like a hand in the bakery until Reuben arrives?"

The question distracted Blaise, and he misjudged the next button, forcing it out of alignment. He glanced down to fix it. "I wouldn't say no." Jefferson's offer made him feel warm and squishy. And loved.

Blaise finished dressing first, heading down to start the fire. Jefferson joined him a short time later, and together they set to work. While the dough rose, they shared a quiet breakfast. By the time the cinnamon rolls were ready, Reuben had arrived to start his workday. Flora bowled in a short time later, eager for her promised pastries.

Then, before they knew it, Jefferson had to head to the stables to meet the rest of the small delegation. Blaise picked up Jefferson's saddlebag, impressed by how much clothing he had stuffed into it.

"I could get that," Jefferson said.

Blaise smiled. "You could, but I want to." He hefted it in one hand. "You have clothes in Nera, don't you?"

"Well, yes, but I needed some for on the road, too," Jefferson pointed out as they strode out the door.

"He wouldn't be caught dead wearing the same clothing twice in a row!" Flora called to their backs.

Jefferson sighed. "I have a certain reputation to uphold." He tucked a hand inside his coat pocket, as if checking for something. The telltale dark blue velvet of the ring box was visible for a heartbeat before the Dreamer eased it back inside. Jefferson caught Blaise's eye and winked.

They drew to a stop outside the stables. Seledora and the other pegasi who would travel with the delegation were already outside, saddled and waiting for their riders. Their coats gleamed in the early morning sunlight, their sleek wings tucked against their sides.

Blaise didn't like goodbyes—they were awkward and uncomfortable. Often heart-wrenching. He wanted to kiss Jefferson, to taste him one more time. But he was painfully aware that they had an audience, so he shifted his weight and rubbed the back of his neck as he tried to figure out how to make this *right*.

"Why are you frowning?" Jefferson asked.

Blaise sighed. "Because the last time I kissed you and we parted ways, things didn't go so well for me."

At his admission, Jefferson stepped closer, warmth in his eyes. "This is *not* like that. But if you want to break the cycle, *I'll* kiss *you*."

Break the cycle. Blaise liked that idea—he was a Breaker, after all. He gave an almost imperceptible nod, but Jefferson was watching for it. The other man swooped in, tugging Blaise into a proprietary embrace. Jefferson paused, aiming a saucy grin at him, lifting a hand to trace the line of Blaise's jaw.

"Remember this." Jefferson's voice was husky with emotion. Then their lips met. For the moment, Blaise's world contracted to only him and Jefferson. He focused on the feel of Jefferson's lean frame against him, the citrus tang of the cologne wafting from his neck.

Someone nearby whooped encouragement, distracting Blaise. *Flora.* Of course, it was Flora. Other voices chimed in, a clamor of appreciation for their show of affection.

"Well, that's mortifying," Blaise muttered, close against Jefferson.

"No, it's not. They're happy for you," Jefferson whispered, gently placing his forehead against Blaise's. He held on to Blaise like he didn't want to let go, though after a moment, he loosened his grip.

Blaise stepped back, ducking his head shyly. He would never be used to being the center of attention, not the way Jefferson was. But Jefferson was right—when he hazarded a glance, those still looking his way were smiling, joy on their faces. Happiness had been in short supply for many of the recent settlers in Fortitude. Blaise supposed he gave them hope.

"Don't forget: this isn't *goodbye*. It's *see you later*." Jefferson touched Blaise's chin, thumb brushing against beard. Then he drew his hand away, moving toward Seledora.

Blaise nodded, though the other man couldn't see it. He allowed a smile to reach his lips. He rubbed his chin where Jefferson had touched him, then pivoted to look for Emrys. Blaise didn't have to go far. The black stallion had come to see the delegation off as well, though he was most interested in Seledora.

<Did you slip sugar cookies into Jefferson's saddlebags like you promised?> Emrys asked, nostrils fluttering.

Blaise reached up and smoothed the stallion's wild forelock. "Yes, and I even left him a note, so he'll know that he's supposed to share with Seledora."

Emrys blew out a contented breath. <She will like that, I hope.> He flicked his ears in Seledora's direction. Blaise smiled. His pegasus was trying very hard to court Jefferson's attorney.

"I haven't met a pegasus yet who dislikes a good sugar cookie," Blaise said with a chuckle. He knew for a fact Seledora enjoyed them, though as with most things, she liked to hide her pleasure. All the same, he had taken notice of the way she peered out of her stall office when she thought he might come around with cookies or some other baked treat.

With one hand on Emrys's neck, Blaise turned to take in the rest of the people gathered. He found Jack there, the outlaw watching his wife with smoldering intensity as she swung into the saddle. Blaise was still getting used to the man Wildfire Jack Dewitt turned into under the influence of his wife. The Effigest lost some of the serrated sharpness that made him prickly to deal with. *Some*—not all. Blaise wondered how Jack was going to cope with his wife gone for weeks, possibly months.

And how am I going to deal with Jefferson being gone that long?

Blaise pushed the thought away, wincing as he recalled Jack's suggestion to travel to Rainbow Flat with him. He wasn't sure he wanted to have the outlaw along for company if he devolved into the snarly, difficult man he often was without Kittie around. But Emmaline was supposed to accompany them, and if he would get his act together for anyone, it was her.

"Daddy, stop making stupid cow-eyes at Mom so she can go," Blaise heard Emmaline say nearby.

Her comment stirred Jack, and the outlaw swung his gaze to her, scowling. "That's *not* what I was doing."

Blaise ambled over, deciding that maybe he should get involved before Jack said something stupid that set back all the progress he'd made with Emmaline. Not that the outlaw would even remotely see it that way. "She has a point. It's either that or it's the same look you have when you're figuring out how to murder someone."

"None of your sass," the Effigest growled, though there was a hint of amusement in his voice. "Besides, not as if you can talk after all your canoodling with that peacock."

"Pot, meet kettle," Kittie called from the back of a chestnut pegasus, looming over them. "He's not the *only* one that's been canoodling, and you know it."

Jack narrowed his eyes, attempting to glare at his wife, who only met his look with a playful grin. "Making me feel outnumbered here."

"You know you love it when the odds are stacked against you," Kittie said, and there was a depth of fondness in her voice that made Blaise smile. "You behave while I'm gone, *Wildfire* Jack Dewitt."

"Not making any promises I can't keep," the outlaw said, which was probably the most truthful response he could make.

"I expect nothing less." Kittie blew a kiss to her husband and daughter, then waved as her pegasus joined the others.

A few moments later, Blaise stood beside Emrys, Jack, and Emmaline as the small delegation receded into tiny specks before they were lost to the horizon. A profound feeling of loneliness tugged at Blaise's heart, as if Jefferson's absence were a physical malady. Emrys bumped his shoulder with his velvet-soft nose, a silent reminder that Blaise wasn't alone.

Boots crunched on the dirt as Jack and Emmaline turned. The Effigest's eyes glinted with a mix of…was that sadness and worry? Jack brushed at one eye, his mouth deepening into a scowl when he realized Blaise was watching.

"So, when are we going to Rainbow Flat?" Emmaline asked, as if she sensed that both Blaise and her father needed a distraction from their messy emotions.

Rainbow Flat. Maybe a trip really would be good for him. And it seemed that no matter what, they were going to encourage him to go. Blaise exhaled a soft breath. "In a couple of days. That'll give us time to pack and get things settled with the bakery and…whatever it is Jack actually does around here."

The outlaw snorted. "What I do around here is more useful than you, cookie."

Blaise hid a smile. He knew exactly what Jack did. Even though the outlaw put on a show that his biggest contribution to Fortitude was the occasional heist he pulled off on Confederation stagecoaches or pack-trains, Blaise knew that he was so much more. Jack was the spider who tended to the web of information that kept them all safe. He was in charge of the sentries, their first line of defense. Jack was *important* to their growing town, even if he pretended to be nothing more than a bandit.

"But yeah, a few days to get things settled is good," Jack murmured.

CHAPTER NINE

A Lack of Hospitality

Jefferson

Flying astride a pegasus was one of Jefferson's great pleasures. He loved every moment, though he would have enjoyed it even more with Blaise and Emrys nearby. He glanced over his shoulder, hoping to see the black stallion bobbing through the air. It was nothing more than a flight of fancy but one Jefferson couldn't help but continue to entertain.

<You have other things to focus on,> Seledora reminded him as they soared through the last of the red rock ravines that gave the Gutter its name.

Jefferson sighed. All of this had seemed more tolerable when he was talking about doing it. Now that it had him apart from Blaise, though? Never had he expected to become so spellbound by someone. In the past, he would have relished this task. It would have given him life. Now? He didn't mind it, but it didn't thrill him as it once might have.

Seledora flew in the lead. Kittie's chestnut pegasus stayed on the grey's right flank, while Mindy's pegasus was on the left. Flora, on the white pegasus, Tylos, who she had flown with before, brought up the rear. Tylos wasn't as robust as the other pegasi, and they had to stop every hour to allow the small stallion a break. Jefferson didn't mind, though. Like Kittie and Mindy, he wasn't accustomed to the demands of a sustained pegasus flight, and the opportunities to stretch were welcome.

During one of the breaks, Seledora caught him fidgeting with the velvet box. <What is that?>

He glanced at her. Of their group, only Flora and Seledora knew about his magic. "Blaise gave it to me." When he was certain no prying ears were near, he explained what the ring did.

Seledora snorted. <That was a good idea. Knowledge of your magic would no doubt endanger this delegation.>

She was right. He knew it in his heart, but he still disliked it. It was a little frightening how quickly he felt like his magic was an intrinsic part of him. Jefferson wasn't looking forward to being cut off from it.

"How much further to the first town?" Kittie called, striding over and interrupting his thoughts.

Jefferson pulled the map out of his saddlebag at her question. This part of their travel was easy—it was simply a matter of following the Deadwood River out of the Gutter. But their evening accommodations weren't something he was looking forward to. The most suitable lodgings he could locate were at Courage's End, a town in the country of Mella that had cropped up in the shadow of Fort Courage. It was that or go well out of their way to a town in Desina, and they would lose too much time doing that.

"At our current pace, we should be there by midafternoon," Jefferson said, tracing his fingers along the blue ribbon of river.

She nodded and went back to her mount. Moments later, their group was airborne again, and Jefferson's thoughts turned to their destination. Of their group, only Flora had been present at the assault that had destroyed the fort. But Kittie's daughter had been held there. And Jefferson's tie to the disaster was more personal than he liked.

As they flew in, the ruins of the fort were like the hulking skeleton of a slain beast. The massive stones of toppled towers and the metal ribs that had enclosed the mighty hull of the *Retribution* grappled as if frozen in the throes of death. Jefferson's breath caught. How had Blaise survived that? By all rights, he should have been crushed, as so many others had been. *I should never have asked him to break the* Retribution. *I could have lost him.*

"Land here, please," Jefferson called to Seledora over the rush of wind.

The grey pegasus alighted near the ruins, the other pegasi following her lead. Flora peered at him, brows arched. Kittie and Mindy studied the destroyed fort. The Pyromancer's mouth was a grim line, her eyes narrow.

"Blaise did that?" Mindy's question was a whisper on the breeze.

"He had to." Jefferson swallowed, thinking of the disasters that Blaise had averted with his magic. And the price the Breaker had paid to do so.

"I know," Mindy agreed, placing a hand on his arm. "I was there when the Salties attacked Itude." Her yellow eyes narrowed, bitter memories no doubt rising to mind. "Maybe I'm only wishing he could have done it sooner." Then she exhaled a whistling breath, shaking her head. "Sorry, that's probably not a thing someone in this delegation should say."

"Don't confuse Ganland with the Salt-Iron Confederation," Jefferson said, smiling as both Kittie and Mindy turned to pin him with sharp looks.

"How can we not?" Kittie asked, gesturing to the battered airship. "Ganland is *part* of the Confederation."

"Let's continue on, and I'll explain," Jefferson said. He had wanted to see the carcass of his airship, and he had. It was a reminder that he had made mistakes in the past, and they'd had consequences. Even though, at the time, he thought it was the right thing to do. And maybe it had been the right thing. The *only* thing.

He shook his head, banishing the unpleasant thoughts. Jefferson was more than happy to explain the intricacies of the Confederation, if only to take his mind off his own guilt. "Think of the Salt-Iron Confederation like a family. United by name and perhaps blood ties, but still full of individuals."

"But the Salt-Iron Council passes on most of the same laws to all of them," Mindy pointed out. "So, it's as if they're no different at all. And Confederation soldiers represent *every* nation."

The Hospitalier was delightfully astute. Jefferson nodded. "Those are both true—to an extent. As far as the soldiers go, each nation also has its own separate military. Some, like Ganland, boast a navy as well. And while the laws are often passed down to all the nations, there is still wiggle room for differences at a national level. Which is why Ganland is overall more friendly to mages." He made a face. "They still must be registered and tattooed, but it's more difficult to force them into an indenture." Difficult, but not impossible. And Jefferson knew only too well that there was a thriving, seedy underbelly of those who would snag mages and traffic them.

"Doesn't spare them if a Saltie Tracker and unicorn come across them, though," Kittie said quietly. "They can overrule the local laws."

"Yes, they can," Jefferson agreed, pressing a hand against the pocket where his new ring nestled. Guilt pulled at him. He would need to put it on soon. He cleared his throat. "Ah, and here's the town where we'll spend the night."

Courage's End was composed of buildings cobbled together from the ruined timber and stone of the fort. Townsfolk silently edged out of their homes and businesses as the delegation entered the outskirts, their expressions grudging. The pegasi had hidden their wings as soon as they approached the town, but the suspicious eyes spoke volumes. They knew who had come to town, and none of the citizens appreciated their appearance. Jefferson was going to have to smooth things over as he normally did: with money. Doubling someone's income could ease mistrust and anger better than words.

The mistrust wouldn't die, though. That would likely never be fully erased from those who had seen the fort fall. Those who had loved ones smashed beneath the fallen airship or crushed by stone. Shot by outlaws. Jefferson wouldn't begrudge them those feelings.

"Someone should stay with the pegasi tonight. Just in case," Kittie suggested, as they bowed their heads close over a table in the town's diner. Mindy had pronounced their food fit for eating. That didn't mean it *tasted* good—it only meant it wouldn't kill them.

"I will," Flora volunteered with a nonchalant wave. "I'll take the last watch."

"I'll take the second," Kittie said.

Jefferson yawned. "I suppose that leaves me with the first."

Flora eyed him. "You're going to fall asleep, aren't you?"

"No." Jefferson crossed his arms, rather offended by her lack of faith in his ability to stay up into the wee hours. "It's waking up that I have a problem with."

"I can take the watch," Mindy offered with a shrug. "I'm not tired yet."

Though the afternoon had taken more out of Jefferson than he cared to admit, he still wanted to contribute to their group. "Are you certain? I'd be happy to take the watch."

The Hospitalier read the bald-faced lie in his words. She waved a hand. "I insist."

Jefferson wasn't going to argue any further. With that decided, he excused himself and found their room. They had to sleep four in a single room. The hosteler claimed he had no other accommodations, although there seemed to be no one else staying at the inn. As much as Jefferson had wanted to argue, he hadn't. Not after the way some of the citizens had stared at their group, hatred burning in their eyes.

The room only had one bed, though simple sleeping mats provided small comfort. Not much, though. As Jefferson undressed, he glanced wistfully at the bed but decided he should cede it to one of the ladies. He doubted even the bed would prove to be that comfortable.

He laid down on a mat, huffing in annoyance at how stiff it was. Even the extra pillow was one big lump, like resting one's head on week-old bread. *Actually, week-old bread is probably softer.*

Fortunately, riding a pegasus all day was tiring, and it wasn't long before his muscles relaxed and his mind drifted to sleep. The dreamscape opened around him like the petals of a flower. Jefferson stretched out his awareness, searching for Blaise. He had never been so physically far away from the Breaker, but he'd decided that if he could still cage Gregor Gaitwood from such a distance, he could locate Blaise.

There. Jefferson found a hint of Blaise, but he wasn't asleep. He had lulled his beau to sleep before, but only when they were close and Jefferson knew Blaise wanted to sleep. So far away, Jefferson didn't want to risk pulling him into slumber during an awkward moment. He would wait and try again later.

He took the time to renew Gregor's dream prison. Jefferson heard the Doyen's angry shouts as he approached. "*Sorcerer!* Let me go!" Something rattled. Hands against the bars on the door.

Jefferson walked up, standing a foot away from the cell. He narrowed his eyes, the carnage of Fort Courage fresh on his mind. *I may have asked Blaise to break the airship, but he wouldn't have had to do it if not for the Gaitwoods.* "No. This is what you deserve. Death is the only other escape, and that's too easy." Jefferson clenched his jaw, silently adding, *I want you to suffer.*

Gregor stared at him, his eyes glazed like a feral beast. "*Deserve? I* don't deserve this. I'm not the *filthy magelover* here. No." The Doyen paused, wheezing. "I'm going to make sure *you* get what *you* deserve."

"Best of luck with that," Jefferson said, finishing his renewal. "Pleasant dreams." Okay, perhaps it was cruel to taunt the nightmare-plagued Doyen—wait, never mind. It absolutely wasn't cruel. Not after all he had done to Blaise. Jefferson turned and stalked away, ignoring Gregor's indignant demands.

That task done, he reached out for the Breaker again, this time relieved to discover that he was asleep. Jefferson was always careful when approaching Blaise in his dreams, as deliberate as he would treat his beau if they were together. Jefferson made the equivalent of a knock at the door, though there was no door. It was difficult to describe, but that was how he thought of it. The way between him and Blaise opened as the other man let him in.

Blaise cocked his head, eyeing Jefferson. "What part of promising to wear that ring did you not understand?"

"*How was your flight, Jefferson? Oh, it wasn't bad, thank you for asking,*" Jefferson parroted, hoping to finagle his way into Blaise's good graces with a reminder of etiquette. "You can berate me after pleasantries."

The corners of the Breaker's mouth twisted up in amusement he failed to hide. "Fine. How was your flight?"

"Missing you," Jefferson admitted, gratified when a genuine smile spread across Blaise's face. "And before you start on your spiel about how disappointed you are that I'm not wearing the ring—I promise I *will.* Tomorrow. You can't fault me for wanting to see you again."

Blaise's shoulders relaxed. "I miss you, too." He glanced around as Jefferson called on his magic, weaving the dreamscape into something new. "What's this?"

Jefferson smiled. "You wanted me to show you places I've been, right? Allow me to show you where I'm going. You've seen my estate outside Nera but not much else. Since you can't be there with me, let me show it to you tonight."

Blaise licked his lips, crossing his arms. "And then tomorrow you'll wear the ring?"

"And then tomorrow I'll wear the ring," Jefferson agreed, though it stung to know it would muzzle his power. He didn't want to be cut off from Blaise.

Blaise smiled. "Show me."

<hr>

To say the hospitality was lacking was to suggest there had been hospitality at all. None of them had slept well that night—but they had slept, and the pegasi were unbothered, which Jefferson considered a victory.

The straw in the pegasi's box stalls had the musty smell of mold, and when Flora asked after it, she was told it was all that was available. For their evening meal, the pegasi had to settle for oats—none of the sweet feed that the equines loved so dearly was anywhere to be found. At least the oats weren't fouled, according to Mindy, whose magic seemed to work for the pegasi as well. Jefferson consoled their steeds by splitting the treasure trove of precious cookies from Blaise that he'd found packed in his saddlebags.

At breakfast, the staff conveniently *forgot* to bring their meals, and by the time their food arrived, it was cold. The scrambled eggs tasted like runny boot leather (or so Jefferson imagined), and the bacon would have made fine shingles, but Mindy whispered they were otherwise fine.

"I don't recall the Mellans being so petty," Mindy commented as they led their fully tacked pegasi out of the stables. None of them had trusted the stable hands to tack up the equines, so had done it themselves.

"It doesn't excuse them, but they have a reason for their poor behavior," Jefferson reminded them softly, casting a meaningful look over his shoulder toward the fallen fort. It wasn't visible from their current location, blocked by the nearby trees, but they understood.

Kittie set her jaw, eyes narrowed, as she laid a hand against the neck of her chestnut mare. She looked as if she wanted to say something, but she kept it to herself. Jefferson found he liked Kittie Dewitt for her spirit and drive. He only knew bits and pieces of her story, much of it gleaned from Blaise. He didn't know what she had endured. From Flora, he'd learned Kittie had once been seen as a threat to the Confederation, called the Firebrand. A fiery woman who spoke out against the oppression of mages. Something had dampened her fire, but she seemed to be slowly regaining it.

<Our tack is secure, and we are ready to be under way,> Seledora informed him.

Jefferson nodded to her. "Very good. I'll settle our bill at the inn, and we'll be off."

He strode into the building, one hand over his coin purse. He wouldn't put it past someone to cut it free. It would be a setback, though nothing insurmountable. The bill he was about to pay was highway robbery as it was. The hosteler watched him approach, face impassive as he leaned against a table.

"I've brought the rest of the agreed-upon payment," Jefferson said as he opened the pouch, drawing out a handful of gold coins. They glittered in the low light.

"You won't be paying in coin," a dangerous voice growled behind him.

Jefferson swallowed, slipping the coins back into the purse and snugging the laces. He turned slowly, dismayed by the trio of burly men edging in to block his escape. They were built like bulls, their arms muscular and chests broad. Former Confederation soldiers? Veterans from Fort Courage with a bone to pick? That was the most likely answer.

"We know who you're traveling with, *magelover*," one of the other men sneered.

"Really? You're using tired old insults like that?" Jefferson asked to buy time. He took a half-step back, though there wasn't much room to maneuver with the wall behind him. "I'm sure you gentlemen can do better than that. Perhaps we should behave like civilized men, since this is a place of business." Jefferson hazarded a glance at the hosteler. The man was watching them with little enthusiasm, though Jefferson didn't miss the plump bag of coins resting on the counter beside him.

His gut clenched. The hosteler was being paid to look the other way. This was a set-up. No doubt they had pegged him as the weakest member of the group. The non-mage. The dandy. They were ready to make an example of him. But he wasn't without options—he only had to buy time, or so he hoped. *Seledora, I hope you're listening. A little help would be welcome.*

Jefferson lifted his chin, drawing on every bit of arrogance he possessed—which, honestly, was bloody hard when he was mere inches from being stomped by this nefarious trio. "I'll ask you gentlemen to step aside one more time so that I can settle my bill, and I'll be on my way."

"You can settle your bill with blood," the stocky man in the middle said, pounding his knuckles into the meat of his palm.

Then they were in motion, flying at him with murder in their eyes. Jefferson barely had time to dodge a beefy fist, though it grazed his cheek, throwing him off balance. A heavy body slammed into him, knocking him against the wall with such force the air whooshed from his lungs. Jefferson's vision wavered as his attacker smashed him against the wall as if he were a ragdoll.

A memory of a time in the past seized him, a time when he thought Jack was about to kill him. The only difference was, to the outlaw, it had been a game, a ruse to test Jefferson's magic. Now it was real. He pulled on his magic with all his might, shoving it at his attacker. *Sleepsleepsleep, please! Sleep, damn it!*

His cast slipped around the brute like a lasso, though it was sloppy, and the man evaded it. Desperate, Jefferson sent out another coil of magic, pulling it taut. He dragged the unwilling man into slumber. Into a blank dreamscape that Jefferson didn't have the time or presence of mind to populate with anything.

The man slumped to the floor with a resounding thud. Jefferson groaned, then tensed when he felt new hands grasp his upper arms, holding tight. Panic rose again, and he flung out his magic, prepared to use it against his new assailants. But just as quickly, he called it back as he recognized Flora and Kittie peering at him with worry in their eyes.

Blood spatter peppered Flora's cheek, though Jefferson presumed it didn't belong to her. The half-knocker's lips pursed as she considered the downed man.

"Are you hurt?" Kittie asked. She reeked of smoke, as if she had spontaneously combusted someone. Jefferson couldn't see any nearby piles of ash.

Jefferson took a gasping breath and nodded, not trusting his voice immediately. He straightened, smoothing the lapels of his mussed greatcoat and brushing a clod of dirt from one sleeve. Let them think he was a preening peacock. He didn't care. In truth, he was shaken up, but he knew from his many years as a Doyen that this wasn't the time to show weakness.

"Who do these goons belong to?" Flora asked, hiking a thumb at the sleeping man. The other two were down as well—one of them was nursing a long gash down the length of one thigh and whimpering, while the other appeared unharmed but was staring at Kittie with wide, white-rimmed eyes.

"Never seen them before in my life!" the hosteler said, holding his hands up. Jefferson noted that the money bag had vanished, secreted away, no doubt.

Jefferson rolled his shoulders. *Ugh, I'm going to have some bruises, but at least I have my life.* "Unbelievable. Such a shame that I can travel to the Gutter and Untamed Territory without so much as a hair on my head bothered, and here I am, attacked on Confederation ground!" Never mind that he had outlaws in Rainbow Flat on his payroll to make certain nothing happened to him. And he had Blaise. They didn't know that. He shook his head and tut-tutted, arrowing a look at the hosteler. "How unfortunate that I'll have to spread the word in Ganland that this part of Mella is *inhospitable.*"

The hosteler swallowed, realizing that the threat was financial more than anything else. *Hit them where it hurts: in the coin purse.* It was an adage that had worked well for him in the past. "Now, don't be hasty, Mr. Cole. All's well that ends well, you know. As I said, I've never seen 'em before." His beady eyes cut to the thugs.

Never seen them before, indeed. But I'll play your game. Jefferson inclined his head. "Then you won't be opposed to us calling our bill fair and settled before I pay the rest. Seeing as they attacked me in *your* establishment, and no one but my companions lifted a hand in my defense."

This demand pained the hosteler, but he knew he was on tricky footing. Requiring full payment now, after this, would only drive home their lack of care and hospitality for guests. He licked his lips as he weighed the options, then ducked his head in agreement. "There's a Healer up the road. Visit her before you leave town. Tell her Ivan sent you and to tend to you at no charge."

"Thank you for the offer, but I'll be fine," Jefferson replied. He wouldn't trust a Healer, not in this town. A Healer could do just as much harm with their magic as they could good.

He strode out of the inn, proud that he didn't limp or move too stiffly, though his body complained every step of the way. Flying would not be fun today, not at all.

Seledora was waiting outside, ears pricked. Her nostrils flared as she read his scent. <I sent the powerful ones in when I picked up the threads of danger in your thoughts.>

"It's appreciated," Jefferson murmured, rubbing her forehead. He hated to consider how it might have turned out if not for that saving grace.

Flora sheathed her blades, gathering up Tylos's reins. "What was that about?"

"I'm not sure. They may be Confederation veterans who have a bone to pick with outlaws," Jefferson answered, wiggling his fingers and toes to be sure everything was intact. Nothing seemed broken, though he had skinned areas beneath his clothing that were going to chafe in flight. And too many bruises to even catalog. All in all, he had been lucky, and he knew it.

Mindy frowned, her pale eyes flicking over him. "I'll figure something out that'll help you feel a little better once we're out of this town."

"Thank you," Jefferson murmured.

"Is this sort of reception going to be an ongoing problem for us?" Kittie asked.

Jefferson winced. It was a valid question. "I don't know," he said, rubbing Seledora's muzzle as he thought. "It may. But we won't let that stop us." *We can't let it stop us because then they'll get exactly what they want.*

Kittie nodded. "Good. We'll have to be more vigilant."

"I let you out of my sight for *two minutes*," Flora huffed.

"I was paying the bill. Completely normal transaction." Jefferson sighed. "Let's put this town behind us, shall we?"

CHAPTER TEN

Grave Dancing

Jefferson

Fortunately, after the dust-up with the thugs in Courage's End, nothing else unusual cropped up to interrupt their journey. Jefferson supposed it helped that on the second night, they stayed in Ondin, the capital of Mella. As soon as they approached the city, he slipped on his ring—as he had promised Blaise he would.

They spent the following evening in Sunrise Harbor, the last major town before they would briefly cross into Petria, and then on to Ganland. Jefferson had mixed feelings about their lodging for the fourth evening of their trip.

Seaside. The pegasi landed a few miles outside the town, and Seledora jigged as she sensed his unease. Flora was watching him closely, too. She knew his long history as a Wells around Seaside. Kittie and Mindy didn't, though luckily, neither of them knew enough to ask. He suspected Kittie knew of his double life, but she was savvy enough to not bring it up. Mindy had no idea, and as much as Jefferson liked the Hospitalier, he was happy to keep her in the dark. The more people who knew his secrets, the harder they became to conceal.

"We'll be staying in the finest hotel Seaside has to offer," Jefferson told them, feigning false cheer as they rode to the town. "It's on the beach, and the sunrise will be absolutely splendid. If you're the sort to wake up that early."

"I will," Mindy said, her eyes bright at the prospect. The Hospitalier had relaxed once they put Courage's End behind them. "I'll have time to go to the beach, right? How many days are we staying here?"

Jefferson smiled at her eagerness. He was glad their excursion would be pleasant for someone, at least. "Three days, and then we'll be on the road again." He glanced at Kittie. "You're welcome to enjoy the beach as well. The afternoons are often balmy in the autumn, and I think you'll find it refreshing. There are swimming outfits we can buy in town."

Kittie had a dubious expression on her face. "I've never gone swimming before. I don't know how."

"You can wade, too," Mindy pointed out.

The two women immersed themselves in a conversation about beach activities. Jefferson fed them additional information when asked but otherwise left them to it. The pegasi hid their wings as they entered the town at Jefferson's request. Overall, he didn't mind people knowing that the Gutter delegation of outlaws and pegasi was coming through. But right here, right now, he didn't want to draw any undue attention to himself.

They found the hotel on the beach, a beautiful stable next to it. The pegasi were enthusiastic about their accommodations, too—especially when Jefferson suggested they might enjoy playing on the beach. Seledora declined, however. He wasn't sure if it was because she was too straight-laced to romp on the beach or because she was worried about him. While he suspected the latter, the grey mare wouldn't admit to such a thing.

Their group settled for the night. The pegasi happily munched on the finest sweet feed they'd had for several days while their riders had a veritable feast at the hotel. Jefferson felt as if something was right in his world again, at least. A good meal in a beautiful setting always did wonders. *The only thing missing is Blaise.*

The next morning, Flora wandered off to *look into some things* while Jefferson showed Kittie and Mindy to the swim shop. Not only did the shop boast an array of outfits designed for the water, but also rubber bladders filled with air, fishing poles, buckets, and sundry items for anyone seeking a day of fun.

Jefferson eyed the swimsuits with appreciation. It had been years since he'd hit the beach in Seaside, and the last time he'd had the chance, full-body wool swimsuits had been the rage. Now…well. Times had changed, and so had fashion, it seemed. The women's swimwear boasted shorter skirts that clung to just above the knee, and bare shoulders were a common theme. The men's swimsuits had pants that ended at the knee as well, with form-fitting, short-sleeved shirts. Jefferson considered a purchase of his own as the ladies shopped.

Kittie held up a sapphire swimsuit while Mindy grinned. The Pyromancer seemed torn, though.

"If it's the price that's stopping you, that's not a problem at all," Jefferson said.

She shook her head. "It's not that. I've never worn something like this before."

"Ah." Jefferson considered the problem. It hadn't occurred to him that Kittie might prefer modesty. Like the other women of Fortitude, she favored trousers over skirts. Jefferson assumed it was because trousers were so much more versatile for the hard life in the Gutter. Perhaps there was more at play, though. "Keep looking. Maybe you'll see something else you like."

But Kittie seemed drawn to the sapphire. While Mindy selected a floral number, Kittie hemmed and hawed over her decision. At last, she nodded and brought it to the counter, though she and Mindy only grudgingly allowed Jefferson to pay since they didn't have enough funds to cover the outfits.

"There, now you'll be properly attired for a day of relaxation," Jefferson said as they walked up the street, heading back to the hotel.

Kittie stared down at the folded swimsuit in her arms. She said nothing, but her eyes narrowed as if she were thinking. Jefferson wondered what was on her mind.

When they made it back to the floor where their rooms were located, Jefferson caught Kittie's attention while Mindy hurried off to change. The Pyromancer frowned, though she followed him into his room when he beckoned.

"Is something bothering you?" Jefferson asked.

Kittie drew her bottom lip into her mouth, chewing it for a moment before sighing. "I don't know if you'll understand."

He shrugged. "I can certainly try. But if you'd rather not..."

Kittie shook her head. "Do you ever feel like...you're trying to be someone you're not? As if you're trying to reinvent yourself?"

Jefferson's brow arched. For a moment, he wondered if she was prodding at his dual identities in a roundabout way, but she seemed... distracted. No, she was thinking this about herself. That was interesting. "I have some understanding of that, yes."

She lifted her gaze to meet his, momentary humor on her face. "I suppose you do. The fact is, I'm trying to figure out who I am now." Kittie rubbed her cheek. "When I was young, I was the Firebrand. Then I lost everyone I cared about, and...well, I can't be that woman anymore. I'm a husk of who I was." Kittie swallowed. "Then I got Jack and Emmaline back. And now I'm trying to reconcile the spirit of the Firebrand with a charred husk."

That is some vivid imagery. I think I see why she was the Firebrand. Jefferson offered her a sympathetic smile. "Can't you be something new?"

"But I have to be the *Firebrand*," Kittie said. "I don't think I'm strong enough to be what I was before."

Jefferson cocked his head, trying to think of a metaphor that would work. "Have you ever seen a forest fire?"

Kittie snorted a laugh. "I've *caused* one. It was an accident, but…" She shrugged and didn't elaborate.

Well, that's concerning. He cleared his throat. "Right. Understand the cycle of the forest. The pines live, they burn, and though the fire destroys, it also makes new life. New trees replace the old."

Kittie opened her mouth to respond, then snapped it shut as if his words had hit her between the eyes. She blinked at him in surprise. "You're a lot smarter than Jack gives you credit for."

Jefferson chuckled. "Thank you. I think. Do you feel better now?"

Kittie smiled, nodding. She glanced down at the sapphire swimsuit. "I do. And now I think I'll see how this looks on me and then head down to the beach."

Jefferson watched as she headed out the door. The irony wasn't lost on him. Kittie was reinventing herself while Jefferson was burying an old part of himself.

* * *

Flora returned that evening, holing up with Jefferson to give him the rundown on what she'd learned. "I made the rounds, and I have a pretty good idea of who's in town for the big shindig."

"It's a *funeral*, not a party," Jefferson muttered, watching as Flora helped herself to the wet bar.

The half-knocker snorted. "You say that, but you wouldn't know it, judging by the so-called mourners. I swear, half of them are here to dance on your—on Malcolm's grave."

Now her errand made a lot more sense. Jefferson hadn't even stopped to consider who might show up for the funeral. No, his mind had been on other things. Which was another point that made him glad for Flora. "Oh?"

"Your Doyen buddies are here. Leonora, Aaron, and Seward. Oh, and Seward's wife, Lizzie." Flora ticked off the count on her fingers, listing several other Doyens before narrowing her eyes. "And Gregor Gaitwood."

Jefferson's mouth went dry at that. He reached over and picked up the glass of wine he'd ordered to enjoy for the evening, taking a restorative sip. "Oh? And how is dear Gregor?" *Was he screaming incoherently? Babbling mindless gibberish?*

Flora tapped a finger to her temple. "Something squirrelly going on with him. I guess a remnant from when you shoved him into the dreamscape and whisked his brains like they were cracked eggs."

Jefferson nodded, not bothering to correct her. The only one who knew even half of what Jefferson had done to Gregor was Blaise. "And yet he maintains his position?"

"Somehow," she agreed, though she was bothered by that, too. "I thought there was a clause that Doyens could be forced to resign if they were unfit for duty?"

"There was," Jefferson said. He pulled his lips taut. "Though sometimes the Doyens have ways of sidestepping rules like that." Odd that the other Doyens hadn't pushed at it. Perhaps it came down to the power of the Mossbacks, the political group headed by Gregor and his ilk. They were likely to band together to oppose the Faedran faction who fought for the mages. They would be reluctant to lose any of their number. Even if one of their number was unwell. "Anything else?"

The half-knocker pushed her red-rimmed glasses up her nose. "Yeah. A bunch of the Wells family *friends* are here, too, if you catch my meaning."

Jefferson rubbed his chin. "I do." That wasn't unexpected. Funerals among the elite were events—even if the elite in question was someone that had been at odds with others among the high echelons of society. Oh, certainly, many of them were there to gloat and metaphorically dance on his grave. That was fine. In his own way, Malcolm still had the last laugh. "I suspected as much, which is why I've been hanging around the hotel and not making any social calls."

Flora's face was grim. "And Alice is here."

Alice. He froze at the name. Jefferson hadn't heard his sister's— Malcolm's sister's—name uttered in years. But he thought of her often, and the way he hadn't stood up for her at the time she'd been traded off as if she were livestock. All because she had developed magic. "I see. How did you find that out?" He had to ask because Flora had never met Alice. His sister had been sent away before he'd ever crossed paths with the half-knocker.

"The usual. I'm incredibly nosy." Flora shrugged. While it was true that she was, in fact, nosy, Jefferson knew there had to be more to it than that. He crossed his arms, pinning her with an expectant look. "Okay, okay. I saw a woman with the…ahem…*Wells look* about her, and when I had time to peruse the hotel registry, I confirmed the name."

The Wells look. Jefferson knew it intimately after staring at it for too many years. Chiseled cheekbones, strong chin, and glossy dark brown hair that gleamed with indigo in the right light. "I see. It's not unexpected that she would come."

"Yeah, but I'd rather you know the lay of the land, so you don't do or say anything stupid," Flora said.

He snorted. "You have such little faith in me."

Flora shook her head. "Nah. It's not that." Suddenly, her violet eyes were the most serious he'd seen them in ages. "You're going to a funeral tomorrow. *Your* funeral. If ever there were a time you might get overwhelmed and slip up, that's it."

"*Malcolm's* funeral," Jefferson corrected stiffly. "Honestly, I've kept up the charade for so long. I know what I'm doing." He took another sip of wine before continuing. "And I don't have to do it anymore. I can just be *me*. The person I *want* to be." His mind drifted to Kittie for a moment, and he hoped she had discovered who she wanted to be, too. And that she could do it. Sometimes, that was the hardest part.

Flora eyed him. "I know. I just hope it will be as easy as you think to be who you are tomorrow."

CHAPTER ELEVEN

Family Matters

Blaise

*B*laise smiled as he finished organizing the pantry. It was the last task he had to complete, and only because he wouldn't be there to help Reuben or Hannah rummage around to find whatever they might need inside its depths. He kept the kitchen in an overall orderly condition. The exception was the pantry, and it had sorely needed attention. It was satisfying to see the spice tins standing side by side like flavorful soldiers ready to be deployed.

But with that done, he couldn't procrastinate any longer. He was supposed to leave for Rainbow Flat in the morning, and even though he wanted to go, he also *didn't* want to go. Blaise took a moment to pull out a flat, stiff-sided carrier he had devised for packing small baked goods in saddlebags. The leather of the carrier was more flexible than a tin, which let it fit into the compartment more easily. He stuffed it with as many leftover cookies and pastries as he could, then set it aside for the next day.

Now I really need to pack. He rubbed his chin, climbing up to the loft. Part of the problem was that he missed Jefferson—gods, why did he miss that man as much as if he'd lost a limb? The loft was a constant reminder of his absence. Blaise shook his head. This was exactly why he needed to go to Rainbow Flat. It would take his mind off things, ease the time away from his Dreamer.

He set about his task, pulling out the few clothing items he figured would fit in the saddlebags. All the while, he wondered what Jefferson would have thought of his choices. Blaise chuckled to himself, suspecting he would have been appalled since Blaise was mostly selecting older shirts and trousers. *This is so last season. Wait, not even last season. Probably last three years.* The teasing mental conversation made him smile.

A solid knock on the door downstairs startled him. The bakery door wasn't locked—Blaise only did that at night. Hinges creaked as the door opened. "Blaise?"

Jack? Something in the outlaw's tone put Blaise on edge. "Upstairs."

"You need to come down. Now."

The Effigest's words brooked no argument. He wasn't being surly or pushy—no, he was being urgent and matter-of-fact, and that was *scary.* Jack became all business when something bad was afoot. Blaise set aside the shirt he'd been about to fold, hurrying down the steep stairs so fast he almost lost his footing.

Jack didn't even comment on his lack of grace. The man's blue eyes were troubled. "Message for you at the post office. You need to talk to Hank."

What? The first place Blaise's mind went was Jefferson. Something had happened to the delegation. Tears stung his eyes, but he shook his head to dismiss them. No use borrowing trouble until he knew what was going on. "Okay." The sound that came out of his mouth was husky and broken. It didn't sound like it even belonged to him.

"C'mon." Jack nodded to the door and led the way, more solicitous than normal. That worried Blaise even more.

The post office was a short distance from the bakery, but it felt like the longest walk of Blaise's life. A handful of citizens were about to enter the building when Jack approached with Blaise in tow. Blaise couldn't see the outlaw's face, and Jack said nothing at all, but the townspeople took one look at him and decided they would visit the post office later. The Effigest shoved the door open and held it for Blaise.

Hank Walker, Fortitude's postmaster, leaned against the counter. He looked pale and tired, as if he'd exerted his magic quickly to travel a great distance. Blaise didn't know the details of his job, though he knew the man traveled to other outlaw towns—and a handful of Confederation ones—to pick up and deliver mail. A burlap sack full of envelopes and boxes lolled nearby. An envelope rested on the counter in front of him.

"Would have come for you myself, but I'm bushed," Hank said, apologetic. He had a difficult time getting around. He'd lost a leg—a parting gift from Lamar Gaitwood. Nadine and a tinker had worked together to create a contraption that served in place of the missing limb, but Hank was still adjusting to it. "I just came back from Rainbow Flat. Stopped my rounds because I needed to get back to tell you."

Rainbow Flat. It wasn't about Jefferson, then. Momentary relief flooded through Blaise until he realized—*Rainbow Flat*. Gooseflesh crawled across his body. "Tell me what?"

Hank tapped the envelope. "This tells you some, but I thought you might want to hear it from me." Something flickered in his eyes. Compassion. Sadness. "Your family there…they got attacked."

Time stood still. Blaise forgot to breathe until his lungs demanded it. He reached a hand out, clawing the envelope over. Didn't even realize he used his magic on it, shredding the envelope to reveal the letter within. Barely registered Jack's sharp intake of breath at the trick. Blaise unfolded the paper, hands trembling so badly that the words jumbled on the page, impossible to read.

"Give it here." Jack's voice was the softest he'd ever heard it. Blaise released the letter. Jack read it aloud, but the things he said made little sense at first. It was like being submerged underwater and hearing someone speak. Garbled. Blaise had to ask him to read it twice more before any of it took hold in his mind.

"The Hawthorne residence was attacked through the night. Daniel Hawthorne was killed in the struggle. Marian Hawthorne is missing, presumed taken. The children hid and are being cared for by a neighbor." The paper crackled in Jack's hand, suddenly the loudest thing in the post office.

Blaise squeezed his eyes closed. Hank spoke, but he didn't hear. Blaise's magic rose, defensive at the bitter grief welling up. There was nothing to guard against, though. Nothing could stop the hurt he felt.

The next few minutes—maybe hours, he wasn't sure—were a blur. He sat behind the bakery in the growing darkness, leaning against Emrys's warm bulk. The stallion was down, legs tucked neatly beneath him. A wing curled against Blaise like a blanket. Emmaline crouched nearby, her face illuminated by a mage-light.

Blaise swallowed. Maybe it had been a nightmare. Jefferson wasn't around to chase them away, after all. But the stricken look on Emmaline's face told him the truth. The awful letter Jack had read was real. A dry sob racked his chest, and Emrys adjusted, craning his head around to nuzzle Blaise. The stallion said nothing, but he didn't need to. There wasn't anything that could be said to make this better.

Emmaline was silent, too. Questions gleamed in her eyes, but she didn't utter them. Instead, she sat down, placing the mage-light between them.

"You don't have to stay," Blaise croaked when he finally found his voice.

"'Course I do," Emmaline said, whisper-soft. "You're hurting, and I'm not about to leave you alone to suffer. That's not what family does."

Family? Her words confused him. His family—they were in Rainbow Flat. They'd been attacked, and he hadn't been there. He blinked as he decoded her meaning. Blaise's breath caught again, but now because of the precious thing she was offering him. He almost couldn't believe he hadn't seen it before. "Family?"

"Yeah," she agreed. "How could you not be like family to me? We're friends. And you...you sacrificed everything to free me." Her voice cracked. They hadn't talked about Fort Courage much. Or at all, really. The memories were too difficult for both of them. "So, what're we going to do?"

"Cry for a while, probably." He was already accomplishing that. His nose was runny, and it took him a moment to find a handkerchief to blow it.

"That stands to reason. I mean after that."

Blaise shoved the soggy handkerchief back in a pocket, not caring about its lack of cleanliness. He looked at her blankly. His mind hadn't gotten that far, not yet. He was still processing the knife's edge of pain that came with the news. But she had a valid question. Blaise mopped his forehead with one hand, brushing his hair back. Lucienne and Brody were all alone. And his mother...

Blaise drew in a deep breath. "I...I suppose I need to get my sister and brother. Make sure they're okay. Get them somewhere safe." Yes, that sounded like the start of a coherent plan. Then, within, something cold and calculating arose like a dragon from slumber. Anger. "Then...then I need to figure out who did this. Who killed my father? Where's my mother?" He pulled away from Emrys, back ramrod straight. "Find whoever did this and make them regret it." The steel in his voice surprised him, and a distant part of his mind boggled that he was the one who'd spoken. No time to think of that now.

He struggled to his feet. "I should go. Now. Emrys, let's go."

The stallion nickered in surprise. <Now?>

"*No*," Emmaline said, firm but soft. She lifted a hand, no doubt seeing the uncharacteristic rage flit across Blaise's face at the denial. "It's night, and it's cloudy. Not safe for traveling. And you're too upset. You shouldn't do that right now."

He shook his head. "I need to *help* them."

"I know." She took a chance, laying a hand on his arm. "But like this, you won't do anyone any good. Emrys loves you, and if you want to go, you know he'll fly in the dark, his own safety be damned." The stallion snorted in agreement. "Look, Blaise. I'm not saying don't go. Just don't go right this instant." She blew out a breath. "Go to bed. Get some rest, and I promise we'll leave first thing in the morning."

"We?" There she went again, confusing him with simple words. He was tired. He hadn't known grief could be so exhausting.

"Yes, *we*," Emmaline said, exasperated. "You think Daddy and I are gonna let you hare off to Rainbow Flat on your own? No way in Perdition. Daddy's finishing preparations."

Blaise closed his eyes. Relief washed over him. He wouldn't be alone. But still… "I couldn't bear it if something happened to you or Jack. This is about my family. It's for me to handle."

Emmaline scoffed. "I know you don't have cotton in your ears. You heard what I said earlier. You're *our* family, too. Even if you try to leave us behind, we'll be hot on your heels."

<I will not leave Fortitude without them, if this is the case,> Emrys said, bumping Blaise with his head. <Because *I* could not bear if something happened to you. Again.>

Blaise sighed, rubbing the bridge of his nose. He couldn't argue anymore. He just couldn't. "Okay. But we leave tomorrow."

Emmaline nodded. "I'll help you upstairs. Do you need someone to stay with you tonight?"

"Emrys can sleep in the bakery," Blaise murmured. It was something the pegasus had suggested before, promising that he would be careful and that he would go outside if he needed to relieve himself.

<I can?> Momentary excitement laced the stallion's voice, though it was quickly dampened. <I mean, I will, if you like. So that someone is close.>

Emmaline pursed her lips. "Guess I'll leave a note for Reuben to mop in the morning. But fine, if that's what you want, your pegasus can bunk in the bakery."

A few moments later, Emrys's hooves clopped as he carefully followed Blaise and Emmaline inside. The pegasus had banished his wings, so only had to be mindful of his bulk and his swishing tail. Emmaline shoved a table out of the way, shooting a glance at Blaise before urging him up the stairs.

Blaise fell into the bed, once again painfully aware of the Jefferson-sized hole in his heart. He squeezed his eyes closed, fearing the nightmares that would come. But thankfully, only dreamless sleep found him.

WHEN BLAISE AWOKE, GROGGY AND STIFF, FOR A FEW FLEETING MOMENTS, he hoped that the previous day was a nightmare. But the hollow thump of hooves on the floorboards below was all the validation he needed. He rubbed his eyes with the heels of his hands, struggling against the surge of heartache.

No. He couldn't function like this, locked down by grief. He had been through difficult times before. Survived horrors that others could only imagine. *I can get through this, too. I just have to take it moment by moment. Even if it's hard.* Slowly, he sat up, fighting off the urge to collapse back onto the bed, into the mindless comfort of sleep.

<Blaise? Are you coming down? I'm hungry. And someone left a tin of cookies on the counter, but I can't get it open.>

Emrys. Right, he was downstairs. Because last night, in the depths of his agony, Blaise had suggested the stallion spend the night in the bakery. He hadn't been thinking straight. "You're *always* hungry," Blaise called, reaching over to flick the mage-light on. Gentle blue light washed across the small room as he tottered out of bed and found a change of clothes.

<I'm an equine. We're designed to eat a lot. And besides, if I were in my stall, I would have sweet hay to snack on.>

Suddenly, Blaise felt a wave of guilt. Did Emrys even have water through the night? He shoved his feet into boots, then made his way down. To his relief, he discovered that someone—probably Emmaline—had filled a bucket of water from the sink and left it for Emrys. The pegasus carefully trod over, snuffling at Blaise's chest to assess his rider.

"Sorry. I should take better care of you," Blaise whispered, leaning his forehead against Emrys's.

<Sometimes it's my job to take care of you,> Emrys said simply. <Now, about those cookies…>

Blaise chuckled, though it came out as a half-sob. He wiped at one eye. He almost wished he were totally alone, like he had been in the Golden Citadel. That time in his life had been terrible, but he had blocked out the trauma and hurt by mentally distancing himself from it. Pretending that things weren't happening to him. Somehow, he didn't think any of his friends were going to let him get away with that.

"Yeah, let me get them for you." Blaise moved over to the counter. Tell-tale teeth marks dented the metal, and one side was sticky and wet with saliva. He arched his brows. "I see you already tried."

<I was hungry, and I didn't want to bother you while you were sleeping.> Emrys was apologetic, though he moved over to sniff at the tin hopefully.

Blaise opened the container, then held it out to allow the stallion to nibble on the butterscotch cookies and almond pinwheels within. Emrys ate with enthusiasm, licking the last crumbs from the container when he was finished. <Thank you. Are there any more by chance?>

There were. Blaise kept stock on hand from the previous days, and before long, Emrys had made another two dozen cookies vanish. If he were a horse, that might have been problematic, but pegasi thrived on sugar. And if they were to set out for Rainbow Flat, Emrys needed all the fuel he could get.

With that thought, Blaise pulled out additional tins to carry to the stable. Then he threw together a simple breakfast for himself while Emrys hovered nearby. Was it odd to have a pegasus lumbering around the bakery? Most definitely. But there was a warm bliss in it, and Emrys was as much a comfort as Jefferson would have been.

Reuben and Hannah arrived a short time later to start work for the day. They greeted Blaise gently, neither of them asking after the news he'd received. He could tell by the pitying looks on their faces that they knew, though. Reuben didn't even say a word about a pegasus in the bakery. He glanced at the note Emmaline had left on the display case, then pulled out another bucket and the mop, ready for when the stallion departed.

Blaise went up to retrieve his saddlebags from the loft, pausing in front of the mirror on the wall. His eyelids were puffy, and his hair stuck up in wild hanks. Not to mention his beard needed a trim—that had been his intent, to take care of before he'd received the soul-shattering news. Releasing a soft sigh, he set about the simple self-care tasks, if only because he knew Jefferson would have urged him to do so.

When he was finished, he looked presentable. Like someone who hadn't had life ambush him once again. Blaise studied his reflection, noting the new hardness of his eyes. Then he shook his head, glancing around to see if he'd forgotten anything before snagging his saddlebags and going downstairs.

"Good luck, Blaise. Take care of yourself," Hannah said as he started for the door.

He paused, turning to look back at her and Reuben. "I'll try."

Reuben offered a grim smile. "Don't worry about the bakery. We'll take good care of it while you're gone."

A lump formed in Blaise's throat. "I know you will. Thank you."

With those goodbyes said, he and Emrys exited the bakery. A pair of gawking children squealed with glee when they saw the ebony stallion emerge from the building, clapping their hands in delight as his wings shimmered back into existence in the early morning sun. When Blaise and Emrys reached the stable, they found Oberidon and Zepheus saddled and ready, their riders lounging nearby. More surprising, however, was the presence of Nadine and her strawberry roan stallion, Leorus.

<Cookies!> Oberidon declared as soon as he spied the familiar tins Blaise carried. Ears pricked with anticipation, the spotted stallion sidled over. <Did you bring us cookies?>

"I did," Blaise agreed, though he handed a tin to Emmaline rather than her pegasus. Then he did the same for Jack, the outlaw giving a curt nod of approval. Blaise glanced uncertainly at Leorus, who was eyeing the last of the tins with a great deal of desire.

"We're coming along," Nadine said, matter-of-fact.

Blaise rubbed the back of his head. "But aren't you needed here?"

"I'm not the only Healer in town anymore. The best, but not the *only*," she answered. Nadine held out a hand, demanding the cookie tin without words. "And the way I see it, you'll want someone you trust to bring your sister and brother to Fortitude while you figure out what to do."

Blaise blinked. He hadn't thought through the logistics of that. And Nadine was a Healer—and she hadn't exaggerated about her ability. She was the best in Fortitude. Maybe in all the Untamed Territory. If Lucienne or Brody were hurt, she could help. And if any threat cropped up with Nadine around…well, she might *look* like a woman approaching her golden years, but she was a force to be reckoned with.

"Thank you," he whispered, handing her the tin.

Nadine popped the lid off, holding it out for her pegasus. Leorus's pink tongue swiped a currant cookie. While the trio of pegasi enjoyed their sugary snacks, Blaise took Emrys into the barn, setting to the familiar task of tacking him up. There was something calming in the simple actions. Over the past few months, Blaise had worked on becoming more comfortable on the stallion's back. And in the air. He didn't think he'd ever be as good at it as Jack, nor as enthusiastic as Jefferson, but he was much better. And this was something he could *do*. Right now, he needed to be *doing*, so this was good. A relief.

With Emrys ready, they came back out to meet the others. Blaise found Emmaline had already returned the empty tins to the bakery to be washed and stored for future use. Jack studied Blaise. The outlaw had been unusually quiet until that moment. "You ready for this?"

No. But I have to do it, anyway. He nodded, hiding the lie. Blaise figured Jack saw it in his eyes, though. "Yeah. Let's go."

CHAPTER TWELVE

Send a Casserole Next Time

Jefferson

The Good Fortune Sacellum was shoulder to shoulder with mourners, all dressed in traditional charcoal grey edged with gold thread. The women in attendance wore outrageous hats of varying sizes, many of them with gauzy, gilded veils that swept over their faces at an angle. Most of the hats had a daunting amount of decoration. Stuffed birds, fruit, and flowers perched above the bobbing heads gave the appearance of a gaudy parade.

"Did they mistake the funeral for the Ganland Derby?" Flora asked, peering up at a hat that indeed had a prancing horse statue atop it.

Jefferson stifled a chuckle at her observation. She wasn't wrong. If not for the mourning colors, the service could be mistaken for the clubhouse at Aspenpoint Downs. True to Flora's assessment, everyone who was anyone had come out for Doyen Malcolm Wells's funeral. *I suppose I should be honored.*

He kept to the outskirts, for once trying to keep a low profile. Jefferson scanned the gathered elite. His former fellow Doyens sat in a cluster near the front, as was their due. A smattering of Confederation leaders were there as well—Madame Boss Clayton of Ganland flanked by underlings from Phinora and Petria. So, Malcolm Wells hadn't warranted the Luminary of Phinora coming herself, but at least she'd sent a representative. That was something.

With Flora at his side, Jefferson slipped into a pew near the rear. Oh, he could have sat at the front, in the rows reserved for friends and family.

But he'd rather not. The old family friends who had claimed the seats were people who had written him off when he'd turned his back on their ways. The powerful elite in Ganland who supported trafficking and other illicit activities. He was loath to rub elbows with any of them.

But he saw a single person who might have been enough to lure him to the front. There was no mistaking the sweep of dark hair, so like their mother's had been in her youth. The woman's back was to him, but Jefferson would have recognized his sister anywhere.

My sister. Unlike the rest of his family in his—Malcolm's—old life, Jefferson couldn't set his sister aside as someone who no longer belonged to him. A surge of anticipation snaked through him at the sight of her. He hadn't seen her in years. She was a woman grown now, so unlike the betrayed teenager she had been. But he would know her anywhere.

Flora elbowed him. "Stop staring."

He frowned. "I'm not."

"You are. Knock it off. It's creepy."

I am not being creepy. He crossed his arms, instead directing his attention to the gold-robed Tabrisian acolyte who strode down the aisle bearing a gleaming copper urn. Soft choral music floated through the Sacellum as the service began.

The acolyte hefted the urn, setting it atop a marble dais at the front. For obvious reasons, there had been no body to bury, only the mishmash of ashes and charred bone in a fire-gutted bedroom. Jefferson heard someone nearby murmur, "Doyen Wells's lapel pin is inside." He set his jaw at the grim gossip, though he knew it was true.

Jefferson leaned into the uncomfortable wood of the pew, listening as the priest led the service. People he had known came up to speak about the things Malcolm had done in his *short, brilliant life,* as one of them put it. Most of the speakers were people he had worked closely with during his time as a Doyen. It was disconcerting to hear about himself in the past tense. But at least he had been well-regarded. *Though I am certain my father was lauded at his funeral, as well.*

When the service ended, the crowd slowly filtered out of the Sacellum. By that time, he was recognized by some of the attendees, and he politely answered questions and bandied about compliments—all the idle chatter one had to endure for the sake of social obligations. Flora stayed nearby, as close as a burr stuck to a pegasus tail, though she was mostly ignored.

"You okay?" Flora asked when Jefferson finally caught a break from social niceties.

"It's been an experience," Jefferson murmured, though he really wanted to say more. Never in his life had he imagined he might attend his own funeral. Disconcerting. "I want to speak to my—to *Malcolm's* sister."

Sloppy. He couldn't be sloppy here. He was off his game, faced with his own mortality. *To be fair, I think that would rattle anyone.*

Flora cocked a pink eyebrow at him. "You sure about that?"

No. "Yes." He cleared his throat. "I should offer my condolences."

Flora snorted. She wasn't an idiot. Of course, she saw through his schemes as if they were a scarf concealing a draft horse. Jefferson didn't care, though. He had so many regrets—he would not let this opportunity pass him by.

A knot of guests blocked his path to her. Just as well. He sidled up against a wall, waiting for more of the mourners to clear out. Flora sighed and turned to scrutinize the stained glass window to their side, tilting her head as she regarded it. Jagged angles of colorful glass depicted the ruby-haired god Tabris from one of the old tales. "What is this?"

Jefferson glanced at the window. "That? Tabris relaxing in his swimming hole filled with gold in Paradise."

Flora whistled. "Maybe I need to find me some religion. No wonder you follow the guy."

Jefferson shook his head at her insight. "You make it sound rather shallow that way."

"Isn't it, though?"

He crossed his arms. "It's how I was raised." Jefferson knew that wasn't much of a defense—it wasn't a defense at all. No time to debate theology with Flora, though. The last of the mourners trailed away, leaving his sister alone in front of the dais.

Flora cocked her head, noticing the direction of his gaze. "I'll give you a few minutes with her. Don't say anything stupid."

Jefferson grimaced, though he was thankful for the illusion of privacy. The sight of his sister was almost enough to make him turn and run. Oh, how she had grown from girl to woman. Her obsidian hair, which had been straight as an arrow in her youth, had been tamed into waves that framed her face and gave her an aristocratic air.

She caught sight of him, her caramel-colored eyes puzzled. "Do I know you?"

Oh, gods. Yes. Yes, you do. I'm so sorry. For everything.

Jefferson swallowed the words, removing his hat as he strode over to her. "No, I don't believe you do. But I was very close to Malcolm." His gaze drifted to the urn, the last physical remnant of Malcolm's existence in this world. Jefferson cleared his throat. "My name is Jefferson Cole."

Recognition flared in her eyes at the name. She cocked her head. "It's a pleasure, Mr. Cole. My name is Alice Dillon."

Dillon. He focused on her surname. She'd been married—sold, really—into the wealthy Dillon family. Jefferson hadn't paid much attention to

Phillip Dillon, aside from a rumor that the railroad baron wanted to dabble in airships. Then he realized he hadn't responded yet, and he dipped his head politely. "The pleasure is all mine, I assure you. You're welcome to call me Jefferson." He sighed. "It's what Malcolm would have wanted."

She considered him, weighing the invitation for familiarity. "You were *that* close to him?"

You have no idea. He offered her a smile and a disarming chuckle. "We were friends, nothing more than that. He was…" Jefferson trailed off, suddenly unsure what to say. All the words that clung to his throat felt like lies. There was nothing he could say that would make amends for the wrong that had been done to her. Malcolm would always be a villain to her, even if she pretended otherwise in the public eye. Unable to form the rest of his sentence, he shrugged. "I seem to be overcome with emotion. Words escape me."

Alice nodded. "Understandable, given the circumstances." Her sharp brown eyes analyzed him. "Unfortunately, I can't be as mournful as you. Good riddance, the way I see it."

As much as he thought he had expected it, her words *stung*. He blinked in surprise, the beginnings of tears prickling the corners of his eyes. *What is wrong with me? Did I honestly think this would be some sort of happy reunion? Well, I suppose that's what I was hoping for.* Jefferson swallowed. "I'm sorry you feel that way. Though I suppose we all cope with loss differently."

Alice narrowed her eyes, shooting a look over her shoulder at the urn. "No loss to me. Only gain. I'm the sole heir of the Wells fortune. This will give me the chance to do exactly what I've wanted to do all along."

Jefferson's mouth went dry. He had known from Seledora that there was a very large inheritance at stake. It wasn't something he needed. Not when any attempt to go after it would lead to suspicion. Anyway, he didn't want that ill-begotten money. He nodded politely. "And what's that?"

His sister huffed out a soft breath, as if she couldn't believe she was having this conversation with someone she just met. For a long moment, Jefferson thought she wouldn't answer. Alice shifted her weight from one foot to the other. "Leave this gods-forsaken wasteland of corruption while I have the chance."

Leave? Oh. Suddenly, he understood. She was a mage—unregistered because their parents had worked the system, but still a mage. She had a spouse among the elite, and no doubt he would try to sink his claws into the inheritance if he had the chance. Alice had never been free. And now she was going to take the money and run.

There was nothing he could say that wouldn't lead down a potential rabbit hole of danger for him. Jefferson settled for an encouraging smile. "Good for you. I hear the Untamed Territory is lovely this time of year."

She gave him a wary look. "That's what I'm counting on." Alice turned to leave. "It's been…interesting, Mr. Cole. I appreciate your condolences, despite my feelings about the deceased."

"Of course," Jefferson murmured. One of the hardest things he'd ever done in his life was walk away from the sister he desperately wanted to repair things with—all without telling her who he was.

He whirled on his heel—and almost ran face-first into the single person he most definitely did not want to cross paths with. Gregor Gaitwood stared at him, though there was a wild gleam in his eyes, like someone being harried to the breaking point. Jefferson took a quick step back, hoping that Flora was nearby if he needed a hand. He didn't think Gregor would try to murder him outright, but…well, there was no telling what the unstable Doyen might do.

"Why, Doyen Gaitwood, I wouldn't have expected you to come to the funeral of a Faedran," Jefferson said, hoping to catch the politician off balance.

Gregor smiled, but it was too wide. Unhinged and wicked. "I would hardly miss it. Not when it would give me a chance to speak with *you*."

Jefferson frowned. "I regret to inform you the feeling is *not* mutual. I suggest you simply send a casserole next time. Now, if you'll excuse me—"

Gregor grabbed his sleeve as he tried to slip away, fingernails digging into the fabric. "No, Cole. You think you've won—that you can get away with these things you've done. That you've taken some sort of gods-damned high road." The Doyen spoke through clenched teeth. "You think you're better—different—from the rest of the elite simply because you think you're right. But you're not. You use others just as much as any of the elite. You *lie*. You *cheat*. Tell me, Cole—does your Breaker know all your deceptions? How you've used him?"

Jefferson's temper flared as soon as Gregor mentioned Blaise. If not for the blasted ring on his finger, he would have drop-kicked Gregor into the dreamscape, consequences be damned. He was taller than Gregor, so he took a step closer, glowering down at the Doyen. "I am *not* using him."

Gregor's smile widened. "Not now, maybe. But I know you. Know what you've *done*." The Doyen took a step back, smug and self-assured, as if he were no longer plagued by nightmares. Jefferson wanted to ask if that was the case, but there was no way he would inquire that of Gregor. He settled for glaring as Gregor chuckled. "You can't escape what you were born to be, Malcolm."

"Malcolm Wells is dead," Jefferson said, voice soft with warning.

Gregor turned on his heel. "We'll see about that." The Doyen cast a withering look over his shoulder before vanishing around a corner.

Flora ghosted up next to Jefferson. He glanced down at her. "Where were you?"

"Watching." Jefferson didn't miss the fact that she had a knife clutched in one hand, as if she'd considered using it. Flora twirled it, then slipped it back in the sheath at her belt. "I didn't like him threatening you, but I figured slitting his throat in a church might be frowned upon."

"More than that, the problem would be a member of the Gutter delegation attacking a Doyen," Jefferson murmured.

Flora snorted. "Wouldn't be an *attack*. It would be straight-up murder. If I go after him, he's dead. No other way around it."

Her words sent a chill through him, and not for the first time, Jefferson was glad she was on his side. He blew out a breath. "Fortunately for us, we can be on our way and put that snake and his venom behind us."

CHAPTER THIRTEEN

He's Tougher Than You Think

Blaise

Blaise wanted to push the pegasi to cover as much ground as they could, but Jack quickly put a damper on the idea.

"You wanna exhaust Emrys and have it take twice as long to get there? That's how you do it," the outlaw said, though there was no rancor in his voice. Only facts. Reluctantly, Blaise bent to the years of experience Jack had in traversing the Untamed Territory.

A chill autumn wind buffeted the pegasi and their riders as they made the final approach to Rainbow Flat at the end of their second full day of flight. The weather had been in their favor—this time of year a freak snowstorm was just as likely to crop up as a heatwave, according to Jack. Blaise was simply thankful that the worst they'd had to contend with was cloudy skies and a stiff breeze.

Rainbow Flat was exactly as he remembered it, an idyllic town overlooking the unfortunately named Tombstone River. Everything about the town was orderly. Its prim and proper appearance brought Jefferson to mind, and for a moment, Blaise almost felt his beau's presence as Emrys's hooves kissed the ground.

The ebony stallion glanced back, his head bare of hackamore. There was no need for the farce that the pegasi were normal horses while they were in the Gutter. Blaise had the sense Emrys wanted to say something or check on him, but the telepath had no doubt been monitoring him as they traveled. Sometimes words weren't necessary. He reached down and ruffled the pegasus's mane to let him know he appreciated the thought.

Oberidon trotted alongside Emrys, Emmaline peering at Blaise. "How're you doing?"

He blew out a breath. All things considered, he was a lot calmer than he would have expected to be at this point. But he'd had so many hours in the saddle—time to mull over his own thoughts and feelings. He had felt so *much*; it was as if he were tapped out. "That'll be a better question to ask later."

She nodded, understanding. Jack and Zepheus moved to take the lead, with Nadine bringing up the rear. The Effigest had a deep scowl twisting his face. "No sentries. I've suggested it before, and still *no sentries*." He shook his head. "That's going to change if we become a nation. Sloppy. That's what this is." He spat in the dirt to fully express his disgust.

Blaise swallowed as he realized what Jack meant. The sentries in Fortitude were the town's first line of defense, a warning system for impending danger. From what Blaise had gleaned, the sentries existed mostly to keep tabs on any potential Saltie incursions. But maybe they could have helped prevent this, too.

"That's something to look into later," Nadine said, keeping them on track. "Dusk is coming, and the priority should be to find the children."

Zepheus drew to a stop as a thoughtful look spread across the outlaw's face. "We have two priorities. Find the children *and* figure out who might have taken Marian Hawthorne. There's enough of us here to do both." His cool eyes flicked to Blaise. "Daylight's burning."

Blaise sighed. "But there's only one of me."

Annoyance slid across Jack's face, but he relented with a nod. Blaise understood what the Effigest had been trying to do. He was concerned about Blaise going to the scene where it had all happened, and...what? Breaking down again, probably. And as tempting as that was, he didn't think he could cry anymore. Icy resolve had replaced the tears. A part of him wondered if this was what had forged Jack into who he was. Had he been so damaged by the circumstances in his life that the only choice had been to become hardened and dangerous?

"Nadine's right. Let's find Luci and Brody first. They can probably tell us more about what happened, too," Blaise said.

Jack's shoulders hunched. "*That's* what I was trying to avoid." He urged Zepheus back into a trot, the palomino springing along with ease. "Kids don't deserve to relive that sort of thing."

Oh. Blaise felt like a heel for the suggestion, but he also knew his sister. Or he thought he did, anyway. "Luci's tough, and she would want us to know." He swallowed. *And talking about it might help.* He knew a thing or two about trauma.

After a few inquiries, they got directions to the Hawthorne home, as well as the neighbor who had taken in Blaise's siblings. The sun was setting as their pegasi trotted to the neighbor's house. Blaise hazarded a look over his shoulder at the home he figured belonged to his family, crouched a quarter-mile away.

A woman with grey hair pulled into a bun peered at them through a screen door. A moment later, two smaller faces appeared, accompanied by a wail of recognition. The door flew open, crashing against the exterior wall as Brody exploded out as only a six-year-old could. His face was red as he raced over to them, yelling Blaise's name.

Blaise didn't even realize he was dismounting until the shock of his heels hitting the dirt ricocheted through him. Brody jumped at him, wrapping his slender arms around Blaise's abdomen with such ferocity it would have knocked him over had Emrys not been at his back.

"I want my Mama," Brody whimpered, his face buried against Blaise's chest.

Carefully, Blaise adjusted to crouch down and hug his little brother. Brody clung to him like he never wanted to let go, and Blaise let him. He looked up as the scuff of feet announced a new arrival: Lucienne, her face pale and void of the spark that had characterized her before. She held something cuddled in her arms, and it took Blaise a moment to realize it was the family dog, Chester. The terrier's face was dark with dried blood, and Blaise's stomach dropped as he saw Chester was missing an eye.

Jack had moved to intercept the neighbor, no doubt hoping to mine her for information as he exchanged what passed for pleasantries from him. Nadine and Emmaline remained on their pegasi, though Blaise knew they were ready to dismount if needed.

Lucienne glanced down at the injured dog. "You're *too late.*"

Emmaline made a sound of displeasure at the vitriol in Lucienne's voice, but Blaise only nodded. He felt the same way. If he had been there, maybe he could have stopped whatever had happened. "I know. But I'm here now."

Lucienne sighed heavily, tears welling in her eyes. But she didn't allow them to fall. She jostled Chester so she could lift a hand, brushing them away. "And what are you going to do about it? Daddy's dead. Mom is *gone.*" She glanced back toward their house. "What are *we* going to do?"

Brody sobbed all the harder as Lucienne spoke. Blaise was quiet for a moment, slowly digesting that his sister wasn't mad at him but at the situation. That it had even happened. That their illusion of safety, of happiness, had been shattered. He knew all about that awful feeling.

Blaise rubbed Brody's back. The child quieted, as if he were exhausted from crying. Blaise's shirt was wet and probably snotty, but he didn't care. "You're going to go somewhere..." He hesitated. *Safe* wasn't a good word right now, not when he had no assurances that such a thing existed. "Somewhere full of people who will do everything in their power to protect you." He lifted his eyes to Nadine. The Healer nodded, expression grim. Blaise decided to have Nadine ask Clover to house Lucienne and Brody. The Broken Horn Saloon had empty rooms, and the Knossan would be a stalwart protector, too.

"You'll take us there?" Brody's voice was so small, Blaise almost missed the question.

"No," Blaise whispered, shaking his head.

Lucienne turned her baleful glare on him again. "Then what *are* you going to do?"

"Everything in my power." Blaise met her haunted gaze. "I'm going to find Mom. And find the people who did this."

At his words, Brody squeaked, burrowing his head against Blaise again, trembling with fear. Lucienne shook her head. "They'll kill you. It's a miracle we survived." Her mouth was a thin line, and somehow she had paled another shade at his declaration.

"They're not gonna kill him 'cause he ain't gonna be alone," Jack announced, swaggering over. Somehow, he managed a combination of self-assured menace that promised doom to whoever had done this while also attempting to not frighten the Hawthorne children. "But even if he *was* alone, give 'im some credit. He's tougher than you think." His eyes glinted. "A real outlaw."

I'm pretty sure Jack just complimented me, and I'm not sure how I feel about that. Blaise ignored it for the present. "Let's go into town and get settled in a hotel. Grab some dinner." He didn't know enough about this neighbor to trust them to extend their hospitality any further. And besides, Blaise now lived in a weird world where all he had to do was mention Jefferson, and he knew he would be well taken care of in Rainbow Flat.

"Then we need to hear what happened," Jack added. Apparently, he had decided they may as well fish for whatever information they could.

Blaise nodded, rising out of his crouch. He glanced from Emrys to his siblings. "Do you want to ride a pegasus?"

Brody's eyes widened, and for a beat, he seemed to forget all about his current circumstance. The question even distracted Lucienne. "We can ride a *pegasus?*" Brody asked.

Emrys lowered his head until his muzzle was at the same height as Brody's head. <You may ride on my back with your brother. Oby has offered a ride to your sister.>

Blaise scratched Emrys's neck in appreciation, glad the pegasi were agreeable. He knew it wasn't good for their backs to bear a double burden for an extended length of time, but they would stay on the ground, and

Rainbow Flat was only a mile and a half away. Blaise hadn't known how else they would get to town, aside from on foot, which seemed unreasonable after everything.

"Give me the dog," Nadine said, brooking no argument. Lucienne offered Chester to her, and before long, the terrier was curled up against the Healer's bosom. The dog looked a little more comfortable, leaving Blaise to wonder if Nadine had a knack for animals she didn't advertise.

A few moments later, Brody perched in front of Blaise while Lucienne sat behind Emmaline, hands around the older girl's waist. Brody reached down and stroked Emrys's mane, and for a short time as their procession rode to town, the Hawthorne children had a bright spot in their overwhelming day.

CHAPTER FOURTEEN

Unicorns Again

Blaise

*B*laise gave silent thanks for Jefferson and his connections. No one so much as batted an eye when they entered the Starlight Hotel and Blaise asked for rooms. In fact, the clerk at the desk inclined his head, full of reverence. "Of course, Mr. Hawthorne. You'll be staying in the suite Mr. Cole has reserved for you. The staff will ensure that your companions are housed nearby."

"I want to sleep with *you* tonight," Brody whined, tugging at Blaise's hand. There was no way he could deny his scared little brother, so he only nodded. Nadine had the mind to ask the clerk to have someone send along additional appropriate clothing, as well.

"I'll stay with you, too. If there's room," Lucienne said.

Their group followed a concierge to the upper floor where they would be staying, promising to bring the clothing soon. Blaise pushed open the door to his suite, the familiarity making him smile. It was the same room Jefferson had put him up in the last time he'd been in Rainbow Flat. The bed was enormous and would easily fit him and Brody. There was a comfortable chaise lounge that would work in a pinch. "Oh, there's definitely room."

Jack and Emmaline had the suite across the way. Blaise decided not to tell Jack that it was Jefferson's personal suite. That fact might annoy the outlaw. Nadine had the room next to theirs. They settled their meager belongings in their rooms.

The concierge returned a short time later with clothes for Lucienne and Brody. She aimed a sympathetic smile at the Hawthorne siblings as she handed the clothing to Blaise. "My children have outgrown these. They're a little threadbare, but they'll serve for the moment, I hope."

No wonder she had been so quick. Blaise's heart warmed at her thoughtfulness. "Thank you, um…I didn't catch your name."

She gave him a surprised look, as if guests seldom asked her name. "Trudy," the concierge said, voice soft. "You're quite welcome, Mr. Hawthorne. Now, if you like, I'll have you and your friends seated for dinner."

To Blaise's surprise, they were led to a private dining room. Another perk courtesy of Jefferson, no doubt. It wasn't long before they'd placed their orders, and all they had to do was wait for the food to arrive.

That meant they had time for unpleasant conversations. Blaise rubbed his cheek. "Can you tell us what happened, Luci?"

She stiffened at the question, then nodded. "Yes."

Lucienne

Frantic yapping, followed by a yelp and whimpering. *Chester?* Luci's eyes flashed open. It might have been a nightmare, but no. It was too real. And too close. She froze beneath her blankets, straining all of her senses to gain some understanding of what she had heard.

Crash. A shout. The sound of breaking glass, of metal instruments hitting the floor. Maybe silverware, it was hard to say. Downstairs. Definitely downstairs. Luci shot upright in her bed, casting around in the darkness for whatever was close at hand. Boots below her bed. Trousers slung over the nearby chair. She pulled them on, trying to stay as quiet as possible.

Once she was dressed, she edged closer to her door and paused by it, listening. She heard people downstairs. More shouting. The percussion of fists hitting flesh. The hiss and sizzle of what was probably an alchemical potion, accompanied by a male shriek. Luci swallowed, nudging her door open enough to peer out. Not far, another door opened, and in the wan light, she saw the gleam of her little brother's frightened eyes.

Brody. She had to get to him. Had to get him clear of whatever this was. Her mother had warned her, instructed her what to do if this ever happened. She—

"No!" Luci heard her father's voice ring out, a strident command. A gun roared in response, followed by his sharp, pain-tinged cry.

"Stop! You're killing him!" Panic filled her mother's voice. "You can have whatever you want. Money, jewelry. But don't—"

Indistinct noises drowned out her words. More chaos, more struggling. A final, gasping shout from their father before he was silenced. Luci trembled. Mama was fighting, that much she knew. She would always fight. Marian Hawthorne had explained to her daughter there was no other option at this point. She was a dangerous—and desired—commodity. An alchemist.

Nearby, Brody whimpered. She refocused her attention, sneaking up the short hallway to him. Luci knelt down to his level, relieved to see that he had remembered the plan. He wore clothing suitable for a quick escape, though his shoulders heaved with every breath, as if he were about to break into a howling tantrum.

"*Daddy*," he whispered, his small face crumpled in despair.

Luci nodded. She wanted to join him in mourning, to curl up with him and cry and cry. But that might end up with them dead or captured again. Neither were options she wanted, especially not when her mother had given her a plan to follow. "I know. I heard. But we gotta go. We can't stay here." His shoulders racked with pent-up sobs. She hustled him to the window at the end of the hallway, propping it open as the sounds of struggle continued downstairs. Their father had nailed wooden pegs into the side of the house below this window to allow them an avenue of escape if it was needed. Luci and Brody had practiced climbing up and down. Luci had hated every minute of it. Splinters bit into her hands, and there were a thousand other things she'd rather be doing. But now, she was grateful for it.

She went first, under the theory that she might catch Brody if he fell. Luckily, it didn't come to that, and they both reached the bottom safely. Luci shivered, glancing up at the setting sickle of moon in the distance. There wasn't much light, but that was good for them. It would provide them with cover that was sorely needed. Her only regret was that it gave her no clue who had attacked them in the middle of the night.

"I want Mama," Brody whined as Luci grabbed his hand.

Me, too. "We can't go to her. The plan. We have to go with the plan." Luci tugged him along, and he reluctantly followed.

Their home was on the far outskirts of Rainbow Flat, and Luci wondered if that had been a mistake. If they lived in town, would they have been a more difficult target? She had no way to know. Luci peered around the side of the house, heart pounding so loudly she feared it might give them away. She heard a pathetic whimpering nearby. Chester. The terrier had limped behind a rain barrel. He turned his head in their direction, whining softly.

"We have to get him," Brody pleaded, pointing at the dog.

"We will." Luci glanced from Chester's position to the closest bush that might mask their escape. "Go over behind that bush and wait for me."

Brody didn't argue. He rubbed one eye, then nodded and scurried across the shadow-pocked ground, diving behind the bush. Once he was safe, Luci slipped closer to Chester. As she moved, she caught sight of their attackers' mounts. Unicorns. Their horns caught the moonlight, gleaming with brilliant malevolence. Luci had no love for unicorns. The last time she'd seen one, it had been the harbinger of their capture by the Salt-Iron Confederation.

Swallowing, she picked up Chester, gasping softly when sticky blood oozed against her. Gore dribbled from one of his eyes. The terrier shivered in her arms, and she cuddled him against her chest. "I've got you. You're going to be okay. We're all going to be okay." It was a lie, but she had to say it.

Luci slunk over to Brody's hiding place. He opened his mouth when he saw Chester, but Luci shook her head urgently, making a shushing sound. She wrapped one hand around Chester's muzzle, afraid the injured dog might bark and give them away.

She didn't know how long they stayed there, too afraid to go any further for fear of being seen. Eventually, the assailants filed out of the house, laughing and joking. Luci couldn't hear what they said, but their growling voices promised nothing good. She studied their profiles in the dim light, trying to figure out who they were. They didn't look like Confederation. The outlines of their clothing were all wrong, as well as their hats. No, they wore the broad-brimmed slouch hats she associated with the outlaw mages who called Rainbow Flat home. But the few outlaws she had seen rode pegasi, not unicorns. One of the men mounted, and something on his hat gleamed like fire.

"They have Mama," Brody whispered. He rose and probably would have run out, spoiling their position, if Luci hadn't grabbed his shirt.

"No," she hissed. "Stay put." *They killed Daddy. No telling what they would do to us.*

The marauders rode off. Luci and Brody stayed where they were, too afraid to move for fear the attackers would return. When dawn tinged the sky with rosy light, Luci gingerly rose.

"C'mon. Let's go to the neighbors and get help."

CHAPTER FIFTEEN

A Man Who's Really Good at Breaking Things

Jack tented his fingers before him. Their food had come during Lucienne's tale, but none of them had touched it yet. Brody cried again. Blaise pulled his little brother onto his lap, though his focus was on the outlaw. "What do you know, Jack?"

"Nothing good," the Effigest admitted with a shrug. Blaise had figured as much from his stony look. "Sounds to me like it's the Copperheads, though they sometimes get called the Unicorn Desperadoes. The hatband gave it away."

"How's that?" Blaise asked.

Disgust crossed Jack's face. "It's the reason they're called Copperheads. Those bands are fashioned from the scales of copper dragons. When they're buffed, they shine like fire in even the dimmest light."

"So, they're outlaw mages?"

"Yep."

Blaise gently put Brody back in the seat beside him, leaning forward with sudden eagerness. "Then that means we can find them and reason with them."

Jack gave him a pitying look. "Not all outlaw mages are the same." He shook his head. "There're outlaws like me and Nadine…and then there're *desperadoes*. They make me look like a choirboy." At Blaise's puzzled look, Jack sighed. "Okay, you know the pegasi are allied with the outlaw mages, right?" Everyone nodded. "Ask yourself why they're riding unicorns, then."

Blaise's frazzled mind was too tired to figure it out, but Emmaline slapped the flat of her hand against the table as it came to her. "The same reason they have the dragon scales on their hats. They don't respect the mystic creatures one bit."

Jack aimed a finger at her. "Got it in one. The Copperheads are more like the Salties than they'll ever admit. They got magic, they're gonna use it to dominate." Then he chuckled. "Though they're a fair bit jealous of us and our pegasi. One of the Copperheads got a pegasus once. Didn't live to regret that choice, though." He reached over and picked up his drink, taking a sip. "Now they got a healthy respect for heights, at least."

"So they're land-bound. We should be able to catch up to them in no time, even with the head start they have," Blaise said, though his optimism waned at the way Jack dropped his gaze to study the untouched plate in front of him. "What?"

"We're hunting a gang of ruthless outlaw mages. They're gonna be guarding against pursuit." Jack looked as if he wanted to say more, but he clammed up on the topic, nodding to their meal. "We should eat. Talk later."

They were subdued as they finished eating. Although the food was no doubt the finest around, it didn't sit well in Blaise's stomach, and it wasn't long before he begged off, heading for his room. Brody and Lucienne tagged along, unwilling to be parted from him now that he was there. He understood their clinginess.

Brody fell asleep almost as soon as Blaise and Lucienne got him settled on one side of the king-sized bed. Chester dozed atop a cozy rug in the corner, dosed with medicine and fresh magic from a local Beast Healer Nadine knew. Blaise dimmed the lights until only a single mage-light illuminated the room. "I'm sorry I wasn't there when you needed me, Luci."

She rubbed one eye, shaking her head at his apology. "I shouldn't have said that earlier. What could you have done against all of them?" Then, as if reconsidering her question, she asked, "Did you really bring down an airship with your magic?"

Blaise sat down on the edge of the bed. "Yes. But it didn't go well." Absently, he rubbed at the pale scar that ran the length of the sensitive underside of his left arm.

Lucienne's eyes went wide as she saw the scar, roving up to the divot on his cheek where a rock had left a mark. "So, you really *are* powerful."

He shook his head. "No. I'm just a man who's really good at breaking things. You're right—I might not have been able to do anything. Bullets can still hurt me." He bore a scar on his arm as a reminder. He didn't mention he'd figured out a way to protect against bullets. Maybe that had only been luck. The fact of the matter was, if he wasn't careful, a bullet could kill him as dead as anyone else. "I bleed, same as you."

She swallowed, worry shadowing her eyes. "And you're going to go after these desperadoes?"

"I have to."

Lucienne frowned. "I don't think Mom would want you to."

Blaise didn't bother to point out that Marian Hawthorne wasn't really his mother. He doubted Lucienne knew a thing about that. And yes, he was still upset over the lifelong deception, but he *loved* the woman he considered his mother. He could still be mad at someone and love them. And want to do everything he could to save them. "Yeah, well, she's not around to stop me." Blaise raked a hand through his hair. "Tomorrow, Nadine is going to take you and Brody to Fortitude. I have a friend there —Clover. She's a Knossan, and she'll look out for y'all until I get back with Mom."

"A Knossan?" Lucienne's mouth hung open in a small *O* of surprise.

"Yeah. You'll like her." Blaise blew out a breath. There was a question he needed to ask but hadn't had the nerve to utter yet. But he was tired and needed to sleep soon. So did Lucienne. "What happened to our father? His body, I mean." He shuddered at the question. Didn't like to think about someone he loved as no longer there. The man who had taught him how to cook. How to *bake*.

Tears welled in Lucienne's eyes again. "Some of the neighbors came around and helped bury him." She scrubbed a tear away. "Under the oak tree behind the house. It's a nice spot. Peaceful."

"Nobody in town looked into the attack?"

She shook her head. "This is the *Gutter*, Blaise. There's no *law* here. No sheriff, no deputy. Nothing."

Lucienne was wrong on part of her statement, but Blaise left it. Fortitude, it seemed, differed from the other Gutter towns. It made him think more about how Jack had said he wasn't the same as the Copperheads. Fortitude didn't have set laws, but there were basic rules that were silently enforced. If something bad happened, it was investigated by one of the Ringleaders—usually Jack or Kur Agur. No wonder Jack had been annoyed by the sentry oversight.

"Time to hit the hay," Blaise said after a moment, reaching over to give her a brief hug. Lucienne clung to him even as he drew away, and though he had hit his limit with touch, he didn't have the heart to shrink back. She heaved a deep sigh and then, at last, pulled back.

"Goodnight, Blaise."

"Goodnight, Luci."

THE NEXT MORNING, THEY BREAKFASTED IN THE SAME PRIVATE DINING AREA. Afterward, Blaise worked with Nadine to make arrangements for the trek back to Fortitude. Emrys had secured the help of two additional pegasi, though Blaise had concerns about Brody flying alone. In the end, they settled for the largest stallion, who assured them he could carry a teenage girl and a child with no issue. Chester was still drugged, and according to Nadine, would do well in her saddlebag.

Nadine, Lucienne, and Brody were on their way by mid-morning, and Blaise felt better with that taken care of. *Now for the part I'm really not looking forward to.*

"Ready?" Jack asked, looking at him from his seat aboard Zepheus.

"Let's go," Blaise said, patting Emrys's neck.

"That ain't an answer." Zepheus and Oberidon's hooves clopped after Emrys. Blaise studiously ignored Jack watching him.

"It's the only one you're getting right now," Blaise replied, shaking his head.

"Fair," Jack murmured.

Truth be told, he was glad to have Jack and Emmaline along. They were quiet as they made their way to the Hawthorne house. The fair weather had receded, and dark clouds hung overhead, as if mirroring Blaise's mood. A light mist fell—not enough to hamper their progress, fortunately.

From the outside, the home looked as if nothing were awry. Their trio of pegasi halted out front, allowing the riders to dismount. Zepheus lowered his head, inspecting tracks that had torn up the grass. <Cloven hooves and unicorn droppings.>

Blaise walked closer, noting that the tracks were, in fact, cloven, like a goat or cow's hoof. Or, he supposed, a unicorn. The tracks were larger than a goat's, certainly. A pile of manure pebbled the ground near the tracks, though the brown was shot through with brilliant hues—vivid reds, greens, yellows, oranges, blues, and even purple. Blaise couldn't rightly say he'd ever seen unicorn scat before, but he figured Zepheus knew more on the topic than he did.

<Ugh, unicorns.> Emrys snorted at the droppings. <They're the worst.>

<Not worse than griffins,> Oberidon pointed out, swishing his tail.

Blaise left the stallions to bicker over the topic. Jack walked in a broad circle around the house. Blaise watched him for a moment, then called, "Can I have a minute alone?"

The outlaw flapped a hand at him, concentrating on whatever he was doing.

Blaise saw the oak Lucienne had mentioned the previous night. He started toward it, though he paused when he heard the crunch of hooves following him, a sign that the minor argument had been abandoned. He almost told Emrys that *alone* meant without him, too, but he didn't have the heart. Blaise approached the tree, slowing at the sight of disturbed dirt beneath its spreading branches. There was no gravestone, but someone had taken a knife and carved *DH* into the trunk. *Daniel Hawthorne.*

Blaise went down onto his knees, digging his fingers into a mound of dirt. "I'm sorry. So sorry I wasn't there for you." Emrys lowered his head, muzzle brushing the ground beside Blaise. "You didn't have to love me like your own, but you did. I never got to thank you for that, so I'm telling you now." *He didn't have to love me, especially with all the problems my magic caused. But he did.* "I won't ever forget that."

He rubbed a tear from one cheek. "I...I have a bakery now. Can you believe it? I hope you're proud of me." Blaise couldn't keep it in anymore. The cool dirt in his hand only emphasized how real this was. A part of him had wanted to deny his father's death. But he couldn't—not now. He choked back a sob as something occurred to him. "And I'll follow your example. You could have turned your back on me, but you never did. I won't turn mine on Mom. Or Luci or Brody. I'll do whatever I can to protect them."

His tears fell with the promise, dampening the dirt. Blaise pulled out a handkerchief, dabbing at his eyes and blowing his nose.

<You would do those things anyway,> Emrys pointed out gently.

Blaise nodded. "I would. But this is a reminder of why I do what I do." He swallowed. "Because someone else did it before me." Then he rose, folding his handkerchief and tucking it away as he rejoined Emmaline, who was pretending to not watch him and failing miserably. "What's your father doing?"

Jack crouched down, studying the pattern of footprints in the dirt. Emmaline shook her head. "I don't know. He's not exactly telling me what he's up to."

The outlaw must have heard their exchange. He lifted his head. "Trying to figure out which mages were here. There were seven of 'em." Jack rose to his full height. "That alone tells me they came expecting trouble."

"How do you figure that?" Blaise asked. *And what sort of trouble were they expecting?*

"Seven's a powerful number."

"Oh, like lucky number seven?" Emmaline's full attention was on her father, no doubt hoping to glean every bit of magical knowledge she could.

"Yep," Jack confirmed. Then he looked Blaise in the eye. "I want to go in and take a look. You coming?"

There was nothing challenging or surly in the question, which was unusual for the outlaw. Blaise didn't like it—didn't like feeling as if he were being coddled. He wanted Jack to treat him like normal—rudeness and all. If anything, it would make him feel less like damaged goods. "Yeah." He strode over to Jack, following him onto the porch. Before the Effigest opened the door, Blaise added, "You don't have to treat me like this."

Jack glanced over his shoulder. "Like what?"

"Nice."

The single word distracted the outlaw from their investigation. He wheeled, scowling. "And why shouldn't I?"

"Because it's a constant reminder of everything I've lost, and it's not like you."

A sort of recognition flashed across Jack's face, as if he understood Blaise in a way. All the same, the outlaw shook his head. "You forget, I've been where you are now. I know the hurt, how it cuts to the bone. All I had to help me back then was Zeph. I'm not being nice to cosset you. I'm doing it because I *understand*."

Blaise blew out a breath, then nodded. "So this...okay." Then, in a whisper, he added, "Thanks."

Jack grunted, pivoting again. He pushed into the home, cursing softly as he moved to open a window. "What's that smell?"

Blaise recognized the rotten-egg smell immediately. "Dragon sulfur." He edged around Jack, taking in the room. It was a small parlor that led to the kitchen and dining area. His family was tidy, but at the moment, the place was a mess. Broken glass and pottery littered the floor. A wooden chair leg was propped against the wall, the rest of the chair on its side nearby.

Light from the window flooded the room. Blaise crouched, gesturing to a broken vial. "She didn't go without a fight."

"Oh?" Jack sounded interested.

"Don't know if she succeeded, but she used Hydra Spit on one of 'em." When the outlaw raised a brow, Blaise figured he'd better clarify. "Not actual hydra spit. It's an offensive potion, probably what the dragon sulfur was in. It burns skin."

"Was gonna be impressed if she knew someone capable of milking a hydra," Jack said, amused at the prospect. "Em?"

"Yeah?" The younger Effigest had followed them inside, though she had been quiet, her lips pursed with concern as she took in the scene.

"Go with Blaise and see if you can cobble together a poppet to track 'em. Marian's the most likely, but if y'all find anything from one of the Copperheads…" Jack chuckled. "Oh, that would be quite the surprise for them."

"Well, there's blood spatter for one, but no way to know who it came from," Emmaline observed, gesturing to a dark spray on the wall Blaise hadn't noticed. He glanced away, wondering if it had been from his father. She stepped closer to him, lowering her voice. "Sorry. But blood would be really good if we knew who it was from."

"I know," he murmured. Blaise swallowed, gathering his resolve once more. "Mom's lab would be down below."

While Jack poked around on the first floor, Blaise picked up a mage-light, and he and Emmaline descended into the basement that had served as his mother's alchemy lab. They found an apron, and Emmaline used a knife to cut a one-inch strip from a string. Blaise was dismayed to see that the lab had been ransacked. The beakers, glass tubes, and ceramic bowls Marian used were shattered on the floor. Metal containers had been dented, as if someone had stomped on them. He went over to a cupboard where his mother would have stored her reagents and discovered that anything rare had been taken, too.

"Now I wonder if they were after her or the reagents," Blaise said.

"Maybe both?" Emmaline suggested. "If you're going for one prize, may as well snag another."

Blaise made a face. "I hate that your idea makes sense." He sighed. "Let's go back up."

Emmaline started up the stairs, but Blaise paused at the base as some-thing caught his eye. A small measuring spoon, not fancy or remarkable, but one he recognized. It brought to mind the time he'd needed to measure something and hadn't been able to find a measuring spoon in the kitchen, so had raided the lab. His mother had been horrified, and Blaise had quickly learned that alchemy and cooking utensils should never cross. He turned it over in his hand, transported to happier memories for a precious moment.

"Blaise? You coming?" Emmaline called.

"Yeah." He tucked the spoon into a pocket.

When they reappeared, Jack's flinty eyes settled on Blaise, as if assessing to make sure he wasn't about to fall apart like a rickety wagon. Blaise was surprised he hadn't, either. The anguish was still there, but now he could try to *do* something about it, and that made all the difference.

Emmaline held up the strip of fabric. "Got something. I'm gonna go put together a poppet."

Jack nodded to her, and Emmaline swept out the door to retrieve materials from Oberidon's saddlebag. "Did you find anything?" Blaise asked.

"Nothing we didn't already know," Jack admitted, gesturing to the surrounding mess. "I thought about dragging a local Necromancer out to see if they could get us anything else, but I reckon it wouldn't be any more than what we have." His lips twisted. "And I'm not eager to disturb the dead."

Blaise blinked. That hadn't occurred to him. "You think my father's spirit is still around? He didn't go to Perdition?"

Jack shrugged. "Sometimes, when a soul dies a violent death, they don't go to Perdition right off. Especially if they got unfinished business." He rubbed his forehead. "But I don't much care for spooks. Rather not invite trouble."

Blaise was tempted to ask for the Necromancer, anyway. Maybe he could at least tell his father he loved him one more time if his spirit was still around. But he didn't want to ask—wasn't sure *how* to ask—for that small favor. He hoped that his moment by the grave would be enough. Instead, he asked, "What do we do now?"

"Get supplies for the road. And pray to Faedra that Em can track them."

CHAPTER SIXTEEN

The Diamond of Ganland

Jefferson

The Gulf of Stars glittered like a rich, azure carpet tipped with sparkling diamonds. After leaving Seaside, they had hugged the coast, and favorable weather meant that it only took a single day to fly to Nera. Jefferson marveled at the speed of their travel. Discounting their stay in Seaside, it only took five days to travel from Fortitude to Nera. *Astounding.* If only the Confederation hadn't forced him to scrap his airship work by turning it into a weapon. Travel could truly have been revolutionized.

The Gannish capitol perched on the coastline a few miles ahead. It was so large that they could see the outskirts from a distance, as well as the lighthouse that helped to guide merchant ships into the harbor. As they closed in on the city, Jefferson hazarded a glance at Kittie and Mindy's faces. Behind the flurry of pegasi wings, the awestruck expressions they wore delighted him as they drew ever closer.

Nera was known as the Diamond of Ganland for good reason. Every building was painted white, with flecks of hematite incorporated into the roofs. It gave the impression that Nera was a sparkling gemstone, the illusion a power play to show exactly what anyone coming in to barter would deal with: wealth, affluence, strength, and beauty.

Jefferson gave Seledora a sturdy pat to get her attention. She flicked an ear back, and he leaned forward, straining against the wind resistance. "Take us down!" She bobbed her head once in acknowledgment, snorting mightily as she began a spiraling descent that the other pegasi soon mirrored.

A few minutes later, all the pegasi were on the ground. Mindy's eyes were still wide, and she glanced over her shoulder toward the city. Jefferson smiled. They would be there soon enough.

He had explained to them before they set off from Seaside how they would need to land in advance of their arrival. It was much too dangerous to fly directly to the Boss's estate, and no one wanted to be shot down by the Bossguard or attacked by a defending theurgist. Everyone agreed, going in on the ground made the most sense.

<Shall we keep our wings out or hide them?> Seledora asked, craning her head around to study him with a single dark eye.

"Keep them out," Jefferson said, though he felt rather bold with the assertion. "It's no secret that we're coming."

"It sets the tone for who and what we are," Kittie agreed, nodding at the logic. "We don't hide it."

Well, not all of us. Jefferson glanced down at the pair of rings on his fingers. One that hid his true visage, and the other his magic. Would a day ever come when he wasn't beholden to one secret or another? Probably not, judging by the way his life had gone so far. He cleared his throat. "Yes, that's another reason. They'll have no way to mistake who we are."

To further that cause, they had dressed in their better outfits for the day. Not their best—Jefferson had cautioned that they save those for when they reached their destination. But they all looked serviceable, and Jefferson fancied he looked rather debonair in his greatcoat with the flight goggles. He snapped them onto his forehead, no longer needing them to protect his eyes from the slicing wind.

They rode toward the limits of Nera two abreast. Kittie stayed alongside Jefferson, while Flora and Mindy rode close behind.

"What's that?" Mindy asked, pointing at a long, sparkling wall that curled around the city. It joined another section that appeared to burrow under the part of Nera closest to the water.

"The seawall," Jefferson replied, glancing back at her. "I don't recall where you hail from. Have you ever experienced a hurricane?"

Mindy pressed her lips together. Many a maverick mage was reluctant to admit where they came from. She shook her head. "I'm not from the coast."

He nodded, knowing that was all he would get from her. And that was fine. He didn't need to know more than that. "Count yourself fortunate. Some hurricanes that come ashore are mild, but others..." Jefferson shook his head. "One of the most destructive forces you can experience and hope to tell the tale of. A hundred years ago, such a storm rolled ashore in

Nera, and the storm surge was so overwhelming, it killed thousands and scoured the city down to nothing."

Even Kittie raised an eyebrow at that. "And they bothered to rebuild here?"

Flora cackled. "Humans can be pretty stupid sometimes. No offense to present company."

"They did rebuild, but after the disaster, they knew the city was too low and would face the same fate if another powerful hurricane threatened it," Jefferson said as they ambled onward. The pricked ears of the pegasi proved they were interested in his tale as well. "This was before Ganland was part of the Confederation, but they petitioned for all the Earth and Stonemages they could get from Phinora. Those pleas set the stage for Ganland to join the Confederation—but that's not the answer to your question." He shook his head to get back on track. "The Earthmages raised the city twenty feet, while the Stonemages created the seawall."

Jefferson could have told them more, but as he considered it, he suddenly didn't want to. They were mages—*he* was a mage—and he didn't want to think about the harm that had been done to the theurgists who helped. The Stonemages had been tasked with using their magic to draw quartz to Nera. It would have been too costly and slow to have it shipped by conventional methods. The effort had exhausted the theurgists, and most of them eventually succumbed to the incredible strain. The Earthmages hadn't been any better off. It was a daunting task to move enough dirt to raise a sprawling city, and six of the seven Earthmages had been found with blood leaking from their noses, dead from the effort.

No, Jefferson couldn't tell them that. Not when they were trying to establish good relations between the outlaw mages and Ganland. He clenched his jaw.

Fortunately, Mindy and Kittie were impressed by the feat and didn't press him for further details as they approached the gleaming quartz wall. A pair of guards rode out to greet them, and while they appeared calm, Jefferson saw by the set of their shoulders they were nervous. Mages on pegasi had a *reputation*.

Time to pull on his charm. He smiled brilliantly at them. "Good afternoon! Always a pleasure to see Nera's finest out here to greet weary travelers."

His greeting caught them off guard. They hadn't expected such exuberance. Jefferson was pleased to see that Kittie, too, offered a friendly smile. The guards studied their group. One man cleared his throat, urging his gelding forward. "Ah, right. You're the delegation from the Gutter?" He spoke incredulously, as if he hadn't expected to be approached by a group of well-dressed, orderly outlaw mages.

"We are," Kittie agreed before Jefferson could say as much. She sat tall in the saddle, her back ramrod straight and head high. As regal as a queen, Jefferson thought. "Boss Clayton invited us to Nera to treat."

The guard who had spoken grudgingly nodded. "We were told to watch for you." He turned in the saddle, gesturing to the gate that would admit them to the city. "The register is there. You'll tell us your names, and if they match our information, we'll admit you." Judging by the way his forehead wrinkled, he seemed to be puzzling out how they would keep a pegasus and its rider out of the city if they wanted to get in.

Once they had identified themselves—including the pegasi—and the guards were content, they were allowed through the gate.

"Do you need a guide to Silver Sands?" the guard asked, referencing the Madame Boss's estate and government offices.

Jefferson smiled and gave a shake of his head. "I'm quite familiar with Nera, though I appreciate the offer."

"That's *Jefferson Cole*, you dolt," a female guard hissed to her helpful counterpart. "He's Gannish. He's been to Nera countless times."

It was nice to be recognized. Jefferson acknowledged her with a wink and led his group into the city.

Many of the older Confederation cities boasted streets that were a confusing knot, as if a child had purposely tangled a skein of yarn. Nera, courtesy of the hurricane, wasn't among them. The streets were laid out in symmetrical blocks, with enough room for carriages to park on one side of the thoroughfare and for wagons or riders to pass by going both directions. Every road bustled with so much activity that even if the pegasi had wanted to land on one of them, it would have been an impossible task at this time of day.

"So many people. So much *everything*," Mindy commented.

"Nera isn't the oldest city in the Confederation, but it *is* the largest," Jefferson said. And the wealthiest. He knew that went unsaid as their heads swiveled about taking everything in.

They threaded through the crowds, and it didn't take long before people were stopping to stare at *them*. Word had already gone out that their delegation was coming, and at first, many of the faces that greeted them were borderline hostile. But that changed as soon as they saw the pegasi.

The equines were a feast for the eyes, their coats and feathers glossy in the warm afternoon sun. They ruffled their wings, extending them when the crowds allowed to show their impressive spans. The pegasi arched their necks, strutting with each step, glorying in the awestruck attention they received.

The Boss's personal guard allowed them entry to Silver Sands, which was nestled in the heart of Nera. It surprised Jefferson to discover Madame Boss Rachel Clayton awaiting them outside the executive stables, her Bossguard nearby.

"I received word you had arrived." Boss Clayton was in her middle years, her short brown hair touched by a few streaks of grey, but her eyes were as shrewd as anyone's. Right now, though, her eyes were wide with the glee Jefferson had seen on many a face of a horse-loving person as they had paraded through the streets. A small boy peered out from behind one of her legs while a girl stood nearby, her gaze on the pegasi, too.

"Mama said we could see the peggy-skies," the boy announced before hiding his face again.

"*Pegasi*," the girl, who was no doubt his older sister, corrected with a long-suffering eye-roll.

Madame Boss Rachel Clayton, who at that moment was also serving in her other important role as a mother, reached down and took her son's hand. "Only if you behave, though. Mama's working." There was a giddy gleam in her eyes, excited at the prospect of meeting the pegasi, too. She cleared her throat, remembering herself. "On behalf of all of Ganland, I offer my deepest greetings to the honored delegation representing the Gutter." She followed the formal words with a slight incline of her head.

"Hiiiiiiii!" The little boy waved enthusiastically.

Jefferson couldn't hold back his grin. Beside him, Kittie had a delighted smile on her lips. The young girl looked mortified by her brother's lack of decorum, but Rachel seemed to have expected it and ignored the behavior.

Jefferson knew Rachel well—he had dealt with her often as Malcolm Wells, but that hadn't stopped him from reaching out to her occasionally as Jefferson. "And we return the greeting to you. We are pleased that our arrival has been a source of wonder."

"Can we pet them now?" the boy asked.

Rachel sighed. "May I present Mary and Romie, my children. If the equines find it tolerable, could they pet them?"

In answer, Seledora and Tylos stepped forward without waiting for their riders. They both lowered their heads, and for a moment, Jefferson wondered if the usually acerbic mare would allow it. But she almost seemed like a different pegasus when faced with the children. Mary reached up and tentatively stroked her forehead while Romie giggled as Tylos sniffed at his chest.

<All a part of our diplomatic work,> Seledora explained to Jefferson privately. Though her mental voice held a contented edge that made him believe she was enjoying the caresses. So, the hard-hearted mare had a soft spot, after all.

A few minutes later, Rachel shooed her children away as a group of hesitant grooms filed in from the depths of the stables, eyeing the unusual equines with concern. Clearly, they didn't know how to comport themselves around the pegasi or understand what the expectations were.

"The executive grooms will see to the care of your pegasi," Rachel announced.

Jefferson pulled the hackamore reins over Seledora's head. He and the mare stepped closer to one of the grooms, a boy who looked to have just come into his teen years. "This is Seledora, and she is to be treated as a guest." The boy's eyes widened at the term. "You may remove her saddle and bridle and then groom her well and bring her any food she may request."

"*Request?*" the lad gulped.

<Yes. Oats mixed with sweet feed would be a good start. Perhaps a rich dessert of some sort. A cheesecake? I am rather fond of those.> Seledora's ears pricked at the groom, who stared at her as if she had sprouted a second head.

The mare had broadcast her suggestion so that others could hear. The Bossguard perked up, suddenly on guard. Rachel was delighted, her face split by a brilliant grin. "I believe our cook was making a cheesecake for tonight. Apple crisp cheesecake, from what I recall of the menu. If that suits the mare, you can bring out as much as the pegasi need, Pip," she informed the stable boy. "I think it likely Seledora isn't the only one who would enjoy it."

The dapple grey mare arched her neck, appreciative. To Jefferson, she said, <I see why you get on well with her.>

The grooms escorted the pegasi into the stables. With their steeds no longer a distraction, Jefferson got down to business. He was going to be the Ambassador, after all. *Might as well own it.* "Madame Boss Rachel Clayton, allow me to introduce our delegation." When everyone had turned to him, he continued.

"Firebrand Kittie Dewitt." At her name, Kittie offered a genial nod, her face a serene mask.

"Hospitalier Mindy Carman." Mindy stepped forward and gave a quick bob before moving back behind Kittie.

"And my aide, Flora Strop." The half-knocker was playing her role well, keeping her features bland. Her hair was pulled back into a severe bun, which made the audacious pink less noticeable. Jefferson knew beneath that facade, she was watching everything, probably entertaining herself with a running commentary.

"It's a pleasure," Rachel said, gesturing toward the expansive residence.

"Please, come in. My staff will help you get settled. I look forward to our dealings."

Jefferson nodded. *So far, so good.*

THE WELCOME DINNER THAT EVENING WAS A PLEASANT AFFAIR, WITH MINDY finding nothing amiss during any of the courses. Jefferson doubted anything underhanded would happen around the Madame Boss, but it did no harm to be cautious. The Gannish Doyens—Aaron Thatcher, Matthew Cohen, and Maude Harrington—joined them. The Board, the group of men and women who appointed the Boss and kept her in check, also attended.

In his time as Malcolm, Jefferson had worked closely with Aaron and, to an extent, Matthew. Maude had been the one selected to fill the seat left vacant in the wake of Malcolm's supposed death. Jefferson liked her feisty spirit—she was young, though not as young as he had been when he first claimed the position.

As the festivities wound down for the evening, Aaron slipped over to him. The red-haired Doyen smiled, though the lines framing his eyes were a clear tell that something was on his mind. "Mr. Cole, I understand you were close friends with Doyen Wells."

Aaron's opening foray caught Jefferson off guard. He had expected many things but not mention of his old, dead self. If he hadn't had years of experience at keeping his expressions unreadable, no doubt he would have made a mistake that would tip Aaron off. Instead, Jefferson gave a small nod. "Indeed. We were distant cousins, actually."

The Doyen's gaze flicked across the room to where Maude was engrossed in a conversation with Mindy. "Someone like Malcolm is difficult to replace. We miss him." Aaron sighed heavily, and Jefferson had to look away to regain his composure. He couldn't help the lump that formed in his throat at the sentiment.

"Yes, I attended the funeral, and I recall you spoke well of him," Jefferson murmured.

Surprise registered on Aaron's face. "My apologies. I didn't realize you had attended. Otherwise, I would have greeted you then as well."

Jefferson shook his head. "It's no matter." He glanced across the room at the members of the Board. One of them was speaking with Kittie, though the expression on the white-haired woman's face was that of someone forced to do something against her will. "Tell me, Aaron, as I've been out of the loop for a while, what is the temperature toward mages in

Ganland now? Do you think it bodes well for an agreement with the Gutter?"

Aaron pursed his lips as he considered the question, his gaze also roving to the Board members. "I'll be honest. It varies. There are pockets of those who don't trust them and will think that allying with the Gutter will lead to our downfall. Others still think we should because the ultimate profit will be worthwhile." He paused, shaking his head. "And others who subscribe to Confederation ways would rather we scour the Gutter."

Jefferson nodded. He'd suspected as much, but it was good to receive confirmation. "Little has changed, then."

The Doyen crooked a finger at one of the Board members. "They're the ones you have to convince. The Board."

"Mmm," Jefferson agreed, having suspected that would be the case. "I appreciate the information. I look forward to more dealings with you in the future, Doyen Thatcher."

Aaron's smile thinned. "We'll see how things proceed, Mr. Cole. I won't lie—we're going to get some guff from the Mossbacks on the Council for even giving your delegation the time of day."

Oh, the Mossbacks. Rub their noses in it, then. Jefferson cocked his head. "Oh? I thought the Faedrans on the Council didn't grovel to that lot."

The Doyen shrugged. "It's been a challenge ever since the Breaker Inquiry." He gave a rueful shake of his head. "Don't get me wrong, we're trying. But so many mavericks are flooding out of the Confederation that it's causing problems."

Problems. Yes, problems like they can't find new mages to subjugate. Such a shame. "Problems for the Mossbacks don't equate to problems for your faction, though." Unless things had changed in the few months that Malcolm had been gone.

"No, you're right on that point, but it has made the Mossbacks grumpy." Aaron shrugged.

"I presume you're being charitable by calling them *grumpy*," Jefferson said, which earned a chuckle.

"You're right. *Unreasonable* is the better word," the Doyen agreed, though he still laughed. Then he sighed. "Anyway, the hour is late, and I have meetings early in the day. As do you, I would imagine."

They said their goodbyes, everyone going their separate ways. Jefferson and his delegation walked to their cluster of rooms together, as they had planned. But as they reached the first door—Kittie's room—the Pyromancer coasted past it.

"Your room is—" Jefferson began, then cut himself off at the look she arrowed at him. "Never mind. I suppose we *should* have a lively discussion." He gestured grandly to the door leading to his room, which he supposed was Kittie's destination.

"You spoke to Doyen Thatcher privately. Why?" Kittie didn't mince words as she flopped down in the middle of the cream-colored, cameo-backed settee. Flora claimed the seat to one side of Kittie while Mindy took the other. It was a clear sign they had all noticed—and wondered.

"I knew he could give me honest insight into what we're getting ourselves into," Jefferson explained. "He's got connections and information the other Doyens don't, so I knew he would be a good one to ask."

"And what did you find out?" Kittie asked.

"We have to win over the Board." Jefferson sighed. "Means more wheeling and dealing. More proving our value."

"As you suspected," Kittie said.

"Yes," he agreed. Jefferson glanced at his saddlebags slumped by the door, a reminder that they still needed to unpack. And take care of other pressing matters. "Tomorrow will be a preparation day before we set to work."

"Preparation day?" Mindy repeated, puzzled.

Jefferson nodded, glancing at Flora. "Yes. Can you make sure our schedule is clear for the day? We need to get to the tailor."

Flora cocked her head. "But you have an entire wardrobe in your house outside of town."

Yes, but it's been a few months since I've been able to treat myself to a proper fitting. He waved a hand, leaving it unsaid. "I need whatever the latest fashion is, and you know it. And we need clothing for Kittie and Mindy, too."

Kittie scowled. "We *brought* clothing." She gestured to the saddlebags. Then, no doubt realizing that might not be sufficient, she added, "*Good* clothing."

Good, but not up to the standards of the Diamond of Ganland. No, Jefferson wanted his outlaws to shine just as brightly. "They're service-able, yes. But trust me on this. We need something better. My treat."

Kittie crossed her arms, no doubt wanting to deny the offer. Conflicting emotions warred in her eyes before she finally relented. "This is part of the plan?"

He grinned. "All part of the plan."

CHAPTER SEVENTEEN

No-Account Greenhorn

"The Untamed Territory is huge and unfriendly. We're gonna need supplies," Jack said.

Blaise stared at the outlaw with disappointment, though in his gut, he knew the pronouncement made sense. They had convened in the stables so that their pegasi could hear their plans, too. Blaise idly scratched Emrys behind an ear, thinking. When they had set out from Fortitude, none of them knew what lay ahead. Now they had a better idea, and with the outlaw's years of experience, Jack knew what they would need to have a chance of success.

"Do we have enough funds to do that?" Blaise asked. He had brought some coin, but probably not enough.

Jack gave him a crooked smile. "Who says we have to use our funds? Throw your beau's name around. Let's see how useful he is."

Blaise frowned, not wanting to take advantage of his connections. He wasn't as embarrassed as he had first been about his relationship with Jefferson—no, he had grown more comfortable with it. But he didn't like using Jefferson's name and influence that way. Would people think that was all Blaise wanted him for, a free ticket?

<He would want you to have the things you need to be successful,> Emrys reasoned, prodding Blaise with his muzzle. <Especially important things like sugar for your loyal pegasus.>

Blaise hid a smile at the stallion's suggestion. "Fine. If we do that, can we leave today?"

Jack pursed his lips, pulling a pocket watch out to consult the time. It was mid-morning, and Blaise thought it couldn't possibly take long to gather whatever they needed. But to his dismay, the outlaw shook his head. "Wouldn't be as smart as making a fresh start in the morning. And Em's still trying to get that poppet to work." Something unreadable flashed across the Effigest's face at that. Emmaline had trekked back out to the Hawthorne home with Oberidon to get another personal item. She'd had no success with the bit of apron they'd snatched the previous day.

Blaise's shoulders tensed with frustration. He wanted to be under way, hunting down the Copperheads. It was hard to tell himself that if Jack thought it was a bad idea to hare off after them immediately, then he needed to listen. "Okay. Let's go shopping, then."

Jack rubbed his hands together. "This'll be almost as good as robbing him."

Blaise narrowed his eyes. "I don't appreciate you talking about robbing Jefferson."

"All in good fun," Jack said with a shrug.

They left their pegasi to start on their tasks. Blaise followed Jack to the Mercantile. The Effigest sauntered in, and the shopkeeper seemed to know him from previous visits. They shot the breeze for a few minutes before Jack hitched a thumb at Blaise and casually dropped Jefferson's name. The woman hadn't recognized him—which had been nice—but her demeanor changed as soon as she knew she was in the Breaker's presence. Her eyes went wide, not from fear but from—respect? Awe? Something like that. Blaise wasn't sure what to make of it. But Jack was right. As soon as the shopkeeper learned who he was—and who he was connected to— she was quick to get whatever they needed. And, of course, Jack was tickled that it went on Jefferson's account.

"Don't think I'll ever get used to that," Blaise muttered as they headed to their next stop.

"What's that?" Jack asked.

"People looking at me like I'm special. Or scary. Or something in between."

Jack snorted. "If it makes you feel better, you're always going to be a no-account greenhorn to me."

It was ridiculous, but that *did* make Blaise feel better. The people who knew him—really *knew* him—understood him. They knew he didn't want to be any of the things others thought of him. There was solace in that.

Blaise rubbed his chin, moving on to another train of thought as they headed to the Dry Goods Store. "Why do you think Em is having trouble with her spell? That strip of fabric definitely belongs to Mom."

The Effigest slowed, that unreadable expression clouding his face again. "Sometimes spells don't take right the first time. Least, not for Ritualists. We're not like you, just touching things and having your magic do its job."

Blaise wrinkled his nose. That wasn't how his magic worked—not at all, now that he understood more about it. Something about Jack's deflection struck him wrong, too. "But that's not what this is, is it?"

Jack grunted. "You're getting more savvy than I like, greenhorn."

So he was on the right trail. Blaise figured there was something Jack didn't want to tell him—but whatever it was would have to come to light eventually if they were to succeed. "If it's not Emmaline's spell itself, then what is it?"

The outlaw moved aside as a laden wagon rumbled by. When it had passed, he stopped and turned to Blaise. "The mages we're going after. I told you they're bad news. I was trying to figure out who came out here but didn't have any luck. But they have magics that can cause us problems."

"Starting with Emmaline's tracking?" Blaise guessed.

"Starting with her tracking," Jack confirmed, grim. "They've got a Dampener—a damn good one, too. That might be enough to block Em, or at least make it difficult. There's also a Warder. One of those who knows what they're doing could send her off the trail without a problem."

Blaise grimaced with dismay, thinking of how expansive the Untamed Territory was. He had been counting on Emmaline's magic. "Finding them is going to be a needle in a haystack, then?"

Jack waggled the fingers on one hand, an indecisive gesture. "Yes and no. We have the advantage of flight, and they're on the ground, so it's possible that we might catch up to them if we can figure out where they are. But the important bit is I know where they're going."

Blaise arched his brows. "And where is that?"

"Thorn," Jack said. "Hank brought news about a month ago that the Copperheads had laid claim to it."

"Oh." Blaise wasn't sure what to make of that, but judging by Jack's expression, it didn't sound good. He chewed on the information for a moment, then realized why knowing where they were going wasn't the best thing. "But it would be in our favor to catch up to them before they get there, huh?"

"Yep," Jack agreed.

After stopping at two more storefronts, the outlaw declared he was satisfied. Everything he'd requested would be delivered to their hotel before dusk. With that task done, they headed to the hotel to meet up with Emmaline, whose attempts at tracking Blaise's mother were still unsuccessful.

Jack waved a hand. "Not worth wasting all your power over."

Emmaline chewed on her bottom lip, glancing at Blaise. "But I want to *help*."

"You are," Blaise assured her, knowing exactly how ineffective she felt. He was about to tell her he felt the same when Trudy, the hotel concierge, approached.

"Excuse me, Mr. Hawthorne. We have a guest who has requested to speak with you. Would you like—?"

"What's her name?" Jack cut in.

Trudy frowned, as if trying to decide if she should answer him or not. Jack smiled at her, though he didn't use his scary smile. No, this time, he used one that Blaise had only seen him use around Kittie. He lifted his eyebrows enough to give himself an open, affable expression as his lips split to show his teeth. It was an *aw shucks*, friendly look that lent him an air of approachability the outlaw didn't otherwise possess.

Emmaline noticed, and her face contorted, a *who are you and what have you done with my father?* sort of look. Jack ignored it as he tried to work his dubious charm on the concierge.

Trudy cleared her throat, then held up a finger as she pivoted and crossed the lobby to the front desk. She conferred with the clerk before returning to their cluster. "The name on the books is Jane Herald."

Not a name Blaise recognized, and neither did Jack from the way his eyes momentarily narrowed. The outlaw shrugged, letting Blaise decide.

"We'll see her," Blaise said.

Trudy smiled and beckoned them down one of the long, ornate hallways. Blaise stayed close on the concierge's heels, with Emmaline behind him. Jack brought up the tail end as if he were guarding their backs.

The concierge halted outside a room and tapped on the door. It opened little more than an inch, blocking any hope they had of seeing the occupant. Trudy conversed with the woman on the other side of the door in a soft voice, then turned back to their group.

"Miss Herald requests that she only meet with Mr. Hawthorne." Trudy spread her hands in apology.

Jack scowled, no doubt suspicious—which, to be fair, was his default. Blaise was conflicted, torn between the safety of the people he knew and whatever tidings this messenger brought. Had she come bearing news about Jefferson and the delegation?

"Up to you," Jack said.

Blaise exhaled softly. "I'll see her." But his eyes were on Jack and Emmaline, shadows of uncertainty in their depths.

Jack grinned at him, slouching with one shoulder against the wall. He pulled out a poppet—not his own, but Blaise's. He didn't particularly like Jack having it, but so far, the Effigest had behaved. "Go ahead. We're not going anywhere."

It was both a promise and a threat to whoever was on the other side of the door.

THE LATCH MADE A SOFT CLICK AS THE DOOR SHUT BEHIND BLAISE. HE found himself in a suite like his own, though while his room was decorated in deep blues and warm yellows, this one was the red of a ripe apple with chocolate-colored accents. It wasn't an unpleasant combination, but it made the rooms appear darker, even in the glow of the mage-lights hanging from the walls.

A woman perched on the edge of a compact loveseat in the sitting room. Her clothing was a mix of black and charcoal, though it was well-tailored. Her long skirt shushed across the floor as she adjusted to study him. "Mr. Hawthorne, I presume." Her voice had almost no inflection.

Blaise paused. Something about that didn't sit well with him, though he decided not to hold that against her. He wasn't a brilliant orator, either. He nodded, then remembered to add, "I am."

Her eyes stayed on him, and she looked as if she either didn't know what to say next or was waiting for him to say something. Blaise shifted his weight, his gaze darting around the sitting room. "Um, Trudy said you needed to speak to me? Should I sit?" *Stop it. Be more sure of yourself. You're not a pushover anymore.* But it was so hard when speaking to someone he didn't know.

The strange woman nodded. "Yes, please sit." She gestured to an armchair diagonal from her position.

Blaise sat. He folded his hands in his lap. "Thanks." He cleared his throat. "You know my name, but I don't know yours." It was a lie, but he hoped she wouldn't know that. Besides, it was simple manners.

"Herald will do," she replied, still watching him intently. "You are friends with Jefferson Cole."

It was a statement, not a question, but all the same, Blaise gave a small nod. Her voice was so odd—she didn't add any emphasis to the word *friends*, as others might if they wished to imply their relationship went beyond that. Just as well, since he didn't want to discuss that with a stranger. "Is this about Jeffer—Ambassador Cole?" Blaise asked.

Herald smiled at that, though no warmth touched her eyes. It was as if she were only going through the motions, mimicking something she had seen others do. "Yes, it is. How close are you to him?"

There it was, though once again, she didn't add any weight to the words. "We're business partners. Is this about the delegation?" As much as her words agitated him, he couldn't take the chance that she might not tell him something crucial.

It was as if his question had opened a floodgate. She swept into action, leaping up from the loveseat in a blur of motion as she dove toward Blaise, a pale hand outstretched. Alarmed, he yelped as she latched onto his arm, hauling him to his feet with more strength than he thought she could possibly possess. He stumbled, unbalanced by the unexpected movement. Herald dragged him upright, his boots scuffing against the floor.

"Stop! Wait! What are you doing?" Blaise tried to dig his heels in, but he still hadn't recovered his feet, and all he could do was valiantly try not to fall on his face.

She pulled him closer to the window—no, not the window. The wall? Outside, there was a pounding and a frustrated roar as Jack hammered on the door. Emmaline shouted Blaise's name.

Herald laid her palm against the wall—and then her hand sank *into* it. Blaise stared. *Did she really*—yes, the rest of her arm followed her hand into the wall as easily as a knife cutting into warm bread. And she seemed determined to drag him along with her.

No. Her magic coiled around him as her left shoulder vanished into the wall. Blaise's own power raced up at his call like a stampede of pegasi. His magic slammed into Herald's, shredding the tendrils that sought to spirit him away. The woman screamed as if the Breaker magic had directly harmed her. Maybe it had. Blaise didn't care at the moment. He just wanted to get *away*.

Herald released him, and Blaise fell onto his backside, grunting as the air whooshed out of his lungs. By the time he had the wherewithal to scuttle away, she had regained her composure, too. Herald pulled her arm back out of the wall, the limb returning with an unsettling sucking sound. She flexed her fingers, preparing to pounce.

"You will come with me," Herald said. "Your presence is required."

"Go lick salt-iron," Blaise rumbled, limbering his own fingers. Silvery wisps of magic played across his skin.

The door exploded inward, falling from the hinges with a resounding crash as Jack and Emmaline hurtled into the room. Jack's face contorted into a snarl, his sixgun out and ready though he didn't fire as he took in the scene. Emmaline's was out, too. She smoothly slid to block Herald's access to Blaise while Jack set his sights on the woman.

Blaise thought he might fire, judging by the way Jack's finger caressed the trigger. "Who are you?"

Herald had regained her stoic composure. She didn't look in the least bit concerned to stare down the business end of a furious outlaw's sixgun. She cocked her head and smiled, then took a quick step to the side, palm extended to—

"Don't let her touch the wall!" Blaise yelled, but Herald moved more quickly than his words. The Effigest cursed as the opposing mage sank into the wall and disappeared.

"Bloody souls of Perdition. What was that?" Jack growled, moving to occupy the same space Herald had been in seconds earlier. He ran a hand over the wall as if searching for a secret door, and Blaise was relieved that he wasn't sucked into it. Jack glanced back at him. "You okay?"

Blaise blew out a breath. "I think so. I was almost pulled into a wall, though." He wanted to sit, but he didn't trust any of the chairs in this room.

"Daddy, what *was* that?" Emmaline asked, her eyes on the wall.

The elder Effigest was quiet for a moment. Then he shook his head. "Don't know. A Walker unlike any I've seen before." Experimentally, he ran his hands over the wall again. "Doesn't mean they can't exist, though. Walkers are like other mages: each one a little different."

Blaise grimaced. He didn't like the idea that someone could just drag him into a wall and off to who knew where. He laughed, and he knew it had a hysterical edge from the look Emmaline gave him.

"What is it?" she asked.

Blaise ran a hand through his hair, no doubt mussing it. He didn't care. "I know Jack said the Untamed Territory would be dangerous, but I can't help but think it may be safer for me than here."

Emmaline canted her head, confused. "Why's that?"

"No walls," he explained, shaking his head.

CHAPTER EIGHTEEN

Turn Them into Flour for a Cake

Blaise

*B*laise hadn't expected the Untamed Territory to be beautiful. Upon reflection, though, it made sense—Jefferson loved it, after all. There was a wild fierceness to the tall grasses that swayed in the wind, interspersed with late-autumn wildflowers in a riot of colors. The terrain was mostly flat, though Blaise saw hints of rolling hills far to the north. Trees were sparse, usually growing in clusters ringing watering holes or small springs. An endless blue sky sprawled overhead, littered with wispy clouds at the highest elevations. It was a little chilly, but Blaise's dark blue duster soaked up the sun, providing all the warmth he needed.

A smile pulled up the corners of Blaise's mouth as he peered over Emrys's shoulder. The stallion tipped an ear back in his direction. <Enjoying the scenery?>

Blaise rubbed the stallion's neck, knowing Emrys would read his pleasure. It surprised him that he felt so…okay. They had a target to pursue, and now that they were giving chase, it soothed the part of him that desperately needed to do something.

And it didn't hurt that it put distance between him and the strange Walker who had tried to whisk him away. He shuddered at the thought. They hadn't spoken of her since that night, but Jack had been so agitated by it, he had declared Blaise would bunk in the same room as him and Emmaline. Blaise hadn't questioned it—he felt better knowing they were close enough to intervene if needed.

He still didn't know what she had wanted. It was possible that she only wanted him because of what he was. As so many others had. Blaise shook the thought away, instead taking in the sights below them. The Untamed Territory was home to so many creatures, many he'd never seen before. Emrys was happy to name them as they flew over.

<Do you see the tan and white deer with the short antlers? They are antelope.> The antelope bounded away in alarm as the pegasi's shadows swept over them, leaving Blaise to observe their white tails flung upwards as they scrabbled away.

Huge, shaggy bovines with humped backs were bison. <Not related to the Knossans. Bison aren't magical, but they can be dangerous,> Emrys advised. <They look small from up here, but they would make even Clover think twice.>

Not long after, they caught sight of a grasscat, a feat difficult to achieve, according to the stallion. The predator stalked a weak bison calf, its lanky feline body low in the grass. It was challenging to make out— Blaise only saw a shadow skulking along, then realized it was a form that looked grassy, covered in wildflowers.

He had a better view of it when the beast leaped at its prey, a blur of vegetation making a terrifying yowl. The calf bleated in dismay as killing teeth clamped onto its neck, and the mother bison bugled her rage. But already, the pegasi were gliding away from the life-and-death struggle, so Blaise would never know how it ended.

He was glad for it, though. Even though the grasscat needed to eat, he didn't want to see the calf torn apart. Emrys snorted agreement when he said as much.

"I can't believe we saw a grasscat!" Emmaline crowed her excitement as they dismounted for their mid-day break at a watering hole shaded by post oaks. "Those are rare to see, aren't they, Daddy?"

Jack was loosening Zepheus's girth to give the stallion a breather, but he turned at the question, pushing his wide-brimmed hat up from his brow. "Yes and no. Most people don't see 'em 'til they're coming at them." He frowned, scanning the area. "And that one was near enough that we have to be vigilant. They usually live in prides, so there're likely more grasscat lionesses with that one."

The news made Blaise uneasy. "Do we need to be worried?"

"The pegasi would hear them before they got too close, right?" Emmaline asked at the same time.

Jack glanced between them. "Yes to Blaise and no to you, Em. They're big cats. They move silent as ghosts, and they smell like grass."

<This is not comforting,> Emrys remarked, which was exactly what Blaise was thinking.

"This is going to be a short break," Jack announced, pulling jerky from his saddlebag. He tossed a chunk to Emmaline and another to Blaise. "Only long enough to let the pegasi rest and eat."

Emmaline loosened Oberidon's girth, then sat down cross-legged beside the small pond. "You ever had to fight a grasscat?"

Jack had a chunk of jerky in his mouth and was busily chewing it as he double-checked his sixgun. Once he'd seated the sixgun in its holster again, he waggled the fingers of one hand, an indecisive gesture. "Fight? No. Escape from, yes." He winced at whatever harrowing memories accompanied his words.

Zepheus had been drinking from the pool, but he lifted his head to regard them, silver droplets falling back into the still water. <We had robbed a Confederation stagecoach. Jack was wounded because—> The stallion stopped abruptly, and Emrys and Oberidon lifted their heads. The trio of pegasi turned, suddenly on alert as they stared to the east.

Jack pulled his sixgun and poppet. Emmaline scrambled to her feet, mirroring her father. Blaise got up as quickly as he could, though he would never match either of the Dewitts.

And then they heard what the pegasi had. A distant bellow, flavored with notes of warning and fear. Jack tilted his head, lips pressed together. "That's a Knossan."

A Knossan? Like Clover? "They sound like they're in trouble," Blaise said, moving closer to Emrys.

<What are we doing?> the black stallion queried as Blaise checked his girth, then put a boot in the stirrup.

"If it's a Knossan, we should see if they need help," Blaise answered.

Jack pivoted, eyes narrowed. "Whatever's after the Knossan, better them than us."

Emrys quivered beneath Blaise, sharing the outlaw's sentiment. But the stallion wouldn't go against Blaise's wishes. Blaise closed his eyes for a moment, gathering his will. Then he shook his head, eyes flashing open. "I won't let someone suffer while I stand by and ignore it." Then softer, he added, "Let's go, Emrys."

The Effigest cursed, then moved to tighten Zepheus's girth. Blaise didn't look back to see if Jack mounted or not. Emrys was already turning, trotting out of the cover of the post oak trees to head in the direction of the bellowing Knossan.

A short distance from their impromptu camp, they found a trio of Knossans. They stood back to back, ringed by grasscats. Only the oddly shifting shadows in the grass told the tale of their impending peril. The Knossans were massive, perhaps ten feet tall at the tips of their long, sweeping horns. Blaise thought Clover was tall, but these bulls would easily dwarf her. They were garbed in clothing made from simple linens and reinforced with leather. One of the bulls had a shotgun, and another had a bow. The third bull was unarmed, blood weeping from a ragged gash down his right arm.

Zepheus and Oberidon pulled up beside Emrys. Jack sighed. "Okay, bleeding heart, now what?"

Blaise watched the ever-shifting grasses that hinted at the felines' movements. "If we scare them, will they go away?"

Jack scowled. "How are *you* going to scare them? Turn them into flour for a cake?"

Blaise licked his lips. *By doing something they've probably never encountered before.* And it wouldn't be pretty. "Something like that."

"Wait, *what?*" Emmaline gaped.

"Emrys, can you drop me by the Knossans?" Blaise asked, ignoring Jack's worried scowl. He tried to pretend like the fact that Jack was *concerned* wasn't worrisome all on its own.

The pegasus cupped his nostrils, snorting uncertainly. <Pardon me?>

"Those cats are going in for the kill any moment. I need to be there to stop them."

"Offering yourself as an appetizer ain't the way to do it," Jack growled. "Can't believe I have to tell *you* this, but don't be reckless."

Blaise swallowed. "I'm not being reckless. If they attack me, I can stop them." He uncurled a fist, silvery wisps of magic wafting from his palm.

The outlaw narrowed his eyes. "You can manifest your magic?"

"Is that what this is?" Blaise asked. He hadn't had a name for it. Just knew it was something that happened now.

"*Yes,*" Jack said, exasperated. He pulled out a poppet, hefting it up. "Go do whatever ridiculous thing you have planned. I got your back."

"Me, too," Emmaline said grimly, sixgun in hand.

Emrys arched his neck as Blaise urged him forward. The stallion vaulted into the sky, though he gained little altitude. <Are we good for a touch and go?>

Blaise hated touch and goes. But they were something he'd practiced since he'd returned to Fortitude. He would never pull it off as effortlessly as Jack or Emmaline, but he could do it. "Yeah, no other choice."

The pegasus circled over the Knossans once. <We are here to help!> Emrys announced, though no acknowledgment came from below. The bulls were too busy keeping their formation against the predators.

As soon as Emrys's hooves touched the ground and his wings mantled, Blaise jumped from the stallion's back. In a great gust, Emrys pushed off and returned to the sky. Blaise botched the landing, his left leg buckling, and he had to throw out his hands to keep from plowing the ground with his face. Something thorny bit into his palm, but he ignored it as he struggled to his feet.

The black and white bull closest to him blew out a breath. "It is not every day one sees a human offer themselves up to the grasscats."

They're about to bite off more than they can chew. Blaise didn't take the time to speak to the Knossan. His gaze flicked over the grasses as they bent and swayed, brimming with nearly invisible cats. He rubbed his hands together, wincing at the gash in his palm. But his magic was there and ready.

Blaise knew that alongside the Knossans, he looked insignificant and weak, like the bison calf. Prey. He held up his hands, willing a thin shield of Breaker magic to take form. It shimmered before him like a heat mirage, almost imperceptible if not for the tiny motes of silver dancing in the sunlight.

There was no warning roar. Something lunged at him. He saw a flash of limber feline covered in a short hide of grass with a mane shot through with flowers. Eyes that gleamed like fireflies. Mouth gaping *wide, wide, wide* with teeth that looked more like sharpened wooden stakes than anything else. Forelegs reaching out, paws tipped with root-like claws.

More shapes were on the move. Blaise only had eyes for the one coming at him. An outstretched paw battered against his shield. For an instant, Blaise feared it would fail, popped like a bubble by the force of his attacker. The grasscat was heavy, and he felt every bit of her weight as she struck.

The lioness yowled, a horrific, agonized cry as his power took hold, unmaking her. The grass shredded, revealing a skeleton made of knotted roots and vines covered in clay-like soil that served as muscles. The wooden fangs fell harmlessly to the turf. The flowers that had been a part of the cat's mane flitted away on the breeze, as if a child had blown the fluff from a dandelion.

The other grasscats in the pride roared, the sound a mix of alarm and outrage. They became visible, heads popping up above the grasses, staring at him with those firefly-eyes. And then they charged.

Blaise lost track of the action after that. Everything was a blur. The bulls were on the move, firing at the grasscats with shotgun and bow. Jack was somehow around, moving preternaturally fast, armed with sixgun and a fat knife Blaise hadn't known he owned. Emmaline stayed at the fringe, and Blaise heard the report of her sixgun when she had a clear shot.

At the end of the dust-up, a dozen grasscats were dead—some of them shredded on Blaise's shield, others hacked by Jack's knife or shot full of arrows or bullets. One of the bulls had taken a bite on the leg, and claws had raked Jack's arm, but otherwise, they were alive, which Blaise thought was something.

He rubbed the back of his neck. "Um, sorry. I didn't know that trick was going to make them come after us like that." Jack gave him a heated look that clearly said they were going to have words about that *trick* when it was safe.

A nearly white Knossan, the one who had the gash on his massive forearm, shook his head. All three were breathing hard from the exertion and seemed on edge. "It was not your ability that spurred them, mage. They were compelled."

Compelled? Blaise blinked, wondering about that, but didn't ask because the black and white bull was staring at him. "You are the Breaker."

Blaise sighed. Great, he had a reputation even this far out. Just what he wanted.

Before he could answer, Jack spoke up. "You say they were compelled? Y'all seen any mages who might do that, by chance?"

The third bull, so dark brown he was almost black, nodded. "Indeed. Two days ago, we came across the Copperheads. They attempted to goad us into a fight." His dark eyes narrowed, no doubt angered by the memory. "But their leader said there was no time. One of the desperadoes said something about sending us to do their dirty work." His hands clenched at his sides.

"*Beastcaller*," the white bull said, disdain in his voice. "He tried to command us as if we were animals. When he could not, he grew angry and used his power to send a swarm of wasps after us. We ran, and as we went, it was as if more and more creatures were sent to hunt us down. We fought those we could, winning our way through. But we were too tired by the time the grasscats came."

"Elementalist," Jack said, seemingly to himself. When the Knossans turned to him, he shrugged. "Beastcaller couldn't have influenced the grasscats. They're not animals, not really." His blue eyes flicked to one of the dead creatures. "They bothered to have two mages send minions to stop you. To stop us." Jack's mouth was drawn, eyes glittering with something indecipherable. "We've got a camp. Join us. We can mend our wounds together and recover."

It was odd to hear Jack downright hospitable, but Blaise figured the outlaw knew what he was doing. Together, their motley group returned to their camp.

Emmaline slipped up beside Blaise as they walked back, their pegasi on their heels. "That was amazing. What was it?"

Blaise shrugged. "Something I learned in the Golden Citadel."

Her eyes widened in understanding. "Oh. I'm sorry I asked but…you should know it was really impressive."

He nodded, knowing that it *was* impressive. No one besides Jefferson and Flora knew he had used the same trick to shatter a bullet. He had practiced it little by little, gradually weaving the shield into something larger. Blaise wasn't sure how he felt about others knowing about that ability, but he knew eventually, it was going to get out. He had to have ways to use his magic to protect himself.

<It was impressive, but I was afraid the grasscats were going to *eat* you,> Emrys said, shoving his head into Blaise's back. <Don't do that again.>

Blaise sighed. He couldn't promise that, and Emrys knew it.

When they reached their campsite, Emmaline pulled a first aid kit from Oberidon's saddlebags. The Knossans tended to their own wounds, and Emmaline helped her father take care of his. Before long, everyone was bandaged, a tentative silence growing between the humans and Knossans.

"You're awfully far from Knossas," Jack observed as he filled his canteen with fresh water.

The dark brown bull huffed. "We travel to the Black Market. It is scheduled to be nearby tomorrow, and there are certain supplies we require." His eyes glittered. "And information."

Information. One of Jack's favorite things. The outlaw cocked his head, though he feigned boredom. "Oh? What sort of information are you after?"

The Knossans exchanged looks, as if debating how much to tell them. After a moment, the white bull spoke. "Precious things have been stolen. Relics." He heaved a long, drawn-out breath. "Younglings."

Jack scowled. Blaise knew for certain the Effigest didn't like that one bit. He was close with Clover, and while Blaise didn't know her history, he could guess. "Young-uns, you say?" The outlaw rose, screwing the cap back on his canteen. "Slocum doesn't traffic."

The black and white bull nodded. "We know this. But he deals with rare items. And he is well-informed."

Jack seemed to chew on that for a few minutes. "We could use a stop at the Black Market, too. Maybe we can travel together."

"There is strength in numbers," the white bull agreed. "We would welcome this."

Blaise frowned, wondering what Jack was up to. With the Knossans, they would be landbound—which Blaise preferred to flying, but they would travel so much slower. But he would trust Jack and hope the outlaw's savvy wasn't leading them astray.

CHAPTER NINETEEN

Attitude is Everything

Zuzanna is a genius, but also a pain in the ass. Jefferson had been giddy at the thought of visiting his favorite tailor in Nera, until he recalled how she enjoyed tormenting him. But the quality of the items she produced was worth it. Zuzanna was more than just a tailor. She was a Fibermage, capable of weaving her power to create amazing outfits. Her designs were unlike anything else.

Most people didn't consider Zuzanna a mage. Fashion icon? Designer? Genius? All of those, and mage last. Jefferson wondered if it was because she was a tailor before anything else that set her apart. Tailors were comfortable. They were *normal.*

Not like Breakers. Or Dreamers, Jefferson considered as he held his arms out while Zuzanna moved around him, making thoughtful little noises and murmuring to herself. Flora waited nearby, somehow looking bored and vigilant at the same time. Kittie and Mindy were speaking with Zuzanna's assistant, going over fabric options since the tailor had finished with them. "I saved the fussiest for last," Zuzanna had informed them as she beckoned Jefferson over.

He glanced at the ring on his left hand, then grunted when Zuzanna poked him in the ribs. "I told you not to move!"

"I didn't," Jefferson muttered. He had barely turned his head at all. But Zuzanna was demanding when she was at work. All a part of her magic, or so she claimed. Jefferson wondered if she just enjoyed bossing the elite around. He couldn't fault her for that.

"You *did*," she insisted, ramming the tip of her index finger into his ribs. "Be still as a statue. Don't move again."

"I have to *breathe*," Jefferson reminded her.

"Oh, I have to breathe, you say? Breathe *later!*" Zuzanna snapped, which sent Flora into a laughing fit.

Jefferson sighed. Yes, she definitely enjoyed playing with the elite. And she still saw him as one, even though she knew he kept company with outlaw mages.

"No sighing!"

"Sweet Tabris, Zuzanna! I'm paying you enough, so at least allow me to *exist*."

She kept her dark-haired head down, though Jefferson suspected she was grinning. "That's an extra charge."

"Then I will pay the existence fee. Gods, I forgot how impossible you could be."

"And yet here you are, and you go to no other. Because you know you will only get the *best* from me," she bragged, stepping back as she took the last measurement. Zuzanna wasn't much taller than Flora, but like the half-knocker, she had a *presence*. Her work had stooped her back, but she was still full of vinegar. "I have everything I need. I'll have your outfits ready by end of day and can send them to you. Shall I send them to your estate?" Her voice turned sly, a sign that she very well knew where their group was staying but wanted him to say it.

"Please send them to Silver Sands."

Zuzanna whistled. "That will be an extra fee."

Jefferson rolled his eyes. "How is that any different from sending it to my estate?"

Zuzanna favored him with a beatific smile. "As I hear it, you call the Gutter home, so foreign shipping. Export fees."

Jefferson's mouth opened to argue, then he snapped it closed. He knew better. The more he said, the more she would tack onto her price because she knew that her shop was the only one he could—and would—turn to. He ran a hand through his hair. "Yes. Fine. It's worth it to be dressed respectably in a Zuzanna Original."

"Of course, it is," she agreed, then put an arm around him to shuffle him toward the door. "And now you must go so that I can begin work before my next appointment. I need time to work my magic." She waved to Kittie and Mindy. "It's been a pleasure, my darlings."

Jefferson nodded, filing out the door with the others. He was quite happy to swing into Seledora's saddle so they could return to their other obligations. And so that he could stop being poked and sniped at.

"How much is Zuzanna milking you for this time?" Flora asked, not even trying to hide the glee in her voice. She enjoyed watching the tailor antagonize him a little too much.

Jefferson sighed. "I don't want to even think about it. Enough that I intend to have this clothing shipped to Fortitude and not crammed in our packs when we're done."

"We're going to look so *good*, though," Mindy cooed. She had taken to Zuzanna right away—Jefferson suspected their magic types were akin to one another. "I can hardly wait. Did you hear what she's making for Kittie?"

The Pyromancer rolled her eyes. "It's going to be ridiculous."

Jefferson smiled. "You'll have attire befitting your station."

Kittie gave him a withering look. "I'll have attire declaring loud and clear that I'm a mage. And not just any mage." She blew out a frustrated breath.

Ah, so that was it. As soon as Zuzanna learned who she was dressing, she insisted on going all-out—as she always did. The tailor had determined she was going to have Kittie declare boldly who she was, insisting that she would design clothes reminiscent of dancing flames. The Pyromancer had argued with Zuzanna at that point, and they'd settled with a handful of different items, including a form-fitting red dress that Kittie seemed to like, though she didn't openly admit it.

"What happened to reminding them who we are?" Mindy asked.

Kittie's cheeks reddened. "It's one thing for them to know I'm a mage. It's another to flaunt the fact that I play with fire."

Jefferson understood. He would feel much the same if more knew about his magic. "You'll have an assortment to pick from. If you really dislike it, no one will make you wear it." That mollified the Pyromancer, and they continued their trek back to Silver Sands.

A few minutes later, they arrived at the gates and found that they weren't the only ones trying to gain entry. A contingent of mounted men and women in the scarlet and gold of the Salt-Iron Confederation milled around, barred by—

<Unicorn,> Seledora warned when the wind shifted to carry the scent. And then the beast turned, revealing the gleaming horn that Jefferson hadn't seen at first, either.

A Tracker, then. Jefferson touched a finger to the ring Blaise had given him, simply as reassurance. He swallowed, the only sign of unease he allowed himself. *Keep up appearances. Not the first time you've misdirected from who you really are.* Kittie and Mindy had seen the unicorn as well, and both knew what it meant. Mindy's yellow eyes were wide, while Kittie's face had paled. Their pegasi drew to a stiff-legged halt, on edge. Except for Tylos. Flora urged him forward, her lips peeled back over her teeth in a threatening smile.

"Do we run?" Mindy asked, breathless.

"That will only make it look as if we have something to hide," Kittie said, though her voice was tight. She glanced at Jefferson for confirmation.

"They have no claim to us," he agreed, though he privately wished they could skulk away and leave the Confederation forces none the wiser. But they had been spotted, and that window of opportunity was lost. That meant he had to move on to their next best option. "Come on. We *belong* here."

Seledora glanced back at him. <We do, but they may still try to detain us.> She started forward anyway.

When they drew closer, Jefferson saw the green and white garbed Gannish Bossguard holding the Salt-Iron Confederation forces at bay. Jefferson smiled when he recognized the guard captain from previous visits to Silver Sands.

"Captain Cerulean!" Jefferson called cheerfully, drawing the attention of friend and foe alike. Cerulean flicked their gaze in Jefferson's direction but didn't budge, arms crossed over their chest as they physically barred the Confederation group. "What seems to be the problem?"

The Tracker aboard the unicorn turned, sizing him up. The unicorn's nostrils flared, drinking in their unfamiliar scents. Its ears pricked forward as it made a throaty nicker, pulling in their direction as it scented the mages. The Tracker suddenly grew more interested in them, narrowing his eyes. "*Mages.*"

"Oh, they're not a problem," Jefferson said, gesturing to Kittie and Mindy. "I do believe you'll find that they're guests of Madame Boss Clayton."

Cerulean scowled. "I've been trying to convince Tracker Norris and his friends of that for the past twenty minutes."

Norris's mouth twisted into an ugly snarl. "We're here by the authority of the Salt-Iron Confederation to apprehend the *outlaw mages.*"

Jefferson leaned forward, resting his arms on the crest of Seledora's neck. "There are no outlaw mages here. Tell me, sir, do you possess a handbill for either of these ladies?" The question was a gamble. Flora had sought any information regarding the Wanted status of both Kittie and Mindy, and had found nothing. Jefferson wouldn't put it past them to fabricate a handbill, though.

Norris ground his teeth as the unicorn tugged at the reins, insistent. "Doesn't matter. They're mages and—"

"They're free." Jefferson held up a hand, ticking off reasons. "They are not Confederation citizens. They are here as delegates and have diplomatic immunity. You have no just cause to hold them as they have done nothing wrong."

Fury tinged Norris's face with scarlet. "They're *mages*." He said it with the same intensity as someone would speak of vermin. The Tracker gestured to the other soldiers. "Take them all into custody."

Seledora flung up her head at the decree, and out of the corner of his eye, Jefferson saw Flora pull out her knives, ready for a skirmish. Kittie's head was high, her eyes burning with anger. Mindy looked ready to ask her pegasus to flee.

Jefferson didn't move a muscle as six soldiers cautiously moved to circle their pegasi. Seledora's ears flicked all around as she surveyed the situation, waiting for direction. Jefferson crossed his wrists over the pommel of his saddle, giving the soldiers a disdainful look. *Attitude is everything.*

"No, I don't think so. Not today, at least." He was quite satisfied by the way the Tracker's jaw hung open at his refusal. The Confederation soldiers shifted, uncertain what to do. "Unless you're certain you wish to cause an international incident."

Norris sputtered something that might have been words if he hadn't been so furious.

Cerulean smiled, stepping forward to break through the circle. "Mr. Cole has the right of it. And I will add, Ganland is a *nation*, not a province of the Confederation. We do not answer to you. If you interfere with the wishes of Madame Boss Clayton, there will be quite an *incident*."

Norris's unicorn edged backward, eyes rolling at the tension in the air. The creature tipped its head toward the mages. Its rider, meanwhile, radiated his annoyance. "Our superiors tasked us with bringing in the outlaw mages. What am I to tell them?"

"How about *no*?" Flora suggested sweetly.

Norris made a sound that fell somewhere between a growl and a frustrated exhalation, yanking the unicorn's head around and digging his heels into the beast's sides. It jolted into a startled trot. The other Confederation soldiers fell away from their circle, turning to follow the Tracker, though they were on foot.

When the Confederation forces had turned a corner and were no longer in sight, Jefferson rubbed his forehead, turning to Captain Cerulean. "Thank you for the support."

Cerulean's gaze was steely. "I was only doing as was right. I won't have the Confederation prancing in here and running rampant like they own everything." They straightened, then turned to gesture to the other guards to open the gates. "Sometimes we have to remind them we are allies, but we call the shots in our own land." Then they chuckled. "Besides, Boss Rachel would dock our pay for a year if we allowed them to snap any of you away in the middle of negotiations." Cerulean cleared their throat. "Madame Boss Clayton, I mean."

Jefferson hid a smile, appreciative that the Gannish leader allowed herself to curry the trust of those around her with familiarity. Sometimes that was an effective way to gain unfailing loyalty. "We're expecting a delivery this afternoon. Will you have someone bring it directly to our rooms?"

Cerulean nodded. "I'll make certain the shift manning the gate later is aware."

With the Gannish guard continuing to monitor the gate, Jefferson turned to survey his cohorts. Mindy looked shaken but was recovering. Kittie looked ready to light something—or someone—on fire.

"I'm not going back to them," the Pyromancer whispered.

"No, you will not," Jefferson agreed. "Neither of you." He aimed an encouraging smile at Mindy. "The danger is past, and we're all safe." He glanced down at his magic-concealing ring. The unicorn hadn't been worried about him at all, only the Pyromancer and Hospitalier. Maybe, just maybe, it was worth the price of inhibiting his magic. He touched the band with his index finger. *Thank you, Blaise. Wherever you are.*

CHAPTER TWENTY

Supply and Demand

"Why are we going to the Black Market?" Blaise asked Jack quietly the next morning as they broke camp. The Knossans had rested nearby, though they kept their own watch as well, wary of any wildlife that might attack in the darkness.

"Because the bulls are right—Slocum gets around. Knows things. I've gone to him often enough to barter for information." An ironic smile touched his face. "Believe it or not, there are times I think information is better'n a sixgun and magic."

Blaise pursed his lips but nodded. "If you think it'll help."

"I do," Jack said simply. He buckled up his saddlebag. "Now, finish getting Emrys saddled before the bulls leave without us."

The Knossans—they had introduced themselves as Gore, the white; Roam, the black and white spotted; and Deal, the nearly black bull—had little to gather and were ready to hit the trail before the outlaws. Moments later, they started on their way. The bulls took the lead, with Blaise and Emmaline just behind them and Jack bringing up the rear, watching for trouble.

By midmorning, they had the first sign that they were near their destination. A faded bandanna hung from the gnarled branch of a half-dead tree, the only tree standing on the horizon as far as Blaise could see. He rose in the stirrups, squinting into the distance as the Knossans implacably continued forward. He thought he saw a dark speck on the horizon, but it was impossible to know if that was their end goal.

Fortunately, it was. As they traveled, it grew larger until it took on the shape of a lone building, standing defiant in the endless emptiness that threatened to swallow it. There were no hints of wildlife anywhere around, not even a scattering of dried buffalo chips. It was as if the animals and magical creatures openly avoided the area.

"That's strange," Blaise said to Emmaline.

Behind them, Zepheus must have overheard. <The Black Market has an aura about it that mystical races dislike, and even mundane animals can sense it.>

Blaise frowned. It had been ages ago, but the family pony Smoky hadn't minded the Black Market. Though Smoky had been there many times and was generally unflappable. "Do you sense it, Emrys?"

<I do, and I don't like it. But I will go there because we must.>

Blaise rubbed his chin. "Why don't we feel it?"

Emrys glanced back. <Please do not take offense, but humans lack the sensitivity to feel it. That includes mages.>

Blaise nodded. That made sense, in a way. In the same way he couldn't track a fox, but a hound could. "None taken."

"That's the Black Market?" Emmaline asked, wrinkling her nose as they drew closer. "For all I've heard about it, I thought it'd look more impressive."

As in Blaise's past experience, the Black Market looked like an abandoned building. This one didn't resemble a saloon but had the look of perhaps a barn. Or maybe a house that had fallen into disrepair. It was difficult to tell. Whatever it was, it was near a natural spring that gave them the chance to drink fresh water and refill their canteens again.

"Lotta powerful things don't look that impressive," Jack commented, then jerked a thumb toward Blaise. "Him, for example."

Blaise ignored the dig, though he recognized it meant Jack was through coddling him. That was good. He was more concerned about the Black Market itself. He hadn't had the best experience on his last and only visit.

The Knossans slowed as they arrived, shifting their considerable weight as if they, too, were nervous around the building. Gore turned to them, dipping his horns. "We will no doubt part ways now that we've reached our destination. Thank you for accompanying us, Scourge of the Untamed Territory." His large eyes flicked to Blaise. "And Breaker of Fort Courage."

Blaise swallowed but nodded, unsure what to say. Thankfully, Jack spoke up. The Effigest touched the brim of his hat. "Best of luck finding your young-uns. Remember that the outlaws of the Gutter ain't half bad unless you're an enemy."

The trio of bulls bobbed their heads, then filed into the building. Blaise thought Jack would follow and was surprised when the outlaw stayed put and dismounted.

"What was that about?" Emmaline asked. "I need to get me a nickname."

Jack chuckled. "You'll earn one, no doubt. But that was all politics." He made a face, as if he'd tasted something rotten. "If the Gutter is a nation, it'll help if any Knossans we come across think well of us."

Blaise arched his brows. "Look at you, learning to play nice with others."

The Effigest snorted. "It's called savvy."

"It's called being diplomatic. Jefferson is going to be so proud."

Emmaline hid a smile behind her hand. Jack glared at him, but Blaise didn't mind one bit. Zepheus must have made a private comment because he nickered his own sort of laughter, butting Jack with his head.

"I'm going in," Jack announced, apparently deciding not to rally against their remarks. "You can stay out here if you want."

As Jack strode toward the door and hauled it open, Blaise swallowed, his mind suddenly back on their current focus. Emrys blew a warm breath against the back of his neck.

Blaise shook his head and plowed toward the door. "No, I'm fine." He wasn't fine, but maybe he would be. *I'm not the green as grass, scared kid I was then.* No, he had come a long way. Endured much. He squared his shoulders and pushed open the door, though he was more mindful of its fragile status than Jack had been. It would only take a nudge from his magic to shatter the hinges.

Jack was leaning against a wall, arms crossed, as he waited for the Knossans to finish their business with the Black Market's proprietor. Tom Slocum, Blaise supposed, was a mage, though he didn't know what sort. The Black Market was unlike anything else he knew—a building that shifted each day, forever cycling through predetermined locations. Maybe some sort of Walker, though Blaise had never heard of one like that.

But I never knew of a Walker who could move through walls. Blaise's eyes widened at the thought, wondering if Slocum knew anything about such a mage. And if their magic was related.

Roam finished speaking with Slocum and lumbered to the door. He paused when he got to Blaise, dipping his horns in farewell. Gore and Deal ambled after, and without another word, the bulls set out on their way.

With the Knossans gone, Jack eased over to the shabby, overturned barrels covered in knotty boards that served as a counter. Slocum's eyes weren't on the outlaw, though. They were on Blaise.

"You're still around, I see, Breaker," Slocum said, his tone somewhere between a welcome and warning.

Blaise moved closer to Jack. "Against the odds, yes."

Slocum nodded, then turned to Jack. "What d'you want, Dewitt?" He leaned both elbows onto the wood, then hazarded a quick glance at Blaise. "No gloves?"

"Don't need 'em."

Jack smiled at Slocum, his expression both friendly and dangerous. "You know what I normally come to you for. Information."

The proprietor nodded. "And what do you have to trade?"

"Coin," Jack said, then scowled at the shake of Slocum's head. "Then what?"

Slocum tilted his head. "I reckon if you've come this far to see me, you're desperate. Coin won't cut it."

"*Slocum.*" Jack's voice was a guttural growl, a promise of violence. Any of the diplomacy that Blaise had teased him about earlier had abruptly vanished.

Around them, the building made an eerie wail. Emmaline's eyes went wide, and she jerked away from the wall she'd been standing near. Blaise felt the rickety floorboards come to life beneath him. *Come to life? How could they? They were dead wood. Rotting wood.*

"You're in my domain, *Wildfire Jack Dewitt,*" Slocum warned.

Amid the sudden flare of power, Blaise's magic roared up, ready to defend or attack. He flexed his arms, balling up his fists to keep it under wraps even as the ceiling overhead made a sinister rumble. Jack was armed, though he held off from taking aim. Emmaline stood frozen, reluctant to incite anything. Outside, the pegasi whinnied a warning.

"Whatever you ask will probably be more than we can give," Jack said, voice gravelly.

Blaise's heart threatened to gallop right out of his chest. They had come all this way, strayed from their trail. No way was he going to let this be a waste. He stared at Slocum. "What do you want?"

"*No.*" Jack didn't even hesitate. He angled to glare at Blaise, his blue eyes stormy with rising anger.

Slocum ignored Jack, relaxing. Around them, the Black Market quieted. They heard the resounding thud of hooves against a decrepit wall as one of the pegasi kicked, but the magical building was sturdier than it at first appeared. Blaise realized that while inside, the pegasi couldn't communicate with them. He was certain Emrys would have queried otherwise.

The proprietor smiled, eyes cutting to Jack. "What do you want to know?"

"The Breaker doesn't know what you demand of him," Jack said, shoving his sixgun back into its holster. He crossed his arms, the poppet tucked neatly into the crook of his elbow.

"The Breaker knows me. We've done business before." Slocum grinned, though it reminded Blaise of the leaping grasscat's maw. A baring of teeth from an apex predator. "I reckon you're here on his behalf. Not yours, Dewitt. Let him speak."

Jack stewed and said nothing. Blaise took a shuddering breath, then nodded. "You know my mother, Mr. Slocum. Marian Hawthorne." It wasn't a question, simply a statement, and Slocum nodded his agreement. "She was kidnapped, and the ones who did it killed my father. We're hunting them down to get her back." He licked his lips, wondering if he should mention the Copperheads. No, because that might be giving up valuable information. "Have you heard where she might have been taken? Do you know anything about those who stole her away?"

Slocum cocked his head, drawing an index finger over the rugged grit of the lumber he leaned against. "I might have information relevant to your questions, yes."

Jack took a step forward before Blaise spoke again. "Relevant? Not good enough, Slocum."

The proprietor chuckled. "More enlightening than you think." His chilly gaze remained on Blaise. "I'll provide the information for a price."

Blaise steeled himself. "What's the price?"

Slocum turned, moving to pull something small out of a box Blaise hadn't noticed at first. It was a clear glass vial, exactly of the sort he'd seen his mother use before for her alchemy. "Fill this with your blood."

"*No.*" Jack was adamant, clamping an arm around Blaise's shoulder to steer him toward the door. "The price is too high. We don't need whatever piss-poor information he has."

My blood. Blaise felt light-headed for an instant, a terrifying vision roaring up. A wicked knife slicing the soft underside of his arm from wrist to elbow. The white-hot pain. The warmth of blood oozing. Dripping. He didn't realize he had slipped away from Jack to stand frozen in the middle of the floor.

"Blaise." The voice was urgent. A new hand was on his shoulder, squeezing with firm but insistent pressure. He blinked, and his eyes focused on Emmaline, peering down at him. Somehow, he'd gone to his knees as an old memory took hold.

"You don't know what you ask, Slocum." Jack's voice was tense, something about it protective, seeking to shield Blaise. "Take mine instead. Wouldn't be the first time."

"The bargain is not with you."

Blaise swallowed, shakily rising. *I'm okay. I'm not there. I have a choice in this.* He was glad that Emmaline remained nearby. *But what should I do?* Blaise knew that the Confederation had taken his blood for some dark purpose, one he never discovered. His mother had told him she had destroyed all the samples she could find, though.

But his blood was different. His magic—this magic he wasn't supposed to have, *shouldn't* have—made him unique. And in his case, being unique was dangerous. "Jack is right. That's something I can't give."

Slocum regarded him with an almost piteous look. "I respect that. A shame, since you're headed into a dangerous situation woefully uninformed."

Jack cursed softly. "Slocum, throw us a bone."

"Nothing in this building is given freely. You know that."

Blaise closed his eyes. If he had been in this alone, he might have turned and walked away. But he wasn't. Jack and Emmaline had thrown in their lots with him. And the pegasi. They wouldn't give up, not after coming this far. Blaise didn't want to put them in any more peril than they were already in. *And Mom. I promised Dad I would find her.*

"Half a vial. That's all I'll offer."

"Damn it, Blaise!" Jack growled. "*No.*"

"Half a vial," Slocum agreed, ignoring Jack's outburst. He held the vial out, and Blaise took it.

Blaise's fingers trembled as they closed around it. The glass was thick, but it would have been a simple thing for his magic to break. He stared at it. "How do you want me to do this?"

Slocum pulled out a bronze cube with a lever attached. "Let me see your arm."

Blaise stared at the unfamiliar device, fighting the urge to edge backward. "What is it?"

"Scarificator. Tool for bloodletting. Most physicians have them." Slocum held it up, displaying eight slits on the bottom of the cube. He pressed down the lever with his thumb, and rows of razor blades flashed out before retreating.

At least it wasn't a knife like at the Cit. Blaise licked his lips, then rolled up the sleeve on his left arm to bare his flesh. When he did so, the pink scar appeared, vivid even in the glow of the mage-lights that lit the interior. Slocum reached down, his other hand returning with a roll of bandages. He studied Blaise's scar but made no comment.

"I'll make the cut. You fill the vial with blood. Half, as we agreed," Slocum said, settling the scarificator on Blaise's tender forearm. He pressed the lever, and quick as lightning, the blades sliced into his skin. Slocum lifted the device away.

The sight of his own blood almost sent him back to the scarring memories. His teeth chattered as he struggled to keep it together. Blaise was aware of the heat of Jack's cloaked anger. Emmaline helped gather the required blood into the vial. She stoppered it, and then in a move that surprised everyone in the room, she put it in Blaise's uninjured hand, wrapping his fingers around it.

"*Your* bargaining chip," Emmaline said, her voice little more than a whisper in Blaise's ear. "*Your* choice."

My choice. With two small words, she had given him the power that the Golden Citadel had stripped away. Blaise tightened his grip, the vial warm in his hand as Emmaline bandaged the slashes on his forearm.

"That blood is mine," Slocum said, tone sharp.

Blaise shook his head. "Not yet. Only after you tell us what you know about my mother. And give me any information you have about a very specific mage." He heard Jack's surprised grunt at the addition.

Slocum narrowed his eyes. "You're demanding a lot for so little, Breaker."

Blaise glanced down at his fist. "You probably know this since you deal with information, but my beau is quite the entrepreneur. He's taught me a few things. Like supply and demand."

The proprietor hissed out a breath. "The Gannish are the absolute worst."

"Something we agree on," Jack said dryly.

Blaise ignored the barb. "What's it going to be? I'm happy to take this with me and toss it in a fire." At least he figured fire would destroy blood. Probably?

"The bargain is struck," Slocum said after a moment, though he clearly wasn't happy about it. He leaned against the improvised countertop. "If you give me the vial, I'll fulfill your requests."

Blaise uncurled his hand and offered the vial. The proprietor snatched it away as if it were a bag of diamonds. He swathed the precious vial in a nest of cotton, setting it in a lockbox. He leaned his bulk against the deteriorating wood planks again, as if it were an everyday occurrence to squirrel away the blood of a mage. Though, judging from Jack's earlier words, it probably was.

"Shame about Marian Hawthorne," Slocum began, giving his head a doleful shake. "Her loss will limit some of the sought-after potions I stock."

Blaise gritted his teeth, suddenly furious. "That alone should have been reason for you to tell me." His palms itched as his magic flared at his agitation.

Slocum gave him a cat that ate the canary smile. "Nah. I said *limited*, not cut off completely." He gave a lazy shrug. "I can charge more, so it's all the same to me. Supply and demand, you know."

"The information," Jack growled, as if he had forgotten that moments earlier, the building they stood in had been ready to attack them.

Blaise was with Jack in that. A dusting of magic played across his skin. He knew that if he looked down, his palms would have a silver sheen as his power manifested. Long ago, Slocum had warned him about those very hands.

Slocum's gaze flicked to Blaise's palms, aware of the unspoken threat. "Marian's wanted, and that's why she was taken."

"Wanted? As in dead or alive, like an outlaw?" Jack asked, the question piercing.

"Nah." Slocum shook his head. "Wanted in the same way you put something on a shopping list. She's lucrative. A brilliant Confederation alchemist out here? Yeah, people are gonna want her."

Blaise frowned, trying to think of why someone would want her. Then he realized he was looking at the situation too closely. He had grown up knowing what she was, though she hid under the guise of an apothecary. When he was a child, her alchemy had seemed commonplace. Unremarkable. Just a part of everyday life. But Slocum was right—Marian Hawthorne was gifted with her alchemy craft, and there were those who would want access to her. *Faedra knows, the Confederation probably wants her back.*

Slocum jerked a thumb at Blaise. "You're on shopping lists, too."

Blaise's gut twisted. "What?" His mouth went dry as more old fears rose.

"Why?" Jack demanded.

At the same time, Emmaline said, "No one's getting Blaise!"

The Black Market proprietor raised his eyebrows, as if surprised he had to explain why someone would want Blaise. "Why? Think about it. What band of outlaws *wouldn't* want a Breaker? Able to crack open any safe. Bust into any jail. Threaten to bring a building down around you." At that, he glanced at the ceiling overhead, as if he were acknowledging the fact that Blaise could do so to the Black Market if driven to it. "Lot of outlaws are mighty jealous of you and yours, Jack."

Blaise gritted his teeth. No time to take offense—he needed to stay focused. "What else do you know?"

Slocum aimed a finger at him. "*I* know *you* know the Copperheads are the ones behind it. 'Cause you're heading to Thorn." A smug look drifted across his lips at Jack's annoyed grunt. "But what you don't know is that the Copperheads have set themselves up a one-of-a-kind auction. Seems a certain alchemist is slated to be the main event, and the buyers are lining up."

"Who're the buyers?" Jack demanded.

Slocum shrugged. "I've told you what I know. Anything else I offer at this point would be a guess. And a guess, even from me, could be a lethal mistake."

Jack nodded. "Fair enough."

"Time's a-wasting, friends. You best be on your way," Slocum said, rising to his full height and picking up the lockbox.

"No." Blaise shook his head. "You still need to tell me about the mage."

The proprietor grimaced, clearly having hoped the information would distract Blaise to the point where he forgot. His shoulders hunched. "Ask."

"You don't have to tell me about your magic—I know we get touchy about that," Blaise began, "but I had a run-in with a Walker who could move through physical *walls*. You know anything about that?"

Slocum cocked his head, studying Blaise for a moment before nodding. "Wallwalker. Freaky offshoot of the Walkers. You're right—not gonna tell you if her power is related to mine. That's a mystery I'm not unveiling to you." He cradled the lockbox against his chest. "Goes by the name of the Herald. From the little I know, she's Gannish but not Saltie."

Blaise wondered if he should ask additional questions, but he didn't know what to ask. He glanced at Jack. The outlaw gave him an approving nod, so Blaise turned back to Slocum. "Thanks. We'll be on our way, then."

"Let's hit the trail," Jack said, motioning for Blaise and Emmaline to precede him to the door. No doubt wanting to guard their flank again.

"Nice doing business with you!" Slocum called in their wake.

CHAPTER TWENTY-ONE

Politics as Usual

Kittie

Kittie had thought coming to Ganland was the right thing to do, but she was having her doubts. Why had she ever thought this was a good idea, a way to find out how she was going to fit into this new world with her family? That this might be the way to find out who *she* was now?

In the past, whenever Kittie unraveled, she went for the one thing she knew would dull the pain and confusion. And now Mindy, that blasted well-meaning Hospitalier, was trying to keep her from it.

"Let me by," Kittie hissed, her voice low and full of warning. "All I need is one little drink."

"No," Mindy said, adamant as she shook her head, curly black hair snaking around her oval face. "That's not what you *need*."

Kittie had been on her way to hunt down one of the staffers with an order for them to bring her brandy. Wine. Whatever they had. Maybe everything they had. Kittie's flask had run dry, and unlike in the few towns they had stopped at on the way to Nera, she hadn't had a chance to leave Silver Sands to secretly refill it.

"How do you know what I need?" Kittie snapped. A part of her regretted the tone, knowing Mindy meant well. But a larger part of her needed a drink to get through their mission, and she wasn't about to let this buzzing gnat of a mage get in her way.

Mindy stood firm. "Because I'm a *Hospitalier*." Her yellow eyes—a rare color in anyone, even mages, Kittie knew—gleamed with determination.

She took a step closer, dropping her voice to a whisper Kittie strained to hear. "I don't *just* know what food or drink will be best for you, or if it's spoiled or poisoned. My magic gives me an inkling of how the things you put in your body might harm you in the long term—"

"You're not the first to tell me to quit drinking," Kittie growled, crossing her arms. She didn't enjoy having this spat in public, so she stepped back into her room. Mindy followed. "But I'm fine. It's not a problem. I can handle it."

Mindy frowned. "You're lying to yourself, and you know it."

Kittie bristled. She hadn't said *you're lying to me*. No, because Mindy was right, damn it. She huffed out a breath, deflating. "I've been trying to stop. Or to cut down. I did, for a little while." Jack had insisted, which had been eye-opening considering he enjoyed a fair amount of alcohol, too. But he didn't *need* it, crave it, the way she did. *Jack.* She thought of him, and Kittie didn't know if she could see this thing that she'd agreed to through. It was so much harder than she'd thought.

The curvy Hospitalier smiled up at her, golden eyes bright. "That's good. That tells me right there you recognize you need to change." Mindy smoothed an errant lock of hair behind one ear. "You've got people back in Fortitude who're worried about you."

Kittie frowned. "Did Jack put you up to this?

"No."

Kittie scowled, wondering who might have interfered if not Jack. Though maybe it wasn't interference—not really. She wanted to quit. Needed to quit, if she could. Kittie thought back to her contentious talk with Nadine. She hadn't asked for help, but the Healer had stuck her nose in, anyway. Probably because she was in the business of fixing people. Nadine had been certain that if she tried, she could succeed. *But you have to want this, Kittie. You can't half-ass it. Throw in an entire donkey train if you must.*

"I've tried," Kittie said after a moment. "I've done the things that were suggested. Get more sleep. Drink plenty of water. Focus on the good things in life." She made a scoffing sound. "All things people should do, anyway. None of it helps. I can't do this."

"Do you want to?" Mindy challenged.

Kittie opened her mouth to snap that of course she did, but it was a lie. She remembered her conversation with Jack, his disappointment that she didn't want this badly enough. Kittie shut her eyes, conflicted. How could she want something so much and not at all? "Yes and no. Maybe if I find something that works."

"*I* can help you, but you have to want it," Mindy said softly.

Kittie massaged her forehead. She really, really could use a drink, but unless she ran roughshod, that didn't seem to be in her future. "How?"

"Do you want to quit?" Mindy asked again, clearly unwilling to commit if Kittie didn't.

The Pyromancer sighed, scrubbing at her face with one hand. "Yes, damn it. I don't want to be this way. But how will what you do be any different?"

"Because I know what you need," Mindy said simply, leaning against the wall. "It's what I do."

"Okay, Hospitalier. What do I *need?*"

Mindy's face lit with a true grin. "I was hoping you'd ask." Her lips twisted, and her brow scrunched, thoughtful. "Caladrius root tea. I can ask if they have any here, and if not, there should be some in town. I saw Caladrius root growing in Ganland on the way here."

"*Tea,* ugh," Kittie groaned. "What did I do to deserve this? Will it help?"

Mindy laughed. "It won't be only tea, at least not to start. I'll mix it with whiskey."

Kittie shot Mindy an incredulous look, certain she'd misheard. "Wait. How's that going to help? I mean, I like the idea, so I don't want to complain, but…"

The Hospitalier smiled. "It's going to be a slow but steady process to wean you from alcohol and onto something not as likely to kill you. Tea is a good replacement—or at least, better than other alternatives."

Kittie pursed her lips. "I've never been much of a tea drinker."

"You'll like it, I promise. The hot water will make the Caladrius root taste sweet. And the whiskey…well, you're familiar with that." She rubbed her hands together in anticipation. "And Caladrius root will do wonders to give you a clear mind for the meeting with Madame Boss Clayton and the Board later."

Kittie sighed. "I hope you're right."

KITTIE RELAXED AGAINST THE CUSHIONED CHAIR. SHE HAD TO ADMIT MINDY was right—the Hospitalier had brought her a cup of Caladrius root tea (with the promised addition of whiskey), and it had done wonders for her constitution. She had more clarity and was less agitated, able to focus on the matters at hand.

Kittie glanced across the table at Jefferson. He was in his element. She knew, thanks to Jack, that the entrepreneur really was the best choice to come along with them. He had lived another life as a Doyen and had rejected that identity. The details behind that were unclear to her, but

Jack seemed to trust him (even if he liked to pretend otherwise), and that made Kittie feel as if she, too, could trust him.

Jefferson leaned forward in his seat, the gleam in his eyes reminding her of someone preparing for a fight. *You can take the politician out of politics, but you can't take the politics out of the politician.* No matter what had forced him to shed his Doyen position, he was eager for this current opportunity.

Madame Boss Clayton sat at the end of the table. Jefferson and Kittie sat to the Boss's right while the five members of Ganland's Board sat to her left. From what Kittie understood, each Board member hailed from a different region in Ganland, appointed by their local leaders. The Board, in turn, appointed the Boss.

And that last bit? It wasn't good news for them, since it meant they could also unseat the Madame Boss, if they saw fit and had a majority in agreement. It seemed some of the Board members were dead set against anything to do with the Gutter, as Jefferson had found out from Doyen Thatcher.

"You're going to provoke the Confederation if you do this," a silver-haired woman protested, shaking her finger at the Madame Boss. She was Sylvia Westerfield. Kittie had spoken with her at dinner and had found the woman incredibly patronizing.

A man with a squat face that reminded Kittie of a hog nodded agreement—Bartholomew Tate. "I've heard talk of Phinora putting a hefty tariff on our goods. We—"

"You pass that on to the Phinoran buyers, then," Rachel interjected before Bartholomew finished his thought. "Don't act as if we haven't done that before when one nation or another sought to strong-arm us."

"But then they'll buy from someone else," Bartholomew grumped. "We'll be too costly."

Jefferson was nearly salivating at the discussion. This, Kittie saw, was a topic he enjoyed. "Then pivot. Sell them goods they can't get from anyone else. Or go to another market." He leaned over the table, more animated than Kittie had seen him the entire trip. "More and more families are moving to the Gutter each day. People who will need goods."

Rachel nodded and was about to speak when Sylvia jabbed a bony finger into the table. "But that's part of the problem right there. Do you not see?" Her finger bent at an angle that made Kittie cringe, but the woman paid it no heed. "The people going to the Gutter are *mages*."

Kittie didn't like the way the old woman spoke. She said it as if it were an epithet. *And here Ganland is the country most favorable toward mages.* "Excuse me? What is the issue with *mages*?" Kittie kept her tone calm, though she wanted to show her outrage at the veiled insult. Her *child*—the people she cared about—would not be slighted.

Sylvia's eyes drifted to her. "The issue is that the Confederation *needs* mages, sweetie." The woman spoke with such condescension, Kittie almost imagined she was getting a swat, like a sticky-fingered child accused of stealing from the candy jar. "Even as we speak, the Confederation is devising ways to keep the mavericks from leaving."

What? Alarm shot through Kittie, and judging by the way Jefferson sat up straighter, he was surprised by this, too.

"Mages—mavericks—are *people*. Not wild horses to be brought in and tamed." Jefferson squared his shoulders as he spoke his heated words. He was no longer entertained by the conversation. "The Confederation has no right to detain them."

A handsome young man who reminded Kittie of a swan shook his head at that. Marcus Funk appeared to be similar in age to Jefferson. "But that's just it. The law of the land still states that mages are not equal to normal humans. Regardless of the dog and pony show that happened with the Breaker."

At mention of Blaise, Jefferson went tight-lipped, his green eyes smoldering coals. Rachel scowled at the trio of Board members, though her eyes darted briefly to the pair who had made no objections yet. She leaned forward as she spoke. "Ganland has always prided itself on being the most hospitable nation in the Salt-Iron Confederation for mages."

Kittie somehow reined in the laugh that threatened to tear from her mouth at that. This wasn't *hospitable*.

"We won't be party to keeping any mages who wish from traveling freely to the Gutter or elsewhere," Rachel declared.

"Even if the Salt-Iron Council issues a decree?" Bartholomew asked. "They're meeting on this very topic when they reconvene."

Kittie hated all this back and forth and posturing. The veiled threats. The derision and condescension. Time to do something about that. "We will, of course, understand if Ganland isn't forward-thinking enough to ally with the Gutter. It takes courage and savvy to do something like that, and, well…" Kittie allowed her words to trail off as she glanced around the table. Was she taking an enormous risk by insulting the lot of them? Probably. But she was *over* being treated as if she weren't equal because she was a mage. Confederation law didn't make that true.

Sylvia's eyes bulged, and Bartholomew's piggy mouth dropped open. Marcus's graceful neck snapped around as he stared at her. Jefferson was smiling, the look on his face that of a cat about to pounce. He seemed to approve of her tactic.

"You make an excellent point, Firebrand Dewitt." When Jefferson spoke, he made her title the honorific it was meant to be. Something to put her on the same level as the Board members. Kittie rather enjoyed it. "That is exactly the sort of gamble I took when I invested in Rainbow Flat, and...well, we've seen how profitable *that* was."

He made no mention that even now, he was investing in Fortitude, all because his beau called it home. Kittie liked that, since she would do the same if she had the resources. But she only had her voice, her mind, and her fierce love. That had to be enough, and she had to use them to help. "And Rainbow Flat will be a part of the new nation. Asylum, too. That would be a boon for trade, would it not?" Kittie didn't know shit about trade, but these people seemed to like it. It felt like the right thing to say.

Jefferson grinned, steepling his fingers before him. Rachel watched him expectantly, as if hoping he would do her job for her. Madame Boss Clayton had an economy of speech and seemed to enjoy seeing others nudge themselves closer to the things she wanted. Perhaps, Kittie reflected, she knew enough of Jefferson to trust him here.

"Not only that." Jefferson's voice was soft, almost seductive. The Board members around the table unconsciously leaned closer to hear what he was about to say. The would-be Ambassador took his time, making certain he had their full attention. "Think of how long the average cargo ship takes to travel from Nera to Thorn. I'm not speaking of a sleek passenger steamer—no, I speak of the lumbering cargo ships. How long?"

"Months," Marcus supplied, though the way his brows slashed down proved he was uncertain where Jefferson was going with this.

"What if," Jefferson began, walking his index and middle fingers across the table as if they were a person, "we could establish an overland trade route?"

"We have those, and the outlaws—" Bartholomew started, then cut himself off as understanding dawned on him. "*Oh.*"

Jefferson smiled, tapping his fingers against the table again. He said nothing. Anything more was unnecessary.

It was brilliant. Kittie had known about the idea, but the way he delivered it was better than anything she could have done. She was no longer the orator she had been in her youth, and she lacked Jefferson's acuity. He'd done his job, and now it was her turn. She pasted on a smile to match Jefferson's. "The Gutter outlaws would have no reason to attack an ally's convoy. And in fact..." She lifted a hand, snapping her fingers. A tongue of flame bloomed to life in her palm, and the gathering of Board members gasped. Rachel's Bossguard went on alert, though they remained in their positions when the Madame Boss gave them a shake of her head.

"Our mage *allies* could help protect the trade route from the dangers of the Untamed Territory," Rachel said. She gestured to Kittie and the fireball dancing in her palm. "As you can see, they have unique skills that a *normal* human lacks."

For a *normal* human, Kittie was beginning to really, really like Rachel Clayton. The Board members were staring, their faces a mix of fear and wonder.

"Is this a threat?" Sylvia asked.

Should it be? Jack would have asked that without hesitation—and a damn good thing she was here and not her husband. *I have tact.* Kittie closed her hand, extinguishing the flame so effectively that not even a wisp of smoke escaped. "No, it's a demonstration. The mages of the Gutter are not lightweights. Do not make the mistake of underestimating us." Okay, maybe that was a little bit of a threat. Unintentional, though.

Rachel smiled. "Thank you for the input, Firebrand Dewitt. Board members, thank you for joining us. As it seems we're only going round in circles, I see fit to table our discussion for the time being so that you might think on it."

The quintet of Board members exchanged glances. It was clear they didn't want to be dismissed, but they were following some protocol Kittie wasn't aware of. They filed out, leaving Boss Clayton alone with the delegation. Once the door closed behind the last Board member, Rachel sank back in her chair.

"That was exhausting. But you made a good show of it," she told them with an approving nod.

"Exhausting for you? We did all the heavy lifting," Jefferson replied with a chuckle, though he seemed in a better mood than when the Board had been ready to disparage Blaise. He turned to Kittie, his face animated again. "We hadn't even planned most of that, but you did an excellent job. You're a natural."

I'm definitely not a natural. She gave a weak smile. "I did what I could."

Jefferson's gaze slid back to Rachel. "Do you think we have a chance?"

The Madame Boss grinned. "When you mention safe transcontinental trade routes, there's always a chance."

CHAPTER TWENTY-TWO
More Than a Breaker

Jack

With the information provided by Tom Slocum, Jack, Blaise, and Emmaline plowed onward. Based on Jack's recollection, the Black Market had been just north of the rough-and-tumble town named Starvation. Their best bet was to cross the Untamed River to the town of Uncertain, and from there, make their final trek to Thorn.

Either the Copperheads had decided not to waste their magic on stymieing their pursuit, or they no longer had a need. Jack didn't like it one bit after their conversation with the Black Market proprietor. "They knew exactly what they were getting when they took your mother. And they had to know you wouldn't twiddle your thumbs," he remarked as they gathered their things after stopping for lunch.

Blaise frowned. "How would they know that?"

Jack snorted to himself, wondering just how *dense* the Breaker truly was.

Emmaline gave Blaise a disbelieving look. "You don't know yourself very well sometimes, do you? Word got out that you only took down Fort Courage to save your friends who were there. To save *me*."

"Oh." Blaise blinked as he took in her words. He rubbed the back of his neck, as if he hadn't equated that with heroics. And to be fair, Jack understood his confusion. Jack wasn't much of a hero, either, but he'd tear down the walls of Perdition to keep the people he cared about safe.

The problem was, folks like the Confederation or the Copperheads would use that drive against someone like Blaise. Or Jack. The more he chewed over the idea, the more certain he was that the Copperheads knew who was on their heels. The grasscats had been a test. Anyone else would have given up. Or died. Now their enemies could bide their time, planning an ambush.

That was something to think about later, though. "We gotta get moving," Jack announced, shooting a look over his shoulder. To the northwest, a wall of thunderheads had built up, the deep blue-grey clouds laced with intermittent lightning. Already, the wind was picking up.

<We can't fly in that,> Zepheus announced, nostrils flared as he drank in the wind.

"Is the wind too dangerous?" Blaise asked.

<Not only the wind, but the lightning,> the palomino answered, pawing at the ground impatiently. <Jack is right, and we must make up as much distance as we can. Perhaps find shelter.>

"Time to stop our jawing and get," Jack agreed. He shoved a foot into the stirrup and swung into the saddle. As soon as his bottom hit the leather, Zepheus surged forward.

"Coming!" Emmaline called, following suit with Oberidon. The spotted pegasus leaped after Zepheus.

<Emrys will not be as fast,> Zepheus observed, one ear pricked back to keep tabs on the other pegasi.

Yeah, Jack knew it. The black stallion wasn't built for speed, even if his rider was more competent now than in the past. "Let them keep pace, but we have to find shelter if we can."

Jack and Zepheus had flown through storms before, but only under duress. As an Effigest, he'd figured out a way around the threat of lightning for himself using a lightning rod spell, but it was harder to duplicate the effort for a creature the size of a pegasus. Maybe something to dabble with in the future, but not now with so many to protect. Never mind that the gusty crosswinds would prove perilous to their passage, too.

Jack glanced back over his shoulder. Oberidon was keeping pace, the spotted stallion snorting with every stride. Emrys was lagging, as expected, but doing his best. He refocused his gaze on the horizon, searching for any sign of shelter. Nothing was visible, aside from a few trees that would only serve as a danger with the lightning.

Then he saw something: a dip in the terrain to the west. Jack tapped Zepheus's neck. "That way!" The palomino angled his head to see where he was pointing, then adjusted his course.

The arroyo Jack had spotted wasn't much. Zepheus slowed as they approached, the outlaw peering down at its depths. In the weather that was coming, the wash would be as much a hazard as a haven. Oberidon jogged up, Emmaline scrambling down from the saddle to see what her father was looking at. Emrys arrived a moment later, lathering between his forelegs from the effort.

"We'll be lower than the rest of the land down there, less likely to be struck by lightning," Jack said, pointing to the dry bed of the arroyo.

Emmaline bit her lip. "But that was formed by flash floods." Her gaze flicked to the growing storm. "Kinda like that."

"Yeah, we're damned if we do and damned if we don't," Jack agreed. "We don't have a lot of time to figure something else out."

Blaise slipped down from the saddle, walking over. He was quiet for a moment, though Jack judged by the look on his face that he was thinking of something.

"If something's brewing in that skull of yours, this is the time to speak," Jack said.

The Breaker looked uncomfortable. "If the flash flood is the bigger concern, I could probably stop it. Or at least slow it."

Jack raised his brows. *"How?"*

Blaise pointed to the sides of the arroyo. "The soil here is dry and hard-packed. I can use my magic to break it into big chunks. Maybe big enough to form a dam to slow the water."

"That's actually not a half-bad idea," Jack mused. Sometimes Blaise was full of surprises, like with that fancy shield of his. "But the flooding is only part of the concern. We won't care about drowning or being washed away if we're struck dead by lightning. But I'm hoping being low in the arroyo will at least offer a little protection."

"I have an idea," Emmaline piped up, though she sounded hesitant. As if she worried that whatever she was about to suggest would be dismissed. Which, Jack realized, he had done before. He gestured for her to go ahead. "Remember when you were teaching me Rising Dread?"

Jack lifted his brows, curious why she was thinking of that spell at a time like this. "Yeah?"

She gained more confidence at his question. "You made a perimeter with it, and the working affects everyone inside." Jack nodded, wondering where she was going with this. "And I was thinking about the wards around Bitter End when I found Mom..." Emmaline paused, brow furrowed with thought.

Jack cocked his head. "A Warder does those." He made it a statement, not a contradiction.

Zepheus snorted nearby, glancing at the darkening sky. <I estimate we have twenty minutes before the leading edge overtakes us.>

Yeah, yeah. Jack gestured to let the stallion know he'd heard.

"Maybe we place a similar perimeter around us. I know you have the effigies in your bag." Emmaline started again, gaining momentum with each word, her eyes bright. "But we alter the spell. Could we make it *protect* what's inside?"

Jack snapped his fingers, thinking of his own lightning rod spell. "Maybe not protect, but divert." Yeah, the more he thought about it, the more he liked it. His previous iteration required affixing the spell to each individual poppet. This would cover a generalized area. He turned and stabbed a finger at Blaise. "Get to work on that dam. We'll set up about a quarter-mile away to give you some wiggle room."

He half-expected the Breaker to look flustered or afraid, but he seemed composed. As if having a purpose, a way to help, was all he needed. Blaise nodded, stepping away from the pegasi and crouching down, laying his palms against the ground.

"C'mon, we'll let him do his thing," Jack told Emmaline, climbing back into the saddle. Easier to fly down to the dry bed than to slide down the steep sides.

They dismounted again when they reached the bottom. Jack moved around to Zepheus's side, pulling an effigy from his saddlebag. He hefted it in his hand, going through the mental calculations. As with cooking, a good Ritualist could make substitutions and tweaks to a spell on the fly to produce something effective and new. The skill in doing so was what set a talented Ritualist apart from others. It had been a gift that made Jack lucrative to the Salties back in the day.

"How do you think we build this?" he asked his daughter.

Emmaline's eyes widened for an instant. Then she nodded with determination. "Um, well, I was thinking about what you told me for the Rising Dread. Set a perimeter of effigies, linking them together. Enhance them with something to protect us or divert the lightning."

"But what?" Jack prodded.

She swallowed as she thought about it. Jack hoped she came to a conclusion quickly. An outlaw mage had to think on the fly to survive.

"Hematite," Emmaline said after a moment. Then her face fell. "But I don't have any."

"I do," Jack replied with a grin, pleased by her answer. He gave a meaningful pat to the pouch attached to his belt, then dug a hand inside until he found the familiar lump of hematite.

Emmaline frowned at the single piece. "Will that be enough?"

"Gonna have to be," Jack said with a shrug. He'd done more with less. "I'm more concerned about the power drain that this working is gonna be on us."

"Oh?" she asked, hazarding a glance at the foreboding clouds. They both jumped as they heard a tremendous rumble.

For an instant, Jack thought lightning had struck nearby, which would force their hand. But he turned and saw a rising cloud of dust further up the arroyo. Blaise stood at the top of the ridge, Emrys beside him, peering down at the makeshift avalanche. Large chunks of soil had broken free to land in a jumble, partially clogging the wash. Jack feared for a moment that Blaise might think it was enough, but the young man climbed onto his pegasus, and together, they flew to the other side.

Content that Blaise had a handle on things, Jack returned to their spellwork. "Yeah, if we can get the hematite to hold, the rest of it is going to be on us to keep the casting up. That's going to depend on the amount of storm we have to hold off."

Emmaline blew out a breath. "We don't have any choice, do we?"

Jack shook his head. "Nope. And we need to get these effigies placed. That squall ain't gonna wait for us to make plans."

The younger Effigest idly rubbed at her cheek, smearing dirt across it. "We should place the effigies at the cardinal directions. The power drain will be relative to the size of the perimeter, right?" At Jack's nod, she grew bolder with her ideas. "And keep it as small as we can. Maybe ten paces apart, with the pegasi in the middle."

"Sounds solid," Jack affirmed, pride surging. Emmaline was going to be a top-shelf mage at this rate. A pattering of fat raindrops began to fall, heralding the coming storm. There was another dull rumble as Blaise dropped more chunks of earth into the arroyo. They were short on time, so Jack took the lead. "You go ahead and place the effigies at north and east. I'll get south and west." He tossed the pair to her, and she moved with determination, counting out the paces.

As Jack and Emmaline worked, Blaise and Emrys joined them. In his peripheral vision, Jack saw the Breaker free their yellow rain slickers from their gear, preparing for the storm.

"Mine are in place. Should I activate them now?" Emmaline called, hesitation in her voice.

"Do it," Jack agreed, doing the same to his. He felt the jolt of his magic racing between his paired effigies. "Then you need to come activate mine, and I'll do the same to yours."

"Can we do that?" Emmaline asked, surprised. "They're already active."

"Layers twine together," Jack said tersely. He didn't have time to explain, not now. He hadn't gotten to the point of teaching her this bit of spellwork, but there was no better teacher than experience.

The air rippled around them as lightning flashed a handful of miles away, followed by a tremendous clap of thunder. The pegasi clustered together in the middle of the effigies, snorting. <Hurry it up,> Zepheus urged.

"Working on it," Jack muttered. "Spell ain't gonna do shit if we get it wrong." He looked at Emmaline. "Key the hematite to the effigies, then go bury it a good distance outside of our barrier."

She nodded, expression grim as she bent down to attune the small stone. If the Effigest had been anyone else, Jack wouldn't have trusted them with the task. Done incorrectly, they were probably going to die. Emmaline finished, then jogged a distance away, hurriedly reaching down to sink the hematite into the dirt before joining them again.

"Now, what do we do?" Emmaline asked, slipping up beside him.

Pray to Faedra that this works. "Pour everything we have into it and hope we can hold off the fury of a storm."

As if summoned by his words, the wind picked up, sudden rainfall battering them. Jack shrugged into his slicker, crouching down beneath Zepheus's neck. The pegasus spread a wing to shelter him from some of the rain but had to tuck it back in when hail began to fall.

"Ouch," Jack heard Blaise grumble as a hailstone the size of a golden eagle coin struck his head, no doubt smarting even with his hat. "I guess whatever you're doing doesn't help with hail?"

"'Course not," Jack snapped. "We're protecting against lightning. What else do you need? Want me to crochet you a fancy doily while I'm at it?" Yeah, maybe it was unfair to take his frustrations out on the Breaker, but he was already feeling the effects of the spell as it chewed through his reserves. Extreme magic drain always made him grumpy.

"I'd like to not get a head injury from a piece of ice the size of my fist," Blaise said, irritation in his voice as a huge chunk of hail struck the ground beside him.

Maybe he had a point—that could take any of them out, or seriously injure the pegasi. Jack hadn't accounted for hail, and that only further annoyed him. "Can *you* do something about it?" Jack grumbled, thinking maybe Blaise would make another one of his fancy shields that broke anything that touched it.

"Maybe." He heard Blaise shift positions. They were cramped within the confines of the spell. "Can I piggyback onto whatever y'all are doing?"

"Sure, why not?" Emmaline said.

"What? No!" Jack growled, but it was too late. He felt the shift as Breaker magic joined the twined forces of Effigest power.

Jack thought for certain that was going to be it for them—that Blaise's destructive magic would chew through their fragile spell, sundering it and leaving them vulnerable to the lightning. But to his great surprise, he recognized the Breaker magic was braiding itself into their working. His breath caught. He wanted to demand to know what Blaise was doing and how he'd learned to do that. And if it would work.

But Jack didn't have such luxuries. They were in the teeth of the storm now, lightning illuminating the dark ribbons of rain around them. Whatever Blaise had done helped with their hail problem—rain got through to them, but in between the nearly deafening peals of thunder, he heard a strange crunching sound that he could only assume was the hail disintegrating. Rain plastered their slickers against them, and Jack hoped that the earthen dam Blaise had created would hold.

Beneath Oberidon's arched neck, Emmaline groaned. "I don't know how much longer I can keep this up."

Yeah, he wondered the same for himself. Their spell was working—lightning danced around them but always diverted to the place where she had buried the hematite. Their exhaustion was in direct relation to the amount of lightning they deflected with the working. Jack opened his mouth to make a response when something new flowed into their spell.

Power. Magic in its purest form, not yet flavored with a type like Breaker or Effigest.

"Take it!" Blaise called.

The Breaker was a continuous surprise. How was he able to share his reserves with them? Ritualists and Effigests could bolster others, but Jack had never heard of any other sort of mage doing so. *I've got questions for you if we survive this.*

Jack felt Emmaline's part of the working grow stronger, no longer threatening to buckle from the strain. In fact, Jack himself felt empowered by the flow of magic. Unstoppable, like a freight train with no brakes barreling down an incline. As if their strange combination of magics were capable of anything. It was a heady feeling, almost seductive. Jack reveled in the sensation.

He lost track of how long they held off the storm. By the time the gusts calmed, and clear blue sky opened overhead, the feeling of immense power had waned. He felt like a husk. Puddles formed around their boots. Rivulets flowed past them, streams of water breeching the dam but not sundering it. The dam held, but for how long? Jack panted for breath, shaking off the paralyzing exhaustion.

"Up. Up to the ridge," he ground out, getting into the saddle. The wet leather squeaked beneath him. Emmaline shook her head, gathering her strength to mount. But it was clear she was too tired, and Oberidon knelt to help her aboard.

Moments later, they were all on the ridge. Jack had a better look at Blaise's dam. Dark water churned behind its confines, pressure building. It wouldn't hold forever, but it had done its job. And Blaise...

Jack whirled to face the Breaker. "What was *that*?"

Blaise leaned hard against Emrys's rain-slicked neck, catching his breath. "Maybe start with, 'Gee, thanks, Blaise, that was really helpful. Now can you tell us what you did because we're curious?'"

Jack snorted. "That's not how I'd say *any* of that."

Blaise sighed. "I know." He struggled upright, rubbing the side of his face. "Can we make camp here? I'm tired."

Jack pursed his lips but nodded. They were all too wrung out to go further. Emmaline was much too quiet, her face pale. She needed rest. Jack dismounted, though he aimed a forefinger at Blaise when the Breaker did likewise. "You're dodging the question."

Blaise took off his hat, shaking out his soggy hair. Curls matted against his forehead. "Look, I only did it because…because I didn't want us to die, okay?"

There was a hint of fear in the young man's blue eyes. "What are you so afraid of?" Jack asked. It was odd, since the formerly skittish Breaker had grown bolder recently. Emmaline shook off her fatigue, moving closer to listen with arms crossed. Oberidon stayed close beside her, helping her remain upright.

Blaise glanced away. "I don't want people to know that…that I can do these things with my magic. It's already bad enough that I'm unique." He licked his lips. "I imagine it would only be worse if they know all of what I can do."

Jack scowled, not understanding. "You ever think that if people know what you can do that they may think twice before crossing you?" But no, of course, the soft-hearted baker wouldn't have such a thought.

Blaise ducked his head. "I have, actually. But I don't want to *be* like that."

"You can be powerful and still kind, you know," Emmaline commented, coming up alongside Blaise. "You don't have to be only one or the other."

Yeah, Emmaline hit the target. That was the problem. Blaise equated flaunting power—his magic—with force. With bullies. Sometimes, it seemed like he'd overcome that, and then others…well, this was a prime example.

Blaise closed his eyes for a moment. "I feel like I can't be both, though. Like when I find the outlaws who took my mother. Who…" His eyes flashed open, and his voice wavered as he said, "Who killed my father. I *can't* be kind then. I *have* to be hard. Powerful. Vengeful."

"Justice and vengeance aren't the same thing at all," Jack pointed out. "And you don't have to change who you are. Yeah, you may need to be hard as steel when we go up against the Copperheads. But then you'll be toe to toe with bloodthirsty desperadoes, not a bunch of mewling kittens.

Don't think you have to show them an ounce of kindness, 'cause they would *never* show you the same."

Blaise sighed, rubbing his hands together. "Okay, I guess you're right." He licked his lips. "I'll tell you what I did during the storm."

"Yeah, you better," Jack grumbled, failing to hide his curiosity.

"The first part, where I added my magic to your spell? That was something I had time to think about when I was…" He swallowed. "When I was in the Cit. When I took down the *Retribution*, there were a bunch of protective spells, all woven together. I don't know who cast them—if it was a single Warder or maybe a group. The part that stuck with me was they were different, but they worked together."

"So you thought you could do the same thing," Jack marveled. It had been an audacious idea, one that could have failed spectacularly. Only it hadn't. That took natural aptitude, something he hadn't thought Blaise possessed for magic. *I was wrong.*

"Yeah," Blaise agreed softly. "As for the other…well, I knew I could lend power." Discomfort crossed his face again. "I learned that when Jefferson and Flora saved me. If I hadn't given some to Jefferson, I would have had too much."

Jack nodded. He recalled that—the potion had overwhelmed Blaise's personal reserve, threatening to shatter him and everything around him if he hadn't bled some off. So he'd siphoned some away to the peacock, and it had worked. Whatever that was about, Blaise had done it effortlessly. Without hesitation, as if it just came naturally.

If they ever caught up to Marian Hawthorne, Jack had questions for her, too. Had she made Blaise into *more* than just a Breaker?

CHAPTER TWENTY-THREE

Plans Are for Outlaws Who've Slept

Blaise

"That wasn't them, was it?" Blaise asked as they lay on their soggy bedrolls, staring up at the clear sky overhead. The sun had set, and the stars were brilliant, though the moon hadn't yet risen.

"The Copperheads?" Jack asked. He kept his voice soft. Emmaline was asleep, worn out from her magical exertion. She had crawled into her bedroll not long after they'd shared a scanty meal of jerky and dried fruit.

"Yeah. Did they summon that storm?"

"Nah," the outlaw answered. "They have a Weathermage, but a storm that size? That's only nature, and it happens this time of year in the Untamed Territory. We're lucky there weren't any tornadoes."

"The hail was bad enough," Blaise agreed, reaching up to rub a tender spot on his crown.

Jack grunted as he stretched. "Yeah. That spell you did, though? That was damned gritty of you. Didn't know you had it in you."

"Are you complimenting me?" Blaise asked, edging up to lean on one elbow so he could see the outlaw's profile better.

"Maybe."

Blaise grinned, and he felt more confident than he had when he'd made the choice to go all-in during the height of the storm. "Thanks." Then his thoughts turned to their purpose. "What are we going to do now?"

"Sleep," Jack said. "The pegasi said they have the watch, so that's what we're supposed to be doing. Really should shut your piehole."

There's the Jack I know. "I mean tomorrow."

"Same plan. Head to Uncertain, resupply, and get any new gossip we can before continuing to Thorn."

"Going to Thorn will be dangerous, won't it?" Blaise asked.

Jack sighed, as if he didn't want to have this discussion now. He probably didn't. But Blaise was too wound up to sleep. "Like whacking a beehive with a stick while covered in honey? Something like that."

"Do you have a plan?"

"Plans are for outlaws who've slept after draining themselves during a damned squall."

Blaise sighed, deciding to let the testy Effigest sleep. He hadn't fully exerted his magic, despite all he'd done. He closed his eyes, dreading what awaited him in slumber. With Jefferson no longer shepherding his sleep, the nightmares had returned.

A dark shape loomed over him. Emrys. <I am not Jefferson, but I am here if you need me.>

Blaise breathed out a soft breath, reaching up to stroke the pegasus's lowered head. Emrys's presence made him smile. He much preferred a stallion in the night to a nightmare.

***

UNCERTAIN WAS A FAR CRY FROM EITHER FORTITUDE OR RAINBOW FLAT. IT seemed to be in a location that would make it prosperous—the Untamed River rumbled in a blue ribbon just southwest of the town. Blaise was surprised that he didn't see docks or boats, as had been common in Rainbow Flat. As their pegasi landed on the edge of town, unchallenged by any sort of sentries, Blaise asked Jack about it.

Amusement glinted in the outlaw's eyes. He jerked a thumb toward the river. "This deep in the Untamed Territory, the local wildlife ain't gonna let a man put a boat in the river uncontested."

That caught Emmaline's attention, too. "But Rainbow Flat is in the Untamed Territory, and they have shipping."

Jack waved a hand. "Any critters in the Tombstone River are more placid than what's here." He held up a hand, ticking off fingers. "You got kelpies, globsters, river serpents, bunyips. People learned real quick that the water 'round here is dangerous."

"I don't know what any of those are, but I'm going to take your word for it," Blaise said.

Emmaline shaded her eyes. "Not even a bridge."

Jack shook his head as Zepheus trotted toward the town. "Nope. Globsters like to attach to 'em and break 'em down. There're a couple of spots where you can ford the river if there's not been heavy rain. Water's too shallow for most of those critters." He grinned. "Made ripe pickings for an outlaw."

No one paid them any heed as they rode into town. Uncertain was almost a ghost town. The buildings seemed to be on their last legs, the paint faded. Some of them had clearly never seen a coat of paint. Honest-to-goodness tumbleweeds rolled down the dusty street. Their pegasi halted outside a small building where Blaise could barely make out the words *Post Office* painted over the door. The elements had scoured away much of the lettering, so it looked like *ost Of ce*. The emblem of an equally faded rampant griffin clutching a letter in its talons, the symbol of mail delivery, was the best clue among the dubious signage.

"Hank travels all this way?" Blaise asked as they dismounted.

"He can go as far east as Thorn, though I imagine that route will get more scarce," Jack said, running a hand along Zepheus's glossy neck. "Only does it once a week or so."

Jack shoved open the door to the post office. Blaise and Emmaline followed him in. They watched as the Effigest made inquiries at the counter, only to discover there was nothing awaiting him. *What's he looking for? A letter from Kittie, maybe?*

Thinking of Kittie led him to thinking of Jefferson. Gods, he missed him. If someone had told him a year ago that he would pine after the egotistical Jefferson Cole, he would have laughed. Yet here he was.

Blaise ran a hand through his hair. They might—no, *would*—be going into a dangerous situation. *What if I don't make it back?* He swallowed the lump that formed in his throat. Blaise knew he shouldn't borrow trouble. But Jefferson didn't know any of what had befallen him. He could send a letter but…Blaise shook his head, dismissing the idea. This was too big, *too much* for a letter, and his predicament would only alarm Jefferson and distract him from his task.

They left the post office, though Blaise was still chewing through different thoughts. "Walkers just get to go willy-nilly into Confederation lands?"

"Walkers are hard to stop if they want to go some place," Jack answered. "Long as they don't get a bullet in 'em or salt-iron on their wrists, they can get away. So mostly the Confederation turns a blind eye to 'em." He shrugged. "And besides, many a Walker provides the same service for the Confederation. Far be it from them to shoot themselves in the foot for something of benefit."

Like the Wallwalker? Blaise didn't want to mention the Herald aloud, fearing that to do so might invite her presence.

They accompanied the pegasi to the town's livery stable. It was downright sad compared to any other stable Blaise had seen, but at least it would be a roof over their equines' heads for the night. There were no grooms other than the gruff stable owner who took more of their coin for the stalls, so they each untacked their pegasi, groomed them, and made sure they had fresh water, clean straw, and a bucket of sweet feed.

That task done, Jack led the way to Uncertain's only diner. The food was palatable, but Blaise was of the opinion that dried buffalo chips might have better flavor. Still, it was food in his empty belly, and he was in no position to complain.

Uncertain's single redeeming feature was the bathhouse. Jack paid for a room—singular, they would have to bunk together—and then they made their way to the baths. Jack and Emmaline made efficient use of their time, but Blaise was in no rush. His sore muscles demanded a good soak after the grueling days of travel.

By the time Blaise climbed out of the tub, the water was cold, and he wished he could have his clothing washed. But there wasn't time for that, so he pulled on his clothes and boots and walked the short distance to Uncertain's sorry excuse for a hotel.

Jack and Emmaline were already in the shared room, though their damp hair was proof they'd only recently come in from the bathhouse, too. Father and daughter were sitting on the bed, and it was obvious they had been discussing something.

Jack pointed to the rickety chair in the corner. "Have a seat. We're making plans."

"About time," Blaise said and dragged the chair over. He hoped it would support his weight. A tendril of his magic told him how brittle the wood was. In fact, that made him decide against it. He pushed it back in the corner and sat cross-legged on the floor. Jack's eyebrows shot up. "It's about to break," Blaise explained.

"You can sense that?" Jack asked.

"Yeah."

The Effigest digested that, probably filing it away as more Breaker trivia for later. Then Jack went back to the matter at hand. "While I soaked, I had time to think. We know that not only was your mother wanted, Blaise, but so are *you.*"

Blaise sighed, rubbing his chin. Briefly, he wondered if he could shave before they left Uncertain. He didn't like when his beard went untended for too long. "Yeah, I'm aware." Nothing new about that, unfortunately.

"I'm thinking that you and Emmaline don't go into Thorn," Jack began, then held up a hand when Blaise opened his mouth to interject. "Not *immediately.* Let me go in, do some snooping around, see what I can learn.

There's an abandoned homestead ten miles outside of town. Should be safe enough for you both to hunker down there."

Emmaline's lips pressed together in an unhappy line. She didn't want to be left behind, either. "Won't it be dangerous for you alone?"

The outlaw hesitated before answering. "Alone, I can go in and keep my head down. Try not to attract attention while I get the lay of the land and dig for information. And besides, one of the engineers for our wind-pump is in Thorn. If nothing else, I can use calling on Creagen as a front." He shifted on the bed. "As long as I don't give 'em reason to pay attention to me, I should be fine."

Somehow, Blaise doubted that was possible. Jack was often quick to take offense, and he didn't back down easily. "Are you saying you'll behave yourself?"

Jack hissed out an offended breath. "I know what I'm about, Breaker. I've been doing things like this since you were in diapers."

Blaise nodded. It wasn't as if he had a better plan. At best, his only idea was to blunder into the town and somehow find his mother and free her. Not much of a plan in the grand scheme of things.

The outlaw yawned. "Anyway, time to hit the hay. Gonna be an early start tomorrow." He rose from the bed, crossing to pick up his bedroll. He unfurled it across the floor and settled down on it.

"Blaise, you want the bed?" Emmaline asked. She patted the mattress, which was about as thin as a pancake and nowhere near as soft.

He shook his head. "All yours. My bedroll dried finally, so the floor will work." He picked up his bedroll and situated it beside the wall. Although the room only had one bed, the hosteler had provided them with additional pillows. That was better than nothing. The pillow smelled funny, like it had never seen a bit of soap or water during the entirety of its existence, but Blaise was so tired he was asleep before he knew it.

A BOOT POKED BLAISE IN THE RIBS. "GET UP, SUNSHINE."

Jack. Blaise groaned, sitting up. There wasn't even the slightest hint of natural light filtering through the window yet. Blaise didn't mind waking up before the sun when he had a morning of baking to look forward to, but the exertions of the last week had caught up to him, and it was nice to sleep somewhere with an honest-to-goodness roof over his head. Factor in the nightmares that had interrupted his sleep, and he wasn't as rested as he'd like to be. "Five more minutes."

"Nope. In five minutes, you're gonna ask for five more. Not gonna happen." The Effigest was adamant. The room filled with the glow of a mage-light. Nearby rustling proved Emmaline had just finished dressing and was pulling on her boots. "Besides, we're gonna go see something before we grab breakfast and get in the sky."

Jack's words had Blaise curious. He reluctantly struggled upright, rubbing at his eyes. Blaise had slept in his clothes, so all he needed to do was pull on his boots and gather his bedroll. After the bath, his hair would probably benefit from a brush and some styling, but those were niceties for another time. He could almost hear Jefferson's exasperated sigh. *My hair probably looks like a bird's nest.* Blaise did steal a few minutes for a much-needed shave, though.

Once they'd gathered the few belongings they'd brought into the hotel, they headed to the livery. In the grey light of early morning, they fed their pegasi. While the stallions ate, Jack motioned for Blaise and Emmaline to follow him.

Rose gold blushed on the distant horizon as Jack led their procession out of town. Uncertain wasn't large, so they didn't have far to go. The morning was quiet, the silence only broken by the nearby rushing of the river and buzzing insects. In the distance, an animal bellowed, a sound unlike anything Blaise had heard before. Splashing accompanied the strange bellow.

Jack stopped on a ridge that overlooked the river. The sun peeked over the eastern horizon, illuminating the water with a pinkish-gold tinge. Emmaline made a small sound of appreciation as they saw what Jack must have wanted them to see.

Creatures were in the river, cavorting in the mist that wafted from the water. Blaise squinted. "Are those horses?"

"Look closer," Jack suggested.

Blaise studied them, observing the fluid way they rose from the water. There were a half-dozen, a small band. A pair of them tussled like juveniles at play, their soaked manes and tails splaying behind them, sending droplets flying. No, their hair wasn't wet. The animals *themselves* seemed to be made of water.

"Kelpies?" Emmaline asked, her voice soft. Jack made a noise of agreement.

"They're pretty," Blaise murmured. *I wish Jefferson were here to see them. He would like this.* "You said they were dangerous. They don't look dangerous."

"Is Emrys dangerous?" Jack asked.

"No," Blaise said automatically, then caught the error in his quick answer. "Oh. I mean, he's not dangerous to *me*. Or anyone he likes." He frowned. "But he *can* be dangerous." Blaise had seen first-hand what Emrys could do when he was motivated.

Jack jerked his chin at the kelpies. "Same for them, but they're wild. They want nothin' to do with humans. And they're carnivorous. Get too close to 'em, and there's gonna be trouble."

"Did you wake us up early just to remind us how dangerous the wildlife is?" Blaise asked.

"Nah," Jack said with a shake of his head. His eyes flicked to Emmaline. "They're pretty. I thought y'all might like to see them, and this is the best time of day to do it."

"I *love* seeing them!" Emmaline whispered. "Even if they *are* murderhorses!"

The golden light revealed the delighted twist of Jack's lips. *He's being a father.* Blaise liked that—he liked seeing Emmaline happy, liked seeing Jack attempt to do something nice. Even if he was rude with his early morning wake-up calls.

"Are there bunyips around, too?" Emmaline asked. "I've never seen one."

Jack's gaze slid to Blaise, as if he were looking for permission. Blaise smiled. "I have no idea what a bunyip is, but I'm game to see one. From a safe distance."

CHAPTER TWENTY-FOUR
The Plan is Don't Get Yourselves Killed

Blaise

They landed at the abandoned homestead late that afternoon. Sad to say, it was in better shape than Uncertain. The barn was dusty and worn, the ground dotted with holes left by various burrowing critters, but it was serviceable. There was a house, too, but Jack warned them to stick to the barn.

"Why's that?" Emmaline asked, curious.

"It's haunted," Jack said simply, as if that explained everything.

Instead, it only filled Blaise's head with more questions. "Excuse me, what?"

"Haunted," the outlaw repeated patiently, as if he were explaining the concept to a small child. "You know, ghosts, spirits, that sort of thing."

Emmaline didn't seem at all daunted by the prospect. "Oh! Do you think we'll see them?"

Blaise sighed. *Of course, Jack is leaving us at a haunted house.* But now, he understood why the homestead was abandoned. "Why didn't the souls go to Perdition like they're supposed to?"

Jack gave them both an amused glance. He nodded to Emmaline first. "You might see 'em later, and you definitely *would* if you dare set foot in the house. So *don't.*" His head swiveled to Blaise. "The poor sods got murdered by the Copperheads, so as you can imagine, they're touchy about that." He rolled his shoulders. "And on that happy note, I better head to Thorn while there's still daylight."

"Let me point out you're leaving us at a *haunted house*," Blaise grumbled.

"The barn is perfectly safe," Jack replied, Zepheus turning in a circle in preparation for departure. "Bed down with the pegasi. Two days. You best give me two days before you get it in your head to come haring off after me."

"Two days," Blaise agreed, eyeing the house. "You're leaving us for two days. At a haunted house. What do we do if you don't come back in two days?"

Jack gave him a wry look. "I figure you two will rush into town with magic a-blazin' despite anything I tell you."

"You're not wrong," Emmaline agreed.

"In that case, the plan is don't get yourselves killed," the outlaw suggested.

"That's not a plan. That's a long-term goal." Blaise shook his head. Not having a plan made him nervous, but there were too many unknowns. No way to plan for every potential scenario.

Jack made no reply. He leaned forward as Zepheus swept into a trot and then a lope before leaping skyward. The stallion's wings flapped furiously as he gained altitude, and before long, the pair were a tiny, receding dot.

Blaise rubbed his forehead, turning back to Emmaline and the waiting pegasi. <We should eat soon,> Emrys suggested.

"Yeah, we should," Blaise agreed, rubbing the whorl of hair on the stallion's broad forehead. Even when staying close to Fortitude, Emrys was always hungry. Though that wasn't his fault—his equine nature required it. And now they were spending five to six hours a day in flight, the pegasi were using more energy than they normally would. They definitely deserved a chance to graze and rest. It made Blaise feel a little bad for Zepheus, having to bear Jack into Thorn, and he mentioned it to Emmaline.

She shook her head as she pulled the saddle from Oberidon's spotted back. "You don't need to worry about Zeph. Daddy will find a stable first thing and make sure he's settled before he does anything else."

They balanced their saddles atop one of the stall partitions inside the barn. Blaise found a dusty bucket and headed out to the well, situated a stone's throw from the barn. That the homestead had access to water made it lucrative, and hard to believe no one else had tried to claim it. Though maybe people had—and had been run off by the ghosts.

He brought the water back for the stallions and found Emmaline pulling out rations of dried jerky and fruit. Blaise was so tired of dried jerky and fruit, and would have given anything for the ability to bake something halfway decent. He eyed the house again, wondering if it was worth braving restless spirits for the chance to bake. *Maybe.*

Oberidon wandered a short distance and lowered himself to the ground, writhing around in the dirt. Too late, Emmaline caught the pegasus's movement in the corner of her eye. "Oby! What in Perdition are you *doing?*"

<Dust bath,> the stallion replied for them to both hear, sounding only a little contrite. <I was itchy. Emrys, come on, it feels fantastic!>

Emrys flicked an ear at the temptation, though his brown eyes were on Blaise. "Oh, go ahead," Blaise told him. "We'll brush you both after we eat."

"I hate when they do that," Emmaline grumbled.

"I don't mind it," Blaise said. In fact, he enjoyed watching the antics of a dust-bathing pegasus. Emrys walked near Oberidon, then pawed at the dirt, raking up clouds of dust. When he had loosened a broad swath, he lowered himself down to his knees, wiggling his body and flapping his wings. He shook himself, ruffling his feathers with the brisk movement. Dust wafted up and away from the pair of pegasi.

"I should let you groom the both of them," Emmaline said, handing a stick of jerky to him.

"I can if you want," he agreed as he took the proffered meat. Anything to stay distracted and keep his mind off his worries. He was so focused on the pegasi and their dust bath that it took him a few minutes to notice Emmaline watching him intently. Blaise raised his brows, wondering if she was staring because he looked like a wild thing. "What?"

Emmaline glanced down at her hands, an unusual move for the young woman who was as spirited as her father. "Can I ask you something?"

He nodded. "Yeah, you know you can."

She took a sip from her canteen and capped it, as if she were stalling. Or like she was figuring out how to ask her question. "I've been thinking long and hard about this. Wondering if Fort Courage broke me, or..." Emmaline wet her lips, then shook her head as if unable to continue her sentence.

Broke her? Blaise leaned forward, his full attention on her. "What do you mean?" He hated to ask. Blaise understood too well the sort of memories that might haunt Emmaline. But his experience was likely different from whatever she had endured, and he couldn't help her without more information.

Emmaline scrubbed at her forehead. "They had a Healer there. Not the good kind. Not like Nadine." She bit off a chunk of jerky and chewed on it as if it had committed a grievous wrong. Blaise didn't mind the break in conversation. He was content to let her take her time to say whatever was on her mind.

"I didn't understand what they'd done to me until I got back to Itude. Until Nadine checked me out and talked to me." Emmaline rubbed her upper arm in the place a geasa tattoo would have been if they'd given her one. Blaise knew that wasn't it, though. She'd never been tattooed as he had. "They do it to women mavericks. Make sure we can't have babies, I mean."

Blaise's mouth went dry at her words, and he hastily uncapped his own canteen and took a swig. If he was following correctly—and as much as he disliked it, he was certain he was—the Confederation had forcefully sterilized her. He reined in the swell of rage that bloomed at the thought of the Salties harming Emmaline. Now wasn't the time for anger—he needed to listen. "I'm so sorry."

"Not your fault," Emmaline said with a wave of her hand, misunderstanding that he meant it as sympathy and not apology. "I never thought about it much before. But after that, I've noticed more and more..." She made a frustrated sound. "Other people my age are pairing up. And..." Emmaline picked up a new piece of jerky and stared at it.

"And they're having cake together?" Blaise suggested, deadpan.

Emmaline snorted a laugh, lifting her gaze to give him an amused look. "Is that what you and Jefferson call it?"

"That's between us," Blaise replied, though he was happy he'd jarred her out of her spiral. "What about it?"

She bit into the jerky, chewing and then gulping it down before speaking again. "I don't find that interesting. And sometimes the new townies ask why I'm not sweet on anyone." Her shoulders rose, as if the very thought irritated her. "They make it seem like that's all I should be thinking about."

Now he understood exactly why she was asking him. "Nothing wrong with being the way you are."

She crossed her arms. "But it doesn't make sense. I like the idea of romance. I think you and Jefferson are adorable. I like the idea of *other* people having that. Shouldn't I want that for me?"

Blaise shrugged. "The cake wasn't only a joke. Some people like cake and would eat it all the time, while others never want it. Some think to have cake when it's offered, or maybe crave it on occasion." He had her full attention, so he continued, "And some people only want to have cake with someone they care about."

Emmaline didn't even try to hide her amused smile. "How'd you come to learn so much about *cake*?"

"I've been paying more attention to people. Trying to figure things out." Emmaline was one of the few people he'd ever admit this to. Jefferson suspected, he was sure. Blaise wanted to understand more of the social cues he'd missed during his formative years, if only to help him navigate his relationship with Jefferson.

"Hmm." She studied him. "I'm never going to look at cake the same way again, thanks to you."

Blaise laughed. "I mean it, though. Your feelings and thoughts don't make you strange." He met her eyes. "Fort Courage didn't break you." It had changed her, just as his time in the Golden Citadel had changed him, but Blaise knew the things Emmaline had described were *normal*.

Emmaline relaxed at his assessment. "I knew you'd understand me." She pursed her lips. "You can't tell Daddy about Fort Courage, though."

Blaise scratched his forehead. It felt wrong that Jack didn't know what they had done to his child. But he knew why she requested it. Jack was fiercely protective of the ones he cared about. If Jack knew, Blaise had no doubt there would be more bloodshed as the Effigest threw himself into the teeth of the Confederation. His fury would know no bounds, and his reckless anger would be the end of him. No, Jack could never know.

"I won't tell him," Blaise agreed. Then he felt compelled to do something he rarely offered to anyone but Jefferson. He wiped the remnants of jerky grease away, then moved over and hugged her. She sank against him, her head nestled against his shoulder.

"Thanks," she mumbled against his shirt. "I wish we could have done laundry. Your shirt stinks."

"We were having a moment. You just ruined it," Blaise said, though he wished the same. He liked the music of her laughter against him. "You don't smell like rosewater and lilies, either."

She drew back, the hint of a smile on her lips. Then she grew serious again. "Thanks for listening."

"That's what friends do. What *family* does." He watched her for a moment, assessing. Blaise wondered how she could look so strong after all she'd been through. "And don't worry about not being like other people. You're better than most."

Emmaline cocked her head. "Be sure to tell yourself that, too." He gave her a self-deprecating smile. Yeah, she knew his woe-is-me tendencies.

Emrys arose from the wallow, dust sheeting off of him as he settled his wings at his side. Emmaline wrapped the remainder of the jerky and shoved it in a pocket. "Time to go groom a certain troublesome stallion."

"I can groom Oby if you want," Blaise offered.

"Nope. I got him," she said, following him into the barn so they could retrieve the brushes from their saddlebags. "Oby, get your tail over here!"

The stallions trotted up, Emrys a dusty grey in the growing twilight.

They settled down to work, brushing the dirt and grime from their coats. Emrys and Oberidon stood side-by-side, each grooming the other's wings with questing lips to make their feathers lie flat. Blaise wished he could have focused his attention solely on the bucolic scene, but he stole glances at the foreboding house every so often.

When they finished, the sun was down, and they were ringed by the warm glow of a mage-light. Emmaline chucked her brush back into her saddlebag. "Why do you keep looking at the house? You're not thinking of going in, are you?"

Blaise glanced at the house again. It didn't look any different from any other home in the darkness. It was in better repair than the Black Market building had been, though not by much. "Jack said the Copperheads killed the people who lived here. Made me wonder if the ghosts could tell us anything useful."

Emmaline quirked a brow. "You thinking about going to have a sit-down and chat with them?"

Blaise shook his head. "I figure nothing good would come of going into a haunted house."

She relaxed. "Good. I'm much more content to sleep in the not-haunted barn. Even if Oberidon does snore like a roaring dragon."

<I do *not* snore,> her pegasus said, stomping a hoof.

<You *do* snore,> Emrys said, earning a nip from the spotted stallion. <And calling it a roaring dragon is charitable.>

<Well, *you* are flatulent!> Oberidon rejoined, and the stallions devolved into trading barbs, while nipping and mock-striking at each other.

Blaise and Emmaline watched them tussle into the furthest reaches of the mage-light. The last few days had been stressful, and the stallions needed to let out some of their tensions. They squealed and spun, but after a few minutes of rambunctiousness, they calmed and trotted back over.

"All better?" Emmaline asked, sugary sweet.

<For now,> Oberidon agreed.

Blaise chuckled, shaking his head. Then they settled in for the long night.

CHAPTER TWENTY-FIVE
Oh, Biscuits

Jack

Thorn was a different town from the last time Jack had gotten this far east. The coastal city had always been a beacon for travelers—it was easily accessible to Eskela, Theilia, and Knossas by ship, which made it a strategic location for the Copperheads to take. Ravanchen wizards traveled overland through a mountain pass. The odd Confederation merchant made their presence known, too.

On his last visit, Thorn had had a laid-back air. The buildings were well-maintained, courtesy of the money changing hands constantly. To the untrained eye, the city looked the same. The buildings were as lovely as before. But the air was charged with tension, as if the citizens who called it home were constantly looking over their shoulders in fear.

Which they probably were with the Copperheads as their new *protection.*

True to his word, Jack behaved himself and kept a low profile. As much as he liked a good fight, he focused on his goal. The frustrating part was that he learned nothing at all regarding the whereabouts of Marian Hawthorne. The trouble was that he couldn't outright ask after her, lest his inquiries cause alarm. Wouldn't do to have the Copperheads come calling on him.

That meant he listened in on every conversation he could, though none of them bore any fruit. Jack didn't really care which bordello boasted the finest entertainment or which saloon served alcohol that was little more than watered-down whiskey. Such topics formed the bulk of the discussions he overheard, unsurprising with the number of visitors.

He discovered that many were in town specifically for the auction Slocum had mentioned. Anticipation rang in every voice that spoke of it, impatient for the day the Copperheads would allow the eager bidders to get an eyeful of the merchandise.

To his surprise, he found that the Knossans they'd come across had made it as far as Thorn, too. Jack was boggled they had reached Thorn so quickly. He spied them sitting across the saloon from him, and he wondered if one of them was also a shaman who might have enhanced their speed. The possibility made it curious they hadn't used magic to fight against the grasscats—unless they couldn't. *Druid, then.* He'd heard the Knossan druids were sworn to not utter a spell against a living thing.

He slipped across the saloon, pausing by their table to tip his hat to them. "Howdy, friends. Got room for another?"

The trio snorted in surprise at his appearance. Roam bobbed his head. "Please, make yourself welcome."

Jack snagged a nearby chair and hauled it over. "The next round's on me." Figured it didn't hurt to be charitable to encourage wagging tongues. "Fancy seeing you lot here."

"We made good time," Deal agreed blithely. Jack suspected the Knossan was smirking, though it was hard to tell.

"Any luck finding your young-uns?"

Gore blew out a soft breath, shaking his horns. "Not yet."

"We suspect we may have more luck soon, when the auction *merchandise* is unveiled," Roam added, his voice low and dripping with disgust.

Jack whistled, scratching his forehead. The server delivered a round of beer, and he waited until she left before he spoke. "You think they're selling *people?*" Jack figured it never hurt to confirm information from Slocum.

"That is what our inquiries have uncovered," Deal murmured. "There is nothing too *exotic* for this auction—that is what the Copperheads say. It stands to reason they mean the mystic races."

And alchemists. Jack nodded, though he was glad he'd taken the chance to chat with the Knossans. This was the most he'd heard yet. "If your young-uns are there, you gonna bid on them?"

Three sets of angry eyes fell on him. "We should not have to buy back our kin," Gore said.

"No," Jack agreed, "and I know you Knossans are fierce but look around." He tipped his head to the other saloon inhabitants. "Lotta these folks gonna take offense to you trotting off without paying." *Not even gonna mention what the Copperheads would do.*

The tips of Roam's horns scraped the table as he dipped his head. "We have no choice. There is no way we could afford the prices this auction will demand." His resonant voice was suffused with heartbreak, and Jack suspected that one of the missing Knossan children was his own flesh and blood.

Damn it. Jack tried to have a hard heart, but he hated trafficking. Especially hated it when it happened to children. And to auction them as if they were a dairy cow? He bared his teeth. "I'll help you get your young-uns back."

The Knossans regarded him with surprise, their ears flicking forward as if they'd misheard him. "You will? How?" Gore asked.

He shrugged. "We'll have to figure out the particulars, but the way I see it, ain't fair to the young-uns for you to not have a shot at freeing 'em."

Deal huffed. "We are not to be taken lightly."

"No, you're not," Jack agreed. "But you're about as sneaky as bison covered in bells. You go charging in, this ain't gonna work." He splayed a hand against his chest. "I'm an Effigest. We can figure something out."

Gore exchanged glances with the other bulls. "We would be foolish to refuse your help. But what do you ask in return?"

Jack pursed his lips. "I suspect there's merchandise in the auction that's of interest to me and mine. If that's the case, all I ask is for your help to recover it. Like for like."

"That is reasonable," Roam said.

A few moments later, the agreement was struck, and Jack moseyed out of the saloon. Twilight was falling across the town, so he checked in on Zepheus and found the stallion relaxing in his stall. Though the pegasus hadn't been idle—he, too, had been listening in on any gossip from those around the stables but had heard nothing new.

Jack found a room for the night. He appreciated a roof over his head and a mattress that was softer than the ground beneath his bedroll, but it made him fret over Emmaline. And Blaise. But he had been right to handle their approach to Thorn with caution. He knew it, but that didn't mean he *liked* it.

Emmaline's tough. She'll be fine. Blaise, though…well, that was the real worry. He wasn't cut out for this, even though he had handled everything well so far. That kid was meant to be in a bakery, not traipsing across the Untamed Territory on a manhunt. Jack shook his head, banishing the thought. Nothing he could do about that.

Blaise

Blaise sat up with a gasp, his heart thundering in his chest. He swallowed, rubbing his forehead as he heard Emrys stir to wakefulness nearby.

<I'm here.> The stallion was an inky form against the void of darkness. Blaise breathed out a soft breath as Emrys moved closer, lipping at his rider's shoulder. <I'm sorry I can't keep the nightmares away.>

"It's okay," Blaise whispered, not wanting to wake Emmaline. He ran a hand along the pegasus's leg, tracing the canon bone down to the feathered pasterns. The equine form was familiar. Comforting. It was enough to anchor him in a better frame of mind.

Sleep was impossible after his nightmares. Emrys drowsed next to him until the distant horizon lightened with the coming day. But as dawn came, a heavy fog rolled in from the east.

Emmaline scrubbed at her eyes as she roused from her bedroll. She yawned and stretched, frowning. "Must be a sea fog."

Blaise glanced at her. "You think so?" He couldn't put his finger on it, but something about the fog unsettled him. Although, it wasn't unusual in the autumn. He'd seen it often enough during his youth in Desina.

"Thorn's on the coast, and we're close enough for it to roll in, I imagine," Emmaline said with a shrug. "May as well eat. Can't do a thing about the weather."

They'd added oatmeal to their supplies when they stopped in Uncertain. Emmaline had foraged and found fresh berries, so they added them to make their meal more appealing. Blaise and Emmaline were sitting down to eat when both stallions came to attention, ears pricked.

Emmaline stopped eating with her spoon halfway to her mouth. "Oby?"

The spotted stallion snorted uncertainly, shaking his mane. <Hoofbeats. We hear hoofbeats.>

<A *lot* of hoofbeats,> Emrys agreed, shifting uneasily.

Oh, biscuits. Blaise's mouth went dry. Jack had said the Copperheads had a weather mage, but not one capable of creating the storm that had assaulted them. That didn't mean they couldn't do something like create this fog.

"We can't ride in the fog, can we?" Blaise asked, his sinking feeling growing. He swallowed, not even bothering to ask if the pegasi could fly in it. It was thick, making it difficult to see the house from the barn, even though the distance wasn't great.

<Not without risk of taking a misstep,> Emrys said.

Emmaline clambered to her feet. "We need to get deeper into the barn. *Now.*"

Blaise picked up his saddlebag, hauling it back into the dark interior.

The pegasi crowded into the furthest depths of the barn, their riders crouching beside them. Emmaline extinguished the mage-light, and they huddled in the surreal darkness together.

In the distance, hooves pounded a foreboding rhythm. The blanket of fog dampened equine squeals and snorts, along with the voices of men and women.

<Unicorns,> Emrys said. <I smell unicorns.>

Blaise's heart raced. The Copperheads had found them. They heard equines milling outside. Laughter. The solid slap of boots hitting the ground from a dismount.

"Breaker! We know you're in there. C'mon out," a gruff voice called.

Unicorns. It had to be the blasted magic-scenting unicorns that had tracked them down. Blaise traded a look with Emmaline.

Emmaline licked her lips, reaching for the sixgun at her side. She pulled it from the holster, metal whispering as she checked her ammunition. "Do we fight?"

Blaise closed his eyes, stomach sinking as he remembered what Jack said about the Copperheads. Emmaline was good. Fierce. But she was only one brave girl, and he—well, he was a Breaker, but he didn't know how to fight. Not when he was surrounded like this. Not when to fight might mean his friends would pay the price. They were woefully outnumbered. He would never forgive himself if Emmaline or one of their pegasi died on his account.

"No," he said, shaking his head as he opened his eyes.

"What do you mean?" she hissed. "They want you!"

They did. And in turn, the Copperheads had something he wanted, too. Maybe, just maybe, he could turn that in his favor, given the time and room to maneuver. Time to leverage the situation.

"Exactly," he agreed softly.

<I don't think you understand what that means,> Emrys said, urgent. He leaned his great head against Blaise's back. <They will take you from me. And they will take *us*.>

That was the part Blaise didn't like. But, in his mind, a peaceful surrender was preferable to being taken by violence and possibly hurt. Or worse. He turned, planting a kiss in the middle of the stallion's forehead. "I know it sounds like a terrible plan. But trust me in this."

<I *do* trust you,> Emrys said, though he was sorrowful. <Now I wish I had run off with you into the fog! I would risk a broken leg to keep you safe.>

But I wouldn't risk you breaking a leg to keep me safe. Blaise shook his head, then glanced at Emmaline. "Are you okay with this?" He knew only too well that she might have horrible memories rearing up of the last time she'd been taken by force.

She tightened her grip on the sixgun. "No. I hate this." Emmaline tried to hide it, but Blaise saw the tremor of her hands.

He took a step closer to her, looking her in the eye—something he did with very few people. "I know. But we can't run, and we can't fight—"

"We *can* fight," she whispered, sounding very much like her father.

Blaise shook his head. He understood her fear. "We can, but *not now.*"

Emmaline made a frustrated sound. "You think they'll give us another chance?"

"I don't know," Blaise whispered. He had to be honest and not sugarcoat the situation. "But we're at a disadvantage here. And I have an idea."

She narrowed her eyes at him. "What—?"

A voice from outside interrupted her. "Breaker! Time's up! Come out now, or we come in by force."

"Later," Blaise promised. "Trust me."

Emmaline sighed and shoved her sixgun back in its holster. Blaise mustered his courage, raising his voice as he called, "We're coming out! Don't shoot."

CHAPTER TWENTY-SIX
Slap in the Face

Jefferson smiled behind the rim of his glass of cider, watching as Kittie flowed through the throng of curious Gannish elite like a hummingbird going from flower to flower. No, not a bird—like a spark prepared to gut a forest. The elite were quite aware of who and what she was, but since she was well-dressed and approachable, she had become a charming curiosity. She seemed to comport herself well, so he contented himself to watch from a distance.

Mindy and Flora were in attendance, too, though they kept lower profiles. Mindy had dressed simply, insistent she didn't want to stand out. She wore a demure black outfit that allowed her to blend in with the staff. Flora was being typical Flora—invisible, but no doubt somewhere nearby.

They had been invited to an early Bounty's Eve gala, hosted by one of the Board members. Bounty's Eve wasn't for another week, though Jefferson and Madame Boss Clayton were optimistic they might sign the declaration that day. It would be symbolic to do so on an important holiday. With that plan in mind, refusing the invitation to the gala had never been an option.

He realized, though, as he watched the elite flow around the great room like schools of fish, that galas no longer excited him as they once had. Or maybe the problem was that he missed Blaise. All the elite with attachments attended with their partners or had brought a guest, which made him feel the odd man out. And it made him a target.

To be fair, in the past, he wouldn't have minded the flirtations of a lovely lady at all. But now? He found it irksome. *Especially* considering the woman who had set her sights on him.

Cinna Smithstone smiled up at him. She was a petite beauty, with wavy tresses such a deep red they were nearly burgundy. She had been the woman Malcolm Wells had been engaged to—not an engagement of love, but one of power. After they had broken it because of Malcolm's wayward inclinations, she had moved on to marry an elderly lecher who had since made the long walk to Perdition.

And now, for Tabris knew what reason, she had attached herself to Jefferson.

It was my fault. She had sat next to him at dinner, and he had held a polite conversation with her. Cinna had taken it as a doorway to monopolizing his time, and no amount of begging off would dissuade her.

"When you're not in meetings, you should absolutely come and walk the Hanging Gardens with me," she nearly purred, threading her arm through his in a gesture he remembered too well from years ago.

Jefferson carefully extracted his arm, simultaneously sliding a few inches away to allow some breathing room. "That is most kind of you, Ms. Smithstone, but my schedule is, as you may no doubt imagine, jam-packed."

She pouted at him. "That's no fun at all!" Then her pout shifted into the alluring smile that used to make his breath hitch. "But you're free *tonight*. No meetings after this, hmm?"

Cinna closed the gap between them again, tracing her fingers down his lapel, nudging the button that kept his greatcoat closed. Jefferson knew exactly what she was doing. Any gamble to win her target. What did Cinna want from someone representing the Gutter? Was it because he, too, was a curiosity? Or did she covet his wealth, hoping to add it to her own? "You're kind to offer, but I'm no longer available for such sport. My heart belongs to another."

She canted her head, baring the pale curve of her neck. "But she's not here, is she?"

"*He* is not," Jefferson corrected, once again wishing that Blaise were there.

Her face contorted with indignation, her mask slipping for an instant. Then it fell back into place as she ran the nail of her index finger around the ridges of his button. "He doesn't have to *know*." She glanced up at him through her long lashes. "It could be our little secret."

Our secret, and one everyone in this room would be privy to. Not that she tempted him. She was a reminder of the life he'd left behind, and he wanted nothing more than to get away from her. But even if she weren't...even if she *were* someone he might find alluring... He shook his head. "I must refuse, Ms. Smithstone. While my beau wouldn't know, *I* would."

An ugly gleam flashed in her eyes at being spurned. Before he could even react, her open hand flew up, slapping him across the face. She spun on her heel and marched off, huffing.

"Oof, that didn't look pleasant," a voice said at his shoulder.

Jefferson rubbed his cheek, wondering if her fingers had left a mark. It wasn't the first time someone had slapped him—but in the past it had been after he'd made propositions of his own. He glanced at Kittie, who had ghosted up behind him. "I assure you it wasn't."

The Pyromancer was watching Cinna, not him, which he found interesting. "Good thing I didn't have to scorch her."

"You what?" Jefferson blinked, thinking he'd misheard.

An amused smile played on Kittie's lips. "Jack told me you're a playboy. He said I should keep an eye out for Blaise's interests."

"I am *not* a playboy," Jefferson grumbled, then sighed when Kittie raised her brows at him. "Okay, maybe a little. But I wouldn't dare go with her. Or anyone else, for that matter." *That life is dead and buried, too. And I'm fine with that as long as I have Blaise.*

"Glad to hear it. So, why was she so adamant, then?"

"You heard? Wait, you *knew* I wasn't propositioning her?" Jefferson uttered a frustrated sigh at Kittie's innocent look. "I don't know why she was so interested. There are many reasons. I *am* quite the catch, you know."

"So I'm told," Kittie agreed. She was about to say something else, but her mouth clamped shut at the sound of heels approaching.

"Firebrand Dewitt! Ambassador Cole!" A young woman with black hair approached them with her arms spread wide. He recognized her from his past. Her name was Tara Woodrow, and her family had been in league with his father. "You simply must join us for the traditional Bounty's Eve toast."

"A bit premature, isn't it?" Jefferson asked. Toasts were often made on Bounty's Eve to encourage a prosperous future, and there were some who reasoned it was bad luck to do so before the proper date.

She flung an arm around his shoulders as if they were old friends. "Oh, Mr. Cole, please don't tell me you're a superstitious sourpuss! In my mind, the more toasts, the better."

"I'm more inclined to ask for Tabris's fortune at the proper time, personally," Jefferson replied, smoothing his lapels and wishing he could shrug out of her grip. But there was no way around this without looking like poor guests. "We won't turn away your hospitality, however."

Kittie gave him a questioning look, and he answered with a slight shake of his head as Tara beamed at them. She scooped her other arm around the Pyromancer. "Wonderful! Come along, then."

Tara herded them to a circle of elite across the great room. To Jefferson's surprise, he noted that they had snubbed the Board members from this gathering. They clustered on their own, flashing suspicious glances at Jefferson and Kittie as they joined Tara and her cronies. Cinna numbered among their group, though she crossed her arms and turned away when she saw him.

Jefferson was troubled by the fact that he recognized many of the group. All people who'd had dealings with Stafford Wells in the past. *My father is dead and gone, along with everything he represents.* Jefferson fervently hoped that had been the nail in the coffin for trafficking, though he doubted it. It made him a little suspicious of the supposed well-wishers, though logically, he knew they may very well support the Gutter if they thought it might fill their coffers.

"Ah, there he is. The good Ambassador." Jefferson recognized the speaker: Phillip Dillon, a man who had close dealings with his father. The very same man who had bought Jefferson's sister as a wife. He bit his tongue to stave off the comments he longed to make.

Phillip picked up one of the shot glasses arranged on the antique table before them. The alcohol in the glasses was a rich amber. As Jefferson drew near, he caught a glint in the bottom of each shot glass. A freshly minted golden eagle, a traditional addition to a proper Bounty's Eve drink.

"Hello, Phillip," Jefferson greeted the other man, feigning a smile he didn't feel.

Phillip grinned at him, then offered a respectful nod to Kittie. "Welcome to Firebrand Dewitt as well! We're honored by your presence, truly." He laid his free hand over his heart, then gestured to the shot glasses. "We wanted to have a toast with you, optimistic that it will help us prosper in all our endeavors."

A deep frown lined Kittie's face. Jefferson didn't understand what the problem was until Mindy slid into their group, sidling alongside the Pyromancer. Mindy whispered something, and Kittie lifted her chin. "I appreciate the invitation, though I won't be able to partake." There was regret in her eyes. And a longing.

Tara scowled, exchanging a look with Phillip. Something about that glance rubbed Jefferson the wrong way, though he couldn't rightly say why. Tara's face shifted back to a friendly smile. "That's no problem. We have other toasting options. Cider?" She removed one of the shot glasses.

Kittie nodded. "That will be fine."

"One for me as well, please," Mindy piped up.

Annoyance flickered on Tara's face, but she feigned the look of a properly polite lady. "Of course."

Jefferson didn't miss the intensity with which Mindy was studying the shot glasses. Tara returned with the two non-alcoholic drinks, offering them to Kittie and Mindy. The Hospitalier murmured her thanks, though her yellow gaze never left the small glasses.

The rest of the elite picked up shot glasses from the table, and Jefferson did likewise. Phillip cleared his throat, lifting his own high. "Now that we're all here, please lift your glasses and…"

Mindy wobbled where she stood, and for an instant, Jefferson feared something was wrong with her. The Hospitalier caught herself on Kittie, locking an arm around the other mage. There was a sharp tinkling as their shot glasses collided, and Mindy made a small yelp of dismay. Everyone stopped what they were doing to stare at the pair as Mindy righted herself.

"Oh, clumsy me. Still getting used to these heels," the Hospitalier said, her shoulders shrugging with embarrassment.

"Did any of the drinks spill?" Tara blurted the question. "On your clothing, I mean. It would be a shame to ruin them." She focused on Kittie, assessing the amount of liquid in the glass.

Kittie recovered, holding her glass in one hand and running her other over the front of her dress, the flame-licked number she'd gotten from Zuzanna. "Luckily, no. Dry as a bone."

Tara nodded, mollified. Mindy continued to look properly embarrassed, though Jefferson had the sneaking suspicion she hadn't been clumsy at all. Her stumble had been deliberate. He frowned down at his own shot glass with concern.

Phillip chuckled. "Now that the excitement is out of the way, let's make this toast properly, shall we?" He lifted his glass again. "To bright futures and fruitful connections!"

"To bright futures!" the others chorused, glass clattering against glass as they chimed together. They drank.

Jefferson followed suit, noticing that Kittie and Mindy did likewise with their ciders. The golden eagles rattled musically, falling against their lips. Dillon had served them a smoky Canenite rum. He wondered if the smoky flavor had been a nod to Kittie or just a coincidence.

"What happened back there?" Kittie hissed, a trace of alarm in her voice as they piled into Jefferson's suite at Silver Sands. Her eyes were on Mindy, demanding an answer.

"Wait for Flora," Mindy said, sounding tired. The ride back had been awkward, full of pensive silence, as none of them dared speak without the assurance of privacy.

"I'm already here," the half-knocker declared as she blew in from the door that led to the bedroom. Of course, she had made it back before them—Kittie and Mindy didn't know about her affinity for salt-iron, but Jefferson had made certain that a tiny swaddled nugget was nestled in the drawer beside his bed to serve as a beacon for her.

Kittie gave a sharp nod, turning back to Mindy. "Explain. You switched our drinks. Why?" Apprehension crept into her tone, and Jefferson realized she wasn't angry at Mindy—she was worried about the young Hospitalier.

"I was watching when the shots were prepared. No one pays much attention to me because I'm not important like either of you." She gestured to Jefferson and Kittie. "And that's fine because it lets me do what I'm here for."

"They put something in our drinks?" Kittie asked.

Mindy's golden gaze flitted between Kittie and Jefferson. "Only yours. I didn't see what they spiked it with, so I don't know what their intent was. But my magic…" She frowned, as if she were struggling with how to describe it. Jefferson could commiserate. "It sat up and took notice. Until I convinced Kittie to order a different drink, I wasn't sure who they were targeting."

Kittie's eyes widened in understanding. "And here I thought you were trying to keep me dry."

Mindy shrugged. "Well, that was part of it. But I thought it odd when that woman took your drink back and dumped it, then replaced it with the cider and added something from a vial to it."

"A vial?" Jefferson asked. "Like an alchemical potion?"

"Or poison," Flora suggested helpfully.

"I don't know which," Mindy admitted. "I only knew Kittie shouldn't drink it."

Kittie crossed her arms. "But *you* did. After you switched glasses with me." Her forehead creased as her eyebrows lifted.

Mindy waved a hand, dismissive. "I'll be fine. Whatever was in your glass won't hurt me." They stared at her. Jefferson cocked his head, the motion silently requesting an explanation. Mindy shifted uneasily. "Okay, I try to keep this quiet. My magic makes me resistant to anything harmful put in food or drink."

Flora whistled. "That's handy."

"It is," Mindy agreed softly. "I'm not comfortable with people outside

Fortitude knowing about my magic, especially that. For a Hospitalier, it's a powerful ability."

I know that feeling. Jefferson offered her a smile. "Your secret is safe with us. So, you won't have any ill effects from whatever they tried to dose Kittie with?"

The Hospitalier winced. "I'm *resistant,* not immune. It depends what was in there. If it was a poison meant to kill, I'll be violently sick and try to puke out my guts."

"I'll hold your hair," Flora offered valiantly, earning a wan smile from Mindy.

"I don't think they would try to kill Kittie," Jefferson said, though he was thinking aloud. "That would be too obvious. All the signs would point back to the gala, unless it was some sort of slow-acting poison. Would something like that work, Flora?"

The half-knocker pursed her lips. "I don't do a lot with poisons." At the looks her words earned her from Kittie and Mindy, she backtracked. "I mean to say I have definitely, positively never killed anyone with poison. So, I can't help you with that sort of information."

Jefferson nodded. "Well, I suppose we'll just have to wait and see what happens."

"How do you feel?" Kittie asked, assessing the Hospitalier.

Mindy rubbed her temples. "I have a headache coming on, but that's not anything unusual."

Jefferson's gaze slid to Flora, but the diminutive woman was already on it. "C'mon. Let's get to your room and get you settled. I'll keep an eye on you."

"If she feels poorly through the night, Rachel should have a Healer on call," Jefferson suggested.

Mindy's eyes widened at that. "No. No Healers. Please. Nadine knows but..." She shook her head, fearful. "I'll be okay. A Healer can't do anything, anyhow."

Jefferson nodded, though the brave face she put on bothered him. Intellectually, he knew the reason she had accompanied them—it was to do exactly what she had done. But that didn't mean he *liked* it. "Is there anything we can do to help?"

She allowed Flora to help her to the door. "Don't eat or drink anything until breakfast for a start. I don't want to worry about you."

Kittie sighed. "We won't. It's our turn to worry about *you.*"

Flora eased the Hospitalier out into the hallway. The Pyromancer turned to Jefferson, her expression like that of a hunting cat. Focused and wary. "Do you have any idea why those in that group would attempt to drug me?"

Jefferson licked his lips. "Without knowing what the drink they intended for you would do, it's hard to say. But I don't think they would kill you." He paced, hands laced behind his back. "Make you ill so you can't attend the next few days of meetings?" Jefferson paused, making a frustrated noise. "Beyond that, my imagination isn't vivid enough to know what they might do."

Kittie rubbed her hands together, a move that reminded Jefferson of Blaise and made his heart pang. Then the Pyromancer spoke, refocusing his attention. "So, we don't know what they're planning or if they're an enemy—though I'm going with enemy if they were spiking my drink."

"I think that's a safe assumption," Jefferson agreed, thinking back to his sister, Phillip Dillon, and his business enterprises. "But until we know more, there's not much we can do."

"So we wait, and we watch," Kittie said. She yawned. "Though first, we sleep."

Jefferson couldn't help it; he yawned, too. Yes, sleep sounded like a good idea. *If only I could Dream.*

CHAPTER TWENTY-SEVEN

Dream or Die

Jefferson

Jefferson rolled over, pulling the sheets around him as something tugged at the corners of his sleeping mind. Whatever it was roused him, and he groaned softly as he rubbed away the grit in the corner of one eye. It had to be the middle of the night, but something had woken him—

Shouts. Running feet thudding down the hallway.

He scrambled into a sitting position, flicking the nearby mage-light on. Its silvery-blue glow illuminated the room, and he unsteadily wobbled to retrieve a pair of pants and pull them on. Jefferson was rising to button them when Flora appeared beside him with the soft pop of displaced air that always announced the use of her magic.

"Get out of here," the half-knocker urged, as serious as he'd ever seen her. "There's a fire."

"Fire?" Jefferson repeated, his fuzzy mind still catching up with the idea that he was awake and needed to take action. Then her words hooked their talons into the primordial part of his brain, and his eyes widened. He let out a soft curse as he snatched up his greatcoat. "Right, I'm going. How's Mindy?"

Flora shook her head. "Not great. Whatever she drank did a number on her stomach."

"Help her to safety," Jefferson said. "Should I get Kittie?" Did a Pyromancer need help to escape a fire? He would think not, but he didn't want to make assumptions.

"I saw her pelting down the hallway toward it," Flora said, her expression grim. "We gotta get out of here fast. The fire's tearing through this place."

Jefferson nodded. "Go help Mindy. We'll meet at the stables if it's safe—"

"They're burning, too," Flora said tersely.

No! The pegasi. Jefferson swallowed, waving Flora away as he pulled his shoes from beneath the bed. By the time he had them on, the half-knocker was gone. He caught the telltale scent of acrid smoke wafting through the cracks in his door. Their rooms were on the third floor, making it a sheer drop to the ground below. Jefferson glanced at the bed. Make a rope with sheets? He'd read of that being done in adventure books, but it wasn't a tactic he wanted to bet his life on.

"Stairs it is," he murmured, hoping that at least one of the two stairwells that served the building was passable. He formed a plan in his mind. Step one, get out of the building. Step two, get as close as he could to the stables to ensure the pegasi were safe. Step three...well, he hoped everyone was safe by the time he reached step three.

Jefferson reached the door and had his hand on the doorknob when it flew open. The hardwood rammed against his face, striking him squarely in the nose, and he staggered backward with a surprised howl of pain. He heard voices, but it was difficult to focus on them through the aching corona that was his face. Jefferson backpedaled until he fell against the bed, sitting down on it, stunned.

"Is this Jefferson Cole?" he heard someone ask. Male.

"Yes."

Cinna. It was Cinna's voice. Why was she here, in the middle of a fire? He heard the tap of feet on the floor, hushing when she reached the rug beside the bed. Jefferson cradled his bleeding nose with one hand, his vision blurring as he stared up at her.

"Don't fight us," Cinna advised him.

Jefferson blinked, struggling to clear his vision, trying to figure out why she might say that. Had she come to help evacuate people from the danger? Two dark shapes flanked her. He blinked three more times, his vision finally clearing enough to see. Cinna fidgeted, and he realized she held something in her hands. A square of fabric. Cinna popped open a small vial and soaked one side of the cloth with the contents.

A vial. Suddenly, his brain caught up with everything. Mindy had mentioned a vial. Someone had tried to drug Kittie's drink.

They failed to take out Kittie, and now they're after me?

Jefferson surged to his feet, fear taking hold. If he could slip past them, make it to the door, maybe he could lose himself in the crowd escaping the fire…

"Don't let him get away! Keep him still!" Cinna snapped. "We don't have much time."

The men loomed over him. Reaching hands grasped for him, clamping around his upper arms. Panic took hold as he bucked in their grip, the men's curses echoing his attempts. Frightening memories of a similar incident flashed through his mind. *Can't let them hold me. Have to get free!*

But there was no way. They were stronger than he was, and his face was a distracting beacon of pain that made it difficult to react. *Think. What advantage do you have?* None. His only advantage was a gutsy half-knocker who was evacuating the ill Hospitalier. Seledora was no doubt escaping the inferno, too. He had nothing.

Nothing except his secret magic, stifled by the precious ring on his finger.

There was no other choice. As the men held him down and Cinna struggled to shove the cloth into his face, Jefferson desperately clasped his hands together, working the ring off his finger. Blaise had asked him not to remove it, but neither of them had expected anything like *this* to happen.

The ring came free, slipping from his fingers to fall on the floor with a metallic clank. Jefferson's heart sank, but he promised himself he would find it later. Once he was safe. He couldn't focus on that right now. As the ring fell away, his magic breathed to life. Jefferson hadn't realized until that moment how much his magic had become a part of who he was. But now it was back and at his command. He was glad for it. *This is who I am now. A mage. The Dreamer.*

He grunted as one man held him down with such force it was difficult to breathe. Or maybe the smoke was drifting into his room—everything was confusing. Jefferson called on his magic, and it roared like a pack of hunting dogs eager to be on the trail. It was damned hard to focus when he was fighting for his life, but he had to. There was no other option. Dream or die.

Jefferson sent a tendril of magic arrowing up at the man who held him down, curling it around him, layering it around his assailant like a parent tucking a child under cozy blankets on a chill winter's night. He felt the man struggle against the drowsiness. Jefferson poured more magic into the effort.

Cinna rammed the cloth into Jefferson's face while he was distracted. She sealed the fabric around his nose, and he tried to sputter as he inhaled the sickly-sweet scent. Jefferson didn't let go of the man with his magic, doing all he could to keep him asleep while trying to twist away from Cinna.

But he had already inhaled too much of whatever was in the cloth. *Why is everything so hazy? Is it the smoke? Is—?*

CHAPTER TWENTY-EIGHT

I Am the Fire

Kittie

Kittie's magic had stirred her from sleep. She was sensitive to fire, but normally its presence didn't bother her. If a hearth held fire in the winter or a stove was in use for cooking, she was aware, but it served as background noise to her senses.

This was different. This was raw, blood-curdling *danger*, like wolves on the hunt. Like a griffin stooping on prey, talons outstretched. *Wrong, wrong, wrong.*

She moved to her window, throwing back the curtains. The world outside danced with gold, firelight reflecting on the nearby hematite-encrusted rooftops. Kittie licked her lips, summoning her magic. She lifted a hand, pushing it out, an invisible spy flitting through the air to bring back news.

She normally used this facet of her power to find easily combustible objects. Kittie could call up flame from thin air, but it was always easier with a source. Her thread of questing magic would also tell her of any neighboring fire, like the town gossip returning with news.

It took only seconds. Her magic retracted, and she chewed on her lip as she took a precious minute to sort through the information. She couldn't describe it to anyone else, but her magic brought back data. How far she was from the fire. The intensity. Natural or man-made. How it was spreading. Kittie assessed it all, her heart sinking.

Someone had set the fire on purpose. It was an inferno, and it was going to *kill*.

Kittie tugged on a robe, tying it around her waist as she pulled on a pair of boots. She had to help. The fire was ravaging the wing Madame Boss Rachel Clayton and her family called home.

The hallway outside her door had turned into a mad rush of people bolting, searching for escape. Someone yelled something indistinct. Men and women crushed together, seeking an exit. Kittie hoped Jefferson, Flora, and Mindy were in their number. Their wing was in danger from the blaze but not as much imminent danger as the Clayton residence.

Kittie gritted her teeth, pushing against the flow of frightened people. They threatened to sweep her away with them like a frenzied tide, but she won her way through their tear-streaked, coughing clusters. Someone grabbed her elbow and yelled for her to follow, but she ignored their plea. No time to explain that she was a Pyromancer and the fire and smoke wouldn't harm her. She didn't *enjoy* breathing smoke, but it wouldn't choke her lungs as it did anyone else.

She thundered down the stairwell closest to the residence. In the distance, she heard a crash as a structure fell beneath the fury of flames. Tongues of fire scorched a garden as she raced through.

In the haze of smoke, she saw movement as figures fell out of a broken window on the lowest floor of the residence, stumbling to catch themselves. Kittie rushed to them.

A middle-aged man and two children rolled onto their backs, coughing. Grime smeared their faces, and dark blood soaked the man's arm. Kittie slid to her knees beside them, recognizing the children from her first day in Nera—the Clayton children, Mary and Romie.

"I'm here to help. Is anyone else still inside, Mr. Clayton?"

The man's eyelids fluttered, and he struggled into a sitting position. Then he moaned and sagged onto his back again. He looked as if he'd suffered burns during their escape, but Kittie couldn't help with that. "Yes."

"Mama's in there," Mary rasped. Despite the soot on her face, the girl was still the spitting image of her mother. Determination and fear gleamed in her eyes. "She promised to get my kitty!"

Romie, the little boy who had shyly hid behind his mother's legs the day Kittie had met him, burst into tears. "Mama! Mama!"

Kittie swallowed, glancing over her shoulder at the fire. She steeled herself, turning back to the frightened family. A searing gust of wind blew hair into her face, and she smoothed it behind her ear. "It's okay. It's going to be okay. You want to hear something funny? *My* name is Kittie. How about I go check on your mama and the furry kitty?"

Mr. Clayton dragged himself onto one elbow. "The Pyromancer." There was a quiver in his voice, as if he feared she was the source of this.

It wasn't the first time Kittie had heard that. She licked her lips. "It's not my doing. But I'm going to help however I can."

"Can you extinguish it?" he asked plaintively.

Kittie didn't have the time to explain that stopping this fire would be the equivalent of jumping onto a wild horse bareback and expecting it to respond to her commands. "I'll do what I can. Get your children somewhere safe."

She rose, stalking toward the burning home as ash rained down. Mr. Clayton called after her, but the symphony of popping flames and crack of failing timbers drowned out his words.

"No, no, no. Not again," Kittie whispered, shaking her head as she drew closer to the home. The crackling dance of flames brought back a rush of memories. She'd lost her own parents to fire. *My fire. No. This isn't that. It's not the same.*

Anyone else would die charging into such a building unless magic of some sort protected them. Black smoke billowed out the doors and windows, trailing up the sides of the structure like thick, inky vines. Kittie crouched low as she prowled inside, her eyes tearing from the smoke.

"Rachel!" she called, though she knew it was futile. If the Madame Boss still lived, she wouldn't hear Kittie over the roaring flames.

She checked every room on the first floor, begging Faedra to reveal the woman lying low beneath the smoke. But she was nowhere to be seen. Kittie was spending all her magic on holding the growing fire at bay, allowing her a path through the destruction. It was the only thing she could do, since she couldn't bring the inferno under her command and quell it.

Stairs. Kittie found them looming in the dense haze of smoke. If Rachel was upstairs, in all likelihood, she was already dead. No one would fault her for turning back now—except they would, she realized. She rubbed ash away from her eyes.

Those children deserved to have their mother back if there was any chance at all.

I am the fire. The flames cannot touch me. Nothing will stop me. Kittie summoned all her courage, all her past regrets, as fuel for her inner fire. *No regrets now.* She had to get up the stairs, but the fire was chewing through them. The Pyromancer gritted her teeth, lifting her hands in a placating gesture. The flames on the stairs paused in their greedy expansion, reluctant to obey.

It was going to have to be enough. Kittie's feet flew up the stairs, the wood groaning and fracturing beneath her weight. When she reached the top landing, she peered into the burning nightmare before her. Impossible to see anything but smoke. She fumbled forward, hoping she would blunder into a door.

And she did. The first was closed, flames licking at the framing around the door. They hadn't breached it yet. Kittie pressed her magic hard against the fire, fighting to hold it back. The blaze strained against her, wanting to consume.

"Later," she promised the fire. *I just need a few minutes. Please.* She opened the door and slammed it behind her, though a belch of smoke followed her in.

A small bed claimed one corner of the room, toys sitting on a table, and books lining the low shelves. A child's room. Kittie was about to turn and continue her search when she spied a dark lump in the corner. It moved feebly, then coughed.

No, she.

Rachel lifted her head, her face dark with soot, eyes streaming tears. She opened her mouth to speak, but another fit of coughing cut it short.

"I've got you!" Kittie called, frantic as she crossed to the woman. Gods, only the fact that the door was closed had spared the Madame Boss's life. There wasn't time to think or explain, only to act. She reached down and pulled the woman to her feet, where she swayed before thrusting a furry mass at Kittie.

The cat.

It was a tiny kitten, and in the face of disaster, it was almost inconsequential. But it was a life, and that meant it mattered. Kittie took it in her hands, the little creature limp though she felt a sluggish heartbeat. Maybe not too late. She tucked the kitten into the large pocket of her robe, hoping it would be safe there.

Now for Rachel. The Madame Boss wobbled on her feet, almost going down. There was no way she was walking out of here. Kittie moved to face Rachel, grabbing her right hand and draping her arm over her own shoulder. It took more maneuvering, but seconds later, she had the Gannish leader slung over her shoulders, Kittie's right arm securing the woman's knees and one of her arms to keep Rachel in place.

Go, go, go. Time was against them. Kittie threw open the door with her free hand, the fire screaming at her impertinence. She shoved her dwindling magic against it, fighting to keep it from advancing on them as she made her way to the precarious stairs.

Later, Kittie still didn't know how she got Rachel out of the home. She only knew one moment they were inside, and then the next, she was lumbering out the door, smoke billowing behind them. Someone yelled. Hands reached out, pulling Rachel from her back.

"Healer. She needs a Healer," Kittie whispered, exhaustion washing over her as a reminder that there was a price for the amount of magic she'd used. Something wiggled feebly at her side. The kitten. "Beast Healer, too." She pulled the furball from her pouch, holding it out as an offering.

Someone took the kitten from her. Kittie staggered forward, away from the inferno, going down to her knees. A blurry form asked her something, but words no longer made sense. Kittie scrubbed at her forehead, her vision going fuzzy, before collapsing face-first into the grass.

———

EVERYTHING WAS TOO BRIGHT. THE HARSH SMELL OF AN ANTISEPTIC POTION assaulted her nostrils. Kittie winced, cracking her eyes into narrow slits.

"She's awake!" Mindy's voice, heavy with relief. Shadows moved closer, blocking out the rude light that assaulted Kittie's face.

She felt the nearness of people leaning over her. The warmth of a Healer brushing fingers beneath her wrist, checking her pulse. "Firebrand Dewitt, my name is Healer Imogene Ames, but you may call me Genie. You're at the Providence Infirmary. You collapsed after magical exertion."

Yeah, I figured. Kittie gave a tiny nod. Her throat hurt, as if the fire had raced down it and tried to burn her lungs to ash. In any other person, it would have. She had a headache and felt shaky, probably from lack of food. A little brandy would hit the spot, but with Mindy nearby, that didn't seem to be in her future. A nurse came in and helped prop her up in bed.

Genie gave her a thorough going-over. The Healer frowned when she finished her check. "You over-extended. You're going to feel the drain for a while, perhaps up to a week."

"Is Rach—Madame Boss Clayton well?" Kittie asked, the words coming out like gravel. She gingerly touched a hand to her throat.

"I'll get you something for that in a moment," Mindy whispered.

Genie offered Kittie a reassuring smile. "Madame Boss Clayton will recover. She had a few burns, but she's doing better than you are." Her words hinted at the fact that the leader had received a dose of healing magic to soothe the burns. It would be her due, after all.

Kittie sagged against the pillows with relief. A few minutes later, Genie and the nurse left the room to tend to other patients. No doubt their beds were full after the catastrophic fire. Mindy eased toward the door, but Kittie raised a hand to stop her.

"What did I miss?"

Mindy swallowed. "You're still weak. I'll tell you soon. I *will*. But let me get you some food and drink. You really need it." Her eyes glistened with helpless tears.

This is all she can do. Kittie nodded. "Okay, I'll wait."

The Hospitalier slipped out the door. Kittie sighed, deciding to enjoy the quiet and the softness of the sheets. She must have been unconscious, as someone had removed her night clothing and robe, cleaned her up, and then dressed her in a cotton shift. She closed her eyes, grateful for the news that Rachel had survived. *Those children still have a mother.* She knew the pain of a shattered family too well and didn't wish it on anyone.

Mindy returned, an orderly trailing her with a tray bearing what smelled like a rich and salty chicken soup. Kittie's mouth watered as the scent wafted to her, and she was more than happy to adjust, allowing them room to place a bed tray over her midsection. A bowl of fresh strawberries sprinkled with sugar and a tea of some sort accompanied the soup. Kittie didn't care too much about the details. Her stomach demanded food, and she set about answering the request.

Once she slurped the last of the soup from the bowl and moved on to the strawberries, she glanced at Mindy. "What's happened?"

The young woman sighed, pulling a chair closer to the bed as she sank into it. "It's...I don't know how else to describe it. A *nightmare.*" Mindy's voice cracked with the word. She sniffled and rubbed at her nose. "Flora got me out, and then by the time I felt well enough to walk, we found you...well, they had brought you here, but there was so much trouble."

"Trouble?" Kittie asked, popping a slice of strawberry into her mouth. It was the sweetest thing she had ever tasted, the flavor parading across her taste buds. "Over what?"

"*You,*" Mindy whispered. "Some of the Board members. They were here, demanding your arrest. Accusing you of setting that fire!" Fury rose in the Hospitalier's voice, her eyes sparking in outrage. "They said since you were a Pyromancer, and the fire was so intense, it must have been you."

Kittie chewed on the amazing strawberry and said nothing as the juices soothed her throat. This turn of events did not surprise her.

Mindy pulled out a handkerchief and dabbed at her nose, which had started to run. "But by that time, the Clayton family was here, too. One of the children heard—the girl, brave little thing! She pulled away from her father and marched over, hands on her hips, and hollered that you had run into the fire to save her mama and nothing more. By that time, Mr. Clayton came over and said that was so, and he was ready to do anything in his power to keep you here to get the care you needed."

Kittie licked a bead of strawberry juice from her lips, heartened by that. "So, they're the reason I'm not in salt-iron shackles right now."

Mindy nodded. "Yes."

"And Jefferson and Flora?"

Mindy stared down at her hands. "I sent a messenger to tell Flora you were awake when I went for the food. I expect she'll be here soon."

She didn't mention Jefferson. Kittie felt the bottom drop out of her stomach at the realization. She didn't feel like eating anymore, but her body demanded it, anyway. Kittie toyed with the rest of the strawberries, eating them slowly to bide her time.

True to Mindy's word, Flora barged into the room a short time later. She didn't bother to knock, as was her habit. The small woman's pink hair was disheveled, and her glasses hung crooked on her face, but she didn't seem to notice. An air of desperation and stark grief clung to her like a second skin.

"Flora?" Kittie asked gently, moving the tray aside and trying to sit up.

The half-knocker swallowed a lump in her throat. "I wasn't there when he needed me." Her head bowed, and her thin shoulders racked with silent sobs. The normally bold, happy-go-lucky, fierce spitfire was broken.

"Tell me," Kittie urged, her voice soft. She knew it would hurt, but her mind was already catching up to speed, thinking. *What would the Firebrand do?* She would gather all the information at any cost. Then use it to decide the next move.

Flora sucked in a ragged breath, then lifted her head. A fat teardrop journeyed down one of her grey cheeks. "He's dead. They...they found him in his room. Must have been trapped, I guess. There...there wasn't much left." She scrubbed the back of her hand against her face, wiping away the tear. Flora uncurled a hand, revealing a ring. "This was near his body."

Kittie's heart sank. No, this couldn't be. Jefferson was a puzzle, but she had come to like his keen mind and boundless determination. What would they do without him?

They would see this through. *This is a tragedy—but we can't let this spell the end for the Gutter. We can't.* She thought Jefferson would want them to continue the fight if he could not.

"I'm so sorry, Flora. I know he meant the world to you." Kittie didn't understand the half-knocker's tie with Jefferson, but whatever it was ran deep. Jefferson's loss cut them all to the core, but Flora the most. "Did the pegasi survive? I saw the stables were engulfed."

Mindy nodded. "Yes. Our pegasi evacuated all the normal horses, in fact. Not a single equine died."

That was a small bit of good news, at least. Kittie would take anything at this point.

"What do we do now?" Mindy asked softly. "Do we…do we go home when you're up to traveling?"

Kittie shook her head. "No. We finish what we came here to do. We do it for Jefferson. And for ourselves." She vowed to see this through if it was the last thing she did. "Mindy?"

The Hospitalier snapped to attention at the sharp query. "Yes?"

"I'm going to need Caladrius root tea. A *lot* of Caladrius root tea."

CHAPTER TWENTY-NINE

Dreams and Nightmares

Jefferson

"Well, it's been a while since I've been here," Jefferson mused as he turned in a slow circle, examining the dreamscape uncoiling around him. It felt *good* to be back—natural. Though, the manner of his return was alarming.

His mind was a little fuzzy, and he wasn't sure if his memories were accurate or if something hazed them. There had been fire. Flora helping Mindy out. A door slamming into his face. A struggle. An old lover from his past. His brain refused to connect any of the dots.

Jefferson frowned, trying to figure out how he had gotten back here. He had *promised* Blaise he would keep the ring on. The only reason he'd be able to reach the dreamscape was if he had taken it off to use his magic. "But *why* would I do that?" As much as he'd missed his magic, his vow to Blaise had been *important*.

He shook his head, frustrated. *Might as well take advantage of my time here.* Jefferson squared his shoulders, calling up his magic. Mists of the dreamscape swirled around him, thickening until they obscured his vision. Then they melted away, revealing the stone hallway that led to the dream prison.

His steps rang out against the floor, echoing back at him. Jefferson strained his ears for any sign of his prisoner, but there was nothing. He quickened his steps, shifting from a jog to a flat run as worry took root. Full of dismay, he drew to a stiff-legged halt in front of the cell that had once held the psyche of Gregor Gaitwood.

It was empty, the door open as neatly as if someone had unlocked it and released the vile Doyen for good behavior. "No, no, *no*," Jefferson murmured, stepping closer to the threshold.

He considered checking the interior but decided against it. He remembered too well the ending scene in the theater production *Song in the Crypt*, where the erstwhile hero had been tricked and bricked into a mausoleum. All the same, Jefferson's heart thundered at the revelation that Gregor Gaitwood was no longer suffering for all the pain he had inflicted.

Gaitwood was free, and he didn't deserve it.

Jefferson balled his fists at his sides, shaking his head. What could he do? Perhaps he could find Gregor and drag him back kicking and screaming, but then what? While that would be satisfying, Jefferson had the uncomfortable feeling that there were more pressing things he needed to worry about.

Was it something to do with Blaise? It almost went without saying that he had his share of concerns for the Breaker. But no, that didn't feel right. Blaise wasn't related to whatever had made him end up in the dreamscape again.

Think. There was the fire. Wait. Am I dead? Is this Perdition? Jefferson didn't like that thought. Though, he would expect Perdition to have a lot more souls. And it stood to reason it wouldn't be something he could shape with his magic. That logic soothed him, and he turned, striding back the way he had come.

"Let's see. Mindy was…yes, Mindy was ill after drinking the shot meant for Kittie." Jefferson decided that mulling it over aloud might help. It wouldn't hurt. "We went back to our rooms. Flora stayed with Mindy." He nodded to himself, hands clasped behind his back as he puzzled through his memories. "I went to bed, but noises woke me. People yelling about the fire."

Jefferson slowed, frowning. "Flora popped in to warn me. I told her…I told her to get Mindy out." He recalled putting on shoes and hurrying to the door—and the hardwood ramming into his face. Jefferson swallowed as his lost memories fell into place. Cinna had been there with two men. She had shoved something into his face as the men held him down.

Oh. He'd removed the ring, hoping to haul one of his attackers to the dreamscape and out of the action. But Jefferson remembered nothing beyond that, except for a too-sweet smell.

"They drugged *me*." He frowned. But why? Jefferson sighed, wondering what his next move should be. He had his magic again, so perhaps he should take advantage of that?

Maybe I could reach Flora? He discarded the idea immediately. Jefferson didn't think much time had passed, and even if it had, it was likely daytime, and he wouldn't find her slumbering. Then a dread thought clutched him. Was he still in his room? Was he going to burn to death while he tried to come up with a plan in the dreamscape?

"That won't do at all," Jefferson murmured. No, it was time to wake up and meet whatever lay ahead in the real world.

———

SILK SHEETS WHISPERED AGAINST HIS SKIN AS JEFFERSON STIRRED TO wakefulness. He kept his eyes closed, ears straining for voices or anything that would clue him in to impending danger. But he would know the cool, smooth feeling of silk anywhere. The pillow his head rested upon was the softest he'd had since his own bed at his estate outside Nera. The amount of comfort was puzzling, though welcome.

His eyes snapped open. He reclined in a dark room, though light filtered in around thick drapes covering the sole window. Jefferson slowly sat up, taking stock of himself. He was a little sore, but that was to be expected. Lifting a hand, he trailed his fingers along the bridge of his nose. It was tender, but no puffiness or traces of sharp pain followed his exploration. No crusts of blood, either. *A Healer must have tended to me.*

Jefferson was bare-chested, though his mystery attendants had left his drawers and pants on. He swung his legs over the side of the bed, then reached over to flick the mage-light on the nearby bedside table, illuminating the room in its glow. A glance around showed a fresh set of clothing laid out on an armchair in the corner. A dresser with a mirror claimed one of the walls, though he was dismayed to discover it held no grooming items. He strode over to the mirror to check his nose.

His mouth went dry when he saw the face in the mirror. No. No, *no, no.* Roguish, dark-haired Malcolm Wells stared back at him, complete with the fading geasa tattoo on his bicep. Jefferson closed his eyes, certain he was mistaken. But when he opened them again, nothing had changed. Swallowing, he glanced down at his hand. His beloved cabochon ring was missing.

"No, this can't be." Jefferson shook his head, moving to take stock of his personal items. He found his pocket watch in the drawer of the bedside table. But of his ring, there was no sign. There had to be a reasonable explanation. He would get it back. Everything would be fine. "One thing at a time, Jefferson," he murmured to himself. "You've been in plenty of scrapes before. This is no different."

After taking a calming breath, he assessed the rest of the room. Beside the door, a small, rectangular wooden panel had a winking sapphire gem embedded in the middle. He raised his brows at that. A call button, either powered by one of the new electrical currents or enchanted with magic.

Where in Perdition am I? Everything about this was puzzling. Jefferson moved to the laid-out clothing. *Well, I may as well be presentable.* He shucked off his pants, setting them aside as he pulled on the replacements. The new clothing was a little large, but not too bad. The provided shoes were the right size, and they were new and unbroken. He knew the logo stamped into the leather. Caesuras. Top-of-the-line shoes, at that.

As he moved, Jefferson's bladder reminded him it needed attending to. His stomach added to the protests. Jefferson pressed the call button. He didn't hear any sort of ring or other response from it, but that meant nothing. It likely sent the ring to somewhere deep in the home, maybe the kitchens or elsewhere the staff might be. Jefferson tried the door but found it locked. Not surprising.

A few moments later, the lock on the door clicked, and a young man in the garb of a well-appointed footman pulled it open. "Good afternoon. My name is Abernathy. May I be of service?"

He had half-expected thugs or a mustache-twirling villain straight out of a theater production on the other side of the door, so the appearance of a benign footman caught him off guard. Jefferson recovered quickly, however. "Yes. I need the quincy and perhaps food, if it's no trouble."

Abernathy inclined his head, then turned. "Your every need will be met." He beckoned for Jefferson to follow.

It wasn't long before his bladder felt relief, and his stomach was pleasantly full. Abernathy had brought a tray to the room, so Jefferson didn't get a chance to wander and figure out where he was. When he asked the footman, Abernathy simply responded, "With the Quiet Ones." Jefferson had never heard the term before, but he decided not to press for more answers. The footman bade him wait and rest in the room.

The Healer returned, though the middle-aged woman said even less than Abernathy. She didn't even give her name. She merely ran her hands over him as if he were a prized racehorse she was assessing for soundness, made a *harrumph* of approval, and left.

A short time later, a knock sounded on the door before it swung open. "The Quiet Ones will see you now," Abernathy said, making a grand gesture for Jefferson to follow.

He didn't know who or what the Quiet Ones were, but this didn't bode well.

CHAPTER THIRTY

Unicorns Are Assholes

Blaise

The Copperheads were a level of bad-tempered Blaise hadn't expected, even with Jack's warning. He'd always considered Jack mean—or maybe ornery was the better term. But the Copperheads? They were something else.

The enemy outlaws had surrounded them, the fog lending them an additional layer of malice. The desperadoes had been ready to claim their prisoners. They relieved Emmaline of her sixgun, reagent bag, and poppets. For the pegasi, they had prepared halters with O-shaped rings made of salt-iron. Blaise clenched his jaw as Emrys squealed at the touch of the metal.

A frowning woman, who the others called Maureen, glared at Blaise as she strolled over. "Where's your weapon?"

Blaise swallowed, lifting his chin. "*I* am the weapon." He flexed his fingers meaningfully.

She gave him a dubious look, as if she didn't think he could possibly be serious. Blaise had to admit it was refreshing to see someone who wasn't frightened or awestruck in his presence. "You look awful soft."

He tensed, stung by her words. It rankled that her assessment bothered him, but it did. Blaise had wanted none of the difficulties life had thrown at him, but he had earned his scars. In his time back in Fortitude, his body had filled out again from the ravages inflicted on him by his time in the Golden Citadel. He wasn't naturally slender, not like Jefferson—he skewed toward a sturdiness reminiscent of Emrys. He narrowed his eyes. "Don't mistake softness for weakness."

He still didn't impress her. Maureen glanced at the leather gloves in his pocket, ignoring his words. "Put those on, Breaker."

To his annoyance, after he slipped his gloves on, another outlaw strode over with a pair of burlap bags, which they tied over his hands. Blaise decided not to point out that the layers of supposed protection would do nothing against his magic. Not even the salt-iron cuffs they had clamped to his wrists. Those surprised him more than anything, though he realized they had brought along an outlaw without a lick of magic to handle the wicked metal.

As before, the salt-iron did little more than irritate his skin and make it impossible to mount. The Copperheads wanted him to ride one of their unicorns, but the temperamental beast refused to kneel to allow him to get aboard. Snorting in frustration, Emrys knelt as a plea to allow Blaise on his back. The Copperheads grudgingly allowed it, though they kept the stallion in the middle of their knot. Oberidon and Emmaline followed along behind, the young Effigest's face a mask of anger.

The Copperheads bantered amongst themselves on the ride back to town. Blaise took the opportunity to learn what he could. It sounded like Maureen had led this expedition, though she wasn't the Ringleader. She had authority, though, and was some sort of Healer.

The unicorns they rode were as rough as their riders. Their scar-crossed coats gleamed with all the colors of the rainbow. Some of them had brands, which made Blaise curious, but he didn't ask. They were all ill-tempered, and the equines enjoyed attempting to skewer the grounded pegasi with their deadly horns. The Copperheads didn't even attempt to dissuade their mounts, and Emrys and Oberidon were soon bleeding from puncture wounds.

Blaise closed his eyes, fighting back angry tears. He had known his plan was a risk to the safety of the pegasi, but he hadn't expected this outright cruelty. His magic itched beneath the layers of bondage. Blaise knew he could break free, but then what? There was nothing he could do to help the pegasi. He couldn't take on a dozen armed outlaws and their belligerent unicorns.

Relief washed over him when the town of Thorn came into view. The unicorns stopped pestering the stallions, more intent on getting back to their stable.

No one paid them any attention as the Copperheads escorted them into town. They threaded through the busy streets, eventually ending up near the docks. The tang of saltwater was heavy in the air, and gulls and other shorebirds cried out as they wheeled overhead. The outlaws didn't stop until they'd reached a building he thought might be a warehouse. It was a three-story affair, constructed from heavy-framed timber with rusted iron cladding. One of the Copperheads dismounted and rolled the massive door open.

Blaise glanced over at Emmaline, but she gave a small shake of her head. She didn't have any better idea of their whereabouts than he did. Their escort urged them inside.

The interior was lit by a mix of lanterns and mage-lights. Sturdy posts of timber supported the high ceiling. Blaise thought the building might be full of ship cargo, but it wasn't. At least if it was, it wasn't anything like he'd expected. Rows of steel cages and stalls took up one half of the vast building. Stacks of crates lined up into long aisles claimed another section. The remaining area looked to be under construction, as if someone were building seats and some sort of staging area.

Oh. Slocum had mentioned the Copperheads were having an auction. *And this is it.*

"Get off, Breaker," one of the Copperheads commanded, taking Emrys's halter and yanking hard on the lead rope. The stallion pinned his ears, eyes rolling as he jerked his head back.

Blaise hissed out a breath. It was clumsy work, but he dismounted without falling onto his face. Maybe his rising anger had given him the grace he normally lacked. "Hurting my pegasus really frosts my cookies."

The outlaw guffawed at the expression, slapping his knee. His eyes glinted with a meanness Blaise had seen in bullies before. "I'll frost your coo—"

Blaise closed the distance between them, lifting his salt-iron-bound hands. He thought about calling up his power to chew through his bonds —and he could. Oh, he could. But that would give away too much, and he wasn't prepared to do that yet.

Instead, he brought the salt-iron shackles up to the man's throat, holding the chain taut against the tender flesh. The man yelped, struggling to twist away, but Blaise followed him, relentless. The outlaw was a mage, as Blaise had thought, and he squealed like a pig as the metal seared his skin. Just as quickly, Blaise yanked it away, though the Copperhead now had a bright red lash across his skin, as if he'd been scalded.

"I'm gonna—"

"You ain't gonna do shit, Calvert," Maureen snapped, sauntering over to them. The wounded man cowered beneath her ire. "The Breaker is not to be damaged."

"But he—"

"I heard what he said, saw what he did, and it's damned clear he knows exactly how to frost *your* cookies." She put her hands on her hips. "If you keep this up, what I do to you will make that salt-iron burn feel like pox from a bordello girl." With Calvert slinking away, she turned to the others. "Sanguine and Cottonmouth, you take the pegasi. Eunice, with me to get the Breaker and young Effigest settled."

A pair of men broke off, each moving to stand by the pegasi. Blaise tensed as one of them took Emrys's lead rope. "If you hurt a hair on either of those stallions, I'll bring the roof of this place down."

"They're not yours anymore," the man said with a shrug.

Blaise gritted his teeth. Nearby, Emmaline stewed, fury lining every crevice of her face. He wanted to argue, but it would do no good. In fact, it might harm the whole reason he had given up so easily.

Emrys rolled a dark eye in his direction, nostrils fluttering. Blaise wanted nothing more than to go to him, so they could reassure each other that it would be okay. *You're my pegasus, and I'm your rider. Nothing can take that from us.* Blaise clenched his fists within his bonds, giving Emrys the smallest of nods. The stallion's hooves echoed hollowly on the stone floor as he was led away.

"Let's move," Maureen said, giving Blaise's shoulder a shove as they started up an aisle.

Maureen and Eunice hustled Blaise and Emmaline into a shared cell at the furthest end of the row. Every other cage had occupants, and he was surprised—and horrified—by the variety. Knossans, Theilians, goblins, knockers, harpies, and more represented the two-legged mystic races. Basilisks, chupacabras, jackalopes, wolves, grasscats, and creatures he didn't recognize occupied others. Blaise glimpsed the occupants of the stalls, too. Bison, antelope, kelpies, bunyips, griffins, unicorns, kirins…the variety was mind-boggling.

The Copperhead women left them in a salt-iron-reinforced cell, along with a bucket in one corner for bodily needs. Blaise and Emmaline waited until they were certain they were alone before they took the chance to speak.

"For the record, I hate this idea," Emmaline hissed, a pained expression on her face.

Blaise winced with sympathy, knowing the salt-iron was leeching magic from her. Maureen had removed his shackles and the sack, so Blaise shucked off his gloves and stuck them in his pocket, flexing his fingers. "I know. I'm sorry, I just didn't know any other way that wouldn't end up with us dead or wounded." It wouldn't take much for this to end the same way, though.

She sighed, rubbing her forehead. "Sorry. Bad memories make me snappish."

"No apology needed." Blaise paced the perimeter of their cell, studying the bars.

"What are you doing?"

He smiled and, in answer, laid a hand against a slat. It wasn't pure salt-iron. He figured that would have cost a fortune, but he felt that they had somehow incorporated it into the steel. Hardly enough to so much as annoy him, though the same couldn't be said for someone like Emmaline. Her eyes widened in surprise.

"We're not as trapped as you think," he whispered.

Emmaline relaxed, sitting down in the middle of the cage, as far from the bars as possible. "What are we gonna do?"

Blaise abandoned his place by the bars and moved to sit beside her. "Still deciding that part. But the way I figure, Jack's going to find out what happened to us."

"The odds of him doing something stupid are pretty high. That move of yours would have impressed him back there, by the way," Emmaline commented, drawing an index finger along her neck.

Blaise grimaced. He wasn't particularly proud of his actions, but it had been the only thing he could think of to get his point across without using magic. Blaise didn't want to hurt other people, but he wouldn't abide bullies, either. That didn't make what he did *right*, though.

Emmaline must have noticed his distress. She bumped a knee against his. "You did what you had to."

Blaise nodded. That was as good a segue as any into what he had to tell her next. "Jack won't let us rot here. You know that." When she nodded, he continued, "And come what may, if you get out, I need to stay in."

She crossed her arms, giving him a stubborn look that was a ghost of her father's. "I am *not* leaving you here with these...these...well, calling them *outlaws* is an insult to outlaws."

He wiggled his fingers, a reminder. "You're not leaving me here. I'm choosing to stay. This is my best shot at finding my mother." Blaise nodded to the expanse of cages all around them.

Emmaline frowned. "You think they have her here somewhere?"

"I don't know, but I intend to find out."

CHAPTER THIRTY-ONE

Malcolm Who-Is-Not-Dead

Jefferson

The footman showed him to a lavish parlor. As he entered, the murmur of light conversation greeted him. Men and women filled the room, some seated and others standing. Staff hovered around the edges, seeing to every whim of the well-dressed elite. His arrival must have served as a signal. As soon as he strode inside, the help slipped out of the room.

Jefferson had little love of being thrown into a situation where he didn't know what was afoot, and he felt vulnerable without his ring. Without his *identity*. Any sign of weakness could very well be like the scent of blood in the air near a murder of chupacabras, and he did his best to hide how flustered he was by the entire scenario. Jefferson doubted he succeeded.

His gaze flicked over the occupants, surprise jolting through him when he saw Cinna in their midst, arms folded across her chest. Jefferson swallowed, realizing he knew everyone in the room. Some came from families his father had dealt with in the past. Others he had come across in his time as a Doyen or in his entrepreneurial guise. A few of them had been in attendance at the gala the previous evening and had taken part in the toast. Familiarity didn't mean he was safe, no matter how well he had been treated to this point.

"Good afternoon," he greeted them, deciding to seize whatever minor advantage he could. "I appreciate the invitation to join you." Jefferson offered a polite nod to the group.

Their eyes fell on him, and he felt a bit like a butterfly pinned down for an exhibit. Phillip Dillon cut through the group like a shark through the surf. A broad smile played on his lips, teeth flashing. *My sister's husband?* "We're pleased you could join us, Jefferson." He paused dramatically, tilting his head. "Or is it Malcolm?"

"Yes, which is it? I feel as if I've seen a ghost," a taunting voice added. *Gaitwood.* Gregor slipped in through a door on the far side of the room, joining the knot of elite.

You did this. Jefferson sucked in an outraged breath. For once in his life, he was utterly speechless. He felt naked, as if they had stripped away every part of his being. And there was nothing he could do about it. Small wonder Cinna had slapped him last night if they had already clued her in to his secret.

"Oh dear, he's overwhelmed." Saccharine-sweet, Tara Woodrow ambled over, offering a wineglass. "Perhaps this will help with the jitters."

Her words snapped him out of it. Jefferson took a step back, glaring at her. "You spiked Kittie's drink."

Tara shrugged. "But this one's fine. Promise." When he shook his head, she took a sip herself. "Your loss."

"Jefferson Cole. Malcolm Wells." This from Phillip, who moved closer, interest etched on his face. "I'm intrigued. I must admit, I doubted Gregor's story, but now that I see it's true…" He pursed his lips as if he grudgingly admired Jefferson's masquerade. "So, *who* are you?"

Remember who you really are. The Dreamer. An entrepreneur. "I am Jefferson Cole."

"He's lying," Gregor said. "You see the proof in his face. Malcolm didn't die in the fire at the Wells Estate."

Yes, he did. Jefferson knew they would never accept it, though. Not with the face of a younger Stafford Wells in their midst. Gregor knew it, *knew* he didn't want to be that person. It took every bit of willpower Jefferson possessed to not let Gregor see how much this was undoing him.

Tara made a frustrated noise. "Are we just going to stand around and hurl accusations? There are perfectly good refreshments going to waste. Ones that are definitely *not* laced with hallucinogens."

"You have a way of making that sound foreboding," Everett Duncan, a magnate from Phinora, observed.

"It's true," Tara insisted. She flounced over to a chaise and claimed a seat, then leaned over to pick up a plate and fill it with her choice of finger sandwiches and pastries.

"Yes, have a seat, Malcolm-who-is-not-dead," Phillip said, sounding almost amiable. "Is there a need for introductions?"

"I believe I'm familiar with everyone here." Jefferson let the weight of his bitter words sink in. They thought they knew him as Malcolm? Well, he had the advantage of knowing *them*, too. He picked out a single chair in the circle, following up the move by filling a plate. Gregor wanted to make him a fish out of water, did he? Jefferson had years of practice having his feet in two worlds. *I can do this.*

He noticed Gregor claim a seat as far away from him as he could. Jefferson smiled in his direction. "Doyen Gaitwood, I couldn't help but notice the bags under your eyes. Not sleeping well?"

Gregor's mouth tightened. "I'm sleeping like a baby now."

"Because babies are notorious for sleeping well," Jefferson said dryly. The rest of the elite had taken their seats and selected refreshments as well. Jefferson took a bite of his sardine sandwich, gulping it down before deciding to make the next move. "I will admit, I'm unclear why I'm here." *And where* here *is. And why you want Malcolm Wells.* Did it have something to do with Alice? Had Phillip discovered his wife had fled and sought to use him to recover her somehow?

The other elite exchanged looks. After a moment, Phillip spoke up. "You're here, Malcolm, because we've decided you would be a worthy addition to our group."

Jefferson bit into his tart to hide the fact that this new information spurred more questions than it provided answers. *Their group? What group?* He recalled his sister's reference to *corruption.* Was this what she meant? After he swallowed the bite of tart, he asked, "Ah, is this a social group? Like a country club?"

Amused titters met his question. Megan Brew, a woman with straight black hair and eyes like a pair of emeralds, laughed as she lifted her glass to him in a toast, as if he had made a jest. "Oh no, Mr. Wells. We're so *much* more than either of those, I assure you."

"We are the Quiet Ones, the true power behind the Salt-Iron Confederation," Phillip added, his eyes glittering. "Seven powerful men and women who drive every aspect of the Confederation." He cocked his head, thoughtful. "Well, six currently. We've had a gap left by the untimely death of Stafford Wells."

"Yes, very sad," Jefferson said. "Anyway—"

"You're his replacement." Tara cut him off with a grin.

Wait, wait. What? Jefferson's brain ground to a halt as he suddenly caught up to their meaning. Stafford Wells had been part of this shadowy group of political puppeteers? How could that be? Stafford had never mentioned the Quiet Ones, even when he had groomed Malcolm as his successor. But maybe this group didn't work like that. Suddenly, things made a lot more sense. Such as how adamant his father had been that

Malcolm would capitulate and undo all the legislations he had worked so hard on. It hadn't been only for the sake of his trafficking rings. It must have been for this group, too.

Jefferson cleared his throat, then took a sip from the glass offered to him. Water, which was welcome, as he didn't know if he could tolerate anything else at the moment. "I'm flattered that I made the top of what I'm sure is an esteemed list of nominees. Though, I'm not sure I would be a good fit."

The pressure in the room seemed to build like a thunderstorm. "An appointment to the Quiet Ones isn't something you can decline," Everett, the magnate from Phinora, said with a shake of his head. "In most cases—such as yours—it's an *inherited* position."

"You either join us, or you're never heard from again," Tara piped in pleasantly, as if mentioning that the weather outside was rainy.

Somehow, Jefferson maintained his composure in the face of such a bald threat. "I'm certain adding me to your roster would have my father rolling in his grave. Or did you forget he disowned me?"

"We have long memories. *Very* long." Cinna leaned forward, her eyes narrowing. "*None* of us have forgotten that, I assure you."

But you're not holding a grudge about it, I see. Jefferson met her gaze, unflinching. "The fact of the matter is, Malcolm Wells is dead. Most of you were at the funeral. You can see how it would be problematic if he..." Jefferson took a breath, correcting himself. "If *I* appeared again."

Phillip nodded. "You're not the only one in this room with secrets, Malcolm. But sometimes, when those secrets come to light, they can be quite helpful."

A chill zinged through Jefferson. They were going to undo all of his hard work; resurrect Malcolm Wells. The one thing he absolutely didn't want. "No." When their icy stares settled on him, he decided he needed to qualify his refusal. "How would that be explained away? It would force too many questions." Questions that he was reluctant to answer.

"Perhaps you had a mental breakdown and wished for time away. And you were quite dramatic about it," Gregor suggested acerbically.

Jefferson gritted his teeth. The expressions all around him showed this was an argument they wouldn't let him win. He tried to think of some way around it, some loophole, but the fear of being forced back into a role he didn't want overwhelmed him. A life he didn't want to lead—a life he had rejected. "What benefit do you even get from Malcolm Wells returning to life?"

"Your seat might have been filled, but your name still has political pull," Tara pointed out, twirling a finger in the air. "We love having politicians in our pocket, as you can see."

Jefferson glared across the room at Gregor. "We don't work well together."

"No one is saying you have to. We know you're Faedran and Gregor is a Mossback. We like playing both sides," Tara clarified.

"And as for why?" Phillip said. "You throw your support behind the Gutter. It's needed to outweigh the Gannish Board."

Jefferson narrowed his eyes. They could have asked Gregor to do that —but no, they couldn't. Gregor would never support such a move, and it would be out of character for him to do so. "What, you don't have Aaron Thatcher in your pocket?"

"Alas, no," Tara said. "He's the sort we don't want privy to our existence."

"So you chose me."

"So we chose you," she agreed with a smirk.

"Because your father was a Quiet One, and his father before him," Phillip explained. "And once we learned you were still alive, it made the most sense."

None of this makes sense. Jefferson shook his head. "The problem with your plan is that Jefferson Cole was in the midst of dealings with Madame Boss Clayton. It would make more sense for me to continue in that guise." *Please agree. Please.*

Gregor made a *tsking* sound. "Oh, you haven't heard? A shame about that. Jefferson Cole died in the fire at Silver Sands. Ironic how history repeats itself, is it not?" He held up something small and shiny between his thumb and index finger. A red jewel winked. Jefferson's pulse raced as he realized it was his cabochon ring.

"You give that back!" Jefferson was up and out of his seat before he even realized it. Then he was on Gregor, grappling with the shorter Doyen. Gaitwood had already slipped the ring onto his finger. Jefferson was grateful the ring was keyed to his blood and would work for no other. Shouts rose from the Quiet Ones around them as Jefferson grabbed Gregor by the shoulders. He didn't strike him, though.

No, he called up his magic, sending it pouring into Gregor as the other man yelped, realizing what lay in store. Jefferson chased him into the dreamscape, furious. He didn't care that the Quiet Ones were probably seeing Gregor go limp in his seat and Jefferson stare at the ceiling as if he were daydreaming. *He. Didn't. Care.*

The dreamscape was formless as Jefferson roared into it, but already his subconscious twisted it based on his emotions. Black storm clouds surrounded him, intermittent lightning striating the darkness. Gregor stumbled backward as Jefferson appeared, grabbing the Doyen by the lapels of his coat.

"What have you *done?*" Jefferson growled. Around them, the shadows took shape, eerie howls coming from them. A great serpentine silhouette lurked at the periphery of Jefferson's vision.

"What I promised I would do," Gregor choked out. "You should have known you would pay the price for your treachery."

"I'm not the treacherous one!"

Gregor laughed, despite his dire situation. "You lie to everyone, including yourself. You think it's not treacherous to deceive everyone by living two lives? And now...oh, Malcolm. Now you conceal your magic. How's that working for you?"

Jefferson huffed a breath, the stark realization like a slap to his face. Blast it all, but Gregor was right—about the last part, at least. Here he was amid the enemy, using his magic. That was a dangerous, sloppy mistake.

"This isn't over between us, Gregor." Jefferson let go of him. "I will free you from the dreamscape, and when I do, you'll return my ring to me."

"I don't think I will," Gregor said, straightening his jacket. "And if you force me to—*or* if you haul me into this gods-forsaken place one more time—I'll tell them about your sorcery. And won't they find *that* intriguing?"

Jefferson fisted his hands, but he didn't have a response. Angrily, he banished Gregor from the dreamscape, then followed him out. He found Tara nearby with a pitcher of water in her hands, clearly about to douse the both of them.

"Oh, whatever palsy has taken them is over. That's too bad." She set the pitcher down with disappointment.

"Have a seat, Mr. Wells," Phillip said with a long-suffering sigh.

Jefferson glared down at Gregor, then stepped away, stalking back to his chair. He ignored the curious looks from the Quiet Ones, as they no doubt wondered what their strange encounter had been about. Neither man enlightened them.

"It should be abundantly clear that you're Malcolm Wells at present." Phillip gestured in his direction. "You'll conduct yourself as such. Like it or not, you serve as a Quiet One now."

Jefferson crossed his arms. "And if I don't? If I act against your wishes?"

"Accidents happen," Cinna hissed. Jefferson suddenly wondered if the death of her first husband had been as natural as had been publicized.

Another thought occurred to him. "The fire. That was you?"

Tara shook her head. "That was the Board's doing. They hope to discredit your delegation."

Jefferson's brow knit. The Board would do something so heinous, an act that would threaten the lives of so many, including the Madame Boss?

Were they mad? Then he considered the company he was currently in. The elite would plumb any depths to give themselves an advantage.

"Come now, Malcolm." Phillip gave him an encouraging look. "It's quite clear you want the Gutter recognized as a nation. That's why you came to Nera, after all. This is what we want, too. Why is this so difficult? It doesn't need to be."

Because I don't trust you. "Why do you want that?" That was what he really wanted to know. It bothered him—everyone in this room had dabbled in trafficking or working to keep mages oppressed and vulnerable. Why would they suddenly support a nation of free mages, especially outlaws?

Phillip shook his head, regretful. "We play a long game, Malcolm. And honestly, none of us are ready to show our hand to someone just joining the game. It could jeopardize years of work."

Jefferson knew he was in an impossible situation. Gregor had his ring, and the Quiet Ones had him exactly where they wanted him. And blast it all, they were right—he would support the Gutter no matter what. No matter the face he wore. Maybe it would be best to concede for now. Buy time to figure something out.

He bowed his head. "I see. I suppose it's in my best interest to work with you, then."

"If you want to live to see another day, it is," Tara agreed, far too chipper.

"Welcome to the Quiet Ones, Malcolm," Phillip said, lifting his glass. Around the room, everyone joined the impromptu toast. The gestures reminded Jefferson of the toast the previous evening. *Fruitful connections, indeed.*

Cinna showed him back to his room after the social gathering ended. She was frosty as she walked beside him, her eyes cutting to him every few strides. "You should have come with me when I propositioned you last night. Your mage wouldn't have been poisoned, then. But we needed the distraction, you see."

Her audacity was boggling. "I'm sorry, I was under the impression you wanted a tryst, not to upend my entire life."

"That isn't your life."

Jefferson ground his teeth, breaking his stride to glance at her. The loss of his identity hurt, and for it to be disregarded as if it were nothing was even worse. "What were you planning to do? Seduce me before drugging me and hauling me off to your Quiet One friends?"

She gave him a sour look. "Don't act as if you wouldn't have liked it. I haven't forgotten all the things you enjoy." Cinna continued onward, her heels echoing down the stone corridor. "We could have been a powerful couple, you know."

Her words surprised him, though they shouldn't have. Back in the day, he had assumed she was simply a gold-digger with a family eager to attach themselves to someone with a good name. "Was your former husband the Quiet One or one of your parents?"

"My mother," Cinna answered with a smirk. "She retired a few years ago. To enjoy her happy golden years."

"How wonderful for her," Jefferson muttered, not meaning it at all.

"Why did you do it, Malcolm?"

He chafed at her use of the name. "Do what?"

She stopped, turning to look at him. Curiosity burned in her eyes. "Give up everything. Become someone else." She gestured broadly around them. "You could have *anything* as a Wells."

Not anything. He swallowed. "You know why. I could no longer tolerate the things my family was doing. I wanted to oppose it." Jefferson shook his head in frustration.

"All things you did as Doyen Malcolm Wells," she reminded him tartly.

He started walking down the corridor, and she hurried to catch up. Cinna would never understand that the simple act of looking at his face in the mirror made him ill. Reminded him of the man who cared more for money and power than his own children. She was right, of course, that he had opposed his father as Malcolm. But the reasons *why* were too personal to explain to someone like Cinna.

"You're not so different from us, you know!" Cinna called.

His shoulders tensed. "I am *very* different from you."

"You're not," she insisted. "Look at you, Malcolm. Doing every unscrupulous thing you can to gain an edge. That's what this Jefferson Cole act was, wasn't it? An elaborate lie, a farce." When he made no reply, Cinna plowed on. "And we're like you. We have pet mages, too."

Pet mages? He whirled at that. "Blaise is not a pet."

She smirked, clearly amused that she'd gotten to him. "We saw your tattoo. The Breaker is the lover you mentioned, hmm? I heard rumors, but I didn't believe that you were really—"

"Don't talk about Blaise," Jefferson snapped, trembling with fury.

Cinna waved a hand. "There's no shame in taking a mage as a lover. Tara even *married* her pet—though, to be fair, he's an alchemist." She shrugged, as if it made no difference. "The fact is that you have a mage at your beck and call. A powerful one. And now so do we."

"I wouldn't ask Blaise to use his magic on my behalf." But it was a lie.

He had. And Blaise had paid the price. Jefferson's stomach turned as he recalled the ruins of the airship at Fort Courage. Gregor was *right*. Cinna was *right*. He was a liar. He had used Blaise. *But I promised Blaise...I promised* myself...*to never do that again.*

She sighed. "Malcolm, don't be so stubborn about this. You can't shirk your responsibilities anymore. We hold all the cards. Don't you see how tenuous your position is?"

The problem was, he *did* see. There was no way out that didn't destroy everything he'd worked for. With a frustrated huff, he stopped in front of the door to his room. "You've seen me to my room. Now leave me in peace, Cinna."

She quirked a brow. "The offer I made you yesterday still stands." Cinna lifted a hand, brushing her fingertips against his chin. "You only need to say the word."

He squeezed his eyes shut at her touch, shivering. Though it wasn't from lust—it was from the shadow of his old life smothering him. "I may not have a choice in many things at the moment, but I have a choice in that. My heart belongs to someone else, and I won't betray him. That's where I draw the line."

Cinna bristled, stepping back. "Your loss." She stormed down the hallway as Jefferson withdrew into his room.

CHAPTER THIRTY-TWO
Legends Aren't Made by Bluster

Jack

Jack grabbed a simple breakfast in the inn's common room before heading out. Zepheus reported that he was fine, and a groom had already visited, delivering a bucket of oats sprinkled with sugar. Satisfied that his pegasus was in good shape, Jack headed to Creagen's Engineering Works to lend some credibility to his visit.

"Well, well, well, if it ain't Wildfire Jack."

Jack narrowed his eyes. *I know that voice.* He paused mid-stride, pivoting and gracing the speaker with a broad smile. "Well, if it ain't Seymour Arce, the outlaw with the most unfortunate name in history." He leaned on the soft C in the last name, drawing it into an *S* sound.

"Arce rhymes with *dark*," Seymour growled.

Jack shrugged. "Honest mistake." They both knew it wasn't. The Copperhead Ringleader had gotten a lot of grief over his name, which was probably what had made him hard enough to claw his way to the top of their gang. Maybe it wasn't smart to beard him, but there were some things Jack couldn't resist. Besides, it would have been uncharacteristic if he hadn't given the outlaw some guff.

"What brings a Gutter Rat out here?" Seymour drawled, clearly wanting to give as good as he got.

"Aw, gotta import your insults from the Salties?" Jack asked. He shrugged a single shoulder, as if he didn't care enough to commit both to the effort. "Oh, you know. Wind-pump's acting up. Thought I'd chat with Creagen." He nodded to the building a dozen paces away.

Seymour's slitted eyes studied him. "That so? Thought you might have gotten wind of the auction." The Copperhead Ringleader advanced a step closer. "We just got something in that may *personally* interest you."

Jack tried not to let his surprise register, but he was too slow to catch it, judging by the smirk that slunk across Seymour's face. His mind whirled, piecing through all the possibilities of what the other man meant. He didn't like any of the conclusions he came to.

"Don't make an enemy out of me, *Arse*," Jack growled. "'Cause it ain't gonna be pretty."

The Copperhead chuckled, reaching out to clap Jack on the shoulder. "Wildfire Jack, I know you think you got stones as big as the Griffin's Crest Mountains, but you forget your place."

Jack's hand brushed against the collar of Seymour's shirt as he ducked out of the other man's grip. "What'd you take?"

Seymour smiled. "The question isn't what, but *who?*"

That confirmed Jack's suspicions. "I'm not gonna rise to your bait like a yearling pegasus to a sugar trap." The Copperhead leader was a bully, and he was no doubt hoping Jack would make a rash decision and take a swing at him. Seymour was a Strength mage. It wouldn't be a fair fight unless Jack pulled a sixgun. As much as he'd love to wipe that arrogant look from Arce's face, he was savvy enough to know this wasn't the time. "Now, get out of my way. I got places to go."

Seymour checked his shoulder against Jack's. "Didn't know you were a coward, Dewitt."

Jack sidestepped away from the Copperhead. "Legends aren't made by bluster. Don't cross me." He trudged past Seymour, heading to the Engineering Works.

"That's right, Dewitt. You should be scared!" Seymour called after him.

Nah, you *should be scared.* Jack flashed a feral smile over his shoulder, smug about his acquisition of the loose hairs he'd liberated from the Copperhead Ringleader.

Jack made good on his false pretense, shooting the breeze with Charlie Creagen before heading back to the stables. Every moment of his visit to the Engineering Works had been agonizing—he wanted nothing more than to race out to see if his fears were founded. But Jack was determined not to blow his cover. He'd come damned close with Seymour as it was.

Zepheus's head was over his stall door, ears pricked as he waited for his rider. The pegasus kept a low profile so he didn't gain the interest of the unicorns ridden by the Copperheads. None were stabled in the livery where Zepheus was, but he wasn't taking chances.

Jack let himself into the stall, crowding close to the stallion. "You got any word?"

The palomino's nostrils roved over Jack's shirt, reading the scents. <No, but you're upset. What is it?>

The Effigest glanced up the stable aisle. No humans were in sight, and mundane equines occupied the rest of the stable—horses and mules. And a donkey, judging by the sudden braying. "We need to fly out to the homestead. Now."

Zepheus peered at him. <What? Why?>

"Ran into Seymour." Jack was already on the move, grabbing the saddle blanket and spreading it across the stallion's back.

<And? What happened?>

"He dropped hints he has Em and Blaise." Jack swallowed, shoving away the fear and anger that threatened to take root. "I need to check before I do something I might regret."

Zepheus nickered with worry as Jack slung the saddle onto his back, deftly tightening the cinches. <You can't take on all the Copperheads.>

"Nah. I just gotta take on *one* of 'em." And in such a manner that would make any of the others think twice. If they had Emmaline and Blaise, Jack had an idea for retaliation. It was dangerous. It was reckless. In short, it was the sort of thing Jack excelled at. "I figure we can make a quick flight, check into things, and then…" He trailed off. Jack didn't need to say more. Zepheus understood.

Moments later, they were underway. Zepheus's wings pumped the air, the stallion pushing himself to his top speed with no urging. The homestead was in view before long, and as the stallion descended, Jack nearly choked when he saw the imprints of cloven hooves that had churned up the dirt all around the house and barn.

"Emmaline!" he shouted, jumping out of the saddle and hoping against hope that she'd hidden. "Blaise!" Zepheus joined him, whinnying and sending out mental queries for any within his range who might hear.

<I don't sense them,> Zepheus said after a few minutes. He rested his chin on Jack's shoulder, an attempt at comfort. <And all the scents they left behind are stale.>

Jack shook his head in frustration, his eyes stinging. He had been foolish to think they were out of the Copperheads' reach here. Seymour Arce and his gang thought they had bested him, but he wasn't done. He would not let this go unanswered.

<What will you do?>
"Get 'im where it hurts." Jack turned and scratched beneath the stallion's forelock. "Let's get back to town. I got some spelling to do."

CHAPTER THIRTY-THREE

Weaponized Crochet

Jack

Two hours later, Jack strolled up the street to his hotel as if nothing was amiss, a paper sack concealing new supplies clutched under his arm. When he reached his room, he took stock of his few possessions, making sure no one had tampered with them while he'd been out. But everything was undisturbed. He pulled a skein of yarn and two crochet hooks from the sack, and an almost-complete project from the bottom of one of his saddlebags.

Only Kittie and Emmaline knew that he'd taken up crochet after the trauma of his experience with Gaitwood in Phinora. He wasn't ashamed of it, but he also didn't want to have to explain himself. That would only end with him stabbing a crochet hook through some Nosy Nelly's eye. The simple act calmed him as he was consumed by creativity. Didn't hurt that he'd figured out how to craft some damned handy poppets.

This project was a good example. With the proper cleansing, it was a simple matter to reuse poppets. Jack was pleased with the design of this doll. It had a pouch in its belly, making it easy to keep binding materials or reagents in place. He didn't want to risk anything disrupting the spells he had planned for Seymour Arce.

Jack removed the hairs from his pocket, stuffing them into the poppet's pouch. Aside from nabbing people Jack cared about, Seymour's biggest mistake had been letting an Effigest within arm's reach of himself. Once the hairs were secure, he stowed the crochet hooks and yarn in his saddlebag. He hadn't planned on bringing the supplies for his new hobby along, but now that he'd spent coin, he wasn't about to leave them behind. Jack tucked the doll into the reagent pouch at his side. He'd have to do additional shopping to complete this specific working.

He stopped by the Mercantile first. Sometimes, especially in the Untamed Territory, a good Mercantile stocked reagents. That wasn't the case here, though. The shopkeeper directed him to a new store that had opened since Jack's last visit, and before long, he stepped into Botanica Magica.

A dryad ran the place, and she eyed him warily as soon as he entered. A trash griffin perched on her shoulder—sort of like someone had the brilliant idea to cross a raccoon with a goshawk, and the result had come out ornery.

"You're not one of our outlaws," the dryad observed, arms crossed. The daisies rooted in her hair swayed as she tilted her head.

"Nah, but guessing my coin is still good here." Jack jingled his coin purse for emphasis.

The dryad might not trust him, but money spoke, and before long, he was the proud owner of flashfire pepper, bittercress, serpent's bite, and a tin of bunyip fat. He took his prizes back to his room to complete the assembly and start the spell.

The working he had in mind wasn't pleasant, but Jack wasn't here to go easy on anyone. In a town full of outlaw mages who would have no problems with sending him to Perdition, he couldn't pull any punches. He held the poppet in the palm of his hand, tightening his grip as he called on his power to activate it. A soft glow washed over the poppet as the sympathetic magic took hold, binding Seymour Arce to the tiny doll.

This was either going to be the power play he needed to gain the upper hand, or it might be his biggest mistake. *Only one way to find out.*

Before heading to his room for the night, Jack paid a visit to Zepheus. The stallion had no new information, though he was curious about Jack's spell. The outlaw had brought the poppet with him, and in the growing darkness, he crouched down to tuck the tiny figure far beneath the manger in Zepheus's stall.

<I smell pepper,> the pegasus observed. <You didn't...?>

"I did," Jack hissed, waving a hand at the palomino. He raked some straw beneath the manger, hoping it would help cut the scent of pepper. A human nose wouldn't detect it, but he worried a unicorn might since Zepheus could. Though, the odds of a unicorn understanding what the pepper meant were low. "I ain't here to be nice."

<This working is quite a bit further south than *nice*. It's downright cruel.>

Jack shook his head. As far as he was concerned, Seymour Arce was already playing dirty and deserved the consequences that were coming for him. With a vengeful smile, he whispered the last words that would activate all the spellwork on the poppet.

With that task done, he retreated to his room. Jack slept with his sixgun and poppet on the bedside table—he wouldn't put it past Seymour to send someone to kill him in the middle of the night. But the night passed without disruption, leaving him to wonder if his working hadn't taken. Did Seymour have protections of some sort in place?

After he breakfasted, he stopped by the stables to check in with Zepheus again. As he was about to leave, the stallion's ears pricked forward. <There's some gods-awful caterwauling coming this way, and someone is screeching your name.>

"Well, that's good news. I was starting to worry I fizzled and didn't know it." Jack stretched, rolling his shoulders to loosen the muscles. A moment later, he heard the same sound: a high-pitched squeal headed their way.

<You're not worried they're going to shoot you on sight or turn you into a toad?>

"The worst Seymour could do is shoot me or rearrange my face with his fist." Though, to be sure, that wouldn't be pleasant. Any blow the Strength mage landed would make one from Jack feel like a love tap by comparison. "But that hex ain't gonna poof if I'm dead." He only hoped that the Copperhead Ringleader understood that very important detail.

<I'm coming with you,> Zepheus said, nosing his stall door open to follow his rider out into the bright morning sunshine.

Jack knew it would be a futile effort to dissuade the stallion. Besides, they were partners. Zepheus had saved his hide many times before. It was good to have him at his back. He simply nodded his agreement, swaggering out into the dusty street in front of the stable.

Seymour stood at the head of a group of Copperheads. Mostly, the rest of the desperadoes did a fair job of looking properly menacing. They either had revolvers or rifles in their hands, or sprites of magic glimmering on their fingertips. Seymour, though…well, Jack had a difficult time not guffawing at the man.

Seymour's face was red, his eyes bulging as he shrilled Jack's name like a piglet calling for a sow. Each step was delicate, as if he were walking across a patch of cacti. Jack's favorite part was the way Seymour frantically clutched his groin.

"What…did…you…*do?*" Seymour finally wheezed the words out amid his extreme discomfort. The rest of his gang fanned out around them, hemming in Jack and Zepheus.

Jack cocked his head. "Looks like you've rolled in the hay with one too many ladies or gents, Seymour. Might wanna think about seeing a Healer."

Seymour made a frustrated rasp. "*Magic.*"

Maureen the Dread Surgeon, Seymour's second, stepped forward. "He saw *me*. And I know a hex when I see it."

Jack had been counting on that. He knew the Copperheads boasted one of the most fearsome Healers in Iphyria. Nadine was scary in her own way but overall had good intentions for her patients. Maureen wasn't the nursemaiding sort, aside from when it came to the Copperheads who rode at her side. Though, maybe not even then. It wasn't healthy to get too close to her. Maureen had earned her moniker after using her magic to amputate key appendages from anyone who got on her bad side.

Jack smiled, allowing some of his own sadism to ooze into the expression. "Then you'll also know I'm the only one who can break it." That was a half-truth. If another Effigest found his poppet, they could cancel the spell. At his words, the enemy outlaws stepped closer, the circle constricting like a noose. Jack crooked a finger at them. "That poppet ain't on me, friends."

Seymour glared at him through watering eyes. Maureen eyed the outlaw leader, and in that long look, Jack knew she was wondering if the time was ripe to take over leadership of the Copperheads. Something to watch. "What do you *want*, Wildfire?" Seymour growled through gritted teeth.

Jack smiled. "Show me the merchandise you think I'll be interested in. Then maybe I'll do something about that pickled pepper pecker of yours."

SHADY WAREHOUSES DOWN BY DOCKS WERE A FINE PLACE FOR AN AMBUSH. Izhadell had boasted a warehouse district, and Jack had seen his fair share of ambushes there. Even conducted some of them himself in his time as a theurgist. Tension laced the back of his neck with every step as the Copperheads showed him and Zepheus to the building that was to serve as their auction hall. The malevolence surrounding them made him downright itchy. *Pretty sure I ain't gonna be welcome in Thorn again.*

He followed Seymour into the depths of the warehouse, surprised by the pungent bouquet of scents that assaulted his nose. The sounds, too. Muted growls, the call of birds, lowing, hisses, and quiet voices. Crying. Moans. It was like stepping into a menagerie. Jack narrowed his eyes.

Beside him, Zepheus flicked his ears, taking in all the sounds. <So

many.> Awe and horror were ripe in his mental voice. Jack felt the same way.

"The pegasi first," Jack suggested, eyeing Seymour lest the man make some sort of double-cross. Jack figured if he got the pegasi, it would be a lot easier to make an escape.

"You don't call the shots here," Seymour said, though he didn't sound very convincing, what with the nasal whimper that punctuated his speech as he continued to experience discomfort in a man's most precious region.

Jack smiled. "Yeah?"

Seymour trudged down a row of stalls, stopping midway along. A snort of surprise echoed in the depths, and a moment later, Oberidon's head thrust over the partition. A rope with glittering beads tangled around his neck, stifling his magic. Jack frowned at the round, weeping wounds dotting Oberidon's flanks. *Unicorns. I hate unicorns.*

Emrys was one stall over. The stallion's head was low, eyes dimmed with depression. Jack's lips pressed together in displeasure. The black stud was taking his and Blaise's capture hard. *Don't you worry, you contrary pie-licker. We're gonna spring you both.*

Jack pivoted on his boot heels. "These two stallions are sentries from out of Fortitude. You release 'em to me, and I'll drop the spell that's making your pecker feel like you dipped it in a hill of fire ants."

Seymour's face contorted at his crass words, while a handful of his compatriots guffawed—including Maureen, who still looked ready to stage an overthrow at any moment. Jack needed her to wait a little longer.

"Agreed. Do it *now*," Seymour snarled.

Jack shook his head. "No can do—or did you forget I don't have the poppet on me? But you have my word that once they're free and I get back to the poppet, it'll happen."

Seymour blew out a frustrated breath. "Then go ahead. Leave and do it!"

"Nope." Jack leaned against the stall, rubbing Oberidon between the eyes to soothe the pegasus. Spotted ears pricked forward, following the conversation. Emrys had lifted his head, too, finally realizing that help had arrived. "I reckon you got something else of interest to me. *Personal* interest."

Tight-lipped, Seymour spun and gestured for him to follow. Jack shook his head. "Nope. Release the pegasi first."

Seymour tightened his fists, and for a moment, Jack feared he'd pushed the man too far. But then the ongoing hex reminded the Ringleader that he needed Jack in one piece. "Get those bangtails out *now*."

Seymour's outlaws hustled to obey his order, and moments later,

Emrys and Oberidon clopped beside Zepheus, free of the infernal salt-iron.

<We're getting Blaise?> Emrys asked, his ears pitched forward and renewed hope in his eyes.

Jack tightened his mouth and gave a small nod. He and the trio of pegasi followed the Ringleader down a new row of cells, and at the end— well, he had to fight back the urge to run to the bars to check on his daughter for himself. Instead, he ambled up as if he had all the time in the world, though his gaze flicked over her, assessing her for injuries. *Faedra help you lot if you harmed my daughter.*

Emmaline appeared unharmed. Blaise was beside her, his steady gaze on Jack as if he were trying to make the outlaw understand something. Jack couldn't figure out what, though. The Breaker glanced at Emrys when the stallion pawed at the ground.

Jack glared over his shoulder at Seymour. "You have my daughter and my—" He paused. *Damn it, Blaise.* "Friend. Let them go."

He saw Blaise's eyebrows lift in surprise at the admission of friendship. Then the young man gave the tiniest shake of his head. Jack narrowed his eyes.

"No," Seymour said, drawing Jack's attention. "You can have the girl, but not the Breaker. You've had him long enough."

Jack saw Blaise's shoulders rise in agitation, then fall back down. The young man was annoyed at the situation and clearly didn't want to be thought of as a possession, but he didn't want Jack to spring him?

Jack clenched his fists until the nails bit into his palms. Even if Blaise wanted to stay here—*why?*—the outlaw needed to make it look like he wouldn't let go of the Breaker easily. "No, he's *mine.*" Behind him, Emrys snorted in outrage. Jack hoped the blasted stud wasn't about to bite him for playing along with whatever Blaise was up to.

Seymour smiled. "I'll cut you a deal, Wildfire." Then he paused, taking a moment to scratch frantically at his groin. "You dispel the hexes on me, and you get the pegasi and the girl. *And* you get to leave town alive." Around him, the Copperheads all took a step forward, as if they had choreographed it. "Quite charitable of me, to be sure."

Jack glowered around at the group, though overall, that was a fair deal. "The *alive* part better include my daughter and the pegasi."

Seymour waved a hand. "It does. We'll be right generous and even let you stay for the auction. We're happy to take golden eagles from Fortitude."

I bet you are. Jack glanced at Blaise. *Hope you know what you're doing, Breaker.* "Deal."

CHAPTER THIRTY-FOUR

It's What I Do

Blaise

I can do this. Blaise closed his eyes, grounding himself. He had underestimated how much Emmaline's presence had encouraged him, but he focused on his relief that she was with her father. And the pegasi were free, too. Blaise wished he'd had some way to explain what he was doing to Emrys. He trusted Emmaline would tell him, but there was a possibility the stallion would be too upset to listen. *This is going to take a lot of apology cakes.*

Blaise spent the late afternoon watching and learning. He noticed that the men and women who patrolled the area where he and the other mystical races were kept weren't gifted with magic. Normal humans— they looked tough, but he wondered if they were simply hirelings and not true outlaws. Security capable of wandering around the salt-iron without feeling the drain and ache.

He also noticed they were lazy. Judging by the routes of the more stringent guards, he figured they were supposed to walk up and down each aisle to check on their charges. But many of them were lax, simply peering down the aisle before moving on, heading off to other entertainments.

The closest prisoners to his cell were a full-blooded knocker and a young Theilian. The white-furred Theilian curled up in a ball in the middle of the cage, trembling. The knocker spent her time pacing, frowning with concentration.

When Blaise was certain no guards were going to sneak up on him, he edged closer to his neighbors. "Howdy."

The Theilian growled and made no other response. The knocker gave him a mistrustful look. "What?"

Blaise glanced at the windows lining the upper third of the cavernous warehouse. Despite the dirt riming the huge panes of glass, he judged by their dimness that night had fallen. Fatigue dogged him, but he couldn't sleep. Not yet. "Do either of you know anything about an alchemist?"

The knocker's frown deepened. "Ew. No, why?"

"Because I'm looking for one," Blaise said. "And once I find her, I can escape."

The knocker snorted a laugh. "You hear that, Furball? This joker here thinks he's going to escape the Copperheads!" She slapped a hand against her knee. "You lost your chance when you didn't go with your friends."

The Theilian lifted her head, uncurling and creeping closer, dark nose quivering. "You're the Breaker." The lupine's voice was soft, reverent. "The howls of your lifesong have made it as far as the mountains of Theilia."

Blaise blinked. "What?"

The Theilian cocked her head. "Your scent was added to the lifesong by the outcast Kur Agur."

That sounded all kinds of strange. Kur Agur, the only Theilian to call Fortitude home, had howled about him? Blaise had a lot of questions and no time to ask them.

"The Breaker?" The knocker edged over. "Okay, I've heard of you. At the very least, this may be entertaining." She rubbed her hands together, and Blaise wondered if she was related to Flora or if most knockers were this eager for dangerous entertainment. "Furball, your sniffer got anything useful?"

"Lirra, *not* Furball," the Theilian corrected with a grumble. She sucked in a deep breath, lips curled and nostrils twitching with the action. "There are too many scents."

"Wait." Blaise dug into his pocket. The measuring spoon. Would it be enough? It had seemed like such a small, inconsequential keepsake at the time. "This belongs to her. Would it help?"

Lirra's eyes lit up. "Yes. Though I will do you little good in a cage."

Blaise grinned. "What if you weren't in the cage?"

"You can do that?" the knocker hissed, incredulous.

In answer, Blaise moved to the rear of his cell. It was darker at the back, and he doubted anyone would easily notice his handiwork if he were careful. He closed his hands around the bottom of a slat, his magic chewing through it. Blaise duplicated the effort at the top, then gently shifted the slat out of the way, concealing it in a shadow. He squeezed through, easing out the hand span of inches between the cage and the wall. It wasn't comfortable, but he managed.

"Guess you *can* do that," the knocker said, eager. "Can you free us?"

Blaise pursed his lips. "In time. First, I have to find the alchemist." He paused outside Lirra's cage. "I'll let you out on the condition that you have to go back in when we finish."

The Theilian growled. "I don't wish to."

Blaise understood. Oh, how he understood. He sighed. "Do you trust me?"

"No," the knocker said.

Lirra whined, her ears flattening. "I don't *want* to, but I know what the lifesong says." She hunched her fuzzy shoulders. "You won't let us be sold?"

"No," Blaise said softly, shaking his head. "I won't." He only hoped he wasn't making a promise he couldn't keep.

Lirra scratched a clawed hand at her throat. "I will work with you and return here when we finish."

With her promise, Blaise set about releasing her. The knocker watched, her jealousy obvious. Blaise hoped she wasn't the petty sort who might call for a guard. Lirra stepped cautiously through the gap he created, then took the spoon into her hands, sniffing deeply.

She gave him a toothy grin. "I have the scent. Are you able to stalk quietly? We don't wish the guards to catch us."

"I'll try," Blaise said.

"Come." And then she was off, her feet whisper-soft on the stone floor.

Blaise hurried after her. Other mystic creatures stirred at their passing, but none called out. Lirra kept to the shadows as best she could, and Blaise mimicked her, though he would never have her grace. As they made their way through the warehouse, he was awestruck by the size of the place—and the sheer amount of *merchandise* the Copperheads had collected.

At the end of an aisle, Lirra paused, stretching as tall as she could with her nose in the air. Her eyes gleamed in the dim light, and she turned again, leading him onward. "We are close."

Blaise hoped she was right. They were no longer in the area that housed the mystic races and creatures, but were surrounded by crate after crate of items. Some of them appeared to hold books—rare ones, Blaise guessed. And...his eyebrows raised. Grimoires? One of them appeared to be bound in leather that looked a bit too much like human skin for his comfort, and he hurried to keep up with the Theilian. Another crate held glittering dragon scales, while yet another had Knossan horns. His stomach turned at the sight.

"Ahead," Lirra murmured, extending a claw down the aisle. She cocked an ear. "The guards have been here recently, so you may have a window of time. I will return to my cell." Her eyes bored into his. "And *you* will return?"

Blaise swallowed, nodding. "I will."

With his agreement, she ghosted away. Blaise turned, quietly slipping down the aisle of crates. He thought Lirra had been mistaken until he saw the cell nearly hidden by stacks of stolen goods. It was like the one he had been in, though it was furnished with a cot. Someone was asleep on it. Blaise crept closer, eyes straining in the low light. Dark curls drooped over one side of the cot. *Mom.* His heart raced, and his magic swelled, ready to be unleashed. *No, we have to be careful. Need a plan.* But first, he had to be sure she was okay.

"Mom." Blaise kept his voice low, and for a moment, he thought he was going to have to speak louder to wake her. But then her head jerked upright, and she stared at him as if he were a phantom.

Marian slowly sat up, the rough blanket falling away from her. "Blaise?" The word echoed off the crates surrounding them, and she winced, dropping her voice. "Gods, Blaise. What are you doing here? You…you came for me?" Her eyes glistened, tears building in the corners.

"Of course, I came for you." Blaise felt tears well in his eyes, too. But there wasn't time for tearful reunions, not yet. They were both still in danger. "You're my Mom."

"Even after…everything?" Marian swallowed, as if she couldn't bear to give voice to the alchemical experimentation she had put him through.

"You'll always be my Mom, even if you did things you regret," Blaise whispered. But did she regret them? The question was on his lips, but he didn't speak it.

She answered anyway. "Not a single day has passed when I didn't wish I could change the things done to you." Marian rose from the cot, stepping over to the bars nearest him. "I wish I could change *everything*." Grief etched the curve of her lips. "Everything I've done has hurt the people I care about the most."

Suddenly, Blaise saw that no matter how angry he was with his mother, she was even more so with herself. Marian Hawthorne wasn't blind to the long-term consequences of her choices. He swallowed, unsure of what to say.

His mother shut her eyes. "Your father is dead because of me. Maybe Luci and Brody, too."

"No," Blaise whispered, shaking his head. "No, they made it." He reached out and placed one of his hands on hers. "They're safe. I got them." Blaise hoped they were still safe, but he trusted Nadine.

Marian's eyes flashed open, hope in their depths. "Oh, Blaise." She shifted her hand, her fingers moving against his. She gave him a light squeeze. "You shouldn't be here."

Relief at finding his mother filled him, replacing the anger he'd felt toward the Copperheads. He didn't need vengeance. He only needed to get her away from here. "I'm going to get you out."

She frowned. "They want you, too. You're not safe here."

"I know. They already got me."

Marian blinked, startled. "What? Wait…you freed yourself?"

Blaise couldn't help his smile. He was ridiculously pleased he was finding uses for his magic. "I'm a Breaker. I broke out. It's what I do."

His mother took a shaky breath, thinking. Then she nodded. "Okay. What's the plan? Are we escaping now?"

Uh-oh. Here we go with people assuming I have a plan. He rubbed the back of his head. "I could break you out, but it's not that simple. It'll take some time. I wanted to be sure I could find you first."

Marian studied him. "Well, you found me." A wavering smile flitted on her lips, and she reached out, cupping his cheek with one hand. "Thank you. You're capable of such amazing things, my Dandelion."

He paused. *Dandelion.* When he had been small, she'd called him that as a pet name—but he hadn't heard it in years. "What do you mean by that?"

She took a deep breath before answering. "Tough. Resilient. Filled with goodness in a way that's not easily destroyed."

Her words and faith warmed him. For a moment, he felt like a small child, safe with his mother. He relaxed against her hand for a dozen heartbeats before pulling away. "I'll be back, Mom."

"Get some rest, Blaise. You look exhausted."

He chuckled, shaking his head. *Still my Mom.*

CHAPTER THIRTY-FIVE

At Least We're Disasters Together

Jefferson

It was ill-advised, but Jefferson had drunk himself into a stupor. It seemed his best way of coping with his current situation. And it was the only thing that helped to send his worried mind to sleep.

At least he had the dreamscape again, though it was little solace. His magic sang as it filled the surrounding void, rolling out like retreating thunderheads as Fortitude took shape. The familiar town made him feel a little better about things, though he knew it was a temporary balm. Then he paused. *Should I?* Jefferson glanced at the cheerful yellow bakery, Blaise's name boldly scrawled over the awning. *Will he be angry with me? Maybe not since the Quiet Ones haven't figured out my magic.*

Besides, Jefferson missed Blaise terribly, and under the circumstances, he would be the easiest person to locate. Finding Blaise, *being* with Blaise, had become second nature.

He reconsidered, though. As much as he missed Blaise, his beau was too far away to help him. Kittie or Flora, though… Yes, he decided to err on the side of being a responsible mage. While he wasn't as familiar with Kittie, he stood a good chance of being able to locate Flora.

Jefferson sent out a tendril of his dream magic, then stopped when he felt it butt up against a barrier of some sort. *Strange.* He tried again, but once more, his magic came up short. Or rather, it was like a seedling trying to break through stone. Not impossible, but quite difficult.

What's stopping me? Jefferson pulled his magic back, assessing the situation. *Oh.* The Quiet Ones must have the estate warded. That made sense

—it would block enemies from scrying their location, too. That didn't bode well for him, though.

Except... He frowned, turning in a circle in the empty dream-streets. It was difficult to describe, but the warding that surrounded him wasn't all-encompassing. There was a tiny crack, allowing something from the outside in. It reminded him of a poorly hung carriage door he'd come across once that had allowed a breath of winter's chill inside.

Jefferson pursed his lips. No, this wasn't a something. It was a *someone*.

Blaise. He nearly laughed with joy. His tenuous connection to the Breaker was a tiny chink in the ward, but it was there, and it was enough. Jefferson hoped Blaise was asleep.

He sent his magic arrowing towards that tiny gap, relieved when he felt it pass through. It was like threading a needle, and Jefferson suspected this would only work with Blaise. *Why? Because I love him? Or because his blood made me what I am? A combination of both? Or is it something darker, like a remnant of our geasa? No, that's long gone.* He didn't know the cause, but he was glad for whatever it was.

Now, he only had to hope Blaise was sleeping. He felt the other man's distant presence, and Jefferson was tempted to crash through to him. But he knew better than to do that to Blaise. No, instead, he approached the dream door that separated them and imagined giving it a polite knock.

Jefferson felt Blaise's response. There were no words, only surprise followed by assent. And then Blaise was there, in the dreamscape, with him. The Breaker closed the distance, throwing his arms around Jefferson and tugging him close.

"Is it really you, or do I just miss you this much?" Blaise mumbled into his shoulder.

Jefferson relaxed, enjoying the feel of Blaise against him. "Can't it be both?"

The Breaker stayed in the embrace but pulled back to look him in the eye. "Have you made it back to Fortitude?"

Wouldn't he know if I'd made it back there? Jefferson blinked at the question. "I...no. I'm still in Ganland." He winced at the admission as Blaise frowned. "It's a long story." Jefferson raised his brows at his beau. "And I take it your question means *you're* not in Fortitude?" He hoped it meant Blaise had gone to Rainbow Flat to reconcile with his mother, as he'd said he would.

It was Blaise's turn to look rueful. "No, and that's also a long, unhappy story." The Breaker sighed, resting his chin atop Jefferson's shoulder. Heartbreak radiated through the younger man.

"Do you want to go to the bakery?" Jefferson asked softly. "We can talk."

Blaise nodded, and together they crossed to the building. The younger mage seemed to shed some of his nerves as soon as he entered, though they both knew it was the dreamscape and not real. But for the moment, it was real enough. Blaise set to work, doing the thing Jefferson could always count on him to do when he was worried: bake.

Jefferson moved companionably beside Blaise. It had taken some doing, but he had learned his way around the Breaker's baking workflow. He banished his greatcoat and then rolled up his sleeves so they wouldn't get in the way.

"Shall I go first, or you?" Jefferson asked.

Blaise swallowed, closing his eyes for a moment. "You."

Whatever had spurred Blaise to leave Fortitude was painful. It almost made Jefferson wish Blaise would share first, but he would wait. As they worked, he explained the chain of events that had led to the kidnapping attempt, the revelation of his identity, and losing his rings.

"Oh, Jefferson," Blaise whispered when he'd completed his tale. The Breaker set aside the ingredients he had pulled out, wiping his fingertips on a towel. Then he closed the distance between them, wrapping his arms around Jefferson. While the dreamscape wasn't real, the reassurance and love in Blaise's embrace *was*. "I know how much you didn't want that ever again."

"The worst part is they killed *me*." Jefferson hissed out a breath. "I mean Jefferson. I can't be who I want to be anymore." *I should have known I couldn't escape the clutches of my family name. All I had was a respite, nothing more.*

"That's not true," Blaise pointed out, reaching up to touch his face. The face he always wore in the dreamscape. *Jefferson.*

"I mean out in the world."

Blaise met his eyes, and for a moment, the Breaker's gaze was like an anchor. "I know. That's what I mean, too. They may have brought you down, but Jefferson Cole is too smart to be done away with so easily."

Blaise's faith made him feel a little better, but Jefferson knew that was an easy thing for his beau to say, not knowing the full gravity of the situation. "But if I can't...if I never get my cabochon ring back..." He would be forever cursed with a Wells family face, no matter the name he used.

"I know it took me a while to come to this decision, but I love you no matter what you look like," Blaise said, leaning in to deliver a soft kiss. "And we'll get your ring back. Somehow." When Jefferson smiled, Blaise continued, "Are Kittie, Mindy, and Flora okay?"

Jefferson shook his head. "I don't know. I certainly hope so. The warding here is too tight, and you're the only one I could reach." Jefferson sincerely hoped the Board had made no new attempts on his friends. It chafed that he wasn't around to do anything to help them. He sighed. "And you? What's happened?"

Blaise went back to the pie lattice he had been constructing, a sure sign he needed a distraction to help him through. As he worked, he recounted the days after the delegation had left. The shocking letter delivered by Hank, and Blaise's frantic journey to Rainbow Flat. Finding his siblings unharmed but afraid, and his father dead. His mother stolen away in the night.

Jefferson sucked in a surprised breath as Blaise continued with his tale. He hadn't thought that anything could possibly be worse than his own situation. But this? It was horrific. *I should have stayed with him.*

"You're not hurt, are you?" Jefferson asked when Blaise finished. He knew of the Copperheads from his travels in the Untamed Territory. They weren't known for being polite. Even Flora would be reluctant to tangle with them, which said something.

Blaise shook his head. "I'm not hurt, though I can't say the same for Emrys and Oby." Anger flashed in his eyes. "But Jack got them out. And Em."

"But not you?" Jefferson asked, curious. Though, he suspected Blaise was someone everyone wanted—and not for the same reasons as Jefferson. Others would want to use him for his power.

"No," Blaise said. "I stayed in the auction warehouse. I found my Mom."

That seemed to be the first bit of good news in the entire awful situation. "And did you free her?"

"Not yet."

"Hmm." Jefferson rubbed his smooth cheek. "So, you're stuck in an auction house run by the meanest desperadoes in the Untamed Territory. I'm stuck in the estate of a shadowy cabal. Fortunes of Tabris, we're a mess, aren't we?"

"We're kind of a disaster," Blaise agreed, sounding much calmer about everything than Jefferson would have expected.

"At least we're disasters together," Jefferson murmured, winning a smile from Blaise. He picked up a towel and dabbed a spot of flour off Blaise's beard. "I don't know how you manage to cover yourself with flour in the dreamscape."

"Would you have me any other way?"

"No. You're perfect as you are," Jefferson admitted, savoring the sweetness of that truth. Then he straightened, returning his attention to their problems. "Do you have a plan?"

Blaise pursed his lips. "Why does everyone assume I have a plan? My plan ended with 'find Mom.' So no." He glanced at Jefferson. "Why? Do *you* have a plan?"

"Finding *you* was my plan," Jefferson said, and Blaise's smile nearly illuminated the bakery. "They unwittingly blocked my ability to get my magic past whatever wards they have set up—aside from my link with you."

Blaise froze, looking at him sharply. "The geasa is *gone*."

"I don't mean the geasa." Jefferson bumped his shoulder against Blaise's in apology. "Maybe it's because my magic spawned from you. Or a connection of a more romantic nature."

Blaise's brows slammed down over his eyes at that. "What?"

Jefferson sighed. "Because I *love* you. Honestly, I thought I'd made that clear on multiple occasions."

Blaise's expression softened. "You have. I was just..." He shook his head, rubbing the back of his neck as he did when he was feeling especially awkward. "You think so?"

"I think love is a sort of magic all its own," Jefferson murmured, meaning every word.

The Breaker paused in his work, all traces of agitation from the moment before gone. He looked as if he were gathering his thoughts, as if Jefferson's simple truth had struck a target. But when he spoke, he did a very Blaise thing: he changed the subject. "Do you think we could find Jack in the dreamscape, like we did before?"

Jefferson shifted closer to Blaise, wrapping an arm around his back. Blaise glanced at him, an apologetic cast in his eyes. Sometimes, Jefferson had learned, his beau was at a loss for how to respond. He was getting better, little by little. *I know you love me. You're just figuring out that bit of magic, along with everything else.*

Jefferson pursed his lips, releasing Blaise from the embrace. The Breaker stayed comfortably close, though he went back to work on his pie. "I don't know. You're the only one I could reach..." He let the words trail off, puzzling through things. "Oh. Do you suppose you're acting as a bridge?" That made sense in a strange way.

"Won't know unless we try," Blaise reasoned, slipping the pie into the oven. "And this time, I know Jack is close to where I am. Physically, anyway. Not sure what that translates to in here." He waved a hand to indicate their current surroundings.

"Would he be sleeping now, do you think?" Jefferson asked.

Blaise shrugged. "Maybe. I think you're stalling."

"Maybe I'm trying to savor every moment I have alone with you."

"Try it, Dreamer," Blaise said, though there was amusement in his tone. It was music to Jefferson's ears.

Gods, I've missed this. Missed him. Jefferson took a deep breath and blew it out slowly, focusing his magic on finding Jack. He came up against the same resistance at first, but then he felt something strange—as if Blaise were guiding his magic. *There.* He found the shape of the Effigest's slumbering mind. Jack was well and truly asleep, though his dreams were troubled, full of worry and anger. Small wonder after what they had been through. It was a simple matter to coil his power around Jack and shepherd him into the dreamscape.

The outlaw materialized in the bakery, frowning at the pair. He glanced around. "This the real thing, or am I so busy fretting I'm dreaming about your damned dreamscape?"

Jefferson huffed. "Of course, it's the real dreamscape. Have some appreciation for the difficulty it took to bring you here." He gestured at Blaise.

Jack cocked his head, turning to the Breaker. "That the real you?" When Blaise nodded, the outlaw's shoulders relaxed, though annoyance carved his face. "This business of staying in the warehouse is a piss-poor idea. I was going to get you out!" In a rare occurrence, Jefferson found himself agreeing with the outlaw.

Blaise grimaced. "It was the best idea I had to find my Mom. And I *did* find her."

Jack snorted. "You got a plan I need to know about?"

The Breaker sighed. "Why does everyone assume I have a plan?"

"'Cause if you've got the balls to sneak out of a Copperhead cage and hunt down your mother, seems like you should have figured out more than that," the Effigest said.

Blaise frowned. Jefferson watched the exchange, realizing what Jack was doing—he was goading the younger man into talking through a plan. The outlaw liked to teach in his own cantankerous way. Jefferson had personal experience with his methods.

"Could you or Em cast Obfuscation on my mother, and we sneak her out that way?" Blaise asked after a moment.

Jack considered it. "I'd need something of her essence."

The Breaker became more animated. "I have one of her old alchemical measuring spoons. We can do this. We can get my Mom out." His relief was almost palpable. Then he glanced away, guilt flashing across his face.

"What is it?" Jefferson asked.

A muscle in Blaise's jaw tightened. "There's so many...so many people stuck here. Other mystic races. I met a Theilian and a knocker." As soon as he spoke, Jefferson understood. Blaise wouldn't leave them behind.

A smirk spread across Jack's face. "Good. I got no tolerance for outlaws who steal *people*." Sometimes, Jefferson decided, the brazen outlaw was downright likable. This was something that he, too, could support. Then Jack's gaze settled on Jefferson. "How's my wife doing?"

Jefferson swallowed. "Ah, she was well the last I saw—"

"What do you mean by *the last I saw?*" The outlaw glowered.

"Another long story." Jefferson sighed, then launched into an extremely abridged version, heavily stressing that Kittie had been doing well until the fire.

Jack waved a hand at that. "Fire ain't gonna hurt my wife. I'm more concerned about the Salties who might blame it on *her.*"

Jefferson blinked. He hadn't even thought of that, though he'd been distracted. He cleared his throat. "I should see her again soon, though. I hope. My captors want to put me back in the action as Malcolm Wells."

"She knows who you are," Jack said bluntly.

Jefferson had suspected as much. He'd doubted Jack would keep that from his wife for her own safety. And she had done well to keep that information to herself. "Just as well in this situation."

"You got a plan to get out of the thorn patch you're in?" the outlaw asked.

Well, now he knew exactly how Blaise felt. "It's a work in progress." Jefferson hoped it was, at any rate.

"You'll figure somethin' out," Jack drawled, in a surprise to both Jefferson and Blaise. "You got more lives than a cat."

"I think you just complimented me. I truly *am* dreaming," Jefferson muttered, earning a laugh from Blaise.

The outlaw ignored him, turning to Blaise. "We can't let the Copperheads see this auction through. This is what I'm thinking…"

Jefferson didn't like the idea of Blaise taking on the Copperheads, but the showdown seemed inevitable. As he listened to their plan formulate, he decided that if Blaise must take on the most feared desperadoes in the land, he had no better ally than the Scourge of the Untamed Territory.

CHAPTER THIRTY-SIX
The Only Idea

Jack eyed the poppet sitting between him and Emmaline. It was Seymour's crocheted poppet, though he'd deactivated the spells as promised. He didn't want the Copperhead leader to have any reason to come after him prematurely. Of course, Seymour didn't know he still had a poppet keyed to him. He'd demanded Jack hand over his poppet, and it had only taken a simple bit of sleight of hand to give Seymour a blank. No way would he ever know the difference.

"You sure about this?" Jack asked, glancing at Emmaline.

His daughter shrugged. "No, but I think it'll work. Hope so, anyway." She picked up the poppet in one hand and a small seashell in the other. Jack had nullified the poppet with mugwort, rendering it a fresh slate for her to work on aside from the hairs still keyed to Seymour. He watched as she carefully tucked a tiny conch shell into her ear.

Jack was antsy to ask if it had worked. She ran her fingers over the poppet, making small, silent adjustments to the spell. Pride soared in him. She was truly becoming a natural at her magic, and it was possible that one day she might even be better than him.

After a moment, she grinned. "I can hear 'em!"

"That's my girl," Jack rumbled, leaning over to kiss her forehead. "I'm gonna go do my part now."

She gave him a thumbs up to show she'd heard, though she was now intent on magically eavesdropping on the Copperhead Ringleader. Jack smirked. *Yeah, this might actually work.*

He slipped out of their shared room, stopping by the stables to update the stallions. Emrys was still upset about the whole mess, pacing a furrow into the straw at his feet. As soon as he saw Jack, he demanded they rescue Blaise immediately.

"Workin' on it," Jack told the impatient stud. Zepheus and Oberidon were more receptive to his news, and they were ready and waiting to do their part. With the equines fully informed, he headed to his next meeting.

The dark alley behind the warehouse stank of rotting fish and shit. The trio of Knossans snorted continuously, as if they were trying to clear the vile odors from their nostrils. Jack almost pitied them, but the alley made the perfect rendezvous point for exactly that reason. Others would avoid it unless they had a compelling reason to go there.

"Let us be done with this place quickly," Gore rumbled, his alabaster tail flicking behind him with clear irritation.

"Yeah, I hear you," Jack agreed. He kept his little trick of an odor-blocking spell on his poppet to himself. As soon as he'd found the alley, he'd whipped it up. "I've got three keys here. Not enough for all of us, but the more of us opening cages, the better."

The Knossans nodded, their horns sweeping with the motion. "That is fine. We will leave Roam unhindered, so that once our younglings are located, he may see them to safety," Deal said.

Jack figured that wasn't the worst plan. The Knossans had been barred from viewing the *merchandise*—clearly, the Copperheads had figured out they were up to something. Jack didn't think it likely they'd be kept from the auction itself, though. The desperadoes were happy to take a coin from anyone, as Seymour had said.

The outlaw handed keys to Deal and Gore, then pointed to Roam. "When it's time, you're with me. I can try to keep you hidden, at least for a short while."

The spotted bull's ears twitched with concern. "Magic?"

"Well, I reckon putting a blanket over your head ain't gonna work," Jack said with a shrug, earning an amused snort from Gore. "I know I got a bit of a reputation as a top-shelf pisspot, but in this, I'm your ally." He glanced at the foreboding, mold-covered brick of the warehouse beside them. "I know the Scourge of the Untamed Territory don't seem the most trustworthy."

"You have proven to be more trustworthy than the Copperheads," Roam said.

"That don't take much," Jack muttered.

It wasn't long before he had a rudimentary poppet with hair from the Knossan. He meant every word he'd told them—he respected the bulls, and he intended to dispose of the hair when all was said and done. Jack finished making arrangements with the trio, then headed back to the hotel.

As soon as he opened the door, Emmaline leaped up, rushing over to him. "Daddy, we've got problems."

He raised his brows. "What kind?"

She chewed on her bottom lip, pointing to the small conch shell she had removed from her ear and left on the bedside table, beside a notebook she'd used to jot down notes as she listened. Emmaline crossed to it and picked up the notebook, thrusting it at him.

Jack scowled as he pieced together her shorthand. "You telling me Marian Hawthorne was never going to be a part of the auction?"

She nodded, moving beside him to point at another line. "Yeah, exactly. They just used her as a draw. An attraction." Emmaline's face grew serious. "And now they have *Blaise* as the star feature."

Yeah, well, neither us nor the Breaker are gonna allow that. Jack nodded. "What's this here?" He ran his fingertips over a handful of words he couldn't quite make out.

Emmaline smoothed a lock of blonde hair behind one ear. "A group from Ravance has offered double the buy-out price for Blaise's Mom, so the Copperheads are going to accept."

"Yeah, that tracks," Jack said. "When is the deal going down over the alchemist? Did you hear that much?"

"The Ravanchen wizards are delivering their payment at the end of the auction."

Jack digested her information, pacing as he mused on how to handle it. It was a delicate situation all around, in a town full of so many dangerous individuals that it was almost ridiculous. He could cast Rising Dread to sow confusion and violence, using the opportunity of chaos to free Marian, but that would make it hazardous for the alchemist. And possibly for Blaise, Emmaline, and the pegasi, too. No, they needed to figure out something else.

"I don't suppose we can sneak in there beforehand and free Marian and Blaise?" Emmaline suggested hopefully.

Jack shook his head. "Nah, with the auction tonight, that would be like sticking our hand into a wasp's nest." *Hmm.* He'd hoped to extract Blaise and Marian in the chaos he planned to create during the auction.

Emmaline gave him a dubious look. "Won't we be cutting it close otherwise?"

He grinned. "Probably."

She swallowed. "Is that a good idea?"

"It's the *only* idea."

Blaise

NO GUARDS STOPPED BY TO DELIVER AN EVENING MEAL. BLAISE SUSPECTED it was because the buyers were already filtering in, claiming their seats around the ring. He heard the clatter of many feet along with rumbling, indistinguishable voices.

"Not much longer now," the knocker commented, her tone gloomy.

"The auction has to happen," Blaise said. "But that doesn't mean the deals are going to go through."

"I hope that is true. We're quite outnumbered," Lirra commented, whining as she spoke.

Blaise shook his head. "We're not outnumbered."

They were quiet after that, listening to the happenings around them. Small groups of guards—or maybe auction workers, Blaise wasn't sure— filtered down the aisles. Some of them removed the more placid creatures. Others carried boxes from the goods area.

In time, they came for Blaise's neighbors. Neither Lirra nor the knocker spoke as the Copperheads hustled them away, though they both shot looks over their shoulders, as if they felt betrayed by his broken promise.

Once they were gone, Blaise heard a soft scuff. He whirled, agitation flaring. Then he relaxed at the lithe, blonde-braided form of Emmaline slipping up beside the cell. Her expression was grim, but she flashed a brief smile at him. "Howdy, Blaise. You miss me?"

"You know it," he murmured. "How's the plan coming?"

"Eh, so far, so good. No one saw through my Obfuscation. Handy spell, that." Emmaline shifted her weight. "We have a bit of a problem, though."

Blaise raised his brows. "What?"

"You're the last on the auction block."

Of course, I am. Blaise rubbed the bridge of his nose. Their original plan relied on his sale being earlier in the auction, giving him time to play his role. "Why'd they do that? I thought my mother was going to be last."

"Yeah, um, sounds like the Copperheads are selling her to someone for an excessive buyout." Emmaline made a face.

"That's not good." Blaise shifted his weight unhappily.

Emmaline gave him an encouraging smile. "Don't worry. We're sticking with the plan. It's a good one."

Bold words, considering how often their plans went sideways. But he *had* to believe this would work. It had to. "This changes the timing." He wasn't supposed to be at the *end*. If anything, he and Jack had thought the Copperheads might put him on the block first. "What if it doesn't work?" Blaise swallowed. When plans had gone awry in the past, he had been the one to suffer. He felt light-headed, and he squeezed his eyes closed to ward off the rising panic.

"*Blaise*," Emmaline's voice was urgent, slicing through the old memories that swelled like a tide. "This was *your choice*. You own this. And you're not alone."

His eyes flashed open. She was right. In the past, those things had been done *to* him. He had been a victim. But this? Blaise had been the one to decide on this course of action. *I'm not helpless. Not anymore.* Blaise hissed out a breath. "Thanks."

"Sometimes, we all need a reminder," Emmaline whispered. "I gotta go before I'm seen. We're gonna do this." Then she opened her fist, revealing a poppet. She whispered something and faded from Blaise's immediate view, though he knew in his gut she was still there. But no one else would. Emmaline slipped away.

CHAPTER THIRTY-SEVEN

Buyer Beware

Lirra and the knocker returned a short time later. Lirra trembled, her eyes wild as the cell door slammed behind her. The knocker muttered curses under her breath. Blaise had no time to speak to them, however, because the guards had come for him.

He didn't recognize them, but they handled the salt-iron manacles with such ease that Blaise suspected if they were outlaws, they didn't boast magic. He allowed them to clamp the shackles to his wrists, then once more placed his hands inside burlap sacks.

"C'mon, you," one man grumbled. "The sooner we get this done with, the sooner I get back to my dice game."

If we do our job right, you'll never get back to that game. Blaise made no response, though. He allowed the men to lead him down the aisle, doing his best to keep calm. His magic awaited his command. *Not now. Too soon.*

The guards brought him up behind the area set aside for the auction, leading him to a large wooden stage—though unlike any stage Blaise had seen before. It was enclosed by a mesh of barbed wire with what he suspected were salt-iron beads strewn throughout. The Copperheads left nothing to chance.

Blaise stepped onto the stage, the door creaking closed behind him. He looked out at the throng of attendees. A makeshift spotlight cobbled together from a lantern and mirrors focused on him, nearly blinding him with its glare. Blaise shielded his eyes with his bound hands, squinting to see the crowd. It was a full house, and every single face in the audience was either unfriendly or covetous. So many races were in attendance, not just humans. Knossans, elves, Theilians, knockers—others Blaise didn't recognize, too. They jostled one another, the crowd's agitation palpable.

"Here he is, ladies, gentlemen, and creatures of all variety! You asked for him, you got him! The Breaker of Fort Courage, a man with such rare magic, you'll never see it again in your lifetime." The auctioneer, a man Blaise didn't recognize, leaned over a podium, enthusiasm in his every movement. "Who will start the bidding at five hundred golden eagles?"

Five hundred golden eagles? Blaise boggled at the number, even as someone in the audience raised a card to place the first bid. No time to wonder how high the bids for him might go, however. He tapped his magic, and it came flooding to his fingers, unhampered by the salt-iron. Blaise let it chew through the sack first, the fabric falling away in jagged strips.

The crowd was loud, and if anyone noticed what he was doing, they wouldn't be heard over the masses. With his hands free of the bags, Blaise wrapped his fingers around the shackles on his opposite hand, pouring more magic into the effort.

The people in the front row saw *that*. A couple of them even rose, waving their cards to get the attention of the Copperheads. Blaise paid them no mind. He hoped Jack, Emmaline, and the Knossans were doing their part. If not, Blaise wouldn't get very far. Here, on the auction block, the enemy outnumbered him.

The bindings fell away from his wrists, landing on the timbers at his feet with a sharp metallic clatter. That made even the auctioneer stop to take notice, and he stared at Blaise, bewildered. Then he found his voice again. "Copperheads! Get this man back in shackles."

The Copperheads and their hirelings advanced on the auction block even as Blaise traced his fingers over the barbed wire, creating a gap. It parted with a twang. The approaching men and women only paused when the first screams rang out from the back of the auction gallery.

A blue and black-feathered anzu soared overhead, its lion's head agape with a guttural roar, talons raking the tops of heads with abandon. Shots rang out as someone tried to take the creature down with bullets, but it was moving too quickly. And it wasn't alone.

Bison bellowed, charging into the crowd with heads lowered, sending attendees scrambling to get out of the way. A pair of harpies shrieked, picking up a crate and smashing it against window after window, creating an escape for the winged creatures. A canine-bodied aralez howled, a rallying cry to the other flyers before bolting through an opening.

More terrestrial creatures and mystic races appeared. Blaise saw the bright flash of Lirra's fur as she wove through the crowd. She wasn't fighting, though—simply trying to find a way to freedom, the knocker close on her heels. Jackalopes hopped around in confusion. Freed bears and wolves streaked through the crowd, growling and clearing the way with calculated bites and unforgiving swipes.

A bunyip appeared, water sluicing from the sleek fur on its warm brown back as it crashed into the hapless buyers. It opened its massive mouth, grabbing a Copperhead and snapping the man's arm in two. A kelpie joined it, whistling a whinny. It fixated on a Copperhead, and the man climbed onto its back. The water horse splashed away with its unwitting prey.

No one paid attention to Blaise. They were too focused on surviving the onslaught of the angry menagerie. At last, he had a large enough gap to squeeze through—though his safety outside of the enclosure was uncertain.

A mighty roar cut through the bedlam. The largest grasscat Blaise had ever seen leaped atop a stack of crates, looking down on the chaos. Sharp claws kneaded the crate before it jumped to the ground to stand before Blaise, leafy tail lashing.

Uh-oh. I hope it's not mad for what I did to the other grasscats. Blaise swallowed. He didn't want to use his magic on the elemental, but he would if it came down to it.

Firefly eyes peered at him, the grasscat so large that it was on a level with Blaise and didn't need to look up to meet his gaze. The beast yawned, displaying serrated, rooty fangs. Then it laid down, giving Blaise a bored look.

"I don't understand," Blaise told the feline. "And there's somewhere I need to be."

The grasscat blinked those gleaming eyes at him, slow and steady. Then he gave a regal nod, as if in understanding. The grasscat made a deep sound, almost a purr.

"I'll be on my way, then," Blaise said, easing around the creature and feeling extremely awkward about the entire conversation.

Suddenly, impossibly, the grasscat sank into the floor. Patches of grass and moss writhed toward Blaise like a shark fin cutting water. Then the grasscat flowed out of the stone beneath him, wood and vegetation reclaiming form. Blaise yelped, pulling on his magic.

The grasscat rose from the floor, Blaise squarely on the elemental's back behind a mane of dandelions and trumpet vine. The grasscat didn't speak, not in the way of a person or even a pegasus. Instead, he sent a series of images and emotions to Blaise. A grasscat leaping at Blaise, then falling to pieces, blown away like chaff on the wind while a malevolent human form watched. A profound sense of sadness tempered with understanding. The scene changed to a peaceful stream, butterflies flitting over it on a sunny day. The grasscat lounging by the water, Blaise at his side, companionable.

Peace. The grasscat sent a message of peaceful intentions. The creature was intelligent enough to know friend from foe. And he didn't blame Blaise for defending himself and others against the compelled felines. Somehow that made Blaise feel even more guilty for having dispatched the others. But now wasn't the time for regrets. It was time for action.

"Can you take me to the alchemist?" Blaise hoped his mother was unharmed in the ruckus.

The grasscat glanced back at him, making a rumble of assent. Then he made an impressive leap, pushing off with powerful hind legs to summit the crates again. The grasscat purposefully stalked along the top, allowing Blaise a better vantage of the warehouse.

Shouts and screams filled the air as men and women stampeded, trying to avoid their attackers as they sought escape. The Copperheads were in disarray, shouting orders to the crowd and one another that no one listened to. Some people were already down, unmoving from injuries they'd sustained. Blaise felt pressure in the air, magic swelling as mages called on it to fight, and mystic races answered with power of their own.

Everyone was too busy fighting or struggling to survive to pay any mind to the grasscat with the mage aboard. Blaise recognized the area they were over, pointing ahead. "That way. I think she's that way!"

The grasscat continued onward. To Blaise's dismay, they discovered that the aisle where Marian was kept bustled with activity. People were trying to claim the alchemist for themselves in the chaos.

Jack was there, too. He must have dropped his Obfuscation spell. There were so many people, he realized the spell would never work as they'd planned. The outlaw attempted to slink around the knots of people trying to slip past each other to get to Marian. The Effigest had resorted to bodily shoving people out of his way.

"Get me down there," Blaise told the grasscat. "Please."

Reluctance shivered through the great cat, but he sprang down. Blaise dropped to the floor, and as soon as he was off, the grasscat whirled away, no doubt eager to make an escape. A dandelion puff floated in his wake. Blaise caught his breath at the sight. *Mom called me a dandelion.*

He swallowed, turning back to the throng. Someone had removed Marian from the cell, gagged and blindfolded, rendering her unable to put up much of a fight—though she was certainly trying, judging by the way she was stomping on insteps. Blaise recognized the men and women directly around his mother as Copperheads. They were no doubt trying to wrest their prize to a safer location.

But others who had gathered were having none of that. "We told you, she's *ours!*"

"Not yours until you make payment," the man who Blaise thought was the Copperhead Ringleader shouted over the cacophony. "We—*stop that man!* Stop Wildfire! He's going to take her!"

Jack had almost gotten to Marian. As one, the surrounding auction attendees turned, all staring at the outlaw. Jack was moving *fast,* but not fast enough. One of the nearby men spun, a book tucked under his arm as he raised a hand and made a grandiose gesture. Jack slowed to a crawl, and Blaise fancied he could almost hear the outlaw's outraged growl. The enemy mage made a gesture that looked suspiciously as if he were lifting a middle finger, and Jack jerked backward, thumping against a wall.

No. The Effigest struggled against the onslaught of magic holding him in place, but he was like a mouse pinned by a cat. The Copperhead Ringleader laughed at Jack's predicament. "I'm gonna enjoy this, Wildfire. You shoulda kept your nose out of our business." Then he cocked his arm back, his knuckles glowing red with power.

Blaise knew what would follow. There was no way he could reach Jack or his assailant in time. But he was close to the mage with the book. Blaise charged at the man.

The mage saw him coming, though. With the book tucked securely in place, he lifted his other hand, and Blaise felt him send the same spell out in his direction. It caught him by surprise as it shoved him back a step. The meaty crunch of a fist smashing into Jack's face split the air. Blaise gritted his teeth and called up his magic, slamming it against the tendrils that sought to drive him back. His power severed the sorcerous threads as easily as if he'd snipped a ribbon. But he didn't stop there. His magic followed the truncated wisps, bridging across to those that held Jack, severing them.

"What?" the mage gasped in surprise as his spell broke.

Jack slumped to the ground, blood pouring from his nose like a grotesque fountain. One of his eyes was screwed shut, but that didn't stop him from lashing out at his attacker now that he was free of the spell. But the outlaw he was fighting was far stronger than he. Another blow from him would do Jack in.

<We're coming!> Emrys's cry filled his mind.

"*Breaker!* That's the Breaker!" someone said excitedly, pointing at Blaise. It was the Copperhead who clutched Marian Hawthorne by the arm.

"Small wonder," the mage with the book huffed, limbering his fingers. "Now I know why my spell failed." He glanced at others who stood nearby. "Get him. He was going to be ours, anyway."

"He ain't yours to claim! He's *ours*," the Ringleader growled, sidestepping an attack from Jack to move into a better position, eyeing Blaise.

The bookish mage shook his head, gesturing for his companions to step closer. "Then you'll have to stop us."

If Blaise thought things were bad before, they suddenly got worse. Magic, bullets, and blades were flying. He crouched, barely able to crawl to Jack, who had pulled himself up onto one elbow, clutching a bandanna tight against his nose.

"You okay?" Blaise asked, though his eyes were on his mother. Her captors were shielding her from the battle, at least. She was too precious to lose.

"Been bether," Jack lisped, spitting blood as he spoke. "Pegathuth coming."

Blaise nodded. "I heard Emrys." All they needed was for the pegasi to arrive—and to extract Marian, somehow. And for no one to get shot, stabbed, punched, or otherwise magically injured. *Easy. Haha, no.*

Jack palmed a poppet, working a spell with a trembling hand. After a moment, the blood stopped running from his nose, so Blaise guessed it was some sort of spell to staunch the wound. "You dithract them."

"What?"

The outlaw glowered, which was a hundred times more menacing when his face was a bloodied and bruised mess. "Dithract!" He waved a hand as if that would help explain what he meant.

"Oh, *distract*."

"That'th thwhat I thaid," Jack griped, clambering to his feet.

Heart thundering in his chest, Blaise stayed low to the ground and wondered what in the world he could do to distract everyone—especially those who held his mother.

<Almost there!>

Blaise swallowed, laying a palm flat against the ground and uncoiling his magic into it. The hard-packed dirt split into great furrows, cracks splintering out from Blaise like a massive spiderweb. People yelled as cages, cells, and stacked crates wobbled and collapsed. Blaise narrowed his eyes, sending a crack toward the Copperheads who had his mother. With a shout, they leaped aside, Marian falling away from them.

Bloody, messy, and glorious, Jack snagged her, tugging her sideways as Zepheus and Oberidon came to the ground, snorting as they struggled to find footing. Emrys landed at the end of the aisle, where he had more room to maneuver. Jack removed Marian's blindfold and helped her climb onto Oberidon's back. As soon as the spotted stallion was airborne, he vaulted onto Zepheus and followed.

<Our turn,> Emrys announced as he charged up the aisle, bulling people out of his way.

Blaise withdrew his hand, pulling back his magic. The ground quieted, though the massive cracks remained. He rose, not realizing the trouble he was in until too late.

A dark-clad hand whipped around him, shoving a square of fabric into his face. Whatever it was, it smelled sickly sweet. Blaise grunted in surprise, trying to twist away but unable to do much of anything.

"I learned from last time," the Herald said, triumphant, as she dropped the cloth and latched onto Blaise's arm.

Blaise wanted to fight back, but he couldn't. It was difficult to even stand, much less try to get away or use his magic. Dark spots swam before his eyes.

He heard an enraged whinny, then the Herald screeched as a large, dark shape plowed into her. Blaise was nearly jerked off his feet by the impact. Too late, he realized it was Emrys, slamming against the Herald to free his rider.

The Herald sank into the wall with a groan, taking Blaise and Emrys with her. Everything went weirdly dark, followed by the sensation of falling sideways.

CHAPTER THIRTY-EIGHT
Crazier Than an Outhouse Fly

Jack

<Emrys and Blaise are *gone!*>

Zepheus's frantic mental cry made little sense to Jack at first. His head still rang from the mighty punch Seymour had dealt, and it was difficult to breathe through his nose. Thank Faedra he'd had enough sense to throw up a weak Stonewall spell, or that blow might have caved his face in. Jack frowned, trying to deduce Zepheus's meaning. *Dead or...?* The palomino was already adjusting his course, retracing his path back to where Emrys would have landed.

<*Gone,*> Zepheus repeated, adamant. <Magicked away!> His tail lashed in his wake.

Magicked away. Anger flooded through the outlaw's veins as he absorbed the information. Who would have taken the pair? And how? Zepheus touched down in the middle of the ruined ground, mindful of the massive furrows Blaise had wrought.

The Salties and Ravanchens were still squabbling with magic and weapons, though few remained on either side. Seymour was face-down in the dirt, blood leaking out from beneath him. Jack reined in the urge to shoot the prone outlaw out of principle; it would be a waste of bullets. And he wasn't one to waste bullets.

<They're growing tired,> Zepheus advised, backing up to stay out of the line of dangerous magics. Jack narrowed his eyes, noting the glossy burn-marks on the nearby wall from arcane magic.

Good. Fancy-pants Ravanchen wizards probably ain't used to a proper magical brawl. And they had shitty aim. Jack glanced around for anything he could use to give him an edge. There was nothing readily available, though the stalls where the pegasi had been held were nearby. He slipped over to them, pleased to discover salt-iron halters and lead ropes. He picked them up, mindful of the salt-iron beads. Jack gritted his teeth against the leeching of his magic.

He returned to the impromptu battlefield. The combatants were breathing hard, sweat glistening on their faces, hair matted against their scalps. They had ignored him until that point because Jack hadn't been fighting them. That was about to change.

The outlaw pulled out his poppet, clutching it tight in his right hand. He dropped the Staunch Wounds spell he'd activated earlier, glad that it had been enough to ease his pain and make it easier to speak. To pull this next trick off, he was going to need as many layers of Speed on his poppet as he could manage. It was going to be a walloping drain on his magic, not counting the slow siphon of the salt-iron.

Jack ignored the blood trickling from his nose as jitteriness washed over him. It was suddenly impossible to stand still. He wanted to *gogogo*. Jack rushed forward, moving so fast his boots barely seemed to touch the ground.

Jack had never layered so many Speed spells on his poppet, and afterward, he vowed to never do so again, without good reason. The sudden, intense burst of speed was like the stoop of a falcon, so quick that his stomach felt like he'd left it behind. Everything around him slowed, as if time itself froze as he flowed forward like living lightning.

He raced to the quartet of attackers who still stood, snatching bits of hair or a dab of freely flowing blood from the pair of Copperheads and attaching them to spare, unattuned poppets he'd kept ready in his pocket. For the Ravanchens, he wrapped the salt-iron halters and ropes around them. *They're going to be pissed.*

That task done, Jack retreated to Zepheus, activating the two new poppets. Then he dropped his own Speed spell and hurriedly threw Paralysis up over the pair.

His spell almost didn't take. Jack felt the magic waver, nearly too brittle to bring the Copperheads to heel. Gods, but that Speed spell had sapped him fast. Jack had a decision to make. If he split his reserves between the pair, they were likely to break the Paralysis quickly. But if he focused it on just one, he stood a better chance.

"Guess I gotta do this the old-fashioned way." Jack drew out his sixgun as he refocused all of his magic on the female Copperhead. He sighted his revolver on the newly freed man, shooting him in the leg to make escape or fighting back difficult.

"Faedra's tits, man!" the wounded outlaw swore, whimpering as he rolled onto his side.

The two wizards from Ravance howled in agony at their salt-iron bondage. They had fallen to the floor, tripped by the ropes, and they writhed as the beads literally burned their flesh. Mages hated salt-iron because it blistered their skin and hurt like the blazes, besides sapping their magic. Wizards were an entirely different thing. The metal was even worse on them. Jack knew he wasn't making friends with anyone here today.

"Which of you assholes are the ones who took the Breaker?" Jack snarled, gaze flicking between the two groups.

The wizards were too busy whining. The paralyzed Copperhead couldn't speak, though her eyes were wide with terror. Good. Jack liked that she was afraid. They should all be afraid.

"Ravance or someone else?" Jack demanded again, swiveling between his captives. "Someone better talk, and soon. I got enough bullets for the lot of you."

"S-stolen from us," one wizard cried after a moment. "Take this off. Take it off!"

Stolen. Blaise was never yours to start with. Jack fought the urge to plant one of the promised bullets in the wizard's skull. But outright murdering wizards from Ravance might cause problems down the road, and he figured it was best to avoid that. The Copperheads, though? They were fair game.

"I want answers, then maybe I'll do something 'bout that." Jack turned to the Copperheads. He loosened the Paralysis spell enough to allow the woman to speak. That was a relief for him as well, using up a little less of his precious magic. "Start talking."

"A Walker took him," the woman rasped.

A Walker. That made sense. But gods, the Walker had taken a *pegasus* too? That would be a huge drain, unless it had been an accident. "Who here has a damned Walker on their side? How did this Walker travel?"

The outlaw shook her head. "Don't know who she belongs to. But she came out of the wall, then back into it. The Breaker and a pegasus went with her."

Jack stared, then cursed softly. The Herald, the same Walker who had tried to get Blaise before and failed. This time, she'd been luckier. And Emrys was with them? *Damn.* At least Blaise wasn't alone with an enemy.

"Any of you lot see that?" Jack demanded of the wizards. One of them whimpered but nodded.

"I've seen her around," the paralyzed Copperhead said. "She was here for the auction, but she'd made inquiries about the Breaker before. Sounded like she got sent to fetch him, no matter what."

"And take him where?" Jack asked.

"Ganland. They—"

Jack hadn't paid attention to the wounded Copperhead, and that had been a mistake. The man had pulled a knife, and he lunged at the paralyzed woman, slitting her throat in a quick motion. Blood fountained, spraying the man and blinding him. Jack growled with renewed rage, sighting his sixgun on the Copperhead and firing. He dropped atop the female desperado, the right side of his face a ruined mess.

The bloodshed made the wizards sob even harder. Jack had learned what he could from the Copperheads. He spun on the wizards. "If I let you up, you gonna play nice?"

They nodded, tears streaming down their faces.

Jack reached down and untangled the halters and ropes, carefully freeing the men. The salt-iron sapped the last dregs of his magic, and he fervently hoped he had no need for it soon. He was done. And damn, but his face hurt, and the blood was becoming more distracting as he tasted it on his tongue. He tossed the ropes aside, his sixgun still out. Not *wanting* to shoot the Ravanchens didn't mean he wouldn't if it came down to it.

The wizards jerked upright. The two men had lost their grimoires in the fall, and Jack took the time to kick them away, far from the pair. Wizards could cast without their spellbooks, but the grimoires strengthened their abilities and made them capable of greater magics than were otherwise possible.

"My father gave me that grimoire!" the dark-haired wizard protested. The telltale signs of salt-iron damage peppered his left cheek. Jack hoped that meant the man would have too little magic left to call the book into his hand.

"Don't care," Jack drawled. "Y'all know anything about these folks in Ganland?"

"N-no," the same wizard gasped. "I promise, we don't. We were only here to purchase the alchemist and the Breaker."

Jack narrowed his eyes. Again, why would Ravance want Marian Hawthorne? As far as he knew, wizards didn't care a lick for alchemy. They figured they were superior to anything an alchemist could whip up. He didn't have time to follow that line of questioning, though. "Get out of my sight. Leave town. If I see you again, I have a bullet with your name on it." Jack glowered at them.

The wizards staggered to their feet, limping over to retrieve their grimoires. Then they turned tail and fled, only glancing over their shoulders to make sure Jack wouldn't shoot them in the back.

Once he was certain they weren't coming back, Jack shut his eyes for a moment. He felt Zepheus move closer, warm equine breath blowing against his face. Jack turned, resting his forehead against the stallion's cheek. "Em and Marian outside with Oby?"

<Yes. Oby keeps demanding to know what's happened.>

Jack's shoulders slumped. He wasn't looking forward to telling Emmaline or Marian Hawthorne that Blaise wasn't coming back with them. Scuffing a heel against the ground, he laid a hand on Zepheus's neck. "Let's regroup with 'em."

"Wildfire!" a voice bellowed. Jack stiffened, expecting to come face-to-face with another of the Copperheads. But when he turned, he saw the white Knossan, Gore, picking his way through the ruined ground. Blood spatter speckled his coat, though Jack saw no visible wounds.

"Gore," Jack acknowledged with a nod of his head.

"I wish to thank you. Our younglings are safe." He snorted, glancing over his shoulder at the surrounding wreckage. "Without your aid, we would have lost them."

Jack relaxed. That was the first bit of good news he'd had, and it was welcome. "Glad to hear it. We weren't as lucky."

"You did not recover the one you sought?"

"We did, but the Breaker got stolen away in the middle of it all."

Gore lowered his horns, his dark eyes somber. "I wish I could assist, but our concern is with our younglings now."

"Nah." Jack waved a hand. "You've the right of it. Get your young-uns to safety." He turned, preparing to mount, though he paused when a thought came to him. "When you go back to Knossas, remember who helped y'all."

The bull surprised him, stooping into a bow so low that the tips of his horns grated against the ruined floor. "We do not forget these things. May Veruc the Great Bull grant you strength." Gore straightened to his impressive full height, turning to plod away.

Jack sighed, swinging into the saddle.

The entire short ride out of the disheveled warehouse, he racked his mind for ways to catch up to the Walker who had stolen Blaise away. What did they want with him? Revenge for Fort Courage? To use him? Or was it a strike against the Gutter? All of those thoughts set Jack's nerves on edge. They were all potential reasons.

Emmaline raced up when they emerged from the warehouse. Marian was nearby, mounted on Oberidon. Good. If the alchemist needed a quick escape, the spotted stallion was their best bet. Emmaline's eyes widened at the mess of his face. Then her gaze searched behind him. "What happened to you? And where's Blaise?"

Jack wiped at the blood trail leaking from his nose. "We'll talk about that some place else." He was painfully aware of the number of people still lurking around the area—and not all would be friendly toward them. He needed to get Marian somewhere secure so that all of this would have been worth *something*, damn it.

Marian stared at him, a lump in her throat. Her knuckles, clutching the pommel of Oberidon's saddle, were white as fresh snow. "They killed him?" Her voice was soft but with a warning rumble reminiscent of a dragoness protecting a clutch of eggs.

"No," Jack answered sharply. *I don't think so, at least.* "C'mon."

They returned the pegasi to the stables. As they walked out, crossing to the inn for a little privacy, Jack froze when he saw a familiar figure looming nearby. Maureen the Dread Surgeon.

She smiled like a crocodile, sauntering over to them, flanked by a handful of Copperheads. They sported a variety of wounds, many of them limping with the effort.

"Wildfire Jack, seems I owe you my thanks," the Dread Surgeon said, cocking her head at him. Jack narrowed his eyes—well, his one good eye. The other was too swollen to cooperate. His fingers twitched, ready to pull his sixgun if needed. "You got rid of Seymour for me, and I didn't so much as have to lift a finger. My hands are clean as a drake's fangs."

He pursed his lips, trying to figure out if she truly was thanking him or if another shoe was about to drop. "I reckon that's not the full truth, but Seymour deserved what he got." Jack shrugged, deciding not to explain that he'd only indirectly been responsible for Seymour's demise. Let them think he was the one who ended the Copperhead leader. More renown for the Scourge of the Untamed Territory never hurt. "Now, if you don't mind, I got things to do."

Jack started forward, though he was still ready to draw if the Copperheads threatened them or made a move to seize Marian.

Maureen held up a hand. "Whatever you may think, I *am* beholden to you for offing Seymour. Let me heal your face, at least."

Jack wondered what Seymour had done to make her so happy the outlaw was dead. And why hadn't she used her own fearsome magic against him to unseat him before? He remembered the shock of Seymour's magic-enhanced fist meeting his face—yeah, that alone might be reason to fear the man. His throbbing face reminded him that he needed to decide. Could he trust the Dread Surgeon? Nadine was one thing. Maureen was something else.

His indecision must have been obvious. She took a step forward. "Wildfire Jack Dewitt, I don't *want* to be beholden to you. But right now, I am—and I'm going to be pissed if I don't get to pay this off with a simple healing."

"I take a life, and you repay me by closing wounds? Seems imbalanced," Jack remarked.

"Think of it as a life for a life," Maureen said, her grin downright threatening.

She's crazier than an outhouse fly. Jack's thumb nudged his holster, debating. But as unhinged as she was, she seemed somehow…sincere? He sighed. "Fine."

She moved over to him almost too eagerly, and Jack had to fight back the desire to strike out as she laid her hands on his face. He'd suffered healing from terrible Healers before, and he figured she might be similar. Jack felt the warmth of her magic flow into him, probing his broken nose, the bruises and battered flesh of his face, and his swollen eye. He prepared himself for the jagged glass feeling he feared might accompany her working but it never came. Instead, her magic was more like being covered by a warm blanket: comfortable and soothing.

So at odds with the woman wielding the power.

When she stepped back, Maureen watched him expectantly. "Well?"

"I'm good, thanks," Jack said gruffly. He decided not to remark on her abilities. She was called the Dread Surgeon for a reason, but her healing was skillful. Nurturing. He suspected she curated the rough reputation to protect herself. "Your debt is paid—as long as y'all keep your grubby hands off the alchemist. She's under my protection."

Maureen nodded. "You have until dusk tomorrow, Wildfire Jack. Any of you and yours who linger at that point are fair game."

"Good enough," he rumbled, pointedly aware that this meant he would no longer be welcome in Thorn. Not unexpected, all things considered. Jack watched as Maureen and her gang sauntered away before turning and gesturing for Emmaline and Marian to head into the inn.

"I was ready to kill her if she did anything to you," Emmaline whispered as they climbed the stairs.

Jack smiled. "Glad you've got my back." He pushed open the door to their room and ushered them inside.

As soon as the door closed, Marian whirled on him. "Start talking. Where is my son? What's happened to him?" Emmaline stood beside her, hands on her hips, the same questions afire in her eyes.

With a resigned sigh, Jack recounted what had happened and the scant information he had learned. "So, Blaise is half a continent away or more." Suddenly, he felt exhausted, as if the sum of his exertion for the day had finally come crashing down on him. But he couldn't stop, not now.

"We have to go get him!" Emmaline didn't even hesitate. She looked ready to bolt out the door right at that moment.

Jack sat on the bed, wishing he could lie down and lose himself to the oblivion of sleep. "We will, but it's going to take time. We have to find another pegasus to hire for Marian. And even then, Zeph and Oby need a break. They're as dog tired as we are." He closed his eyes. "Or we could find a ship, but…" That would allow all of them a chance to rest and recover, but a voyage by sea, even aboard a fancy steamer, would take too long. It was far from a direct route.

"If you think you know where he is, one of you could take us there. You're mages, after all," Marian said.

Jack cracked an eye open, scowling. "We're Effigests. Neither of us can manage a spell like that." And even if that *was* in an Effigest's bag of tricks, a working that size would take the collaboration of a coven.

"You're *mages*, and you *can*," Marian insisted.

He wanted to argue that she knew nothing of mages or what they could or couldn't do, but that wasn't right. She *did* know mages. She had *made* a mage. Jack glanced at Emmaline, who shrugged. She was as uninformed as he was on this idea, at least. "Explain."

"What separates a mage from a wizard?" Marian asked.

Jack pressed his lips together, annoyed that she would stall with a question. "Mages specialize in magic that comes naturally to them and takes minimal training—sometimes none." When she nodded, he continued, "Wizards don't have any specialties, can only cast a couple of spells without reading from a grimoire. But their pool of magic is deeper than a mage's."

The alchemist snapped her fingers. "There were grimoires in the warehouse."

Jack cocked his head. "You think we can cast a travel spell if we find a grimoire with one?" He didn't like the sound of that—it seemed awfully risky.

"Yes."

Hope gleamed in Emmaline's eyes at the simple word. "We should try, Daddy."

Jack shook his head. "I'm wrung out—no way would I have the reserves needed to cast a wizard-class spell. Even if you bolstered me."

Marian sat at the foot of the bed. "Do you remember the potion that Doyen Gaitwood used on Blaise?"

Immediately, Jack turned, eyes narrowed. "That was *you?*" The potion had almost been the Breaker's end, threatening to tear him apart and take everyone nearby with him. Would this woman's evil never end? Gods, had it been a mistake for Blaise to come after her?

"I didn't have a *choice*," Marian said hotly, arms crossed. "They had my family. And I didn't know they were going to use it on *Blaise*." Her voice broke when she said his name, frustrated tears glistening in her eyes. She raked a hand through her curly hair. "Gods, do you think I *want* to hurt him?"

"Didn't stop you the first time," Jack growled, ignoring the way Emmaline's eyebrows slammed up in surprise. He forgot there were some things she wasn't privy to.

"That's not an argument for here, but I'll be damned if you think I haven't regretted every moment of suffering that I've caused him." She trembled. "No matter what anyone may think, I'm his *mother*. I *love* him." Marian's face crumpled, helpless tears streaming down her cheeks.

Jack almost felt sorry for making her cry, but not fully. Blaise didn't deserve a lick of what had happened to him. He was just another soul thrown into the hungry maw of the Confederation, as Jack had been. "Fine. Tell us about your *potion*, then."

Emmaline offered Marian a handkerchief, and it was a moment before the alchemist composed herself enough to speak. She swallowed. "It's the Elixir of Overwhelming Magic. They gave Blaise a modified version because they…" Marian shook her head. "They didn't care if it killed him in the end. It floods the mage who takes it with a deep river of magic, replenishing anything used as quickly as it's spent."

"What's the cost?" Jack asked. There was always a cost, some detrimental side effect.

"When the effects wear off, the mage is exhausted and helpless."

Ha. Already there. Jack frowned. "And you think it'd be enough to power a wizard spell?"

Marian rubbed her forehead. "That was part of the ultimate goal."

Jack bit back a comment at that. Sounded like the Confederation was hoping for their own wizard-class mages. *Small wonder Ravance was so interested in Marian. They wouldn't want magical competition from the Confederation.* "There's a reagent shop in town."

The alchemist shook her head. "This isn't your run-of-the-mill potion. It's specialized. It requires rare reagents." She gave a grim smile. "Reagents that I'm fairly certain are in that warehouse."

Jack rose from the bed. "Sounds like we better get back to the warehouse, then."

CHAPTER THIRTY-NINE

Globetrotter

Blaise

Blaise didn't know how long he fell sideways into the darkness. He knew he was screaming. Someone else was screaming, too— the Walker who had grabbed him. And there were snorts and throaty sounds from Emrys, the clatter of hooves failing to find purchase on... wherever they were. *Emrys.* Blaise couldn't let the stallion come to harm.

He wanted to slam his power against the Herald's, shattering her hold on them. Blaise tried to call on his magic, but it was sluggish. Slippery, like trying to catch a minnow from a stream. Out of his grasp for the moment.

"Let go of me, or I'll make sure you get turned into glue!" the Walker howled as they traversed the void of miles.

Suddenly, they stopped. Blaise was breathless, as if he had run the distance they'd covered himself. He fell down onto the ground—*grass*— panting and rolling onto his side. He felt dizzy, his muscles non-responsive from the sweet-smelling fabric.

Wherever they were, the sun was still up. Emrys was a dark, thrashing shape, snorting and shrilling his anger. Blaise groggily fought to sit up, to go to the stallion, but a hand grabbed his arm—

"No!" Blaise wailed. He was about to be dragged back into the Walker's world, and he had no way to fight back. Then the Walker went flying, releasing his arm.

A shadowy form loomed over him. Blaise was vaguely aware of Emrys trying to talk to him, but his mind was too clouded. He felt as if he'd been spinning in circles. His stomach lurched with nausea, and he fought dry heaves for longer than he liked. Eventually, he rolled onto his back, staring at the sky.

They were outside. They must have traveled westward—the sun was still up, though it was low. Emrys stood over him, a protective bulwark against the unknown. Blaise groaned.

<Can you hear me now?>

"Yeah," Blaise grunted, slowly easing into a seated position. The movement agitated his nausea again, and he had to take a deep breath before he trusted himself to speak. "Sorry."

<Are you okay?> Emrys asked, head lowered as he sucked in Blaise's scent. <You smell ill.>

Blaise nodded, then regretted that, too. "I think if I stand or move, I'll throw up. Or if I do...anything." He wanted to curl into a ball and sleep, but he was afraid if he did that, he would never wake up again.

The stallion made a concerned rumble. <Then stay still. I'll watch over you until you can move.>

That made Blaise feel a little better. He was somewhere far away from Jack, Emmaline, and...oh gods, his mother. He swallowed, tears stinging his eyes. *No, don't dwell on that. I'm not with my friends, but I have Emrys. I'm not alone.* All the same, he couldn't shrug off the utterly helpless feeling.

"What happened to the Walker?" He had seen no sign of her.

<I kicked her into the wall of the barn, and she vanished.>

Well, at least he hopefully wouldn't have to worry about the Herald coming after him any time soon. Not unless she wanted another attack from the pegasus. "Do you know where we are?" Blaise whispered, squeezing his eyes shut. He felt less queasy when his eyes weren't open.

<Not yet. A farm, maybe? Lots of grass. Rolling hills. I smell cows and pine trees in the distance.>

Cows and pine trees. "Desina, maybe?" Blaise couldn't help but feel hopeful at the prospect. Just thinking of Desina made him homesick. Made him think of his mother...

A velvety nose brushed his face, and a rough tongue swiped his cheek, catching a salty tear. <I don't know. But stop with those thoughts, whatever they are. We are together. We are safe for the moment. I will let no one hurt you or take you away from me.> Blaise imagined the stallion had his ears laid back flat against his head at that fierce declaration.

"Thank you," Blaise murmured. Gods, he didn't know what the Walker had planned to do with him. *Don't think, don't think.* He focused on breathing and taking in everything his senses told him. The evening wind tousled his hair, carrying the earthy fragrances of the countryside to him.

Grasshoppers sang, and sandpipers trilled. It was peaceful, and in other circumstances, he would have enjoyed his surroundings.

Night had fallen by the time Blaise trusted himself to stand. Clutching Emrys, he shakily got to his feet, momentarily proud that he no longer wanted to puke. But then he realized they were alone in the dark, with no idea where they were or if there was a safe place to spend the night. Or get food, when his stomach felt like keeping something down.

<I am saddled, and your canteen is still attached. There may be food in the saddlebags, too,> Emrys reminded him. <If you get on my back, we can start traveling and perhaps orient ourselves.>

That wasn't a terrible idea. Blaise didn't have any better ones. He took a swig of water, checking the saddlebags. Emrys was right—there were a few scanty rations, mostly dried fruit and jerky. But it would do, when food appealed to him. *Things are looking up.*

Emrys hid his wings, and a few minutes later, had found a road. Even with the moon out, it was dark. Blaise couldn't see a thing, but the pegasus assured him he could see well enough.

They didn't find a town, but Emrys located a clearing off the beaten path that would serve for the night. Blaise wished his bedroll had been packed along with the rest of his gear, but he was exhausted, and honestly, he had slept in worse conditions.

Jefferson didn't visit his dreams that night. Blaise was so tired that not even nightmares invaded his sleep. He had hoped for the Dreamer, though. While he knew they could do little for one another with the distance between them, there was much to be said for finding comfort in the one you loved.

In the morning, Blaise's stomach felt better. He kept down a handful of dried fruit before setting off with Emrys again.

<I wish I dared to fly. That would be the easiest way to figure out where we are,> Emrys said as he trotted along.

"Not worth the risk," Blaise agreed. Then he raised his brows when Emrys slowed, nostrils flared. "What is it?"

<Salt and surf.> He flicked an ear. <We're near the coast.>

But the coast of where? Though a coast was a good sign—they were more likely to run into fishing villages or ports. As they continued on, they came across wooden signs listing the names of a few small towns, though Blaise didn't recognize any of them.

"Could be Desina. Maybe Mella? Even Ganland." His breath caught. What if they were in Ganland? But the odds of that were slim.

<If we are in Desina, it would be a simple thing to fly to the Gutter,> Emrys reasoned. <I don't think we're in Mella. I would smell the mountains, and we would see them to the north.>

True enough. They plowed onward, and all the while, Blaise worried about what they would do. He didn't have any coin, so it wasn't as if he could pay for food once his meager supplies ran out. Or lodgings. He was so busy mulling through his limited options, he didn't notice the sound of hooves approaching them.

A pair of riders came into view—local wardens, judging by their clothing. Green and white: the colors of Ganland.

Blaise swallowed, nodding to the wardens as they loped past. The riders vanished down the road, no doubt on pressing business that had nothing to do with Breakers who had been spirited far away. "We're in Ganland." He wasn't sure if that was fortuitous or not. If they ran across a Salt-Iron Confederation contingent, they'd be in trouble. But Ganland also meant people he knew. Flora, Kittie, and Mindy. And somewhere, *Jefferson.*

<I saw. Should we follow the wardens and ask for help?>

Blaise shook his head. "No." He wasn't sure who he could trust. "I'd rather find our people. Let's get to a town and ask for directions to Nera."

Emrys arched his neck. <Sounds like a plan.>

EMRYS'S NAVIGATION INSTINCTS WERE THEIR SAVING GRACE. BLAISE NEVER came across anyone he felt confident asking for directions to Nera, but it wasn't long before the stallion recognized their surroundings from their previous ill-fated trip to Ganland.

<This is the road we traveled from Seaside to Nera,> Emrys insisted with certainty, though Blaise didn't feel so sure. He didn't recognize the scenery at all, but that was no surprise. The last time he had taken this road, his murky future had distracted him.

But Emrys was right. By mid-afternoon, Blaise's breath hitched at the welcome sight of Jefferson's ostentatious estate situated outside the city. The gate from the road to the house was open, and Emrys trotted up unhindered. Though, the pegasus drew to a stiff-legged halt when he heard a throaty whinny.

Emrys's nostrils flared, his head held at attention. Then he surged forward. <Seledora is here!>

Seledora? Did that mean Jefferson was here, too? Blaise's heart galloped along with Emrys's hooves as the stallion bolted toward the stables. The grey mare appeared in a paddock, though it took her little effort to flit over the fence and greet them. A groom walked out of the stable, scratching his forehead in puzzlement.

"Wasn't expecting any visitors—oh, it's you." The groom's eyes went wide when he recognized Blaise from his last visit, though it had been several months. He straightened. "You have my condolences, Mr. Hawthorne."

Condolences? Blaise frowned at the confusing words as he slid out of the saddle. "Um, thanks. Can you see to Emrys? Give him a good rubdown and some oats—though make sure he doesn't eat them too quickly."

"Of course," the groom agreed, giving a deferential nod.

Emrys was busy catching up with Seledora. The mare was still frosty toward the black stallion, but she was curious, wondering how—and why —they had come to Ganland. She flicked a black-tipped ear at Blaise, then turned to him once Emrys followed the groom into the stable to be pampered.

Seledora's eyes gleamed like amber in the afternoon light. <What is this Emrys tells me of a Walker dragging you across half a continent?>

Blaise sighed. "That's a story I'd rather not recount multiple times. Is Jefferson here?"

The mare lowered her head, and Blaise got the sense that she was mourning. But why? <He is...not. But Flora, Kittie, and Mindy are.> She paused again, ears pricked toward the house. <I've told them you are here, and Mindy is directing one of the staff to bring refreshments to the parlor. Ask them to open a window for me.>

"Okay," Blaise agreed, too worn to do anything else. He turned and strode to the house, but he didn't get far before Flora appeared at his side.

The half-knocker looked as rough as Blaise feared he did. Her pink hair, which was normally well-kempt, was scraggly, with flyaways framing her face. Her eyes were red, as if she'd had little sleep or had cried a lot...or both. Flora's mouth opened, and Blaise half expected some catty remark, but she closed it again, shaking her head.

"Flora, what's wrong?" Blaise asked, bothered by...well, everything. It was so un-Flora-like.

She swallowed a lump in her throat, stopping to look up at him. "I know we should wait until we're inside, but...oh gods, Blaise. I'm so sorry." Flora surprised him by wrapping her long, slender arms around him in a hug. She released him quickly, sniffling. "Sorry. Forgot you don't like that." Flora wiped away a tear.

"It's okay," Blaise murmured. He was still shy of touch from most people, but he felt safe around Flora. "I've never seen you like this. What's going on?"

Flora sighed heavily. "There's no good way to tell you. Jefferson's dead."

Her words chilled him to the core. Blaise staggered backward as if he'd been physically struck. "What? How?"

"There was a fire."

Oh. Blaise immediately relaxed. His foggy brain had forgotten that not everyone knew what he knew. "Jefferson's not dead."

The half-knocker reached out and patted his hand, and Seledora bumped him with her nose, as if offering her own form of support. "I know you don't want to think that, Blaise. But there's no way he could have survived. We found a body. I thought you'd heard, and that was why you came."

Blaise shook his head. "That's not why I came. And he's *alive.*"

Flora gave him a pained look. "I wish he were, too. But if he were, we would have found him by now. Some Healer would have brought him forward."

Gah, Blaise hated trying to explain things to people. Especially when he was as exhausted as he was. "Let's go inside and talk." That would give him a little breathing room to puzzle out an explanation.

Flora nodded, leading the way into the elegant home. Everything about it was Jefferson, from the fine artwork adorning the walls to the plush rugs lining the hallways. They filed into a parlor where Kittie and Mindy awaited, the promised refreshments laid out on a table. Kittie watched him closely when he walked in, questions bright in her eyes.

"Hi, Blaise," Mindy greeted him, though her usual warmth was missing. The trip had been hard on her, too, it seemed. She frowned at the food, then glanced at him. "The ham and mustard sandwich. That's what you need."

"Howdy. And thanks," he replied, sinking down onto the softest couch in the room. Oh, what he wouldn't give to peel off his boots, stuff his face with food, and then sleep. But that had to wait. He appeased his stomach by loading a small plate with food—complete with Mindy's sandwich recommendation—before turning back to the matter at hand. "Seledora was hoping someone would open the window for her." At his request, Flora pulled one open, and the mare thrust her head inside.

"You're a long way from Fortitude," Kittie said, her tone neutral yet somehow still bristling with questions.

"And that's a long story for later," Blaise replied. First things first. "Like I was telling Flora, Jefferson's *not* dead."

"How do you know?" Kittie asked sharply. Almost defensive, as if she were protecting herself.

<The dreamscape?> Seledora asked, nostrils flared as she made the private query. <He dreamed to you?> Then, before he could even think to reply, she snapped her teeth. <Wait, say nothing.>

Blaise winced. He had forgotten that of those present, only Flora and Seledora knew about Jefferson's magic. It wasn't his place to divulge that secret, even among friends. Too late, he realized it would have been wiser to make his explanations outside to Flora and Seledora. His brain raced for a plausible explanation and failed entirely.

"I just do," he said, though he knew he sounded like a petulant child, unwilling to acknowledge the truth of the matter. "It's *Jefferson*. He's cunning."

"Even the most intelligent people die," Mindy said, staring down at her plate of food as if she'd lost her appetite.

Blaise glanced at Kittie, and an idea came to mind. "Everyone thought *you* were dead for years. But Jack never gave up hope."

The Pyromancer's eyes narrowed, and her mouth curled as if his words made her thoughtful. "You're not wrong about that. For your sake, I'll hope that you're right." She leaned forward. "Now, will you tell us what you're doing here, hundreds of miles from where you're *supposed* to be? And why do I suspect my husband is tangled up in it?"

As much as he hated being the center of attention, Blaise recounted the entire mess to them. Kittie didn't seem surprised that both Jack and Emmaline had accompanied Blaise, but the pride that glittered in her eyes was unmistakable when Blaise spoke of their deeds.

When he finished, Kittie crossed her arms. "So, what will Jack and Emmaline do now that they've rescued your mother?"

Blaise shook his head. "I don't know." By now, they had to know he'd been stolen away. How would they react? Would Jack come unglued? Or after the chaos they'd sowed at the auction, were they fleeing from Thorn for their lives? He couldn't even imagine what they would do now. He hoped they'd go back to Fortitude, where they would be safe.

But this was Wildfire Jack Dewitt, and when had he ever done something that would guarantee his safety? Still, perhaps he would—if only for Emmaline. And maybe Marian.

"You've been through a lot," Flora announced at the tail end of his accounting. "Blaise, you look like you need a good soak in the tub and then rest in a decent bed."

"I do," he agreed, and he rose from his seat with a groan. His muscles were happy to remind him of everything he'd been through the last few days. A soak in a warm tub sounded downright amazing. He bid Kittie and Mindy goodnight and followed the half-knocker to the suite of rooms reserved for Jefferson.

Flora wasn't lying about the bath. She called for a staff member to prepare one, and the man hurried off to see to the request. But when the door closed behind the staffer and they heard the distant sounds of preparations, she held up a hand. Flora marched over to a window and hauled it open, revealing Seledora. Mare and half-knocker eyed him. "Start talking. How do you know he's alive?" Hope clung to Flora's words like the last golden leaf on an autumnal tree branch.

"The dreamscape," Blaise whispered. "He pulled me into it..." He paused, trying to figure out what day it was. "Not last night. The night before, I think? Anyway, not more than three nights ago. When was the fire?"

"Four days ago," Flora replied, pensive. She traded looks with Seledora. "How certain are you it was him? And that you weren't just dreaming *about* him?"

"Absolutely certain," Blaise answered without hesitation. "He told me he lost the ring I gave him, and I was mad at him for that, but also sort of glad because I missed him. And *no*, before you ask again, I didn't just dream that. I know it was real because we brought *Jack* into the dreamscape, too. That was how we planned the auction escape."

Seledora laid back her ears. <If that's true, then why hasn't he shown up? Is he hurt? What happened?>

"He said a group called the Quiet Ones have him," Blaise said. No recognition flared in Flora's eyes at the word, and with chagrin, he realized they truly were a shadowy organization. "They attacked him during the fire, and he took his ring off so he'd stand a chance against them."

"Then why hasn't *he* tried to tell me any of this? He's pulled me into the dreamscape before," Flora pointed out, as if she were reluctant to believe him.

"He can't," Blaise said. "Wherever he is, it's warded. And somehow he can only get to me because..." He shrugged. "I guess because my magic broke a crack in the ward?"

She stared at him. "All of that sounds absolutely unhinged, and that makes me think you're probably right."

"Er, thanks." Blaise rubbed the back of his head. "One more thing, though. The Quiet Ones are forcing him to be Malcolm again, declaring Jefferson dead in the fire. They took his cabochon ring away."

Anger flashed across Flora's eyes. "*Schist.*" She shook her head, plainly understanding how painful that would be to Jefferson. Seledora made a fierce rumbling sound, shaking her head. "But you say the Quiet Ones will send him back to Nera? To continue to campaign for the Gutter?"

Blaise nodded. "That's what he said."

Flora chewed on her lower lip, thinking. "Okay. I'll figure out something to tell Kittie and Mindy."

A knock sounded on the door, and the steward returned, eyeing their odd group. "Mr. Hawthorne, your bath is ready. Do you need help undressing?"

Flora bit back a laugh, which made Blaise suspect she was feeling a little better about things. Meanwhile, he kept the horrified look off his face that would normally crawl across it at such a question. "Um, no, thank you, I'll be fine."

"As you wish." The steward slipped out.

The half-knocker released a long sigh. "I'll let you get cleaned up. You look like you really *were* dragged across half the continent. Then get some rest." She paused at the door. "You think you'll see Jefferson tonight?"

I hope so. But there was no way he could guarantee it. "I don't know. He wasn't in my dreams last night." He paused. Was it last night? He'd lost track of time.

<Jefferson is a man of many surprises. We won't count him out,> Seledora said, withdrawing her head from the room.

Flora ran a hand through her mussed hair. "Yeah. Get yourself cleaned up now. You stink." On that note, she left him to his privacy.

Blaise sighed, then shucked off his boots, leaving them by the door. He had learned from his previous visit that Jefferson's steward would no doubt slip in, remove his worn clothing, and replace it with something fresh. Any other time he would have thought that intrusive, but he welcomed it now. Blaise was glad that he was nose blind to himself, figuring that Flora was probably right about the smell. He piled his clothing in a stack beside the boots, then headed to the bath.

The warm water and suds were so delightful he nearly fell asleep as he relaxed and washed away grime. If only the troubles that dogged them would be as easy to wash away as the dust of travel.

CHAPTER FORTY
Portal Fantasy

Jack

They weren't the only ones with plans to loot the ruined warehouse. Other outlaws and thieves had fallen on the damaged structure like carrion birds to a rotting carcass, and Maureen's Copperheads had their hands full trying to dissuade the interlopers.

"That's gonna be a problem," Jack grumbled as he, Emmaline, and Marian huddled outside the building. If he had the magic for it, he could use Obfuscation again on himself, and Emmaline could do likewise. But he was too depleted to cast it on himself, much less Marian, and he didn't want to suggest Emmaline cast on the alchemist.

"No, it's not," Emmaline said, stepping forward. Jack's brows shot up, and he caught her arm. She stiffened, looking over her shoulder at him. Defiance and self-assurance gleamed in her eyes. "Daddy, let me do this. I can be a distraction."

Inwardly, he growled. He was the one who wanted to take risks, to be the distraction. But Emmaline was coming into her own, trying to show that she was capable. And damn it, she was. Jack would only cause more harm by denying her this chance. Besides, he had done a thousand more feats of derring-do by the time he was her age. "Don't do anything I'd do."

"Nah, I'll be smart about it," she quipped, flashing him a grin as he released her arm.

Be careful. I love you. He watched her stride off, the words unspoken but on his lips. But she knew, he hoped.

"That's a good girl you've got there," Marian remarked.

"The best," Jack agreed, voice gruff. He cleared his throat, shifting his weight from foot to foot as he waited. Emmaline would need time, but he was impatient. He wanted to get this going.

After several minutes, he heard shouts and the steady thump of boots on the ground. Jack took that as their signal, and he and the alchemist slipped inside the warehouse. The interior was dim, many of the mage-lights broken during the havoc they'd created. As they walked down the long aisle of overturned cages, dark remnants of blood spatter were visible.

"There," Marian whispered, pointing at the toppled crates in the far corner of the warehouse, near the location where the Copperheads had kept her.

Some of them had come open, the contents spilled across the floor. Gems glittered amid dried herbs, cracked vials of powder, and harvested bits of once-living creatures. Jack recognized the flexible, feather-like scales from dragons, gleaming like sun-fired copper. The spiraling horn of a unicorn. The tanned skin of a chupacabra, the runic patterns dull on the musty hide. He curled his lip as Marian crouched down, picking through the items.

"Awful, all of it," Jack muttered.

The alchemist glanced up at him. "Plenty of blood on your hands, or so you've told me." He fought the urge to sneer at her comment. "You should look for a grimoire."

The grimoires. Jack didn't like being told what to do, but the sad fact was he'd been distracted from his purpose, and Marian was right. But that didn't mean he had to acknowledge her rightness. He made a face and spun, heading over to a promising area that held a jumbled collection of scrolls.

Something caught his eye on the way over. Jack diverted from his course, eyeing the small upside-down crate. He shoved a mess of scrolls out of his path, crouching to right the crate. Jack recognized the rising sun insignia painted neatly on the box, and he wondered if he dared believe it was legitimate.

He pried the top open, whistling when he saw its contents. *Rare.* A single fire pot nestled in a protective cover of phoenix feathers, a strip of dragonhide wrapped around the feathers to keep them together.

"Can't believe they got their grimy hands on one of these." Jack wondered if the Copperheads even knew what they had. It was likely they didn't. He carefully closed the top of the crate again, then picked it up. Though his primary mission was to find a grimoire, he saw nothing wrong with liberating a little something extra. He rose, returning to his original search.

It was downright strange that the Copperheads had snagged grimoires for their auction. From what Jack knew, wizards didn't let go of their spellbooks easily. The Ravanchens gifted grimoires to young wizards when they showed an aptitude for magic, and they kept the book with them for the rest of their lives. *Grave robbers, maybe.* When a wizard died, their tome went to the grave with them.

Jack found a toppled crate of grimoires, the books a disheveled mess. He pursed his lips. The magic wafting from the tomes was palpable, akin to holding a hand over a flame and feeling a halo of warmth. The outlaw crouched down, studying the pile of books. He reached out, snagging the nearest one to pull it closer, nose wrinkling at the musty bouquet rising from it.

He frowned at the tome, expecting it to be warded against use by anyone other than the owner. But he was able to open it without issue, and he thumbed through the contents, searching for something helpful. *Damn cocky wizards, leaving their grimoires where any old cuss can read 'em.* Jack wasn't going to look a gift pegasus in the mouth, though.

Footsteps announced Marian's arrival, a heavy bag slung over her shoulder. "Any luck?"

Jack kept his eyes on the page, unwilling to admit he'd been distracted on his way to the spellbooks. "Not yet, but there's more to go through."

The alchemist shrugged the bag from her shoulder, resting it on the floor. "I could have a look, too." She reached for one of the nearest books.

Inwardly, Jack cringed at an alchemist handling anything magic-related. It was just plain *wrong*. But he wasn't about to turn down an offer to go through the mess of grimoires. Besides, it wasn't as if she were unfamiliar with mages—she'd raised one. "Have at it."

"I'll look, too."

Jack nearly jumped out of his skin, sixgun at the ready, when he realized Emmaline had snuck up on him courtesy of her Obfuscation spell. She wore a broad grin, no doubt enjoying the opportunity to toy with him. Emmaline had the invigorated look of someone who had stirred up trouble and had a grand time doing it.

"Son of a bat-eared harpy, don't *do* that." Jack glowered at her, then gestured to a stack of grimoires. "Get to readin'. I take it you had luck?"

She nodded, not contrite at all, as she picked up a tome. "Yeah, we have maybe twenty minutes."

Twenty minutes. It would have to do. They set to work, flipping through the grimoires on the hunt for the right spell. One of the books was devoted entirely to turning people into different animals, while another seemed to be some sort of magical cookbook. The cookbook made him think of Blaise, which only served to further his irritation as book after book proved useless.

"This one, maybe?" Emmaline asked a few minutes later, her fingers tracing the handwritten words.

Jack set his book aside and scooted closer, leaning over her shoulder. His excitement grew as he scanned the words. "Portal. Yeah, that's exactly what we need."

"Good, because I don't think this one was even a grimoire," Marian said, shoving her current read aside. "Unless there's something magical about treating toenail fungus."

"This is solid," Jack murmured, nodding with satisfaction. He still wasn't convinced they *could* cast the spell, but it was certainly worth a shot. The only problem was the amount of power drain that would come with it. The note at the very bottom of the page gave him reason to suspect that this portal would bankrupt even a wizard.

Marian tossed a canvas sack over to them. "Stow it in that."

Jack nodded. He held the sack open while Emmaline carefully tucked it inside. Then he glanced at the stack of other grimoires, debating if they should try to run off with more. No telling what might happen if they fell into the wrong hands.

"We should go," Marian said, turning at the sound of boots treading their way.

"Yeah, let's get out of here," Jack agreed, though he scooped up an armful of additional grimoires as they hurried out of the warehouse.

JACK STEEPLED HIS FINGERS, STARING AT THE GRIMOIRE SITTING ON THE bedside table. It was almost dusk, and they needed to get out of Thorn before Maureen made good on her promise.

He straightened to alertness when the door creaked open, but it was only Emmaline and Marian. They had gone outside to allow the alchemist to make the final touches on her potion—she feared that the fumes from her creation might make them ill if she continued to work in the small room.

"All done?" Jack rumbled, eyeing the flask in Marian's hand.

"Yes," she answered, though she traded a glance with Emmaline.

They'd been scheming away from him, no doubt. He frowned. "Out with it."

"Daddy, I think I should be the one to cast the portal spell," Emmaline said, her words coming out in a flurry. "And I know you don't want me to, but it makes sense. We're traveling more than half a continent away.

Marian says the magical draw is gonna be huge, and whoever casts it is probably going to be unconscious when we arrive." She held up a hand when Jack opened his mouth to interject. "It can't be you. *First,* you're still wanted in the Confederation, and you'll be impossible to defend if you're senseless. *Second,* you've been to Ganland—and my single rescue trip there doesn't account for much." She sucked in a breath. "And if Blaise is in trouble, you stand the best shot of helping him."

Jack pursed his lips, shaking his head. "You don't give yourself enough credit, daughter of mine." The smile that bloomed on her face warmed his heart. And damn, he didn't want to allow this, but it made sense. His reservoir of magic had refilled a bit, but he wasn't at full power yet. Emmaline was fresher than he was, and with the potion, she would be a veritable locomotive. "You got this."

Her eyes lit up, and she turned to take the flask from Marian. "I won't let you down, Daddy."

"I know you won't." Gods, but he was so proud of her. And scared. But mostly proud. Jack swung his gaze to take in the room. Most everything was loaded in the saddlebags. He watched as Marian stuffed the grimoire back in its carry sack. "Let's get down to the pegasi."

Together, they went to the stables. Zepheus and Oberidon were already tacked up, raring to go. The stallions pranced out of their stalls, heads high. The palomino snorted at the sun dipping on the western horizon. <Running out of time.>

"Yeah, we're getting to it," Jack muttered, patting Zepheus's glossy neck.

Emmaline studied the spellbook, worrying at her lower lip. "This says I need turquoise to anchor it."

Jack nodded. He had studied the spell to know what Emmaline was up against. Judging by the way the spell was written, the wizard liked to use an actual door with a turquoise-inset frame. But the caster had apparently made it work without the same set-up as well. The grimoire's owner had jotted notes in the margin, detailing that without a doorway, the turquoise had to be placed north and south. Jack dug in his carry pouch and pulled out a pair of the blue-green stones, passing them to Emmaline.

"Didn't know you carried these," she remarked, then crouched down to place them in position, about six feet apart. Emmaline's goal was to create a portal large enough for the pegasi to pass through, so they would leave no one behind.

"I—" Jack began, then a braying laugh cut him off.

"Wildfire Jack! I thought you would have left town by now," Maureen called, standing in front of the livery. She was flanked by a half-dozen other Copperheads, all spoiling for a fight.

Emmaline's eyes widened. "Marian, give me the flask." She held out a hand, and without a word, Marian thumped the flask into her palm, its contents sloshing.

Jack turned away from his daughter and the alchemist, though he desperately wanted to make sure all went according to plan. But he had to trust Emmaline in this. The pegasi moved to flank him, presenting a unified front. Jack made a show of lazily pulling out his pocket watch. "Huh. Judging by my watch, we still have a few minutes." He hazarded a quick glance behind him. The lowest edge of the sun touched the distant horizon.

Maureen put her hands on her hips. "Cutting it close, aren't you?" She smiled. "It'll be fun to play with you and your pony."

Zepheus snorted at the insult, mantling his wings.

C'mon, Em. "We had a bargain, Maureen."

Behind the pegasi, Emmaline made a gasping retch. *Must have drank the flask.* Jack fought the urge to spin and make sure she was okay. He narrowed his eyes, keeping his attention on the Copperheads.

Maureen tilted her head, taking a step forward. She smiled, but it wasn't a pleasant expression. "Time's running out for you."

"'Scuse me, Maureen, but looks like that girl has a *grimoire,*" a gap-toothed Copperhead pointed out.

Shit. Jack grimaced, exchanging looks with Zepheus and Oberidon. "Stampede, boys."

The pegasi surged forward, charging at the formation of Copperheads. Fearsome they may be, but in the face of a pair of 1,200 pound animals plowing toward them, the men and women broke ranks with a yelp. Self-preservation was like that sometimes. Zepheus and Oberidon stirred up a dust cloud with their hooves and wings, obscuring the Copperheads' vision.

"We gotta go!" Jack growled, whirling to check on the status of the working.

Emmaline's back was straight as a fence post as she stood between the turquoise stones. Her hair was swept back, as if blown by a gale—and most alarmingly, her eyes glowed like the moon through clouds on a starless night. Jack had seen the shimmer of magic on the hands of some mages but never had he seen it in their eyes. No, that was a *wizard* thing. Gooseflesh crawled across his arms as he stared at his daughter.

The *bang* of a revolver caught his attention, and Jack turned back to their assailants. He pulled out his sixgun as the pegasi surged back to join him. Jack caught sight of a grey shape in the cloud and fired, satisfied when he heard a yelp and saw a man stagger to the ground.

Suddenly, the air behind him howled and rippled with the force of the spell being wrought. A shockwave burst forth from Emmaline, forcing Jack to stagger backward and the stallions to stumble. Jack's ears rang, but he righted himself and found Emmaline. Her eyes had stopped glowing, the color cooling back to her normal green as a slit of radiant light opened in the air before her. There was a great tearing sound, as if someone were ripping a piece of fabric. The opening yawned wider, revealing a verdant, well-manicured garden.

"She did it," Jack whispered.

"Let's go!" Marian shouted, pointing at the portal.

<We'll guard your back,> Zepheus announced, half-rearing, wings flared out dramatically.

Jack didn't even argue. He put an arm around Emmaline, wincing as she sagged against him from exhaustion. Her eyelids fluttered.

"Just a little longer, darlin'," Jack murmured to her, watching as Marian slipped through. When the alchemist seemed to be on the other side and no worse for wear, Jack followed. Crossing through the portal was unlike any sensation he'd felt before. For the heartbeat it took to step through, it was as if someone had jabbed thousands of needles into his flesh. He hissed against the unexpected pain, though it vanished just as quickly. Jack glanced down at his daughter. Emmaline shifted against him but made no other sign of discomfort as he guided her onto a gravel path.

Even through the portal, he heard the sounds of the Copperheads. Zepheus and Oberidon stormed through. "Close it, Em. We're good." Hopefully, none of the Copperheads planned on following them through. Jack grinned at the idea. Well, if they did, they'd be fish out of water.

Emmaline's head lolled, but not before she closed the portal. It made a soft pop and faded from existence. Then she sagged against him, unconscious, just as Marian had predicted.

CHAPTER FORTY-ONE

Don't Press Your Luck

The water in the tub trembled. Blaise had been relaxing, motionless with his eyes closed as the warm water eased his tension. His head whipped up at the sudden, strange sensation that rolled through the air. Something like the change in pressure from an incoming storm, only not that. His magic came alive, on edge.

Blaise stumbled out of the tub, dripping as he grabbed the fluffy towel awaiting him. He barely mopped up any of the water trailing down his body before he wrapped the towel around his midsection, barreling into the bedroom proper. As he'd suspected, the steward had replaced his worn clothing with a new set. He tugged on pants, shoved his feet in boots, and shrugged the shirt on, attempting to button it as he raced out of the room.

Ahead, he heard pounding feet and exclamations of surprise. He broke into a run, barreling out of the house, across the expanse of the wrap-around porch, and then down a short flight of stairs. He heard whinnies and cursing.

Blaise followed the sounds into the garden and stopped in surprise, his magic dissipating at the tableau.

Jack stood there, propping up Emmaline, who drooped against him as if she couldn't walk. Kittie was already rushing over to her with a sharp exclamation of worry. Zepheus and Oberidon were there, too, though they stepped aside, crushing a bed of marigolds as they made room for the humans.

My mother. Marian Hawthorne was there. Her eyes found him, and she gasped with surprise, then jogged over to him, wrapping her arms around him.

"Blaise, Blaise," she crooned, holding him as if he were a small child and not a grown man. "You're safe. You're here? But how are you *here?*"

"I have the same question for you," he replied, utterly baffled. Flora appeared nearby, eyes wide as she took everything in.

"It's complicated," Marian said, not releasing him from the embrace.

"Usually is with this group," Blaise agreed, though he couldn't help the sense of relief that his mother was here and safe. Far from the Copperheads, at any rate.

Kittie ushered Emmaline into the house with Flora's help. With his daughter in someone else's care, Jack turned to Blaise, his eyes glinting dangerously. "Didn't expect to find you here. What happened?"

His mother released him at last, and Blaise took a step back. He glanced down and realized that every button on his shirt was off by one, but he decided not to care. "It was the same Walker who tried to get me in Rainbow Flat. The Herald. She latched onto me, but Emrys bit her and didn't let go." He ran a hand through his soggy hair, raking it back until he hit a snarl.

<And I'll do it again if she dares to show her face around Blaise,> Emrys declared, pawing at the ground. He and Seledora had come to see what the fuss was about.

"Yeah, I figured it was that blasted Walker, but how did you get *here?*" Jack asked.

"We ended up somewhere in Ganland, and Emrys kicked her away. Didn't see her again after that." Blaise gestured around to their current location. "Emrys figured out we were close to Nera. To Jefferson's estate."

"Is the peacock here?" Jack asked gruffly, no doubt recalling their last conversation with him.

"No."

The outlaw nodded. "Was afraid of that. Well." He turned in a circle before facing Blaise again. "Glad you're safe."

Blaise raised an eyebrow. "Were you worried about me? As in, you cared if something happened to me?"

Jack made a face. "Don't press your luck, Breaker." He waved a dismissive hand. "I'm gonna go check on Em and catch up with my wife. I trust you can have one of your beau's grooms see to the pegasi." Without waiting for an answer, Jack stalked to the house.

"He *was* worried about you," Marian murmured.

Blaise smiled. "I know."

CHAPTER FORTY-TWO
Everyone Loves a Mystery

"Ou'll make your triumphant return to Nera tomorrow," Phillip informed Jefferson at breakfast the next morning.

He stopped eating, raising an eyebrow at that. The very idea made him lose his appetite. He didn't want to go, didn't want to be Malcolm Wells. "Must I?"

"Yes," Phillip said, making a sour face. "We would have preferred more time to indoctrinate you to our ways, but it can't be helped. The Board is attempting to unseat Madame Boss Clayton."

Jefferson didn't even try to hide the show of surprise on his face. "What? Why?"

Phillip sighed. "They've been attempting this since the fire. They're declaring her unfit to govern and recalling her, citing *hysterics.*"

Jefferson narrowed his eyes, offended on Rachel's behalf. "Rachel Clayton has never been hysterical a day in her life."

Phillip nodded, and it felt odd to have anything at all in common with the Quiet One. "If they succeed, the Board will seat one of their own in her position and scuttle any hopes of recognizing the Gutter." His lips puckered as if the idea left an unpleasant taste in his mouth. "Your job will be to return to Nera and help ensure Madame Boss Clayton wrests back control."

Jefferson frowned. "And how am I supposed to do that?"

Phillip shrugged. "That's up to you. You have a good head on your shoulders. And more than that, people trust you."

"Who's going to trust a man coming back from the dead?" Jefferson asked, once more hoping against hope that Phillip might see the sense of his argument.

"Everyone. They're going to eat up the sob story you and Cinna will feed them—"

"Cinna?" Jefferson set down his spoon, the metal rapping sharply against the surface of the table. "I don't need a nanny, especially her." The very thought of his ex-fiancée accompanying him turned his stomach.

Phillip waved a hand, dismissive. "She's part of your cover story, Malcolm. After your breakdown at the traumatic loss of your parents, you faked your own death and sought an old flame to heal your shattered heart. And then, when it became apparent that Ganland needed your leadership once more, you rose to the challenge." He had the nerve to back up his words with a smile. "It's hopelessly romantic. People will eat it up."

The disgusting thing about the narrative was the fact that it *was* romantic. Exactly the sort of thing that made a compelling story and would earn him favor once more. "I don't want Cinna. Pick anyone else."

"She's the only one among us that makes sense, Malcolm. Regardless of your opinions, she is going with you." The Quiet One laced his fingers together. "You go in there, help Madame Boss Clayton keep her authority, and then push the Gutter's recognition through."

Something about that rubbed Jefferson the wrong way. "And after that?"

"That's none of your concern."

Jefferson straightened in his seat. "If I'm to be a Quiet One, then it absolutely *is* my concern."

Phillip raised a brow, gesturing with an index finger. "I like your spirit, but I don't trust you. Not yet. You're ours to use as we see fit until you've proven your value."

Jefferson's hackles raised. He stared Phillip down, drawing on every bit of haughtiness he possessed. "And what will happen if I don't prove my value?"

"The same fate as anything without worth." The calculated glint in Phillip's eyes made Jefferson's stomach churn. "But don't worry. I'm certain you'll live up to our expectations." Then Phillip smiled in a manner that telegraphed he had one more nugget of information to dole out. "Oh, and Malcolm? Once Ganland recognizes the Gutter, you'll need to hold a celebration."

Jefferson frowned. "I don't have a home in Nera." Not as Malcolm, anyway.

Phillip gave a bored shrug. "Use the Cole estate. I have it on good authority that's where you stay when you're conducting business in Nera. Everyone knows you were so *close*." He chuckled. "And now we know why."

Jefferson clenched his fists beneath the table, annoyed at being commanded. But holding such a celebration in his own home made things more promising. He might, just might, wrest back control of this horrible situation. "The Cole estate it is, then."

———

To Jefferson's frustration, the windows of the carriage conveying him to Nera were covered in heavy drapery, making it impossible to gain his bearings. If he so much as twitched in the direction of a window, Cinna adjusted her grip on the pretty little pistol she had produced from the folds of her dress.

She sat across from him in the carriage. Cinna had tried to sit beside him, but he had made a point to move when she did so. The Quiet Ones might have forced her along with him, but that didn't mean he had to tolerate her. Though Cinna seemed to have other plans, judging by the mostly one-sided conversation she kept up.

"You know, Malcolm, it wouldn't be such a terrible thing if we wed," she said. "We don't have to do it for love, only our combined might. You can keep your mage to warm the bed if you like." Cinna smiled. "Though I wouldn't mind warming it as well."

"I will *not* marry you," Jefferson insisted, crossing his arms. "You're out of your mind."

She leaned forward, a swell of cleavage peeking out of her bodice. "You will if the Quiet Ones demand it." Though, he didn't miss the brief stricken expression on her face, as if his declaration had actually stung.

Jefferson huffed out an exasperated breath. First, the Quiet Ones had stripped him of his preferred identity, and now this was a possibility? He hated it. Had to come up with some way for that to *never* happen.

Cinna shifted, the fabric of her long skirts rustling as she recrossed her legs. She glanced down at the pistol, then back at him. "For this venture, you *will* treat me as if we are engaged again."

Jefferson stared at her, wanting to argue but realizing that to do so would only put him in more jeopardy. Cinna was watching every move he made and would report back to her cohorts. He *had* to play their game to have any chance to escape. "Very well."

Mollified by his agreement, Cinna peeked out the curtained window. She made a satisfied sound and drew it open, revealing the pristine beauty of Nera. "Your public awaits."

"What do you mean?" Jefferson leaned over to get a glimpse of his own, though he was disappointed they were in Nera. He had no clues that would lead to where he had been held. He blinked when he saw curious citizens lining the road to Silver Sands. "All these people want to see me? Why?"

"Everyone loves a mystery." Cinna smirked. "It doesn't get more mysterious than a beloved politician they thought to be dead returning to the scene."

He hated how right she was. Jefferson stared down at his bare fingers. He fervently wished for his ring. Both of them, actually. He wanted to *look* like Jefferson, and he wanted to be safe from any potentially snooping unicorns and Trackers. But he had neither and would have to carry on without.

The carriage rolled up to the Silver Sands entry gate. Captain Cerulean strode over and spoke to the driver before coming around to the side. The guard pulled the door open, peering inside.

"They claimed you were Malcolm Wells, and I had to see for myself," Cerulean said, their eyes wide. The guard captain was familiar with the former Doyen and didn't even attempt to hide their surprise. "Is it truly you?"

Jefferson had no choice but to incline his head. What else was he to do, claim that he'd been kidnapped as Jefferson Cole and returned as someone thought to be deceased? "It is."

Cinna reached out and placed a hand on his knee, as if in comfort. "He's had a long and challenging road." She smiled warmly at the guard.

Cerulean raised their brows, curious but unwilling to ask. "Go on through." They shut the door and motioned for the driver to continue once the gates were open.

As the carriage rolled in, Jefferson got a better view of the damage wrought by the fire. The residential wing was a burned-out husk of tumbledown brick and charred timber, the guest wing bearing similar damage. The only building that seemed to have suffered minor damage was the executive wing. Their carriage halted outside.

A footman approached, opening the door to see them out. As soon as she could, Cinna snagged Jefferson's hand in hers, claiming him. She smiled demurely as the Bossguard approached to guide them through a throng of gawking Gannish politicians and staffers.

Their escort left them in a small parlor, along with a selection of brunch items. Jefferson wasn't hungry. He was still trying to puzzle through how he was going to play this. Cinna sat nearby, loading a plate as if nothing were wrong.

The door opened without a warning knock. Flora hustled inside, staring before rushing over, throwing her arms around him. She hugged him fiercely, as if she would never let go. Cinna stopped eating, eyebrows lowering with disapproval at the spectacle.

"Don't you ever make me think you're dead again," Flora whispered in his ear.

Jefferson chuckled. "It wasn't my intent. But I'm glad to see you, too." It improved his outlook to have Flora back on his side.

"Malcolm, why is your creature here?" Cinna asked, setting the plate aside as she locked eyes with Flora, no doubt attempting to overpower the half-knocker with her air of superiority.

Jefferson squeezed Flora's wrist, a silent plea for her not to verbally or physically attack. "Cinna Smithstone, allow me to introduce you to Flora Strop, Jefferson Cole's aide."

"And *problem solver*," Flora added, baring her teeth in an aggressive smile.

Cinna scowled, connecting the dots. Clearly, she disliked what she found. "I know what she is. You may greet Malcolm and then be on your way. We're here on business."

"As is Flora," Jefferson snapped, unable to hold his temper at her dismissal of his oldest and dearest friend.

"If I were you, I'd take an extended trip to the powder room," the half-knocker advised the Quiet One. Cinna stared, unsettled at the demand from someone she towered over. Flora pulled out her butterfly knife, the one she liked to toss around for show. That helped Cinna decide, and she retreated from the room.

Jefferson relaxed as soon as she left. "What have I missed?"

Flora grimaced, looking up at him. "I could write an entire book about what you've missed. But first, *how are you not dead?* There was a body in your room!"

"Ah, that was probably one of the men Cinna brought along to kidnap me." He hadn't gotten a good look at the man, but the fire might have only left enough behind for his friends to believe that any corpse in the room had been Jefferson.

Flora gave him a long look, no doubt reading the subtext that he had used his magic. She knew him too well—Jefferson wasn't a scrapper, wouldn't have been able to fight back against those odds. "Gotcha. Well, to answer your question, the Board is trying to unseat Rachel and discredit our delegation. Blaise somehow got to Ganland, and Jack and Emmaline appeared not long after—"

"Wait. Blaise is *here?*" Jefferson asked, hope rising again. He was almost certain he'd misheard her. Guilt pulled at him—he'd been too depressed about his own situation to seek Blaise out in the dreamscape.

Jefferson knew Blaise had his own difficulties, and he had no desire to add to them.

"At your estate. Jack, too. That's a long, weird story," Flora confirmed with a nod. "Blaise is the one who told us you were still alive. And that you had to be…" She waved a hand to encompass his body. "This."

Blaise is here. That knowledge soothed him more than anything else. If things went well for the day, he could retire to his estate and see Blaise. He slouched against his seatback. "I heard about the Board's machinations. But I also have it on good authority *they're* the ones who set the fire."

Flora looked up at him. "Do you have any proof?"

He shook his head, voice still low. "None aside from the word of someone who will see me dead if I don't do as I'm told."

Flora scowled. "Not while I'm around."

Oh, he had missed her spirit and fierce protectiveness. He thought about trying to dissuade her, but he knew it wouldn't do much good. "I want to meet with Rachel as soon as I can."

Flora sighed. "That's going to be difficult. The Board's had her locked away 'for her own good,' they say." She made a face, gritting her teeth. "Ever since she refused to implicate Kittie as the source of the fire, they've been dogging her heels."

Kittie? Jefferson paused, then recalled Jack had suggested this might happen. Of course, the Board would be the ones responsible for the fire—and attempt to pin it on an outlaw mage. That would have guaranteed Ganland cutting ties with the Gutter. Instead, it seemed Rachel had doubled down on her determination to acknowledge the Gutter. Jefferson grimaced. He had a vested interest in the Gutter's nationhood, but it annoyed him he would be doing exactly what the Quiet Ones desired if he stayed the course.

Maybe they're not so bad, a distant, niggling part of his brain rationalized. *There's always going to be some group vying to be at the top, to be dominant. Why not be among that group?* After all, wasn't that exactly the game he had played as a Doyen? But that had been different. He had been the one calling the shots, crafting the policy. The Quiet Ones…well, he wasn't sure what their end game was. Maybe he would have gone along with them to see where things led. But now he had too many people he cared about who might suffer if things went awry. No, he would figure something out.

"Do you think I can see the Board, then?" Jefferson hazarded after a moment.

Flora gave him a toothy grin. "As a matter of fact, you can." Without even asking, she tugged out his pocket watch and checked the time. "Yep.

In a half-hour, the Gutter is on their docket again. As soon as the rumor mill brought word that you were coming, I took some liberties with their schedule." She snapped the watch closed. "I penciled Malcolm Wells into their meeting with Kittie."

"You are a true wonder, Flora," Jefferson chuckled, shaking his head. He took back his watch and replaced it in his pocket, smoothing his lapels. "Oh. Do you have my ring? The one Blaise gave me."

Her face softened. "Yeah." Flora dug it out of her pocket and offered it to him. "For a while, I thought that was really all I had left of you. What is it with you and leaving jewelry behind?"

"Not a trend I hope to continue," Jefferson said wryly. He held the ring in his palm, debating if he should slip it on or not. His magic might be the only ace he had, and it was worth protecting. Wrinkling his nose, he slid the ring on, shivering at the sensation of his power abruptly cutting off. Flora watched him, curious, but didn't comment on his choice. "Where's Kittie? We should get ready to go shark fishing."

CHAPTER FORTY-THREE

Hostile Takeover

Jefferson

"So it seems the tales of your demise were exaggerated, Mr. Wells," Board member Sylvia Westerfield commented as they took their seats at the long table. The rest of the Board stared at Jefferson with beady eyes. Despite their *heartfelt* greetings and feigned relief at his appearance, he wasn't welcome. Neither was Kittie, who sat beside him, sipping a cup of tea as if her life depended upon it.

"Yes, well, everyone needs time away from the limelight," Jefferson said with a shrug. "I had some issues to work through."

"Most people would just step down or retire," Board member Marcus Funk muttered.

"I'm not most people," Jefferson shot back, thinking that was the most profound truth he'd ever spoken. "But I didn't travel all the way to Nera to justify how I spent my secluded time. Let's move on to the matters at hand."

"As you can understand, Pyromancer Dewitt and Mr. Wells—"

"Doyen." Jefferson had no qualms about interrupting Bartholomew Tate. "Even when we no longer hold the position, we keep the honorific." As much as he disliked the role he had to play, he wasn't going to allow any slights from this group.

"*Doyen* Wells," Tate corrected through gritted teeth. "We must table the request by the Gutter to be recognized as a country. Ganland is a leaderless nation at the moment, a ship without a rudder—"

"You've put the ship in dry dock, and it hasn't even sprung a leak," Kittie interjected, narrowing her eyes.

Jefferson braced his elbows on the table, steepling his hands together. "You must admit, it is offensive to refer to our Madame Boss Clayton in nautical terms. Makes it easier to dismiss her, I suppose." He smiled at the tense glances the rest of the Board traded.

"Now see here, Doyen Wells, we have nothing but respect for Madame Boss Clayton," Tate retorted, crossing his arms. "Her health has been delicate since the fire. Surely you, of all people, understand that."

"What I understand is that this Board has tried all the lowly tricks in their power to undermine the Gutter delegation from the day they crossed the border into Confederation lands." Jefferson chose his words carefully, remembering his role. Malcolm Wells had not been at the attack, but he *could* pretend to have heard tales of it.

At his accusation, even Kittie's head snapped up. This wasn't something he'd discussed with her. No, the pieces had only now fallen into place. He was more certain than ever that the Board was responsible for the attack near Fort Courage. "The Board isn't working for *Ganland,* is it? You're working on the Confederation's behalf."

All around the table, Board members sputtered in indignation at the allegation. "That is malarkey, Doyen Wells! Ganland is a part of the Confederation." Funk slammed a palm against the table.

"As long as we stay in lock-step and bow to the Confederation's whims, we are," Jefferson agreed. Yes, that was something he had been painfully aware of as a Doyen. "You think you stand to lose too much if mages have a chance at freedom in their own land. So, you hired thugs to take out Jefferson Cole the first night he and his delegation were in Mella." Memories of the attack stirred him to anger, and he shook a trembling index finger. "And when it became clear Madame Boss Clayton was willing to break with the Confederation—potentially jeopardizing Ganland's standing—you couldn't bear it, could you?"

"What are you on about? This is ridiculous!" Westerfield protested, shrill with outrage.

Jefferson grinned savagely. He wasn't done, not yet. "You're the ones behind the fire. You sought to discredit Pyromancer Dewitt, to cast doubt on the delegation." He debated his next words. *Should I?* At the moment, he was doomed to his identity as Malcolm Wells, so what did he have to lose? Jefferson slammed a palm against the table. "You killed Jefferson Cole."

Tate's face reddened. "Doyen Wells, you are out of line. We understand the Pyromancer may not have caused the fire. It may have just been an accident. A terrible accident."

Kittie rose from her seat, placing her hands flat against the table and leaning over them. "It wasn't an *accident* that someone stacked oil-soaked bales of hay against Silver Sands. Nor an accident that someone set them ablaze."

"It sounds as if you know exactly what started the fire, Pyromancer. Are you confessing?" Funk asked.

"Knowing the *source* of the fire doesn't mean I *set* it," Kittie shot back.

Tate gestured to the nearby guards, who came to attention as if this had been planned. Jefferson suspected it had been. "Arrest Pyromancer Dewitt. Cite that she has confessed before the Board to setting the fire."

Kittie recoiled, eyes widening with horror. "What? No!"

"She did no such thing!" Jefferson growled. The guards in the room closed ranks around them. Jefferson narrowed his eyes. "So, this is how it's going to be? Staging a coup?"

"Not a coup. We're acting within our rights as the Board," Tate said tightly. "Guards, arrest Doyen Wells on the charge of conspiring with an outlaw mage."

Well, this escalated quickly. Jefferson stood, shoving his chair away to block the nearest guard. "Stand down, man. This is madness. You really think the lot of you will get away with this?"

"I *do* think so because we *are*," Tate said with a grim smile.

Jefferson sighed. "Very well. This is all on you, then." He squared his shoulders as if he were about to make a speech before a crowd. "The Gutter is allied to Ganland, and thus Madame Boss Clayton, the rightful leader. As such, we'll rise in her defense." As soon as the words left his mouth, he realized he had spoken as if he were Jefferson. No one seemed to catch his mistake, though. Everyone focused on the rising tension instead.

"Good luck with that. You're outnumbered," Funk sneered.

"Outnumbered, perhaps. But not outmatched." Kittie glanced at Jefferson as she spoke. They hadn't made any plans to handle a hostile takeover. He trusted her instincts, though. They couldn't allow the Board to arrest them. Not only would it sink their plans for the Gutter, but they would likely end up in the Confederation's clutches.

The Firebrand snapped her fingers, a circle of flame blooming to life around them, cutting off the guards. Jefferson didn't particularly *like* being enclosed in fire, but he trusted Kittie could handle it. The Board took her display of power as a new threat.

"She's going to burn us all! Just as she tried to do to the Madame Boss!" Tate yelled, doubling down on his accusations against Kittie. "Shoot her! Don't take her alive!"

"I don't think so," Kittie murmured, lifting a hand as the guards aimed revolvers at her. Jefferson didn't see exactly what she did, but she gestured, and an instant later the guards dropped their weapons, yelping as if they were hot coals. A single revolver misfired as it struck the ground, the bullet punching through the ceiling.

But the guards had Jefferson and Kittie hemmed in, and it wouldn't take long for the Board to bring in reinforcements if needed. Kittie glanced over at him. "What now?"

Good question. His mind whirled through the possibilities, but none of them seemed likely. Except for one, in which he made a display of his own magic. Gods, were all his secrets to be forced into the light now? He didn't see any other way around it.

"Now it's my turn," Jefferson said softly. He worked the ring off and slipped it into his greatcoat pocket for safekeeping. His power breathed to life. *Sorry, Blaise. I tried.*

He called on his magic, and the dreamscape boiled up in his subconsciousness, ready. Jefferson focused on Tate, curling a tendril of magic around the man, luring him into slumber. His body hit the ground hard, and a guard cried out, moving to pull his limp form away from the ring of fire. "They killed Board Member Tate!"

"Oh, for Tabris's sake, he's sleeping like a baby," Jefferson muttered. Then, one after the other, he dragged the rest of the Board into the dreamscape.

Never had he forced so many to slumber against their will. Sweat beaded his forehead at the exertion. He was going to pay the price for this later, but at least that might mean he *had* a later in which he wasn't behind bars. When he finished, all five Board members lay dozing on the floor or slumped across the table, some of them snoring. The guards stood over them, uncertain.

Kittie kept up her wall of fire, though her forehead wrinkled when she looked at Jefferson. "Was that you?"

He wanted to deny it, but there was no use. She was a mage and would no doubt see through his lies. And he couldn't afford to alienate any allies. "Yes."

"You and I are going to have a talk later." She set her mouth in a thin, determined line. "Once we figure our way out of this mess."

He winced. "That's fair." Jefferson turned to the guards. "Put your weapons down!"

"You're not in command of us," a guard snarled petulantly.

The door swung open. "No, but I am." Madame Boss Clayton strode in, frowning at the sleeping lumps of Board members, then at Kittie's fire shield. Flora and Mindy were a few paces behind her. Jefferson had wondered what the half-knocker was up to. Springing the Madame Boss with the help of a Hospitalier, it seemed. "Stand down."

"But—"

"I said *stand down*," Rachel repeated, firm. "As you can see, the Board is incapacitated. And as such, *I* am the only authority." Puzzlement was clear on her face as she tried to figure out why her treacherous Board members had taken a nap in the middle of a meeting. Her eyes flicked to Jefferson—to *Malcolm*, as that was who she saw. "Put the weapons away, or I'll relieve you of duty. Permanently."

With a grumble, the guards did as she commanded and moved back to their defensive positions. Kittie dismissed her fire, the smoke curling away and dissipating into nothing. Jefferson glanced down. The floor and furniture didn't bear so much as a single scorch mark. She was *good*.

"So, what did I miss?" Rachel asked. "Aside from the miraculous return of former Doyen Malcolm Wells." Her eyes were sharp, as if she were trying to peel back the layers of lies and half-truths.

"That's a topic for another time," Jefferson said stiffly, hoping it was a conversation that would never happen. But he knew better. He gestured at the Board. "They were planning a coup, from the sound of it. Discrediting us, overthrowing you. You know, the usual."

Rachel raised her brows. "What happened to them, anyway?"

"I suppose I bored them," Jefferson said with a shrug that didn't fool anyone.

"Explanations later," Rachel murmured, and Kittie smirked in agreement. Then she turned to the guards. "Arrest the members of the Board on charges of treason."

"And arson," Kittie added without hesitation. She picked up her cup of tea, peering into the golden liquid before taking another sip.

Rachel nodded. "Arson." Her face darkened with anger as she understood the true meaning behind the charge. "Attempted murder."

Kittie shook her head. "Not only attempted."

The Madame Boss tensed at that, bowing her head with such grief that a wave of guilt washed over Jefferson. "I stand corrected. Charge them with the death of Ambassador Jefferson Cole."

Jefferson turned away so no one would see the flicker of remorse in his eyes. He wanted to yell at them, to declare that Jefferson Cole stood before them. He puffed out a frustrated breath.

The guards were reluctant to do her bidding, and Rachel seemed painfully aware of this. She strode into the hallway and had one of her staffers run off on an errand, and moments later, her Bossguard arrived on the scene. They hauled the sleeping Board members into custody as Jefferson strained to keep them in the dreamscape. He knew they were confused about where they were and how they'd gotten there, but he didn't much care. A part of him wished he could spare enough focus to give them reason to regret their actions.

Once the Board had been cleared from the room, Rachel released a haggard sigh. She turned, giving Jefferson and Kittie a grateful smile. "I appreciate what you did. You took a significant risk for me. For Ganland."

Kittie inclined her head. "Doyen Wells proclaimed that the mages of the Gutter are your allies—Ganland's allies—and that much is true. The least we could do was stand firm."

"And then some, it seems," Rachel murmured, eyeing Jefferson. "It's time for an explanation, isn't it?"

Jefferson sighed. "I suppose it is."

"Tea. I'd drink a whole kettle right now," Kittie muttered, massaging her forehead with her thumb and index finger.

"I've got you covered," Mindy said, pushing a fresh cup in front of the Firebrand. Steam rose from it, and the rich, sweet scent drifted across the table to Jefferson. Kittie sighed and took another swig, as if the tea were a balm for her soul. Jefferson didn't know what was going on with her, but he suspected it was. If only tea would help his situation.

They sat around a table in a small assembly room that Rachel had commandeered—a room that gave them the privacy they sorely needed. Jefferson didn't enjoy it one bit, despite the snacks delivered to them by a perky staffer.

"Where do you want to begin, Doyen Wells?" Rachel prompted.

He swallowed, reluctant to unearth his secrets. Not that he wanted to mislead anyone—there were some secrets that simply needed to remain buried. But now, he had no choice if he wanted to stay in their good graces. And he would need every advantage against the Quiet Ones. His stomach twisted as he ignored Flora's persistent attempts to catch his eye.

Jefferson looked up, meeting the Gannish leader's eyes. She wouldn't like what he was about to say, but he saw no way around it. "Let's begin with the fact that you also know me as Jefferson Cole."

Rachel's mouth dropped open, then snapped shut as she absorbed the news. Her cheeks flushed with anger. "I'm sorry, *what?* Jefferson Cole, as in the man whose death we just accused my former Board members of?"

Mindy's lips tightened, as if she, too, felt betrayed by this new information. The Firebrand kept her mouth shut, wisely concealing the fact that she was very aware Jefferson Cole was alive and well when she'd made the suggestion.

"Yes, *that* Jefferson Cole," he agreed, wishing he were anywhere but here. Well, maybe not anywhere. He certainly didn't want to end up back at the Quiet Ones' estate.

"How is that even possible?" Mindy asked, the hurt clear in her tone.

Jefferson didn't meet her eyes. He liked Mindy, and he truly had not wanted to hurt anyone with this. "It was a lot of work, I assure you." He rubbed the bridge of his nose, thinking. "I don't want to get into the details, but trust me when I tell you I am also Jefferson Cole."

"What game have you been playing with us?" Rachel asked. "Malcolm Wells is supposed to be dead, too. Yet here you sit, telling us that somehow, you are *two* people." Her voice rose with each word, her frustration getting the better of her. "I should have you arrested for this."

Jefferson sighed. "Please don't. There was no game. Everything I have done, I have done to *help*." Inwardly, he winced, knowing he hadn't always been so virtuous. "I know this doesn't look good, but I had my reasons for this masquerade."

"Ones that you won't share with us?" Rachel needled.

Jefferson thought back to his family's wicked ways and how he'd tried to separate himself from them. He didn't want to recount any of that at the moment. It was punishment enough that Malcolm Wells stared back at him in every mirror he passed. "Perhaps in the future, but not today, with so many other things afoot."

"Just as well because *I* have questions about what you did to the Board members," Kittie said, fire in her eyes.

"Yes, do tell us about that," Rachel agreed.

Jefferson rubbed his forehead, debating how much truth he could tell them. He felt Flora's gaze on him but still refused to meet her eyes. "I'm a mage."

Kittie cocked her head. "I've never heard of a mage who puts people to sleep."

"I'm unique, and we need to leave it at that," Jefferson said. He might have to bare every aspect of himself to them, destroy his lifelong web of lies, but he refused to betray the secret of Blaise's blood.

"And when, exactly, were you planning to share this information with us, Malcolm?" Rachel prodded, her eyes flinty as she stared Jefferson down.

He'd withstood her withering gaze before. And he'd be damned if he would cringe under it now, though her use of his old name stung. "To be quite honest, I was never planning to share it with any of you." This admission earned him nothing but deepening scowls, and Jefferson flapped a hand. "Not because I'm trying to deceive you—I'm *not*. But..." He shook his head, struggling to figure out a way to explain his situation without connecting his magic to Blaise. "I was *not* previously a mage. And you must understand that magic showing up at this stage in life is problematic."

"On so many levels," Rachel agreed. She shifted to match Kittie's cross-armed stance. "You were gunning to be the Ambassador as *Jefferson Cole*. How can I trust you with such a position after keeping this from me? I'll need to consider someone else."

No. His eyes widened at that. Blast it, but he wanted that position! It was perfect in every way for him, for his goals. To be with Blaise and still do something meaningful. But the Quiet Ones would use him...*wait, the Quiet Ones*. He was safe behind the Madame Boss's walls, with her Boss-guard, wasn't he? With his outlaw mage allies around him.

"You can trust me because I'm about to tell you something I shouldn't." Flora jerked upright at his words, her eyes wide as she no doubt wondered what he was about to say. "The night of the fire, I tried to escape like everyone else. I was attacked and kidnapped, held against my will."

"What?" Rachel's voice went gravelly with stark disbelief, and Kittie's brow furrowed. Mindy blinked in surprise. "Who would do such a thing? At Silver Sands, of all places?"

I hope they believe me about the next part. "There's a powerful group of elite called the Quiet Ones. They seek to set things in motion, to fall in place to their design." Jefferson licked his lips. "They said that I had to join their group as Malcolm Wells and ensure that Ganland recognize the Gutter as a nation."

"So, they like mages?" Mindy asked, uncertain.

"Mages are useful to them, and they see value down the road in having the Gutter tightly allied to Ganland." Jefferson rubbed his chin. "I don't know what their long game is. They didn't seem overly concerned about the Confederation taking umbrage to any of this."

"Why is this the first time I'm hearing of this group?" Rachel asked.

"Because they operate behind the scenes," Jefferson said. "They're shadows, lining things up just so. I may be in dire straits for telling you this much."

"And you're joining these Quiet Ones?" Rachel frowned.

"I have little choice," Jefferson said, his shoulders tense. "I have to do what they tell me, or..." He shook his head, averse to telling them how truly grave his situation was. "They sent Cinna Smithstone along with me to make sure I stick to their plan."

"I wondered why she was with you," Rachel murmured. "I knew that engagement was broken years ago."

"Cinna and the rest of the Quiet Ones don't know about my magic. It has to stay that way," Jefferson said urgently.

Rachel frowned, clearly reluctant for the secrets to continue. "If they're as connected as you say, they're going to find out."

"I would rather they find out from me," Jefferson replied. "On my terms."

"Well, you and Kittie stood up for me and for Ganland, so I'm grateful for that. I'll keep the secret of your magic, though note that I'm *not* happy about that," Rachel said. She stared at him for a dozen heartbeats, then straightened as she moved to a new topic. "I believe tomorrow I can arrange a time to sign the declaration recognizing the Gutter as a nation…and Ganland's newest ally. It will be noteworthy to do so on Bounty's Eve."

Kittie made a soft gasp. Jefferson's shoulders sagged with relief. "Just tell us when, and we'll be there."

CHAPTER FORTY-FOUR
Flair for the Dramatic

"It was still stupid, even if you think you had no choice," Flora pointed out, dogging Jefferson's steps as they crossed from the Silver Sands executive wing to the portion of the stables that had been untouched by the fire. The half-knocker had made arrangements to delay Cinna, and Flora was clearly determined to use every moment to her advantage.

He stared straight ahead as they walked. "It was the only thing I could do that might give me some power back. And offer protection."

She scowled. Jefferson knew he had just insulted her—Flora considered herself his protection. And she was, but there were some things even she couldn't guard against.

"The more people who know, the harder your secrets are to keep." Her voice was soft, the words meant only for his ears.

Oh, how he knew. "No sense dwelling on what's done."

"I'm only dwelling on how *stupid* it was."

"Oh look, there's Seledora," Jefferson said, deciding a change of subject was best. He was glad to see his pegasus attorney—it meant he wouldn't have to ride a mundane horse back to his estate.

<Why did I hear Flora say you did something stupid?> the dapple grey mare asked, ears pricked forward.

Jefferson sighed. *And here I thought perhaps you missed me.* "No reason."

Seledora must have broadcast to the half-knocker as well. Flora harrumphed at his response, though she glanced over her shoulder. Cinna Smithstone strode toward them, not yet near enough to overhear. "Dreamer here flaunted something he should have kept to himself."

<She's right. That's stupid.>

"It's quite unfair that you outnumber me," Jefferson complained as he swung into the saddle.

"Malcolm, you wouldn't leave without me, would you?" Cinna asked as she finally caught up. A Silver Sands groom led a glossy bay gelding out for her. She frowned at the animal. "Wait. Where is the carriage?"

Jefferson stroked Seledora's sleek neck. His attorney fluffed her wings, settling them against her sides. "No carriages. I prefer the saddle." Carriages were for *Malcolm*. Riding Seledora was a spark of defiance. A subtle nod to who he wanted to be. "I'm certain Madame Boss Clayton's staff would find accommodations for you if you don't wish to join us."

Cinna crossed her arms, glancing at the pegasi. "I'll take one of those, then."

"One does not simply *demand* to ride a pegasus," Jefferson said, happy that in this, at least, he had the upper hand. "However, since you don't have the advantage of flight, we'll keep to the ground." He nodded to the bay gelding. For a fleeting instant, Jefferson entertained the idea of flying off into the sunset, leaving this mess behind him. If only it were so simple.

Cinna narrowed her eyes and, assisted by the groom, got into the saddle. She joined Kittie, Mindy, and Flora who were already waiting on their pegasi.

"Ready?" Kittie asked, glancing at Jefferson.

"We may proceed," Cinna said with a nod.

"So very ready," Jefferson agreed, meaning every word. *I'll get to see Blaise soon. And I'll be in my own home.* Though Blaise was definitely the best part. His only worry was what Blaise would think of Cinna's presence.

Dusk was falling as the open gates of the estate came into view. Magelights illuminated the windows, lending the home a cheerful glow. Jefferson had missed this sight.

Seledora trotted to the stables, allowing Jefferson to dismount. The rest of the delegation, plus Cinna, did the same.

As soon as she was on the ground, she sidled up next to him. "Shall we go inside?" She reached over to snare his hand.

Jefferson jerked away from her. "You presume too much."

She closed the gap between them again. "No, *you* do. You forget yourself, Malcolm."

I most certainly do not. But she was right. In public, even here on his own estate, he had to pretend. The realization tied his stomach in knots. Cinna linked her arm through his, aiming a victorious smile at him. Reveling in her power over him.

He turned back toward the house. The front doors were already open, with some of the staff filing out to the wrap-around porch. Jack, Marian, and Blaise were there, too, watching their arrival.

Blaise glanced from Jefferson to Cinna. Recognition flashed in his eyes, along with something else. *Disappointment.* Before Jefferson could climb the steps to greet him, to offer any sort of explanation at all, Blaise stepped back inside.

Blast it all. He knew exactly what Blaise was thinking. He was Malcolm Wells again, and Blaise knew he'd been engaged to Cinna. *I should have asked Seledora to pass word to Emrys of this farce.*

When Jefferson reached the top of the stairs, he glanced at the staffers. He frowned—he looked like Malcolm Wells, which meant he technically couldn't command them to do anything. But he could ask politely. "Good evening. Could you prepare one of the guest bedrooms for Ms. Smithstone?"

Cinna tittered, as if it was a jest. "That's unnecessary. I'll be staying with Malcolm."

The muscles in Jefferson's jaw ached from how tightly he clenched his teeth. "I wouldn't wish to sully your reputation during our engagement." He gave her a polite smile and a gallant half-bow. They both knew he had a prolific history as a rake, but she could hardly make that argument when he mentioned an *engagement.* "I'm certain the staff will find satisfactory accommodations for you."

The Quiet One opened her mouth, no doubt hoping to find a loophole. But Jefferson was already untangling his arm from hers, uncomfortably aware of Jack's furious gaze. He hoped he could get to Blaise before the outlaw murdered him.

Jefferson left Cinna staring after him as he hurried to the suite where he suspected Blaise would be. He tapped on the door, but there was no response. Gently, he turned the knob and pushed it open.

The mage-lights were dim. Blaise sat on the bed, his face in his hands. He looked up when he heard the door close.

"Blaise," Jefferson said softly. "Please talk to me."

The Breaker quivered. "I don't *understand.* You…" He shook his head as if he couldn't bear to complete whatever thought had crossed his mind.

Jefferson moved to the bed and sat a few feet away from Blaise. This wasn't the reunion he'd hoped for. "Let me help you understand."

Blaise lifted his head, meeting his gaze. "I know who she is. What she was to you."

"*Was,*" Jefferson agreed.

Confusion sparked in the Breaker's eyes. "I thought..." He paused, then rubbed the back of his head. "Oh. I jumped to some conclusions I suppose I shouldn't have." Blaise relaxed, though now he looked embarrassed.

At least this crisis was averted. Jefferson scooted a little closer to the Breaker, though he still gave his beau room to shift away if he needed. "I will *always* choose you over her. No matter what it looks like. No matter what she forces me to do." He took a ragged breath. "That is a promise."

Blaise lifted his head, meeting his gaze. "What do you mean what she *forces* you to do? Why is she here?"

Jefferson grimaced. "She's one of the Quiet Ones. And since we have a history, they sent her along to make sure I behave." He was suddenly tired of this. Tired of the Quiet Ones and the Board. Tired of everything. "You're the only one I love. I hope you can believe that, even when I wear this face."

Blaise closed the distance between them. "I do. I was just..." He shook his head. "I recognized her and thought..."

That I would abandon you for her? Jefferson shook his head. "Never. I missed you. Gods, you don't know how much I missed you."

Blaise huffed. "You could have *done* something about that. You haven't bothered to see me in the dreamscape the past two nights."

Jefferson rubbed his forehead, mentally kicking himself because Blaise was *right*. "I was in a bad spot, and I didn't want to bring you down with all you were going through." He had a thousand questions for Blaise. How had he gotten here? What had happened in Thorn? It didn't matter, though. He was *here*. That was what mattered.

Blaise was quiet, staring down at his hands. "You helped me through one of my hardest times. Don't you think I'd want to do the same for you?"

"I know you would, but..." Jefferson trailed off, deciding how to phrase his next sentence. "You've been hurt so many times. I feared adding to it."

Blaise bumped Jefferson's shoulder with his own. "We're stronger together, you know."

Jefferson sighed. Blast it all. He *should* have sought Blaise out in the dreamscape. "Forgive me for being stupid?"

A ghost of a smile touched the Breaker's lips. "I forgive you." Blaise looked as if he were about to add something. Instead, he leaned in, claiming Jefferson with a heated kiss. The Dreamer melted into the familiarity, into the love the gesture offered. Blaise was warm and comfortable, a bulwark against the horror that was his current life. For those precious seconds, Jefferson could pretend like nothing was wrong.

When at last they parted, Blaise murmured, "That was nice, but now you should probably tell me more about what's going on."

Jefferson rubbed the side of his face. "Madame Boss Clayton knows who I really am…and about my magic." At Blaise's blank look, he realized the Breaker had no clue who he was referring to. "The leader of Ganland. Oh, and Mindy knows, too."

He'd thought Blaise might be more alarmed by the news, but the younger man merely shrugged. "I trust Mindy. And I assume you had a very good reason to tell them."

"I didn't know what else to do." Jefferson recounted the meeting with the Board. Hard to believe it had only been hours ago. It felt like ages. He pulled the magic-concealing ring out, turning it over in his hand. "You didn't want anyone to find out about it."

Blaise curled his hand over Jefferson's. "No, I wanted you to be safe. There's a difference." He sighed. "And none of that turned out as I'd hoped."

"Neither of us could anticipate the nest of vipers I walked into." Then Jefferson winced, recalling that Blaise had dealt with snakes of his own. The Copperheads weren't to be taken lightly. "Ah, sorry. Wrong turn of phrase."

The Breaker brushed the words away with a shake of his head. "Maybe it's time your era of secrets came to an end."

What? Jefferson's first instinct was to say no. His secrets had been too large a part of his life, a layer of protection he had relied on for years. "I don't want to be Malcolm Wells."

"You don't have to be," Blaise said, as if his simple words made it true. Maybe they did.

I'm Jefferson to him, no matter what. He swallowed the lump in his throat —he hadn't anticipated how much that would mean in this moment. Blaise understood. But the Breaker was only one man, and to everyone else, Jefferson would forever be Malcolm Wells. "Everyone else thinks Jefferson is dead."

"So was Malcolm Wells. You had a funeral and everything. You do have a certain flair for the dramatic."

Was Blaise teasing him at a moment like this? Jefferson blinked, taking stock of the twist of Blaise's lips and the glint in his eyes. *He is.* "What do you mean? About my secrets, that is."

"Be Jefferson. Be a mage. Just be unapologetically *you.*" There was a fire in Blaise's voice, stoked with determination and love. The Breaker was thoughtful, looking down at his palms as if they held an answer. Maybe they did, for all Jefferson knew. "You said Gregor has your ring. Do you think he'll attend the signing tomorrow?"

Gregor. Jefferson bit his tongue to stave off his anger at the enemy Doyen's name. "No, I don't think the Quiet Ones would want that. Gregor opposes the mages, and it would be strange for him to attend."

"Do you think he's still in Ganland?"

"He was at their estate when I left this morning. I suspect they may keep him there in case he's needed. There's no Salt-Iron Council sessions for another month, so his time is his own."

A determined look settled on Blaise's face. "We need to find out where this estate is."

Jefferson's shoulders slumped. "It's warded, and the carriage windows were covered, so I couldn't see a thing."

Blaise cocked his head. "That's not the only solution, you know."

Jefferson frowned, puzzled. He couldn't think of any other way. "What do you mean?"

"If your ex-fiancée is so eager to be here, we may as well make her useful."

Jefferson still wasn't following Blaise's train of thought—mainly because he wanted nothing to do with Cinna. "What?"

Blaise sighed, leaning over to give him an exasperated kiss before pulling back to explain. "Bring her into the dreamscape and interrogate her. The dreamscape is real to you...and to me. But she wouldn't know that. And didn't you tell me you used it to change the memories of the guards who had..." Blaise drifted off, suddenly unable to finish his question.

Jefferson knew exactly what he meant, though. "I did. I mean, at least I think I did, based on the reports Flora dug up about the incident afterward." Now that Blaise mentioned it, he was warming to the idea. "That's brilliant. I'd much rather do that than the alternative."

"What's the alternative?"

Gods, he didn't *really* want to tell Blaise, but he'd asked. "Seduce her. Though, to be fair, I would have to put little effort into it so it wouldn't be much of a seduction." When the Breaker's brows shot up at that, Jefferson gently took his hand. "And I'd rather *not.*"

"I'd rather you not, too," Blaise agreed, fingers tightening around Jefferson's. There was a veneer of possessiveness over his tone that Jefferson liked.

Jefferson glanced down at their twined fingers, savoring the contact. "What will we do with the information I get from Cinna?"

Blaise leaned over and kissed his cheek. "Leave that to me."

———

Jefferson disdained the idea of hosting Cinna in the dreamscape, but Blaise was right—it really *was* a good idea. And if he did it just right, she would never know what she had divulged to him. It was a stroke of genius.

He curled up beside Blaise in the partial darkness, a single mage-light casting its pale glow over them. Jefferson stole a glance at the Breaker's profile. To the observer, he seemed to be asleep, but Jefferson's magic told him he wasn't. All the same, Jefferson relished seeing Blaise relaxed, as if the world hadn't come crashing down on them.

"You're delaying," Blaise muttered, cracking one eye open. "You really don't like her, do you?"

"No," Jefferson admitted.

Blaise opened his other eye. "Can I ask why you ever liked her?"

Jefferson snorted. "Explaining that to you will cause another delay." Not that he minded.

"I'll allow it," Blaise murmured, rolling onto his side. "I know why you don't like her *now*, but that doesn't explain the past."

Jefferson sighed, very aware that everything he was about to explain would sound exceedingly shallow to someone like Blaise. "Let me preface this by saying I was a different person back then."

"Literally or figuratively?"

"I suppose only figuratively, considering how I look at the moment." Jefferson chuckled, suddenly feeling more at ease when Blaise rested a hand on his side. "I told you before that the elite seldom marry for love."

"You did," Blaise agreed, sounding sleepy but content.

"We were betrothed in our teens. I saw nothing wrong with it—or her—at the time." Jefferson made a face. "She *is* quite beautiful. And as often happens with young men, I was enamored with her...ahem...*physical* features." To further illustrate, he sketched an hourglass figure in the air with his hands.

"I mean, she's pretty, but is that enough to...?" Blaise trailed off, sounding baffled.

"Past Me was quite stupid, so yes, at the time it was enough." Jefferson shook his head. "When she wants to be, she can be quite charming. And in some ways, she is *not* vile. Cinna has a soft spot for birds. She has a lovely aviary where her people nurse injured wild birds back to health." He laughed nervously. "And now I'm babbling. None of this probably makes a lick of sense."

"No, it does," Blaise said. "I only saw the woman who wants to use you, and I couldn't imagine why you would ever like her. This makes more sense." He cuddled closer to Jefferson. "Thank you for explaining. Now I won't delay you any longer."

Jefferson reached over to touch Blaise's cheek, dragging his fingers gently through the fringe of his beard. "I wouldn't *mind* if you delayed me."

The Breaker leaned into the caress. "I know. But you need to do this while she sleeps, since neither of us like the other option you proposed."

"You raise a valid point." Jefferson drew his fingers away from Blaise. He shifted beneath the sheets, easing onto his back. "Goodnight."

"It is. I'm with you," Blaise whispered, leaning over to kiss Jefferson's cheek before snugging a blanket up to his chin and shutting his eyes.

Jefferson wanted to reach out and take Blaise's hand, wanted more contact with the one he truly cared about, but that would only distract him from his task. Blaise was right: he needed to do this, and the sooner he set about it, the better. He closed his eyes, calling on his magic.

The dreamscape swirled around him, a grey void of mist. Jefferson tilted his head, considering the best way to lower Cinna's guard. He crafted a lavish bedroom, complete with candlelight to add an air of romance. He was ready to seek out Cinna and drag her to the dreamscape when he remembered one critical detail.

He looked at himself in a mirror of his own creation, shaking his head. In the dreamscape, he was *always* Jefferson. He had total control over his visage in his domain. *But Cinna won't want Jefferson.* Not if this was to be a believable dream for her, anyway. He wrinkled his nose in distaste, watching as his features melted into those of Malcolm Wells.

With the transformation complete, he sought Cinna. She wasn't difficult to locate. Because of their history and her proximity, she was in his periphery. Carefully, so as not to flaunt his magic, he pulled her into the dreamscape bedroom.

"Oh, Malcolm," she murmured with delight as soon as she laid eyes on him. Cinna stepped up against him, resting a hand on his chest. "You truly *are* the man of my dreams."

Her words sent a shock through him. Had Cinna loved him? Or had it been only lust—for power, for status, for a handsome man on her arm? But there was something genuine in her tone, as if she had let her guard down. Which she probably had. That was the whole point of this exercise. All the same, it made him a little sad to know she may have loved him, but he would never love her in return. *No wonder she slapped me.*

Jefferson gathered her up in his arms. Music played softly in the background, and he led her into an intimate dance. "Hello, Cinna. It's been a long time."

She smiled up at him, her face radiant. "It has. I missed this. Missed *you.*"

I am truly the worst person ever. Jefferson met her smile with one of his own. He leaned over, taking her hand in his and trailing kisses up the length of her too-perfect arm. "You are as lovely as I remember."

Cinna shivered beneath his touch. "Malcolm," she whispered, blissful. "If only you were like this outside of my dreams. Oh." She moaned softly as he reached her shoulder. "If only you'd choose *me* over that mage. I don't know what you see in him."

Jefferson held his tongue. He had a role to play, and as much as he wanted to defend Blaise, this wasn't the time. "I'm here now," he said instead, kissing her neck.

Cinna closed her eyes. "We would be such a powerful team, Malcolm. How can I convince you? Two Quiet Ones, united. Nothing would stand in our way. Think of the romantic stories that would be told of us. How I healed you with my love from the depths of your despair."

Lies. All lies. But now, Cinna was moving closer to the topic he wanted. Just a little nudge, and maybe he could end this farce. "Perhaps so. Tell me, if we were to wed, could we hold the ceremony at the Quiet Ones' estate?"

Her eyes flashed open at the mention of marriage. "Anywhere your heart desires."

"The Quiet Ones' estate," Jefferson murmured, nuzzling her ear, kissing the tender skin beneath it. "Where is it, by the way? I've been so curious."

She sighed, relaxing into his embrace. "Not far. A few miles west of Nera. There are orange groves all around it, which have served us well to keep anyone from snooping and trying to break through the wards." Cinna twisted to look at him. "But if we wed there, it would be a private ceremony."

"Indeed," Jefferson whispered. While it wasn't an exact location, from what Blaise had told him of his plan, that would be enough for an aerial description. It seemed to check out from his memory of the carriage ride to Nera—it hadn't been as long as he'd thought it would be if the estate was further away.

Now that he had what he needed, it was time to extract himself from the dream. This was going to be more challenging than the time he'd twisted the memories of Blaise's guards, however. He had to make Cinna believe he was still there when he wasn't. Jefferson held her close as he concentrated, willing a likeness of Malcolm into existence, layered over him. Then he took a step back, satisfied when the ghost of himself remained with Cinna.

Dream-Malcolm took Cinna's hand, a roguish smile slipping across his face. He gave a gentle tug, pulling her toward the bed.

Cinna's eyes widened with surprise, then she tilted her head, coquettish. "Oh, *Malcolm,* I knew you'd come around."

CHAPTER FORTY-FIVE

Reconciliation

Blaise

Breakfast the next morning was an awkward affair. The staff who ran the household did their best, but their heart wasn't in it—they believed Jefferson, their employer, was dead. And they were probably worried about what would happen to them in the coming weeks.

Cinna's presence didn't help, either. When they came down for breakfast, she attempted to sit beside Jefferson—though Kittie must have seen it coming because she smoothly claimed the seat she was aiming for, and Blaise was already on his other side. Stymied, Cinna instead chose the seat directly across from Jefferson.

Blaise didn't like the woman, and not only because she wanted Jefferson—well, Malcolm. She seemed eager to get between him and Jefferson any way she could. But after last night, Blaise knew Jefferson wouldn't allow it. He'd been too quick to judge the situation when he'd first spied the woman walking with Malcolm. Blaise had forgotten that no matter the face he wore, he was Jefferson. *And Jefferson is mine. And I'm his.*

No one said much at breakfast except for Cinna, who seemed to enjoy the sound of her own voice. Jack hadn't come down, instead choosing to stay with Emmaline, who was still recovering from the portal spell. Blaise's mother was there, though, and he suspected she was plotting the best way to go about poisoning Cinna Smithstone. Her cutting looks at the woman almost made up for all her past hurts to him. She truly loved him and wanted to protect his heart.

When the meal was finished, Jefferson rose, getting everyone's attention. From their earlier conversation, Blaise knew what was at hand. Knew the role he had to play.

"Today is a momentous day for the Gutter. Ganland will recognize it as a nation, and at last, mages will have a land to call their own." This wasn't news to anyone at the table, but they all nodded in agreement. Then Jefferson continued, "And in celebration, we'll host a gala here this evening."

Marta, the cook who had formerly served Malcolm in Izhadell before moving to Nera at Jefferson's behest, stopped in her tracks, narrowing her eyes at her former employer. "And you're just telling us *now?*"

Jefferson momentarily withered under her question. Blaise recalled that Marta was a tough one. Jefferson cleared his throat. "Ah, yes. But I have faith that you and the others will do an admirable job."

"I can help," Mindy piped up.

"Yes, please do," Jefferson agreed. Blaise wondered if he wanted Mindy for her magic or simply to help the frazzled kitchen staff. Possibly both. "Kittie and Cinna will accompany me to Nera for the signing." He didn't mention Flora, but Blaise knew for once she wouldn't be accompanying her boss. Jefferson had called her to their suite in the grey hours before dawn, telling her their plans.

Cinna aimed a triumphant look at Jefferson as if she had won something. Maybe she thought she had since Jefferson was taking her instead of Blaise. He was fine with that. Let her think she'd won. She wasn't the one who had woken up beside Jefferson that morning.

Jefferson, Kittie, and Cinna finished their preparations and headed out. Once they were gone, Marian slipped over to him, frowning. "Is that horrible woman trying to steal Jefferson away?"

Ah, so he *had* interpreted her look correctly. "Um, she's trying. It's not going to work." Blaise shrugged.

Marian pursed her lips. "I could poison her."

"Mom, *don't,*" Blaise warned. They didn't need an overzealous alchemist ruining their plans.

"I could give her warts?"

"*Mom,*" he said, exasperated. Though, he appreciated her drive to protect him. He took her hand. "Walk with me. Let's talk." Blaise needed to talk to Jack, too, but that could wait. They had hours before his part of the plan needed to take action.

He led her outside, near the paddock where Emrys was grazing with Zepheus and Oberidon. It was peaceful, downright pastoral. Blaise leaned against the white fence railing. "I was going to Rainbow Flat to work through things with you. I want to understand."

Marian slouched against the rail, her eyes on the pegasi. "What part do you want to understand?"

"All of it. But mostly…" He paused, uncertain what he really wanted to know. What could heal the wounds except for time? Blaise shook his head in frustration. He had so many questions, and suddenly they were difficult to ask. "Why did you run away with me?"

She glanced at him. "I loved you from the start, even though you had to be a part of the experiment. I don't know what it was—I could think of all the other children as little more than test subjects. But you? I was the only one who could hold you and get you to calm down. To feel safe."

Blaise nodded. It was true; he'd always felt safe with his mother. *Always.* "And that changed things?"

"A little, though I obviously went forward with the experiment." Marian waved a hand to encompass him. "But then when all the children became ill and started dying…" She shook her head. "You were so sick, and it physically hurt *me* to know what I'd done to you. I did everything I could to help you pull through. And I vowed that if you lived, my days as a Confederation alchemist were over."

"So you left," Blaise whispered. *She left because she loved me.*

Marian smiled. "I did. I took you and ran as far as I could. You…I knew they would want you because of what you are. The only surviving alchemical mage, a Breaker. But you're so much more than that."

Her statement led to his next question almost too easily. He looked her in the eye. "Why alchemical mages?"

His mother traced a whorl in the wood with her index finger. "Imagine the power that comes with being able to control the variety of mage you can create. Not only that but one *superior* to natural-born mages."

Blaise wrinkled his nose at that. "*Superior?*" He'd never felt superior to anyone else, even if his brand of power did intimidate others. "How would an alchemical mage be superior?"

"You have a deeper magic reservoir than the average mage. You may not have noticed. And you…" She swallowed a lump in her throat. "Your magic is *different.*"

The old, familiar dread of being different stung Blaise, but only briefly. He frowned. The way his mother emphasized it hinted at something more. "Not only because I'm a Breaker."

"No, because you *are* a Breaker." Her voice was soft, a whisper on the wind. "There's a lot the average person doesn't know about Breakers.

Things that the Confederation and the wizards of Ravance don't want to get out."

Gooseflesh crawled across his skin. The Ravanchens had wanted him. Gregor Gaitwood, too. And the Quiet Ones. He worried at his bottom lip, thinking back to all of his conversations with Jefferson—really, Malcolm. The Doyen had connections, but there were limits to his knowledge. With his support of mages, he would no doubt have been denied crucial information.

"What do you mean?"

Marian rubbed her forehead. "I thought for years if you didn't know… if we hid…I thought no one would remember. Things are forgotten. But when it comes to power, the ones in control have a long memory." She hissed out a ragged sigh. "Words matter. Names matter. Your variety of magic is called Breaker to make it sound destructive and unpredictable."

"They're not wrong," Blaise pointed out, his tone even.

His mother locked on him with a fierce look. "They *are* wrong. Your power breaks all of the rules. *That's* what makes you a Breaker." Blaise wanted to speak, but there was something urgent etched in her expression. She leaned in closer. "Never think you're less. You're *more*. You have the potential to do things with this magic that others can only dream of. Only you could spawn an entirely new sort of mage. And that portal your friend Emmaline created? *You* could do that without breaking a sweat."

He stared at her. Emrys stopped grazing, striding over and thrusting his head over the fence to nose his rider. Blaise absently rubbed the stallion's forehead. He wanted to refute his mother's bold statement, but he couldn't. Not after what he'd done during the storm.

"Oh." It was the only thing he could think to say.

<None of this changes who you are,> Emrys reminded him, as if Blaise needed an anchor to keep him moored. He *did* need that.

"How many know all this? That I'm…" He shook his head, unable to think of how to end the sentence. *Powerful* didn't sound right, even if it was true.

"Special," Marian finished for him, fondness in her voice. Love. "I don't know. But even if they never realize the sum of what you are, the legend of Breakers is enough to make you interesting."

He digested her words. This was a lot—more than he'd bargained for, in fact. But there was a sort of freedom in finally knowing the truth of himself.

"I'm sorry for the pain I've caused you. For all the hurt. For making you something you never wanted to be." She hesitated, turning to look at him. When she spoke, her voice was a whisper. "I can take it away if you wish. I know how to make a potion that strips magic."

He blinked, startled by the offer. Years ago, he would have accepted without a second thought. But now? He shook his head. "No. I'm okay with being…this. I wouldn't be where I am today without magic." Blaise paused. "Well, I don't mean *here*. This is a weird situation."

His mother laughed, swiping away a tear with one hand as her tension shattered. "I understand. Does this mean you forgive me?"

"I had already forgiven you," Blaise admitted. "I only wanted to understand why you would do those things. And what I am." And he had wanted to be certain that she loved him, that it hadn't been an act. "I needed to know I really had a family."

"You do. Always." Marian put an arm around him, tugging him into a sideways hug. "There was never a day when I didn't think of you as my son. That's why I got a little touchy about the idea of someone stealing your beau away."

Blaise relaxed in her embrace, a feeling of ease settling over him. As if something inside him that had been broken was repaired. He had family. He had Jefferson. Well, he had Malcolm. That was something to fix. "I have to do something that might be dangerous later."

She eyed him. "I'm honestly not surprised. Do you need anything from me?"

He thought for a moment. It wouldn't hurt to be prepared. "Maybe some healing potions. But I'm not sure what you can make here."

"I picked up a few essentials in Thorn. If my son wants healing potions, he gets healing potions."

Jack quirked a brow. "I'm sorry, say that again?"

Blaise sighed. "I need you and Em to come along and do outlaw things."

The barest hint of a smile tweaked the Effigest's lips. Jack had finally left Emmaline's side when the younger mage felt well enough to sit up in bed and was asking for food. Blaise had found him taking a tray from the kitchen to the room Emmaline was using.

Jack pushed open the door to the room, and Blaise followed him in. Emmaline's skin had a porcelain cast to it, and she looked exhausted, but her eyes brightened when she saw Blaise. "You're here! I didn't know you were here." She shot an annoyed look at her father. "*Someone* didn't tell me."

"You were sleeping, and things have been busy," the outlaw muttered in his defense.

Blaise smiled at her enthusiasm, moving to sit at the end of the bed while Jack settled the tray on the bedside table. "Yeah, long story, but I'm here." He watched as Emmaline frowned at the tray, clearly displeased with the selection of bland food. "Heard about your portal. Pretty impressive."

She snorted. "Yeah, but I don't think I want to do that ever again." She poked at a piece of toast. "Can't I have something else? Bacon? Eggs?"

Jack shook his head. "Not according to Mindy."

Emmaline sighed, leaning back against the pillows and picking up the toast, gnawing off a side of crust. "What did I miss?"

"Blaise wants to do outlaw things. Ain't that cute?" Jack said, unable to hide his amusement.

Blaise rolled his eyes, though he wasn't about to ruin Jack's good mood. Emmaline looked up from her food. "What are you up to?"

Emmaline didn't know any of the happenings in Ganland, so Blaise gave her a quick overview, including Jefferson's true identity. She scowled at that, probably unhappy they had left her out of the loop for so long, but didn't comment on it.

When he finished, she nodded and summarized his plan. "So, now you wanna go to this enemy's territory and get Jefferson's ring."

Jack had listened to the whole thing, a thoughtful expression on his face. "I like it. Shows they're vulnerable." He grinned, rubbing his hands together. "We'll teach 'em not to mess with outlaw mages."

Blaise nodded. He'd surprised Jefferson with his idea to get the ring back. Blaise wasn't the type to carry the fight to someone. But he'd thought more about the point Jack had made during their travels, that sometimes letting others know the sum of your strength might dissuade them in the future.

"And I get to go?" Emmaline asked, her eyes cutting to her father, as if she assumed he would immediately deny her. They all knew he would have in the old days.

"We don't know how many enemies we're likely to run across," Jack said grudgingly.

"Flora will be coming along, too," Blaise said. "I hope three outlaw mages and a half-knocker are enough." It felt strange to count himself as an outlaw mage, a fighter. But he was. He'd made that abundantly clear in Thorn.

"Do we know who has the peacock's ring?" Jack asked.

"Gregor Gaitwood."

Jack cracked his knuckles. "This reckoning is overdue."

CHAPTER FORTY-SIX

Making History

The huge crowd gathered to witness the historic signing didn't surprise Jefferson one bit, though he knew a fair number had come just to see *him*. The miraculous return of Malcolm Wells had made him something of a curiosity, and while once he wouldn't have minded it, he minded it *very* much now.

The gathered celebrants were no doubt curious to see how the proceedings would unfold without the presence of the Board. Jefferson knew rumors spread like wildfire through a city such as Nera, and he was certain many had come to see what Rachel would do. She had made it clear that she no longer wanted or needed a Board of any kind to oversee her, which was a sort of coup in itself. Fortunately, her popularity made a healthy portion of the populace willing to overlook her audacious move. Jefferson was glad that this, at least, was not a headache he had to concern himself with.

The Silver Sands staff had done an admirable job preparing the grounds for the ceremony. It was fitting that the rubble and soot-stained buildings served as their backdrop, a reminder of what might have been lost on the fateful day of the fire.

Jefferson scanned the crowd. Cinna sat in the front row, and she waved enthusiastically to him, blowing a kiss. He inwardly cringed, remembering only too well their time in the dreamscape. It rankled him, even though he knew nothing had happened between them. But that wasn't what she remembered. Jefferson noticed the rest of the Quiet

Ones were in attendance, as he'd hoped. At least something was in their favor.

Kittie stepped onto the dais beside him, wearing a Zuzanna original and looking every bit the Pyromancer she was. It was the one Kittie had resented at first because of the flames decorating it, but now she embraced it. As she should. She was the Firebrand, after all. There was a rumble from the throng at her appearance, a combination of approval, skepticism, and outright hostility. There were still those among the population who had little love for mages, much less outlaws, and blamed Kittie for the fire.

"Are they all accounted for?" Kittie asked. Jefferson had taken the time to apprise Kittie of their situation while they saddled their pegasi that morning.

"Yes," Jefferson said, watching as Madame Boss Clayton arrived, flanked by the Bossguard.

No one was taking any chances with her safety, not after what the Board had attempted. Her children and husband filed in after her and sat in the front row, though not on the same side as Cinna. Little Romie and his sister Mary beamed and waved wildly to Kittie. The Firebrand winked at them.

Rachel nodded to Jefferson and Kittie as she took her place on the dais. An ornate wooden table separated them, a parchment squarely in the middle, along with a trio of pens. One of Rachel's aides made a quick check to ensure everything was as it should be, giving the Madame Boss a sign that all was well.

Rachel moved to the front of the platform, standing in front of the table. A pair of Bossguard stood stoically to the side, ready for action.

"People of Ganland, I thank you for joining us on a truly historic day." She paused as a few cheers surfaced from the crowd, along with murmurs. Everyone wondered how the Salt-Iron Confederation was going to react.

"I'm joined by Firebrand Kittie Dewitt of the Gutter—the very mage who saved my life."

True cheers rang out at that. Rachel was beloved by most of the populace, and they appreciated her rescue. Kittie bowed her head, accepting the accolades. The Madame Boss waited for the clamor to die down before gesturing to Jefferson. "And I'm also joined by former Doyen Malcolm Wells, who—in legendary style—returned for this historic signing."

This time, murmurs rippled through the crowd again, no doubt rumors flying around about the life and death (and life again) of Malcolm Wells. Jefferson stared straight ahead, keeping his head high and regal, playing the role of Malcolm Wells once more. If all went well for Blaise, he only had to endure this farce a little longer. Gods, he hoped Blaise was successful.

"Today, we sign a declaration recognizing the Gutter as a true nation, not only for the benefit of the mages but for ourselves," Rachel said. "We are allying with those who rooted out the evil within the very Board who should have supported me. The mages of the Gutter have proven to be worthwhile allies, and I hope that we have a long friendship and fair trade."

The crowd whooped at the mention of trade. Rachel said a few more words, then gestured for Kittie and Jefferson to join her. Kittie signed the declaration first. Then it was Jefferson's turn. He paused, taking a moment to recall his signature as Malcolm. He hadn't written it in so long.

When he finished, Rachel added hers with a flourish. Then she lifted the parchment high for all to see. "Today, on Bounty's Eve, the most fortuitous of days, we recognize the Gutter, our new ally."

The atmosphere turned to sheer revelry after that. The Bossguard escorted Rachel, Kittie, and Jefferson off the dais. They filed into a reception room in the executive wing. Rachel was grinning, invigorated by their success.

"That could not have been more perfect," she said.

Jefferson smiled, wishing he could share her enthusiasm. But he needed to focus on what was still to come. "We're holding a celebration at the Cole estate this evening. You're welcome to attend if you like."

Rachel nodded. "I would like that. I'll be there." Then one of her staffers called her name, and she turned away. "Excuse me."

Jefferson watched her go, rubbing the back of his neck. Kittie studied him, curious. "Being Malcolm Wells really makes you itchy, doesn't it?"

"You have no idea," Jefferson said, catching his dark-haired reflection in the glass of a picture frame. *But hopefully, that will change tonight.* Cinna slipped into the room, her smile broad as she approached.

"Malcolm, you were *magnificent.*" She leaned up to kiss him, and Jefferson shifted to the side, so she only caught his cheek.

He crossed his arms, taking a step back. "I thought you were going to deliver the invitations to tonight's gala."

Cinna waved a hand. "I already did. It wasn't a difficult thing." She closed the distance between them, as if she thought to win him over by sheer proximity.

He gave a sharp nod, aware of Kittie watching them. Jefferson recalled her previous words about protecting Blaise's interests. "Good. We should head back to the estate to make preparations."

CHAPTER FORTY-SEVEN

Showdown

Blaise

<I smell citrus,> Emrys announced, wings stuttering as he dropped altitude. <Reminds me of the orange meringue pies you made for Vixen's birthday. Those were good.>

Blaise shook his head at the stallion's tangent. He peered over Emrys's shoulder. The shadows of late afternoon were long, darkening the landscape, but he saw the trees dotted with oranges below. Emrys, Zepheus, Oberidon, and Tylos flew over the groves, seeking some sign of where the shrouded estate might be.

Blaise had never come up against a warded area before, but Jack had. He'd described it as feeling like an absence. Most people wouldn't think twice about it unless they knew to be aware. The pegasi flew in a pattern over the groves. Blaise spotted a few dirt roads weaving through the trees, but he supposed a theurgist might be able to hide roads as well.

Finally, Jack had luck. <We are going down,> Zepheus announced, since there was no way the riders could hear Jack with the wind whipping his words away. They followed the palomino down to the ground.

The stallions landed nimbly, tossing their heads in anticipation. Now that they were close to the ward, Blaise understood what Jack meant. It reminded him a little of the time a Dampener had muted all the sounds in the forest during an attack. An odd feeling, one that he might have otherwise ignored. That wasn't the only spell that imbued the ward, though. It tried to repel them, sending out a *wrongness* that made Blaise's stomach churn. When he took a step backward, the sensation eased.

Jack looked to be affected by it, too. His lips peeled back over his teeth, and he was armed and ready. "Get on with it. I hate this thing."

Emmaline frowned, squinting at it. "It's like the one I broke at Bitter End, but worse."

"How'd you break that?" Flora asked with interest as she fidgeted with her butterfly knife.

<Sheer stubbornness,> Oberidon commented, then pinned his ears when Emmaline swung her head to glare at him. <What? Where's the lie?>

The younger Effigest swept a loose lock of hair behind her ear. "I guess Oby's sort of right. At the time, I was tracking Mom, and my drive to find her overrode the magic of the ward." Her nose scrunched at the memory. "It wasn't pleasant, though. Be careful, Blaise."

Blaise planted his feet in a wide stance and bit his bottom lip, hoping he truly could break through the ward. *Jefferson is counting on me.* He reached out a hand, surprised when he felt very real resistance in what appeared to be empty air. The magic of the ward pushed against him, trying to force him away.

"C'mon, Blaise," Jack growled, though he took another step back as if he couldn't help it. The stallions also retreated a few paces, snorting loudly and pawing at the ground in irritation.

Well, now I know where the ward is, at least. Blaise took a deep breath, calling up his magic. Silver pooled on his skin as he sought the barrier again.

The ward pulsed with a flash of white light as soon as his magic came into contact with it. Blaise gritted his teeth, suddenly aware that the Warder had built fail-safes into it for just such a situation. Much like the protections he'd fought through on the *Retribution.*

But he was stronger than he'd been back then. His magic had grown, as had his confidence and ability to wield it. He layered his power against the ward, feeling it crack and then shatter beneath the inexorable Breaker magic. There was another brief flash, and then his shoulders sagged with relief. He no longer felt the urge to back away.

Jack heaved a sigh, coming closer. He waved a hand through the air the ward had occupied, satisfied with the lack of resistance. "That was a heavy-duty ward. Whoever made it is gonna be pissed."

"I think that's an understatement," Blaise muttered. He looked at his friends, worried about them. "You still want to do this?"

"We already knocked on the door, too late to play a game of ring and run with 'em," Flora pointed out, the most cheerful Blaise had seen her since his arrival in Ganland.

Jack grinned in agreement. "Yeah. It'll be fun." He spun his sixgun, clearly in his element now that he had free rein. "Let's see if anybody's home." They heard the baying of hounds, and the quartet of pegasi went on alert, nostrils flaring.

"Someone's home," Emmaline said as running footsteps and shouts carried to them. A line of trees blocked them from view of the buildings on the distant estate, but it was only a matter of time. She looked to Blaise. "You want one of us to stay with you?"

As much as he did, Blaise had concluded he could get into the estate house quietly on his own. Especially if his friends were providing a prominent distraction.

He shook his head. "I think I'll be okay. But be sure the pegasi let me know if someone gets hurt. I have the potions." Blaise patted the sturdy pouch at his side.

His mother hadn't been exaggerating about her stock of reagents. She'd put together three healing potions for him to carry in the event someone was wounded. Their strengths ranged from minor to a potion that would quite literally freeze the victim to give them time to reach a Healer for a life-endangering wound.

Jack shrugged. "We're gonna get some scrapes. Goes with the territory." He swung into Zepheus's saddle. "Time to stop jawing and get to business." Emmaline followed suit, though Flora stayed on the ground. The half-knocker patted Tylos and pointed to a dark grove nearby. The small white stallion wasn't prepared to fight like the others, though he'd been happy to transport Flora to the scene.

<Be careful.> Emrys bumped his nose against Blaise, his eyes full of worry.

"You, too," Blaise said with a fond smile, scratching the stallion behind the ears. "I'll be out as soon as I can."

Blaise waited as Zepheus and Oberidon vaulted into the air, only to descend on the other side of the treeline with their riders whooping and yelling to attract attention. The stallions tore across the grass, turf flying in their wake. A moment later, Emrys pushed through the trees and brush to forge a path for Blaise. He followed the black stallion's trail, glancing back to see what Flora was doing.

Her head was cocked to one side, thoughtful. "They have salt-iron in the house. Not a lot." Flora pushed her glasses up on her nose.

"Maybe to control their mages," Blaise suggested, to which Flora nodded. Jefferson had made no mention of salt-iron, but if it was a small amount and not near him, he was likely to have been unaware.

"Yeah. I'm gonna pop inside and take a look around. Holler if you need me!" Flora waved and vanished.

Emrys arched his neck as he turned to Blaise. <Call if you need me, too.>

Blaise gave a curt nod, and the stallion trotted off to join the others. The sound of fighting carried to him as Blaise kept to the late afternoon shadows, not wanting to attract attention. He had dressed in dark colors, anticipating the need for stealth.

Every few moments, the curtains in one window or another in the home twitched back, revealing a worried face peering out. Every time Blaise glimpsed the movement, he paused, hoping to recognize the person. Mostly, he saw young women dressed in what looked like formal uniforms. Household staff, he presumed.

Then, on the first floor, the curtain pulled back, and he knew the face. He'd seen it far too often in the Golden Citadel, trying to bring him under control.

Blaise froze as unexpected panic welled at the sight of Gregor Gaitwood. His heart raced, and he fought off the drive to run, to flee. Magic danced across his palms at his sudden fear. Blaise closed his eyes, swallowing as he tried to master himself. So much for thinking he'd worked through the dark memories.

But he wasn't trapped in the Golden Citadel now. Blaise clenched his jaw, strengthening his resolve. It was *good* he'd seen Gregor—he had Jefferson's ring, after all. Blaise huffed out a breath as he released the last of his anxiety. He needed to get inside, find Gregor, and reclaim the ring. It was the whole reason he'd come.

Blaise slipped through a garden and eased up to a side door. It was locked, which was sensible for a place that had found itself under attack. A locked door couldn't dissuade him, however. It was a simple matter to use his magic to break the lock and gain entry.

When Blaise slipped inside, he expected to be greeted by guards or... someone. But the corridor that stretched before him was empty, which made him think the defenders had gone to meet the threat presented by the outlaws. Anyone inside the structure was probably hiding and reluctant to fight. Blaise was glad for that since he shared the sentiment.

Now he had to figure out which room Gregor had been in. He sighed, frustrated with himself. Fear had paralyzed his brain when he'd caught sight of the Doyen, and he hadn't noticed which window Gregor had been in. All Blaise remembered was the first floor. *Maybe somewhere around the middle?* He rubbed his cheek, wishing he'd had the presence of mind to count windows.

He set about trying nearby doors. The first two rooms were empty. He had more luck in the third room. Blaise came across a trembling maid huddled in the corner; her face was burrowed against her knees. This was the part Blaise really hated: scaring innocents who had no part in this.

"Are you okay?" he asked.

She looked up, cringing at his question. Her back slammed against the wall as a reminder that she couldn't get very far. "Leave me alone! Don't hurt me!" She clutched a letter opener in her hands, probably the only nearby item she had found to defend herself.

"I'm not here to hurt you," Blaise said, which was the truth. He hoped she believed him. He held his hands up, palms open and bare of magic. "But I *am* looking for someone. Do you know which room Doyen Gaitwood is in?"

Blaise feared she wouldn't answer, locked down by her terror. But after a moment, she swallowed, nodding. "Three doors down."

Close by. That was good. "Thank you." He retreated to the threshold. "If you stay in here, you should be safe."

"Who…who are you?" she asked, her voice cracking.

This was it. He had to make it absolutely clear who had broken the Quiet Ones' defenses. Who they should think twice about crossing if they came after Jefferson again.

Blaise leaned against the doorframe, feigning ease as he answered. "The Breaker." Then he turned, shutting the door behind him and striding up the hall.

He found the door the maid had mentioned easily. Blaise wasn't at all surprised to discover it was locked. His magic took care of it once again, and he shoved the door open with his shoulder.

Gregor yelped as Blaise breached the door. But the Doyen had prepared for the inevitable. He held a revolver in his trembling hands. Gregor's eyes narrowed when he realized exactly who had forced his way into the room.

"*You!*" Gregor snarled, pulling the trigger.

Blaise was ready, too. He had his hand up, a gossamer-thin shield of Breaker magic flowing out to protect him. The first bullet struck it, the casing shattering, powder raining down. Gregor made a strangled sound, clearly not believing his eyes as he fired again.

Blaise's shield had weakened from the first hit, but it was a small matter to reinforce it. The second bullet met the same fate. The acrid scent of gunpowder bit the air, tickling Blaise's nose. "*Your* people are the ones who taught me this trick, Doyen Gaitwood."

Gregor took a step backward, glancing down at his ineffective gun. His eyes were wild. "I don't want your nightmares anymore!"

Of all the things the Doyen might have said or done, Blaise hadn't expected to be met with fear reminiscent of his own. "What?"

"Nightmares," Gregor whispered. "Your nightmares. For months, that blasted turncoat has been siphoning your nightmares to me, in a prison of dreams." He panted, as if he couldn't handle his terror. "The *bleeding*. The *pain*. The *fear*. The airship failing. I don't want any of that!"

Blaise blinked. He hadn't had nightmares for months, aside from his recent time apart from Jefferson. Had the Dreamer been feeding Blaise's trauma to Gregor as a form of torture? Blaise knew Jefferson's goal had been to make Gregor pay for his deeds, but he'd never gone into the details of *how*. Blaise only knew it involved the dreamscape. Now things fell into place, and he wasn't sure how he felt about Jefferson taking his experiences and giving them to someone else—even if that someone else was Gregor Gaitwood.

Blaise pursed his lips, thinking. He didn't want to fight the Doyen, despite all the terrible things he'd done. "I'll make you a deal. Give me Jefferson's ring, and I promise he won't torment you with my nightmares anymore."

Gregor stared at him. "Jefferson Cole is *dead*. He has no need of the ring anymore." He backed up his words with a cackle that told Blaise this man was far from well. "I *told* him. Told him he would pay for ruining my life. So I ruined *his*."

On second thought, maybe he does deserve my nightmares. Blaise clenched his fists. "Give me the ring."

"No." Gregor shook his head. "Even if I wanted to, I couldn't. I don't have it."

"Who does?"

"The Black Market. Sold it to Slocum this afternoon." Gregor bared his teeth in a too-wide smile.

The new information hit Blaise like a rock. He had to get that ring. He pivoted and headed for the door, though he paused before leaving the room.

"I'll ask Jefferson to stop giving you my nightmares on the condition that you leave us alone. If you make a move against either of us, I'll find you and show you what I can do with my magic." For emphasis, he touched a finger to the door. As he turned away, the wood groaned, spiderweb cracks forming.

"Blaise!"

Flora dove against him, knocking him down as a bullet whizzed past where Blaise had been standing only a heartbeat ago. He fell hard, his right arm wrenching beneath him in a futile effort to catch himself. There was the gut-twisting snap of bone as he landed wrong. Pain radiated through his forearm, sudden dizziness rocking him. He rolled onto his side with a whimper, tears stinging his eyes.

The half-knocker scrambled off of him, cursing as she leaped into a defensive stance with her knives out. Blaise stayed on his side. Every slight movement jostled his arm and made the pain worse. Spots swam before his eyes. *Can't black out. Not here. Not now.*

With his uninjured left hand, he fumbled for one of the small, cotton-wrapped vials in the pouch at his side. Even moving his left hand hurt. Glass rattled against his fingertips as he pulled a healing potion out.

Blaise didn't take the time to read labels—didn't think he could *read* a label at the moment, anyway. He uncorked the vial with his teeth, then poured the contents over the break with a trembling hand. An icy chill seemed to blanket the injury, and he couldn't feel his hand or the lower part of his arm anymore. At least he no longer felt as if he might black out from the pain.

Flora was staring down Gregor Gaitwood like a mouse against a rattlesnake. Though in this case, Blaise would bet on the mouse. "He's lying," Flora hissed, her eyes locked on her adversary. "He has the ring."

It took Blaise a moment to understand her words. His mind was fuzzy as the potion worked to mask the distracting pain of his injury. The Doyen had the ring. He'd hoped to distract Blaise and kill him when his back was turned. A new wave of nausea rose, and he didn't know if it was from his broken arm or the realization that he'd almost been shot with no defense against it.

"Lamar was right. You cause too much trouble to live," Gregor spat, his eyes glassy. "Every plan I make, you somehow interfere!"

Blaise rose to his feet, unsteady. His right arm felt like it was no longer connected to his body. And it was *cold*—so cold. But he would focus on that in a moment, he promised himself. Blaise shook his head, wishing that he hadn't threatened to end the devious Doyen only moments earlier. Now he had to see it through. If he didn't, Gregor wouldn't stop until Blaise was dead and Jefferson was ruined.

It was a horrible thing. Something he didn't want to do. Blaise squeezed his eyes shut as he tried to gather the courage to do something that went so far against his nature. He felt Flora's eyes on him, waiting. And Gregor's, full of malice.

Blaise's magic had killed before, but never on purpose. But for this, he had to. To protect the people he cared about. All the same, he knew this was a cliff's edge he could never come back from.

"I know you won't do it. You're too scared. *Weak*," Gregor said, then laughed his high-pitched, unhinged laugh.

The piercing *bang* of a bullet shattered the air. One moment Gregor was upright, and the next, he lurched to the ground, crimson blossoming from the center of his chest, staining his clothing. Startled, Blaise jumped aside, nearly stumbling into Jack.

The outlaw glared at the dying Doyen. "Blaise ain't *weak*. Nothing about him is weak." He spat in Gregor's direction, holstering his sixgun. "Did you get the ring?"

Blaise shook his head. In fact, he'd almost forgotten about the ring. He shivered. "No."

Jack and Flora set about searching Gregor's body for the ring. Blaise eased over and sat on a nearby chair, shaking. The cold was seeping up his arm into the rest of his body. He wanted a blanket and a warm fire.

"Got it," Jack announced, holding up a familiar cabochon ring. The outlaw glanced back at Blaise and cursed. "Gods damn it, why didn't you say you got hurt?"

Blaise wrapped his fingers around his broken arm. He couldn't feel anything aside from a weird, rubbery sensation. "We were busy. I'm okay."

"Faedra's tits, you are *not* okay," Jack swore.

"That was kind of my fault," Flora said, wiping her blood-slicked hands on Gregor's jacket. "I made him fall, and he landed wrong, but it was better than getting shot in the back."

Jack rose with a heavy sigh. "We're not gonna hear the end of this from that black stud." He moved over to Blaise, gently tucking the ring into his shirt pocket. "You hold on to that. Can you walk?"

"Yeah," Blaise whispered, getting to his feet. At least he could still feel his feet. That was a good sign, wasn't it? Jack put an arm around him to keep him upright, and he barely felt the outlaw against him.

"You're cold," Jack muttered. "What did you use?"

"Um?" was all Blaise managed through chattering teeth.

Flora picked up the empty vial and held it up. "He used something called Chill of Death. That doesn't sound foreboding or anything."

Jack huffed out a breath. "Blasted alchemy potions. You used the wrong damn one, Blaise. C'mon. We'll get you out of here and set to rights."

Oh. Blaise blinked. If he didn't feel so numb, he'd warm with embarrassment over using the most extreme potion. Chill of Death was going to slowly and inexorably freeze him until he reached a Healer. On the plus side, at least his arm didn't hurt. Nothing hurt aside from the smothering cold.

Blaise let Jack help him out of the estate, Flora guarding their backs. "Th-thank you," Blaise said. "I d-didn't want to k-kill him."

"Shut your piehole. I know." Jack whistled, and the pegasi stallions swept over to their location at a lope. Emmaline was astride Oberidon and looked none the worse for wear, though she scowled when she saw Blaise leaning on her father.

<Blaise!> Emrys snorted in alarm as soon as he saw his rider. <What happened?>

"Broken arm," Jack grumbled. "It looks worse than it is 'cause he used the wrong healing potion to stop the pain."

Emrys shook his mane, then knelt to allow Blaise to clamber into the saddle. Blaise groaned, clutching the saddlehorn with his left hand. He couldn't feel the leather, so he kept his eyes on his hand, worried that he might let go without realizing it.

"Blaise, I am *so* sorry, but I really didn't want you to get shot," Flora called up to him. "I'll pop ahead and try to get Jefferson's Healer to the stables."

"Do it," Jack said with a nod. The outlaw looked over at Blaise. "Hang in there. Flying ain't gonna be fun."

Jack was right. It wasn't fun at all with a broken arm, his body slowly icing over.

CHAPTER FORTY-EIGHT
The Truth Is a Weapon

Jefferson

The guests arrived at seven, including the Quiet Ones. From what Jefferson saw, most everyone invited would be in attendance, Quiet One and elite alike. He hoped Blaise was successful. This was his best chance to get what he wanted, to be *who* he wanted to be.

Cinna stood in the grand entryway, greeting guests as if she were already Malcolm Wells's wife. It grated at Jefferson, but he let it be. He only had to endure a little while longer.

Kittie was there, reprising her role of the Firebrand, along with Marian Hawthorne, though the alchemist kept to the outskirts, doing her best to remain anonymous. Jefferson had the feeling she was keeping an eye out for him, protecting Blaise's interests. He'd had mixed feelings on the topic of Marian Hawthorne. Jefferson wanted to be angry at her for hurting the man she called her son, but she truly seemed to love Blaise.

Jefferson circulated through the room, exchanging pleasantries here and there, artfully dodging questions from the curious inquiring about the faked death of Malcolm Wells. Madame Boss Clayton arrived, which was a relief as she ended up garnering most of the attention for a while.

Although cool fury burned in Jefferson's veins, he maintained the mask of a pleasant host preparing for an evening of revelry. His steward announced it was time for food, and the guests filtered into the dining room.

Jefferson stood behind his chair, aiming a smile that he didn't feel at his guests. "What a pleasure it is to have all of you here, celebrating the historic act of the Gutter becoming a recognized nation." His gaze flicked to Phillip Dillon, and the other man gave a nearly imperceptible nod.

"In honor of this, I'm gruntled to tell you that Mindy Carman, a talented Hospitalier from the Gutter, has had a hand in preparing tonight's meal." Jefferson noted the puzzled looks of a handful of Quiet Ones and elite who weren't familiar with that strain of magic. "Hospitaliers are a sort of mage who can suggest the best sort of food for you, and they are *never* wrong."

"Interesting," Tara murmured from her seat beside Phillip, her dark eyes settling on Mindy as the smiling young woman made a loop around the room, studying the guests.

Mindy paused when she reached the end of the table near Kittie, offering a stiff half-bow to their guests. "Because of the personalized nature of the meal, there will be a brief delay in service. I hope none of you will mind."

"We'll make do," Quiet One Megan Brew said, waving a hand in obvious dismissal. The nearby elite nodded in agreement.

Jefferson turned to Phillip, who had chosen the seat beside him. "I think this will be a night to remember."

A satisfied smile settled on the older man's face. "I think it will be, Malcolm. You've done well, and I think you will be the perfect replacement for your father."

Jefferson's jaw ached from clenching it. *Bide your time. Play along.* "I'm glad to hear that my performance was satisfactory."

Conversation at the tables turned to different topics, much to Jefferson's relief. The price of salt-iron per ounce, which was ridiculously expensive, though Tara had heard rumors of new veins discovered in the aptly named Salt-Iron Range. That pricked Jefferson and Kittie's attention —that range butted up against the Gutter. He filed it away for later—a potential reason the Quiet Ones had so much interest in the new nation. Jefferson had to catch up with the conversation when Everett Duncan waxed on about his newest racing unicorn, a colt that he claimed would sweep all the classics the next season.

"He's a certainty for the Triple Crown," Everett bragged, lifting his glass of water as if making a toast.

Megan snorted. "Only because you'll hustle the other owners to make it happen. If I had a colt or filly to aim at the classics, I'd make certain it wasn't so easy for you. Perhaps next year."

Of course, they would even rig the races in their favor. Jefferson's brow wrinkled at the new information. How far did their claws dig into everything within the Confederation? Were they like a vine clinging to the stone walls of a building, working their tendrils so deep it would be impossible to dig them out without damaging the whole structure? It was sounding more and more like that—which granted him more certainty that the plan they had come up with was the only course of action.

Mindy strode in a half-hour later, accompanied by the kitchen staff bearing the evening meal. Jefferson had to admit that it all smelled wonderful. His stomach rumbled at the first savory scent of roast chicken, which made him feel downright traitorous to think of food amid their precarious situation. *Well, best to do battle on a full stomach.*

Up and down the table, a variety of plates clattered into place before the guests. Garden-fresh salads, cuts of lamb, roast chicken, pork roast, mashed potatoes. Mindy, Marta, and the rest of the kitchen staff had truly gone all-out for their part in this. Jefferson was fiercely proud of them. None of them were powerful, but they were doing their part. He made a mental note to grant them all a considerable bonus when he was back to being himself.

Phillip eyed Jefferson's meal. "Trade with me."

Jefferson arched his brows. "Do you think we're poisoning you?" He kept his voice innocent and incredulous, though he was delighted that Phillip suspected him of treachery. Their Hospitalier was the perfect misdirection.

"Something like that."

Jefferson shrugged. Mindy stood by the door that led to the kitchen, and a muscle ticked in her cheek, though he knew it was only annoyance and nothing more severe. Jefferson reached over and lifted Dillon's plate of lamb and fresh green beans, swapping it with his former entrée of chicken breast and steamed broccoli florets.

"Just as well," Jefferson said. "I do so hate when the florets get stuck in my teeth with company over. Embarrassing."

His comment gave Dillon pause, and the other man hesitated before doubling down, lifting fork and knife to saw at the chicken only after Jefferson did the same for his lamb and took a bite.

The dinner course continued smoothly. Light chatter peppered the room, and Jefferson did his best to listen in on the surrounding conversations while maintaining his own. He watched everyone at the table closely. Midway through the course, he glimpsed a shock of pink hair in his periphery. Marian slipped out of the room, though no one else paid her any mind. Flora had called her out, but why? Jefferson hated that all he could do was sit and smile politely.

As the staff removed their plates, Seledora's mental voice tickled against his mind. <They're here. Blaise was injured, and Flora summoned your Healer to tend to it.> The mare must have sensed his sudden alarm since she continued, <It is not bad. A broken arm, nothing more. Your Healer is tending to him now, and his mother is here, too.>

That didn't matter. Knowing that Blaise was hurt sent a tremor of guilt and worry through Jefferson. He rose from his seat, glad for all his years of practice at controlling his expressions. "I believe we have some entertainment lined up to go along with the dessert course. I'll be back in a moment." He excused himself and hurried out to the stables.

TRUE TO SELEDORA'S WORD, HE FOUND BLAISE SITTING ON A BALE OF HAY IN the stables, his face almost as grey as Flora's skin. Jefferson's Healer, Agnes, gripped his arm in her hands as Marian Hawthorne stood on the other side, her face crinkled with worry. Jack and Emmaline were seeing to the pegasi, though they shot furtive glances at Blaise. Emrys was still tacked and in the stall across from Blaise, his attention never leaving his rider.

"Oh, Blaise," Jefferson whispered, hurrying over. He crouched in front of the Breaker, though he gave Agnes room to work. "What happened?"

Flora peered around from behind Blaise, guilt etched on her face. "It was me, but it was an accident. I'll tell you later."

"Why is he so cold?" Jefferson asked, touching Blaise's face gently. Blaise's eyes were closed, and he never stopped shivering. The Breaker hadn't even acknowledged his presence yet, which was worrisome.

"I sent along healing potions," Marian explained, voice soft. "Blaise picked the wrong one. The Chill of Death potion is intended for grievous wounds."

"It's doing its job, though," Agnes murmured, giving Jefferson an encouraging look. "I'm almost done mending the break, and he should warm up after that."

Jefferson glanced back at the house. If he lingered too long, the odds were good someone would come looking for him. Probably Cinna, and that would ruin everything. He eased over to Jack. "Did he get the ring?"

The outlaw gave a curt nod, then tapped a hand over his own shirt pocket and pointed to Blaise. Jefferson appreciated the Effigest's candor. Agnes didn't know his secrets, though he wondered at this point if it even mattered.

The Healer made a satisfied sound, rising. "He's going to be tender, but he'll be right as rain before long. Shall I help him to bed, Ms. Strop?"

Jefferson had forgotten that at the moment, Flora had command of his home. The half-knocker's lips pressed into a frown, no doubt aware that the current plan didn't include anyone convalescing. "We'll take care of him. Thanks, Agnes." The Healer nodded and headed out.

As soon as she was out of the barn, Jefferson slid in front of Blaise again. The Breaker's skin had regained a little of its color, though he still shivered. "Blaise?"

The Breaker cracked his eyes open, lifting his good hand to pull something small from his pocket. The cabochon ring gleamed up at them. "Got it."

Jefferson wanted to protest that he didn't care about the ring, that he cared about *Blaise*, but it was a lie. He needed that ring, needed it so that he could live with himself. He hoped Blaise understood that. Jefferson's need for Blaise was on a different level, but it was just as pressing. Gingerly, Jefferson reached for the ring, surprised when Blaise closed freezing fingers around his wrist.

The Breaker lifted his chin, plaintive eyes meeting Jefferson's. "No more secrets."

Jefferson's fist curled around the ring, and he was shocked by how chill both the metal and Blaise's flesh were. He reached out and cupped his beau's cheek with his free hand. "My secrets are a sort of armor."

"The truth is a weapon we can wield," Blaise whispered, and there was no doubt he was completely lucid in that moment. He squeezed Jefferson's wrist, then released it. "No more secrets. Or you'll never be free."

Jefferson swallowed. "But—"

"Go," Blaise whispered, teeth clacking with the effort. "Your guests are waiting."

Jefferson huffed with frustration. "I love you. I need you to be okay." Then he leaned in and kissed the Breaker on his freezing lips. *Please be okay.*

"We've got Blaise," Jack said, pointing toward the house. "Get in there and make your point, or this will all be for nothing."

Jack was right. Jefferson nodded, clutching the ring in his fist. Blaise didn't look like he should go anywhere except to bed, as Agnes had prescribed. The Breaker met his eyes, and Jefferson couldn't overlook the intensity in their depths. Blaise wouldn't be denied this. Jefferson swallowed. "See you soon."

He slipped the ring into his greatcoat's interior pocket and headed for the house, glad to find Flora tagging along. "I'm really, really sorry," she said, jogging to keep up with him. "I didn't mean to break your Breaker."

Jefferson couldn't help it; he had to chuckle at the absolute madness of the situation. *Gallows humor, I suppose.* "I know you didn't. What happened?"

Her expression tightened with anger. "I popped into the room where

Blaise was and saw Gregor about to shoot him. Blaise didn't know—he had his back turned. I was closer to him than I was to Gregor, so I tackled him."

Jefferson drew to a stop, trembling. "Gregor tried to kill Blaise?"

"Gregor's dead now," Flora said, steel in her voice. She stared ahead of them at the house where the Quiet Ones and the rest of the elite were awaiting his return. But they could wait a few moments longer.

"Was it Blaise? Or you?" Jefferson hated to ask it, but he had to know. Not that he was unhappy to hear of Gregor's death—no, he was more concerned with the psychological weight of such an action on Blaise.

"Neither of us. It was Jack."

Jefferson relaxed at the news. He knew that if it came down to it, Blaise would do what needed to be done. But he would suffer for it. At least he shouldn't have to worry about that in this case. Jefferson buried those concerns for the time being. He needed to see this through to the end.

He paused outside the entrance to the dining room, clenching and then loosening his hands a few times to work out some of his tension. Flora patted his arm and ghosted away, as she always did. Jefferson pasted a brilliant smile onto his face and pushed the door open. The waitstaff were delivering slices of cake to each of the guests. The dessert was a delicious chocolate confection with a topping of fruit, so tempting that it had distracted most of the attendees.

Jefferson returned to his place at the table, though he wasn't hungry for the beautiful slice of cake. Phillip slid a curious glance his way, but the cake did its job, and the Quiet One was more concerned with eating it than worrying about Jefferson. But to maintain appearances, he poked at the cake with his fork, taking a few half-hearted bites while he thought about Blaise sitting in the stable, chilled to the bone.

<Blaise and Emrys are ready,> Seledora informed him. <And I'm right outside.>

Jefferson breathed a sigh of relief. Finally, something was falling into place. He waited another minute before pushing his plate away and rising from his seat. He crossed to the front of the room, which put him comfortably near the recessed entryway. It would give him the clear exit he needed.

"May I have your attention, please?" Jefferson called above the dull roar of conversation. The soft murmurs continued, most guests unaware that he had moved to speak.

A ball of flame roared up into the air, vanishing as quickly as it had come. Kittie stood across the room from him, smiling. "Sorry, but you must admit that was very effective." By the look on her face, she wasn't sorry at all. "Malcolm Wells would like to speak." She nodded to Jefferson, returning to her seat with satisfaction. He was glad that Kittie had found her way as the Firebrand.

All eyes in the room fell on him. Jefferson took a deep breath. This was it, a moment that he knew would define the rest of his life. He thought he'd done difficult things before as a politician, but this? It was overwhelming, and he knew he wouldn't have the tenacity to do it without Blaise and his friends.

"Thank you all once more for joining us this evening. Bounty's Eve is a special holiday in Ganland, a time for reflecting on the gifts granted to us by Tabris's grace." Murmurs from the crowd agreed with his sentiment. "And I'm quite glad to say that over the past months, I've been given a windfall. But it's not gold or fine goods, not the sort of thing you would expect."

Confused whispers rose at his words. Rumors taking wing. Cinna, seated a dozen yards away, beamed as if he meant her. Jefferson didn't miss her reaction, and his mouth pulled into a thin line as he plowed onward.

"By now, you have all heard the stories." Jefferson gestured to his guests, many of whom nodded. "How the distraught Doyen, overcome with grief, faked his own death. And while, as with most wild stories, there is a grain of truth to it—that's not what actually happened." He thought about Blaise, curled close beside him. Blaise astride Emrys, smiling as they went out together for a ride. "In truth, I had a second chance at life. At love."

The crowd grew noisy once more, women enchanted by the idea of such romance and men whistling in appreciation. Cinna rose from her seat, as if to accept their accolades. He almost felt bad about what was to come, aware it would crush Cinna's hopes. But not really, knowing that his own happiness was at stake.

He pulled out his ring and clutched it in his hand. "Not the way you think, though. Not at all."

Jefferson rolled the cabochon ring between his thumb and index finger before slipping it onto his customary ring finger. He felt the glamor wash over him, erasing Malcolm Wells and shifting him into the man he truly wanted to be. Cries of alarm and confusion rose from the crowd, along with a few nervous titters, as if some thought this might be an elaborate prank.

"Malcolm Wells is *dead*," Jefferson declared, his voice ringing out. "I'm Jefferson Cole, and I'm an outlaw mage. I won't be taking questions at this time."

Chaos erupted at his announcement, men and women trying to get out of their seats to accost him, to demand answers. Jefferson caught sight of Phillip trying to break free of the mass to come after him. Cinna stood in the middle of it, shock etched across her lovely face.

Jefferson caught Kittie's eye and gave her a grateful nod, then slipped out through the nearby exit.

CHAPTER FORTY-NINE

Dragons Aren't Scared of Other Dragons

Jefferson

"Are you well enough for this?" Jefferson asked, frowning at Blaise. The Breaker clung to Emrys's saddle, his skin as pale as moonlight.

"Better than I was," Blaise assured him. He sounded stronger, at any rate. "You're not leaving without me."

Jefferson nodded. In this, he knew the younger man wouldn't be dissuaded. Truth be told, Jefferson wasn't particularly inclined to argue. His world had just been turned upside-down—even more than before. If ever there was a time he needed Blaise, it was now.

<Where shall we go?> Seledora asked.

"The beach, then north. There's a little cove there where we can lie low while the ruckus dies down." Jefferson sighed, relishing the idea of peace.

The two pegasi took to the air, the stars overhead lighting their way. Seledora soared over the breaking waves once they reached the beach, and Jefferson guided her to the cove. The pegasi trotted through the surf to reach it.

Blaise and Jefferson dismounted, moving to sit on a log that had washed up in a storm and then been partially buried in sand. "What now?" Blaise asked.

"I don't know," Jefferson said softly, taking Blaise's hand. It was much warmer now. "But it's okay because I'm with you. I'm sorry you were hurt on my account."

"I was hurt because I'm the most accident-prone mage in history," Blaise pointed out. "I'm very talented at hurting myself. If I hadn't landed wrong, I would have been a little bruised and nothing more."

"Well, the fact remains that you *were* hurt, and I don't like that," Jefferson murmured, looking down at Blaise's right arm. It looked better, though. Agnes had done an excellent job. She wasn't Nadine, but she was skilled. "Flora told me what happened."

Blaise stared out at the silver-capped waves as they reflected the starlight. "Why didn't you tell me what you did to Gregor?"

Oh, not that. Jefferson didn't want to think about that right now. But Blaise deserved an answer. The Breaker's tone was neutral, but Jefferson knew it wouldn't take much to tip him over into anger. As much as Blaise disliked conflict, there were some things he would stand up for, and Jefferson suspected this was one of them.

"I was so angry about what he'd done to you. I wanted him to suffer, to understand on an intimate level every moment of pain that had been inflicted on you."

Beside him, Blaise sighed. "I know *why* you did it." His voice was so soft it was difficult to hear over the lapping waves. "But those were *my* fears. *My* experiences. *My* pain. You can't just give away those pieces of me. They're part of what's made me who I am."

Damn, Jefferson hadn't even realized he'd done the equivalent of stealing from Blaise. When he put it like that... He winced, shaking his head. "But it's *my* fault you had to suffer those things at all."

Blaise looked as if he'd been ready to say something else and paused, narrowing his eyes. "What do you mean it's your fault? Gregor was the one who held me there. Not you."

"*I'm* the reason you were captured in the first place," Jefferson said, recalling the sight of the mangled airship and destroyed fort. "If I hadn't asked you to use your magic to—"

"I would have done it anyway."

It was Jefferson's turn to look surprised. "What?"

Blaise edged closer, his shoulder brushing Jefferson's. "I would have destroyed the *Retribution* anyway. Flora told me I didn't have to. That you would understand if I didn't." He hazarded a glance before continuing, "I knew what I was getting into. Have you been blaming yourself for that all this time?"

"Obviously," Jefferson said, boggled. It had never occurred to him that it might have been *Blaise's* choice. He'd been so certain the kind-hearted Breaker had only done it at his behest.

"And you've been trying to make up for it ever since?" Blaise guessed.

"*Obviously.*" Jefferson rubbed his cheek as he considered this new information. "I made a grievous miscalculation, using my magic as I did. I should have told you."

"You should have told me," Blaise agreed. Then the Breaker reached over and took Jefferson's hand. "But we all make mistakes. Some bigger than others. I know you thought you were protecting me, but I'm tougher than I look."

You are, aren't you? Jefferson squeezed the Breaker's hand, glad for the warmth that had returned. "Did you work things out with your mother?" Jefferson asked gently.

"Yeah." Blaise was quiet for a time, leaving the only sound around them the wash of the tide and the occasional swish of a pegasus tail as they rested nearby. "I understand more about her. More about me." His words hinted at new revelations, but Jefferson didn't press. He was confident Blaise would tell him when he was ready.

"I didn't get to properly tell you, but I'm very sorry for the loss of your father," Jefferson said. "He was proud of you."

Blaise's fingers tightened on his as the Breaker turned to face him. "Wait. What do you mean? You met my father?"

"He sought me out the last time I went to Rainbow Flat." He'd been mindful of Blaise's temporarily strained relationship with his family, which had been challenging when he had to check on his interests in the other outlaw town. "I know you asked me not to speak with them, but I could hardly be rude when he was the one to find me."

"That sounds like something he'd do." Blaise nodded. He licked his lips, as if uncertain about his next words. "Why did he speak to you?"

Jefferson chuckled. "He didn't come out and say it, but I suspect he heard about me from your mother. I got the impression he wanted to see if I was worthy of his son."

Blaise glanced at him. "You are, even if you do stupid things sometimes." It seemed he wasn't going to forget about Gregor anytime soon. Fair enough. "What else did he say?" There was a hunger in his voice, as if he were seeking out a precious connection to a lost loved one. Jefferson wondered what that was like, to have such a bond with a father.

"He asked me how you were doing. He worried for you, I think. Wanted you to be okay. So, I told him about the bakery. And oh, I wish you could have seen the way his face lit up. There was so much pride in his eyes."

"I can imagine it," Blaise said. He swiped at one eye with his free hand, and Jefferson heard a soft sniffle. Then he cleared his throat. "So, that was quite an exit you made. And you sidestepped my earlier question. What's next?

Jefferson wet his lips. He'd avoided answering because, for the first time in his life, he didn't have a plan of any sort. Didn't even have another identity to fall back on. "I don't know what tomorrow will bring. But I think for now, I'd like to watch the stars with you."

Blaise squeezed his hand again. "I'd like that, too."

Jack

THE CONFUSION THE PEACOCK HAD SOWN AT HIS FANCY GALA WAS A SOURCE of endless entertainment for Jack. The gobsmacked looks on the faces of the elite as they realized Cole had pulled one over on them was satisfying. It was enough to make Jack think Jefferson Cole wasn't so bad after all.

The aftermath, though, had been a whole other mess. Many guests thought it was an elaborate joke. Others were angered, demanding that Cole pay for his treachery.

Courtesy of Flora, Jack had found a good spot to watch the crowd. He wanted to see these so-called Quiet Ones for himself, to assess the threat they might pose. Jack didn't like their interest in the Gutter. He would feel far more comfortable if they *didn't* want the Gutter to be a nation. That seemed more normal for the Confederation.

After a few minutes, he'd figured out who the Quiet Ones were among the guests. It wasn't a difficult task since he was familiar with the little rattlesnake named Cinna. She had been quick to seek out others, and Jack observed how they interacted. *Quiet Ones.*

Many of the guests went home, while others stayed to take advantage of the free-flowing alcohol. Jack waited until the Quiet One he wanted was alone, then slipped over to him as silent as a shadow.

"Phillip Dillon." He allowed a hint of a threatening growl into his voice, his favorite way to let someone know they were on his shit list.

Dillon turned, eyes wide as he took in the looming outlaw. "Who... what do you want?"

Jack stalked closer, allowing his feral smile to slide into place. "Wanted you to know we sent a message to your home, but I'm sure you didn't receive it yet." He folded his arms across his chest, meeting Dillon's gaze.

The Quiet One scowled. "What?"

Jack stepped closer until mere inches separated them. He leaned over to Dillon's ear and whispered, "Gregor Gaitwood is *dead.*"

Dillon reeled away, mouth twisting in disbelief. "But...how? Wait. *You're* the one who got the ring back to Wells!"

"Nah," Jack said with a shake of his head. "That was all the Breaker. I only settled the score." He took a step back, allowing a little more space between them.

Dillon made a whistling noise as he exhaled through his nose. "And is he the one who killed my Walker? Or was that you?"

His Walker? Jack hadn't expected the question, and it took him a moment to connect the dots. The Wallwalker. Emrys's kick must have done her in. Jack decided this man didn't deserve an answer to all of his questions. Instead, he gave a too-wide smile. "I'll let you and your buddies get going. As I understand it, there's a bit of a mess to clean up." Jack's pale eyes bored into Dillon's until the other man broke the stare.

Dillon swallowed. "We're not afraid of you."

Jack chuckled. "Dragons aren't scared of other dragons. Even when they should be." With a lazy shrug, he pivoted and ambled away, though a large part of him hoped that Dillon would either try to attack him or call him back. But the Quiet One did neither, much to his disappointment. Maybe the man had a sense of self-preservation.

He slunk back into the shadows, watching as the rest of the guests left over the next few hours. It was the middle of the night by the time only Cole's staff and the outlaws remained.

Kittie rubbed her forehead, yawning. "Can we sleep now? This has been a day."

Jack slipped alongside his wife, curling an arm around her. Yeah, he figured hitting the hay was a good idea. Even better with her at his side.

"Where did Jefferson and Blaise go?" Emmaline asked, frowning with concern.

"I have a pretty good idea where they went," Flora said. "I'll get 'em in the morning."

"Better get shut-eye now while we can," Jack agreed. "With the shit-storm Cole left behind, the next few days ain't gonna be simple."

CHAPTER FIFTY

Ambassador

Jefferson

Two days later, Madame Boss Rachel Clayton paced across the front of the assembly room, pausing occasionally to shake her head and give Jefferson a bewildered look. He had the good sense to stay quiet. Jefferson knew the only thing standing between him and a long vacation in the darkest hole of a Gannish prison was the simple fact that he'd stood up for Rachel against her Board.

"What are we going to do about this?" Rachel sputtered at last, slapping her palm against the tabletop. "We have elite out there demanding to break all ties with the Gutter because of you...because of this..." She seemed unable to decide how she wanted to end her sentence and simply shook her head, eyes narrowed with frustration.

Jefferson wet his too-dry lips. "I'm willing to take all the blame, Rachel. But don't let this destroy things with the Gutter. Please."

She frowned, pulling out a chair and dropping into it. "You've heard the Confederation is demanding we hand you over to them, right?"

He nodded. "Yes." Was her plan to trade him off to the Confederation, in order to let the declaration with the Gutter remain in place? That might be the only way to placate the Confederation in a situation like this: hand over the treasonous former Doyen.

"I've told them no."

Jefferson blinked. "What?" He was certain he'd misheard her.

Rachel braced her elbows on the table, leaning over them. "I won't pretend I agree with everything you've done. But I can see you have a good heart, and you're trying to do what you think is right." She sighed. "And besides, I have need of an Ambassador, and who better than a mage from Ganland with deep ties to the Gutter?"

His mouth dropped open in surprise. He was sure he'd lost all hope of his ambassadorship, but it had been a worthwhile loss in the grand scheme of things. "But...how?" His mind whirled, trying to figure out how she would make it work.

A hint of a smile touched her lips. "I'm being quite stubborn about the whole thing, honestly. And without a Board, no one can naysay me." Rachel shrugged. "Even if they could, who would be a better selection?"

Jefferson cocked his head. "I know for a fact you have *many* diplomats who would fit the bill." Many who would be eager to work with the Gutter, on the hunt for future profit margins.

"And none of them who have a working relationship already," Rachel reminded him. Then her expression softened. "Besides, that's the safest option for you at this point. Outside of a Gannish prison to atone for your fraud, anyway."

"I'll happily keep that off the table, thank you," Jefferson agreed, though he deflated at the reminder. It had only been two days since his announcement, but it had been a whirlwind. And during much of it, he'd kept a low profile to avoid answering questions. He was vilified in the newspapers, and he wondered at Rachel keeping him on as Ambassador.

Worst of all, though, the Quiet Ones couldn't harm him physically. They moved in another way sure to hurt him. Despite his insistence that he was Jefferson Cole, couriers had begun to deliver letter after letter declaring that his accounts were being closed and access to his funds denied. There was no proof that he existed, which Jefferson knew was false. When he'd first taken on this identity, he'd been very careful to create a trail proving his validity. The Quiet Ones were scrubbing away every trace, still intent on denying him this life.

"Are you going to be okay?" Rachel asked, her voice gentle.

Jefferson rubbed his face. "I will be, in time. I appreciate your support."

The Madame Boss nodded. "*You* supported *me*. It's high time I returned the favor."

CHAPTER FIFTY-ONE
Rich in the Only Way That Matters

Blaise

"Mama!"

Brody and Lucienne pelted out of the Broken Horn Saloon, throwing up clods of red dirt in their wake as they sprinted toward the group of pegasi coming in for a landing. Chester yapped in their wake, ears flapping.

Blaise pulled up his flight goggles, snapping them against his forehead as he watched his mother dismount. It had been a long road to get back to the Gutter—they hadn't dared go overland, concerned they might pose too tempting a target for the Confederation to snatch up.

Of their group, only Jack's face was on handbills, but they hadn't wanted to take any chances. Madame Boss Clayton had chartered a steamer for them, and they made the arduous journey across the Gulf of Stars and into the Jewelled Sea. None of the pegasi had enjoyed the crossing, forced to spend much of their time below decks in the hold as they trundled through late-season storms.

But they were back now, and that was what mattered. His siblings swarmed around their mother, Brody alternately laughing and crying with delight. It wasn't long before he was babbling about the wonders of the Feast of Flight. Blaise smiled at his little brother's enthusiasm, though he was disappointed he'd missed it. They'd had to celebrate it amid a hurricane-force gale on the steamer.

Clover ambled up, watching Blaise's siblings fondly.

"Hope they weren't too much of an imposition," he called to her as he dismounted.

The Knossan shook her head, moving closer to Emrys and Blaise. "They were not a problem. I was happy to provide them with a roof over their heads and the safety they needed." Her warm brown eyes studied him. "Did you have your vengeance?"

Blaise rubbed his cheek. "Turns out that wasn't what I needed."

"That is often the way of things," Clover agreed, her hooves crunching the dirt as she shifted her weight. "Will they be staying in Fortitude?"

"Yes," Blaise answered. Even if the Hawthorne house in Rainbow Flat hadn't been in a shambles, he would have wanted it so. He didn't want so much distance between him and his family—in more ways than one.

The Knossan nodded, content. "That is good."

Emrys trotted to the stables, flicking an ear back as Blaise dismounted. More of the pegasi from their group filed in, some with riders and some without. A handful of grooms hurried out to greet them.

<Will there be celebratory cake?> the pegasus asked, nosing Blaise's shoulder. <Or, at the very least, apology cake?>

Blaise chuckled. Emrys's dream of sugary treats had sustained him during the interminable time at sea. "I'll start working on the cake tomorrow. I suspect we'll have a town celebration for our return, but you can help me sample them to see which flavor is best."

<All the flavors.>

"Not going to happen," Blaise told the stallion, giving him a fond scratch behind the ears.

He went about the business of unsaddling Emrys and rubbing him down, making sure he had fresh water and sweet feed. Blaise was happy to handle the tasks again. For the longest time, his friends had taken care of Emrys for him. Despite Agnes's effective healing, he'd been treated like a porcelain doll. Blaise had grudgingly allowed it—he was surrounded by people who *cared* about him. Family, even if he wasn't related to a single one by blood.

Emmaline walked with Oberidon to a nearby stall, then came over to hang on the partition outside Emrys's. "Same time at the bakery tomorrow?"

Blaise yawned. As much as he was looking forward to a return to normal, he needed a little rest. "You can go in whenever you want, but I may sleep in for once. Might do some baking for fun when I get up and about."

She nodded. "Sounds good. I'll tell Reuben and Hannah they're in charge tomorrow." Emmaline waved, then hurried off.

Blaise glanced up the aisle, noticing Jefferson outside Seledora's stall, murmuring to the mare. He walked over to join them.

Seledora's ears pricked in his direction, and she spoke privately to Blaise. <He's telling me I'll have to go elsewhere for work because he can no longer afford me. Your mate is oblivious.>

Blaise's mouth twitched. He really wanted to tell Seledora that Jefferson was *not* oblivious—she just refused to come out and say the obvious: that she liked Jefferson enough to claim him as her rider.

Jefferson turned at Blaise's approach, a smile sliding onto his face. But it wasn't genuine. Blaise read the worry behind it.

"Stop trying to fire your attorney," Blaise suggested.

"She told you, did she?"

"Yes."

Jefferson sighed. "I'll go into bankruptcy keeping her on retainer. Wait, I'm *already* in bankruptcy."

Blaise shook his head. "You don't owe her anything, Jefferson."

Jefferson's green eyes narrowed in confusion. "What do you mean?"

Blaise crossed his arms. "Tell him."

Seledora's sides heaved with a great breath. She raised her head as if she were going to pull away, angling it to give Blaise a nasty look. The mare raked the straw with a forehoof. <You are my rider.>

Jefferson swallowed as if he dared not believe it. He placed a hand beneath Seledora's jaw, as if he feared she was an illusion that might vanish. Then he rested his forehead against hers.

"You're only bankrupt without love," Blaise said.

Jefferson pulled away from Seledora, a smile illuminating his face. "Then I'm rich in the only way that matters."

<hr>

Jack

"Seems you made a good showing for yourself, Firebrand." Jack's boots clattered against the stairs as they left Ringleader HQ. The meeting they'd just gotten out of hadn't been the most pleasant, but hadn't been the worst, either. Jack was going to be sorely glad when he didn't have to worry about meetings for a while. Kittie had presented herself and the delegation well, though. "I'm proud of you."

Kittie beamed at her husband's words. "I was with good people who helped to see it through."

Jack shook his head. "Didn't mean the delegation, though I'm proud of you for that, too. I mean your habit. It hasn't escaped my notice that you're dry as the Deadwood Forest in fire season."

"It's true for that, too," Kittie said, though she glanced away as if embarrassed. "Mindy helped figure out what works for me."

Her penchant for Caladrius root tea hadn't escaped him, either. Jack had watched her carefully since he'd arrived at the Cole estate, and he'd been surprised that, despite the cock-ups, she hadn't wavered. Whatever Mindy had figured out had been effective. "You should be proud of yourself, too."

"I am." Kittie lifted her chin, meeting his eyes. Mischief glinted in hers. "And it seems you didn't do half bad with our daughter, either."

Jack raised his brows. "Only trekked across the entire Untamed Territory with her."

"Took on the nastiest desperadoes on the continent," Kittie added, crossing her arms. She hadn't been enthused about that, though Jack wondered if it was only because she hadn't been there.

"Then portaled across half a continent." Jack didn't mean to sound so smug about it, but he couldn't help it. That was something no mage had ever done before. Then he paused, wondering if he'd misspoken. "Wait, this an ambush? You mad at me?"

Kittie eyed him. "Should I be?"

He frowned, rubbing the back of his neck. "I had an easier time fighting the Copperheads than figuring you out about this."

Kittie laughed. "No, I'm not mad at you. I'm proud that you treated Emmaline like the brilliant young woman she is."

"She's gonna be an outlaw," Jack said, his voice so low it barely carried to his wife's ears.

"Is that so bad?"

Jack pursed his lips, thinking. He liked being an outlaw. Enjoyed the danger. No two days ever the same. But was that the life for his daughter? He turned the idea over in his mind. What did he expect her to be, a townie? A woman settled down like a broody hen, only worrying about children and a household? That wasn't right, either. Kittie wasn't any of those things. Then he thought about Blaise, how the Breaker was an outlaw—and also wasn't. *Maybe Em can be like that.*

"Nah, I reckon it's not," Jack admitted, setting those thoughts aside for later.

He cocked his head. "I got something to show you."

"Jack Dewitt, did you bring me a gift?" Kittie asked, her face alight with pleasure. "And you've been sitting on it this long?

"I needed to wait until we were in the Gutter."

She linked her arm through his. "Now you're being mysterious."

"Yep." Jack grinned, revealing a carry-sack he'd concealed in his duster. He carefully drew out the box containing the firepot. He'd hung onto it, waiting for the right moment once they were back in Fortitude and the dust had settled a little.

"What is it?" Kittie asked, studying the box.

The outlaw carefully opened the box, displaying the firepot wrapped in dragonskin. Kittie's eyes widened as Jack drew the small earthenware jar out. "Somethin' you don't see every day. And what comes of it is up to you." Something rattled within the earthenware. "Hmm, we should go to the fire pit behind the house."

Kittie regarded him with great curiosity, and together they walked from HQ to their house. There was little more than ash in the fire pit, but Jack didn't think that mattered. He held out the firepot. "For you."

Kittie accepted it, frowning uncertainly at it. "You can start explaining any moment now."

He chuckled. "Open it up and pour the contents into the pit."

Kittie did as he suggested, watching as what looked like uncut red gemstones clattered into the fire pit. A pair of gleaming black stones winked in the afternoon light. Kittie crouched down, getting a better look. "Is that fire opal? And obsidian?"

"Yep."

"*Jack.*" Kittie sounded exasperated. "You forget, I only know a fraction of the arcane dragonshit you do."

He hid a smile at her frustration. "Set 'em on fire and watch."

"If you're tricking me into releasing a fiery demon from Perdition that we have to fight, so help me—"

"It's not a demon. I mean, not really."

Kittie gesticulated at him with both hands. "What do you mean *not really*? I should set *you* on fire, Jack Arthur Dewitt."

"Damn, you used my entire name," he said with a laugh. Then he grinned, stepping closer to her. "I'd never trick you. This really is something special. Promise." He followed his words by planting a kiss on her lips. She didn't reciprocate, not at first. Probably too annoyed at him playing coy. But then she relented, and he had a few sweet moments to enjoy the smoky taste of her.

Kittie pulled away first, giving him another dubious look. "Guess I'll see what ridiculousness you've gotten up to."

She stood beside the fire pit and snapped her fingers. A spark appeared in the cold ashes. She gasped as the fire—*her* fire—took on a life all its own. A brilliant flash blinded them for an instant, and Jack took a step back, wondering if he'd been mistaken. Then he heard the sharp rap of hooves on the ground and a snort.

"What?" Kittie gasped, a hand to her mouth.

A chestnut mare stood over the fire pit, her eyes shining like obsidian. She pawed at the ground, arching her lovely neck. Her long mane and tail tousled in the breeze like living flames. The mare stared at them, nostrils distended as she assessed them. She tossed her head, skittish, and tried to back away, but the invisible constraints of the fire pit bound her. The equine snorted out a fearful breath, ears flicking back and forth.

"Jack..." Kittie didn't dare look at him, her entire focus on the mare. "What in Perdition am I looking at?"

"She's an aethon," Jack said. "A horse born of fire. She was trapped in the firepot, and only arcane flame could free her."

"I freed her or trapped her again?" Kittie asked, voice sharp. She no doubt had noticed the aethon couldn't leave the pit.

"The pit is a safety measure. Couldn't exactly release a fire spirit in the middle of a flammable town." Jack watched the mare, marveling at her beauty. "Once we know she won't run off and burn down the first building she trots by, you can release her."

Kittie made a frustrated sound. "And how do I do that?"

Jack shrugged. "Touch her. Like knows like. Let her know we'll release her either way, but if she hurts this town, there'll be trouble."

His wife paused at that, glancing at him. "You brought her here so I could free her, knowing that doing so put Fortitude at risk?"

That wasn't quite it, but Jack didn't want to explain himself at the moment. "She was imprisoned, and I didn't like it. See if she'll let you touch her."

Kittie pursed her lips, then held out a hand. The aethon tossed her head, blowing out a nervous breath. Then the mare took a hesitant step closer, nostrils sucking in Kittie's scent. The fire spirit made a soft rumble. The next thing Jack knew, the aethon had shifted so that Kittie's palm pressed against the equine's broad forehead.

"*Oh.*" Kittie's voice was breathy. "She understands. And she wants to stay."

Jefferson

"So, tense meeting, huh?" Blaise asked.

Jefferson glanced over his shoulder, watching as Blaise picked his way through the scrubby brush that sprung up around the rim of the canyon. A frigid wind whistled past them, and Jefferson tugged his greatcoat closer. He'd wandered out of town to think at the end of yet another meeting with all the stakeholders of the Gutter. "It was tense, yes, but I'm used to that."

Blaise studied him for a moment, then moved to sit down beside him. "Look, you've been pretty quiet the last few days, so I gave you some space. But quiet and introspective is *my* thing. What's wrong?"

Everything. Jefferson sighed. He wanted to tell Blaise that he was fine, but it was a lie. "I feel unmoored. The life I had…" He blew out a breath. "Everything's just *gone.*" Jefferson snapped his fingers. "Like that." Flora had stayed in Nera to salvage things, but he'd received correspondence that morning bearing word that she couldn't save his estate. He'd already lost his business assets, despite Seledora's work to find loopholes. Nothing had worked—the Quiet Ones were utterly relentless.

Blaise narrowed his eyes. "Not *everything.*"

Jefferson blinked, suddenly realizing how awful he sounded. How pathetic and ungrateful. "I said every*thing.* You're not a thing. You're in here." He tapped a hand over his heart.

"Nice recovery," Blaise said, bumping his elbow against Jefferson's side.

"It's the truth," Jefferson murmured.

"Anyway, everything's not *gone.* Just different," Blaise said, settling a hand on Jefferson's knee. "We have the bakery." He tried to keep a straight face and failed. "I'm the breadwinner now."

Jefferson snorted. "You've been waiting to say that, haven't you?"

"Maybe." Blaise grinned, and the expression was infectious. Jefferson found he couldn't resist matching it. "Anyway, I *know* you. And Jefferson Cole may be down, but he's *not* out."

Blaise's faith made Jefferson's breath hitch. "Oh? You think so?"

The Breaker continued, "You have more lives than a cat, and somehow you land on your feet. This is just one more inconvenience."

Inconvenience. Jefferson made a face. "It *is* rather inconvenient to be missing most of my wardrobe." The bank would no doubt sell everything in his Ganland house at auction. "How can I be a respectable Ambassador when I only have a choice between four different greatcoats?"

Blaise looked away, though the hint of a smirk touched his lips. "You can borrow one of mine."

Jefferson's brow furrowed at the suggestion. *How do I gently decline this offer without—wait.* "You're *teasing* me."

The Breaker turned back to him, chuckling. "Maybe. Though the offer stands if you need something from three seasons ago."

Three seasons? Blaise truly had no idea how behind on fashion he was, but Jefferson wasn't about to break it to him. Besides, he knew his beau was trying to rile him from his melancholy. He pretended to look affronted. "I would rather go naked."

Blaise laughed, the sound music to Jefferson's ears. "Somehow, I doubt that."

"Is that a challenge?" Jefferson *had* to ask.

Blaise eyed him. "I doubt that would go over well with the Ringleaders." Then he sobered. "What happened at the meeting?"

Jefferson sighed. It had been the first big meeting since the Gutter had gained nationhood, which meant that not only had the respective mayors of Asylum and Rainbow Flat attended, but anyone who might be a major stakeholder. Men and women who held the larger outlying farms and ranches were there as well, and Jefferson had become all too aware that word of his antics had spread far and wide.

"Let's see. I received a sound verbal thrashing for all of my deceptions, which has become a depressingly normal turn of events." Jefferson shook his head. "Not to say I always thought I'd avoid such a fate, but..." He shrugged. "Anyway, it seems they'll still tolerate me as Ambassador since Madame Boss Clayton already agreed to it."

Jefferson didn't dare mention that several had spoken against him, suggesting he should be banished from the Gutter for his misdeeds. To Jefferson's surprise, Jack had been the first to rise to his defense, insistent that *while the man's a righteous piss goblin, he did what had to be done*. No one seemed inclined to argue with the outlaw.

"Isn't it a relief, though?" Blaise asked, his voice little more than a whisper. "No more secrets. No more entanglements to keep straight."

Jefferson chuckled. "I don't even know what that's like anymore." He fiddled with the cabochon ring, the only bit of jewelry he wore, though he kept the ring from Blaise in his pocket. "Oddly enough, that makes me feel more like an impostor than ever."

Blaise put an arm around him. "You get to decide who you want to be now. That's what you always wanted, right?"

"Yes."

Blaise raised his brows, giving him an expectant look. "So?"

"What?"

"Tell me who you want to be. You're at rock bottom, and this is your chance."

Jefferson made a face. "I could have done without the reminder." Blaise gave him a stern look. "Right." He took a deep breath, eyes on the red stone of the opposite canyon wall. "I'm Jefferson Cole. Ambassador. Dreamer. Maybe entrepreneur again someday." He glanced at Blaise. "And outlaw mage."

PERSUADER

Author's Note

Fantasy books take us to another world, but that doesn't keep them from serving as a mirror to our own. Because of that, there are topics in this story that may prove difficult for some readers—and if that's you, please be gentle with yourself. *Persuader* includes blood, death, drinking, kidnapping, forced captivity, guns, murder, PTSD, mention of suicide, violence, abusive relationship, anxiety, profanity, stalking, physical abuse, and weapons.

Pronunciation Guide

Words are fun. Below is a rough guide to the pronunciation for words you'll find in this book. If your brain disagrees, that's fine. Language is malleable, so you do you!

Argor – ARR-gor
Asaphenia – Ass-uh-FEE-nee-yuh
Blaise – BLAY-z
Canen – KAY-nun
Chupacabra – CHOO-puh-cah-bruh
Desina – Dess-EE-nuh
Effigest – Eff-IH-jest
Emmaline – Em-uh-LINE
Emrys – Em-RISS
Faedra – FAY-druh
Faedran – FAY-drun
Ganland – Gan-LUND
Garus – Gair-USS
Garusian – Gair-OO-shee-un
Geasa – GESH-uh
Hospitalier — Hoss-pih-tal-yer
Itude – Ih-TOOD
Izhadell – Iz-UH-dell
Knossan – NOSS-uhn
Knossas – NOSS-us
Kur Agur – Kur Ah-GRR

Leonora – LEE-oh-nor-uh
Lucienne – Loo-SEE-ann
Marian – Mayr-EE-uhn
Marta – Mahr-tuh
Mella – Mell-UH
Mellan – Mell-UHN
Nadine – Nay-DEEN
Nera – NEER-uh
Nexarae – Nex-UH-ray
Oberidon – Oh-BEAR-uh-don (alternate: Oby – Oh-BEE)
Ondin – Onn-dihn
Oscen – Oss-KIN
Petria – Pet-RIA
Phinora – Fin-OR-uh
Ravance – Ruh-VAN-s
Ravanchen – Ruh-VAN-chen
Reuben – Roo-ben
Rhys – Reess
Seledora – Sel-uh-DOR-uh
Seward – SOO-urd
Tabris – Tab-RISS
Theilia – Thee-LEE-uh
Theilian – Thee-LEE-uhn
Theurgist – THEE-ur-jest
Zepheus – Zeff-EE-us

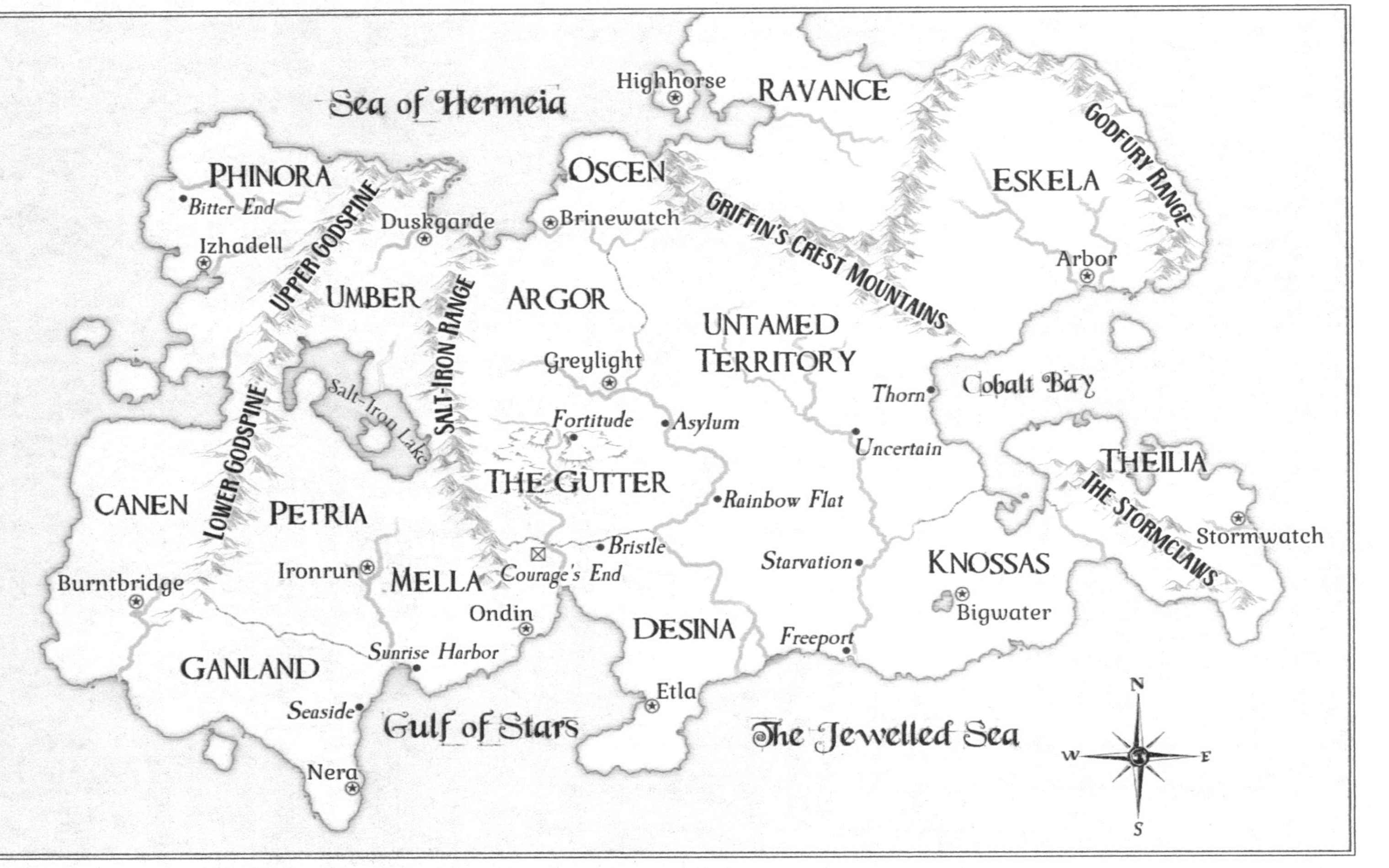

Sea of Hermeia
Highhorse
RAVANCE
GODFURY RANGE
PHINORA
Bitter End
Izhadell
UPPER GODSPINE
Duskgarde
OSCEN
Brinewatch
GRIFFIN'S CREST MOUNTAINS
ESKELA
Arbor
UMBER
SALT-IRON RANGE
ARGOR
Greylight
UNTAMED TERRITORY
Thorn
Cobalt Bay
LOWER GODSPINE
Salt-Iron Lake
Fortitude
Asylum
Uncertain
THEILIA
CANEN
PETRIA
THE GUTTER
Rainbow Flat
THE STORMCLAWS
Stormwatch
Burntbridge
Ironrun
MELLA
Bristle
Courage's End
Starvation
KNOSSAS
Ondin
Bigwater
DESINA
Freeport
GANLAND
Sunrise Harbor
Etla
Seaside
Gulf of Stars
The Jewelled Sea
Nera
N
E
S
W

CHAPTER ONE

Piss-Poor Name Choice

Vixen

"Y ou've been nursing that same drink for the past hour."

Vixen sighed as Clover slid down the bar closer to her. She should have known better than to linger at the Broken Horn, especially feeling as she did. But it had been comforting to come here, to be surrounded by the familiar sound of pool cues striking billiards balls, the slosh of whiskey being poured, the hum of voices and braying laughter.

Aside from Vixen's pegasus, Clover was the one who knew the most about her. Or at least hints about her. But some self-destructive behavior declared Vixen needed to be near those who would nudge her down the road she dared not tread of her own accord. "Got some things on my mind."

"Hmm." The Knossan flicked an ear, tilting her head. She was fishing for more information, and normally the Persuader would speak freely. But not about this. Not now. "I suppose I have to guess. Is it Raven?"

Vixen huffed out a breath. Raven. Things with him were complicated, but that was tiny by comparison to what was currently on her mind. She shook her head. "Guess again, cowgirl."

Clover drummed her stubby fingers against the wood of the bar. Her fuzzy ears flipped forward. Newcomers to town who had never come across a Knossan before were often intimidated by the bovine race, but Vixen had known Clover for years. "I have heard rumors of problems with the Confederation."

That was closer to the target. But the problem went beyond that even. Vixen scraped a fleck of gunk from the top of the bar with a fingernail. "Not just problems. Odds are good, they're going to come knocking."

The Knossan snorted out an unhappy breath, understanding that *knocking* would involve battle and blood. Like Vixen, Clover was a survivor of the assault that had claimed so many lives in their town, formerly known as Itude. That attack had been orchestrated by one man with a grudge. What would happen if the entire might of the Confederation came at them? It was horrifying to even contemplate. And that didn't take into consideration the shadowy cabal Jefferson claimed was working behind the scenes. Vixen longed for the days when the most she had to worry about was if Jack would catch her cheating at cards.

"You do not have to stay, you know," Clover said, her voice gentle. "After what happened, no one would begrudge you."

Clover was giving her permission to turn tail and flee. Vixen rubbed absently at her cheek. If only it were that simple. Clover, and probably others, thought she was still traumatized over what had befallen her at Fort Courage. And while in a way that was true, that wasn't the sum of her issues. "I'm not turning my back on the Gutter. Not when I can do something about it."

"Ah," Clover murmured, though there was a wagonload of meaning in the single syllable. "Your magic, then?"

Vixen laughed, though she knew it held an edge of borderline hysteria. Yeah, her magic would play a role, no doubt. And it was still amazing she'd gotten it back. She chalked that up to the walking miracle that was their Breaker. "Sort of. I…" Vixen faltered. It had been a bad idea to come here. What was she thinking? "I gotta go, Clover. Add this to my tab?"

"Of course," Clover agreed, watching as she pushed up from the stool and headed for the door.

Vixen wove through the crowd of regulars, none of them paying her much mind. Her presence in the Broken Horn was a natural thing, and no one would blame her for leaving in a mood with the pall of current events hanging over them.

But there was one who would call her bluff. She heard the cadence of wingbeats announcing her pegasus's arrival. Alekon wheeled overhead and let out a trilling whinny—his way of catching her attention, the arrogant bastard. She watched him head for the stables, where he would no doubt alight in the area the pegasi dedicated to departures and arrivals.

<I may have been on patrol, but you know we pegasi gossip like old broodmares,> Alekon remarked as he trotted around the corner, dust roiling before him. He drew to a stiff-legged, snorting halt, his onyx mane tossing artfully around him. Alekon was a bright bay, his coat a

rich red-brown with mane and tail like black satin. He lacked the flashy white markings some of the other pegasi bore, but made up for it with flair.

"Yeah, I'm well aware, you pest," Vixen complained, batting at his neck.

Alekon whacked her in return with his nose. <We should go for a flight.>

A flight. With her mind abuzz, that wasn't a bad idea. "Yeah, let's do that."

She pulled herself onto his back, unable to hide the surge of joy that flooded her. No matter how many times she rode a pegasus, she would always feel the same. There was freedom here. Freedom she wouldn't find anywhere else.

Alekon craned his neck to make certain she was secure before breaking into a fluid trot and then a lope. Vixen clung to his barrel with her legs, and her hands twined through his mane as he took to the air. She could count on one hand the number of outlaws willing to ride a pegasus bareback. It wasn't a safe endeavor by any means, but there was something in the act of defiance, in throwing caution to the wind, that she loved.

With a high-spirited snort, Alekon threaded through the network of canyons that made up the Gutter. His wings pumped with the effort, pouring on more and more speed until Vixen wished she'd remembered to swap her tinted glasses for her flight goggles as the wind whipped beneath the frames, making her eyes tear. But she wasn't going to let that stop her. She squeezed her eyes shut, whooping as she clung to her stallion's sleek back. The early summer sun's warmth offset the chill of the wind, further invigorating her.

She felt his wingbeats slow, evening out as he changed course. Vixen's eyes still stung, so she kept them closed when Alekon's hooves rang against stone as he landed atop the canyon rim. Vixen shoved a hank of hair out of her face, opening her eyes at last. They were several miles from Fortitude on a cliff overlooking the Deadwood River.

The sound of new hooves on stone drew her attention. Vixen twisted, looking behind her to find a familiar palomino pegasus pacing toward them, a rider on his back. She frowned. "Jack? What are you doing out here?"

The Effigest glanced at Alekon, then at her. "Wanted to talk to you, and I figured you'd want this discussion as far from town as possible." He stroked Zepheus's neck. "Keeps us away from so many busybodies."

Vixen froze, not liking where this was going at all. "Don't see any reason for that." Maybe she could bluff her way out of this conversation. What did the wily Effigest know about her? Too much, she feared.

"I think you do," Jack shot back, almost too quickly. "I'm downright ashamed at how long it took me to figure you out."

Damn it. Jack knew. Or he thought he knew something, at any rate. Didn't mean it was right, though with the way he prided himself on his web of information, the odds weren't in her favor. He had trapped her nicely—if she stormed off she would confirm his suspicions. Vixen lifted a hand, adjusting the fit of the glasses on her face, the ones that kept her magic from inadvertently affecting others. Jack met her gaze, his cool blue eyes almost daring her to try him. He knew what she could do.

But he had come on his pegasus, and Zepheus would know if she used her power on him. It was generally frowned upon for her to use her magic against friendly outlaws without good reason, and she doubted anyone else would agree this was a good reason. Vixen settled for crossing her arms. "What do you think you know?"

He chuckled, shaking his head. "Valerie ain't your last name. Ain't your first name, either."

She couldn't help but roll her eyes at that. "You already practice these lines on Jefferson?"

At the mention of the Gannish ambassador, Jack's eyes narrowed with keen calculation. "No, but I have a notion you got more in common with him than you let on."

Vixen had half a mind to use her persuasive magic on the Effigest to force him off the trail of her past. She licked her lips, peering at him over the top of her smoke-lensed glasses, hoping he read the warning. "I reckon you should let it go."

"Yeah, can't do that when I'm looking at every angle to keep our fat from the fire." He looked away, his gaze falling across the golden walls of the canyon. A hawk soared over the nearby rim, wings skimming the air as it gained altitude.

"I told you to *let it go*," Vixen hissed, brow furrowing with frustration. "You don't know a lick about me."

"I do." He turned, eyes snapping to her face, as if daring her to use her power. "I know you're Valoria Kildare, the Spark of Garus, second only to the Luminary." Jack's lips curled at the title. "And I'm the idiot who didn't connect Valerie and Valoria for years, despite your piss-poor name choice."

Vixen bristled. "I was only fourteen! I had to come up with something!"

Jack laughed, and belatedly she realized he'd baited her into the confirmation. Gods, he was insufferable. Beneath her, Alekon shifted uneasily. The pegasus was the only one in the entire Gutter who knew her secret. She hadn't even told Raven. Which, upon reflection, was one of the smarter things she'd done.

<I did not tell Jack,> Alekon said apologetically. <He only asked me if his suspicions were true and said it was important.>

Yeah, Jack would say just about anything was important. And what could Vixen say? She could argue, could say he was being ridiculous, that he was wrong. But he wasn't wrong. She swallowed. "And I guess it ain't a coincidence you're asking after me now."

He gave her a look that she couldn't quite discern. There was something almost sad about it, but she didn't know why. "Nah, it's not. You know what's at stake. You survived the Battle of Itude and Fort Courage." His voice hitched at the last sentence, confirming his strong feelings on the subject.

"What do you expect me to do, Jack? I can't just walk back to my old life and demand the Confederation stand down." She shook her head. "I'm a mage. An *outlaw mage*. I'm not what I was."

He looked away, gaze roaming the ruggedly beautiful lands around them once more. "There's still part of what you used to be buried deep. It's buried, not lost."

Buried. "The Spark is dead."

Jack snorted a laugh. "Yeah, so was Malcolm Wells." He tilted his head. "And then Jefferson Cole. And then he wasn't, and he's still a pain in the ass. If anyone can help you reclaim your old life, it's the peacock."

"What if I don't want to?"

He gave her a look. "Yeah, ain't that the question?"

Did Jack know how frustrating it was to talk to him sometimes? He surely knew because why else would he do it? "I'm sayin' I'm not keen on the idea."

To her surprise, he nodded. "That's fair."

She blinked. "What?"

"You heard me." He shifted in the saddle. Zepheus blew out a bored snort. "Vixen, I ain't gonna force you to do something you don't wanna do. Even if it's the best shot we got at keeping clear of war. Nobody should have to give up the life they wanna live."

Vixen pursed her lips. Damn, but he was a manipulative bastard. If she wanted to be selfish and stay hidden, others would suffer. But if she put herself out there and reclaimed her birthright…he was right. She would lose the life she loved. There was no way she could win this, no way that everyone ended up happy.

"Have you told anyone else?"

Jack clucked to Zepheus, and the stallion pivoted to move away. "Nope."

"Are you going to?" she called after him.

"Nope. That's on you."

Vixen huffed in annoyance. Bastard. Now she felt terrible about the whole thing. She buried her face in Alekon's ebony mane. "What do I do?"

Alekon arched his neck, eyeing her. <All you have to do is the next right thing.>

The next right thing. She sighed, ruffling her stallion's black mane. The feel of the coarse hair grounded her, made her feel as if she weren't adrift. Yes. She would have to talk to Jefferson.

CHAPTER TWO

As Serious as a Smoking Sixgun

Jefferson

That Vixen wanted to meet with him privately was both concerning and intriguing. Jefferson didn't know as much as he'd like about the flame-haired outlaw, aside from the fact that Blaise trusted her. Come to think of it, that said volumes about a person. Blaise was reserved and preferred to keep to himself.

What was strange about the whole thing was the way the pegasi conspired to make it happen. Seledora was the one who told him Vixen would like to meet, and the grey mare then made a point to fly him out to a distant precipice where the Persuader awaited him.

There wasn't much grazing to be had on this part of the rust-colored rim overlooking the Deadwood River, but Alekon made a show of pretending to browse on the stubby growth. Seledora rolled her eyes at his theatre and simply moved to the questionable shade of a scrubby mesquite, cocking a hind hoof in a stance of relaxation. The bay joined her a moment later, and they stood nose to rump, using wings and tail to swish flies from each other as they relaxed.

Vixen stood near the edge. Heights didn't scare Jefferson, but even he would have been hesitant to stand so close. She angled toward him, lips curling into a smile of greeting. "Thanks for coming."

Jefferson shrugged. "I don't think I had much say in the matter. Seledora seemed determined to bring me here. And anything that makes her so intent is intriguing to me."

Vixen's expression shifted, as if she didn't wish to be the source of any intrigue. "Yeah, *intriguing*. I suppose that's the word."

"May I ask why we're so far from town?" Jefferson asked, eyeing the gorge below. "You don't have plans to dump my body down there, do you?" He was only half-joking, though he knew there were people out there who would happily do exactly that.

<I would not have brought you in that case,> Seledora reminded him, mental voice drowsy.

The Persuader huffed. "I'm not *Jack*."

"Wait, has Jack actually done that to someone? And you think he might do that to me?" The thought was disturbing. And it did, in fact, seem like something the tempestuous outlaw might do.

"Not that I know of, but no telling with him," Vixen admitted. She licked her lips, and Jefferson realized she was nervous. She had neatly evaded explaining why they were so far from town.

Jefferson didn't have Flora out here—since their run-in with the Quiet Ones, he'd asked the half-knocker to keep an eye on Madame Boss Rachel Clayton, the leader of Ganland. Clayton knew about their enemies, which meant they might come for her. Blaise didn't know he was gone. Only Seledora was here. Was this a set-up of some sort? He took a step backward, readying his magic in case he needed it.

Vixen must have noticed his sudden tension. Her brows knit. "Oh, damn. You think I'm up to no good, don't you?"

Jefferson kept a firm hold on his dream magic. He was relatively certain he could use it on her if needed, but he didn't want to without reason. "The last year has been rough, so forgive me for being cautious." *Longer than that, honestly.*

Her shoulders slumped. "Sorry. Sometimes I forget I'm not the only one who's been through things that would make the demons of Perdition think twice." She gave him a rueful smile, gesturing to the nearby outcropping. "No, I didn't ask you out here to kill you and dump your body in the Deadwood. Alekon asked Seledora to bring you because out of all the people in Fortitude, you may understand what I'm about to tell you the most."

Why do I have the impression I'm going to regret this conversation? Jefferson walked over to a chunk of stone that looked like it would make a serviceable seat. As a bonus, it was a healthy distance from the edge. "I have my suspicions about why you think I'm the best person to come to. I'm listening."

Vixen blew out a breath, ambling closer to where he sat, though she didn't join him. "I'm not the person I appear to be."

Bullseye. As soon as she'd said he would understand, he had thought it might be something like this. He offered her an encouraging smile. "I suppose I do know a little something about that. Though I doubt it's any worse than being a Salt-Iron Council Doyen in an outlaw town."

Vixen laughed, a hollow sound. She flipped a lock of brilliant red hair out of her face. "That's a bet you would lose, Doyen."

"I prefer *Ambassador*," Jefferson said mildly, if only to dampen the rising tension.

"Ambassador," Vixen agreed with a good-natured shake of her head. "I still don't know how you sweet-talked your way into that. You're not even a Persuader."

"I can be quite charming, but I was lucky," he admitted, since it was true enough. Odd that she was once again straying from the original topic.

<She's nervous,> Seledora told him privately, ears pricked in their direction. <This truth scares her.> Jefferson knew a thing or two about that, too. Revealing the truth made a person vulnerable. He would always see falsehoods as armor, even if Blaise disagreed.

Vixen watched him as she mulled over whatever thoughts meandered through her mind. Jefferson let her, knowing better than to push. She picked at a thread in the seam of her trousers, as if it had suddenly become far more interesting than anything else. "This thing I'm going to tell you...I'm only telling you because it directly affects the Gutter. The threats against the Gutter, I mean."

Jefferson nodded at the earnestness in her voice. He noticed she'd dropped the drawl she often used. All a part of her act, he mused. "I understand."

"And I may need your help with it."

That sent a flash of shock through him. "My help?"

Vixen smiled. "You're our ambassador to a Salt-Iron nation. And you were a Doyen. You have connections and influence that may be necessary."

Jefferson cocked his head, uncertain. He wasn't sure if he liked where this was going. "I think you underestimate how royally I've burned bridges with my stunt in Nera."

"That'll change when you return to the Confederation with the Spark."

Jefferson stiffened, and even Seledora let out a whicker of surprise, proof that Alekon had left her in the dark, too. As an attorney, the mare knew a little more about the hierarchy of Confederation nations than the average pegasus. Garus was the patron god of Phinora, and the Luminary served as his vessel—with the Spark as an heir. Not only that, but the Luminary acted as the head of state. Vixen was *far* more important than

Malcolm Wells had ever been. Jefferson swallowed. "Please tell me you're joking."

"I'm as serious as a smoking sixgun," Vixen said, rubbing her forehead.

Jefferson closed his eyes. He wished this was a nightmare—he could influence those. Change the outcome. This truth Vixen had revealed was dangerous. Not only to him but to every single person who called the Gutter home. There were zealots who would turn the Gutter into dust to get her back if they thought the outlaws were involved. Which raised the question…

"Lamar Gaitwood had you. How in Tabris's name did he not know who he had at the time?" Jefferson asked.

Vixen shook her head. "How would he know that Vixen Valerie, outlaw mage, was worth the time of day? The Spark is dead."

Assumed dead, Jefferson suddenly realized. He sighed. "I suppose we do have a lot in common, you and I."

"Unfortunately," she agreed.

"What are you proposing?" Jefferson asked.

"I need to go back. To Izhadell."

To Phinora. To the heart of the Salt-Iron Confederation. Vixen was asking him to help her get to a place that was dangerous to both of them. To use the gossamer-thin strings of his tenuous ambassadorship to ease the way there. "What do we gain by doing this?"

Vixen straightened her shoulders, as if donning a mantle of boldness. She met his gaze. "Come on, Ambassador. You're well aware that the Confederation's considering an attack on the Gutter."

The breeze rippled through Jefferson's hair as he grimaced at the dire reminder. "Yes, that's been keeping me busy with—*oh*." He'd been almost too preoccupied to see what she was getting at, but now he did. "You could stop it."

"I could stop it." Vixen glanced back toward town, lips pursed.

Damn, it sounded far-fetched, but she was right. It might work. He tilted his head in a side-to-side rhythm, puzzling through how he could make this happen. "Very well. I'll help you."

"When we travel, my identity remains a secret," Vixen said, her tone sharp. "Until I can figure out the best way to let the Luminary know."

Jefferson shook his head. "I can't keep any more secrets from Blaise. Especially not one this big." And one that would put him in direct peril.

Vixen chewed on her lower lip, conflicted. Then she nodded. "I trust Blaise. He won't…" Her sentence died, unfinished.

Oh. This was deeper than Jefferson had thought, perhaps even a worse tangle than his own mess of identities had been. "Anyone who hates you for finding out your truth was never your friend to begin with."

She made a soft scoffing sound. "That works for simple things, yeah. But I'm the heir to the Luminary, the living avatar of Garus. Thanks to the Confederation's invocation of Garus, mages don't exactly like that god very much." Though the feeling was mutual. Followers of Garus hated mages just as much, happy to subjugate them as little more than tools.

Jefferson cocked his head, thinking. "But nothing has changed in the two minutes since you've told me. You're still the same person."

Vixen's smile was tight. "Because you understand. You've always been you, no matter if you were Malcolm Wells or Jefferson Cole."

He stepped closer, not invading her space, but near enough to be a firm presence. Proof that she had not alienated herself from him, at least. "Whether you are the Spark or Vixen Valerie, you're still you. The woman who cheats at cards and taught the Breaker how to wield his magic."

At the accusation of cheating, she pulled away. "I do *not*—" Vixen paused, then made a soft laugh. "Fine, I get it. You're saying even if I'm the Spark, I'm not so high and mighty to people who know me."

"Exactly," Jefferson agreed, pleased that she understood.

"So, what do we do now?" Vixen asked.

Ah, that was the question, wasn't it? A large part of Jefferson wanted to pretend this conversation had never happened. A tiny part of him wondered if hurtling himself off a cliff might be a cleaner fate than whatever might happen if he went to Izhadell as a liar and a mage—with the Spark in tow, no less. But he said none of those things. "I'll speak with Blaise, and once I've felt him out, we'll form a plan of action."

Vixen nodded, relaxing. She looked more like herself: the confident outlaw mage who knew her mind and took no guff. "There's one more thing you might help with…"

Tabris's sweet golden ass, what next? "And that is?"

Vixen sighed. "I need to hide my magic for as long as I can."

"Ah." He understood why she'd made that request. Word had spread about the unusual ring Blaise had gotten for him. Jefferson always carried it when he went out and about, not only because it could be useful, but because it was a reminder of Blaise's regard for him. The ring had cost the Breaker an enormous sum, and all to protect Jefferson. It was the next best thing to a proposal from the Breaker, which he knew was unlikely to come. He fished it out of his pocket, the inset nub of unicorn horn glinting in the light. "This infernal thing is rather precious to me, you know."

Vixen's gaze fell on the ring cupped in his palm. "Blaise gave it to you."

Jefferson nodded. "Yes. He gave it to me, to protect someone he holds dear." He extended his hand, the nullifying ring jostling with the movement. "But I also know he considers you a dear friend."

She reached out to take the offered ring, but paused. "We can wait and ask him, if you prefer."

Jefferson chuckled. "You and I both know Blaise's kindness. He would want you safe as well."

Vixen took the ring, holding it gingerly in her palm as she studied it. Then she slipped it on her finger, wincing at the sensation of her magic being cut off. Jefferson knew exactly how awful it felt, but it had come in handy before. "I can't believe you wore this for an extended time," she muttered as she shucked it off again.

He chuckled. "You get used to it after a bit. I suppose it wasn't as hard on me, since I haven't had magic for as long as you." But even in that short time, it had become an intrinsic part of his fiber. He hadn't felt whole without his magic.

"Do you want it back for now?" Vixen asked.

Jefferson shook his head. "No, hang on to it. I presume, since you've revealed your truth to me, you'll have to stay the course."

She rubbed the ring between her thumb and index finger, then stuck it in a pouch at her belt. "Thanks, Jefferson."

He was going to regret this, he just knew it. But if what Vixen had told him was true, then she was right. It might head off any aggressions if they handled the situation delicately. "Don't mention it."

CHAPTER THREE

Play to Win

Blaise

*B*laise stared at Jefferson blankly. "She's what now?"

Jefferson sighed, running a hand through his hair, the scarlet gem on his precious cabochon ring winking with the motion. "Not a *what*, more of a *who*."

That didn't really help, as far as Blaise was concerned. Sometimes Jefferson forgot how little he knew about all things Confederation-related. And while he understood Jefferson was trying to explain something of great importance to him, he really had no concept of why there was any importance to it at all. "Again, Vixen being the Spark of Garus means about as much to me as declaring Emrys the Prime Minister of Pies."

Jefferson snorted a laugh at that, though he made it look elegant and charming. "Fair enough. I don't enjoy feeling as if I'm talking down to you."

Blaise shrugged. "You're not, since I really have no context for any of this." It wasn't as if, during his stint in Phinora, anyone had bothered to explain their favorite god or political structure. No one would stoop to explain such things to a prisoner.

"I suppose that's true," Jefferson mused. He stared at the board arrayed before them. The Dreamer had laid out a game of chess, though they hadn't begun gameplay. The pieces stood at the ready, like armies carved from wood. Jefferson picked up the white queen. "Imagine this is the Luminary."

"Now I see why you picked chess," Blaise remarked, studying the pieces. "The Luminary isn't the leader, then?" He pointed to the king piece. Honestly, Blaise had never connected the Luminary to Garus, but then again, he'd only ever heard the title and nothing more.

"Well, yes, though there's also a Clergy Council that makes decisions," Jefferson said. He set down the queen, exchanging it for a bishop that he waved around as he spoke. "What I'm getting at doesn't align with the rules of chess, though. Which of these pieces has more power?"

That was easy. "The queen."

Jefferson nodded. "That's the Luminary in a nutshell. She is not only the voice of a god but runs the theocracy, for the most part."

It had never occurred to Blaise that the gods and goddesses might be anything more than stories. He knew Jefferson was a follower of the Gannish god Tabris, but they hadn't discussed it much. "Um, do you think the Luminary really *is* an avatar?"

Jefferson smiled, setting the piece back on the board. "I suspect you really mean if I think Garus is real. That I can't answer." His face shifted to what Blaise thought of as his cunning expression, when Jefferson was looking to reap the highest rewards. "But I do know that belief is a powerful thing and might be something we can use to our advantage."

"How does Vixen factor into all of this?" That was what Blaise really didn't understand.

"Ah." Jefferson picked up a pawn from the board. "She's something like this. What happens when this pawn makes it across the board?" He gestured to the spread in front of them.

"It becomes a—oh." Blaise glanced from the pawn to the queen. "So you're saying Vixen will become the Luminary? The avatar of Garus?"

"She has the potential, yes," Jefferson agreed. "For the past few centuries, the Luminary position has been hereditary."

Blaise frowned. Vixen had kept a huge secret from all of them, though he suspected she had good reason. He still remembered talking to her what felt like ages ago, when he first realized he wasn't the only mage with a hard-luck story. Then the puzzle pieces fell into place in his mind —Vixen was a mage. She had been in an important position in Phinora, beholden to a god notorious for disliking mages. Or that was what Blaise understood, at any rate.

"No wonder she hasn't told anyone," he whispered.

Jefferson nodded, no doubt having already made all those connections. "I see you understand."

Blaise did, but now he had other questions. "She told you all this… why?"

The sudden tautness around Jefferson's eyes spoke volumes. "As the

Spark, she'll be in a position of power. If I understand her correctly, she believes she can convince the Confederation to stand down from attacking the Gutter. Phinora always has the most say in the Confederation's actions."

Jefferson was evading the question, dancing around it as if he were back in his politicking days. Blaise crossed his arms. "And this involves you how?" He had an idea, but he wanted his beau to confirm it.

"She would like me to use my position and whatever's left of my influence to help her return to Izhadell for an audience with the Luminary." Jefferson watched him closely, as if waiting for Blaise to refuse the idea outright.

And Blaise wanted to—he really did. He didn't want Jefferson anywhere near Izhadell. Not after all they had been through there—or rather, what Blaise had been through. But the place was just as much a threat to Jefferson, possibly even more so now, since he had openly declared he was a mage. Blaise cocked his head. "The fact that you're telling me this leads me to believe you've already agreed to it."

Jefferson nodded. "Yes. I think Vixen has the right of it. That this is worth trying, for the sake of the Gutter and all the people here." He looked the gravest Blaise had ever seen him, his green eyes alight with a fire of determination. Jefferson believed in this, despite the potential for danger.

"Will your ambassadorship provide any buffer for you?" Blaise asked.

"Look at you, being strategic. Fair question," Jefferson mused, a tiny smile gracing his lips. "Technically, it should, but that entirely depends upon if the rest of the Confederation feels like further poking Ganland. And they may, considering Ganland isn't on the best terms with the other nations at the moment."

"That's not really encouraging," Blaise commented, crossing his arms and hoping he gave Jefferson a look communicating how much he disliked this idea.

Jefferson shifted the game board, rising from his chair to move to Blaise's side of the table. His eyes were earnest as he gestured to Blaise's lap. "May I?"

"You think I'm going to be mad at you," Blaise guessed, though he nodded.

The Dreamer shot him a wounded look as he lowered himself to sit sideways on Blaise's lap, slinging an arm around the Breaker's shoulder. It was a comfortably intimate position; Jefferson's slender form nestled against his. "Not mad, no. Worried." Jefferson angled to plant an apologetic kiss on Blaise's forehead. "After my past mistakes, I have a better understanding of how I may accidentally make you mad versus what worries you."

Jefferson was right—everything about this worried him. He appreciated his beau's foresight in coming to him. Something about Jefferson grounded him, staved off the panic that constantly threatened. Blaise didn't know what to say. He knew Jefferson, knew that this man he loved would do what he could for the mages of the Gutter. And Blaise loved him even more for that, even as it terrified him.

"I'm not defenseless, you know," Jefferson murmured, peering down at him.

"Neither was I," Blaise reminded him, finding his words at last. "And you're vulnerable to salt-iron."

Jefferson's nose wrinkled in distaste. "An unfortunate allergy, like most mages."

Blaise licked his lips. Vixen would be vulnerable to it, too. Vixen was a friend, someone he cared about. And Jefferson was going.... There was only one response to any of this. "I'm going with you."

He felt Jefferson's shiver of surprise. The Dreamer shifted to straddle him, leaning in to rest his forehead against Blaise's. Jefferson tenderly lifted a hand to cup his cheek. "I can't ask that of you."

Blaise closed his eyes. "You're not. I'm asking this of *me*."

"I see," Jefferson murmured, looping his arms around Blaise's neck.

Blaise wasn't sure he did, though. He looked up at Jefferson, debating how he could explain his tangle of thoughts. How he wasn't willing to risk Jefferson going without him. And he wanted to go, wanted to defeat his fear of everything Phinora represented in his mind. But by the way Jefferson smiled down at him, maybe he did understand.

Blaise cleared his throat. "Besides, you'll need a place to stay while you're there. And it just so happens I have one."

Jefferson chuckled. "Oh, you don't say? I suppose we'd make poor guests to go calling there when the master is away."

"Can't have that," Blaise agreed. He had given little thought to the Wells estate that he'd inherited from Malcolm's alleged death. Now it was one of the few assets of Jefferson's that had evaded the machinations of the Quiet Ones, the shadowy cabal of elite pulling the strings within the Salt-Iron Confederation. He didn't mention that was his other motive for accompanying Jefferson. Blaise feared the Quiet Ones might move against Jefferson within the Confederation boundaries. He would not allow it.

"You're too kind," Jefferson said. "To tell you the truth, I'm happy that you want to go along for purely selfish reasons."

"And what are those selfish reasons?" Blaise asked.

Jefferson glanced away for a beat, blowing out a soft breath. "Ah..." His green eyes darted back to Blaise. "Because of how I feel about you."

"I don't think love is selfish."

"Perhaps not, but it feels like it sometimes," Jefferson admitted, canting his head. "And I know I can be a bit much." He brushed the fingers of his right hand along the ridge of Blaise's jaw, then rose to move to his own side of the table once more.

Blaise's gaze followed Jefferson. "Sometimes I like when you're a bit much."

"Do you?" Jefferson raised his eyebrows.

"You generally get that way over things you're passionate about," Blaise said, picking up a white pawn and tossing it from one hand to the other.

A smile softened Jefferson's face. "I do have strong feelings regarding you."

And I feel the same about you. Blaise held up the pawn. "If you win this match, you can be a bit much with me later."

Jefferson narrowed his eyes. "I hope you don't intend to lose on purpose to humor me." The skin between his eyes creased into a V of concern.

"First of all, I intend to play to win. But even if I didn't, it's not *humoring* you." Blaise placed the pawn back on the board. "I love you and like seeing you happy."

"I'll be happy with you regardless," Jefferson murmured.

Blaise smiled. "I know."

⸺

Jefferson

JEFFERSON SHOULD HAVE KNOWN THE MEETING WOULD GO SOUR. HE'D BEEN too optimistic after his pleasant evening with Blaise the previous night. Still, it had been nice to entertain the idea that everything would go smooth as silk.

"So, let me get this straight." Jack tilted his head, eyes darting from Jefferson to Vixen. "Not only do the both of you want to go to Phinora unannounced, but you want to take our Breaker with you."

"That's the long and short of it," Jefferson agreed, though there was something about the way the outlaw worded the statement that didn't sit right. As if it were some sort of bluff. Odd. Did he know about Vixen?

"It's not for nothin'," Vixen insisted, crossing her arms. Jefferson noticed she was careful not to meet Raven Dawson's gaze. Not because of her magic, no. She kept her tinted glasses firmly on the bridge of her nose. Jefferson knew they were old flames, though he didn't know how they'd parted ways.

Kur Agur, the wolfish Theilian, drummed his furry fingers against the table, claws clicking with each movement. His nostrils flared. "It seems like too great a risk. Why would we send you to the enemy's heart? Especially when there are whispers they may come to us." A growl rumbled in his throat.

"By then, it will be too late," Jefferson said. This argument, at least, he was prepared for. "When we get to Izhadell, we can get an audience with the Luminary. If we can convince her, the odds are good that the Salt-Iron Council will also scrub any potential thoughts of attack." He hoped no one planned to ask for the details on how he'd arrange an audience with the Luminary.

"Why the *Luminary?*" Raven asked, his emphasis on the word as sharp as the knives sheathed at his hip.

Vixen had an answer ready. "Garus represents wisdom. If we can convince his avatar that it would be wiser to work with us than fight us, we stand a chance."

Raven's eyes narrowed, clearly unconvinced by her response—but he didn't argue.

Jack was studying Vixen, his frigid blue eyes calculating. His lips pursed as he considered. Jefferson watched the outlaw closely. The more he saw, the more he was convinced the Effigest was play-acting. "You're planning to use magic, yeah?"

Vixen crossed her arms. "I reckon, if it's necessary."

Mindy looked uneasy about the plan. Jefferson knew the Hospitalier was no coward—she had been an integral part of their mission to Nera last year. "You think waltzing into Izhadell and using magic is a good idea? What makes you think it won't have them come after the Gutter even harder?" She swallowed. "And we wouldn't have any of you here if that happened."

Jefferson traded a look with Vixen. This was an uphill battle, and it was quickly becoming apparent the vote was going to go against them. If only he could figure out Jack's angle. Jefferson suspected that regardless of the outcome, Vixen was going to Phinora. Her mind was made up. *I'm going to have to put a spin on this—*

The door to the meeting room creaked open. "It's a show of strength," Blaise said, all eyes falling on him as he stood framed in the threshold. He leaned against the lintel as if all that attention didn't unnerve him. Jefferson knew different. The Breaker's gaze settled on him as if he were the only person in the room, a solid rock to grab onto amid a river of discomfort.

<I told him the discussion was not going well,> Seledora reported from outside. Ah, so his pegasus attorney had stuck her nose into the meeting. She was quite handy to have around.

The other Ringleaders frowned at the Breaker. "I thought that was the last place you would want to go, Blaise," Mindy pointed out, her voice gentle.

Out of reflex, Blaise rubbed the tender underside of his left arm. No one could see it beneath the blue-checked, long-sleeved shirt he wore, but all of them knew of the long scar that marred his skin. Jefferson knew it intimately. "I'm not the same man I was the last time I was in Izhadell. I was a victim then. A prisoner." The corners of his mouth tightened, and Jefferson knew Blaise was thinking of what else he had been considered. A criminal. A murderer. There were times he still grappled with the guilt of what happened at Fort Courage. He was quiet for a long moment before continuing. "I'm not those things now. And after the Inquiry, I have *standing* in Phinora." He shrugged. "At least that's what Jefferson tells me."

"And a lot of people there are gonna want you dead," Jack added amiably. "Or just want you." Jefferson arrowed a glare at the outlaw.

Blaise shook his head. "That's true no matter where I am." His voice held a note of sadness. Jefferson wished he could change that reality for Blaise, but he was right. They could pretend to have an idyllic life in Fortitude, but it would take very little for their bubble to not just burst, but shatter. "This is our best shot to protect the place and people I care about before it comes to that. If we let them march on the Gutter, innocents will die." His fists clenched at his sides, a sheen of silver wafting from his closed palms.

"You're not invulnerable," Kur Agur rumbled, flattening his ears.

Blaise pursed his lips. "I'll be the first to agree with that. But I think it's a chance worth taking. With Vixen's persuasion and Jefferson's..." He paused, and for a moment, Jefferson feared his love would inadvertently reveal his magic. "...diplomacy, I think we stand a good chance."

"What are you gonna do? Bake them a cake?" Jack asked, sounding amused. Jefferson continued to be perplexed by the outlaw's stance. What game was he playing?

Blaise smirked at that. Actually *smirked*. Jefferson couldn't hide his own smile. "Yeah, if it comes to it."

"I can't believe any of you are actually warming up to this idea," Raven said, his eyes dark with barely concealed anger. "It's reckless. It puts three of our mages hopelessly far into enemy territory with no assurance of their safety."

"We make our own assurances, thank you very much," Vixen shot back, arrowing an irritated look at her former beau.

"Vixen, you're a *Ringleader*," Raven growled, testy. "And despite his theatrics, Jefferson is an *ambassador*. You have responsibilities to the Gutter."

"And you can't just mosey into Phinora and claim to represent the Gutter without our say-so," Mindy agreed.

"We *do* have responsibilities to the Gutter," Vixen said. "Do you think we want to go to Izhadell for some sort of pleasure holiday? We know what's there."

"We're going because it's the right thing to do. The only way we see to stop an attack before it starts," Jefferson added.

Blaise's voice was soft when he spoke. "I wasn't here to help at the Battle of Itude. At the very least, I want to do something before this town is attacked again." His blue eyes raked the room, and for a moment, Jefferson feared old memories had reared up to capture the younger mage's attention. Then Blaise shook his head, as if flinging those memories away. "We should at least try."

"What's going to happen when the Confederation captures you?" Raven asked, voice tight as he fidgeted with a knife. *Damn him.* Jefferson's jaw tensed, too aware the Shadowstepper had asked to goad Blaise. His panic attacks were common knowledge among the Ringleaders.

"They won't." The Breaker's words were almost inaudible. There was a feral underlying growl, like a cornered wild animal. Blaise would not be held by the Confederation again, not without a significant cost. He would fight.

"Have a little faith in us," Vixen said, perching her hands on her hips. "None of us are greenhorns."

Kur scratched his chin. "As much as it pains me, I see the wisdom of their gambit. It is better to be the hunter than the prey."

Jack nodded at that. "We're outlaws. We ain't prey." He rapped his knuckles against the table, though there was a strange glint in his eyes. As if the Effigest knew something, but was keeping his cards to himself. "Y'all have my vote."

Mindy's gaze flicked between Raven and the other Ringleaders. The Hospitalier mage shifted in her seat, then nodded. "Faedra knows we've done more audacious things. I'll back it."

Raven hissed out a breath of frustrated dissent. Jefferson caught Blaise's eyes, aiming a grateful smile at the Breaker. *Majority rules.*

CHAPTER FOUR

Never Yours to Lose

Vixen

"What in Perdition was that about? You can't be serious about going to Izhadell!"

Vixen had known Raven would come after her, critical of their plan. She'd seen it in his eyes, in the set of his jaw. Even so, she was annoyed that he had. Better for him to just let them do it. Did he think he had the chance of a snowball in a dragon's maw of convincing her otherwise? She spun on her boot heel to face him. "You were at the meeting. I know you don't got cotton stuck in your ears."

She expected to see the same anger from the meeting lining his face, but it had been replaced with something else. Concern. Worry. Even a dash of defeat, if she was reading him right. "I only know the things you and Cole spoke aloud. But I know you. I know to read between the lines, and I can't." He swallowed, his dark eyebrows low, shadowing his eyes. "Let me start over. Can we talk?"

Vixen tilted her head. She appreciated he was trying, but it wouldn't change anything. Still, talking wouldn't hurt. "We can. I was going to the shop. I've got some work to do." When Fortitude had been rebuilt, she'd cleaned up her ways—at least a little. She'd taken up work that was more honest than cheating at cards, opening her own tailoring shop. Through necessity, she'd learned to mend and sometimes fashion her own clothing, and over time had found that she was good at it—and enjoyed doing it.

He nodded, falling into step beside her as they made their way up the street. Raven wisely didn't speak as they walked, holding his silence until they reached the shop. Vixen had flipped the sign on the door to *closed* while she attended the Ringleader meeting and now realized it would be closed for an extended time when she left. In fact, she might never open it again. That bothered her more than she'd thought it would. Vixen had become attached to her little shop and understood a bit of why Blaise loved his bakery.

Raven cast a glance around her shop, past her work table by the massive windows that lined the front, to the organized swathes of fabric, lace, and spools of thread. A mannequin bore an almost-complete dress that Vixen had been working on for herself—though it wasn't fully a dress. The skirt was much shorter than any respectable woman would wear, reminiscent of a saloon girl's. For good reason, that caught Raven's attention.

"What's that?"

"A little something I've been working on," Vixen said. She was proud of it and thought it was going to be a lovely piece when she was done.

"Isn't it a little...um, short?"

She scoffed. As if he had any say in what she did or wore. But it was a valid question—it was shorter than what she usually wore. Though, to be fair, she favored trousers. "If it were worn alone, yes. But that's not it. Let me show you." She moved to the worktable, picking up the other part of the outfit and holding it up to reveal dark trousers that would be form-fitting, the hem at the end of each leg edged with ornate black lace. "See, I was making something sensible that could be worn while riding."

Raven cocked his head. "I'm not sure how *sensible* it is."

"Says the man who's never had to consider riding in a dress," she shot back, earning a chagrined look. "Trust me. It's very sensible." She folded up the trousers and set them aside. "But we didn't come here to talk about my work."

"No," Raven agreed, taking another turn around the shop. Since it wasn't large, it didn't take him long at all. He blew out a breath. "Look, I know this is the last thing you want to hear from me, but..." The Shadow-stepper paused, as if deciding on his next words. "I don't know what your history is in Phinora, but I know you have one. And I know you never wanted to tell me, so it must be painful. That's why it's a mystery to me why you'd want to go back."

Vixen weighed her options. With the trajectory she was on, her secret would come out and he would learn soon anyway. But that didn't mean she wanted everyone to know. Once word got out, no one would look at her the same. And Raven...well, he was the son of a theurgist. He wouldn't look kindly upon anyone from the upper echelons of the Confederation.

"I don't owe you an explanation."

Hurt registered on his face. "You don't. You made that pretty clear when you turned me down the day I proposed to you."

Her hackles raised at that. Vixen wished he hadn't brought it up. Turning him down had been one of the hardest things she'd done in her life, but she'd known it was the right thing for both their sakes. And not just because of her past, but because, while he loved her, she didn't feel the same for him. Two people bonding over the shared pain from Fort Courage didn't make them compatible in the long run. She saw that plain as day, but he didn't.

"Drop it, Raven," she advised him.

"Why can't Jefferson and Blaise go without you? Why is it so important for you to go?" he asked.

"Blaise is only going because Jefferson is. And this is something Jefferson can't do alone." For more reasons than she was willing to state aloud. They both knew Blaise was a good man, but he wasn't a diplomat. He was too anxious, and being the center of attention was one of his worst nightmares.

"Someone else could go," Raven suggested.

Vixen snorted, ticking off the options on her fingers. "Sure, we can send Jack. Wait, no we can't—his mug is still on wanted handbills all over the Confederation. Oh, we could send Kur. Never mind, we can't because the Phinorans would take offense at a wolf in their sheep-like presence. And while Mindy went to Nera with the delegation, she kept to the fringes for good reason. Who's left? You?" She knew her words were a challenge. Didn't care.

He scowled. "You know I can't. I meant someone like Kittie."

"I wanna see you suggest that to Jack. Makes me wonder if he has a poppet of you yet," Vixen drawled. From what she knew of Jack, there was no way in Perdition he'd keep his peace if Kittie went to Phinora for any reason. The fear of losing her again would be too much for the man.

Raven shook his head, unwilling to admit defeat. "Fine. It doesn't have to be Kittie. We've had lots of new arrivals. Might find someone suitable among them."

Vixen canted her head. "Do you think I'm such a poor choice for this?"

He blinked in surprise, then took a step back as if he only now realized what his suggestions sounded like. "No, but I don't want to lose you."

"I was never yours to lose, Raven." She couldn't help the annoyance that crept into her voice. She had told him no. How hard was that to get through his thick skull? "I could decide to up and move to Starvation tomorrow. Would you follow me across the Untamed Territory?"

The jut of his jaw proved he would consider it. He sighed. "I can't help how I feel about you, even after..."

"Yeah, well, I can't help it either," Vixen shot back. "And now, if you don't mind, I have work to do. With luck and time on my side, maybe I can finish this before I leave." She nodded to the almost-complete outfit.

Raven rubbed his forehead. He looked as if he wanted to say something else, but maybe he realized it was a lost cause. He gave her a final, wounded look and strode out the door.

Vixen huffed out a breath, shaking her head. Relationships were messy things. From here on out, it would just be her and Alekon. No more humans to pine after her. Pegasi were better than people.

———

Jefferson

"JEFFERSON! A MOMENT, PLEASE!"

He paused at the familiar voice, turning to see Kittie trotting toward him on a chestnut mare. Though the Firebrand's mount was no mare of flesh and blood—somehow, after their return to Fortitude, she'd come into possession of an equine fire elemental. Jefferson assumed Jack was likely involved, though he didn't know how. All the same, he had a great deal of respect for the mare. Even though she was horse-shaped, some instinct in the back of his brain held a healthy fear of the elemental. Didn't help that he had rather unpleasant memories of being kidnapped during a fire. He took a breath to compose himself. "Afternoon, Kittie."

The woman slipped out of the saddle. Like the pegasi of Fortitude, there was no need for Kittie's steed to wear a bridle in the town. The mare eased to the side, so she didn't crowd her rider, while staying protectively close.

"Do you have a moment to speak?" Kittie asked, her eyes flicking to the nearby bakery.

She knew he was headed home and had intended to intercept him. Curious. But Jefferson liked Kittie a great deal after his work with her in Ganland. She had a good head on her shoulders—and she hadn't turned her back on him for his duplicity. He was rather thankful for any allies he had. "Absolutely. Would you like to come to the bakery? I'm certain there would be a treat we could enjoy." That was an unfair trick. Elemental she may be, but Kittie's mare loved Blaise's sweets as much as any of the pegasi. The mare's nostrils widened at the prospect, her head craning toward the bakery.

Brief annoyance crossed the Pyromancer's face, and she shook her head. "I was thinking perhaps a walk around the outskirts of town." The elemental heaved a disappointed sigh.

Poor mare. Jefferson hadn't meant to distress her. He paused, glancing at the creature. "I'd be happy to speak with you, Kittie. And if your mare would like a snack, I'm sure Blaise would see to it. She only has to go around to the back window."

The equine rocked on her heels, as if ready to bolt away. But she waited, lambent eyes on her rider. Kittie nodded. "Go on, girl. You deserve it." And with that, the mare whinnied and trotted to the bakery, tail swishing in her wake. The occasional spark flickered in the dust after her passage, but nothing caught fire, and that was what mattered.

Jefferson allowed Kittie to lead their stroll. She didn't speak for several minutes, until they were out of earshot of most anyone else, perhaps save a pegasus. "I've heard of your plans to travel to Izhadell."

It was a statement. Jefferson wasn't sure if she expected a response or if her intent was to add more. But after a few steps, when she made no additions, he said, "Yes, that's the goal."

Kittie frowned. "I don't believe for a moment that you're only going to convince Phinora to keep the Confederation from waging war against us."

Jefferson should have been insulted, but he wasn't. Partly because Kittie was right. And he was also impressed that she had picked up on facets of him that Blaise hadn't. "To be fair, that's most definitely part of why I'm going. The Gutter is my home now. And there are people here I care about." And it was more than Blaise. He liked Clover, the Knossan bartender, a great deal. And Flora's uncle, Jasper. And Blaise's family lived here now, too. They were all worthy of protection.

The Firebrand blew out a breath, a lock of hair flipping out of her face. "But that's not all, is it?"

He swung his hands behind his back, threading the fingers together as they continued to walk. "In truth, no. Flora hasn't been able to find out how deep the Quiet Ones have burrowed into the Confederation."

"Are you planning to use yourself as bait?"

Jefferson sighed. "Not as bait, exactly. But I'm hoping to flush them out. They've done all the damage they can to me from a distance." That was depressing to think about. His enemies had drained his vast fortune, stripping him of every fiscal advantage he had.

Kittie crossed her arms. "According to Jack, parts of the Confederation want you."

"Ah, that." That was nothing new. As soon as the truth of his dual personas had come to light, the Salt-Iron Confederation had become exceedingly interested in him. "And that is why my attorney will accompany me."

The Pyromancer scoffed. "Jefferson, this is *serious.*" Worry reflected in her eyes. "You don't know what they do to mages."

"Actually, I do," Jefferson retorted, his voice suddenly frosty as his brows slammed down. He remembered only too well the things Blaise had revealed at the Inquiry. The way Gregor had stripped Jack's will and used the Effigest like a weapon. There wasn't a day that passed when he didn't reflect on the horrors visited upon mages in the Confederation. "I know many people think that everything I've ever done has been a sham. But I have always—*always*—fought for mages. Even before I became one." He ran a hand through his hair, turning to face her. "I know what they do to mages. And I know there is the potential it could happen to me." Gods, he hoped not. "I also know what will happen if we let the might of the Confederation rain down on the Gutter. That's not a fight we can win."

Kittie was quiet for a moment, thoughtful. As if she were calculating their own strength against the relentless Confederation onslaught. It would be a bloody, horrible thing all around. Jefferson knew without a doubt that they could inflict terrible losses on the Confederation. But magic, even power like Blaise's, had limits. The Confederation boasted multiple nations. Even if Ganland stood down—bloody Perdition, even if Ganland *helped*—it still wouldn't be enough.

"Do you believe the Quiet Ones would engineer this? I thought they supported the Gutter," Kittie said at last.

"That right there is the thousand golden eagle question," Jefferson murmured. "Whatever game they're playing, it's a long one." He grimaced. "And I believe I've scuttled some of their plans. I wonder how they're regrouping. And how deep their claws are into the upper echelons."

Kittie nodded. "You're risking a lot by going there."

Oh, he knew. And the thought of what he might walk into was enough to twist his stomach. "I won't be alone." That was the only thing that made him think he could do this. That he had half a chance.

Kittie cast him a side-eyed glance. "Does your beau know about this angle?"

"We haven't spoken of it, but Blaise has his concerns," Jefferson said, looking over his shoulder toward the distant bakery. "Unlike our trip to Nera, I have a better idea of what I'm getting into. They no longer have the advantage of surprise."

"I hope you're right," Kittie murmured.

CHAPTER FIVE

Family Fun

Blaise

"At least take this one." Marian Hawthorne shoved a potion into Blaise's hand, closing his fingers around the glass and its sloshing contents.

"Mom," he protested, freeing himself from her grasp. Blaise glanced down at the label on the bottle. His mother had been experimenting again, and he never knew what to expect. She was always happy to foist potions on him if he had plans to leave town for any reason. "*Polymorph?* Do I even want to know what this does?"

"Emptying the contents on a person will turn them into an animal. Temporarily." She smiled at him as if that were a completely normal thing to offer her son.

As a child, he hadn't thought twice about his mother's work. Now that he knew how uncommon alchemists were and how gifted his mother, in particular, was? It was a little frightening. Scratch that, it was terrifying. "How do you even know if it works?"

"Your brother wanted to be a dog."

Blaise rubbed his forehead. Maybe he was fortunate that his mother had made him a mage and not a dog.

"He got better," Marian said, frowning at him. "Do you honestly think I'd leave Brody as a dog?"

The question stung. And that wasn't how Blaise wanted to leave Fortitude, frustrated with his mother. He didn't know what to say, didn't know how to voice the words he feared would hurt her, either.

In the end, he didn't need to. She blinked, then made a soft hissing sound, her expression crumpling. "That was the wrong thing to say. I'm sorry, Blaise. I'm worried about you going to Izhadell, and I wasn't thinking." She was shorter than he was, and she closed the distance between them, reclaiming the potion in the same motion as she wrapped him in a hug. "I love you."

Blaise relaxed against her. "Love you, too. And I'll be okay." Nearby, Jefferson was speaking with Lucienne and Brody—and Blaise's younger brother was definitely not a dog. Brody laughed at something Jefferson said. "Can you maybe not experiment on family members, though?"

"That's part of being an alchemist," Marian said, her mouth close to his ear. Blaise realized she was revealing something that wasn't meant for others to hear. "We're able to experience the effects of our potions for a short time without suffering ill from them."

He made a soft, surprised sound. "I never realized..." Blaise licked his lips as he thought. Did that mean that for a brief time, long ago, his mother had Breaker magic like him? No wonder she had known his magic was dangerous, but not that it had other uses. Other possibilities.

"Alchemist's secret," she whispered.

Blaise tilted his head. "I'm not an alchemist."

"No, but you're my son. And I don't want you worrying about the things I'll be teaching Luci and Brody." Marian pulled back, her expression serious. "There's no one else to teach them, and though we live in a town surrounded by outlaw mages, they're alchemists by birth."

He didn't fully understand alchemy, but he understood that denying them the chance to learn it was akin to leaving a mage ignorant of their magic. And he knew what that felt like. Blaise smiled. "I'll take potions, but please only send normal ones. I don't want to explain to anyone why I'm a Breaker armed with offensive potions."

"Simple answer. Because you're *my son*," she said, sounding smug. "Give me a moment."

While she stepped into her apothecary shop, which was a stone's throw from the stables, Blaise ambled to join his siblings and Jefferson. When they turned to look at him, Blaise pointed at Brody. "A dog? *Really?*"

The boy grinned. "It was the best! I could pee on everything outside, and no one could be mad at me."

Jefferson's eyebrows flew up, a mix of curiosity and confusion. "Do I even want to know about this conversation?"

"Mom made a potion that turned Brody into a dog," Lucienne offered helpfully. Brody dropped down on hands and knees in the dirt, growling at his sister.

Blaise rubbed the bridge of his nose. "Temporarily, at least."

"Ah." Jefferson threaded his hands behind his back. "Remind me not to get on your mother's bad side."

"You'll be on my good side as long as you treat my son as he deserves," Marian said, coming up behind them. Jefferson jumped at her voice, though he did a good job of covering his surprise by pretending to adjust his cuffs.

"I wouldn't imagine treating him any other way," Jefferson said. The certainty of his own words must have put him back at ease, as he aimed a dashing smile at Blaise.

"Here." Marian shoved a leather bag into Blaise's arms. "Perfectly normal potions."

He frowned, freeing the laces to peer inside. "Please tell me there's no Chill of Death or Faedra's Embrace." Blaise pulled out one bottle, sighing when he saw the name of another unusual potion. "Mom! This is *not normal.*"

"There's no Chill of Death. I don't want to risk you with that one again." Marian shook a finger at him. "You know better than to administer potions to yourself when you're bad off."

She was trying to change the subject. He wasn't going to let her. Blaise pulled the cobalt blue bottle out, pointing to the label. "Incognito? Why?"

"Why not?" Marian asked, as if it were perfectly reasonable.

"What's it do?" Jefferson asked, curious. "I'm going to assume it doesn't turn you into a dog, at the very least."

"Oh! Oh, can I show them?" Brody asked, bouncing to his feet.

Blaise sighed as his little brother snatched the potion from his hand. "Why can't I have a normal family?"

"I don't think there is such a thing," Jefferson said with sympathy. Then more softly, he added, "But let me assure you, this is a breath of fresh air."

Brody held the bottle in his hand, poised to open it. "Can I show you? Pleeeeease?"

How could Blaise say no to that? It was good to see Brody excited about something. "Go ahead."

The boy unstoppered the bottle, taking a sniff. "It smells and tastes like peppermint." That was good to know. Too often, alchemical potions tasted awful. Brody took a tiny swig, then shoved the stopper in again. As he swallowed, an effect rippled across him, reminiscent of when Jefferson's glamor fell into place. A moment later, Brody no longer looked like the brown-haired, fair-skinned child he had been, but now had bright red hair and a generous smattering of freckles across his face.

"Oh, so it's like an alchemical glamor." Jefferson crouched down to peer at the boy, appearing far too interested. He glanced at Blaise. "We should take that."

"See?" Marian asked, grinning at the Dreamer.

"Fine, we'll take it," Blaise relented. "Better to look like another person than an animal, I guess." He accepted the bottle from Brody. "But how do you remove it?"

"The duration depends on how much you ingest," Marian said. "There's no reversal for it aside from time."

Blaise didn't like that, but he had an idea. "Brody, come here."

His brother cocked his head. It was odd to see him with such red hair. "Wait, why?"

"I want to see if my magic will work on it."

"No way, that's no fun!" Brody pulled something out of his pocket—another vial. He took a step backward.

"Brody Hawthorne, don't you dare," Marian warned.

He drank the potion, shrinking into an orange tabby. The bottle fell to the dirt with a clatter as the cat meowed and darted off, paws pattering against the dirt. Blaise sighed. "Really?"

"Well, you mentioned getting a cat for the bakery." Jefferson was far too jovial about the whole thing.

"He is so grounded." Marian put her hands on her hips, looking at her daughter. "Luci?"

"On it." Before Blaise could even ask what she was doing, his sister scooped up the bottle, grinning at him. She tapped her forehead. "Sometimes, to catch an alchemist, it takes an alchemist. Try to keep up." Then she sipped from the bottle as well, shifting into a fawn-colored hound.

"Your family is so much more fun than mine ever was," Jefferson observed. "Are they always like this?"

"Only when they're flaunting their alchemy," Blaise grumbled. He picked up the bottle and handed it to his mother. "We'll be back." Then he broke into a reluctant jog after Luci. The hound had already bolted after the cat, her nose low to the ground as she picked up the trail. She bayed, the sound so deep it rattled Blaise's teeth.

In her canine form, Luci was much faster than either of them. Blaise didn't even attempt to keep up. Attracted by the strange doings, Emrys came over to see what was going on. Like Jefferson, he was amused by the whole thing and took up the chase with them. That worked in Blaise's favor, allowing him to climb onto the stallion's back. Seledora joined them a moment later.

<I hear baying toward the eastern trail,> Emrys said, turning to trot in that direction.

"How far do you think a little cat can run?" Jefferson asked.

"When that little cat is an alchemist, there's no telling." Blaise shook his head.

Ten minutes later, the pegasi homed in on the hound, discovering that Luci had Brody treed. The orange cat clung to a branch, hissing at the dog. Luci's tail wagged with fiendish glee as she leaped up, snapping at the cat. She wasn't big enough to reach him, though.

Blaise eyed the tableau. "Brody, come down."

The cat meowed, digging his claws into the branch. Blaise assumed that was a no.

"What's the plan?" Jefferson asked. "I've never hunted an alchemist-turned-domestic cat before. This is out of my wheelhouse."

Blaise cocked his head, thinking. He wasn't about to climb the tree, and even aboard Emrys, he couldn't reach the branch. His magic was more than a match for the tree, but that move was too extreme. No, sometimes the simplest solution was the answer.

"If you come down from the tree and let me try my magic on the glamor, you can eat as many cookies as you want before dinner."

Luci whirled with a snarl, fangs bared.

Blaise shrugged at her. "I'll take it up with Mom later." He peered up at the cat. "Best I can do."

<I think the kid is getting the better end of the deal.> Emrys snorted, arching his neck.

Brody must have agreed. He eased toward the trunk with a mewl, ears flattening when Luci barked at him.

"Luci, let him down," Blaise called.

The hound backed off with a whine, moving beside the pegasi. Her whip-thin tail wagged as she watched the cat tentatively make his way down. When Brody hit the ground, his feline form rippled, and he returned to the shape of a boy with oddly red hair.

"Hey, how'd you do that?" Blaise asked. "Did the polymorph potion run out?"

"Nah." Brody shook his head. "I'm an alchemist. I ended it." He raised his brows. "You promise about the cookies?"

"Yes."

"I want in on the cookies, too!" Luci demanded, reclaiming her human shape. "It's not fair."

"Mom's going to kill me," Blaise muttered. "Fine. Cookies for you, too. Now, Brody, let me see you."

Blaise slipped down from Emrys's back. Brody obediently came over, though he still wore a mischievous smirk, and Blaise half expected him to bolt. But he held still as Blaise rested his palm on Brody's arm. This was where he needed a delicate touch with his magic—without control, he could just as easily shatter a bone as remove the potion's effect. But he was beyond that now. Taking a breath, he focused his magic, feeling out the layer of potion that overlaid Brody's skin.

He had to admit, the potion was intricate. It was almost impossible to find where the glamor ended and Brody began. Blaise persevered, though, and before long, he sent his magic into the thin shell of the glamor. His power ate away at it, and a moment later, brown-haired Brody grinned up at him.

"Is it cookie time?"

"Yes, I guess it is," Blaise agreed with a rueful shake of his head. "I'll meet you both at the bakery." With a whoop, the Hawthorne children dashed off. He turned back to Emrys. "Now it's time to go ruin everyone's dinner and face my mother's wrath."

<Can my dinner be ruined, too?> Emrys asked.

"I don't think it matters at this point." Blaise hoped he had enough left-over cookies in the bakery for this. He had a sinking feeling that his surplus inventory was about to take a hit.

Jefferson chuckled. "I do love your family."

Blaise couldn't help but smile. "Yeah. Me, too."

"Your mother can't be too angry, you know," Jefferson reasoned as they made their way back. "What with us leaving tomorrow and all. And she was the one who suggested the potions."

<Listen to Jefferson. He has a good defense,> Seledora agreed, easing into a trot.

<If she's too angry, just offer her cookies.> Emrys bobbed his head at the sage advice. <It's impossible to be mad in the face of cookies.>

Blaise chuckled. "I guess it's worth a try."

CHAPTER SIX

Nobody Here Likes Unicorns

Blaise

Traveling with Jefferson and Vixen was almost pleasant. For a little while, Blaise could pretend as if they weren't on the trail to head off another crisis. He didn't even mind that they had to dodge inclement weather that slowed their progress to Ondin, the capital city of Mella.

He knew everything would change once they reached Ondin, however. Jefferson had sent messages ahead, working with his connections in Ganland. Through Flora, he'd gotten in touch with someone who worked with Madame Boss Clayton to secure their passage on a train that would take them all the way to Izhadell.

"Are you looking forward to the train ride, Blaise?" Vixen asked as their pegasi approached the station.

He made a face at the question. "I'm not overly excited. But it'll be nice to dry out, at the very least," Blaise said, shaking the sleeves of his yellow rain slicker. It wasn't raining in Ondin, but they had come through another shower as they'd approached, and now they stuck out like sore thumbs in their bright raincoats. Well, he and Vixen did, at any rate. Jefferson's raincoat was a deep blue, and the raindrops beading on the fabric made him look as if he were garbed in bejeweled finery.

"What?" Jefferson asked, glancing back and noticing Blaise's eyes on him.

"I was just thinking you're the only one of us that doesn't look like a drowned rat."

The Dreamer grinned. "Oh, you think I look good, do you?"

"That's not what I said."

"But it's what you meant."

Vixen snickered at their banter. Blaise hissed out an exasperated sigh. Better to change the subject than let Jefferson continue to needle him. He wondered if Jefferson had made his flirtatious sally as a distraction. His beau knew he was nervous. "Where do we go?"

"We're going to be riding in a private car, or so Flora assured me." Jefferson pointed to a train hunkered down on the nearest set of tracks. Unlike some of the other iron behemoths, the engine and cars belonging to this train appeared to be freshly painted and in good repair. "And the pegasi will have a livestock car to themselves."

Seledora pinned her ears, snapping her teeth. <We are not livestock.>

Her rider was quick to stroke her neck. "No, you certainly aren't. I suppose we'll have to call it the pegasi car."

The train station was bustling with activity. That should have come as no surprise to Blaise—Ondin itself was a riot of people, as he supposed a capital city would be. It wasn't as busy a place as Nera in Ganland, but nonetheless, pedestrians, wagons, and riders clogged the streets. The calls of vendors selling wares rose above the din of voices and hooves on hard-packed ground. A rumbling blast from the train on the farthest rail split the air, giving Blaise a start, but all around him, the mass of people carried on as if nothing were amiss.

With Seledora and Jefferson leading the way, they threaded through the crowd. The pegasi had their wings hidden, so aside from their rain gear, no one gave them a second look. Jefferson had Seledora pause every few steps as he scanned the area, seeking someone.

"Cole! Jefferson Cole!" a voice rang out. Seledora swung in the caller's direction. Blaise followed Jefferson's gaze to a woman standing on the stairs to the station, waving enthusiastically at them. "Over here!"

"And that would be our contact," Jefferson said, glancing back at Blaise and Vixen.

They followed him over to the woman, who looked a few years older than Jefferson. She was dressed in a black frock coat over a long striped skirt and gleaming ankle boots. Blaise didn't think she had the look of one of the elite but perhaps a bureaucrat. A man stood a few paces behind her, wearing a dark red wool coat with gold braiding over tan trousers. The colors of the Confederation. Blaise froze up when he saw the uniform.

Emrys balked, sensing his unease. <Do you want me to back away?>

Blaise swallowed. He noticed that Vixen's eyes had gone wide, and she was staring at the uniformed man, but not with the same gut-clenching fear that Blaise was experiencing. Jefferson seemed oblivious to the both of them, intent on connecting with the other diplomat.

"Monica Bremner, I was not expecting that you would be the one to meet us," Jefferson said, sliding out of the saddle to land on the balls of his feet with flawless ease. He flashed her a charming smile, only then seeming to note Blaise's unease.

The woman, Monica, returned the smile. "The Madame Boss isn't playing games. We don't want a war any more than you do."

"So she sends the best." Jefferson chuckled.

The uniformed man watched their exchange with polite interest and little more, though he hazarded the occasional furtive glance at Vixen. Not at Blaise—which was fine with him.

Monica spread her hands. "Let's just say she's trying to prevent a powder keg from going off. We're a little nervous about outlaw mages going to parley with Phinora."

Jefferson's eyes flicked to the Confederation man. "I see."

The Gannish woman's mouth tightened. "Allow me to introduce your escort. This is Tracker Rhys Kildare. It was thought prudent to send along additional security."

To protect us or to protect others from us? Blaise kept the thought to himself.

"A Tracker?" Jefferson's brow furrowed. He clearly had misgivings about this, too.

Rhys stepped forward, arms uncurling. "As Diplomat Bremner said, I'm here in the capacity of security. I'm not here to conscript you as theurgists or anything else you may think."

"I see." Jefferson paused. Blaise wondered for a moment if he was about to call the whole thing off. Being accompanied by a diplomat was one thing. But a Confederation Tracker? That was something they had not prepared for. It was almost a threat.

"It will be fine," Vixen said suddenly, her words confident. She glanced at Blaise and Jefferson, giving them both a nod.

<Alekon doesn't have specifics, but Vixen has reason to trust the Tracker,> Emrys advised Blaise. <He believes we do not need to worry.>

Blaise chewed on his bottom lip, forcing his shoulders to relax. He trusted the pegasi—and Vixen. He caught Jefferson's eye and nodded.

Jefferson studied him for a moment before turning back to the others. "Excellent. In that case, we should make our introductions."

Vixen

IT WAS DIFFICULT TO FEIGN THE COOLNESS SHE SHOWED, BUT VIXEN HAD years of gambling experience to draw on. Alekon sensed her inner turmoil, though, and she knew he was assessing her rush of emotions. Rhys Kildare was the last person she had expected to run into upon her return to the Confederation.

She noticed that the sight of the Tracker distressed Blaise, and even with his impressive level of control, no one wanted an upset Breaker. Vixen was thankful Alekon had passed on a message to calm the others while she tried to decipher what this meant.

Monica showed them to the livestock car that was reserved for the pegasi. It was a fancy thing, painted a glossy red with the words *Bull's Eye Stables* painted in a swirl of letters.

"Is this car on loan from a racing stable?" Jefferson asked when he saw it, apparently recognizing the name.

Monica nodded. "Yes. The stalls in this car are wider than the standard livestock cars. I thought it might be necessary." She twined her thumbs together and wiggled her fingers, hinting at wings.

"Ah," Jefferson murmured.

The broad door to the boxcar was open, a long ramp leading the way inside. The pegasi paused at the base, ears flicking. Alekon tossed his head, uttering a loud snort. <There's a unicorn inside.>

Given Rhys's presence, that wasn't a surprise to Vixen at all. A unicorn was part of a Tracker's kit. But Emrys's last experience with unicorns had been traumatic, and the black stallion shied backward, his rider not even attempting to stop him. Since he'd likely told Blaise what manner of creature was inside the boxcar, the Breaker no doubt understood his response.

This wouldn't help their trip at all, though. Vixen jumped down from Alekon's back, springing over to Emrys and snatching the loose reins. The stallion rolled his eyes at her. "Emrys, shhh. You have reason to be upset, I know. But trust me. If this unicorn is who I think it is, it's okay." She kept her voice low, only carrying to the black stallion's ears.

Emrys's neck was slick with sweat from his anxiety. <I don't *like* unicorns.> He pawed at the ground, massive hoof scraping at gravel. <*Nobody* here likes unicorns.>

Vixen looked up at Blaise. They couldn't let old fears derail their mission. True, she and Jefferson could go on without Blaise, but she doubted either of the men would allow such a thing. "Can you do something?"

The reluctance on her friend's face was clear. With a sigh, Blaise slipped out of the saddle and moved to Emrys's other side. "You know what the unicorns did to him and Oby out in Thorn."

She glanced at the black stallion's hindquarters, his sleek hide pocked by scars. "This one is different," Vixen whispered, and she hoped she was right. But a gulf of years spanned between the last time she'd seen Rhys and his unicorn. Things could have changed.

Blaise nodded, placing a hand on Emrys's forehead. "Go along with this, and when we get to the house in Izhadell, I'll bake you whatever pie you want."

Emrys snorted, lowering his head as he considered the offer. <A pie *and* a cake.>

The Breaker chuckled, scratching beneath the stallion's forelock. "Deal."

<I would like a cheesecake,> Seledora added.

Blaise blew out a breath. "Okay."

Alekon twisted in Blaise's direction. <If you're taking orders, I'll have a tray of sugar cookies.>

Vixen rolled her eyes, turning back to her stallion. "The lot of you are ridiculous." But she was pleased that, once again, Blaise's baked goods would win the day for them.

Unaware of the bribery afoot, Rhys had already climbed the ramp and waited at the top, no doubt prepared to show them to their pegasi's accommodations. Vixen had so many things she wanted to ask, but this wasn't the time. All the same, she was the first to escort Alekon up the ramp, meeting Rhys's eyes when they stepped into the car. If he recognized her, he gave no sign.

Four large box stalls took up most of the livestock car, though there was a makeshift area that served as a tack room and storage for feed. A cot huddled along one wall in the small room, a blanket laid across it and a knapsack tucked beneath.

"Is there a groom staying here?" Vixen asked, glancing at the cot.

Rhys's expression was neutral. "That's where I'll be staying."

Well, that answered that. Whatever his purpose, the Confederation or Ganland hadn't ponied up the fare for him to have a proper stay on the train. Or maybe it was more pragmatic—it wasn't a bad idea to keep someone near the pegasi on a train full of unfamiliar people. Still, Vixen had mixed feelings about Rhys staying in such conditions.

An equine head Vixen hadn't seen in years thrust over the only currently occupied stall. The unicorn was a blue-grey that might be mistaken for a standard grey horse at a glance. But the spiraling silver horn on his forehead stamped him for what he was.

"Darby," Vixen whispered when the unicorn flared his nostrils in her direction. He made a huffing sound, almost an affirmation. Alekon bumped into her with his muzzle, feigning envy. "You have no reason to be jealous."

<You're the one making sugar-sweet eyes at the unicorn,> Alekon retorted, then pricked an ear at the open stall door. <Oh no. I'm going to be stabled next to him?>

"Grow up," Vixen muttered, urging the bay stallion into the stall. Better Alekon than Emrys, at any rate. As it was, she saw Blaise making sure the black stallion stayed as far from the unicorn as possible, which was wise. Then she set to removing his saddle and hackamore. She stowed the tack but kept her saddlebags right outside the stall door, ready to take with her to their own accommodations.

That done, she regrouped with the others. Jefferson was chatting with Monica while Blaise hovered nearby, looking awkward and uncertain. Vixen very much wanted to find an excuse to talk to Rhys, but this didn't seem the time. But if he was staying in this car, she figured she'd have ample excuse to do so later. So, she focused on Blaise, slipping up beside him.

He relaxed slightly at her appearance. Blaise's saddlebags were perched over his shoulder, though he seemed unbothered by their weight. "Will Alekon be okay?"

Vixen nodded. "He'll behave." She hoped so, anyway. Wooden slats separated the stalls. If Darby was so inclined, he could poke his horn through it to annoy his neighbor. She didn't think Darby would do that— at least, she hoped he wouldn't. Such antics would give Alekon reason to respond, though.

Monica finished whatever she was telling Jefferson and turned to them, a bright smile on her face. "Well, now that the pegasi are settled, allow me to show you to your car!"

CHAPTER SEVEN

Respect the Name

Blaise

*B*laise was thankful that, while it appeared they were being given one of the more luxurious cars, their quarters were not at all reminiscent of his only previous train experience. Monica showed him and Jefferson to a master bedroom, a compartment with seating that folded out into beds. There was also a washstand and a toilet. Jefferson seemed pleased by the accommodations, so Blaise decided he was, too.

To his relief, Vixen would be nearby, so their group would stay together. She laid claim to the next compartment over with a similar set-up, though smaller and designed for a single person.

Jefferson had already unpacked his meager belongings. It was odd to see him travel so light, but he seemed to have adjusted to his new reality. Blaise still marveled at the way his beau had cobbled together a new wardrobe piece by piece after being decimated by the Quiet Ones. Jefferson was resourceful, though, so it really shouldn't have been a surprise. And fashion was one of his priorities.

"What do you think?" Jefferson asked, gesturing to their quarters.

Blaise raised his brows. "What's there to say? It's about the same size as the loft back home."

Jefferson chuckled. "I suppose so." He shifted closer, his green eyes going soft. "I'm glad you're coming with me."

Earlier, Blaise had felt like an afterthought while Jefferson chatted easily with Monica. Now, this admission eroded all of his anxiety. "Me, too."

Jefferson smiled—not his roguish smile, not the one that charmed so many. It was all warmth and love, a smile meant only for Blaise. The sort of smile that communicated a wealth of emotions. "I will admit, I've been hoping to take you on a proper train ride. The last one didn't count."

Blaise couldn't help but laugh. Jefferson had the worst of it the last time they'd been on a train, spending the entire trip paralyzed by Jack while Gregor Gaitwood taunted him. Blaise had spent most of it drugged and asleep, which upon reflection, he decided was preferable. "I guess we can scratch this off the list."

"Indeed." Jefferson pulled out a pamphlet he found tucked against the window, opening it to show a diagram of the train. "Here, this is the layout. In the normal configuration, there's an observation car, but that was removed because of the pegasi." He stabbed a finger to show the car at the end of the line. "Our quarters are here." Jefferson pointed to the car adjoining the pegasi car.

Blaise had figured that much out, at least. The boxcar for the pegasi had a door and connector that allowed them to travel between the pair of cars. He liked knowing the pegasi were nearby. "And these other cars?"

Jefferson traced a hand over them. "There are two more sleeper cars in front of this. There's also a lounge car and a dining car." He tapped the dining car. "I expect, aside from this car or the pegasi car, that is where we'll spend most of our time. Unless you'd care to socialize?"

He meant the lounge car, no doubt. Blaise made a face. "With people?"

"That answers that," Jefferson said, though his eyes danced with amusement. He'd known Blaise wouldn't enjoy the idea. "Sometimes, on a train such as this, the lounge car will have entertainment in the evenings."

"You want to go, don't you?" Blaise asked.

"Is it that obvious?"

He chuckled. "Only because I know you." Jefferson was a social butterfly, the polar opposite of Blaise. He still didn't know how they got along at all, considering their differences. "Find out more about it, and let me know."

Jefferson's brows shot up. "You'll go with me?"

"I'll consider it." Blaise figured it didn't hurt to needle his beau a little.

The Dreamer grinned, heartened by the statement. "In that case, I'll most definitely find out."

Vixen

THE TRAIN PULLED AWAY FROM THE STATION MID-AFTERNOON. VIXEN discovered that their contact, Monica, didn't intend to travel with them, entrusting them to Rhys's care as she waved goodbye. Once they got underway, Jefferson and Blaise made their way to the dining car. Blaise wasn't as excited by the prospect as Jefferson but went along anyway.

That gave Vixen her chance. She told them she would check on the pegasi and make certain they were comfortable, then catch up.

She negotiated the accordion connector between the cars, the door to the pegasi car creaking as it opened. Snorts greeted her, along with the unmistakable sensation of Alekon touching her mind.

Emrys swung his head over the stall door, nostrils cupped to drink in the scents that wafted into the car. <Is Blaise coming?>

Vixen paused at his stall. "No, he went to the dining car. I'm sure he'll stop by later."

<Perhaps with treats,> Emrys commented, though Vixen knew a suggestion when she heard one. She'd have to remember to tell Blaise.

Rhys had come to the door of the tack room, leaning against the frame. He watched her, eyes intent. The Tracker looked as if he wanted to say something but was keeping it to himself.

Vixen had no such inclinations. She strode over. "Rhys Kildare, what in Garus's name are you *doing* here?"

At her use of his name, he blew out a breath. "I should ask you the same thing. I thought..." Rhys trailed off, glancing toward the unicorn's stall. "You said you would never come back."

She had said that, hadn't she? It felt like an eternity ago. "That's what I thought but..." Vixen turned to Alekon. The bay stallion craned his head toward her, and she closed the distance to stroke his forehead, smoothing his silky forelock. He sighed with contentment, though his dark eyes were watchful. "Things changed."

<Who is he to you?> Alekon asked, curious. <I know he is important, but you have not mentioned him before.>

Emrys and Seledora weren't watching, but she knew they were both eavesdropping. Besides, they would find out sooner or later. Might as well be sooner. "Rhys, allow me to introduce you to my pegasus, Alekon. Alekon, Rhys is my brother."

The pegasus blew out a breath of surprise. <You never told me you had a brother.> And to Rhys, he said, <I am pleased to meet you.>

Yeah, Vixen knew that at some point, she was going to have to explain their convoluted relationship. She wasn't looking forward to that. Life had been so much simpler when she only had to be an outlaw.

"I've never spoken to a pegasus. It's good to meet you, Alekon," Rhys replied, hesitant. He tilted his head as if Alekon were a puzzle to be deciphered.

<Then you're missing out. We're a treat.>

Vixen snorted at that, shaking her head. Time to get back on track while she had the chance. "How is it you're the one who came?" It seemed too contrived to be a coincidence. Vixen feared someone was positioning them like game pieces.

Rhys shook his head. "I was given orders. I didn't know it would be you. I was told to accompany three outlaw mages and their pegasi. The Breaker, the Traitor, and…" He gestured to her.

"The *Traitor?*" Vixen frowned.

He winced. "That's what Ambassador Cole is called in…certain circles."

It was also a testament to the fact that the Confederation didn't know what Jefferson's magic was. That probably scared them, so they sought to belittle him with a moniker like Traitor. Well, it wasn't Rhys's fault for repeating what he had been told, so she set that aside for now. "And all you're supposed to do is serve as security?"

Rhys nodded. "Yes. To protect the public from the outlaw mages, and the outlaw mages from anyone else."

If the Confederation had sent another Tracker in his stead, Vixen would have been concerned. Trackers had unique training that gave them the upper hand when dealing with mages. And all Trackers were immune to direct magical attacks—a closely guarded secret that Vixen only knew because of her relationship with Rhys. That ability, combined with combat training, made them more than capable of taking on most mages one-on-one. But as small a portion of the populace as mages were, Trackers were even smaller. Maybe it really was a coincidence.

She glanced at Darby. Trackers rode unicorns just as many outlaw mages rode pegasi, but that was where the similarities ended. Some Trackers had a strong working relationship with their unicorns, but that was rare. Most unicorns were trained under cruel conditions and treated afterward just as poorly. But not Rhys's unicorn. In the past, she'd seen her brother treat the blue-grey stallion with the same regard she showed Alekon. Darby watched them with liquid brown eyes full of intelligence. Unicorns couldn't communicate in the same way as pegasi, but they were smart. Vixen didn't doubt that Rhys and the stallion were prepared to neutralize mages, if necessary.

Rhys was watching her. "And why are you here?" He paused, brow knitting. "What do I even call you?"

"Vixen," she said automatically, which earned an amused look.

"You must be kidding."

She made a face at him, and for a moment, it was like the gulf of years between them vanished. "I'm not. Respect the name—I'm rather fond of it." With a shake of her crimson hair, Vixen rubbed her forehead. "I'm here because I'm afraid I may be all that stands between the Gutter and an attack from the Confederation."

He raised his brows. "You're going back? To Izhadell?"

"Unless I'm on the wrong train."

"You know what I mean." Rhys blew out a breath. "When you left, it seemed pretty final. Besides, how are you going to even do that? You're..." He gestured to her, then paused. His eyes narrowed. "Except I don't feel your magic."

Ah, yes, the other, better-known ability of Trackers. They were sensitive to magic, able to detect when it was in use. A good Tracker knew when a mage was around, though it took a unicorn to pinpoint one in a crowd. Vixen pursed her lips, deciding if she should reveal the ring or not.

While she considered, Rhys spoke again, excitement growing with each word. "Are you not a mage? Was there some sort of mistake? Is that why you're coming back?"

Vixen ground her teeth. There it was, the old Confederation bias that magic was wrong. In her heart, she knew Rhys hadn't meant it that way, but it galled her regardless. Worse, she realized with a sinking feeling that she could have come back after Lamar Gaitwood's forces had stripped her magic at Fort Courage. But she hadn't even entertained the idea. Why?

Because even on her worst day, she loved being an outlaw and living in the Gutter more than her best day as the Spark in Izhadell.

Decision made, she lifted her hand, rubbing her index finger over the curl of silver. "I'll never stop being a mage, any more than you can stop being a Tracker. It's part of my soul. This is hiding my magic, for now."

His expression crumpled at her declaration. Rhys leaned over to peer at the ring, then nodded. "I still don't understand why you're returning to Izhadell."

"There are innocent people back in the Gutter who deserve a chance at a peaceful life."

He relaxed at her words. "That's why you're coming back? Not to... usurp the Luminary's position?"

Vixen snorted at the very idea. "Gods, no. That sounds terrible. I don't know exactly how I'll handle things with mother, but that's not my goal." Ridiculous, that's what it was. Then she pointed to his cot. "Who'd you tick off to get stuck with this detail?"

His shoulders went rigid. "No one. I'm not important enough to warrant anything better."

She scowled. "I strongly disagree with that." It was unfortunate her room wasn't larger, or she would have invited him to sleep in comfort befitting his lineage. Though that wouldn't work, either—people would make the wrong assumption about them. And right now, she couldn't take such a risk.

Rhys sighed. "I'm just a Tracker."

"That's dragonshit." He blinked in surprise at her language. Oops. Vixen was going to have to remember to curb her outlaw tongue. "Do you get to go to the dining car, at least?" she asked, to distract from her slip.

"Only if there's someone here to keep tabs on them." He pointed to the equines.

Vixen figured, at the very least, Blaise would be happy for the excuse to come here later. "I think I can make that happen. Let me go catch up with the others, and I'll make sure there's relief for you here soon."

CHAPTER EIGHT

On Time is Late

Jack

Jack despised meetings, but they were part and parcel of his position as a Ringleader. He was glad that, aside from the times when something came up requiring an emergency meeting, they otherwise only met once a week. That was far too often, in his opinion.

He ambled over to his customary seat in the meeting room at HQ, eyeing the others who had already assembled. Mindy was there, chatting with Kur Agur. With Vixen on the mission to Izhadell, that meant all they were missing was Raven.

Jack frowned. It wasn't like Raven Dawson to be late. He was usually the first to arrive for all of their meetings. The Shadowstepper assumed the unofficial role as the chair of their ragtag council. The outlaw pulled out his pocket watch, checking the time. Two minutes until the agreed-upon start time. Dawson wasn't officially late...yet.

The silver flash of Jack's watch snapping shut caught Kur's eye. The Theilian twitched an ear. "Do you need to be elsewhere?"

"Nah," the Effigest said with a shake of his head. "Was just thinking it's odd that Raven's last to arrive."

Mindy pursed her lips. "Come to think of it, he didn't eat at the Jitterbug last night like he normally does." She paused. "Though he might have gone to the Broken Horn instead."

That was reasonable, but Jack suddenly had a terrible feeling in his gut. And he'd been around long enough to know when he needed to trust his instincts. He couldn't remember the last time he'd seen Raven. Days ago, at the very least. "I'm gonna see if Zeph knows anything from Naureus."

Mindy raised her eyebrows. "Is that necessary? He's not late yet."

Jack was already at the door. "On time is late for Raven."

"I will go check his home," Kur volunteered. "Sniff around and see what I uncover."

"I'll stay here in case he comes and you miss him," Mindy said.

Jack nodded, hurrying out with the lupine close on his heels. Kur loped off in a cloud of dust as Jack broke into a jog, heading for the stable.

His first stop was the stall that housed Naureus, Raven's buckskin pegasus. It was empty, but that meant little. Most of the stalls were unoccupied at this time of day. Jack whirled, marching up the aisle on the hunt for any of the five grooms who worked at the stables. The pegasi paid the young humans to muck out the stalls, refill their buckets with sugar water, and feed them morning and evening. The youngsters had a good handle on the comings and goings of each pegasus.

A scrawny kid with dark, tousled hair hauled a water bucket into the stables, pausing at the sight of Jack. From what the outlaw recalled, the kid was one of the new arrivals, the son of a maverick mage. He stared and looked like he was ready to flee, but stood his ground as Jack stalked up to him.

"You know anything about Naureus?" Jack demanded, pointing toward the vacant stall.

The boy followed Jack's gesture, swallowing. "Um. He's not here?"

Jack reined in his frustration. He tried to save his moments of intimidation for those who deserved it, and this greenhorn groom didn't. Taking a breath, he did his best to keep his voice reasonable. "What I mean is, has he been here recently?"

"Oh." The groom blinked. "It's been a couple of days. Why?"

Jack waved a hand in dismissal. That was what he wanted to know. It lined up with his own last sighting of Raven. "Thanks, kid."

A quick stop by Zepheus's stall revealed that, like most of the other pegasi, the stallion was out. Jack stopped by the tack room to review the posted sentry schedule. Yeah, Zepheus was out covering the northern canyons, so wouldn't be close.

He felt a sudden rush of warmth. He spun, knowing what that meant. Kittie's aethon steed stood uncomfortably close behind him, mane whipping like a windswept flame. The fire elemental looked like a horse most of the time, and though she was an embodiment of magic, she couldn't communicate with him the way a pegasus could. But she was intelligent in her own primal way.

She snorted in his face, acting far too much like a spiteful mare for his comfort. A spiteful mare who could turn everything around her to cinders if she chose.

Jack didn't have time for her drama. "What is it, Najaria?"

The aethon turned to the paper schedule on the door. For an instant, Jack feared she was going to burn it. But she didn't—she tapped it with her velvet-soft nose, then pawed the ground, her hooves sparking.

What in tarnation? "You got something I need to know?" Her red equine head bobbed in agreement. "Is it about Kittie?" A snort of disagreement. Jack paused, thinking. "You know something about Raven or Naureus?"

Najaria retreated a step, head rocking up and down in assent. She turned, ears pricked toward the exit.

It would be really helpful if she could communicate with him. Kittie could understand her in a limited way through their shared affinity for fire. Jack moved to follow the elemental. "Lead on."

The mare broke into a trot, showing him to a fire pit on the far side of town. The ashes in the pit were cold, and nothing about it looked unusual to Jack until the aethon adamantly nosed something stuck to a stone along the edge of the pit. It was a charred scrap of paper. He reached down and plucked it up, frowning. The remnant was no bigger than his thumb, and it was mostly scorched, though he knew there was some sort of writing on it.

He shook his head. "Sorry. I don't know what this clue means."

Najaria snorted in a manner that communicated she thought he was quite the stupid human. Which, yeah, that was true sometimes, but in this matter, it was hardly fair.

Jack tilted his head, considering. If the elemental knew something, he didn't want to miss out. "Would you be able to tell Kittie?"

The mare approved of the idea. She spun on a hind hoof and then moved like a living blaze. She was there one moment and gone the next, leaving only a charred hoof track. Wisps of smoke drifted from the imprint. Jack crouched down to study the fire pit while he waited.

That scrap wasn't the only paper. There were more tiny bits, though he assumed the bulk of the writing had become ash. Why had burned papers made the aethon suspicious?

Najaria jogged up a few moments later, Kittie astride her bareback. Jack had to admit, Kittie looked damn good on that mare. Though, if he were honest, it didn't take much for Kittie to look good in his eyes. She was the fire that warmed his heart. The Pyromancer raised her brows at her husband. "So, you must be why Najaria is riled up."

Jack snorted. "No, she's got *me* riled up. Trying to figure out where Raven is, and your horse dragged me over here."

Najaria made a dangerous, primal noise at being called a *horse*, reminiscent of the roar and crackle of a growing inferno. Jack raised his hands in apology.

Kittie rolled her eyes at the exchange, then slipped down from the mare's back. "You want me to translate, is that it?"

"Would be helpful, yeah."

Kittie pursed her lips, turning to the aethon. "What do you want Jack to know?" She laid a hand on Najaria's forehead.

As Jack watched, Najaria's eyes closed to a blissful, half-lidded state. A smile curled Kittie's lips as they communed. A small part of Jack was jealous, but he knew he had a similar relationship with Zepheus. Well, with a lot more snark and hard-headedness.

"Mostly, she just shows me simple images," Kittie relayed after a moment. "Raven was here, reading papers. Letters, maybe. Then he burned them." She paused, sorting through new information. "She says he was…hot? No, that's not the right word. Upset. Angry, perhaps. Elementals don't translate emotions very well."

Upset or angry. And then he had burned whatever might have inspired those feelings. He then didn't show up for a meeting. Letters from Vixen, perhaps? Jack knew the pair had parted ways, and the Shadowstepper hadn't been happy about it. But his gut didn't think it was anything from Vixen. That didn't feel right. "We need to find Raven." Jack feared they wouldn't find him in Fortitude. Or even in the Gutter.

WHEN JACK REGROUPED WITH THE OTHER RINGLEADERS, KUR REPORTED that Raven's house was vacant, filled with only stale scents of the man. As expected, Mindy hadn't seen him come to HQ, either.

Zepheus returned from his patrol, trotting up at Jack's call. <What is wrong?>

"You heard anything from Naureus?"

The palomino shook his mane. <Regarding anything in particular?>

"Yeah. His rider is missing."

The pegasus's head snapped up in startlement. <What?>

Jack gave him a brief run-down on their findings so far. Further inspection of the tack room revealed that Naureus's saddle and hackamore had been left behind. While it was normal to go without the hack-amore around the Gutter, the saddle was a different issue. Jack couldn't imagine why anyone would go out without a saddle for an extended time —especially if they had made plans to skip town. He said as much to Zepheus.

<Perhaps he would not take a saddle if he didn't plan to stay with his pegasus,> Zepheus reasoned after considering the question. And Jack hated to admit it, but that made a level of sense. If that was the case, it meant Naureus might come back to Fortitude, unless Raven had asked him to keep a low profile. Either was a possibility.

Jack rubbed his forehead. "Yeah, the pegasi are gonna hate me, but this might be important. Ask all available sentries to go out and fly a grid pattern, searching for Naureus or Raven. If they find both, that's prefer-able. Have them work the grid in pairs."

Zepheus pricked an ear. <What do they do if they find them?>

The outlaw assumed Raven didn't want to be found. "One sentry tails them, the other passes the message to us with their last known location as soon as possible." He turned, another idea coming to mind. Yeah, he was going to use every resource at hand. "Can you get the sentries on that? I need to find Em."

<I will. You know this will require bonus pay.> Zepheus snorted. Jack waved a hand in agreement.

Jack found Emmaline at the bakery. The thing Jack liked about her work with the Breaker was that she stayed out of trouble, and he knew where to find her half the time. She, Reuben, and Hannah were cleaning up from their morning work. The bakery seemed somehow emptier without Blaise there—the Breaker wasn't an outgoing man by any defini-tion, but he had a presence in the bakery. It was his domain, the one place in the world the young man never doubted himself. Even Jack had to admit he made damn good desserts.

The trio looked up at his entrance. Emmaline narrowed her eyes, no doubt immediately reading the tension that lined his face. "Daddy?"

"Need your magic, Em." He jerked his head toward the door, a silent command for her to come with him. Though she had the same flavor of magic that he did, Emmaline had different strengths. And right now, he could use them.

Emmaline glanced at the other two. Reuben had a healthy respect for Jack and made himself busy sweeping the floor, desperate to steer clear of the elder Effigest's attention. "We're fine. Go do what you need to do."

Emmaline blew out a breath. She didn't enjoy being ordered around by her father, and Jack realized he had misstepped by blustering in and making a demand. He cleared his throat, deciding he needed to correct that. With anyone else, he wouldn't give a damn. But he still walked a thin line when it came to Emmaline, and he didn't want to chase her away. "You can do something I can't, so I'd appreciate your help."

His daughter gave him an incredulous look but nodded and headed for the door. When they were on the porch, she said, "Sometimes you really *can* be a reasonable person."

Jack snorted at the comment. "We both know I'm a piss-goblin at heart." Then he sobered. "You got a spare poppet on you?"

"Yeah." Emmaline patted the back pocket of her trousers. "Small one. Does that matter?"

"Shouldn't," Jack said.

"Are we looking for someone?" Emmaline asked.

She knew very well her specialty and why he might come to her. "Yeah. Raven."

Emmaline sucked in a surprised breath and didn't speak as they headed for Raven's home. The door was unlocked—even though it was a town of outlaws, it was rare for them to steal from one another. Any outsiders who came in to do such a deed would soon discover that the outlaws defended their own swiftly and brutally. Jack tugged the door open, studying everything.

As far as homes in Fortitude went, it was tiny. Raven lived alone and had needed little—it was a single room with a bed, a rudimentary kitchen that would have given Blaise conniptions, and a table. A chest stood beside the bed. Jack stalked over to it, pulling open a drawer.

Emmaline watched him, brow furrowed. "What are you looking for?"

"Something for your poppet." Jack wanted to make certain whatever they used was tied to the missing Ringleader.

After a moment, he located a black bandanna that he knew for a fact the other outlaw had worn. Even better, since it covered his nose and mouth, it would have a deeper tie to Raven's essence. Silently, he handed it to Emmaline.

She accepted it, winding it around the poppet. Emmaline moved over to the bed and sat down on its edge, cupping the tiny doll in her hands as she whispered words not even Jack understood, activating the poppet. The air over the doll rippled with magic as she began her spellwork.

Emmaline had tried to show him how to cast this spell, but it seemed the sort of magic one had to have a knack for. Jack couldn't do much with it—he could use a poppet to sense if someone was alive and well, but not where they were located. It was a potent ability, and one more reason to make sure the Confederation never got their hands on his daughter.

Ten minutes passed before she rolled her shoulders, which had surely grown stiff. Emmaline groaned. "He's west of here."

"Close?"

"No. I think…I think he's past the mountains."

"Which mountains?"

Emmaline met his gaze. "All of them."

CHAPTER NINE

She's Not My Girl

Raven

It had been a long, long time since Raven had willingly set foot on Confederation soil. Unlike Jack, he wasn't fool enough to constantly risk his neck. He might not have the bounty on his head that the Effigest did, but he was a wanted man. And yet, here he was in the back alley of a restaurant in Ondin, doing the unthinkable.

He sighed, glancing up at the stars that salted the velvet night sky overhead. Coming here was a risk, yes, but so was not coming here. Shadows surrounded him. As long as no one got the drop on him, he had the advantage. He brushed his fingertips against the knives sheathed at his belt, his preferred weapons. Sixguns got the job done, but so did a good blade. The greenhorn who coined the adage *don't bring a knife to a gunfight* had never come across a Shadowstepper.

"Come on, I don't have all night," he murmured, turning in a slow circle. Raven felt naked here by himself. Out of necessity, he'd left Naureus back on the farthest fringes of the Gutter. Raven's insistence had displeased the buckskin stallion, even more so when Raven couldn't say when he'd be back.

Or *if* he'd be back. He just didn't know. There was too much at stake. And he wasn't willing to tangle Naureus in this web.

Somewhere nearby, a door opened with a chilling creak. Raven tensed, fighting the urge to leap into the safety of the nearest shadow to watch and wait. But he was expected here, and if he ran and hid every time his contact came to look for him, he'd get nowhere.

"Mr. Dawson?" Someone shuffled into the light. A middle-aged man, human. Dressed like a waiter from the stuffy restaurant, judging by the attire.

Raven took a step forward. "Yeah?"

"They'll see you now." The man ducked his head. Raven couldn't tell if it was a tic or deference. "Follow me, please."

The Shadowstepper frowned. "Not until I know who's summoned me."

His guide didn't look back, only shuffled over to the door. "I don't know. I was only told to come out back and fetch a gentleman by the name of Dawson."

Gentleman. Raven was the farthest thing from that descriptor, but he let it go. Full of mistrust, he followed the man inside. They entered through the kitchen, the staff bustling, busy at various stations. Raven didn't have time to goggle about and look, instead following his guide through into what looked like a pantry but opened into stairs that led down. A cellar, perhaps? Raven had no choice but to follow. He kept his magic at the ready—just in case.

His escort led him into a room flanked by so many mage-lights, it was almost as bright as day. Raven winced, his eyes still adjusting after being outside. When his vision cleared, he found a man and woman studying him.

They were well-dressed, the man in a fine greatcoat, crisp trousers, and polished shoes. The woman appeared to be similar in age to Raven, though her attire was more a match for the man accompanying her. She wore a burgundy ruffled blouse and smart black boots that disappeared beneath the voluminous floral skirt. *Confederation elite.* Raven stilled, heart thundering. He could magic himself away. It wasn't too late. "Who are you?"

The man was the older of the pair, his salt-and-pepper hair catching the light. "Consider us…potential benefactors, Mr. Dawson."

Raven frowned. "Benefactors?"

"Yes," the man continued. "We have quite an interest in the Gutter and the people who call it home."

Raven had sat through enough Ringleader meetings to know that any outsider expressing an interest in the Gutter usually meant trouble for the outlaws. He shifted his weight from one foot to the other. "Whatever you want with me, it's nothing I can give."

"I wouldn't be so certain. Wouldn't you agree, Tara?" The man smiled at his counterpart.

The woman, Tara, shrugged. "Depends if Mr. Dawson wants to spare his friends, Phillip." She moved to pick up something from the table that separated the pair, the move like a languid afterthought. At first, Raven thought the table held nothing of importance—maybe only mail or magazines—but he lost confidence in that as Tara flipped through a few pieces of paper. "Ah yes, there it is." She pulled out a slip. "This one, in particular."

Tara held the paper out for Raven. With misgivings, the Shadowstepper accepted it, swallowing when he realized it was a sketch of Vixen. The worst part was, he knew exactly what it was from. When they'd been taken to Fort Courage, sketches had been made of each imprisoned outlaw to go with their records. They knew about Vixen and had connected her to him. And while she might not love him, he didn't feel the same. He hated that this pair knew. Would use that as leverage.

"Like I said, whatever you want is probably not something I can give."

"That's too bad." Tara clucked her tongue, taking the sketch back and settling it among the other papers. Almost idly, she removed another one, shifting it into the light just so. It was an image of Raven himself. "You were at Fort Courage, were you not, Mr. Dawson?"

Raven bristled. His instinct told him to get out of there, but another part told him to stay. These elite were an implied threat against the Gutter and the people there. "I was."

Phillip whistled and shook his head. "Nasty business all around, that attack on the outlaw town and then the mess with Courage." He aimed a smirk at Raven. "It would be a shame if it happened again."

Raven gritted his teeth, suddenly glad Vixen, Jefferson, and Blaise were striking out to prevent that. "Not if we can stop it first."

Phillip nodded at that. "Oh yes. We know about Cole and the Breaker." Was it Raven's imagination, or did the man's voice grow sour when he spoke Jefferson's last name? *Definitely wasn't my imagination.* "Your girl is with them, too, hmm?"

"She's not my girl." The words hurt to say. They were true, but that didn't ease the pain. Gods, he loved Vixen, and the knowledge that she didn't feel the same way was almost a physical wound.

"No?" Phillip asked with an interested quirk of his brow.

"No," Raven confirmed through clenched teeth.

The well-dressed pair exchanged knowing glances. Phillip reached across to Tara's assortment of pictures, picking up Vixen's. He lifted it, his gaze flicking to Raven. "But you wish she was, don't you?"

Raven felt his cheeks warm, hating the man picking at a festering wound. He could just disappear into a shadow—that would be the safe thing to do. But how did they know so much about Vixen? There were many things she hadn't told *him*.

"He does," Tara confirmed with a soft laugh. Raven arrowed a glare at her. "Don't try to hide it. We can see it in your eyes."

"She could be yours, you know." Phillip's voice was a seductive whisper. He rose from his seat, hands behind his back as he walked in a circle around the room, as if the action helped him think aloud. "I know what it's like to love someone. To lose that person because of the machinations of others." His words became heated, leaving Raven to wonder who had come between this powerful man and his love.

Tara frowned, waving a hand to draw attention back to herself. "Your friends can't win. Surely you know this."

Raven swallowed. As much as he hadn't wanted Vixen to go, he understood their task was important. He read the undercurrents easily enough —this pair was determined to stop them. And for some reason, they'd set their sights on Raven. Maybe he could do something about it, though.

"What do you want with me?"

Phillip smiled, composed once more. "You have a special set of skills that would be useful to our cause."

They wanted to use him. He narrowed his eyes. "What makes you think I'd betray my friends? I'm a Ringleader, for Faedra's sake."

Tara smirked. "Because if you work with us, you can get your girl back. If those outlaw friends of yours succeed at their task, you'll lose her forever."

Raven stiffened. "She doesn't love me."

"But she *could*," Tara insisted, her voice almost a purr. "We have the means to make it happen."

That couldn't be true…could it? Indecision warred within. His need to have Vixen as his own pitted against the knowledge that she was a spitfire who knew her mind—and ultimately, that was what he loved about her. But he *loved* her.

As if sensing his conflict, the woman rose from her seat and crossed the room, moving to a collection of stoppered bottles. She made a contemplative sound, then selected one with a flourish. "Alchemy has progressed by leaps and bounds."

Alchemy. As a mage, he detested alchemy, but…what if it was true? Raven swallowed. It was tempting to refuse to work with these brash elites, but if they were plotting something, wouldn't it be better to be on the inside? Maybe he could scuttle their plans.

And if it meant he had a chance to win Vixen back, wouldn't it be worth it? Raven closed his eyes. "Tell me what I need to do."

CHAPTER TEN

Jefferson's Favorite Party Game

Vixen

Their train made an afternoon stop in the Gannish town of Aspenpoint two days later. Jefferson discovered it would be a longer stop than normal, allowing them a chance to let the unicorn and pegasi disembark to stretch their legs and graze.

The Godspine Mountains were visible in the distance, looming on the horizon like jagged teeth. The train depot at Aspenpoint bordered a verdant field, and their group appreciated the convenience as they accompanied the equines there. The sun glared overhead, making Vixen regret leaving her smoke-lensed glasses packed in her things. With the ring, she didn't need them to temper her magic, but they were handy against the sun.

<I wish we could fly,> Alekon lamented to Vixen, his liquid brown eyes on the fluffy clouds overhead, ears pricked. <I want to go fly in the mountains. Maybe startle some goats. It would be fun.>

"You're land-bound for the time being," she replied, patting his warm shoulder at the point where his wings would be, had he not shrouded them with the camouflaging magic unique to pegasi. "But it's a lovely day, and there's nothing to stop you from flying with your hooves."

Alekon arched his neck, snorting at the sentiment. <That will have to do.> He swung his head away when she freed him from the halter—they had committed to the farce that the pegasi were horses, which meant all the normal equine trappings. As soon as she stepped back, he bolted across the turf to join the others, who had already been released.

Vixen watched, a smile curling her lips as Alekon raced alongside Seledora and Darby. Emrys rolled in the grass nearby, grunting and snorting his contentment. The pegasi had become more accepting of the unicorn, though Vixen wouldn't quite call them friends. They were tolerant but wary of each other, which was all they could ask under the circumstances.

"They're quite the sight, aren't they?"

Vixen turned at Rhys's voice. Darby's halter and lead rope were slung over his shoulder as he ambled over to lean against the fence.

"They are," she agreed, relaxing at the spectacle of the jubilant equines. While the train was luxurious, it was still a confining box of metal and wood. Vixen had grown far too accustomed to open skies and the freedom to do as she pleased. Her gaze skated over to where Blaise and Jefferson sat beneath a shady tree, relaxing. The Breaker's back rested against the bough, with Jefferson laying down, hands pillowing his head which rested in Blaise's lap as they spoke quietly.

Rhys followed her gaze. "You're rather fond of your friends."

She nodded. "Blaise has had some hard times. It's nice to see him happy. He's been a good friend."

The Tracker leaned over, plucked a flower, and twirled it between his index finger and thumb, thoughtful. "Everyone says he's dangerous."

Vixen scoffed, shaking her head. "The people who say that don't understand his magic. Folks are always going to think the things they don't understand are dangerous." She'd had a lot of time to think about that. Vixen thought this was why the Confederation felt as they did about magic in general. That, and also those without were desperate to grasp whatever power they could.

Rhys nodded. "That's true." He tossed the flower aside, bending to pick a new one. "Do you—?"

Darby interrupted him with a shrill cry. The unicorn skidded to a halt, grass flying beneath his cloven hooves. Seledora and Alekon continued to gallop, though they swung in a circle, coming around behind the unicorn, also on alert. Darby ignored them, moving into a high-action trot, nostrils flaring as he drank the scents on the wind. Every few paces, he swung his horn from one side to the other.

Rhys's brow furrowed. "I'll be back. He's signaling something."

A mage. Vixen knew that only too well. She watched as Rhys broke into a run, the halter flapping against his arm as he rushed to keep up with the unicorn. She shaded her eyes. Darby stopped at the edge of the field, allowing Rhys to catch up.

She wasn't sure what passed between them. Vixen scowled, straining to see what might have set off the unicorn. People were coming and going at the station house, with a few new passengers boarding their train. Were there unbound mages among the incoming passengers? Unicorns were trained to scent the difference between a maverick and a mage with a tattoo, whether or not they were geasa-bound.

Blaise and Jefferson ambled over to Vixen, their idyllic peace interrupted by the unicorn's alarm. "Do you think we need to be worried?" Blaise's voice was soft but laced with nerves, his shoulders tensing.

Vixen glanced at Jefferson. He edged closer to Blaise, subtly capturing the Breaker's pinky finger with his own. It was a sweet gesture, a kindness that made her smile. Like others, she'd been suspicious of Jefferson at first, but he was undeniably good for Blaise. "No. Unicorns are extremely sensitive to the scent of magic, that's all." She twisted the ring on her finger, wondering how Darby would react if she removed it.

"Luckily, I know firsthand how well that lovely piece of jewelry works," Jefferson said with a smile, tipping his head toward her. Blaise had relaxed at her words and Jefferson's proximity.

Vixen nodded, shifting her gaze to the unicorn. Darby had his head slung over the distant fence, nostrils distended. "Sorry your quiet moment got interrupted."

"As am I," Jefferson murmured.

Blaise rubbed the back of his neck. "It was nice while it lasted."

A few minutes later, Rhys made his way back, though Darby kept pausing, twisting around to peer over his shoulder. The Tracker had a deep frown etched on his face.

"What was that all about?" Vixen asked.

Rhys shook his head. "I'm not sure. There must be a mage over there."

"A theurgist?" Blaise asked, not as schooled in the nuances of unicorns as Vixen was.

"No. A maverick or outlaw," Rhys said.

"Do you have to go after them?" Tension lined Blaise's eyes, and Vixen knew the Breaker was dangerously close to a resurgence of old memories. Jefferson must have known, too, since he brushed his fingers lightly against Blaise's arm.

Vixen didn't know if Rhys sensed Blaise's turmoil. He smiled and shook his head. "That's not my current job, so no." His easy words made Blaise relax almost immediately. Rhys slipped the halter back onto Darby's head. "I think I'll put this troublemaker back in his stall. He's going to be too distracted now." He gently smacked the velvet of the stallion's nose. "That's not the work we're doing right now, you great pest."

Jefferson consulted his pocket watch. "We'll follow shortly. We need to have the pegasi back aboard within the half-hour." Rhys and the unicorn headed toward the station. When they were out of earshot, Jefferson cleared his throat. "Care to share with us how you know the Tracker?"

Vixen spun at his question. Blaise had moved to lean against the fence, watching the pegasi. Jefferson climbed the fence to perch atop the rail, a behavior she wouldn't have expected of the dapper ambassador. Somehow, he made it work and looked good doing it. She was sure he knew that. "We have a history."

"And that is?" Jefferson asked, tone mild, as if he were making a polite inquiry at a dinner party.

Vixen watched as their pegasi settled back to grazing. Alekon stayed nearby, though, the hide at his shoulders twitched like a memory of his wings. "Rhys and Darby are the ones who figured out I was a mage."

Blaise made a soft sound of surprise. "So, he knows about you?"

"Yes, but he won't betray me." Vixen paused. "At least, I don't think so. He didn't when he had the opportunity years ago."

"How is it he's the one saddled with our group?" Jefferson asked.

She shrugged. "I asked him, and it sounds like it's just a coincidence."

"Hmm." Jefferson rubbed his chin, twisting to glance over his shoulder in the station's direction.

"You don't think it's a coincidence," Blaise guessed.

"I don't," Jefferson admitted. "After everything I've been through with the Quiet Ones, I wouldn't put it past them to manipulate his placement somehow. He might even be in their pay."

Vixen shook her head. "No! Rhys wouldn't." Jefferson aimed a cool look her way, which gave her pause. She frowned. "I mean, he wouldn't because…" She faltered. "Because it's complicated."

Jefferson cocked his head, reminding her of a hunting hound on the trail of a scent. "Were you lovers?"

"What? Ew, no," Vixen blurted, failing to hide the revulsion the very idea incited.

Her response only intrigued Jefferson further, though. He leaned over, and it was a surprise he didn't fall off the fence. "Oh? That's a shame. He looks like a treat."

"Hey," Blaise protested, jabbing his beau in the side. "Check yourself."

Jefferson chuckled, though he shot a fond look at Blaise. "I'm allowed to make observations, love. And the Tracker does have rugged good looks." His green eyes arrowed back to Vixen. "So what is he, then? I'm prepared to make more equally scandalous guesses. This is one of my favorite party games."

Vixen blew out a frustrated breath. "He's my brother. My twin."

"Oh." Jefferson's eyes widened at that. "But you don't look alike."

Oh, how she knew. That was perhaps the most remarked-upon aspect of their family growing up, aside from their status. Rhys had hair that gleamed like oiled bronze in the sunlight, a sharp contrast to Vixen's red.

And their eyes differed, too. Vixen's were a light grey like liquid silver. Rhys's were brown.

"He favors our father, and I take after our mother," Vixen explained.

Blaise raised his brows. "Then why is he a Tracker? Why isn't he...?" The Breaker stalled, licking his lips. He waved a hand in Vixen's general direction. "Whatever you are?"

Vixen fiddled with the ring on her finger. Though he hadn't been clear, she understood Blaise didn't mean a mage. "There was an uproar when we were born. Never in memory had the Luminary birthed twins." She stared off in the direction Rhys had gone. "Historically, the Luminary only has a single child, so we were quite the scandal."

Jefferson snapped his fingers. "Yes, now I recall! I had forgotten that since the Spark was supposedly..." He cleared his throat with a look of sudden discomfort.

"Dead?" Vixen suggested.

"Well, yes." Jefferson studiously stared at the distant mountains, possibly to forget his own dalliances with alleged death.

"Doesn't explain much of anything to me," Blaise said, reminding them he had precious little context for their conversation. "Does this mean your father is a god or...?" He chewed on his bottom lip, brows furrowed with confusion.

"Oh, no," Vixen said with a shake of her head. "Our father was as mortal as anyone else." She swallowed the lump that suddenly formed in her throat. Her father hadn't crossed her mind in ages, and for that, she felt a pang of guilt. "He died when we were little, so I don't remember much about him."

Blaise's expression closed. He was thinking of his own father, Vixen suspected. "I'm sorry."

She waved a hand, deciding to refocus on the question Blaise had asked earlier. "The reason Rhys isn't the Spark is simple. Garus chose me." Vixen recalled the weighty sensation of a deity pressing into her skull. She had been twelve and, at first, hadn't understood what was happening. For most of her life, Garus had just been a big idea to which her mother dedicated most of her waking time. Things had changed when he made his presence known, wrapping her in a brilliant beam of golden light that not even the most skeptical of clerics could deny. All of that was why she'd been so confused when her magic manifested two years later.

"But shouldn't he be something else important?" Blaise asked.

"Trackers are important," Jefferson observed.

Vixen nodded. "At around the same time Garus chose me, we discovered..." She hesitated. Should she tell them? Perhaps she owed this knowledge to them—they were going into a dangerous situation. If Vixen was to serve Garus, then she would arm her friends with information. "I need you both to keep a secret."

"Oh, I'm good at keeping secrets." Jefferson grinned. Blaise elbowed him again. "I don't mean from *you*."

"I don't like secrets, but I know sometimes they're necessary," Blaise said, voice soft.

She trusted them. "This is particular to Trackers, and it's not common knowledge. Rhys is immune to magic—all Trackers are. They're also sensitive to when it's being used around them."

"I thought unicorns were needed to sniff out mages?" Blaise asked.

Vixen wiggled the fingers of one hand in an indecisive gesture. "A unicorn can pinpoint a mage in a crowd of people, or a mage who's not actively using their magic. That's why Trackers have them."

"Magic immunity," Jefferson mused. "That makes sense. I'd always assumed it was the unicorn and combat training that gave them the upper hand against a mage."

"That's what they want everyone to think." It was a fine bit of sleight of hand. Most maverick mages didn't have the training to fight someone, and when faced with a Tracker, they relied on their magic. The tactic fell apart quickly when faced with a Tracker immune to their power. Vixen wet her lips. "So anyway, that's the story of me and Rhys."

"The god of wisdom chose a Spark with magic." Jefferson's green eyes were on her, calculating. "He chose you. Why did you leave?"

"I ran away." Vixen decided this was a good time to look elsewhere. She reached down and snatched up a flower, methodically plucking the petals and flicking them away. "Rhys and Darby were the ones who discovered my magic. At first, we thought maybe I could hide it..." She ripped the head of the flower from the stem, tossing it aside. "It didn't take long for me to figure out I couldn't. I'd seen too many mages hang. I was scared."

She had fled. Not for a minute had Vixen even considered taking the new development to her mother. The Luminary despised mages because magic was an abomination of wisdom. Vixen had only seen all the ways she would be hated. Ostracized. Maybe even killed for something beyond her control. Garus had been absent from her life since he'd chosen her— she assumed he'd realized his mistake.

"Huh," Blaise murmured.

"Rhys helped me escape from Izhadell," Vixen whispered. "And that's how I know we can trust him."

Blaise's eyes softened at that. She knew he would understand, based on his own past. "I think, even if he weren't your brother, we could trust him."

"Why's that?" Jefferson peered at his beau, curious.

Blaise gestured to the pegasi. "Emrys said he takes good care of them. He doesn't treat them like horses."

<He does not,> Alekon confirmed, lifting his head. <He treats the unicorn well, and he makes certain our needs are met. Even talks to us.>

Vixen raised her brows at that. "That's good to hear. Rhys always had a way with the unicorns." Even better if he knew to treat the pegasi as more than a normal horse. The unaware often made that mistake.

Jefferson pulled his pocket watch out, consulting the time. "I think our break is at an end. We should make our way back before we miss our ride."

<I'd be happy to never get in that box again,> Alekon admitted with a snort, ambling over.

Vixen scratched him between the eyes. "Just a little longer. We'll be in Izhadell before you know it."

And then the real work would begin.

CHAPTER ELEVEN

The Accountant

Jefferson

The train was the luxurious sort that Jefferson was accustomed to on the occasions when he had taken this mode of transportation, all polished wood panels, ornate brocade draperies, and gleaming brass fittings. The other passengers were exactly the sort he would expect to see in such a setting—the Confederation elite, though he spied a few he suspected were high-class merchants on the cusp of elite status. They fluttered around the elite like moths to a flame.

That meant it was also the sort of setting where Blaise felt most awkward. This was exacerbated by the fact Jefferson wasn't comfortable giving out his name (or Blaise's) in their present company. As it was, there was always the chance someone might recognize Jefferson from his affluent past. He didn't mind adopting a temporary moniker, though Blaise certainly did. The Breaker had only grudgingly agreed to the idea.

The dining car boasted beautiful booths that were spacious enough to hold large parties. None of them were designed for intimate meals, but to accommodate as many people as possible. They'd been fortunate so far and had been able to keep to themselves when they ate, but that didn't seem to be on the cards tonight. Every booth held at least two occupants, many of them completely full.

"We must have picked up additional passengers in Aspenpoint," Jefferson murmured.

"We have to sit with other people?" Blaise asked, voice soft as he took in the crowded car.

Jefferson gave his hand a surreptitious squeeze. "If you prefer, we can take a plate back to the room."

The Breaker eased, as if the option gave him more clarity of mind. He glanced at Jefferson. "We can eat here." There was something he left unsaid, but Jefferson suspected he knew. Blaise understood Jefferson would enjoy this, and he wanted him to be happy. It was no small thing, and it made him want to pull Blaise in for an appreciative kiss, but that would only embarrass his beau in their current situation. He settled for flashing Blaise a smile that he hoped communicated all that and more.

A group of four diners rose from a booth in the corner. Jefferson touched Blaise's elbow, and they moved to claim it. Blaise scooted in to sit beside the broad window—it would provide the Breaker a chance to focus on the scenery more than those around him. Jefferson sat comfortably close beside him.

A well-dressed man and woman approached, obviously on the hunt for seating. The gentlemen gestured to the empty bench opposite Blaise and Jefferson. "May we?"

Jefferson inclined his head. "Be our guest." He supposed Blaise would regret his concession, but they couldn't be rude and deny fellow passengers a seat. The Breaker nodded, but he didn't turn from the window to acknowledge them otherwise. Jefferson knew he would come around after a few minutes.

The newcomers bobbed their heads and made a show of taking their seats, expensive fabric rustling with their movements. It reminded Jefferson of a flock of birds preening. "Excellent. Allow us to make introductions. I'm Barnabas Inman, and this is my lovely wife Antoinette." The man smiled. "We own a modest number of fish factories on the Canen coast. And you are?"

The Inmans. Jefferson had heard of them, but fortunately, didn't know them. But if he gave his name, this pair of elite would know exactly who he was. If they hadn't known him as a wealthy entrepreneur, they would most certainly know him after the mess at Nera. He was spared from having to come up with an immediate answer, however, as a new woman appeared. She was a brunette with close-cropped hair, and while she dressed respectably, she was a step down from the Inmans.

The woman gave them a bright smile. "Hello! The other tables are all filling up. Could I impose on you?"

Ah, bless her for the interruption. Jefferson met her smile with a brilliant one of his own. "We'd be delighted for your company. Please, have a seat. We were just introducing ourselves."

She bobbed her head as she sat. "Of course. I'm Holly Lewis, traveling home to Phinora." Holly's gaze swept over everyone at the table. Was it

Jefferson's imagination, or did she linger on Blaise? Wonderful. As if he needed another person to worry about on this train.

The others were looking at him and Blaise for their own introductions. Jefferson could feel the discomfort radiating from his beau. Blaise, no doubt, was worried about what would happen if people knew who he was. That put Jefferson in a difficult position. Blaise also disliked deceptions. But sometimes, like now, they were necessary.

Jefferson cleared his throat. "I'm Jeffrey Hawthorne. An accountant." Blaise made a soft, surprised sound at the use of his last name, but Jefferson decided he rather liked it.

"Jeffrey the Accountant," Antoinette repeated, as if tasting the words. As if she were trying to decide if he could possibly be monied enough to be in their presence. It wasn't even a bald-faced lie. He did most of his own accounting these days, what little there was to be done. And he handled the books for the bakery, to Blaise's benefit. "And this is Blake Cole. He's a pastry chef."

Blaise shot him a look that was a mix of annoyance (probably at the last name) and optimistic joy. Jefferson had given him something he could have a level of proficiency about in conversation. Blaise murmured a greeting, then went back to looking out the window.

"An accountant and a pastry chef," Antoinette mused. "How quaint."

"I believe we saw you load the horses that are in the livestock transport," Barnabas commented, keen interest in his voice. "Are you somehow connected with Bull's Eye Stables, then?"

That was something Jefferson hadn't accounted for. His mind raced, seeking plausible connections. The current unicorn racing meets were taking place in western Ganland, but that wasn't their destination. He thought it likely Monica would secure a boxcar that wouldn't be too out-of-place going to Phinora, however. It was possible there was a stud or training stable there, though for the life of him, he couldn't recall. Time to bluff. "Indeed, we are."

At that, Blaise elbowed him. *Hard.* He didn't like lies, even needful ones. And he clearly didn't appreciate Jefferson including him. It was likely the Breaker would take the rest of his meals in their room after this. And perhaps that wasn't the worst idea.

Barnabas nodded. "So, you'll be working with Tara Woodrow, then. And you're escorting new bloodstock?"

"We are," Jefferson agreed without batting an eye. "It seemed expedient." But the name immediately put him on edge. Tara was one of the Quiet Ones. She must own Bull's Eye Stables. If so, that was worrisome for many reasons.

Holly had been quiet until that point, either polite or calculating. She fussed with her flatware, which was still rolled up in a linen napkin. "So, you're a pastry chef, Mr. Cole?"

Perhaps it had been a miscalculation to swap last names. Jefferson made the mistake of opening his mouth to speak before realizing the question was meant for Blaise. To his credit, the words *pastry chef* had snared Blaise's attention, and he nodded.

"I am," Blaise agreed, sounding confident. As he should, Jefferson thought with pride.

"I didn't know Woodrow would hire a no-name chef," Antoinette said with a sniff.

That was a flat-out insult. Jefferson wished he could argue against it. Blaise, however, simply shrugged. "I like to think that I'm up-and-coming."

The server came, bearing their meals, which gave them a much-needed break from conversation, allowing Jefferson a chance to mull over Woodrow's potential part in whatever plot was afoot. Perhaps it was merely a coincidence—Monica would have no way of knowing she was the enemy. But in this case, Jefferson didn't like coincidences.

Vixen's reappearance spared Jefferson from further contemplation. The Persuader paused when she saw the others seated at the table, her lips pressed together and silver eyes narrowed. It seemed she was making a threat assessment, too. She motioned for Blaise, and the Breaker squeezed out of the booth. She whispered something in his ear that Jefferson couldn't quite make out, then slipped in to claim the spot the young man had vacated.

Blaise smiled. "If you'll excuse me, there's been a..." He hesitated, eyebrows raised as he chose his words. "Pastry emergency."

"A pastry emergency?" Antoinette repeated, boggled. She glanced toward the kitchen compartment, as if expecting Blaise might venture there next.

Blaise laid out a linen napkin and scooped a handful of scones into its middle, creating a bundle. "Yep. And I always rise to the occasion."

Jefferson could barely conceal a chuckle at his beau's pun. He watched as Blaise beat a retreat out of the dining car, clutching the precious scones against his chest. Then Jefferson returned to his dining partners and did what he could to suss out any connections they might have to the Quiet Ones.

"Blake *Cole*? Of all the possible names, *that's* what you choose?" Blaise crossed his arms, sitting on the couch that folded out into a bed. He had returned to the room before Jefferson and Vixen, and it appeared he had been planning his ambush for some time.

Vixen's lips pinched together as she fought back a laugh. Jefferson, meanwhile, shrugged. "What? I thought it had a very nice ring to it."

The Breaker blew out a breath. "At least you didn't make me an accountant."

Vixen's glance shifted between them. "Sounds like I missed out on some fun."

"It was not fun. It was mostly just awkward," Blaise muttered.

Jefferson sat down beside his love, so close their shoulders brushed. "If you'll forgive me, you know why I didn't offer our true names."

Blaise breathed out a long sigh, slouching back. "I understand why. I just don't *like* it."

At that, Jefferson smiled and patted Blaise's knee. "It's only for the duration of the train ride. Not much longer." Then he updated Vixen on their temporary personas.

When he finished, the Persuader nodded. "Yeah, that was the right thing to do." Her mouth twisted into a frown. "Though if they figure out who you are, I could probably use my magic to convince them otherwise."

And I could do similar. Jefferson didn't dare say it aloud. Instead, he said, "But we need to keep your magic hidden."

She made a face, fiddling with the ring. "If we need it, though, it's there."

Her words nudged a smile from Blaise. The Breaker reached over for the train's information pamphlet and unfolded it, scanning its pages. "You want to go to this?" He pointed at something on the schedule.

Jefferson leaned over to get a better look. "Oh. That's a recital." He raised his brows, hope stirring. "You would go to that with me? Even after how dinner went tonight?"

"As long as there's no music about *me*." Blaise's expression soured at the thought.

"You *do* recall me telling you that one of the songs in the musical about you won an award, yes?" Jefferson asked, almost unable to hold back a smile. Having his friend Lizzie Jennings pen a musical about Blaise's extraordinary life had ended up as quite the coup that had helped them gain favor during the Inquiry that would have otherwise spelled their doom.

"No songs about me," Blaise repeated, adamant. "Just because I didn't die of embarrassment before doesn't mean it won't happen now."

"If there are any songs about you, I promise to whisk you away to the confines of this room immediately," Jefferson said gravely, earning an amused snort from Vixen.

Blaise relented, his shoulders relaxing. "Okay, I'll go with you. But only because I figure there will be less chance for awkward introductions since, hopefully, I won't be the entertainment."

And because you know I would enjoy it. Jefferson smiled. He suspected Blaise would like it, too. Jefferson could count the number of concerts his beau had seen on one hand. Blaise had never really had the opportunity to enjoy them like a normal person.

"Yes, there is that," Jefferson agreed. He vowed to set aside his suspicions for the rest of the evening, if only to allow himself and Blaise the chance to be normal. Jefferson turned to Vixen. "Would you like to come along?"

She waved a hand. "Three's a crowd. I'm going to check on the pegasi and then explore the rest of the train. I've never been on one before." They all knew she really wanted to spend more time with her brother. Jefferson felt an age-old pang, the old scar that flared up whenever he wished he had a better relationship with his sister. Or a relationship at all.

"Have fun," Jefferson said instead. He pulled out his pocket watch to check the time. "As for us, we should head out soon, or we may not get a seat."

CHAPTER TWELVE

Outhouse Surprise

Jack

It was a full day before anyone came across Naureus, and even then, it was the elemental mare who ended up locating him. According to Zepheus, Najaria threatened to scorch the buckskin stallion's wings if he didn't return with her. Jack wasn't sure he wanted to know how the aethon had communicated such a threat.

Raven's pegasus alighted on the edge of town, the tips of his wings singed but otherwise intact. Jack studied the equine as he trotted up, head hanging. Naureus knew that none of this looked good for him or his rider.

Most of the human citizens suspected nothing, but the pegasi certainly knew. The Fortitude flight had grown over the past year and now boasted around fifty of the equines. Most of them lined the street leading to the stables, ears laid back because they didn't understand what would have made Naureus and his rider part ways. It made them fearful.

Jack glanced at the ranks of pegasi, then turned to Zepheus. "They ain't gonna make this any easier. Can you get 'em out of here?"

The palomino bobbed his head in agreement. <Yes. Do not begin with Naureus until I am back, though.> With that said, he surged forward, ears flat against his skull, shrilling a cry that broke up the knots of pegasi. They bolted away, turning tail as Zepheus chased them off.

Naureus watched quietly, then ambled into the shade of the stable, heading to his stall as if he were an old plow horse. Jack frowned, having seen pegasi behave like this before. Naureus was worried about his rider, and when that happened, a pegasus often went off their feed and lost weight. It could lead to a whole mess of health problems that weren't easy to treat.

Zepheus returned, folding his wings as he quick-stepped over to where Jack waited outside Naureus's stall. With the palomino back, the outlaw nodded, giving the stud permission to lead the questioning. He figured it made sense, seeing as they were the same species.

Zepheus regarded Jack with surprise for a beat, then turned to the buckskin. <Where is your rider, Raven Dawson?>

Naureus sighed heavily, digging at the straw with a forehoof. <I do not know. He would not tell me where he was going, though I have my suspicions.>

Jack frowned. That made little sense. "But you took him somewhere." Then he winced, realizing he had intended for Zepheus to do most of the questioning.

<Only as far as Desina. Then he instructed me to stay away from Fortitude.> Naureus gave them a mournful look. <I told him I wanted to stay with him, but he said where he was going, it would be too dangerous for me. I tried to follow him but...> The stallion's black-tipped muzzle touched the ground. <When Raven wants to lose someone, it is easy for him.>

Jack nodded. Raven was one of the handiest sorts of Walkers, since shadows were everywhere. Small wonder Naureus wouldn't have been able to follow. He grunted in agreement.

<Do you know why he left?> Zepheus asked.

Naureus lifted his head. <No.>

"You think he might have gone after Vixen?" Jack figured it was a likely possibility.

The buckskin snorted. <Perhaps, but that is not the sum. He had become more distant over the last few months. Secretive.>

Jack and Zepheus traded looks. That wasn't a good sign. Jack loved his secrets, but Zepheus was privy to them. It was a foundation of their partnership. Outlaw and pegasus had to trust one another, or things went sour fast.

<Did you pick up anything unusual from him? Emotionally?> Zepheus asked.

Naureus blew out a breath. <His relationship with Vixen has been like a stone in his hoof. But that does not seem unreasonable when pursuing a mate.>

Yeah, that was true. But from what Jack understood, there was no more pursuing Vixen. Raven had proposed. She'd said no. Jack was one of the few in town privy to that bit of information. He rubbed his chin, thinking back to the fire pit. "Had he been communicating with anyone new?"

<There were letters he read, but that did not seem strange. Every human in town receives mail occasionally.> The buckskin paused. <Though Raven seldom received any previously.>

Jack pursed his lips. By itself, it wasn't strange. But with Najaria considering burned bits of paper suspicious, it took on a new light. "Letters from the post office or from elsewhere?"

Naureus arched his neck, suddenly thoughtful. <Not from the post office.>

That's what Jack had thought. Raven's only family were far, far away in Confederation lands. And from what the outlaw had gleaned, they were unaware of Raven's whereabouts. The odds of the letters being from a doting mother were low.

<Could it be from another mate?> Zepheus asked.

Naureus considered the question, then shook his inky mane. <No. I never picked up on any passionate emotions, nor scented any musk.>

Jack raised his brows at that. Naureus's statement left him wondering exactly how much Zepheus picked up from him when he was around Kittie. He didn't want his pesky pegasus sticking his nose where it didn't belong. But Zepheus's line of questioning inspired one of Jack's own. "Did he keep any of the letters, or burn 'em all? Do you know if Raven has any hidey-holes?"

The buckskin twitched an ear. <I don't know if he kept any. But yes, he has a stash.>

Zepheus traded looks with Jack. <Can you take us to it?>

Moments later, they were back at Raven's house with Naureus. Jack frowned—he thought he'd done a solid job of checking the inside for clues. The pegasus didn't lead them to the house, but instead around to the back, where an outhouse stood solitary vigil.

Jack wrinkled his nose. "You gotta be kidding me."

Naureus nudged the wood on one side of the outhouse. <There's a false wall. I have not seen inside, but from what I understand there is a latch that will open a compartment out here.>

Jack sighed. Of course, a damned pegasus had no need for an outhouse, which meant *he* had the privilege of exploring the interior. Silently cursing Raven, Jack entered. There was no mage-light to brighten the inside, but ample light flooded the cracks in the walls. As Jack groped around, he wished he'd had the presence of mind to cast the working that would shield him from the stink.

Then his fingers brushed something to the left of the rough wooden seat. It was, in fact, a lever of some sort. Jack pulled it. "That do anything out there?"

<Yes. Naureus is right. There is a compartment, but it's in the eaves.> Zepheus's golden bulk was visible through the cracks.

Jack came out, sucking in a lungful of fresh air before peering up. With the false door open, the stash was quite obvious. But when it was closed, it was nearly invisible in the shadow of the eaves. Jack couldn't quite reach it, but climbing aboard Zepheus gave him the height to pull out a bound wad of envelopes.

<What are they?> Naureus asked, ears pricked forward with interest—and a hint of optimism, as if hoping that the contents might vindicate his rider.

"Let's find out," Jack murmured, slipping from Zepheus's back so that he'd have an easier time perusing the find.

The first few letters were ones Raven had written, but never sent. They were all addressed to Vixen; the contents ranging from anger at her dismissal to poems professing the depths of his love. Not very good poems, but poems, nonetheless. Jack scowled as he flipped through them, then froze when he came across half of a torn letter with crisp handwriting that didn't belong to Raven.

> *—last time we will make this offer. Meet us in Ondin on—*

Ondin? Jack nearly crumpled the paper. Meet the author in Ondin *when?* That part was missing, but flipping the correspondence over showed a date from a little more than a month ago. He tried to make sense of the rest of the letter, searching for clues, but the closing had been torn away as well.

<Jack?> Zepheus nudged him. <We cannot read.>

Jack hissed out a breath. "Doesn't matter. This doesn't tell us shit."

<But you are still upset with my rider.> Naureus's ears flopped to the side.

The outlaw tilted his head, thinking of how to express his frustrations without hurting the buckskin any further. A good pegasus was loyal to their rider—even when that same rider had abandoned them. "Yeah. This mentions Ondin, and that has me on edge."

<Ondin. That is where Vixen's group got on the train.> Zepheus pawed at the ground, catching some of his rider's unease.

"Yeah. And I don't like coincidences."

<Perhaps we should go to Ondin and investigate?> Zepheus suggested. Jack flipped to the next letter, eyes widening. "Nah, not Ondin. Izhadell." He traced Raven's precise scrawl with one finger.

Stay out of Phinora, Jack.

CHAPTER THIRTEEN

Colorful Past

Jefferson

The train pulled into the station outside Izhadell, hissing as it came to a stop. Jefferson watched as Blaise peered out the window, his face pinched with worry. Sinister memories had plagued Blaise's dreams the past two nights, and Jefferson didn't know how the younger man would have fared without Jefferson's magic to chase them away.

Maybe bringing Blaise along had been a mistake. Maybe they were wrong in thinking that coming back here would heal him. Jefferson feared that, if anything, it might make him worse. He didn't tell Blaise that, though. He didn't want his love to bear any more worries than he already carried.

"There's so many people. I don't remember there being this many people," Blaise murmured.

No, he wouldn't remember. Blaise had either been in the Golden Citadel, on Malcolm's estate, or ferried to the Salt-Iron Confederation Council building. In fact, once they had freed Blaise, Jefferson had made it a priority to shield the young man from the outside world however he could. He took Blaise's hand. "There are. But here, you're just like a drop of water in a stream. No one will even think twice about you."

Blaise pressed his lips together, uncertain. His blue eyes were doubtful. "They will when they know who I am."

"Perhaps," Jefferson agreed, voice soft. "Though I suspect you'll be of much less interest than Vixen." *Or myself.*

The Breaker huffed out a breath. He looked as if he wanted to say something but didn't know how to put it into words. Jefferson slung an arm around him.

"Remember, you came of your own free will. This is not like last time. You decided this. *Your choice.*" Jefferson sank as much conviction into his words as he could, hoping it would ease Blaise's mind.

Blaise swallowed, then nodded. He sighed. "You're right. Sorry. I shouldn't borrow trouble, especially when I know we're bringing our own."

Jefferson raised his brows, noting the weak smile on his love's face. "Was that a joke?"

"A terrible one," Blaise said, though now his expression had bloomed into a genuine smile, as if he were feeling better.

"Not that bad." Jefferson chuckled. This was good. Perhaps he could keep Blaise in a positive frame of mind. "We'll disembark soon. We should make sure we have everything."

Really, it was just a distraction ploy—Jefferson knew they had everything packed. He'd triple-checked, in fact. But it was busywork, which Blaise needed. Though it didn't stop Jefferson's mind from wandering. Their travels on the train had been mostly uneventful. Jefferson had only caught fleeting looks at the woman who'd shown interest in Blaise at the dinner. Perhaps she'd only found the Breaker comely. Jefferson couldn't fault her for that.

By the time they made their way back to the pegasi car, Blaise was calm, behaving as if nothing had bothered him. Their saddlebags slung over their shoulders, they joined Vixen and Rhys with the pegasi and unicorn. Alekon and Darby were already saddled. Blaise and Jefferson set to tacking up Emrys and Seledora—another diversion for the Breaker.

A few minutes later, the car door rolled open, afternoon sunlight streaming in. Rhys led Darby to the threshold, glancing back at them. "I'll go first."

They watched as Rhys and the unicorn made their way down the ramp. Someone called to the Tracker, and he turned in their direction. He strode over to a group of men wearing—oh, damn. That was not a good sign. Salt-Iron Confederation uniforms.

No need to worry. Not yet. Rhys is a Tracker, and nothing has gone amiss with his presence. Jefferson hoped his faith wasn't misplaced. He glanced at Blaise but found the Breaker was facing Emrys, murmuring to the stallion.

Rhys gestured, the lines of his body growing tense. Vixen slipped beside Jefferson. "This doesn't look good," she whispered.

"It doesn't," he agreed, voice just as soft. Jefferson had suspicions about what was afoot. Well, there was no sense in delaying the inevitable. He took a steadying breath, patting Seledora's shoulder before going down the ramp with her. "I may need you as legal counsel."

The mare's dark eye found his. <Not surprising. How lucky for you I'm here.>

When they reached the base, the soldiers were there to greet them. A man with a bushy mustache stepped forward. "Doyen Malcolm Wells, you are under arrest. You'll come with us."

The name made Jefferson freeze, a flash of shock racing through his veins. His breath hitched, but he recovered quickly and offered them a smile. "I beg your pardon, but you seem to have me confused with someone else."

"Malcolm Wells, alias Jefferson Cole," Mustache Man clarified, to Jefferson's dismay. He pulled a folded piece of paper from a pocket. "Our orders list both names, so it's all the same to us."

<On what charges?> Seledora asked. Jefferson was gratified that her mental speech startled the entire group, and they took a step back as if someone had slapped them, glancing around to look for the speaker. The mare advanced, head high as her wings shimmered into view. <I am Counselor Seledora, and I represent Mr. Cole.>

Mustache Man swallowed, staring at the pegasus. For a moment, Jefferson thought he was too stunned to speak. Then he remembered himself, clearing his throat. "Identity fraud."

That was sadly unsurprising. The Quiet Ones loved to attack his identity, trying to force him back into the person he didn't wish to be. His brow furrowed. Jefferson opened his mouth to speak, but Seledora nonchalantly rammed her shoulder against him. <Say nothing to refute this. We both know it is the least of things they can hold you for.>

But Jefferson didn't *want* to go with the soldiers. He turned, staring up the ramp to where Blaise stood beside Emrys. The Breaker was watching the proceedings, and even from this distance, Jefferson read the emotions on his face: fear and worry. Damn it all, this might spiral Blaise into a panic attack.

It didn't look like a fate Jefferson could avoid, though. He took a breath, addressing the soldiers. "I need a moment."

"No, you—"

"Give him a moment." This demand came from Rhys, who had ambled over to stand with arms crossed. "He's not going to escape."

Ignoring the soldiers, Jefferson walked back up the ramp to Blaise. The Breaker was trembling, and his face had grown pale. He leaned heavily against Emrys.

"Blaise, I have to go with them," Jefferson said, voice soft.

The Breaker stared at him, his expression hollow. "You can't. What if...?" He swiped a hand at one eye.

"Listen to me." Jefferson wrapped his arms around his beau, pulling him into a tight embrace. He felt the tension in Blaise's body, like a tightly coiled spring ready to snap. Jefferson didn't fear the Breaker would lose control of his magic—but he didn't want those men to know exactly who Blaise was. *They* would fear a potential loss of control, and if they moved against Blaise, it very well could become a self-fulfilling prophecy. "I'll be okay. I suspected this might happen, and the charge they're bringing against me is one Seledora and I can easily fight."

At that, Blaise pulled back just enough to look at him. "You *knew* they might arrest you?"

Jefferson's face warmed with chagrin. "Well, considering my colorful past, yes."

"And you didn't tell me?" The Breaker's lips drew into a taut, pale line.

Blaise was mad, which meant it was in Jefferson's best interest to be honest. "No, because you would worry." *And we both know you've had enough on your mind.*

Blaise gave Jefferson a look that was all annoyance, which was preferable to him shutting down. "I hate that you're right."

Jefferson smiled, then reached up to cup Blaise's cheek. "I'm not defenseless, and neither are you. I promise they won't keep me."

"They'd better not," Blaise agreed. "I'll fight the entire Confederation for you if I must."

The words, a long-ago echo, struck Jefferson like an arrow. He had said nearly the very same to Blaise when the Breaker had been imprisoned at the Golden Citadel. Meeting his beau's eyes, he realized Blaise had intended it. It was the most heartfelt declaration anyone had ever made him, and it warmed Jefferson in ways he couldn't explain. Ways that cemented how he felt about Blaise.

"Malcolm Wells!" mustache man called.

"That's not your name," Blaise whispered, voice rough with slumbering anger.

"I know. They're being rather obtuse," Jefferson murmured, relieved that Blaise had traded his momentary fear for other emotions. While an angry Blaise was hazardous, it was better than when the mage was locked down by panic and the burden of memories. Anger granted Blaise renewed determination.

Vixen, who had been watching their interaction from beside Alekon a few yards away, said, "I'll be with Blaise. We'll be okay."

"I should go," Jefferson said with regret, though he flashed the Persuader a grateful look.

"Wait." Blaise's voice was so soft Jefferson almost didn't hear it. But that didn't matter as the Breaker lifted his chin, lips brushing against Jefferson's. *Oh.* Jefferson hadn't expected that, but it was easy to lean into the kiss, to lose himself to the sweetness of a blissful moment with Blaise.

But it was over far too soon. Jefferson smiled as he stepped back, then pivoted to start down the ramp. He paused midway down to call back, "You know, conjugal visits are a thing."

Blaise stared at him for a moment before the press of his lips showed further annoyance. "You're insufferable."

Privately, Jefferson counted that a victory. He'd calmed Blaise and succeeded in distracting him. Jefferson strode down the ramp, summoning up every bit of snootiness he possessed. He gave the soldiers a condescending look. "I suppose I'm ready to go with you."

Blaise

Blaise's mood darkened after Jefferson's arrest. He had been naive to think they could travel to Phinora and everything would be fine. Gullible to believe it was as easy as Jefferson made it sound. He should have known that for them, nothing was ever easy.

Things didn't improve when they reached the estate. *His* estate. That didn't sit well with him, either. It felt wrong in a way he couldn't put his finger on, so it became one more thing bringing him down. Not even Emrys could stir him from his dour mood.

"Looks like the groundskeeping has been lacking," Vixen commented from beside him. She had made a point to take up Jefferson's place at his side. Blaise didn't like that, either, but he knew why she did it, and he valued her too much to snap at her for the imposition.

At her observation, Blaise frowned, his gaze sweeping the land before him. She was right. He hadn't noticed immediately because of his mood, but the garden was overgrown. A top rail of one of the fences had come loose, and the home's windows had a haze of grime. None of that had been in evidence when it had been Malcolm's estate. Jefferson had told Blaise funds had been set aside for the upkeep of the house and grounds. Something wasn't right.

Had the Quiet Ones gotten to this cache of money, too? The thought roused Blaise's fury even more. They were relentless in their campaign against Jefferson.

"Howdy to the house!" Vixen called when Blaise said nothing. He knew he was being uncharacteristically prickly, but he had good reason.

A moment later, a teenage boy ducked out of the barn, eyes widening when he saw them. He hurried over. "Mr. Hawthorne?"

<He means you.> Emrys prompted when Blaise made no response.

Oh. Right. Blaise had been so distracted he'd forgotten that he was an authority here. "Um, yes. That's me." Gods, would he ever be able to act like a normal person?

"We got the letter that you'd be coming. Didn't think you'd actually come," the boy remarked, then winced when he no doubt realized he'd spoken private thoughts aloud. Well, at least Blaise wasn't the only awkward one.

"*We?*" This from Rhys, who had been quiet as they traveled, seemingly lost in his own thoughts. Blaise had forgotten the Tracker was even there.

When the boy caught sight of the gleaming unicorn's horn, he faltered. Was it Blaise's imagination, or did he pale a shade or two? "Um, well, it's just me now. Everyone else is gone."

"What happened?" Blaise asked. Jefferson would have made certain the estate had adequate staff, of that Blaise was sure. That made him suspect something had happened here that his beau hadn't caught wind of yet.

The boy dug a toe into the dirt. "They all up and left. Better pay elsewhere, I suppose."

Blaise didn't believe that for an instant—unless someone had maliciously hired them away, which was a possibility. "Why did you stay?"

The boy hitched a thumb to the barn. "The horses here can't take care of themselves, sir."

That said something for the boy's character, and Blaise gave an approving nod. "What's your name?"

"Tristan, sir."

"You can call me Blaise."

Tristan goggled at him. "Yes, sir. I mean, Blaise. Sir."

Blaise sighed. He swung out of the saddle, Vixen following suit. Blaise looked at the Persuader's brother, who was still mounted. "There's enough rooms here if you'd like to stay." Whether they were suitable for habitation was a whole different issue.

Rhys shook his head. "I appreciate the offer, but I have my own place. I should get Darby back to the stables and make my reports."

Reports? Blaise didn't know if he liked the sound of that.

The Tracker's unicorn edged closer to Vixen as he continued to speak. "And I'll see what I can find out about your friend. I expect they'll have to bring him before a magistrate in the next day or two. I'll be in touch." Rhys smiled, and tapped two fingers to his forehead in a little salute before Darby turned and trotted off.

"Well, suppose we should see to the pegasi now," Vixen said.

"Pegasi?" Tristan squeaked. As he spoke, Emrys's purple-tinged wings shimmered into view, the feathers whispering against Blaise's arm. The boy looked torn between running for the hills and coming closer to stare with admiration. He split the difference by stumbling backward until his back rammed into the white fence surrounding a paddock.

<We're harmless to you,> Alekon advised the boy with a jaunty tilt of his head. He shook out his mane as his own wings swept into view.

Blaise studied the boy, the only person apparently still in his employ at Hawthorne House. "You've been taking care of everything here on your own?"

"Best I can," Tristan agreed, though he seemed worried that Blaise might reprimand him. "It's hard to do much with this place alone."

Blaise nodded. "Thank you for what you've done. I'll see to it you get paid extra for doing so much more than you were hired on for." It was the least he could do, and it seemed reasonable. Blaise would figure out how to make that happen later.

They took care of their pegasi, and he discovered that there were, indeed, horses. Two light grey carriage horses, though they were caked a muddy brown from a recent wallow. Blaise didn't remember them from his previous visit, though Emrys assured him they had been there.

Blaise moved alongside Tristan, who had been watching them with a high level of bemusement, as if he didn't know what to make of them. "Is the kitchen stocked?"

The boy cringed. "With only the most basic things, sir."

"It's *Blaise*. And if you had the funds, could you fetch more?"

Tristan blinked at him. "Yes, sir. I mean Blaise. Yes."

He arranged the matter of coin for the boy. While Tristan headed off to the nearest market riding one of the carriage horses bareback, Blaise and Vixen made their way into the house.

Blaise only had fleeting memories of the place. He remembered the master bedroom because...well, it wasn't the time to think about that. His cheeks warmed at the pleasant memory. And he remembered the kitchen —that was where he and Malcolm had worked together on Blaise's plan to win public favor with baked goods. His recollection of the rest of the house was murky.

"How are you doing?" Vixen asked.

His shoulders slumped at her question. "Jefferson said he'd be okay, but I can't help it. I'm worried about him." He rubbed the back of his neck. "He's a *mage*. Not just the politician he was the last time he was here."

The Persuader settled a hand on his shoulder, her touch light. "You know we're not going to let them keep him, right?"

Blaise nodded. He didn't want to say it, but if it came down to it, he'd use his magic to free Jefferson. He'd tear the Golden Citadel down to its foundations. Blaise huffed out a breath, feeling tension pool at the base of his neck.

Vixen seemed to have her own thoughts on the matter. She lifted her hand from his shoulder, fiddling with the ring on her finger. "I know what you're thinking. It won't get to that. I can use my magic or my name."

He frowned. "You'd show your cards so soon?"

She smiled. "Might be no better time to tip my hand. Besides, what kind of friend would I be if I kept my magic hidden when it was needed?"

Her words and friendship warmed him, doing much to improve his mood. Blaise wondered if she knew how much it helped him. Knowing Vixen, she did. She was good at reading other people. "Thanks."

"You can repay me by whipping up something sweet once Tristan gets back."

"That's the plan."

CHAPTER FOURTEEN

Straw Man

Jefferson

The Golden Citadel was the last place Jefferson wanted to see on his return trip to Izhadell. But he wasn't all that surprised to discover that was where his escort intended to leave him. He was a mage, after all.

Seledora followed for as long as she could, determined to represent him. But when they arrived at the Cit, he knew she would have no choice but to leave and rejoin the others. His guard had allowed him a moment to speak with her before she flew off.

Now Jefferson reclined on a lounger that was a decade out of fashion. He was lucky, or as lucky as anyone imprisoned in the Cit could be. Because of his former position as a Doyen, they'd jailed him in one of the more luxurious cells. That was fortunate, since it was a far cry from his memory of Blaise's cell—and the panic he'd felt when they'd arrived to free the Breaker and discovered it empty.

While the cell had comforts, that didn't mean it was comfortable. Like the rest of the complex, the walls had salt-iron incorporated into them. The metal didn't agree with Jefferson at all. He had the beginnings of a headache, and it would only get worse. If he was truly unlucky, it would turn his stomach.

"You've got a visitor!" The scrape of a key and click of a lock followed the announcement.

Jefferson straightened. He set aside the book he'd been reading, rising as a guard entered and motioned for him to come over.

"Who's visiting me?" Jefferson asked, then hissed in pain as the guard slapped salt-iron cuffs onto his wrists. "Blessed Tabris! Give a man some warning next time." He'd love to have Blaise's resistance to the vile metal.

The guard shook her head, saying nothing. She gestured for him to walk beside her.

With a resigned sigh, he did as she required, determined that he would be on his best behavior. He didn't want to give them any cause to mistreat him or otherwise find a reason to keep him there. Perhaps Blaise had somehow come to visit him? No, this would be too soon. Blaise and Vixen would be settling into the estate. At least, he hoped. Though a small part of him wished it was Blaise. While he'd only intended to shock Blaise out of making a mistake with his suggestion of conjugal visits, Jefferson desperately wished for a visit from the man he loved. As unrealistic as that was.

She showed him into a visitation cell. Like his own cell, it was a much nicer affair than anything Blaise had experienced during his stay. He sat down in the chair, waiting for his visitor to arrive.

The door opened a moment later, and another guard showed in a man who made Jefferson's hackles rise. Most definitely not Blaise. Jefferson's eyes narrowed as soon as he saw the well-dressed elite. His hands tightened into fists. "Phillip Dillon. You're quite far from Ganland. To what do I owe the displeasure?"

The Quiet One waited until the guards shut the door behind him, the locking mechanism grating. Phillip smiled, then ambled over to sit across from Jefferson. "I heard you came all the way to Phinora, and I thought I owed you a visit." He made a show of looking around the visitation cell, lip curling with disgust. "Though I certainly wasn't expecting to find you *here.*"

Like Perdition you weren't. He was certain that Phillip had known exactly where he would end up. Most likely had orchestrated it. "Yes, well, these accommodations would be much more fitting for you, I'm sure."

Something dangerous flickered in Dillon's gaze. "Tread carefully, Malcolm."

"Do I look like Malcolm Wells?" Jefferson growled. He was so very tired of people calling him by that name.

"No, but underneath all this, you still are." Phillip gestured to him. He folded his hands in his lap. "You have seen how far our reach extends, haven't you?"

Jefferson scowled, knowing exactly what Phillip was referring to. The Quiet Ones had systematically eviscerated his persona as Jefferson Cole, destroying all of his years of hard work to establish himself. Then they drained his bank accounts and holdings, leaving him destitute.

Without Blaise, he would have been lost. His pulse sped at the reminder.

"Yes, very impressive job of destroying a straw man," Jefferson said. "If you came to gloat about that, then your work here is done." But even as he said the words, he wished he hadn't. He had come to Phinora to root out information about the Quiet Ones, after all. And this meeting could unearth a few precious nuggets, though it wasn't something he'd prepared for.

Phillip smiled. "It's not time for me to take my leave. Not yet. I'm here for a purpose."

"I thought I'd made it quite clear I want nothing to do with any of you," Jefferson said, pulse racing.

The Quiet One leaned in, reminding Jefferson of a predator. "Rest assured that I want nothing to do with you as well. But I have a vested interest in you for other reasons."

That was puzzling. "If you didn't come to convince me to take up my father's mantle, then why *did* you come?" As much as he despised Phillip, maybe Jefferson could tease information from him. That might make this incarceration worth a damn.

"Because I want to know where *she* is," Phillip said, his voice a rumble.

Jefferson blinked. Of all the things the Quiet One might have said, that was not what he'd expected. Though, Jefferson realized with chagrin, perhaps that was an oversight on his part. Phillip was an enemy for more reasons than simply being a member of the shadowy group who'd taken so much from him. Dillon had *also* bought Jefferson's sister Alice as a bride, simply because she had developed magic.

"You think I know where Alice is?"

Phillip pressed his lips together so tightly they were pale. "You spoke to her at your own funeral."

As far as sentences went, it was certainly one that would have been nonsensical to nearly anyone else. Jefferson eased back in his seat, trying to act as if the blasted salt-iron shackles didn't chafe his wrists. "Correction: I, Jefferson Cole, spoke to Alice Wells at the funeral of Malcolm Wells. What makes you think she would have told me anything? She doesn't know me." That last bit stung to admit, but it was true. He wondered if word had reached her of his duplicitous nature.

Phillip stared at him. "Then you're useless to me."

"Even if I knew, what makes you think I would tell you?" Jefferson asked.

The older man studied him for a moment. "Because you have a softer heart than your father, Malcolm. And I have it on good authority that with the proper motivation, you have a tendency to make things happen."

A surge of fury washed through Jefferson. "Let me assure you that though my heart is soft, I can still be every bit as hard and cruel as Stafford Wells ever was." And even as he spoke the words that made his gut clench with dread, Jefferson wasn't about to back down from them. "Consider yourself warned."

Phillip made a dismissive gesture. "I appreciate it, but at the moment, I imagine you'd have a difficult time following through." He made a show of rising from his seat slowly, his gaze meeting Jefferson's. "I'll offer you something in good faith, however. Perhaps it will inspire you to help me find Alice."

"I don't want whatever you have to give." Jefferson didn't wish to be beholden to this man. It would only be trouble.

"It's advice." Phillip stood over him. Jefferson rose so that they were on equal footing. "Keep your nose out of Phinoran politics."

Damn it. Did this mean Phillip knew their purpose in coming—did he know who Vixen was? *Maybe I can squeeze an admission from him.* "That's like advising the sun to not rise in the morning."

Phillip shook his head. "I'm trying to help you. Stay clear of the politics. Cool your heels here until..." He gestured to the surrounding chamber, though his words faltered.

"Until what?" Oh, Jefferson was so close to an answer.

The older man gave him an assessing look, then heaved a sigh. "I'll see that you're released, in due time. Remain here. And I'll see if I can use my influence to protect your Breaker, too."

The reference to Blaise made Jefferson's pulse race. But not at Phillip's offer to shield him. No, Blaise wouldn't tolerate Jefferson staying in the Golden Citadel for very long, of that he was certain. And even if Blaise would allow such a thing, Jefferson didn't like the idea of relying on Dillon's charity. Not to mention, doing so would leave Vixen vulnerable.

The smart option would be to agree and perhaps go the route of malicious compliance. Jefferson considered it for a beat, but erred on the side of keeping clear of his enemies. "I don't need your protection."

Phillip pursed his lips, making a frustrated sound. "Let me put it plainly: the Quiet Ones have goals in Phinora. If you thwart us, you *will* regret it."

"Funny, I was about to say the same to you." Jefferson aimed a charming smile at him.

The sour look on Phillip's face proved that even though Jefferson didn't feel confident inside, at least he sounded confident. Jefferson watched with disinterest as Dillon stalked to the door, rapping on it to get the guard's attention.

Well, that could have gone worse. Jefferson watched Phillip slip out, then took a moment to wince at the blisters on his wrist. *Blasted salt-iron shackles.*

CHAPTER FIFTEEN

Stolen Fair and Square

Jack

Jack stared down at the paper in his hands. Most people thought he was impulsive and rash—and yeah, sometimes he was. But at times like this, when something big and important lay in the balance, he took his time to think about things. And he kept coming back to the problem that Raven Dawson was currently a wild card.

More than that, he'd suspected Jack would find his stash and had left a warning. There had been no mention of Vixen aside from the unsent letters that seemed to predate the other correspondence. Zepheus suggested that if Raven told Jack to stay clear of Phinora, it might be wise to heed the advice. Whatever was afoot had to be more than a scorned lover. And it spelled trouble that Raven mentioned Phinora when Vixen was headed there, too.

"What's that?"

Damn it. He had been so caught up in his own thoughts he'd not been paying attention and had missed Kittie slipping into their bedroom. She snugged an arm around him, resting her chin on his shoulder as she peered down at the paper.

He was tempted to snatch it away and hide it, but that would only make him look suspicious. Or guilty. And he was neither of those things, not right now. Besides, this was his wife. If there was anyone he should be honest with, it was her. "A copy of the portal spell Emmaline used."

Kittie made an interested sound, then rested one of her hands atop his. "And you have this why?"

Jack glanced at her. "'Cause the grimoire with the original is in the bakery. And I figured it didn't hurt to have a copy."

"Hmm." Kittie regarded it with a critical eye. "So, not only have we stolen grimoires from Ravance, we now have a copy of one of their spells."

Jack snorted. "I stole it from the Copperheads fair and square." It was splitting hairs, but it was true. She had a point, though. If the Ravanchens had a way to hunt down their missing grimoires, they'd be angry to discover them in the hands of an outlaw mage. Jack assumed that the former owner of Blaise's grimoire was likely dead, though. With a little luck, no one was missing it.

"I suppose the question I should have asked is why you're staring at it right now," Kittie clarified.

At that, he nodded. It was a better question. "Because Vixen, Blaise, and Jefferson don't know about Raven." Jack had revealed the information contained within Raven's stash to Kittie, as well as the other remaining Ringleaders.

Kittie narrowed her eyes. "Jack…" She looked away, her gaze falling on the porcelain doll with long, brown locks settled atop their dresser. "You're not considering portalling to Izhadell, are you?"

He grimaced at her tone. "It'll take Hank days to get there, if he even gets that far." And anyway, what would he even put in a letter? *Howdy Vixen, hate to send you this in the post, but your old flame is headed your way, and I suspect he's up to no good.* That wasn't the sort of thing to commit to paper.

The Pyromancer crossed her arms, moving to sit on the bed beside him. "Why does it have to be you? Can't someone else do this? Someone else could go."

Jack shook his head. Few in town knew about the grimoires, and he was happy to keep it that way. The people who knew weren't ones to flap their jaws about it. Emmaline could cast the spell—she had done it before —but the thought of her in Izhadell again twisted his stomach in knots. Especially since the spell would leave her vulnerable.

"It ain't a simple spell. And I'm gonna have to ask Marian for a potion to even have a chance at casting it. Unless…" He paused, thinking back to the way Blaise had empowered him and Emmaline before. By Perdition, Blaise could probably cast the portal spell without breaking a sweat. Jack knew that some Ritualists worked in covens, combining their magic into something powerful. He wasn't one to work well with others, though. It was something to consider for later. A coven might be what they needed in the end. But that wasn't something to dally with now.

Kittie raised her eyebrows, waiting for him to continue. "Unless?"

Jack frowned. "Nothing. The alchemist can make what I need to pull this off."

The Pyromancer sighed. "Jack, *I* could help you do this."

The words struck him like a bullet. He shivered at her suggestion. How could he explain to her that this was his greatest fear? Kittie back in Phinora, falling into the hands of the Confederation again. It had been bad enough having her in Ganland with the ambassadorial delegation. But he knew he couldn't explain all that and have it make sense. She would think he didn't believe in her to do the task. But that was wrong—Jack knew she could do it. Kittie could do anything she put her mind to.

He bowed his head, almost crumpling the paper in his hands. "No." Jack swallowed, hating how raw his voice sounded. "You're one of Fortitude's strongest defenders, with Blaise gone. I'm good, but you're better."

She canted her head, giving him a skeptical look. "I don't believe for a second that's your reason."

Jack scowled. "It's reason enough."

Kittie sighed, moving in to press a kiss against his forehead. "You're scared of me going to Phinora."

"I ain't scared," he grumbled, but they both knew that was a lie. The Effigest closed his eyes, savoring her affection even as he dreaded what might happen to her.

He felt her hand move lightly along his shoulder to rest against the back of his neck. "How do you think I feel about you going there? Your handsome face is still on handbills."

Yeah, and he still had the same wanted posters tacked to the bedroom walls as proof. His humbling reminder. Jack's eyes opened. "What if we came to a compromise?"

Kittie made a soft sound of consideration. "What sort of compromise?"

"You cast the spell, and I go through."

She frowned. "It should be the other way around."

"Nope," he said, voice gravelly. "This is the best I'm gonna offer. That spell wipes out the caster. Ask Em about that. This will let me arrive in Izhadell without being an unconscious lump."

"You're insufferable," Kittie accused.

Jack chuckled. "Yep."

Kittie blew out a breath, pulling away from him. "Am I to assume that if I cast the spell and go through, you would just be a stubborn ass and go as well?"

He grinned. "What do you think?"

"You're a jackass."

Jack closed the distance between them again. "That's me. So you'll do it?"

Kittie rubbed her forehead. "I'll do it. I won't like it, and I'll worry about you as much as you'd worry about me, you know."

Jack knew, but there was no help for it. "I'd expect nothing less."

CHAPTER SIXTEEN

The Bread-Locomotive

Blaise

The kitchen was a chaotic mess of mixing bowls, pans, measuring cups and spoons, and a variety of other items. Blaise surveyed his domain, inhaling the calming aroma of cooling cookies and cake. Vixen had chipped in to help with his baking frenzy, but after a while, had withdrawn when it was clear she couldn't keep up with him. She'd stayed nearby to watch, though.

"Gotta check the quality," Vixen said as she pried a still-warm chocolate chip cookie from a nearby cooling rack.

"None of the work and all the reward. I think there's a children's fable about that." Blaise aimed a mock-stern look her way. They both knew it was bluster. He'd relaxed considerably since first descending into his baking frenzy.

Vixen hefted the crumbling cookie at him. She nimbly caught part of it in her free hand before it hit the floor, then shoved it into her mouth. "Right, but I *tried* to help. I just bowed out to give the master room to work."

He smiled, glad that he felt more like himself. Baking always served as a bulwark that offered him a literal sweet release from stress. But later would be an entirely different matter. He couldn't stay up all night and bake—well, he *could*, but it wouldn't be wise. He had to sleep sometime, and that was when he'd really feel Jefferson's absence.

Blaise swallowed, rising to collect a basket from a countertop. "I'm going to take some treats out to the pegasi." Then he forced himself to pretend that he would be okay. "I'll tell you what. Clean up the dishes and kitchen, and we'll call it even."

The Persuader eyed the mountain of dishes Blaise had left in his wake. "This seems about as fair as a one-legged donkey in an ass-kicking contest." Vixen grabbed a towel and moved to the sink. She was lucky—Doyen Malcolm Wells had been extravagant enough to install plumbing in the house before his untimely false demise.

Blaise slung the basket over his arm and made his way into the cool night air. A gentle breeze tousled his hair, and night insects sang nearby. Not the screaming cicadas from the Gutter, at least. That was a pleasant change.

<Seledora is coming,> Emrys informed him before Blaise even reached the stable. The stallion had his head over the stall door, ears pricked.

True to his word, the dapple grey mare landed with a musical ringing of hooves a moment later. She tossed her head, folding her wings to her sides before striding into the barn.

"How's Jefferson?" Blaise blurted as soon as the pegasus was near. Then he realized he was being rude and pulled a cookie out of the basket. "And welcome back, by the way." He offered the treat in apology.

The mare lipped it from his palm, her dark eyes assessing him. <They've jailed him in the elite wing of the Golden Citadel. All we can do is wait until he has his chance before a magistrate.>

Blaise's stomach clenched at her mention of the Golden Citadel. It brought back too many awful thoughts. He stumbled over to Emrys, his breath ragged as he rested his forehead against the stallion's neck.

<Breathe,> Emrys reminded him, blowing out a loud breath of his own. <Seledora would not have left her rider there if she thought he would come to harm. Right?> One of his ears flicked toward the mare, uncertain.

<I cannot just go in and take him out,> the mare replied, swishing her tail with agitation. <Not even as his attorney.> Then her mental tone softened. <But I do not believe he is in danger of being mistreated. Even as a mage, he is too high-profile.>

She had a point. Jefferson Cole—or Malcolm Wells—was both famous and infamous. Blaise sighed, relaxing a little again. And Emrys was right, too. Now that Seledora had declared Jefferson her rider, she wouldn't want him jailed for long. Pegasi bonded with their riders, and it was difficult to be parted for too long. Though there was no telling if that was the case with Seledora—she was unconventional.

Blaise distracted himself by doling out the basket of treats, having made certain Seledora was properly untacked. He checked to make sure her stall had fresh water and gave her a ration of sweet feed. He even spared a few cookies for the draft horses, who had been taking in the excitement with stoic calm.

<You will see him tonight in your dreams, will you not?> Emrys asked, crunching another cookie. Crumbs tumbled to the straw.

Blaise's hand was sticky with sugar and pegasus saliva. He needed to rinse it off in the water trough soon. "The Cit has salt-iron. I don't think his magic can get past that."

<Salt-iron does very little to *you*, though,> Emrys pointed out.

Blaise frowned at that. "But Jefferson is the one who has to reach out to me."

The stallion considered him with bright eyes, nosing him for another treat. <Your magic does not follow rules. I heard your mother say you can do almost anything with your power.>

Blaise blinked in surprise. Was Emrys insinuating that he might be able to use dream magic? His face scrunched as he considered that. He didn't know how Jefferson used his power, and had never thought to ask because it didn't feel similar to his at all. But Jefferson's magic had spawned from Blaise's. And more than that, they shared a bond that he didn't quite understand. Jefferson had used the thread that connected them, a sliver of Breaker magic, to get through a ward before. Blaise rubbed his forehead.

"You might be right."

<Of course I am. And now, am I right to think you have strawberry tarts?>

An hour later, after the trio of pegasi were sated and content with their sweet treats, he headed back to the house for bed. It was already late, and Blaise wondered if Jefferson had been trying to reach him. Or if he… No. Blaise shook his head. Jefferson was fine. He had to be fine. Seledora had said so.

Blaise climbed into the king-sized bed, gaze lingering on the empty spot beside him. The place Jefferson should have been. He whooshed out a breath to steady himself and then laid down.

Blaise always had a difficult time going to sleep unless he was flat-out exhausted. Too often, he would drift, only to be startled awake by the beginnings of a nightmare. Jefferson was the one who eased him past the nightmares and into sleep. But the Dreamer wasn't there. Blaise clenched his teeth, willing sleep to come. If he could just get to sleep, he had a hope of seeing his beau.

After tossing and turning for far too long, he finally drifted. At first, his mind took over, sending him into a strange dream. He was at the station in Ondin, waiting for their train to arrive. Blaise was alone, except for a black bird that hopped on the ground behind him. Every time he turned to look at the bird, it hopped behind something to obstruct his view. That was odd, but he didn't worry about it for long. A sound that reminded him of the jingle of the bell over his bakery door announced the train's arrival. The locomotive pulled into the station, though it looked more like a loaf of bread than a train—

Blaise frowned as something tickled his mind. A memory. He was missing someone.

Jack appeared out of nowhere. "You're missing a peacock." Then, with a grin, he vanished.

Jefferson. Right, he was supposed to reach the Dreamer, if he could.

He was dreaming, but was he in the actual dreamscape or his own mind? Or were they the same? Blaise didn't know. But he had to try before he lost this precarious grip on his slumbering mind. Already, he felt how easy it would be to flow back into a deeper sleep. He was in the grey area between wakefulness and slumber.

Blaise sought Jefferson, though he felt as if he were floundering in a vast ocean. Jack appeared again, reaching down to pick up a thread as thin as spider silk. "This what you're looking for, kid?"

"Why do I include your insults in my dreams?" Blaise asked as he plucked the thread from the outlaw's outstretched hand. Then he paused, a thought occurring to him. "Wait. Are you the real Jack, or...?"

The Effigest shook his head. "Nah. You ain't good enough to track down the real me, Breaker." He vanished again, leaving Blaise alone with the thread and the bird.

"I kind of prefer *my* magic to this confusion," Blaise muttered, focusing on the thread. Strangely enough, Dream Jack was right. This wisp led to Jefferson.

He turned, tugging on it with both hands. The thread widened in his grip until it was a rope. Blaise heard a confused exclamation, and Jefferson appeared.

The rope tangled around the other man's waist like a lassoed calf. Jefferson glanced down at it, then at Blaise. "Oh. That was *you?*"

"Yes," Blaise mumbled, though he felt the fist of deepening sleep tighten around him.

The bells of the bread-locomotive chimed again, claiming Jefferson's momentary attention. "Of course, you would have a train made of rye. I suppose I'd better do something before I lose you."

"Don't want to lose you," Blaise echoed with a yawn. The scenery flickered around him like a guttering candle.

"No, no, you can rest once I have control of this place," Jefferson murmured, slipping up beside Blaise and putting an arm around him.

Jefferson's touch roused him. Blaise shook his head. "Sorry. This is hard." So hard. And sleep was such a welcome temptation.

"I know. I'm going to use my power, so you don't have to do all this. But it's a challenge." Jefferson blew out a breath.

Blaise felt the brush of Dreamer magic against him, but it stuttered as if Jefferson were having difficulty. He heard Jefferson make a soft, pained sound and realized that somewhere far away, salt-iron was sapping his beau's magic. Blaise pulled him close and lent him power. Jefferson inhaled sharply, eyes widening as he broke free of the salt-iron drain. All around them, the dreamscape sharpened and gained a new semblance of order as Jefferson took command.

"Ah, that's better. Thank you." Jefferson straightened, composed once more. The gossamer rope hung at his waist like a fashionable belt. "Now you can rest."

The words had weight to them. Blaise felt the pressure of Jefferson's magic release him into a true sleep. He relaxed, though he stayed in the dreamscape. He no longer had to fight to remain in the liminal space between dreams and wakefulness. "That's really hard. I don't know how you manage it."

Jefferson chuckled. "Practice. Lots of annoying practice. How in Tabris's name did you do that? I didn't know you could."

"I didn't know I could either. Emrys suggested it." Blaise watched as the rye train wavered, shifting into a locomotive of gleaming dark metal. "Don't think I'll be doing it again unless I really have to."

"I'm so glad you tried." Jefferson's voice was gentle. He touched Blaise's chin with one hand, as if he feared Blaise might vanish.

"Are you okay?" Blaise asked, deciding to move on to his chief concerns. The sooner he and Jefferson addressed them, the better. "Seledora came back."

"I was hoping she'd made it back to the estate without issue." Jefferson kept an arm around him, though he tugged Blaise a little closer. The Dreamer was a warm, solid presence and smelled lightly of peppermint. "Aside from the salt-iron, I'm fine. I have enough social standing that they've put me in a posh cell. If not for the bars on the windows and the fact that I can't leave when I wish, you'd think I'm a guest in a fine hotel."

That was good news to Blaise. "No one's hurt you?"

Jefferson made a soft sound of understanding. "No one has harmed me." He moved to sit on a nearby bench that looked like it was made of pretzels. Jefferson waved a hand, and it became polished wood. "I did, however, already merit a visit from a Quiet One."

"Already?" Blaise sat down beside him.

"Yes, they're not wasting any time." Jefferson sighed. "It comes as no surprise, though. It was Phillip Dillon." As he spoke the name, the atmosphere of the surrounding dreamscape darkened for a beat, a sign that the Dreamer was unsettled.

Blaise glanced at him. "What did he say?"

Jefferson's gaze fell on the black bird, which had persisted through the change of dreamscape management. It hopped closer, peering at them with glassy eyes. "To stay out of their affairs. He said if I behaved and stayed in the Cit, he would make certain I was released later."

"*No,*" Blaise said without hesitation, his heartbeat racing.

"He promised protection for you as well, if I stay out of matters," Jefferson added, voice soft.

Blaise shook his head. He had come to terms with the idea that he might never be truly safe, and he wasn't willing to rely on the dubious *protection* of a member from the group that had damaged Jefferson's life. "No," he repeated, firm. He wanted to say more, but his throat constricted with emotion.

"That's what I told him, too." Jefferson put a hand on Blaise's knee, patting it.

Blaise hissed out a breath, relaxing. He should have known Jefferson would refuse. "Was that all he came to tell you?"

Jefferson squeezed Blaise's knee. "Oh, there was a bit of classic melo-dramatic villain drivel. I've heard more threatening lines at a third-rate play."

"I doubt you've ever seen a third-rate play."

The Dreamer grinned. "On that, I'm guilty as charged."

Blaise frowned. "Aren't you worried about what this means for you? For us?"

Jefferson pressed his lips together, quiet for a moment. "They want to take me out of play like a captured pawn. More than that, they want you to stay out of matters as well. They're afraid of us. We have the upper hand."

Blaise wasn't so certain that was what any of this meant, but who was he to dispute it? Jefferson had more experience with these adversaries than he did.

"Did you bake?"

Jefferson's question caught him off guard. It took Blaise a moment to catch up with the change of topic. "Um, yes. I am, in fact, that predictable." And that reminded him… "I think the Quiet Ones targeted the estate."

Jefferson tensed at the suggestion. He frowned. "What do you mean?"

"All the staff are gone. Well, except for one."

Jefferson swore softly, shaking his head. "Blast. I hoped that with the estate in your name, they'd keep their claws out of it. But they found another angle to attack."

Blaise rested his head against Jefferson's shoulder. "It'll be okay. It's dusty, and the garden would horrify you, but it's nothing that can't be fixed."

At that, Jefferson smiled. "You're right. We'll get past this."

Somehow, Blaise knew Jefferson meant more than just the issues with the house. He sighed, but this time with contentment. Jefferson might not be physically with him, but not even the Golden Citadel could keep them apart. And together, they could make things right.

CHAPTER SEVENTEEN

Magic Theory

Jack

The problem with Kittie casting the portal spell was that the locations she knew in Phinora differed from those Jack knew. Ideally, he would arrive straight at Hawthorne House, with no one the wiser to his appearance. But Kittie had never been there. Emmaline had also never been there, so it wasn't as if he could ask for her to assist with that, either.

Kittie crossed her arms as they mulled it over. "I should be the one to go."

"No," Jack snapped before he could stop himself.

"Why don't you cast it together?"

Jack growled, spinning to see Emmaline leaning against the door frame behind them. "How long have you been listening in?"

She grinned shamelessly. "Long enough to know what you're up to."

He glared at her, but he knew he had no one to blame but himself. It was exactly the sort of thing he'd do, after all.

"What do you mean, cast it together?" Kittie asked.

Emmaline became animated at the question. "I've been thinking about this ever since I cast the portal spell back in Thorn. Daddy, remember the lightning rod spell?"

He pursed his lips. "Yeah. But what does that have to do with this?"

She moved closer, peering down at the paper. "You copied the spell? That was a good idea. Anyway, it has everything to do with this. That lightning rod spell I cast with you was modified from Rising Dread."

Jack frowned, uncertain. "That was a modification of a mage spell."

Emmaline's eyes were bright. "I don't think they're that different. Look, there are parts each of you could cast, and then you bring them together. Just like we did with the lightning rod."

Kittie looked thoughtful but not convinced. "You're both Effigests. That makes it easier for you to work together."

"*Blaise* worked with us, too," Emmaline added.

Yeah, because the Breaker can do impossible things with his magic when he puts his mind to it. Jack studied the spell. Was he being too close-minded about this? It was possible—sometimes, he got stuck on an idea and had a hard time getting beyond it. But what Emmaline suggested was awfully close to his earlier thoughts. "You think we can combine two disparate magics like a coven."

Emmaline nodded. "That's exactly what I think. If not you and Mom, then who?"

"She's got you there," Kittie said, failing to hide an amused smile.

Jack folded the paper and shoved it in his pocket. "Fine. You may be on to something. I can cast the location part of the spell while Kittie powers the travel portion."

"When do we try?" Kittie asked.

Jack rose from the bed. "As soon as I make sure I have enough ammunition and reagents."

Kittie's hand shot out, grabbing his upper arm in a firm grip. "Jack Arthur Dewitt, you are not haring off on this half-cocked."

Her voice was so harsh and earnest that Jack paused. If there was anyone who could get him to slow down, it was Kittie. "Yeah, fine. I get it. I'm just champing at the bit." He shook his head, itching to make his move. But Kittie would be involved in a spell—a wizard spell—she'd never cast before, which meant they needed to be careful. And they still required an Overwhelming Power potion from the alchemist. "I tell you what. You go talk to Marian Hawthorne and make arrangements. I'll make my own preparations, and we'll cast it tomorrow. How's that sound?"

"Realistic," Kittie said, and this time there was amusement in her eyes. "Was that so hard?"

Yes. It was incredibly hard. No one understood the urgency he felt, the drive to do what he could to protect Fortitude and the people he cared about—especially now that Kittie was here. But instead of admitting all that, he kissed her, pleased when she reciprocated.

"Guess it'll give me another night with you," he whispered.

"Ugh." Emmaline rolled her eyes. "Let me know when you're done mauling each other."

CHAPTER EIGHTEEN
One Headache at a Time

Blaise

"You're looking more chipper than I'd expect this morning," Vixen commented as Blaise joined her for breakfast—much later than he'd intended. Once he'd found Jefferson in the dreamscape, he'd given himself permission to rest and relax, which included sleeping past the time his body normally woke him to start a day of work at the bakery.

But Blaise couldn't tell her he felt better because he'd spent the night with Jefferson. Vixen didn't know about the Dreamer's magic, and it wasn't Blaise's place to tell her. He eyed the uninspiring spread of food. Dry toast and scrambled eggs. He brought over a tin of muffins he'd made in his flurry of baking last night and popped it open, offering Vixen one.

"A good night of sleep helps," Blaise finally said, which he decided was close enough to the truth. He nibbled on the muffin, deciding that the next batch needed some additional flavor. Blueberry? Maybe strawberry? "How soon do you think we'll hear something?"

Vixen sighed. "Hard to say. I assume Jefferson's high profile enough that he won't sit around very long."

And that could be good or bad. "But we'll find out in time because he needs his lawyer…right?"

She made a face. "I don't know. There's going to be a bias against him as a mage. And for…" Vixen waved her half-eaten muffin around. "All the other general lying he's done."

Blaise clamped his jaw. It wasn't lying, exactly. Though, he'd be the first to admit Jefferson had a habit of obscuring the truth. "What does this mean for what you came here to do?"

Vixen glanced away, momentarily evasive. "I won't approach the Luminary 'til we have things ironed out with Jefferson. One headache at a time, I think."

If it took too long to free Jefferson, they'd have to reconsider—Blaise didn't know how much time they had before the Confederation moved on the Gutter.

A clatter at the door interrupted his thoughts as Tristan came in, already rumpled from seeing to his work. "Thought you should know your Tracker from last night is coming up the drive." His face was pinched with worry.

Vixen's eyes widened. "Rhys." She dropped her mostly eaten muffin on a plate, rising to head for the door.

Blaise got up as well, but he paused, studying Tristan. The teen was more nervous around the Tracker than seemed normal for a Phinoran. Unless… "Tristan, are you a mage?"

The boy's eyes widened. "N-no," he stammered.

Another reason, then. "You have mages in the family?"

Tristan swallowed. "Something like that, sir—I mean, Mr. Hawthorne."

Blaise sighed. Maybe *sir* was better than *Mr. Hawthorne*. "You don't have to be scared of Rhys. He's on our side." At least, Blaise hoped that was the case. Would things change once Vixen presented herself as the Spark?

Tristan gave him a dubious look. "In my house, they taught us not to trust a Tracker. But if the Breaker does, then maybe I will."

Yeah, okay, Mr. Hawthorne *or* sir *is definitely better than* the Breaker. Blaise rubbed his cheek. "I'm going to go greet our visitor. Are you hungry?" He gestured to the remaining muffins.

"I'm always hungry." Tristan stared at the muffins with a covetous look.

"Enjoy," Blaise urged him, then hurried out to join Vixen.

The three pegasi were out of the stables, and predictably they had flown over the fence so they could join the conversation. Rhys dismounted from Darby as Blaise approached, looking only slightly bemused by their presence. The Tracker nodded a greeting to Blaise.

"Rhys found out when Jefferson's going before the magistrate," Vixen updated him.

Blaise licked his lips. "When?"

"At three this afternoon," Rhys said. He shook his head. "But he's going before one of the worst possible magistrates."

Of course. If the Quiet Ones were pulling the strings, nothing would go in their favor. "In what way?" Blaise asked.

The Tracker rubbed his forehead. "Magistrate Hooper is well known for his anti-mage stance. And he declared this morning that he wouldn't tolerate any *animals* in his court."

Seledora snorted at that, flattening her ears. <I am not an *animal!* I am an attorney.>

Blaise's heart sank. The mare was their best shot at helping Jefferson. His mind raced through other options. They could try to break Jefferson out. However, not only would that be difficult, but it would wreak havoc on their reason for coming to Izhadell in the first place. And Blaise didn't know if he could trust himself to set foot in the Golden Citadel without panicking. The very thought made his heart race and his breath hitch.

Vixen waved a hand in front of his face. "Blaise?"

He blinked, then cleared his throat. "Um, sorry. What?"

The Persuader's silver eyes flicked over him. "I was saying Seledora may not be able to go in, but we can."

Immediately, Blaise shook his head. "I can't." Not because he didn't want to. Though, to be honest, he didn't want to. There was no way he would do anything but stumble over his words in front of the magistrate. "Whether or not I like it, people know who I am. That won't help Jefferson."

Vixen nodded. "Yeah, that's true."

<He doesn't have my training, but with his background in politics, Jefferson stands a chance at defending himself,> Seledora suggested, thoughtful. Her ears twitched. <And if he is not bound by salt-iron, I might even offer him guidance.>

The mare had a good point. Jefferson stood a better chance than any of the rest of them—especially if the pegasus attorney could get through to him. "You think so?"

Seledora bobbed her head, then shifted to face the house. <Yes. But we need to prepare.> She trotted around the side of the manor. <Come along, Blaise. I'll need your hands.>

Vixen gave him a baffled look. "What's she going on about?"

He shook his head. "I don't know, but I'm going to find out." He followed the grey mare toward Hawthorne House.

CHAPTER NINETEEN

I'm Not Judging

Marian Hawthorne crossed her arms, pinning Kittie with a look as only a mother could. It was an expression Kittie understood all the way to her core. "Is my son in danger?"

"He's in *Izhadell*," Kittie said.

The alchemist snorted from her place behind the counter in her apothecary shop. Kittie wasn't sure why Marian continued with the farce that she was a simple apothecary. Everyone in town knew she was an alchemist. "Fine. Is my son in additional danger?"

That was more like it. Any mage traveling to Phinora was going to be in some level of danger. The remaining Ringleaders had kept Raven's disappearance quiet, and from what Kittie had observed, most of the citizens thought the Shadowstepper had simply left to follow Vixen like a lovesick puppy. She had Jack's blessing to explain more of the situation to Marian Hawthorne, and so she did.

When she'd finished, the alchemist's lips pinched into an unhappy line. "Their task was already hard enough without a rogue mage causing problems." She paused, arching a brow. "And I assume you're telling me this for a reason?"

Kittie nodded. "Jack wants to portal to Izhadell to nip any problems in the bud."

"Does he, now?" Marian's tone was somewhere between impressed and derisive. "Is that wise? Even I know he has quite a record. And he's been foolish enough to risk himself on Confederation land before."

"Multiple times," Kittie agreed. She wasn't going to comment on the wisdom of Jack's decision.

"Hmm." Marian turned, making a circuit around the interior of her shop. It wasn't large and took only a matter of seconds. "I suppose he wants Overwhelming Power, then. You know it will leave him as weak as a day-old kitten afterward, right?"

Kittie swallowed. "We're going to cast the spell together so that he can go through."

"Only him?" Marian arched a single brow, the other remaining firmly in place. Kittie wondered how she managed that. Her own brows kept a united front and only moved together.

"Well…" Now it was Kittie's turn to pause, studying one of the nearby bottles filled with an amber dust.

"I'm not judging." Marian came around the counter, clutching something in her hand. A vial, Kittie supposed, when she saw the slight bulge. "But all I'm saying is I've lost my husband. I know you've only recently reunited with yours, and it's not been easy."

Kittie nodded, thinking of her own travels to Ganland, which had kept her from her husband. Meanwhile, he'd hared off on another dangerous adventure, taking their daughter with him. Marian Hawthorne understood how fragile life and love could be. "I don't *want* him to go, but he's stubborn."

The alchemist extended her hand, a potion cupped in her palm. "This one's on the house. So that you can go help my son and his friends." Marian smiled. "Your husband doesn't have to be the only stubborn one, you know."

Kittie met Marian's smile with one of her own. "He's not."

CHAPTER TWENTY

Exhibit A

Alekon tossed his head, glancing back at his rider as they wove through the press of traffic. <This place stinks. I thought we were already in Izhadell at Blaise's house. Is the whole place this crowded?>

"That was well outside the city," Vixen murmured to the stallion's cocked ears. "And yes. Welcome to the city."

<Zepheus told me it stank. I didn't believe him.> Alekon blew out a snotty breath in disgust.

Izhadell was much as Vixen remembered it. Well, she didn't remember the landmarks all that much, but the press of people? That, she recalled. They had constructed new buildings since she'd left, and the streets almost seemed to have narrowed, but perhaps that was because she had grown.

"You really think this will work?" Rhys asked. He had traded his uniform for clothing that allowed him to blend in and had left Darby behind. Seledora had agreed to serve as his mount, which Vixen considered rather progressive for a pegasus. But Seledora prided herself on not being like other pegasi.

Vixen wet her lips. "It's worth a try. What other option do we have?"

He gave a long-suffering sigh. "I already told you the Luminary has the power to pardon someone like your friend."

She had the power, but would she do it? Jefferson was a mage. And more than that, many of the elite despised him. There was no guarantee that her mother would free the ambassador. Besides, Vixen didn't want her first act upon reuniting with her mother to be to beg her for a favor. That wouldn't do.

"I'm not running to mother with my tail between my legs."

"That's not even close to what I'm suggesting!" He shook his head. "It would be really helpful if either of you pegasi would back me up here."

Alekon angled his head to look at Rhys. <You must be new to how pegasi loyalty works. I will always side with my rider. Unless I have a better idea.>

<I remain unconvinced the Luminary would pardon Jefferson,> Seledora said, swishing her tail with agitation. <And I have a saddlebag full of evidence for our case.> As far as Vixen knew, this was true. She hadn't seen the contents of the folders Blaise had packed into the saddlebag, but she knew they'd found something.

Rhys rubbed the bridge of his nose. "This is the most ridiculous circus I've ever been a part of."

"You haven't been around outlaws long enough." Vixen couldn't help but laugh. With everything else going on around them, laughing felt good. She quickly sobered, though, as she caught sight of familiar architecture in the distance. The Asaphenia, the main cathedral built to honor Garus, towered above the other buildings on the horizon. She hadn't realized how close the courts would take her. She tore her gaze from it. "And you didn't have to come along with me."

"I'm your escort." Rhys bristled.

"Yeah, to Izhadell. We got here. Job done," she drawled. "Good work."

He sighed, shaking his head. "No. Your friend shouldn't have been arrested. So my job isn't done." Rhys swallowed. "And besides, you're *you*."

Vixen knew he was avoiding her real name and title, but all the same, his words annoyed her. "If you're going to treat me like a delicate flower, let me just stop you right there. Not interested."

He raised his brows at that, then, in a surprising move, laughed. Rhys nodded. "Your spirit hasn't changed from when we were kids." He gestured to the dour brick building to their right. "We're here. And I suspect your friend is already inside awaiting his turn."

Vixen followed his gaze to a jail wagon parked further up the street. Alekon flattened his ears. <Salt-iron bars on that monstrosity.>

There was a place to tether their *horses* off to one side of the building. As Vixen dismounted, she murmured to Alekon, "Give me a warning if you find any unicorns in the area."

The pegasus snorted, flicking an ear at her with curiosity. <Do I want to ask why?>

"You know me. I'll cheat if it'll give us a win," she whispered back, meaning every word. She rubbed the silver ring, hissing out a breath.

<I heard that,> Seledora said, sounding righteously insulted.

Vixen sighed. She hadn't meant it as an insult to the mare. Vixen didn't trust anyone they were dealing with in Izhadell, and she would much rather be prepared.

After Vixen collected the folders from Seledora's saddlebag, she followed Rhys inside. He walked with confidence, and she realized he must have come here before. She vaguely remembered that sometimes, Trackers brought mages accused of crimes before magistrates. That explained why he knew of this one's biases.

The court was in session with another case. Rhys found a bench to sit on, and she settled beside him, listening as the magistrate heard the defense of a man accused of using magic to kill his neighbor's orchard. The problem, as Vixen saw it, was that the accused wasn't even a mage. Though as the case progressed, she discovered that the man's teenage son had come into power. As the accused spoke, she realized that, while there was bad blood between the neighbors, the arboricide had been accidental as the young mage grappled with learning to control his magic while trying to stay hidden.

"The court orders you to pay the plaintiff ten thousand golden eagles for damages. In addition, the accused mage is indentured to the Salt-Iron Confederation immediately." Magistrate Hooper's eyes gleamed with malevolent glee at the declaration.

The father gasped at the mighty sum, but at the mention of his son, he wailed. "For how long? He's my only son—I need him to help with my—"

"Indefinitely." Hooper took great pleasure in cutting him off.

Vixen's heart sank. Murmurs arose from the gallery as the bailiff led the dejected father out. She had known that this magistrate was unfriendly to mages, but she had forgotten how cold many in the Confederation were towards her kind. She took a deep breath. That was why she was here. To do something about that.

Rhys nudged her. Vixen shook her head, having missed the introduction to Jefferson's trial. The Ambassador strode into the courtroom, his head high. He scanned the assembly, no doubt looking for a familiar face. His gaze settled on her and Rhys, and she didn't miss the disappointed crinkle tug at the corner of his eyes when he realized Blaise wasn't there.

***

Jefferson

IT HAD BEEN UNREALISTIC TO EXPECT BLAISE TO COME TO THE COURT. Jefferson knew that, but all the same, he had hoped. He gave a tiny shake of his head, refocusing. *Think about Blaise later. Better still, be* with him *later.* Yes, that was the goal. Focus on this. Win.

"Doyen Wells, do you have representation?" Magistrate Hooper asked.

Hooper. Jefferson knew this judge. He had an uphill battle ahead of him, and Seledora was nowhere in sight. Vixen caught his eye, and she held up a package—no, a folder. Jefferson smiled, hoping that the contents were what he thought they might be. "I'll be representing myself in this matter." He inclined his head to the gallery. "I'd like to request that my team join me."

Rhys scowled at him. *Well, I suppose he's not Team Jefferson.* Maybe it was best not to have a known Tracker at his side for the moment.

Magistrate Hooper's gaze roved to Vixen, but he nodded. "Proceed."

The Persuader slipped over to him, sliding the folder onto the table in front of Jefferson. "Seledora had Blaise gather some documents for you."

"Outstanding," Jefferson murmured. He looked up at the magistrate. "Would you be so kind as to allow a brief recess?"

"Denied," Hooper barked. "Doyen Wells, you stand accused of identity fraud. How do you plead?"

Jefferson pursed his lips. Correcting Hooper on the name would get him nowhere. Possibly contempt of court, which wasn't what he needed right now. "Not guilty."

The magistrate stared at him as if he'd turned into a tap-dancing cockatrice. "Doyen Wells, are you aware that in this court, you're compelled to convince *me* otherwise?"

"How in Perdition are you going to manage that?" Vixen whispered.

Jefferson met his gaze. "Magistrate Hooper, as I understand it, I'm charged with fraud because there is reason to believe that Jefferson Cole is not my identity. However, I believe—"

"I don't have all day, Doyen Wells. Present your evidence."

Jefferson's jaw snapped closed. He did, in fact, have all day if needed. That was the way court worked in Phinora. But that didn't mean Hooper abided by the rules. Most likely, Hooper already planned to strike down any evidence Jefferson provided. He hoped that whatever Seledora had sent along was ironclad.

Swallowing, he opened the folder and thumbed through the pages. A sense of calm settled over him. Yes, he knew these forms. *I could just kiss that mare.* The only thing better would be if she could also guide him, but the salt-iron shackles on his wrists prevented it. Jefferson pulled out a handful of papers. "As I was saying, I've been charged with identity fraud. The burden is upon me to prove that I am, in fact, Jefferson Cole."

Hooper looked bored already. He leaned on an elbow. "Then do so."

And I will. Jefferson smiled. "Exhibit A: this notarized form from

Rainbow Flat, where Malcolm Wells established Doing Business As paperwork for Jefferson Cole." That form was a closely guarded secret, which was why it had been filed originally in Rainbow Flat, a town indebted to him. Afterward, to guard his dual personas, he had stored the paperwork in a safe in the library at Hawthorne House. Seledora knew of it and must have urged Blaise to retrieve it.

The magistrate shrugged. "Jefferson Cole is a business, not a person."

He knows exactly how to annoy me. Jefferson huffed out a breath, pulling out another paper. "Exhibit B: this contract between two parties. One, Blaise Hawthorne, and the other, Jefferson Cole, for the joint establishment of a bakery in Nera." *Blast, and I told myself I wasn't going to think about Blaise.*

"Phinora doesn't recognize contracts made with mages." Hooper smirked.

Jefferson almost crumpled the contract in his fist. "May I remind the court that Breaker Blaise Hawthorne is currently the only land-owning mage in the Confederation? Thus, the contract is valid."

"And I will continue not to recognize it," Hooper shot back.

Jefferson straightened. It was time to call the judge on his dragonshit. The other defendants couldn't do it, but maybe he could. "Magistrate Hooper, you've set me the impossible task of changing your mind when it's clear that you intend to refute every piece of evidence I set forward. How is any mage expected to have a fair trial under these conditions?"

Hooper's eyes glittered. "You have yet to provide irrefutable evidence that you didn't commit fraud by taking the identity of Jefferson Cole."

"You can't win," Vixen whispered. "He won't let you."

Jefferson swallowed. She was right. He couldn't. Every scrap of evidence Seledora and Blaise had gathered wouldn't be enough for this man. "Leave me, Vixen." He hated to say it—he would lose the case. Phillip Dillon was making certain Jefferson didn't go free. Hooper would sentence him to time in the Cit. Possibly indenture. No, it wouldn't come to that. Blaise would come. He would tear the Golden Citadel apart.

"Not going to happen." Vixen tucked a lock of brilliant hair behind one ear. Jefferson glanced down to see her work the ring from her finger. Before he could caution her against it, she had it caged in her fist as she stepped around the table, smiling at Hooper.

Jefferson couldn't hear what she said, but it didn't matter because he knew her words weren't for him. He saw Hooper's full attention fall on Vixen, snared by her power.

"No magic!" a voice bellowed.

Jefferson blinked in surprise. It took him a moment to realize it was Rhys. He turned and saw the young Tracker standing at the front of the gallery, fists clenched, as he glared at Vixen. The Persuader whirled, jamming the ring back on her finger.

Hooper shook his head like a dog shedding water. "What? Magic?" His glare fell on Jefferson first, then snapped to Vixen. "Tracker Kildare, I didn't recognize you out of uniform. Thank you for your intervention. Bailiff! Remove these mages from my court!"

Vixen stared at her brother, her expression desolate. She didn't put up a fight as a bailiff hooked a hand around her arm and led her to the exit. Jefferson balked when another bailiff came for him.

"I will not allow my documents to remain here," he told the woman, which he felt was very reasonable. She crossed her arms but allowed him to gather them up. Jefferson looked at Rhys. "Could you at least get these back to the house for me?"

The Tracker's mouth was set in a grim line, but he nodded. Jefferson suspected he felt guilty for ruining Vixen's gambit.

A moment later, he was loaded back into his least favorite form of transportation, the salt-iron reinforced jail wagon. Though, unlike his first trip, he was no longer alone. Vixen sat beside him.

"Sorry, but I had to try," she said.

"I know," Jefferson murmured. He rubbed the back of his neck, uncomfortable from the metal enclosing them. "It was never a trial I could win, not even with everything Seledora brought. And now I don't know how we're going to get out of this mess."

Vixen sighed. "I do."

"It's not Blaise taking apart the Citadel brick by brick, is it?" There wasn't a hint of humor in Jefferson's question. They both knew it wasn't an exaggeration.

The Persuader shook her head. "No. But I'd almost prefer that."

CHAPTER TWENTY-ONE

An Army of Gladiatorial Poultry

Blaise

He had to get out of the house. Guilt at abandoning Jefferson to his fate with the magistrate ate at Blaise—even though he knew he'd made the right choice to stay behind. With Vixen gone, the house was far too empty, and even the kitchen reminded Blaise of the jailed Dreamer. He needed a change of scenery, and he needed it now.

He almost jogged from the house to the barn. Rhys's silvery blue unicorn stallion grazed in the nearest paddock and lifted his head, nostrils flaring as the light breeze carried the scent of Breaker magic to him. But Darby did little more than read the scent before settling back to grazing. Blaise strode into the barn, heading for the tack room.

<What are we doing?> Emrys peered at Blaise curiously as the Breaker hauled saddle blanket, saddle, and hackamore out.

"I need…" Blaise hesitated as he balanced the saddle on the aisle floor, horn and pommel down. "It's hard to stay here doing nothing."

<We're going for an outing?> Emrys brightened. <Or must we stay on the estate?>

Blaise had the distinct impression that Emrys, too, was eager to leave the confines of Hawthorne House. "There's a market nearby, according to Tristan. I was thinking we could go there. See what they have." He opened the stall door, and the pegasus ambled out, standing square in preparation for being saddled.

<Oh, markets are good,> Emrys agreed, trying to sound nonchalant but failing. His interest in the potential for future treats was too strong.

As if summoned by the mention of his name, Tristan strode into the stables, whistling. "Mr. Hawthorne, I was thinking...since you're new around here, maybe I should show you how to get to the market."

Blaise hadn't even thought of that. He nodded. "Sure. I'd appreciate that."

Tristan grinned, hurrying to grab a saddle and bridle for a draft horse.

It wasn't long before both the pegasus and the draft horse were tacked up and ready. Blaise gave Emrys's girth a last tug before swinging into the saddle. The stallion ambled out of the stable, wings shimmering out of existence as he took on the guise of a normal horse. Tristan made a soft sound of astonishment at the trick.

Tristan tapped his heels against his mount's rounded barrel, the big beast lumbering ahead of Emrys. "Let's go. Follow me!"

Blaise took a deep, refreshing breath as Emrys's hooves rang on the gravel of the road, easily keeping up with the drafter. Maybe for a bit, he could relax and just...be. He could master his slumbering fear of Phinora, of the Golden Citadel. Of everything he'd endured on his last trip to the city. Blaise listened to the cheerful birdsong in the trees lining the road; watched the play of shadows across Emrys's dark neck. A hint of a smile tugged the corners of his lips.

Emrys glanced back at him. <We should have done this sooner if it makes you happy.>

Blaise agreed. He forgot how liberating it was to ride Emrys without having to worry about anything. All he had to do for the moment was stay astride as Emrys kept pace with Tristan's mount.

They followed the twists of the road, Blaise enjoying the simple peace of being with Emrys out in the world. He held the reins loose in his hands —there was no need to guide the stallion. But he still had to uphold the farce that they were a normal horse and rider.

"Not far now!" Tristan crowed, turning to flash a grin back at Blaise.

And he was right. Emrys's ears pricked forward, catching the buzz of sounds from the market. They followed a bend in the road, and then it spread before them: an assortment of tents and cobbled-together stalls that looked like a scene more at home in the Untamed Territory than the outskirts of Izhadell.

The marketplace reminded Blaise of home. Not Fortitude—but Bristle, his original home in Desina. Stalls lined pathways, makeshift tables set up to allow men and women to hawk their wares. It was a veritable feast for the eyes. Brightly dyed bolts of fabric vied for attention with artfully designed canisters of spices, fresh vegetables, hand-tooled leather goods, furs, and more that Blaise couldn't take in.

<Busy place,> Emrys commented, though he didn't sound pleased. The tight quarters meant he wouldn't be able to stay near his rider.

"Yeah," Blaise agreed, though for once, when he encountered a mob of people, he didn't feel fear—he felt a frisson of anticipation. No one turned to look at him as if he were unusual. No one knew him at all. There was a strange sense of freedom in that.

"There's a place for the...er, horses...over this way," Tristan said, guiding his mount to the right and aiming an apologetic look at Emrys. Blaise was glad the boy had erred on the side of caution.

Blaise found a hitching post where he made a show of tying Emrys, though he used a knot Jack had shown him—one Emrys could easily pull loose with his dexterous lips if needed. The stallion sighed heavily as Blaise put the finishing touch on it. Blaise scratched Emrys beneath his forelock. "I'll pick up a treat for you."

The pegasus perked up. <I would like that.> He blew out a contented breath.

"I have to run an errand while we're here," Tristan declared, though he shifted his weight as if nervous. "Is that okay?"

Blaise nodded. "Sure. I'm going to wander and take in the sights before I decide what I'd like to buy."

With that decided, Blaise parted from Tristan and wound slowly through the organized chaos. He kept one hand near the pouch at his belt, on guard against pickpockets. This was the first time he'd shopped anywhere outside of Fortitude in ages.

Blaise meandered through the market, smiling as merchants tried to draw his attention to their wares. He made a mental note of the locations of the spices and fresh fruits—those would be worth another visit before he left. There was a confectioner with tempting candies, too.

It took an hour, but he finally made a full circuit of the place. The market was lively and charming. Blaise liked it and hoped he could return to visit again. He stopped by the spice merchant and treated himself to canisters of allspice and cinnamon, even chatting with the young woman when she asked how he planned to use them. She was interested to hear of his baking and asked if he was thinking of opening a stall at the market in the future.

The suggestion was a shock—and a thrill. Blaise loved his bakery in Fortitude and missed it. It was tempting to consider renting a stall, even for a short time. He knew Jefferson would tell him to do it. Blaise told her he'd think about it, and she gave him the contact information for the man who ran the market in case he wanted to pursue the idea.

As he rounded a corner, a vendor he had overlooked captured Blaise's attention. The jeweler's setup wasn't as flashy as others. But there were artfully crafted loops of gleaming rings with intricate etchings, delicate chain bracelets, and metal necklaces hammered into different shapes.

The artisan was busy with another customer. Blaise leaned over to inspect a row of rings nestled on a layer of velvet. They were simple pieces, a far cry from the gaudy grandeur of Jefferson's cabochon ring. Blaise smiled at the thought, pulse racing as a realization occurred to him.

Gingerly, he picked up one ring. *He makes me happy. Wouldn't this be the next step?* Blaise swallowed. The next step, perhaps, but a big step. One that was a little scary. But was it more frightening than the thought of life without the Dreamer? That was a straightforward answer. *No.*

"See something you like?"

Blaise almost dropped the ring. He'd been so deep in thought he hadn't noticed the crafter shift over to his side. He settled the ring back in place, his face warming. "Um, your work is nice." It was the weakest compliment possible, and Blaise knew it. *Ugh.*

The vendor, an older man with a great bristle of silver brows, peered at him as if he were a curiosity. "Thank you. If you like that ring, it's yours."

What? Blaise took a step backward, shaking his head. "No, I couldn't possibly."

The artisan smiled. "Did you see what I etched on the sides?" He winked.

If he was so proud of it, then why would he want to give it away? Blaise frowned. A part of him wanted to flee, but a larger part found this man disarming and curious. Blaise licked his lips, picking up the ring again to study the delicate engraving. At first, he thought it was a pattern of galloping horses, but then he noticed the fanciful wings. Pegasi. This man, so deep in Confederation land, had etched a ring with pegasi. Blaise knew enough to understand that was unusual.

"Are you a mage?" Blaise asked.

The man picked up a polishing cloth and a nearby bangle. "There are those who say what I do must be magic. But it's all good, old-fashioned know-how." He set the cloth aside, shifting the bangle so it caught the light. A moment ago, its surface had been as smooth as butter. Now it boasted a similar etching to the ring.

A maverick. This man was a mage. "I should go."

The artisan mage put the bangle down beside the cloth. "Wait. Please take the ring you were admiring, with my thanks. It would honor me."

He knows who I am. Of that, Blaise was certain. But what could he do? If Blaise denied it, he might only draw more attention. Relenting, he stepped closer to the booth. "Thank you." He plucked the ring from the velvet, hardly believing this maverick was gifting it.

The vendor pulled out a small cloth carry-sack, holding it out. "So you don't lose it." When Blaise moved to accept it, the man continued to speak. "I was advised to watch for you." The jeweler glanced past Blaise's shoulder. "You should know there are others watching you, too. Those who work against you."

A chill threaded down Blaise's spine. "What?"

"You heard, Breaker. But there are also those who will back you. You're not alone." The mage thumped a fist to his chest.

Swallowing, Blaise pulled back. He shoved the bag with the pegasus ring deep into a pocket. "I need to go." He almost missed the artisan's grave nod as he pivoted to head back down the aisle.

He was six rows from Emrys when two men stepped into his path. If they had been in the crowded section of the market, Blaise would have thought they'd had no choice but to be jostled into the way. But this aisle was empty, the stalls vacant. Their looming appearance drew him up short, clutching his purchases.

"You made a big mistake," one of the men rumbled.

Don't panic. Blaise sucked in a deep breath, struggling to master himself. He frowned, doing his best to stay calm despite the way his heart had broken into a gallop. His brain scrambled to make some sort of response, and he blurted the only thing that came to mind. "Did I insult a local baker?"

His question confused the men momentarily. They paused, trading befuddled looks. But they weren't alone. Another man stepped up behind Blaise. "We know who you are, *Breaker.* And you're coming with us."

No. Panic surged, and for a brief, terrible moment, he was back in the Golden Citadel, tied to a chair, completely at the mercy of his captors. He froze—right until one of the men reached out, grabbing his arm.

The sensation of rough fingers biting into his flesh snapped him back to reality. *No. Never again.* Still clutching his spices in the crook of his right elbow, he reached up with his left hand, wrapping his fingers around his assailant's wrist.

"*Let go.*" Blaise almost didn't recognize the snarl as his own voice. It sounded too deep, too rough. Downright feral. But the man didn't let go, instead digging his fingers in to tighten his hold. Blaise sent a jolt of Breaker magic out, intending only to cause discomfort and make his point.

The man screamed as a sick crackling, snapping sound filled the air. He jerked away from Blaise, his wrist and hand flopping uselessly, the bones shattered by the force of Blaise's magic. Pulse thundering, Blaise shrunk back as the injured man shrieked, falling to his knees as he hugged his broken arm against his chest. Gods, he hadn't meant to do that. He'd only wanted the man to release him.

An old memory reared up. Heathcliff, a guard at the Golden Citadel. Heathcliff grabbing Blaise's arm to force him into the room where Gregor Gaitwood tortured him and tried to bind him with the geasa. Blaise's panic overcoming him. Heathcliff's scream as Breaker magic shattered his wrist.

<Blaise? Blaise!>

Emrys's mental voice roused Blaise from the suffocating memory. He shook his head. He hadn't succumbed to the panic for long—the remaining pair hadn't closed the distance to him yet. But one of them had drawn a revolver, and now the weapon was trained on Blaise.

"No more tricks. You're coming with us," the armed man said, voice low.

"No, he's not!" Both men whirled at the voice, and it took Blaise a second to realize it was Tristan. The boy threw something at the man with the revolver. It was a baked apple or perhaps a rotten one. Whatever it was, the teen's aim was true. The fruit hit the man in the face and splattered into a blinding, saucy mess. "Mr. Hawthorne, go!"

Even with Tristan's appearance, the men were undaunted. The one with the revolver cursed, wiping fruit from his face and lifting his weapon to aim at the teen. Blaise dodged his other assailant, tripping the man, though it was mostly unintentional. He dove at the man holding the gun, ripping the weapon from his hand with a growl.

Tristan pelted the downed man with more fruit. The disarmed attacker spun toward Blaise, hands reaching out like claws, seeking the weapon. "Give that back!"

The rhythmic thunder of Emrys's hooves heralded the stallion's arrival. Blaise took a few steps back, glad that the man couldn't see clearly with the apple grit in his eyes. He glanced down at the revolver, pulse pounding as he realized the only way out of this. "You want it back? Catch."

Blaise sent a tendril of magic into the weapon, this time mindful of what he did. Not panicked, as he had been when the first man grabbed him, but this time as deliberate as baking a cake. A precise expenditure of magic.

Emrys skidded up, dust swirling behind him like a miniature tornado. Blaise shoved a foot into the stirrup, looking at Tristan. "Get out of here!" By the time he spoke the last syllable, his bottom thudded against the saddle, the ebony stallion whirling to dash away from the market.

Ten seconds later, a sharp *boom* reverberated behind them. Emrys shied to the right at the unexpected sound, ears flattened. <What was that?>

"A warning," Blaise said, voice grim. He wasn't proud of anything he'd done back there. His stomach churned at the memory of snapping bone. Blaise tried to tell himself it had been necessary, even if it was an accident. That those men would have done far worse to him. He hoped Tristan had gotten to safety.

And it wasn't over. Not yet. Riders broke out of the cover from the side of the road, their horses surging to cut Emrys off, blocking the stallion. Emrys's hooves tore into the ground as he slid to a stop, abruptly shifting backward.

<I'm going to fly,> Emrys warned. Blaise was fine with that. Whatever got them out of this mess.

There wasn't enough room ahead for Emrys to take off, so with the riders closing in, he pivoted and galloped back in the direction they had come. His huge hooves rang out like thunder as his speed increased, wings rippling into existence.

Magic sizzled as something shot out of the ground a half-dozen strides ahead of them. Emrys was going too fast and could do little more than dodge to the left to avoid the construct. Blaise didn't see what it was —but he certainly felt it when something clamped around his right leg, jerking his foot from the stirrup.

For a gut-wrenching second, Blaise thought his boot would tangle with the stirrup and he would be dragged alongside Emrys. But that *something* had a tight grip on his leg, tearing him free of the saddle, the pegasus squealing in rage as he lost his rider.

The world spun around Blaise in a confusing jumble. Breath whooshed from his lungs as he struck the too-hard ground. He rolled before coming to a stop. Everything hurt, and his lungs desperately tried to suck in fresh air. Blaise was distantly aware of Emrys's frantic mental pleas, but his brain was too dazed to understand.

There was a peal of thunder, and Blaise thought maybe there was a storm—but no, it was hooves as a dozen riders moved to ring him. No, not a dozen. When he blinked, there were fewer. Maybe six.

A muddle of voices added to his confusion. Emrys's shadowy form was a blur in the corner of his vision as the stallion swung around, pawing at the ground as he prepared to charge at their foes. Blaise shook his head, the world slowly returning to focus.

A pulsating black chain wrapped around his right leg, anchoring him to the ground. It didn't hurt, not like Lamar Gaitwood's wicked cage had, but Blaise knew this had to be the work of another Trapper. Wincing, banged-up parts of his body complaining about the motion, he sat up. He'd torn one of his sleeves, and the sticky warmth of blood oozed from a gash on his elbow. He dismissed that as unimportant for now.

Blaise focused on the manacle. Magic pooled in his hands, and it only took the barest of touches to shatter the arcane chain.

Emrys had moved in front of him, blocking their pursuers, but the Trapper hadn't left the stallion unhindered. A pulsating fetter wrapped around the stallion's right hind leg, tethering him in place.

Blaise swallowed, assessing their situation. Five men slowly circled them, and a sixth, who was surely the Trapper, stood stationary as he focused on his targets. Another chain snapped out of the dirt, seizing Blaise's left leg. It was more an annoyance than anything else, and with a flick of his wrist, he shattered the magic.

<Free me, and let's get out of here!> Emrys's eyes were ringed with white as he tossed his head.

Blaise nodded, expression grim as he studied their enemies. They outnumbered him and Emrys, and Blaise knew he would have to leverage everything he had to win. He drew on his observations of Jack, channeling the Effigest's ruthless swagger. "Leave while you still can."

<Oh, that was good. Very intimidating. Let me try.> Emrys pinned his ears, snaking his head and snapping his teeth in warning. The stallion squealed, the sound echoing with fury.

At Blaise's words, the men paused, then guffawed. Their laughter was cruel, reminiscent of the bullies Blaise had encountered all his life. "You talk big, but you're only one man, Breaker," a burly man to Blaise's left said.

"That's what your friends back at the market thought, too." Blaise tasted the salty tang of blood in his mouth, and he spat it out. His tongue hurt. He must have bitten it during the fall.

His bold words didn't have quite the effect he'd hoped for. Or maybe they were too effective. The Trapper summoned more chains in quick succession. They lashed up from the ground with blinding speed, wrapping around Blaise's forearms before he could react. The chains pulled taut, forcing him down to the dirt. Gravel bit into his palms. He heard the telltale rattle and felt more wrap around his legs, waist, and then his neck, pinning him down.

<Blaise!> With his face pressed against the dirt, facing away from the pegasus, Blaise could only hear Emrys's mental cries and the sound of his hooves grinding against the gravel.

"You're coming with us, Breaker," another of the men said.

Dirt had gotten into his mouth, and Blaise spat it out. He couldn't let it end like this, for him or for Emrys. Maybe he couldn't get a grip on the arcane chains, but he wasn't ready to give in. His fingers clawed into the ground as he channeled his power.

"Let him go!" It was a voice Blaise had heard before, but he couldn't place where he knew it from. Female. He was too frazzled to think beyond that. Too busy trying to force his magic to undermine the chains anchored to the ground. Shouts and curses burst around him, followed by what had to be a skirmish.

His magic broke a great furrow into the road beneath him. The chain holding his right arm flew loose for an instant. It flailed like the tentacle of some great kraken, then dove downward as if it sought to root itself again. But Blaise's hand was free, and that was all he needed. When he moved, everything hurt, but he grasped the fetter on his left wrist and used his magic to snap it. Then he repeated the same for the opposite hand before the right chain found purchase again.

"No!"

Blaise was fairly certain that outraged howl came from the Trapper, who then yelled something he couldn't quite make out. Blaise staggered to his feet, his abused muscles complaining, accompanied by the damp sensation of blood trickling down his right leg. A downward glance revealed that he'd shredded the fabric at his knee in his fall, and the flesh beneath wasn't much better.

His attackers squared off against a trio of newcomers. Blaise had seen them before...on the train. He swallowed as he realized the woman was the same one from the dining car.

Blaise limped over to Emrys, crouching to free the stallion from his fetters. His power crackled against them, and they dissipated into a fine, dark mist.

<Thanks. You don't look good. Do you think you can mount?> Emrys bumped his soft nose against Blaise's shoulder, blowing out a worried breath. The stallion's ears flicked back and forth as he followed the sounds of fighting.

"No," Blaise whispered. Not without Emrys kneeling, at any rate. And he couldn't leave his mysterious rescuers to fight his battles. Even if he really, really wanted to run away.

The stallion seemed to follow his thoughts. <They're here to stop your capture. If you stick around and end up caught, it's going to make all this for nothing.>

A good point, but Blaise didn't want the assailants to see him as a coward. As easy pickings. Better to dissuade them from coming after him again. He sucked in a breath, then took a shaky step forward.

Blaise didn't get very far, though. And he didn't end up rejoining the fight at all. Blaise saw the woman—Holly, that was her name—dance out of the fray as a huge rooster strutted onto the scene. She reached down to pick him up, her lips moving as if she were crooning to the fowl. In her arms, the rooster's bulk almost hid the woman from view. The rooster's head reared back, and he crowed, the sound slicing through the grunts and dull thuds of fighting.

<Um, are you seeing what I'm seeing?> Emrys snorted in alarm.

Maybe Blaise had hit his head. Surely he wasn't seeing a veritable flood of chickens running toward them. Their taloned feet rasped as they found purchase on the gravel, heads swiveling this way and that as they clucked and grumbled. Blaise was used to chickens, having raised his share of them in the past, but he'd never seen so many moving as one, like an army of gladiatorial poultry.

The rooster crowed again, and the chickens joined the fray.

The former attackers shouted as birds shot toward them, pecking with their sharp beaks and harrying with talons, wings flapping. A man lashed out savagely, and a hen fell away with a broken squawk, feathers blowing loose in the wind. More of the birds fell, but it didn't matter. Three more arose for every one that shrieked as a killing blow landed.

With shouts, the attackers scrambled for their horses. Hens launched onto their backs, beaks latching onto ears as they beat at the humans with their wings. The assailants rode off in disarray, leaving behind a sea of milling birds.

The rooster crowed again, and just as quickly as they had arrived, the chickens retreated, hurrying away to their...well, Blaise assumed they must have come from nearby farms. There was no other explanation he could come up with.

Emrys shook his head and neck, mane flying with the movement. The stallion positioned himself between Blaise and the unfamiliar mages, snorting a warning.

"We're on your side," the woman hoisting the rooster called around the bird's feathery bulk.

Blaise swallowed, placing a hand on Emrys's side. That was a mistake —his ravaged skin complained at the touch. "Thanks." He probably should have said more than that, but he wasn't sure what. He might not have walked away from that fight without their help, and he didn't like that thought.

The pair of male mages accompanying Holly moved to either side of the woman. "Blaise Hawthorne?" one of the men asked. He had sandy hair and a shadow of stubble on his jaw. The other man was bald and had a silver earring. Blaise had definitely seen him on the train.

Blaise nodded, but the approach of new hooves interrupted them.

Emrys blew out a worried breath, but relaxed at the sight of the grey drafter rounding the bend. Tristan was perched on the gelding's back.

"Tristan!" Holly called as the teen reined the horse to a halt, dropping from the saddle. As soon as he hit the ground, she jostled the rooster in her arms to make room for the boy, pulling him into a hug.

Blaise raised his brows at that. "Tristan, is there something you want to tell me?"

The teen grinned, shrugging out of the woman's embrace to hike a thumb in her direction. "Yeah. She's my mom."

CHAPTER TWENTY-TWO

Maverick Underground

"We're called the Maverick Underground," said the sandy-haired man, who had introduced himself as Ryan. He was a sort of mage Blaise had never heard of before, specializing in cleaning. As they'd left the scene of the attack, he'd joked that he would have been more of an asset in the battle if he'd had a mop and broom handy.

They sat in the kitchen at Hawthorne House. Blaise had decided that whatever was afoot needed to be explained somewhere private, and the house seemed the best bet. It had provided a chance for him to clean and bandage the worst of his wounds before bringing out leftover cookies and tarts. He wanted to use the healing potion his mother had sent along, but decided to wait until he was alone.

The trio of mavericks made their formal introductions. Holly Lewis, the self-styled Chicken Mage and Tristan's mother, was really a form of Beastcaller. The balding man's name was Daniel, and he was a Greenmage specializing in roots. Blaise's stomach had clenched when he'd learned the man's name. His mind had wandered to his deceased father, who shared the name, but Ryan's words brought him back to the conversation.

"What's the Maverick Underground?" Blaise asked. "I know what a maverick is, but I haven't heard the rest of it."

Holly smiled. "Good. If people knew about us, that would be a problem. We're mages who are tired of our treatment by the Confederation."

Daniel leaned forward in his chair, pinning Blaise with an intense gaze. "My brother was in the Cit when you were there." Blaise's pulse sped at the mention of the Golden Citadel, and he took a breath to calm himself so he could focus. "After the Breaker Inquiry, they freed him along with the rest of the mages who had been abused."

"Oh." Blaise had given little thought to the other mages who had been in the Cit, mostly because he did his best to forget everything about it. He licked his lips to settle his rising nerves. *This isn't about me.*

The Greenmage's gaze dropped to the table, where a half-eaten tart rested on a plate before him. "I thought with his release that everything would be okay. I knew he'd been hurt—he had the scars to prove it. But he wasn't the same after..." He shook his head, pushing his plate away.

Blaise's stomach twisted. He understood that far better than he wanted to admit. "What happened to him?"

Everyone else in the kitchen was silent, even Tristan, who had been munching on a piece of crunchy toast. Daniel's voice shook when he spoke. "My brother was an Animancer...sort of a mix between a Healer and a Greenmage. Not as rare or powerful as a Breaker, but unusual enough to be interesting." He took a ragged breath. "Shawn knew that his freedom would be fleeting, and he begged me to help him leave the Confederation. So I did what any brother would do. Together we set out, traveling overland because it's the only safe path for a maverick."

Blaise swallowed. He didn't know if he wanted to hear any more of this story. He already knew it couldn't end well. But everything about this sounded important. Blaise nodded in encouragement.

"We were almost to the Godspines when a Tracker and unicorn caught our trail. I told Shawn I'd distract them and he should go ahead, find a place to hide. Greenmages like me are a copper a dozen. And I thought...I thought we were going to be okay." Daniel swiped a tear from one cheek. "I did distract the unicorn and Tracker. But by the time I found Shawn..." The Greenmage's shoulders quaked. "He was so afraid of being caught. Shawn swore he'd never go back. I guess...I guess that's why he took his own life."

Blaise's breath caught. Daniel stared at his hands, as if expecting Blaise to ask why his brother had done that. He didn't have to ask. No, he knew those dark thoughts. The desperate idea that death offered the only freedom and safety. He'd never entertained those thoughts for long, but he understood.

"I'm sorry," Blaise whispered. Tears stung his eyes.

Daniel sighed. "I didn't tell you this for your sympathy. I told you because you know the torment he went through. Not only that, you didn't let it destroy you."

This mage had no idea how wrong he was. The Cit had damaged

Blaise in ways few understood. But there was no use trying to explain that now.

"*You* are why we formed the Maverick Underground," Holly said, picking up where Daniel left off. "Because you gave us hope that if only we can get our fellow mages and mavericks to a safe place, they can heal."

Jefferson's long-ago words came back to Blaise: *you're not the only one hurt by the Cit. Be the voice for the voiceless.* And now it seemed he was the hope for the hopeless. It should have been flattering, but Blaise had never felt as if he were someone people should look up to.

"So, what does that have to do with all of this?" He gestured around them, though he meant more than just the kitchen. "You were on the train. And Tristan was somehow the only person left working here."

Ryan nodded at that. "The Maverick Underground is more than just the three of us. We're a network of mages throughout the Confederation. This allows us to ferry mages out safely, with the added benefit of netting information."

"As soon as we intercepted the letter saying you were coming to Izhadell, we set to work. We'd been watching this house and knew that all the help had been hired away." Holly nodded to her son. "I made sure Tristan was employed here while we ferreted out how you were traveling to Izhadell."

Blaise had mixed feelings about this. The group's network was impressive—and Jack would be most interested in the informational aspect—but Tristan was, in essence, a spy. What if he had been working for the Quiet Ones instead of the Maverick Underground? "That was how you ended up on the same train," Blaise guessed.

Holly nodded. "Yes. We wanted to be certain you made it here without incident."

That brought Blaise back to the earlier battle. "How did you know to come help me?"

Tristan was the one with the answer to that. He had a guilty look on his face as he explained. "I've been keeping the MU updated on you. When we got to the market, I sent a message by chicken that you were there, and they were the closest to come keep an eye on things."

Blaise frowned, crossing his arms. He quickly regretted that—the skin on his arms was scraped up from his earlier fall. "I don't like being spied on."

The three mages exchanged regretful looks. "I'm sorry we couldn't tell you sooner. But if the Confederation knew that mages were working together like this..." Holly trailed off.

She had a point. The Maverick Underground would be squelched if they were known. "I can imagine." Blaise worried at his lower lip. "But why so much interest in me? It sounds like you have a lot on your plate."

They gave him incredulous looks. "Because you're the *Breaker*," Ryan said, as if it were that simple.

"As brave as you are, you wouldn't come to Izhadell without reason." Daniel studied him, as if searching for the ghost of his lost brother in Blaise's visage. "You've done so much. And we're here to help you in any way that we can."

Blaise had been ready to refute the first point—he was anything but brave. But Daniel's last sentence brought him up short. "Wait, what?"

"The Maverick Underground is at your service."

***

AFTER THE DAY HE'D HAD, BLAISE WASN'T ALL THAT SURPRISED WHEN Seledora and Alekon returned to the estate, minus their riders. Judging by Seledora's perpetually pinned ears, Blaise figured the pegasi hadn't had the best day, either. The equine attorney's pride had been stung in more ways than one.

<You're taking this news well,> Emrys noted as Alekon and Seledora completed their tale. The black stallion had stayed close, attentive.

Blaise scratched the whorl of hair in the middle of Emrys's forehead. He was still bruised and banged up, but he'd used a potion his mother had labelled *USE THIS ONE BLAISE* to speed the healing on the worst of his wounds. But as with every potion, it had a cost. It sapped his strength to accelerate the healing, and before long, he'd have no choice but to sleep.

He was about to respond when Seledora slammed a forehoof into the ground. <I hear that thrice-damned unicorn coming. I'm going to give that Tracker a piece of my mind.> She bared her teeth, proving that it might not only be her sharp mind that attacked Rhys.

Blaise hurried out of the stables, though he had to take it easy since his muscles were still complaining. He hadn't noticed that Darby had even left the estate, but he must have gone during the market misadventure. Maybe to avoid the incoming mavericks. Whatever the case, he'd found his rider.

Rhys had dismounted and held his hands up in a placating manner as Seledora shook her head at him, unleashing a barrage of telepathic frustration. She lifted one of her hind hooves, as if she wanted to kick something. Or someone. The Tracker stood still as he weathered the onslaught, though the mare kept it private, so Blaise didn't know what she said.

When at last she finished, Rhys nodded. "I deserved that." His grey eyes settled on Blaise. "I came to apologize and tell you I'm going to make things right. I also brought back Jefferson's papers. They're in my saddle-bag." Then he paused, noticing the bandage on Blaise's hand. "What happened to you?"

Blaise didn't feel like recounting his afternoon. He waved away the question, focusing on the more pressing problem. "You betrayed your sister."

<That's one of the many, many things I said.> Seledora snorted.

Rhys winced. "I'll understand if you don't believe me, but I couldn't help it." He waited a beat, as if expecting Blaise to argue. When he didn't, Rhys sighed. "Look, I don't know how much you know about Trackers…"

"I know enough to consider you bad news." Blaise couldn't keep the layer of frost from his words. He'd had a rough day, so he figured it was warranted.

"Ouch," Rhys murmured, but he nodded. "That's fair. I know you have good reason to think that." The Tracker blew out a breath. "This will sound like a sorry excuse, but I can't help reacting when I feel magic being used around me. It's like hearing wood scrape against stone."

The notion of wood scraping stone gave Blaise a sympathetic chill. He wondered if this was unique to Rhys or if all Trackers felt the same. But that didn't matter at the moment. Vixen and Jefferson did.

"Valoria—I mean, Vixen—told me about you. That you're one of the best people she knows, and you'd do anything for your friends," Rhys continued. The words came as a surprise to Blaise, and it took him a moment to absorb them. "I didn't want you to do something rash because of my mistake."

So, the Tracker thought Blaise might make a bid to free Jefferson and Vixen himself. He wasn't up to it tonight, but if they remained in the Cit, all bets were off. Eventually, the drive to help them would be too much, and he'd have to do something. "What are you going to do to fix this?"

"I'll get them out, I promise. It might take a little time. But I wanted you to know before you do anything you might regret."

Blaise studied the Tracker. Rhys seemed earnest and guilty about what he'd done. Could Blaise believe him after this? Trust him? He idly rubbed the bandage on his hand. "Vixen is right. I love my friends, and I'd do almost anything for them." He'd come to Izhadell, a place crawling with terrifying memories, for Jefferson's sake. "You know what I am. And you know what I can do." Blaise felt a little too much like Jack in that moment, veiling his words with threats.

<Maybe you aren't taking this news as well as I thought,> Emrys amended. Then, worried, he added, <I don't want you going near the Cit.> Blaise lifted his unbandaged hand to absently stroke the stallion's nose.

Rhys stiffened. "I'm well aware of what happened at Fort Courage and have heard reports from Thorn. That's what I'm trying to avoid."

"Then we understand one another," Blaise said. Yeah, he sounded a lot like Jack. He didn't really like it but had to admit it was useful. Exhaustion pulled at him, a reminder of the healing potion's price. He stifled a yawn.

"I'll be on my way." Rhys inclined his head in a show of respect. "Have a good evening, Breaker Hawthorne."

"I will once my friends are out of the Cit, Tracker Kildare," Blaise said. Two could play the formal titles game.

Rhys swung back into the saddle, and moments later, the silvery unicorn trotted out of view. Blaise rubbed his forehead, sighing.

<You sounded very tough.> Emrys nudged him with his soft muzzle. <I know that was hard for you.>

"Yeah," Blaise mumbled. He rubbed at his eyes. "I need to get to bed. It's been a day."

He headed for the house but paused when he heard the sleepy cluck of a chicken. Blaise frowned. The estate didn't have chickens. Climbing onto the porch, he discovered the hen nestled beneath a rocking chair. It wasn't the safest place for a lone hen—too easy for her to be snapped up by a fox or feral cat.

"Come here," Blaise said with a yawn, gathering her up. The hen gave a mild protest before settling in his arms. Blaise trudged out to the stable, nestling the hen in a manger in the empty stall next to Emrys's.

<What is that?> the stallion asked, peering over.

"I'm pretty sure this means the Maverick Underground is watching me."

And since Blaise was alone on the big estate with only the pegasi and Tristan, that made him feel a little safer.

CHAPTER TWENTY-THREE
Family Reunion

Vixen

Vixen had never set foot in the Golden Citadel before. As with everyone raised in Izhadell, she'd seen it, though usually from a distance. It was the glittering, golden facade that reminded the masses that maverick mages went in and loyal theurgists came out.

If they came out at all.

Probably because of her association with Jefferson, she'd ended up in a cell that resembled a shabby boarding house room. Blaise never spoke of it, but Vixen knew in her gut that he hadn't been held in anything like this. Though maybe after what Jefferson and Blaise had done, mages were no longer treated like livestock at the Cit. For her sake, she hoped so.

She had a sleepless night and spent most of it replaying her own foolishness of the afternoon. *I shouldn't have risked that. Should have known better.* But what else could she have done? The magistrate wasn't going to let Jefferson go free any other way. He'd been doomed from the start.

The salt-iron embedded in the walls didn't help her situation. When the guards had brought her in, they'd made her remove the ring, though Vixen had seen Rhys pocket it. That was good, at least—no telling if she'd recover it if the guards took it. But without the ring, she was susceptible to the relentless power drain of the metal, and it left her with a headache.

One day passed, and then a second. Vixen was having her doubts that she would be released soon. Wouldn't Rhys have gone to their mother? Maybe Blaise had been right to be nervous around him. He was a Tracker, and she was a mage. Two opposing forces, like fire and ice. And they had been apart for so many years. Maybe blood didn't matter when your twin was a mage.

She was mulling through those dark thoughts when the door to her cell creaked open. Light flooded in, accompanied by the sound of raised voices. One voice telling someone not to go in. Another voice, familiar through the haze of years, responding that she answered to a higher power and would do as she saw fit.

Vixen had been lying on the thin mattress of the bed and jerked upright, heart pounding. The woman framed by the light was achingly familiar. Emotions warred within Vixen. She wanted to get up, to run to her. But part of her stayed rooted, horrified and afraid that her mother would reject her.

"You have a visitor." Rhys entered first, coming over and taking Vixen's hand. He turned it over, pressing something cool into her palm. The ring. "Put it on. Quick." His voice was so soft she almost missed the words, but she did as he said. Rhys wasn't in his Tracker uniform, instead dressed in muted greys and browns that would hide him in shadows and make him look unremarkable.

The Luminary strode into the cell, statuesque as ever. Vixen's mother had always commanded a room with her presence—she assumed it was some facet of being the avatar of Garus. And, in that moment, this woman wasn't her mother. No, she was the Luminary through and through.

The Luminary studied Vixen with keen grey eyes. She wasn't clad in her usual gold and white regalia, marking her as the avatar. No, like Rhys she wore drab grey clothing, a robe that reminded Vixen very much of the sort worn by the clergy. It was a similar design, though the Garusian priests wore either all white or all gold, depending on their rank. But even in the dull robe, she looked regal and otherworldly. The Luminary stood there, as if drinking in Vixen's essence with her eyes.

The woman chewed at her lower lip, and in that gesture, Juliette Kildare replaced the Luminary. "It's really you, isn't it?" Her voice was husky with emotion.

Vixen peered up at her, feeling like a lost little girl. She hadn't realized how much she had missed her mother. Now the dull ache of their time apart roared up, as wide as the canyons that made up the Gutter. "Yes."

Juliette took a shuddering breath, then closed the distance to envelop her daughter in a hug. Vixen froze for a second out of instinct. She had never imagined she'd see her mother again in this life, much less hug her. But she couldn't hold back. Vixen returned the hug, drinking in the scents she associated with her mother—honey and whatever incense had most recently wafted through the Asaphenia.

After a moment, her mother pulled back. "I thought you were dead."

"I know." Vixen had wanted her to think that. She had wanted no one to come after her, to discover what she was. At the time, it had been unthinkable.

Juliette swallowed. "When Garus refused to choose another Spark, I hoped…" Her intense gaze flicked over Vixen. "In my heart, I had hoped the reports of your death were wrong, since we never found a body."

Of course, the god of wisdom wouldn't select a new Spark. The Luminary might not have known Vixen was alive, but Garus knew. But he knew she was a mage, too. He couldn't possibly want her.

Could he?

Vixen would have to ponder that later. She needed to focus on getting herself and Jefferson out of there. She heaved a breath. Well, Vixen had planned to reconnect with her mother. Perhaps not quite in this way, but…she'd have to play the hand the circumstances dealt her.

She gave a wan smile. "I'm back. And I need a favor."

CHAPTER TWENTY-FOUR

Unexpected Guests

Jack

Kittie frowned at the glass of rose-colored liquid. "So I drink this, and it will give me the power boost I'll need for the spell?"

Jack stood beside his wife on the back porch of their home, which blocked them from the view of most curious citizens. Zepheus stood nearby, saddled and ready to go. Emmaline perched atop the railing, legs dangling as she lazily swung them. Jack had included her so that she could help her mother into the house once the portal was cast.

"Yeah. It tastes like brine and old boots, and you're gonna feel like you got trampled by a horse when you're done," Emmaline piped up.

The Pyromancer glanced from the potion to her husband. "You're going to owe me for this."

He grinned, closing the distance between them. "Sure. Anything you want. Name it."

Kittie met his eyes, hers steely with determination "Take me with you."

Gods damn it. He couldn't believe she was trying again. Jack's mouth went dry, and he shook his head. "We've been through this. I told you why you can't go." But he saw the flicker of doubt in her eyes. She didn't believe any of his reasons were worth a damn.

Her mouth tightened. For a moment, he thought for sure she would argue. But Kittie simply lifted her chin, eyes narrowing with disapproval. Yeah, she was pissed at him. But he could live with that if it meant he had a wife to come back to.

"Hand over the spell, you selfish piss-goblin," Kittie growled. Emmaline blew out a breath, mouthing the words, "You are so dead," to Jack.

He stuck his hand into the pocket where he kept the portal spell but didn't remove it. "This ain't gonna work if you cast while you're mad."

"You should have thought of that sooner." She glared at him.

Jack sighed. He put a hand on Kittie's shoulder, expecting her to jerk away. She didn't. He met the burning anger in her eyes. "I know you think I'm a jackass for wanting you to stay behind. But there ain't a lot in this world that scares me shitless. The thought of losing you again is one of 'em, though." Jack swallowed, hoping that she'd understand.

She shook her head, brushing the hair back from her face with one hand. "And don't you think I feel the same about you?"

The outlaw's lips drew into a thin line. It was the same old song and dance. "Nah, I know you do." He took her hand in his, lifting it to his lips. Jack kissed her knuckles, savoring the ever-present scent of smoke that clung to her. Not an unpleasant sort of smell, but the scent he associated with cheerful bonfires and good times. "There ain't many people I'll beg, but I'm begging you to stay here."

She sighed. "Let's see the spell."

Kittie hadn't agreed, but he figured she was stewing about it, and this might be the closest he'd get. He pulled the spell out, unfolding it before handing it to her. "You get to do the set-up."

She took the paper, frowning as her gaze flicked over it. Then she stepped back to look at the framing of the porch, which they were going to use as the basis for their portal. "This is outside of my magical expertise."

Jack smiled, moving in again and wrapping an arm around her waist. "Nah, you're just not accustomed to thinking about your magic like this. That's all. The idea behind this is magic is magic, no matter the source."

"Doesn't matter if it comes from fire or ritual?" Kittie asked.

"Doesn't matter," Jack agreed. At least, he hoped that was the case. It was what they were betting on, at any rate. Marian Hawthorne said Blaise could work a spell such as this, and his magic was pure chaos. Jack wondered if, at its root, all magic started the same, and it was the strengths of the practitioner that defined it.

Kittie nodded. "All right. I'll try it." She uncorked the potion bottle, taking a swig. The Pyromancer made a face at the taste, then drank the rest of it down. She wiped her mouth with the back of her hand. "Em, I'll take some tea later. When I'm up to it."

Emmaline grinned. "Got it."

Then Kittie limbered her fingers, focusing on the spell. Jack held it where she could read it. The casting called for turquoise, and Jack had already placed the stones. "Here we go."

He felt the pressure of her summoned power. It was like the rumble of distant thunder, something palpable in the air. A vibration magnified by the alchemical potion. Kittie made a soft exclamation. She snapped her fingers, and tongues of flame roared to life on her palms. Jack stepped aside, cautious around the might of her fire. He had a healthy respect for the destructive force, and though she wouldn't intentionally harm him, there was no telling what might happen under the potion's sway.

The flames leaped from her hand to the columns that supported the porch. Emmaline yelped, jumping down and skittering back a safe distance. The fire crackled, the white paint on the wood blistering. But the wood itself didn't catch fire. The flames simply skimmed along it like an insect skating atop a still pond. Kittie's hair blew back in a rush of magical wind, her eyes glowing with power.

Jack swallowed. "Kittie?"

She didn't look at him. "Almost done."

The flames danced along the wood until they framed the entire rectangle, creating a blazing doorway. Jack studied it, nodding. He supposed it made sense that a Pyromancer would make a portal of fire. "Ready for me?"

"Yes." Kittie's voice resonated with something almost otherworldly.

Jack handed the spell to Kittie, watching as she folded it and tucked it away for safekeeping. Then he took her hand, his breath catching at the intense heat of her skin. He shouldn't have been surprised—she'd been holding fire in her palms, after all. It was like touching a cooling stove. Still hot and uncomfortable, but possible.

He clutched a poppet in his left hand, using it as a focus for his contribution to the working. Like Kittie, this was something he'd never done before. But Emmaline had done it—and she was right. It shared some basic pillars in common with a spell like Rising Dread, or the lightning rod spell they had cast together. It was just a matter of twisting magic in a new way.

Jack felt the poppet in his grip activate. He formed a vision of his destination in his mind's eye. The peacock's home, though now it belonged to Blaise. The stables, he decided, would be the safest place. Close to the house, but hopefully clear of anyone who shouldn't see his arrival.

Amid the door of flames, the scenery wavered from the other side of the porch to the aisle of a faraway stable. He heard Kittie's soft intake of breath. Jack grinned. "We did it."

Beside him, his wife wove on her feet. "I don't know how long I can hold this."

Jack nodded. He leaned over to plant a quick kiss on her lips. "Thanks, darlin'. Come on, Zeph." The Effigest leaped through the portal of flames, feeling the momentary disorientation and discomfort of traveling so far in a short time.

The clatter of hooves proved Zepheus had made it through. Jack rubbed his temples as he recovered from the portal, squinting. Flames licked along his vision, evidence the magical gate was still open. Why? Kittie should have closed it.

Footsteps and a soft, pained groan. Jack shook his head, fighting off the effects. He knew that voice. When his vision fully cleared, he found Kittie clinging to Zepheus's mane, her eyelids fluttering. Her fingers loosened their grip, and she reeled. Jack lunged to catch her as the drain of the spell fully caught up to her. He cursed, gently easing her down, though he adjusted to cushion her head with his lap.

"Why did you *do* that?" the outlaw asked, unable to mask the tremor of confusion and fear in his voice.

<She did not wish to be left behind,> Zepheus said, lowering his head to nudge his rider. <You treat her like the porcelain doll that is her poppet.>

Jack didn't feel well enough to deal with this. A distant part of him knew Zepheus was right—that Kittie was right. She was a capable woman, and he should trust that she could handle herself. But the void of the years she had been missing from his life was still a gaping wound in his heart, and his fear of that happening again was too strong. Jack knew he wouldn't survive a second occurrence. Frustration burned his stomach. What had he done to be saddled with such a glorious, strong woman? He'd done nothing to deserve this sort of love.

He shook his head, wishing with his entire being that he had the power to send her back to the Gutter. To safety. But was the Gutter safe at this point?

A pair of pegasi had their heads over stall doors, ears pricked as they watched the scene with interest. Jack recognized Emrys and Alekon, which meant he was in the right place. He smoothed a lock of loose hair back behind Kittie's ear, then looked up at the pegasi. "Can you tell Blaise we're here?"

<Already have,> Emrys replied.

The Effigest breathed a sigh of relief. He still wasn't on the best of terms with the black stud, so he appreciated Emrys doing that much. Jack cupped his wife's cheek in one hand, mind whirling as he waited for the Breaker. He hoped Emmaline would be okay. Kittie wasn't the impulsive type—which meant she'd likely warned their daughter about this. Damned women, conspiring against him. But that conclusion made him feel a little better. Emmaline would stay with Clover, as she had in the past.

He adjusted his position, still cradling her head. "Damned persistent woman." But he smiled. He wouldn't trade her for anything in the world.

***

Blaise

WHEN THE STRANGE SENSATION OF MAGICAL PRESSURE RIPPLED THROUGH the house, Blaise knew exactly what it was. He'd felt it before in Ganland. It was the pulse of a portal opening. But who would use that to travel here? He had a few suspicions, but he knew better than to fall prey to them.

"I can't catch a break this week," he grumbled. With Jefferson and Vixen still jailed, he wasn't in the best mood. He had several tins of cookies and pans of pies to show for his efforts to distract himself. Blaise had made plans to have a pity party with the pegasi that evening. The equines were looking forward to gorging themselves on the treats.

<We have company in the barn,> Emrys informed him. The stallion didn't seem bothered, which was a good sign.

Blaise closed up the bag of sugar he'd been about to use and put away the butter. He had a cake in the oven, but he had about twenty more minutes before taking it out. Time enough to see what was going on, or so he hoped.

He stalked onto the porch and down the stairs. The resident hen pecked at the grass nearby, her head snapping up as he passed. She trailed after him as he hurried to the stables.

Tristan must have arrived only seconds before him. The lad was nearly boiling with fury, fists clenched. "Unhand her!"

Unhand who? Blaise came around the corner in time to find Jack holding a sixgun, the muzzle trained on the boy. Zepheus stood behind him, watching everything with his usual calm demeanor. Blaise pulled up short when he noticed the woman prone on the ground. He blinked, recognizing Kittie.

"Whoa, whoa, whoa." Blaise held up his hands. Tristan didn't turn, still staring at the outlaw with more courage than sense. Jack's cool gaze flicked to Blaise for a heartbeat, then back to Tristan.

"I found an intruder, and he's harmed this woman!" Tristan announced, reminding Blaise of a terrier facing down a bulldog.

Jack's chin jerked up at the accusation, his eyes narrowing as an atmosphere of impending danger bloomed. Blaise stepped in front of Tristan. He was pretty sure Jack wouldn't shoot him. Probably. To be on the safe side, he had his magic at the ready. "Tristan, it's not what you think. These are friends of mine." Blaise angled so that he could see the boy in his periphery. "Howdy, Jack. Wasn't expecting you."

The outlaw was kitted out as if he'd come prepared for a fight, a bandolier bristling with cartridges across his chest and a reagent pouch attached to his belt. "Yeah, didn't exactly have time to send a message." Jack's hand swept across Kittie's brow. A mixture of worry and defensiveness shadowed his face.

Blaise suspected Kittie must have been the one to cast the portal spell. Had his mother made a potion to give the Pyromancer the extra jolt of power necessary? He'd have to ask later. He looked at Tristan. "Can you prepare a guest room? Please?"

Tristan frowned but nodded, scurrying off.

Jack's shoulders relaxed. "Thanks. That's exactly what she needs."

Blaise smiled. "Do you need help to get her to the house?"

The Effigest shook his head. He shifted, holstering his sixgun and retrieving a poppet. "Nah. I'll give myself a little extra strength. Should do the trick."

Blaise chewed on his lower lip, though he let the outlaw do as he wished. He stayed nearby, just in case the other man ended up needing a hand. Jack was so intent on doing things on his own sometimes. And he was clearly worried about his wife. Blaise busied himself by settling Zepheus in a stall beside Alekon, filling a bucket with fresh water mixed with sugar and another with sweet feed.

A short time later (after Blaise had removed his cake from the oven), they had Kittie settled on a bed. She had roused as Jack carried her up the stairs, though her skin was as pale as porcelain, as if the magic had drained all the color from her body.

"Can I bring you something?" Blaise asked.

Kittie's eyes were slits, as if she were struggling to stay awake. Blaise remembered the exhaustion that came with expending too much power too quickly and had an idea of how she felt. She sighed, her breath barely a whisper. "Later. Sleep now." Jack sat at the foot of the bed. Kittie opened one eye wider. "Go away."

The outlaw scowled. "No."

"I'm not why you're here," she murmured.

Jack's face hardened, every line on his face taut with displeasure. The conflict he felt was clear. Kittie made a good point—she *wasn't* why he had traveled so far. Blaise saw the stubborn twist of the Effigest's lips and knew he was going to ignore his wife's wishes unless he had some other distraction.

"Why *did* you come?" Blaise asked, deciding that was as good an opening as any.

The distraction worked. Jack's gaze pounced on Blaise. "You seen Raven Dawson?"

Raven? Why would Jack ask about the other Ringleader? Blaise frowned. "No?" Then he coughed, hating that he made it sound like a question. "No."

The Effigest's lips thinned. "Not surprising. Where's Vixen?"

"Um, it's complicated."

"And the peacock?"

"Same complication."

The Effigest made a frustrated sound. "You gonna explain, or do I gotta torture it out of you?"

Blaise scowled. The odds were good that Jack was only venting, but Blaise didn't appreciate his tone. The outlaw was obviously upset, though he was unlikely to admit it. Blaise gave him a pass. "We ran into trouble as soon as we arrived in Izhadell. Jefferson was arrested." He blew out a breath, distancing himself from the distressing thought of the man he loved imprisoned. Even though he'd twisted his magic to visit Jefferson last night, it was a poor substitute for the Dreamer's freedom. "According to Seledora and Alekon, Vixen's bid to free Jefferson went sour. She ended up arrested, too."

Jack stared at him, as if he couldn't believe that things had turned to disaster for them so quickly. Blaise had to agree. It was impressive. "So, why are you sitting around here? You got the magic to break them out."

Blaise huffed. "I think you know exactly why I can't do that."

Jack winced, then nodded. "Yeah, yeah, I suppose I do. You'd be shot full of holes like Ravanchen cheese." He rubbed his cheek, gaze flicking to Kittie before settling on Blaise again. "You okay?"

Blaise moved over to the window, resting a hand on the sill. It was a good sign that Jack had calmed enough to think of someone else. The Effigest wasn't the most empathetic. "Yeah. I've been able to talk to Jefferson, even through the salt-iron. He's okay. I just..." He gazed into the distance, studying the outstretched canopy of trees. "It's the Golden Citadel."

The outlaw made a sound of agreement. Blaise knew he didn't need to say more than that. Jack understood Blaise's feelings about the place. Jack had his own history with it as well.

"That's not what I meant, though." The Effigest gestured to Blaise as if that explained it. Jack must have realized it didn't. "You're banged up. You got a bandage on your hand."

"Oh." Blaise rubbed the back of his neck. "I'm okay now, but I almost wasn't." He licked his lips, self-conscious, before Jack's intent gaze. "I was attacked when I went to the market."

"Why in Perdition would you go to a market in Phinora?" Jack asked, his tone somewhere between incredulous and condescending.

"Because I wanted to be normal for five minutes!" Blaise hadn't realized he snapped until he caught the way Jack cocked his head, looking at him as if he had turned into something dangerous. He sighed. "But you're right. It was a stupid thing to do."

"Nah," the outlaw said, to Blaise's surprise. "I get it. Maybe I was too hasty in what I said." That was the closest he'd come to an apology. Jack's eyes narrowed. "What happened?"

Blaise pursed his lips. The chicken had wandered into the yard below the window, pecking at the grass as she hunted for insects. "People knew who I was. There were mages there—mavericks. One of them warned me I was being watched, so I tried to leave, but then another group attacked me." He recounted the rest of the encounter, including the appearance of the Maverick Underground.

Jack's eyes flicked to Kittie. "Maverick Underground. Never thought I'd see the day."

"There's more. They knew I was coming—that we were coming. They intercepted the letters."

The outlaw cursed. "Damned Walkers. If you can't trust them with the post, what in Perdition can you trust them with?"

Blaise decided not to point out that he knew Jack made a habit of checking the correspondences that came through Fortitude. But the mention of Walkers reminded Blaise of Jack's earlier question. "Why were you asking about Raven?"

"Damn, I'm as distractible as a mewling jackalope." Jack shook his head. "He skipped town. Even ditched his pegasus."

"He abandoned Naureus?" Shock threaded through Blaise. He couldn't imagine doing the same to Emrys.

The Effigest grunted. "That, and more." Jack studied his wife, as if to reassure himself she was okay. Then he told Blaise what Naureus had said and about the stash of correspondence in the outhouse.

Blaise stared at him. "He *literally* told you not to come to Phinora. Why are you here?"

Jack cocked his head, lips pressed together. "'Cause he doesn't want me stopping whatever he's up to."

Jack and Jefferson are more alike than either care to admit. Both were determined to be stubbornly defiant. "You could have sent a letter."

"Too slow."

It wasn't worth arguing about—Jack was here, and that was that. Blaise abandoned that track. "So Raven is around doing who knows what. Jefferson and Vixen are jailed, and I get attacked." He sighed as he finished the summary, uncertain about what to do for any of it.

"Stinks of a plot," Jack commented.

Blaise frowned, rubbing at his bandaged hand. "You think it's all connected?" It wasn't something he wanted to consider. Each incident by itself was bad enough.

Jack nodded. "Someone's going too hard for it to be a coincidence. At this rate, you're lucky something didn't happen on the train."

The train car belonged to a Quiet One. Blaise swallowed, new worries mounting. "I don't know what to do about it—besides stay here and hope Jefferson and Vixen get free soon." And then what? Well, he supposed he would figure that out later.

Jack rose from the bed, pacing the short distance across the room. "You got any leads on the assholes that went after you?"

Blaise gave a hesitant nod. "The Maverick Underground might know something. I could go ask the chicken."

Jack stared at him. "Ask the chicken?"

"Yeah. Let me go do that." Blaise didn't feel like explaining that it would take Tristan longer to get the message to the Maverick Underground than it would to have a conversation with the hen, who would report back to her Beastcaller mistress. Blaise glanced over his shoulder to find that Jack had taken his boots off and had moved onto the bed beside Kittie, taking her hand in his.

CHAPTER TWENTY-FIVE

Last Gasp of Freedom

Vixen

The Luminary had the power to pardon whoever she liked—a power that was seldom used. Only a handful of staff at the Golden Citadel seemed aware that the Luminary was in their midst, garbed as she was in a drab robe. It meant that no one gave Vixen a second look as she accompanied her mother and brother out of the infamous building.

Vixen's mother didn't even have to give a reason for the pardons, which meant Vixen could leave the facility with no one any the wiser to her true identity. No doubt that would change soon, but at least she had a brief reprieve. Jefferson was another matter—everyone knew him, which meant that when he accompanied them out, the former Doyen was met with a host of hostile glares. Vixen imagined the gossip to come from his release would be astounding.

Jefferson had been respectfully quiet once they'd collected him. Vixen saw the questions brimming in his expression, but he was too cunning to spring them early. Their unusual group slipped out to a coach with the fox-head symbol of Garus emblazoned on the side in gold filigree.

Jefferson's brows raised when he saw the emblem, his gaze sliding to Vixen. He made a soft exhalation as he realized exactly where she'd gotten her outlaw name from. She bit her lip. Yeah, she hadn't been all that creative years ago. But she'd been scared and hard-pressed to think of something. It had been the first thing to come to mind.

As soon as they were ensconced in the coach, Juliette's shoulders relaxed as she shed the veneer of the Luminary. "I have many questions about why the Spark is in the company of a trait—of you, Jefferson Cole." Her lips pinched as if she had eaten something sour. Vixen didn't know if it was because of Jefferson's duplicitous past or because he was a mage. Maybe both.

"He's here because of me," Vixen said before Jefferson could speak. She took a breath before plunging onward. "I needed someone who..." No, she couldn't explain that Jefferson understood the awful position she was in. "I thought someone with political savvy would be good to have along."

"Fat lot of good I've done so far," Jefferson murmured.

Vixen gave her head a small shake. It wasn't his fault their enemies were doubling down on their attacks against them. In fact, she couldn't imagine coming here without Jefferson and Blaise.

Juliette remained tight-lipped, her expression pensive. "I'm curious about why you'd need his skills, but that's a discussion for another time." She glanced out the coach window at the city scenes flashing by. "But my more pressing concern is *you*, Valoria. When Rhys told me you were here...that you were in the Cit, I didn't believe him. I thought you were dead. Where have you been all this time?" Her gaze cut to Jefferson. "Did the mages kidnap you?"

"*No,*" Vixen shot back immediately. "No, what happened to me is complicated and..." She faltered, struggling with what to say next. *Some Persuader I am.* But she didn't want to reveal her magic to her mother, not yet. The old fear returned. What if her mother rejected her because of it? "I'll explain later. But I'm back thanks to Jefferson Cole and Blaise Hawthorne." When questions flared in her mother's eyes, Vixen added, "The Breaker."

Juliette frowned, looking at Jefferson. "I'd heard rumors he was back in Phinora. I suppose you're behind that?"

"Blaise is here as my *friend,*" Vixen cut in before Jefferson could respond. She hoped her mother would think of the Breaker favorably if she associated him with Vixen.

"Hmm." Juliette leaned against the wall of the coach. "Curious. And Rhys tells me he was assigned as your escort by an unknown superior." Her gaze slid back to Jefferson. "You have connections. Was that you?"

The Ambassador's brows raised. "I didn't know of Rhys Kildare until quite recently, so this is none of *my* doing."

Juliette's eyes narrowed, shrewd. "I see. This is too convenient to be coincidence. Someone knew you were coming back to me, Valoria. Even before *I* knew." Claws of concealed anger prickled in her words.

"We have enemies," Jefferson said.

Juliette scoffed. "As if I don't?" Then she released a long sigh. "For more than a decade, there's been no Spark. Garus ignored me every time I asked him to choose another. No heir in the event something happened to me." She stared out the window again. "There are those among the elite who would be happy to have Garus select the next Luminary from their family line."

Vixen frowned at the thought. Was that truly possible? She could imagine some greedy elite coming up with creative deceptions to rig the selection process.

"But that doesn't matter. You're here. You're *back*." Juliette's tone lightened. "We'll have to have a ceremony to reclaim you as the Spark." Her fingers drummed against the wood of the coach's side panel. "A gala to formally announce it and then the ceremony, most likely. I'll have one of my priests arrange it."

"Ooh, a gala," Jefferson said, unable to hide his glee.

"We'll invite my friends, of course," Vixen said quickly. She needed them by her side as much as possible. Though, she feared that her opportunities to be with them were about to be greatly reduced. Unless... "And maybe we should keep my presence here a secret until the formal announcement. There's a place I can stay with my friends."

Juliette stared at her. "You won't stay at Dawnlight? You still have a room there."

I want just a last gasp of freedom before I give it up. Vixen twisted the ring on her finger, longing to remove it. "I will—after the announcement."

"I'll vouch for the mages." Rhys's voice was soft. "I think I'd trust them more with Valoria than I would some of my fellow Trackers."

Vixen scowled at him, wondering how much of that was because they would sniff her out for the mage she was. In response, he gave her a one-shouldered shrug.

Juliette rubbed her forehead. "Very well. I can't believe I'm saying this less than an hour after getting my long-lost daughter back, but...I'll allow it. Temporarily."

A thrill of victory zinged through Vixen. *A final hurrah of freedom.*

CHAPTER TWENTY-SIX
A Thug and a Cheat

Jack

Jack had thought maybe Blaise had finally been through too much and had cracked like a dropped ceramic dish, but the Breaker had, in fact, spoken to a chicken. That had been strange, but a half-hour later, a woman ambled through the cypress trees that stood vigil on the north side of the estate. Blaise seemed to expect her, which led Jack to believe maybe there was something to this chicken business.

It had surprised him to discover she was a maverick. The woman—Holly—was mistrustful of Jack at first, apparently having heard of the Scourge of the Untamed Territory. But Blaise's opinion won her over, and before long, she spilled what she knew.

"We recognized the Trapper mage," she began. The words *Trapper mage* made Jack twitch, thinking back to Lamar. But Lamar was dead. Jack had made certain of that. "Name's Jeremiah Jones. He and some of the others are locals. Jones keeps his magic off the books by doing shady jobs for the elite." Jack grunted, familiar with that sort of arrangement from his days as a theurgist. "He works at the slaughterhouse."

Jack scowled, glancing at Blaise. "Slaughterhouse, eh?" What had the attackers planned for the Breaker? And were they tangled up with the Quiet Ones, or was this some other group after Blaise for his unusual magic? Or, since they were in Phinora, it might just be a group of mage-hating assholes. Jack knew there were many who resented Blaise after the Inquiry.

Thankfully, Blaise must not have reached that conclusion. Jack wasn't about to enlighten him. The kid had enough on his mind.

"Yes," Holly said with a nod. She put a finger to her lips, thoughtful. The huge rooster that shadowed her made a rumbling sound. "Jones and the ones he runs with aren't easy marks. We only ran them off because we got the jump on them."

"The hundred or so chickens didn't hurt, either," Blaise said.

Jack shook his head, still not quite believing that chickens could turn the tide of any fight. "Yeah, well, I intend to get the drop on 'em, too."

As soon as he said it, Blaise groaned. "Jack, no. Can't you even cool your heels for five minutes before running off?"

"Best to go after the trail while it's still warm." Jack crossed his arms, turning to the Beastcaller. "Got a few more questions for you, if you don't mind."

He picked her brain for a few moments longer, trying to get a description of his quarry. When he was done, she and the rooster vanished back the way they had come.

"What?" Jack asked when he saw the frown on Blaise's face.

"You're going to hunt this Trapper down and just...leave Kittie here?"

Jack didn't like the way Blaise made it sound, as if he were abandoning her. That was the furthest thing from the truth. "I'm entrusting her to *you*."

The Breaker hissed out a long breath. "And what exactly do I tell her when she wakes up mad?"

"That her husband is an asshole who went and followed a lead without her."

"Well, at least it's the truth," Blaise grumbled. He shook his head. "I know you won't listen to me, but...just be careful, okay?"

"You're as bad as a broody hen." Though, Jack couldn't blame him. The Breaker had been through the wringer. "Look, all I plan to do is find this Jones and squeeze him for information. Simple."

Before long, he had Zepheus tacked up and ready. The stallion's banded wings stayed hidden as they trotted down the drive, leaving Hawthorne House. The name made Jack snort. *Hawthorne House.* It sounded so damn uppity and nothing like a place Blaise would willingly own. Yet here he was.

Back in the day, Jack had known all the ins and outs of Izhadell and the surrounding area. But he had been gone a very long time, and things had changed. When he reached the market Blaise had visited, he stopped to ask for directions to the slaughterhouse.

It wasn't hard to find. He and Zepheus simply had to follow their noses. They were downwind of the building, and the reek of death, shit, and smoke carried to them on a stiff breeze.

Zepheus shook his head, exhaling a mighty breath. <I don't like this.> His ears flicked backward, and he stomped a hind hoof in agitation.

"You don't like it because it stinks," Jack pointed out.

<That is only part of it.> Zepheus sidestepped as they drew closer.

The slaughterhouse complex was huge. Pens of animals surrounded the abattoir, filled with beasts aware of their fate. Cows lowed and shifted nervously, some of them pressing against the fences. Pigs squealed and shoved one another. A pair of old horses, their backs swayed with years, huddled together, their heads drooping so low their muzzles brushed the ground. Watching them, Jack understood why Zepheus didn't like it. The telepath faced a wall of fear and despair.

"Hang in there," Jack murmured, patting his pegasus's neck to offer some small comfort.

He found a secluded copse of trees near the slaughterhouse to stow Zepheus. It was clear of the worst smells but still close enough for the stallion to keep tabs on his rider. Though that would be difficult, the further away Jack got.

<How are you going to do this?> Zepheus bumped Jack's shoulder with his muzzle.

"Sneakiest way I can," Jack murmured, pulling out his poppet.

<Obfuscation?>

"Yep."

The stallion pawed at the ground, restless. <Don't do anything stupid.>

"Too late. I already came to Phinora." Jack grinned, starting his cast. The spell settled over him, hiding him in plain sight. As long as he didn't bump into anyone, he would have the advantage.

The outlaw headed for the building, smirking at the sight of one of the side doors gaping open as men loaded meat onto a wagon bound for market. Jack crept up to the group to eavesdrop and find out if any of them were his mark. Once he'd discovered they weren't, he made his way inside.

Jack wandered the building for longer than he liked. At this rate, he was going to have to accost one of the workers and bully them into telling him Jones's whereabouts. He toyed with the idea of trying this tactic on one of the men slaughtering the animals. The brute handling the lambs enjoyed his job entirely too much, torturing the innocent creatures before they died. Jack had a cruel streak, and he'd happily eat meat, but he wouldn't draw out the suffering of an animal the way that man was.

But that wasn't why he was here. He had to keep his focus. Jack trudged invisibly across the slaughterhouse floor, though he didn't notice until he walked onto a clean section that his boots were covered in blood, and he'd left a spattered trail of red footprints.

Shit. Jack stepped back onto one of the dirty sections of the floor. *Shouldn't have let the asshole distract me.* Jack shook his head. What were the odds someone would notice a new pair of bloody bootprints? The workers weren't paid for their attention to the finer details.

Besides, Jack didn't have much choice. He had to get a move on.

"—don't think we'll be able to do that, Jer." A voice echoed down a nearby corridor. Jer? The odds were good it was short for Jeremiah. Jack stayed where he was, cocking his head to listen.

"I don't want to hear it. No one's going to know we're selling meat from glandered horses. We do the job, we get our money," another voice answered.

Well, not only is my pal Jeremiah a thug, he's a cheat. Jack gritted his teeth. Glanders, that was a gods-awful disease. It would kill the horses slowly and painfully, and it could spread to other livestock or humans. Even pegasi. In the Gutter, if any of the outlying farms that provided meat tried to pull such a stunt, they'd suffer swift consequences. Not so in a bloated city like Izhadell.

Not a thing Jack could do about that except make Jeremiah Jones extremely uncomfortable. He crept forward again, following the voices. The complainant stormed off, leaving Jones alone.

Jack stalked closer, finally rounding the corner. He found the man inside a broad room filled with rows of carcasses hanging from hooks. Most of them appeared to be cattle. There were a few on the far side that might have been from the mystic races. One had the unmistakable look of a griffin, though it had been skinned. Jack's lips curled. *This place is evil.*

Silent as a cat on the prowl, he slipped into the room, sneaking behind Jones. Jack clutched his poppet in his left hand, willing a speed spell into it as he pulled his sixgun, dropping his Obfuscation at the same time that he leveled the muzzle at Jones's head.

"Howdy," Jack whispered. Jones tensed, muscles bunching. The Effigest nudged him with the sixgun. "I've got questions, and you're gonna answer them, real quiet-like. If you get loud...well, this sixgun is pretty loud, too."

Jones swallowed. "Who in Perdition are you?"

"Nope, I'm the one with the questions," Jack said. "You went after the Breaker. Who are you working for?"

The man shifted to glance back at Jack. "I don't know what you're talking about."

"You need a refresher?" Jack murmured.

Jeremiah's head reared back at the question, nearly slamming into Jack's nose. The outlaw still had his speed working up, though, and narrowly avoided the painful move. He cursed and lifted his sixgun again to aim—

A black chain shot out of the floor, snapping around Jack's wrist and jerking his arm down. The sixgun flew from his grip, skittering across the cold floor with a metallic clatter. Growling, Jack banished his speed spell and cast strength. He felt the immediate drain of the working as he tugged against the chain, the arcane metal snapping beneath his might. But as quickly as he broke it, another chain flew up around his left wrist, leashing him again. *Gods-damned Trappers!*

In quick succession, more chains rose. In seconds, Jack was tethered in place. With a snarl, he flexed his right arm to snap the new chain.

A knife whispered beneath Jack's chin. The outlaw froze, painfully aware that so much as twitching the wrong way could end with his throat slashed. He knew the glint of the nine inches of steel, knew that the wielder was better with a blade than with a sixgun by necessity.

"Couldn't stay home, could you?" a familiar voice whispered.

"Howdy, Raven," Jack murmured, the words pressing his tender skin perilously close to the knife's edge.

He heard Raven's soft exhalation. Every muscle in Jack's body tensed against the threat. Jack wanted nothing more than to put a comfortable distance between himself and the rogue Ringleader, the room to work magic or snatch up the fallen sixgun. This was about the last place he'd expected to find Raven. The Effigest had a flurry of questions, and he was certain that even if the other mage gave him a chance to ask, he would receive no answers.

"This the one you were talking about?" Jones asked the Ringleader, keeping his chains in place.

"Unfortunately," Raven confirmed. "You can go, Jones. I'll handle him from here."

"You sure? He's a right bastard."

You got that right. Jack glared at him for good measure.

"I'll be fine," Raven answered. Yeah, not if Jack had a say in it. "I guess this means you found my stash. You should have paid attention to my warning," Raven said after a moment, regret shading his voice. "But sometimes you really *are* predictable, no matter what you may think."

Jack gritted his teeth. "You *baited* me." He wanted to say more but didn't dare risk it. Jack had seen what that blade could do in a fight, and he couldn't defend against that. Not like this. "Whose side are you on?"

"You're not going to delay me with questions," Raven said, annoyingly pragmatic. "And know this is nothing personal."

Before Jack could react, the knife slipped away from his neck. But Raven wasn't removing it, wasn't giving him any sort of quarter. Instead, it slashed against the top of the outlaw's upper arm, slicing through his duster and shirt like butter. Jack hissed as the steel bit into flesh. As quick as the knife was in, it was out again, a fine spray of blood salting the air as Raven stepped away. It joined Jack's bloody footprints on the ground.

Out of reflex, Jack clapped his hand to the wound, as if he might soothe the hot corona of pain. His fingers came away sticky. And more than that. A sickening realization struck him as fire raced through his veins.

"Go lick salt-iron," Jack growled as he went down to his knees, unable to stand against the wave of agony that surged through him. Raven hadn't only cut him. The blade's edge had been coated with poison. Jack had been cut before. None of those instances had ever felt like *this*.

Raven looked down at him, the younger man's eyes the coldest Jack had ever seen them. The Shadowstepper didn't move, just watched as Jack's breath rasped while he struggled to shrug off the poison.

The Effigest's fingers twitched. If he could get to his poppet, he might stand a chance. He knew workings that could dull pain or temporarily staunch wounds. The odds were slim they would work against poison, but Jack was willing to try. But his hand behaved as if it were no longer his to command, fingers flexing into a pained fist.

"Raven." Jack tried to load the single world with the certain promise of retribution, but his tongue was thick and spongy in his mouth. Panic seized him. He tried to thrash, tried to fight, but nothing worked. After a moment, it was all he could do to collapse onto his side, panting for breath.

The Effigest closed his eyes, trying in vain to gather his thoughts, to figure out some way around this. He was going to be pissed if this gods-damned traitor was the one who ended him. Poison was a coward's tool. That thought gave Jack pause. Raven could have killed him easily, could have slit his throat and been done with it. But he hadn't, instead nicking Jack's shoulder with a poisoned blade. Why?

The obvious answer was that he didn't want Jack dead. At least, not yet. Which meant that while the poison was damned inconvenient and bloody frustrating, it likely wouldn't kill him.

Whatever Raven was up to wasn't good, but Jack knew that as long as he lived, he had a chance. And that was all he needed. Now all he had to do was endure the gods-damned Perdition this poison was putting him through.

CHAPTER TWENTY-SEVEN

We're Being Serious Right Now

Blaise

Kittie showed no signs of waking. Blaise alternated between checking on her and puttering around in the kitchen. He had thought about staying with Kittie until she woke, but it wasn't long before that was downright awkward, and he'd retreated to the kitchen to busy his hands and his mind.

Jack had been gone for several hours. Blaise wasn't sure if he should be worried or not. But Emrys advised him not to concern himself too much, since Zepheus was with him. Of all the pegasi, Zepheus was the most level-headed.

Blaise had just slid a pot pie into the oven when Emrys called to him. <There is a coach approaching. Alekon and Seledora say that Vixen and Jefferson are aboard!>

Jefferson? Blaise's pulse raced at the mention of his beau, almost weak with the relief that he was no longer imprisoned. He hurried outside, a wave of uncertainty rolling over him at the sight of the unfamiliar coach. Blaise stayed on the porch, worried it was some sort of trap.

The trio of pegasi stood at the fence nearest the coach, their wings hidden. Emrys must have picked up Blaise's nervousness. <If there is any threat, we are here.>

Blaise didn't need to worry, though. As soon as the coach drew to a halt, Jefferson didn't wait for the footman to set out the block of stairs. No, the door flew open, and the Dreamer leaped down, followed by Vixen. Jefferson's green eyes settled on Blaise, assessing him with every stride as he drew near. Blaise kept his still-bandaged hand behind his back, self-conscious.

Blaise trotted down the porch steps to meet him. As soon as Jefferson was within arm's length, he reached out and pulled his beau into a desperate embrace. The Dreamer opened his mouth to say something, but Blaise didn't give him the chance. He crushed his lips to Jefferson's. Blaise savored the assurance that the man he loved was here. Jefferson was okay. He was free.

Jefferson seemed surprised by the move for a beat, but he wasn't one to shy away from affection. He looped an arm around Blaise, his hand resting against the nape of the Breaker's neck. Comfortable and *right*.

"Y'all act like you were apart for a year," Vixen observed from somewhere nearby.

Blaise pulled away, glancing at her with feigned annoyance. He was glad to see her, though. "It was long enough." Then his gaze snapped back to Jefferson. "Howdy."

"I do so enjoy your greetings," Jefferson murmured, lips twisting with pleasure. Then, his voice even softer, he added, "I'm okay. I'm here, and I'm okay."

It was no surprise that Jefferson knew the heart of Blaise's response to his return. The old fear that even though things were different now, he might have been mistreated, as Blaise had been. Blaise nodded, heaving out a breath.

Mischief gleamed in Jefferson's eyes. "Though if you wish to give me a *thorough* examination later, I wouldn't refuse."

The corners of Blaise's mouth twitched. He should have known the Dreamer would say something like that. "We're being serious right now."

"You think I'm not serious?" Jefferson asked with a wink, though he released his grip on Blaise and took a step back. His flirtatious humor meant that he really *was* okay, which did much to put Blaise at ease. Then Jefferson cleared his throat, making a show of straightening his clothing, which honestly hadn't been mussed at all by their embrace. "I suppose we have some catching up to do."

That was an understatement. Blaise paused, wondering if Kittie was awake yet. Gods, they didn't even know about Jack and Kittie's arrival. He rubbed the back of his neck.

Vixen cocked her head. "What are you not telling us?"

"Um, Jack and Kittie are here. Well, Jack's not *here* here, but..." Blaise waved a hand. "It's complicated."

Jefferson and Vixen stared at him, baffled. Clearly, neither had expected that bit of news. Jefferson heaved a dramatic sigh. "Sounds as if my examination will be delayed. More's the pity."

Vixen stifled a laugh, shaking her head as she headed for the house. "It's a miracle Blaise puts up with you."

"It actually is. I'm quite thankful for it, though," Jefferson agreed, moving to follow the Persuader, though he glanced back at Blaise, grinning. He was acting the part of a rake, but Blaise couldn't even pretend to be annoyed because he knew it meant Jefferson *cared*. About *him*. Blaise couldn't express how precious that was.

The savory scent of baking pot pies greeted them as they entered, which served as Blaise's much-needed reminder to check on them. He hurried to the kitchen and pulled them out of the oven, pleased to discover they hadn't burned.

"I thought I heard voices."

Blaise looked up and saw Kittie at the base of the stairs, though she leaned heavily on the railing. She was still exceedingly pale, her dark hair stark contrast to her complexion. She reminded Blaise of the porcelain doll Jack used as her poppet. "Should you be up?"

"I'm up," the Pyromancer said, voice as fiery as her magic. Blaise wasn't at all surprised that Kittie was as stubborn as her husband. "And I'm hungry."

Jefferson, ever the gentleman, hurried over and offered her his arm. "Good afternoon, Kittie. I certainly wasn't expecting to see you here." His voice was warm and full of welcome as she took his arm, leaning against him for support. "I suppose your trip here was *taxing*."

"You could say that," Kittie agreed as she sat at the table.

Vixen claimed a seat beside the Pyromancer as Blaise dished out the piping hot pot pies. She flashed him a look of thanks before focusing on Kittie. "Blaise said you and Jack came here together?"

Mention of the Effigest prodded the Firebrand to glance around. "Where *is* my meddlesome husband, by the way?"

"Um." Blaise set the empty bakeware aside, then turned back to their inquiring gazes. "That's a long story, but the quick version is someone attacked me, and now Jack is hunting down one of the men who did it."

Jefferson went still, staring at Blaise's injured hand. A thousand questions crossed his expression, but he left them unspoken. Instead, he nearly growled as he said, "Someone *attacked* you?"

Blaise nibbled his lower lip, nodding. Now everyone's attention was on him, as intent as cats waiting to pounce. Their focus was so overwhelming, he turned to face the counter. "I'm okay." Blaise didn't realize Jefferson had risen, moving close to him until he felt the light touch of a hand on his shoulder.

"Jack went off without me?" There was a distinct twang of disapproval in Kittie's tone.

"Honestly, not all that surprising," Vixen drawled. "It's a very Jack thing to do."

"And I'm still mad at him for it," Kittie retorted. "That *man.*"

Blaise was fairly certain she'd considered adding some colorful language but had held her tongue. Now that the focus had shifted from him, he turned back, though he shot a grateful glance at Jefferson before moving to claim a seat at the table. "Kittie, can you tell them about Raven?"

Vixen went on alert at her former beau's name. "What about Raven?"

The Pyromancer gave her a sympathetic look, then explained what had spurred her and Jack to portal such a great distance. Kittie spoke slowly, her words deliberate—Blaise saw the exhaustion in her every move. She really should have stayed in bed, but he wouldn't risk the suggestion. Not now.

When she finished, Vixen looked utterly baffled. "He can't...he wouldn't..." But she frowned, as if realizing that he could and he would if he had reason.

"Do you have any idea why he's behaving in this way?" Jefferson asked, tone neutral as he sank his fork into the flaky crust in front of him.

Vixen shredded her own pot pie until it was more crumbs than anything else. "We didn't part on the best of terms."

"Do you think he's come to spite you?" Kittie asked.

Vixen shook her head. "No. Raven's many things, but he's not spiteful. If anything, he's doing it because he thinks it's a way to win me back. Or protect me." She made a face at that.

"Would he jeopardize the Gutter for you?" This from Jefferson, whose green eyes had turned serious and contemplative, all of his earlier flirtations brushed away.

Vixen hesitated, licking her lips. "I want to say no, but...if it came down to the Gutter or Blaise, what would you pick?"

"I already made that choice once before, but it wasn't the Gutter that was involved," Jefferson replied, his words crisp. The matter-of-fact statement made Blaise's heart squeeze. *Jefferson chose me above everything else.* "Regardless, when it comes to someone you love, you'll go to great lengths for them."

"Without fail," Kittie murmured.

Vixen visibly bristled. "However he feels for me, it's not mutual. Gods-damned idiot man." She tapped her nails against the table in irritation.

Blaise decided it might be time for a change of subject. And besides, he was curious... "How did the two of you get released?"

Vixen's silver eyes darted to Kittie, uncertain. The Firebrand smiled. "Jack may try to run off without me, but he doesn't keep secrets from me."

The Persuader nodded at that. Kittie knew who and what she was. "The Luminary pardoned us." Her tone was neutral, though Blaise suspected there was a wealth of emotion behind that simple statement.

"Did something happen? Why are you back here?" Blaise asked Vixen. He had assumed that the Persuader wouldn't have been allowed to leave once her mother realized she was back.

"Since only mother knows, she let me leave." Vixen pursed her lips, looking very much as if she'd bit into a lemon instead of a savory pot pie. "But there will be a gala tomorrow night to announce my return."

"We're invited," Jefferson added cheerfully.

"Wait, what?" A gala was about the last thing Blaise had expected to pop up in this conversation.

"The Luminary is hosting a gala to announce the return of the Spark. Vixen made sure we'll be on the invite list." Jefferson's eyes gleamed at the prospect.

Now it was Blaise's turn to look as if he'd eaten a lemon. "But I'm a *mage.*" *And I don't want to go. There will be people there.*

"You're not just a mage," Jefferson reminded him, voice gentle. "You're the Breaker, the mage who had an Inquiry end in his favor. You're a landowner, which is remarkable for a mage in the Confederation. And you're one of the mages who returned the Luminary's daughter."

Blaise glowered at the logic. "No one told me when I came that I'd have to be *social.*"

Jefferson's green eyes danced with mirth. "You're welcome to attend and be mysterious and taciturn. That will only make you more interesting to everyone."

Blaise huffed an annoyed breath. "Can I just bring a plate of cookies, throw them on a table, and call it a day? You can go without me, right?"

Kittie rapped lightly on the table with her knuckles, drawing Blaise's attention. "You have the option to be left behind. Ask yourself if you want to be."

He swallowed at her words. She was right—Blaise didn't want to be left behind, not where Jefferson was concerned. He turned, meeting Jefferson's rich green eyes. "I've never been to anything like that before." He knew it was ridiculous to be scared to go for that simple reason. Blaise had done harder things—but sometimes the fact that he'd survived harder things made the small ones seem just as daunting.

"You won't be alone," Jefferson reminded him, smiling.

Blaise nodded. "Looks like I'll be coming to your party, Vixen."

"*Gala,*" Jefferson whispered. "It's a *gala.*"

CHAPTER TWENTY-EIGHT
The Elite Event of the Season

Jack

His shoulder burned. With a grunt, Jack's eyes flew open. He tried to roll his shoulders to relieve the throbbing pain, only to discover his hands were bound behind his back. Not only that, but someone had tied his legs and torso to a chair. Jack had a moment of disorientation, his memories of how he'd gotten into this situation murky.

Someone had stripped off his duster. Crusts of drying blood stained his shirt. *Raven.* That traitorous bastard had worked with the Trapper. Which meant the shadow-stepping asshole really was associated with the attempt to snag Blaise. And what else?

"Oh good, you're awake."

He didn't know the speaker, but the outlaw recognized the polished, *I'm-better-than-you-so-I'll-rub-it-in-your-face* speech of one of the Confederation elite. A woman circled around him, hands clasped at her waist as she peered at her quarry. She was dressed in fine clothing that probably would have made her the talk of the elite social circles, but Jack didn't give a shit where this woman bought her glossy boots. She was an enemy, and that was all that mattered.

"So, you're the fearsome Wildfire Jack," the woman said, tone bright. "The so-called Scourge of the Untamed Territory."

Jack glared up at her. Something about this woman was vaguely familiar. "You know me, but you must not be worth a unicorn's rainbow shit 'cause I sure as Perdition don't know you."

She clucked her tongue, as if she were disappointed. *"Manners.* You were a theurgist; I know you had manners once upon a time."

Theurgist. The word turned Jack's blood afire. "I'm a far cry from a lapdog now."

"I suppose you are," she agreed, her chin tipped to a jaunty angle. "Well, you may not have manners, but I do. I'm Tara Woodrow. Pleased to make your acquaintance." Somehow, she managed to make her words both welcoming and sardonic.

Tara Woodrow. That name tickled the recesses of Jack's mind. How did he...? Oh, yes. Woodrow was one of the Quiet Ones. Jack had likely seen her in Nera when the peacock had made his grand announcement refuting his old name and declaring himself an outlaw mage.

Now, how could Jack use that nugget? He didn't see any use for it, not yet. "Yeah? Well, it ain't mutual."

Tara's lips twisted into a pout. "A pity. At the very least you should have a bit more respect for your situation. I hope you enjoyed the poison that immobilized you. Alchemy really is a modern marvel, isn't it?"

Alchemy. That explained the coating on Raven's blade. "Can't say I agree."

She shrugged. "Agree to disagree. But we should get to business." Tara's calculating look slid over him. "When you threatened Phillip Dillon, you threatened *all* of us."

Jack allowed himself a lazy shrug, though the gesture was difficult with his hands bound behind the chair. The movement made the fire in his injured shoulder burn brighter, a blaze of pain in his skull. "Glad to hear he understood it for the threat it was. Sometimes y'all ain't that smart." He backed up the words with a feral grin that promised bravado he currently didn't have.

A muscle ticked in Tara's jaw. Yeah, Jack was definitely getting to her. Good. Maybe she'd get sloppy, and he'd figure out some way to take advantage of the situation. There was no sign of his sixgun, poppet, or reagent pouch, but Jack wasn't going to let those inconveniences stop him. Not if he had half a chance.

Woodrow took a step back. "You may talk big, but you're at our mercy now. Phillip will be pleased to hear of your capture." She angled a coy look at the outlaw. "I'm sure he'll want to attend to you *personally* before your hanging."

The blood in Jack's veins froze. He'd faced the threat of the noose countless times before but had always dodged it. A small part of him knew at some point his luck would run out. And it might be now.

No. He couldn't let those thoughts, the potential for despair, weigh him down. That was what this woman wanted. Jack tamped down his fear, summoning up his swagger. He wasn't dead yet, and as long as he drew breath, he had a chance. It wasn't as if he was in Phinora alone. Blaise, Vixen, and the blasted peacock were here. Zepheus, too. And so was Kittie, though fresh fear rooted in him at the thought of her swinging beside him.

"All that fuss for me?" Jack asked. "Nice to know my death will be the elite event of the season."

She met his snark with her own, beaming. "Yes, I plan to wear my finest gown. It'll be quite the occasion. And your death will serve as a warning to other outlaws."

Jack met Tara's gaze with his own frigid glare. "That so? I don't think you know outlaws all that well. Your *warning* will be your end."

The Quiet One frowned, as if Jack's words made her uncomfortable. Good. Tara turned, snapping her fingers. "Raven, darling!"

Raven slipped into the parlor, his jaw clenched. The Shadowstepper refused to look at Jack, nodding to the Quiet One as if he were subservient.

Traitor. Jack's gaze burned into the other Ringleader, a man he had once considered a friend, as he thought of all the things he'd do to Raven if given a chance.

"I'm bored with him. Take him away," Tara commanded, gesturing to Jack. "Somewhere that his friends won't be able to get him."

Jack frowned. What did they intend, the Golden Citadel? A hidden dungeon? Raven didn't know Kittie was here. And Jack figured Blaise wouldn't let this stand. Yeah, if they thought Jack was powerless, with no one to help him, they had another thing coming.

Raven nodded to the Quiet One, moving over to Jack. Almost too fast for Jack's gaze to follow, the Shadowstepper pulled a knife and slashed the ropes binding Jack to the chair. He clamped a hand onto the outlaw's shoulder, right over the inflamed wound. Jack snarled at the pain, rocking beneath the other mage.

"Don't fight me," Raven cautioned, his tone flat.

Jack didn't fully understand what happened next. He felt the pull of magic and the parlor seemed to twist around them, warping. There was a sensation of motion, vertigo clawing at him. His stomach lurched, and for a few seconds, he was in danger of retching up the contents. He squeezed his eyes closed, inhaling through his nose to gain control over his body. Jack's stomach settled after a moment, and his eyes flashed open.

Where was he?

It was like a room but also nothing like a room. His chair had vanished, and it was only Raven's grip that kept Jack from a tailbone-jarring fall, hands still bound behind his back. Jack sank to the ground as he tried to make sense of where he was. It was all darkness except for a puddle of dim light. Jack couldn't figure out where the light came from. There was no sun. No mage-lights. No lanterns. Pitch black fringed the area for as far as he could see, which wasn't far. The air was still but not stale, the climate temperate.

"Did you bring me to Perdition?" Jack asked drily, though it wasn't fully sarcasm.

"You and the Breaker aren't the only ones learning new tricks with your magic," Raven said, though he sounded distracted. He shifted uneasily, as if grappling with the enormity of what he'd done. Good. Jack hoped the betrayal tormented him. Raven pulled a knife from a sheath at his belt, the blade making a soft *skree* as it came free. Not one of his standard knives—Jack could tell by the hilt. The Shadowstepper sank it blade-first into the strange, spongy ground. "I don't know what to call where we are. This is the in-between, the realm between shadows. One of the few places I suspect our friends won't be able to reach you."

Our friends. Interesting choice of words. Raven still counted himself as an outlaw mage, despite whatever he had done. "Why are you working with the Quiet Ones?"

Raven clenched his jaw. "You wouldn't understand. I know you, Jack. By now, you only see me as one thing: a traitor."

The other Ringleader knew him well, which was unfortunate. "Then convince me you're *not*."

For a moment, Jack was sure Raven would give in, would unpack whatever had led him down this road. Instead, the Shadowstepper shook his head. "What does it matter? You're not the one I have to convince."

"Did they bind you?" Jack asked. He couldn't help it. He had to know. "You got a geasa tattoo? Did they make you a theurgist?"

Raven's lips thinned. "There are more ways to bind someone than the geasa." Suddenly, the other man looked older than his years. Jack didn't know Raven's exact age, but he figured he was about as old as the peacock. But now, he looked as if the worries of the world had added years to him. "I'll be back to check on you. They'd be unhappy if you died in the shadows before they had the chance to make a spectacle of you." He winced, as if the words were as sour on his tongue as they were to speak.

Raven pursed his lips, then pulled something from his back pocket that was rounded and no longer than his index finger, setting it on the ground. Jack frowned, realizing it looked like one of the smallest mage-lights he'd ever seen, though it wasn't illuminated. "Don't think to attack me here. This is *my* realm."

Without another word, Raven melted into the shadows and vanished. Jack glared at where the other mage had stood, then sighed. His shoulders and arms hurt from being tied. He licked his dry lips, assessing the surrounding area.

Raven had left the knife. Jack's eyes widened as he realized what that meant. It was an outlaw custom from the times they robbed a stagecoach or pack train. They often tied up their victims—at least the ones who hadn't chosen death by fighting—but made a point of leaving a knife where the victims could retrieve it once the outlaws left the scene.

"Hmm." Jack thought about that. Raven had said the Quiet Ones didn't want him dead yet. But there were ways to keep a man alive and captive. The Shadowstepper had made a very deliberate choice in leaving the knife. And his warning not to attack.

Somehow, Jack had the idea Tara Woodrow wouldn't want him to be untied, to have any sort of freedom in this shadow prison. Raven was dissenting in a small way the elite would likely never know about.

The outlaw heaved in a deep breath. Time to see about getting to that knife.

* * *

Zepheus

AT FIRST, ZEPHEUS THOUGHT JACK HAD SIMPLY SLIPPED PAST THE RANGE OF his telepathy. As one of the oldest pegasi living in the Gutter, over the years, he'd honed his ability to a hoof knife's edge, able to keep tabs on his rider as long as he was in the vicinity. The number of other minds in the area affected Zepheus's accuracy, too. It didn't help that he was so close to hundreds of minds ripe with terror and despair inspired by the slaughter-house. Zepheus was careful as he sifted through the different thoughts, seeking Jack. He shuddered as he brushed the mind of a heifer in line for slaughter.

Where was Jack? The pegasus snorted, shaking his head as he swept past the auras of the dying. He hated it, but there was nothing he could do except focus on his rider.

There. He found the bright spark of his outlaw, the warmth he associated with Jack. Zepheus sensed his mage was stalking someone. He must have found his prey.

Alarm flared in his mind like lightning. Something was wrong. He felt a jolt of momentary chaos and calculation as Jack struggled against some-one. Zepheus pushed his telepathic power harder, burrowing deeper to get a better idea of what was going on. Sometimes, if he strained, he could almost see through his rider's eyes, hear through his ears. The stallion poured all he had into the connection, but he failed when instead, he was struck by the white-hot sensation of agony in his shoulder.

Something had happened to Jack. Zepheus weighed his options. He could go back to Hawthorne House for help, but he might be too late. The stallion pawed a furrow in the grass beneath him. He'd gone after Jack before and gotten him out of hairy situations—even in Confederation lands. Not that he was eager for such a thing. But he would not leave Jack behind, not if he could help it.

Dusk was falling, and he observed the workers leaving the slaughter-house and new ones arriving. Zepheus understood that meant they worked in shifts, thus the abattoir was always serving its brutal purpose. The slaughterhouse was a dangerous place for an outlaw or pegasus— Zepheus knew it would be a simple thing for him and Jack to end up in a sausage, and no one else the wiser.

He shoved that grim thought aside. Zepheus was certain he would know if they had killed Jack. He had sensed Jack's near-fatal injury when he'd been shot by Lamar Gaitwood, despite the salt-iron ropes that had dampened his flight and telepathy. Jack was not dead. He couldn't be. Zepheus refused to believe in such nonsense.

The stallion picked his way out of the cover that had concealed him. It wouldn't be long before someone spied the loose *horse* and tried to catch him. He was going to have to work quickly—and probably reveal his true nature. It was a sacrifice he was willing to make.

He broke into a trot, approaching a gaping open door to one side of the slaughterhouse. The closer he got, the more pungent the reek of death and fear. Zepheus flattened his ears, snorting out great, huffing breaths. He got farther than he'd expected before someone realized he was unac-companied by a human.

"Get that horse!" a cry rang out, followed by the slap of booted feet breaking off from other tasks.

Zepheus blew out a breath, shaking his head against the stench. The carcass of a steer hung nearby, blood dripping into a massive metal bucket beneath the corpse. Men circled around him, but Zepheus ignored them, scanning the area for any sign of Jack.

He wasn't there. It was as if he'd just…vanished.

A man held up his hands, whistling softly at the sight of the golden stallion. "Easy there, boy. Did you throw your rider? You look like you're worth a load of coin." The man took a tentative step closer, though his fingers curled in anticipation of snagging the hackamore reins.

Three more men flanked him. Zepheus spun, bugling a challenge. He lashed out with his hind hooves at the man who'd tried for his reins, catching him on the shoulder and sending him flying backward with a grunt.

"Get him!" one of the other men urged his counterparts as they inched closer.

Zepheus snapped his teeth at them, unfurling his wings as he did so. The trio gaped, then had no choice but to dive away as he stampeded toward them. He extended his wings, sweeping the slowest of the men away with a flick of his long primaries.

Then he was out in the darkening evening. More shouts rang out behind him, but he didn't care. He was fast and had the advantage of flight. All he had to watch out for was griffin riders. Zepheus bolted into the sky.

He was a little disoriented, but as he flew low over the land, he sought familiar minds—his fellow pegasi. Blaise. Kittie. *Mother of Mares, what will Jack's mate think?* He wasn't looking forward to that conversation.

It wasn't long before he found the fire-bright mind of the Firebrand. Zepheus adjusted his course and moments later alighted in the driveway of Hawthorne House. Emrys, Seledora, and Alekon immediately peppered him with questions, but he ignored them. The palomino stood stock still in front of the house and whinnied, pushing out a commanding mental call. <Kittie! Blaise!>

Kittie was the first to come out, though she was quickly followed by the Breaker and—Jefferson and Vixen had arrived while he was away. Zepheus noted that but focused on his current need. He hurried over to Kittie, shoving his head against her chest. Zepheus sensed she was still weak from the magic drain, but she was up, and that was what mattered.

"Zeph?" Kittie asked, rubbing his glossy neck right behind his ears. "Where's Jack?"

He huffed out a distressed breath. <I don't know. He was there one moment, then gone the next.>

The Pyromancer went still, and Zepheus felt a wave of fear and anger wash over her, focused at Jack for leaving her behind once more. But just as quickly, she set it aside. "Where did you last detect him?"

<Deep inside the slaughterhouse.> He pulled away from Kittie, looking at the other outlaws.

Vixen frowned. "That doesn't sound like a good place to go missing."

<I went inside. He was not in there.> Zepheus didn't mention that scenting the man would have been impossible. So much death. So much pain and terror.

The Persuader heaved a sigh. "We'll figure something out. I know we will."

Yes, Zepheus knew they would. They had to. He turned to look at

Jefferson. It was fortunate the man was here. Zepheus kept his next request to only Kittie, Blaise, and Jefferson. Vixen didn't know of the Dreamer's power. <You will search for him tonight?>

Surprise crossed Jefferson's face at being addressed, but he gave the tiniest of nods. Zepheus relaxed. They would find his rider. They would.

They had to.

CHAPTER TWENTY-NINE
Night Terror

"I'm happy to announce I've completed my examination, and you seem to be fine," Blaise said, leaning his head against Jefferson's bare shoulder.

Jefferson savored the gesture, though Blaise's beard tickled his skin. "Are you sure? I might need another going-over." He most definitely wouldn't mind more of Blaise's attention.

The Breaker snorted at the suggestion. "It's getting late." Though he delivered another spate of kisses up Jefferson's neck, every single one bringing the Dreamer closer to melting.

Jefferson hissed out a breath. He treasured every private moment with Blaise, but it wasn't enough. It would never be enough. And then Blaise went and did something like…well, like he was currently doing.

"I fail to see how you think I'll sleep after you cover me in kisses," Jefferson murmured.

Blaise pulled back, though he regarded Jefferson with a smile. "Because we have work to do. You promised Zepheus." He flopped onto the goose-down mattress.

"So I did," Jefferson agreed, sobering. With a soft sigh, he reclined beside his beau.

Blaise rolled onto his back, yawning. "It's the middle of the night. If Jack's asleep, this is the best time to find him. And it's better if we're not exhausted in the morning."

"But we don't have to wake before dawn. You're not running a bakery right now." Jefferson propped his head up, gaze lingering on his beau's shadowed profile.

The Breaker placed an index finger against Jefferson's lips. "You're just being contrary to stall."

Jefferson was rather pleased that Blaise knew him well enough to notice that. He kissed the finger, chuckling when his love pulled it away with an annoyed huff. "Can you blame me?"

Blaise's enchanting blue eyes softened. He knew that Blaise didn't fully understand why Jefferson was so captivated by him. Sometimes Jefferson didn't, either. All he knew was that Blaise made him happy, made him feel complete and grounded like no one ever had before. Jefferson was determined never to take that gift for granted.

"No." Blaise's voice was whisper-quiet. "But we still need to find Jack."

"We do," Jefferson relented, turning onto his side. He shifted, adjusting his position until his back was flush against Blaise's chest, as close as a pair of the Breaker's favorite measuring spoons.

Blaise tensed. "*Jefferson.*" His voice was husky.

"What? I'm not being improper. Not at the moment, anyway." He glanced over his shoulder. Jefferson couldn't help that he wanted Blaise so close. However, he knew Blaise may not feel the same. Sometimes his beau needed space. "But I can move away if you prefer."

Blaise slung an arm over Jefferson's side, splaying his hand against the Dreamer's stomach. "I'm not saying *that.*"

Jefferson grinned, content. Blaise never admitted it, but he was a cuddler—at least, with Jefferson. He awoke some mornings to discover Blaise snuggled against him, as if they were a pair of kittens. It was another heartwarming sign that the shy younger man was comfortable with him, a detail that made Jefferson ridiculously happy.

"Mmm, good. Now, let's get some sleep and track down a surly outlaw." Jefferson savored Blaise's warmth behind him as he summoned his magic to send them to the dreamscape.

Moving into the strange realm of dreams had become second nature to Jefferson, along with drawing Blaise into it. The Breaker never fought it, too aware that without Jefferson, he was likely to succumb to the nightmares that plagued him.

The bakery took shape around them, one of the easiest locations for Jefferson to create. It was the place he knew Blaise would always feel most comfortable. The dream town of Fortitude was empty of its citizens and structures, aside from the yellow-and-white building surrounding them. Jefferson wouldn't bother with those details tonight. They had work to do.

Blaise pulled out a chair at the small table in the corner. "Do you need me to help find Jack?" He sat.

Jefferson pursed his lips. "Possibly. If he's not nearby, I might have difficulty finding him, since we're usually not on the best terms."

"I doubt he's nearby," Blaise said. And that stood to reason. If he was, Zepheus would have certainly found him.

Jefferson nodded, accepting his beau's offer. It was hard to explain how Blaise melded his magic with Jefferson's. It might have been some component of the unusual Breaker power, a side effect of their dead geasa bond or their relationship. Jefferson secretly hoped it was the latter.

With their magic combined, they searched for the Effigest. Often, when Jefferson was left to his own devices, it felt like looking for a specific book in a library that had no organization to it. Blaise usually had more luck, for some reason. But this time, the Breaker came up short, unable to find the outlaw.

"That's strange," Blaise murmured, shaking his head. "Even if he's not asleep, I would think we'd feel some hint of him."

Unless he's dead. Jefferson didn't want to suggest it, though he thought Jack was too stubborn to die. He would probably fight off the demons that hoped to drag him to Perdition. "Hmm. Maybe I should see if Kittie can help us locate him."

Blaise cocked his head, thoughtful. "Would it worry her more that we can't find him?"

"We'll have to tell her regardless," Jefferson reasoned.

"Then we may as well bring her in," Blaise said.

With the Breaker's agreement, Jefferson sent out his dream tendrils, roving through the house for Kittie. She was nearby, easy to find. Simple to draw into the dreamscape. In her dreams, the Pyromancer ran from something with many legs and gnashing teeth. Parts of it were mechanical, metal and gears clanking and rasping. As Kittie ran, the footprints left in her wake glowed with red-hot embers.

Jefferson dissolved the bakery around them, though he left Blaise's chair. The Dreamer lifted a hand, curling it into a fist. He gritted his teeth as he seized the nightmare creature with his power. The horror roared and struggled against his magic, thrashing as it tried to go after the Pyromancer.

Blaise rose, moving to stand beside Jefferson. "Do I need to do something?"

"No, I've got it. Wasn't expecting a nightmare." Sweat beaded Jefferson's forehead. Whatever Kittie feared, it was powerful. Sometimes the things that haunted dreams made no sense, except to the sleeper. He was used to handling Blaise's nightmares and was prepared for those. Jefferson focused on the terror, raising his other hand, making another fist.

Kittie had stumbled and lay nearby, panting. She stared up at them, her eyes wide. "Jefferson? Blaise?"

"Might need your help with this, Kittie." Jefferson strained as the night terror nearly snapped through his restraints.

Kittie swallowed. "What do I do?"

"Kill it with fire."

Jefferson had expected that she might incinerate it. But Kittie didn't do that, not exactly. She lifted her right hand, and a long spear flickered into existence. A spear made entirely of fire, flames licking up the shaft and ending in a point made of molten metal that gleamed as fiercely as a tiny sun. Kittie hefted it as if the spear was her weapon of choice. Perhaps she understood that in the dreamscape, if she wished to be a mistress of spears, she could be.

The Pyromancer drew her arm back and then sent the fiery spear hurtling through the air. It struck the night terror square in the...well, Jefferson wasn't sure if it even had a chest. The spear caught it in its midsection, causing the nightmare creature to wail as tongues of fire consumed it from the inside. It shrieked, writhing free of Jefferson's magic. But it didn't matter. Kittie's spear worked, reducing the terror to ash that drifted away on a phantom wind.

"Huh," Blaise said, eyebrows brushing against a curl of his copper hair.

Kittie shook her head as if clearing her mind, then turned to them. "Are you real?"

Jefferson waggled his fingers, wondering why every new person he brought into the dreamscape asked the same question. He was never certain how to answer. "We're...ah, something. This is the dreamscape."

At that, the Pyromancer nodded, as if it made some level of sense. "Thanks. I was worried about Jack. Wasn't sleeping well."

"You're welcome." It was something to think about later, but Jefferson wondered if there was a way he could help her sleep, too. With his magic, he didn't *like* when people he knew suffered in their dreams. Well, unless they were an enemy. Then they were fair game. "I'm happy that I could help you banish the night terror, if only for now." Jefferson cleared his throat. "Ah, we brought you here for a reason, though. We can't find Jack."

Kittie pursed her lips. Something flickering in the depths of her eyes. "You can't? Is he awake?"

"We'd be able to detect him," Jefferson explained. "You know I can pull people into the dreamscape if needed." Kittie had witnessed it before, when she had first learned of his magic.

She huffed out a breath. "What are the other options? Dead? Unconscious?"

Jefferson nodded. "Those are unfortunate possibilities."

"Wards could block it," Blaise mentioned, drawing their attention. "Or salt-iron."

"Ah, that is true." While they weren't ideal, Jefferson appreciated that there were options beyond death and loss of consciousness. "But in the event it's something else, I thought your connection to Jack might help our search."

Kittie tilted her head. "What do I do?"

Jefferson blinked, then glanced at Blaise. This was where it became difficult to explain out loud something that came naturally. It was like explaining how to walk. There was so much more to it than putting one foot in front of the other, but Jefferson wasn't certain if it would make sense to someone else.

"Just think of him. You have a stronger connection to him than either of us," Blaise said. Jefferson breathed a sigh of relief, shooting him a look of gratitude.

Kittie's brow furrowed with determination, and with a start, Jefferson realized Blaise was correct. He could feel her thoughts influencing the surrounding dreamscape with her own perspective of the outlaw. Jefferson wrapped his magic around the Pyromancer's thoughts.

It was no longer like searching inside a disorganized library. Now, his magic was like a pack of hounds on the trail of a rabbit, seeking the Effigest. His power roved over miles and miles, almost as if they found traces of Jack but not the man himself. The last hint of the outlaw felt like it was in a home.

"I don't understand. He's there, but not there," Jefferson murmured.

"This place. Is there a way we can figure out where this is?" Kittie asked, gesturing to the indistinct landscape around them. It was ever-shifting, taking on the aspects of various houses, none of them the same.

"Not that I know of. I don't know how much the dreamscape over-laps with the physical world. If it does at all." Jefferson felt as if they had traveled miles to search for Jack, but he wasn't confident they actually had.

"Are there slumbering minds here?" Blaise asked.

Now, that was a good question. If nothing else, perhaps Jefferson could glean something from another sleeper. But that would require more power, and after fighting Kittie's night terror and searching for Jack, he was nearly spent.

"Yes, but I don't think I can sustain this much longer."

Blaise caught his eye. "Do you want my help?"

Always. Jefferson smiled. "Whatever you wish to give."

The Breaker didn't move, did nothing at all, but Jefferson felt the power siphon from Blaise and into him. The magic seeped into his being, and he felt like a ship catching a stiff wind after days in the doldrums. Jefferson hissed out a breath in relief.

"Thank you. That will do," Jefferson said. "Let me take a peek into the slumberers."

It was definitely an estate of some sort. Jefferson touched the minds of some of the staff, finding a cook who was nearly awake to start her day. He skimmed her thoughts, trying to find out more about where this was, but she was distracted with thoughts of all she had to prepare. Jefferson left her alone, though she reminded him of Blaise, and he very much liked that.

He latched onto another sleeper, and this time he knew he had struck gold. It took some effort to sift through the layers of dreams wrapped around the man. They were filled with darkness, despair, and something like self-loathing. Jefferson dug a little deeper, his breath hitching.

"What is it?" Blaise asked.

"Raven. I found Raven."

* * *

Blaise

"Wake up." Blaise nudged Jefferson's shoulder. The Dreamer groaned softly, rolling over and showing no outward signs of waking. Blaise sighed. "Jefferson, wake up."

In response, Jefferson buried his head under his pillow and muttered something indecipherable. Blaise retaliated by pulling the sheets away.

"Mrmph!" The lower half of Jefferson's face appeared from beneath the pillow. "What was that for?"

"It's time to get up."

"I disagree." One of the Dreamer's hands groped for the missing covers.

"Told you we needed more sleep last night." Blaise shoved the covers as far from his beau's reach as possible. Under other circumstances, he would have let Jefferson sleep. He'd expended a lot of power through the night, and Blaise knew that true slumber would help Jefferson recover. But they didn't have that luxury at the moment. "We have problems."

The Dreamer yawned, but at Blaise's statement, he shoved the pillow off his head. He rubbed his eyes, and Blaise realized Jefferson had never looked so rough. Under normal circumstances, his beau seemed immune to anything that made him look less than dashing. Red-rimmed his eyes and his golden hair tangled. It was enough to convince Blaise to send him back to sleep—almost.

"I'm just so tired." Jefferson rose into a sitting position. "Last night was more difficult than what I usually do."

Sometimes it was easy to forget that magic was new to Jefferson. The man was so self-assured in all he did, it was almost as if he'd been born a mage. But he hadn't, and in many ways, he was less experienced than Blaise. The Breaker scooted closer to him. "I know. You did good, though." Blaise swept an arm around Jefferson.

A sleepy smile drifted across the Dreamer's lips. He yawned again, then shook his head. "You're right. I'm going to need a nap before the Luminary's gala, though."

The gala. It had slipped Blaise's mind with everything else they had discovered through the night. Ugh, he still wasn't enthused with the idea of going, but it seemed he would have to tolerate it. But that was a concern for later.

"I think we need to tell Vixen what we discovered. But the problem with that is we have to tell her about your magic," Blaise said.

Jefferson said nothing, and for a moment, Blaise thought he might have drifted back to sleep. Then the Dreamer sighed. "Yes, we can tell her. I believe she'll keep it in her confidence."

But would she keep it a secret from the Luminary? That was Blaise's concern. Vixen might be an outlaw, but she also had deep, deep ties to Phinora and the Confederation. The same Confederation that would be extremely interested in Jefferson if they caught wind of his magic. A Dreamer, a completely unknown magic type, would be lucrative.

"What?" Jefferson asked.

"Just thinking," Blaise said.

"About your lack of clothing?" Jefferson cast a flirtatious sidelong glance at Blaise.

Blaise snorted. "And suddenly, you're much more awake." Besides, he had pulled the covers over himself. He was nowhere near as naked as Jefferson. Though, it was likely Jefferson intended to point that out in a sneaky, roundabout way.

"Mmm, yes." Jefferson stretched, then combed his fingers through the mats in his hair. "I stand by my nap idea, though. I really am quite bushed."

"I know." Blaise leaned over, brushing a kiss against Jefferson's brow. "We'll make sure you get one. I can plan our outfits for the gala while you rest."

"You most certainly *will not*." Jefferson's eyes widened, then he frowned. "If you're trying to get a rise out of me, there are other ways I prefer you go about it."

Blaise rose from the bed, moving to the dresser and pulling out clothing. He put little thought into matching any of the items, too busy focusing on other things. Like Jefferson and his rakish ways. "Maybe. But now you're motivated to get out of bed and dressed."

"Quite unfair." But Jefferson joined him in donning clothing. The Dreamer gave a pained sigh at Blaise's mismatched attire. "You are adorably *frustrating*."

Blaise smirked. "I know. Now come on, breakfast isn't going to make itself."

They padded down to the kitchen to discover that Tristan had scrambled a skillet of eggs, though he somehow made them both runny and burned. Vixen was there, too, looking like she'd just awoken. She gave them a half-hearted wave and rubbed her face, staring at the empty pot. "I'll make coffee." Vixen gave her red locks a shake as she groped for the bag of grounds.

"I know exactly what I'll make," Jefferson said, puttering over to a counter and opening the breadbox.

Blaise eyed him. "You're not going to mistreat my bread, are you?"

"Wouldn't dream of it." Jefferson still sounded tired, but at least moving around seemed to have roused him. Blaise decided not to begrudge him the bread. He edged over to the stove to see if he could help salvage the eggs.

They worked in companionable, sleepy silence as they assembled the makings of breakfast. Kittie appeared midway through and lent her talents. Her hair was bedraggled, and she had dark circles under her eyes, as if whatever terror she had defeated with Jefferson had come back for another round. Before long, they plated their food and sat to eat.

Blaise's brows rose as Jefferson brought his contribution to the table. The Dreamer shot him a smug look. "I present to you medium-rare bread with a buttered glaze."

The Breaker made a strangled sound. "Toast. This is toast."

"It's so simple, yet so elegant." Jefferson offered a piece to Blaise, barely hiding his smirk. Yes, he was definitely more awake now and trying to lighten the mood. Kittie and Vixen were amused by his antics, so maybe it was worthwhile.

Blaise accepted the toast, biting off a corner. When he finished it, he nodded. "Careful, or I'll have you help in the kitchen more."

"Don't threaten me with a good time." Jefferson winked at him. The simple statement made Blaise feel fluttery inside. He really *did* like it when Jefferson baked with him. His preferred activity, in fact.

Once Tristan finished his plate and skulked out, Kittie's gaze sharpened, flicking between Blaise and Jefferson. There was a question in her eyes, one she wasn't willing to voice because she, too, knew that Jefferson's magic was a private affair.

"Vixen, there's something I have to tell you," Jefferson said without preamble, pushing aside his half-eaten plate of scrambled eggs. Sadly, Blaise hadn't been able to salvage them as much as he'd have liked. The flame-haired outlaw's eyebrows rose, an invitation for Jefferson to continue. "I've kept this quiet to protect myself, but we're at the point where you should know about my magic."

That piqued her curiosity. "I know what it means for another mage to share that information with me," Vixen said, her tone soft.

Jefferson smiled, then explained his Dreamer magic as best he could. The Persuader listened, asking a few questions for clarity. When she nodded with understanding, Jefferson moved to the next component. "Last night, I used my magic to look for Jack. I wasn't able to find him. But I did find Raven."

CHAPTER THIRTY
What Could Possibly Go Wrong?

*R*aven. Even now, his name brought a rush of confusing emotions. If Vixen had known parting ways with him would be so hard, she'd have never given their relationship a chance to begin with. But that wasn't fair. She'd deserved a chance to try. She blew out a frustrated breath. But had her dalliance jeopardized their bid to protect the people and the land she cared about? Vixen wouldn't allow that—not if she could help it.

She heaved a sigh. "Where is he? Who is he working with?"

Jefferson shook his head. "Those are things I couldn't quite pinpoint with my magic. Not to mention that by the time I found him, I was wrung out."

Vixen nodded. The ambassador had shadows under his eyes, which was unusual for him. "I'm not sure how we can use this information. Especially since you didn't actually find Jack."

Kittie pursed her lips. "We may not have found Jack last night, but I'll see what I can do about that today."

Blaise looked at the Pyromancer in alarm. "Is that a good idea?"

Kittie regarded the Breaker with a cool look, and when she spoke, her tone was gentle. Proof that she understood Blaise's nerves. "He's my *husband*. What would you do if Jefferson vanished without a trace?"

There was a time when Vixen knew it wouldn't have occurred to Blaise to go after the other man. But that time had come and gone. The Breaker didn't hesitate. "I'd search for him from one sea to the other."

"So, you understand," Kittie said, to which Blaise nodded, though he still didn't look happy about it. She turned to Vixen. "If I can find Jack, I suspect he'll have ideas about Raven. He might have even learned something."

Vixen didn't doubt that. The problem was she feared the Firebrand might not find Jack. They couldn't rely on the missing Effigest to be of help in any of this. But she also recognized it was a fool's errand to dissuade Kittie.

"Right. Kittie will search for Jack." Vixen blew out a breath. "And we'll attend the gala tonight."

She didn't enjoy thinking about the gala. Vixen stood on the precipice between her old life and her outlaw life. She touched a hand to the pocket that held the enchanted ring. After tonight, she wouldn't stay at Hawthorne House with her friends. And she didn't know what she would do about Alekon. Vixen couldn't bear to part with him, but he was a pegasus. He was in danger if he stayed in Phinora long term. A pegasus would be a tempting addition to an elite menagerie.

"Vixen?"

She blinked. Kittie had risen from the table to head off on her quest to find her husband. Jefferson and Blaise had been speaking and must have asked her something. "Sorry. I was distracted. What?"

"I asked if you knew who's invited tonight. I would assume all the Phinoran elite, but since this is secular..." Jefferson drifted off, waving a hand.

Right, even though Jefferson hailed from the Confederation, he wouldn't know all the ins and outs of the Luminary's traditions. "Yes, this will be celebratory, so most of the guests will be elite or dignitaries." Gods, Vixen didn't like the thought of being around the elite. If they knew about her magic... She wet her lips, setting that worry aside. "The Reclamation Ceremony will be held in the Asaphenia, and everyone is invited to that, regardless of station." Entry to the ceremony would be a frenzy, but that wasn't something she had to worry about.

She'd have a front-row seat.

"Do we have to go to that?" Blaise asked, his voice almost a whine.

The Breaker wouldn't like the Reclamation Ceremony. If they kept to tradition, it would involve the spilling of blood. She saw Jefferson was about to speak, but she shot him a look to quell his tongue. "You don't have to go to the Reclamation Ceremony if you don't want to."

Blaise rubbed his arm, the one with the dead geasa tattoo and the long, pale scar. "I feel like an awful friend, not wanting to be there for you."

Vixen shook her head. "You came here all the way from the Gutter, and you didn't have to. You're a damn good friend."

He gave her a wan smile. She didn't miss the way his gaze flicked to Jefferson. Vixen knew Jefferson was the real reason Blaise had come, and she didn't begrudge either of them. She stood by her words. Blaise *was* a damn good friend.

"But we *will* be at the gala," Jefferson said. "And this may be one of our best opportunities to learn about any ongoing plots."

"How are we going to find out anything?" Blaise asked.

Jefferson grinned. "You forget, I can be quite charming."

"And you attract trouble," Blaise added.

The Dreamer slung an arm around Blaise's shoulders. "It's a gala. What could possibly go wrong?"

CHAPTER THIRTY-ONE

Slaughterhouse Tour

Kittie

Kittie's strides were resolute as she headed to the stables. She still wasn't at her best, but there was no way in Perdition she was going to sit around like a fragile flower with her husband missing. Especially after that same husband had left her in the dust. *Jackass.*

All four pegasi were out in the paddocks, grazing together. Their heads lifted at her approach, swishing their tails. <Jefferson did not find your mate,> Zepheus said, voice mournful. Kittie supposed Emrys or Seledora had already shared the news.

"No, he didn't," Kittie agreed, the old pain of loss searing deep inside. A reminder of the time she had thought she'd lost her family forever. A time when losing herself to the oblivion of alcohol had been the answer. And damn, that was tempting at the moment. Oh, what she wouldn't do for a cup of caladrius root tea right now. She shook her head, refocusing. "But I'm going to go after him."

The palomino's ears swung toward her with interest, though indecision warred in his rich brown eyes. He wanted to go with her, but his instinctive fear of fire won out. Kittie understood, though her heart twinged once more at the pegasus's fear of her.

<I'm sorry.> Zepheus lowered his head. Kittie noticed a sheen of sweat on his neck. He was agitated, and going with her wouldn't help, even though he wanted Jack returned as badly as she did.

"I won't be alone." She patted her pocket, then pulled out an earthen fire pot. "I have Najaria."

At that, the pegasi shifted nervously. They had a healthy respect for the aethon's potential inferno. <An elemental in Phinora may be a risk,> Zepheus said after a moment.

Oh, she knew. But Kittie also had a lot of faith in her unusual equine. "She'll keep to her harmless state, I'm certain." Unless they needed fire. "As far as anyone who sees us will know, she's only a chestnut mare. And I need her to help me find Jack." Kittie's mind drifted back to Fortitude, where the aethon had led them to the fire pit with the burned papers. Najaria knew something.

Kittie picked up additional information from Zepheus about the slaughterhouse. Unfortunately, Jefferson hadn't been able to figure out where the estate house was, so the slaughterhouse was the best place to start. Once she had gleaned everything from the palomino that she could, Kittie opened the fire pot to release the mare.

A plume of smoke curled over the lip, billowing into the form of a pawing chestnut mare. Najaria regarded Kittie with bright eyes, twisting her head around to snap her teeth at the pegasi.

"Behave," Kittie murmured, stroking the elemental's sleek neck. "You'll have to wear a saddle and bridle." The mare snorted in annoyance.

<I believe there are spares in the tack room,> Seledora said. Of the pegasi, she was the least nervous around Najaria. Perhaps because they were both mares.

The Pyromancer headed for the tack room, Najaria clopping alongside. Seledora was right. There were saddles and bridles there, though they were not at all the sort outlaws used. Jack called them pancakes, as they were flatter and more rounded than the outlaw saddles, and they lacked the horn. Fortunately, Kittie was quite familiar with the Confederation saddle, so it made little difference to her.

The elemental hated being saddled. The entire time Kittie tacked her up, the mare's ears lay flat against her skull, and she stomped a rear hoof to display her agitation. Kittie knew Najaria would settle once the task was complete. She found a bitless bridle, and a short time later, Kittie and her aethon set out on their hunt.

Kittie wished Emmaline had come with them. The young Effigest had a talent for finding people, and Kittie felt certain her daughter would have been able to narrow down Jack's location. But as it was, Kittie would have to go about things the old-fashioned way: making inquiries and using every trick she could think of to get results.

While they didn't know where Jack was, Blaise had given her a name to work with: Jeremiah Jones. Kittie repeated his name over and over in her head like a mantra. Maybe if she thought about him enough, he'd be easier to locate.

A mundane horse might have grown nervous approaching the slaughterhouse, but not Najaria. The reek of death clung to the area like a fog. Livestock milled in the pens, their anxious sounds filling the air. There wasn't a pig, sheep, or cow on the premises unaware of their fate. Kittie swallowed as she rode past a bleating sheep, keeping her eyes focused ahead.

The slaughterhouse was so much larger than she had expected. It was a massive building with stockyards butting up to it. The building had a lovely stone facade topped with dainty cupolas, as if the architect had tried to make the building of death into something classy and modern. They had tried but ultimately failed.

A man came out of the slaughterhouse gates. He squinted at her. "It's not time for tours, miss."

Tours? Kittie flicked a glance at the slaughterhouse. Who in their right mind would seek to tour a slaughterhouse? But she answered her own question—she knew. There were many in the Confederation who would see nothing wrong with witnessing the spectacle of slaughter. While Kittie had no issues with eating meat, she disliked the idea of the process turned into some sort of deranged entertainment.

Burn. Najaria pawed at the ground. The aethon couldn't communicate like the pegasi, but she had a way of getting across her ideas. And right now, the mare was very interested in the idea of burning the slaughterhouse to the ground. A picture flashed in Kittie's mind of the aethon fully engulfed as she raced through the structure, setting it ablaze.

As tempting as that was, it wasn't their purpose. Kittie cleared her throat, drawing on all the bravado her younger self had possessed. "I'm not here for a tour. I'm here to see Jeremiah Jones."

The man frowned. He scratched his forehead and inadvertently left a line of dirt on his brow. "Huh. Didn't know he had any business today. You can come in."

"No, I won't be leaving my mount," Kittie said quickly. Then she cleared her throat, realizing she had spoken too forcefully. "The stink of death makes her nervous."

Najaria snorted, annoyed by the lie. The man appeared not to notice and nodded. "Right. I'll see if he'll come out."

A few minutes later, a man strode out to meet them. Kittie licked her lips, keeping her inner fire under wraps. She had dismounted while she waited, and now she pasted a pleasant smile on her face. Let him think her soft and weak. "Mr. Jones. Thank you so much for meeting with me."

He regarded her with curiosity. "You're welcome. I wasn't expecting anyone today. Are you here for a contract?" Jones nodded toward the slaughterhouse.

"I'm here to make a deal, yes," Kittie agreed. She glanced away. "Could we walk a bit? I need to stretch after being in the saddle."

"Of course, Miss...?"

"Larue," Kittie supplied, using her birth name. "Kittie Larue."

So far, so good. Kittie started at a sedate walk, Najaria trailing along as if she were a stolid pony. When they were a healthy distance from the abattoir's entrance, Kittie started. "I'm here to speak with you because I have it on good authority you can provide the information I need."

Jones hesitated. "I'm not sure what you're after. I run the slaughterhouse."

"Mmm, you do." Kittie turned, looking at the modern facade in the distance. "And yet, I suspect there's more here than meets the eye."

He scowled. "Are you a reporter with the *Izhadell Tribune*? I've already told you people, I have nothing to say about my business. Especially after the last reporter *disappeared*."

A chill threaded down her spine. There were so many horrifying ways a slaughterhouse worker could make someone disappear. That only solidified her suspicion that this man was up to no good, especially if he didn't want a journalist looking into his work.

Kittie shook her head as she started walking again. They passed a pen of milling cattle. "No. I'm looking for someone who's missing, and you're one of the last people he saw." It was a guess, but she figured it was a worthwhile bluff.

The slaughterhouse worker laughed, turning to lean against the stockyard fence. "That so? This wouldn't be the first time someone has accused me of running a troublemaker through the works."

Her rage wanted to roar up like an inferno, but Kittie kept it corralled like a cheerful hearth fire. If Jack had met his end inside this slaughterhouse... No, she couldn't think that. He wasn't dead. Couldn't be dead, not to a man like this. Jones was trying to prod her into making a mistake, and she couldn't allow that.

"I'm looking for a man with blonde hair. Mid-forties. Dresses like an outlaw and has an attitude to match."

Jones's bravado wavered for a beat, a clear tell that he knew who she meant. Then he shrugged. "Can't say I've seen anyone who looks like that."

"I think you have," she challenged.

He moved fast, closing the distance between them and grabbing Kittie's wrists. A dark chain shot up from the ground, wrapping around her right leg. His face twisted into a snarl as Najaria flung up her head, nostrils flaring in alarm, issuing a warning whinny. Jones ignored the mare, focusing on the person he hoped to intimidate. "Listen, woman—"

Kittie bared her teeth at him. "No, *you* listen. You don't know who you're dealing with." His dirt-encrusted nails gouged her skin, but she didn't break his grip. Not yet. She glanced over his shoulder, catching sight of a steer that stood nearby, tail swishing away the cloud of flies that harried it. The Firebrand's brow furrowed as she focused on the tiny insects.

The steer bellowed in terror as the swarm of flies turned into a mass of burning embers. The nearby cows heard the cry and caught the scent of smoke. They rushed to clump on the far side of the pen, pressing against the boards of the fence, the lumber groaning under the pressure. Jones twisted to look over his shoulder, eyes widening when he saw the smoldering flecks that had once been horseflies.

"What?" he gasped, voice almost a squeak.

"Tell me what you know about the outlaw, or I'll burn you from the inside out," Kittie growled, her eyes sparking with anger. She snapped her fingers, almost an afterthought, and sent a gout of flame into the arcane cuff Jones had used to bind her. The metal fell away like slag.

He released her, stumbling away. Jones trembled, and for a moment, he looked like he might consider fleeing. But Najaria stood nearby, pawing the ground, eager for a chase. No living man could escape the aethon's flashfire, and Kittie had a decent range on her fire. He would be ashes before he made it to the safety of the slaughterhouse.

"The outlaw...he was here. The other mage nabbed him, though." Jones swallowed, his eyes wide with terror.

Good. He had a respect for fire. "What other mage?"

Jones shook his head. "I don't know. Black hair. Didn't say much, but he's working for the same woman I am." Then the slaughterhouse worker realized he'd said too much, biting down on his lower lip.

"Who do you work for?" Kittie demanded.

"I don't know the name. I just know she has money. One of the elite. Rents a house nearby. The boys took the outlaw there."

Kittie's pulse raced. That was just the sort of lead she'd been hoping for. "Take me there."

Jones shook his head. "No. I can't."

Kittie pulled on her magic, lifting her right hand. Flames danced in her palm. She curled her fingers around them, then smiled as they lazily licked up the length of her arm like a fiery snake. The flames settled around her shoulders like a brightly burning shawl. Kittie said nothing, just watched him while the fire crackled cheerfully.

"I...I can tell you how to get there," Jones hazarded.

She canted her head, considering. Kittie glanced at Najaria. The mare bobbed her head. Maybe she was right. Traveling with this man might be more trouble than it was worth. "Do that."

Moments later, Kittie had directions. She met Jones's eyes before she dismissed him. "If these directions are wrong, if you have betrayed me, I'll burn this slaughterhouse to the ground with you inside of it, hanging from a meat hook. Do you understand?"

He stared at her in disbelief, then anger clouded his face. No doubt hazing his healthy fear of her. "You bitch—"

Najaria pinned her ears, her mane and tail igniting. Fire caressed the edges of her hooves, dangerous sparks lighting her eyes. Her head snaked toward the man, teeth bared as she bit his shoulder, lifting him up and shaking him like a terrier with a rat. Jones screeched in agony and fear, collapsing in a whining heap when the aethon released him.

Kittie stood over the fallen man. "Consider yourself lucky she only bit you. We both could have done much worse. This is a warning." She turned to mount as Najaria's mane and tail returned to thick horsehair, and once she was in the saddle, she glanced back at the man who was staggering to his feet. One arm was clapped to his wounded shoulder. "Thank you for the information and directions, by the way."

Najaria was already on her way when he shouted a litany of curses in their wake. Kittie smiled, satisfied. She knew well that the man's pride was battered, in addition to his flesh.

An hour and two wrong turns later, they found the residence Jones had described. Najaria ambled down the road outside it while Kittie considered what to do. She couldn't get inside. But the aethon was another matter.

Kittie asked Najaria to move off the road, into a copse of trees. She had an idea. "You are fire. Can you become part of the fire that's in the house, possibly eavesdrop?"

The mare tilted her head, ears flicking with uncertainty, telegraphing that she didn't understand the question.

Right, fire elementals had little knowledge of something like this— especially one like Najaria, who had been imprisoned for so long. "That means you would go in there and listen. Or look, if you can. I don't know what it's like for you when you're pure fire. Can you see?" Najaria bobbed her head to say that she could. "Good. Perhaps if they use any lanterns instead of mage-lights, you can keep an eye out for Raven? Or whoever the elite is that he's working with?" Though how Najaria would communicate that, she didn't know.

The mare blew out a soft breath, then turned to nudge the leather of the saddle. Oh, good plan. Wouldn't do to burn up the tack when she went full flame. Kittie hurriedly removed the saddle and bridle, stowing them nearby.

"I'll wait here."

Najaria nuzzled her affectionately, then stepped away, arching her neck. The mare reared, her body dissipating into a puff of smoke. The smoke wafted away on the light breeze, though it didn't follow the course of the wind. It undulated toward the fence surrounding the house and then flitted up to the chimney.

CHAPTER THIRTY-TWO

Passive Aggression

Once they finished making plans, Jefferson drifted back to bed, his handsome face lined with exhaustion. Blaise transitioned to a flurry of nervous baking, which Vixen didn't complain about because everything he made was mouth-wateringly delicious and filled the house with sweet, yeasty scents. Nibbling on an assortment of cookies, muffins, and tarts was a pleasant distraction from what was coming.

Mid-afternoon, Blaise headed upstairs to rouse Jefferson so that they could dress for the gala. Vixen went to her own guest room, sighing as she regarded the lovely dress that had been delivered late that morning. It was a striking emerald green, a color that would bring out the vibrant red of her hair. But the fact remained that it was a dress, and Vixen didn't much care for them. Trousers were much more comfortable.

She chewed on her bottom lip, reconsidering. While she might have to return to her former life, Vixen had changed—and wouldn't it be fitting for some of those changes to come with her? With a nod, she decided she liked the idea. Her reintroduction was going to cause a ruckus, so she may as well run with it in her own way.

And in that case, she had just the thing. Vixen grinned as she popped open her travel trunk. In all the chaos of their arrival, she hadn't even unpacked. She dug around and pulled out the outfit she'd finished back in Fortitude shortly before they'd left. The fabric of the corset had wrinkled, but that was something she could fix.

"Gods, this will be almost scandalous," Vixen murmured to herself, running a hand over the silky ruffles of the short skirt. But something about it felt right. As the Spark, she'd always been told to trust her gut. That Garus had given her the wisdom to find her way. There had been many times she'd doubted that after she'd discovered she was a mage. But now, in this moment, Vixen wanted to believe that the god she'd been born to represent approved.

She remedied the wrinkled fabric, then set about dressing. Vixen paired it with some flattering striped trousers she'd brought along. They clung to her shape in a manner that a proper Confederation woman would disdain. *I'm not a proper Confederation woman, though.* That thought made her smile.

To complete the outfit, Vixen pulled out her knee-high riding boots. They were dusty and scuffed from use. That wouldn't do—if she showed up with footwear in such a state, she'd lose any advantage this was giving her. She visited Blaise and Jefferson's room to inquire after boot polish. With her prize in hand, Vixen headed back to her room to clean and polish the leather until it gleamed.

Once the boots were on, she saw to her hair and rouged her lips. Then she studied her reflection in the floor-length mirror, swallowing. The creature staring back at her was a cross between the Valoria of old and the Vixen of now. She lifted her chin, deciding that she liked the woman staring back at her. A blend of Phinoran and outlaw.

She stepped out into the hallway and headed downstairs to where Blaise and Jefferson waited in the parlor. She heard them discussing the Breaker's ensemble—Blaise was apparently unhappy with the puff tie his beau had selected for him.

"But it completes the *look.*" Jefferson gestured to encompass all of Blaise as she entered. He glanced over his shoulder at the sound of her boot heels on the hardwood floor. His eyebrows lifted with appreciation. "Well, *hello* there. That's quite a striking outfit."

Vixen grinned. "I decided that even if I'm returning to my old life, I'm a different person now, and I should remind everyone of that."

"It works," Jefferson said, his voice husky. Blaise jabbed him with an elbow. "What? You don't need to be jealous."

"I'm not *jealous,*" Blaise grumbled, in exactly the manner of someone who was, in fact, a little jealous. Or maybe not jealous, Vixen decided. *Anxious.*

Jefferson heard it, too. His focus shifted to Blaise, stepping closer to take his hands. "Good, since you have absolutely no reason to be jealous. You look magnificent, puff tie and all."

"The word *puff* should only be used with pastries." Despite his observation, Blaise seemed mollified.

"Noted," Jefferson said, eyes twinkling.

Blaise tugged at the offending puff tie, though now his gaze had fallen on Vixen. "I guess he's right. You *do* look nice."

Vixen grinned. From Blaise, that was high praise. He didn't concern himself with how other people looked all that often, not like his beau. Now, if she'd been bearing a tray of cupcakes, then she'd have his complete attention as he dissected how they were made and what he thought about them.

"She'll be the talk of the town by the time the night is done," Jefferson said. Then he cocked his head. "Our coach will be here soon. Are you ready for what's coming?"

"No. Can I stay here?" Blaise asked.

Jefferson nudged Blaise's side. "You very well know I wasn't talking to you."

Vixen was going to miss their banter. She took a breath to steady herself, then nodded. "What other choice do I have?"

"You always have a choice." Blaise's voice was soft, almost a whisper. Jefferson had a contemplative look on his face, but he nodded in agreement. "If you don't want to do this, we can figure something else out."

Vixen shook her head. "It's too late for that now." She heaved a breath. "But I can do this. I have my friends beside me."

Her words influenced Blaise. She saw his spine straighten, a determined jut in his jaw. "You do."

<There is a coach coming up the drive,> Alekon informed her, his tone neutral. Vixen knew he wasn't happy about being unable to accompany her to the gala, though the pegasus was relieved the other mages would be with her. <Will you come see me before you go?>

His request was heartbreaking, as if the bay stallion expected to never see her again. Like she was abandoning him. Vixen swallowed a lump in her throat, knowing she would do everything in her power to prevent it, but it may not be enough.

"Our ride is here, but I need to stop by the stables for a moment," Vixen said.

"There's a tin of cookies on the kitchen counter," Blaise offered.

"Thank you. I'll be at the coach shortly." Vixen headed out, her boot heels ringing on the floor as she went to snag the cookies that were the only solace she could offer her best friend right now.

Blaise

"Now I know how the animals in a menagerie feel," Blaise murmured to Jefferson as yet another elite couple drifted away after a stilted conversation instigated purely so they could goggle at the Breaker.

"Not that it will make you feel any better, but at a gala like this, everyone is on display to some extent. Not just you," Jefferson said, voice soft. He pressed a reassuring hand against the small of Blaise's back.

"Do you have any good conversation stoppers?" Blaise asked, trying to hide a grimace as another couple strode toward them.

"Don't you mean starters?"

"No. Definitely stoppers." Then Blaise had no choice but to paste on a smile as the approaching woman cooed about meeting *the* Breaker. Maybe he should take another look at the Ravanchen grimoire. There had to be an invisibility spell, right? Or maybe he could figure out how Jack cast his Obfuscation spell.

When they had arrived for the gala at Dawnlight, the official residence of the Luminary, attendants had whisked Vixen off to meet with the Luminary. Guards in the gold and white uniforms of the Luminary's Lightguard escorted Blaise and Jefferson to the front entry, where Blaise discovered that this was an important enough affair to warrant an announcement of each guest's arrival. Or at least the guests who mattered, according to Jefferson. Apparently, *they* mattered. Blaise had hated every second of those eyes on him, and he had definitely entertained the idea of running away to live the rest of his days in the surrounding swamps. Swamp hermits didn't have to endure the predatory gazes of a hundred elite men and women.

Jefferson had been right about one thing: the other elite barely tolerated the Dreamer's presence there. Whenever they approached, they shot cutting looks at him. The worst part was that they were mostly civil to Jefferson, but there was a level of antagonism to their words and gestures that even Blaise—who knew he still sorely lacked in his understanding of social interactions—could detect.

"Why are they behaving like that to you?" Blaise asked.

"Like what? Oh." Jefferson linked an arm through his, starting on a casual stroll. "They're being passive-aggressive."

"I don't like it."

Jefferson chuckled. "Nor do I, but their words and pettiness can't harm me anymore. They're not—" He stopped walking. "Blast."

"What?" Blaise felt the sudden stiffness of Jefferson's biceps against his as the Dreamer's muscles tensed.

Jefferson stared across the vast room. "Tara Woodrow is over in the far corner speaking with Phillip Dillon."

The names were vaguely familiar to Blaise, but he hadn't seen either person before, so only knew of them from Jefferson. "Quiet Ones?"

"Yes." Jefferson pursed his lips.

Nothing set them apart from the other attendees at the gala. If Jefferson hadn't pointed them out, Blaise would have thought they were just another set of wealthy blowhards. He chewed his lip as he thought back to the things Jefferson had told him about the Gutter delegation's time in Nera. Woodrow was the woman who had dosed Kittie's drink in a bid to have the Firebrand blamed for a deadly fire. And Dillon? He was the one who had orchestrated the campaign that had drained Jefferson's fortunes, poking holes in his preferred identity. He was dangerous in a way Blaise didn't understand, wielding power, wealth, and influence.

"Should we leave?" Blaise asked. He disliked the idea of Jefferson being around people who had hurt him in a manner Blaise could do little to fight.

Jefferson shook his head. "No, we need to be here. They haven't even introduced Vixen yet. Besides, if we leave, they win."

Blaise considered this. He didn't enjoy backing down, but sometimes it was the safest idea. But Jefferson had a better grasp of the undercurrents of the gala, so he trusted in him.

He didn't have long to ponder. Someone squealed nearby. "Blaise Hawthorne! I *thought* I heard them announce your name!"

When Blaise turned, he couldn't help but smile because he knew the woman hurrying over to them—and more than that, he *liked* her. Lizzie Jennings grinned at him, her eyes dancing. "Oh, howdy, Lizzie."

She gave him a friendly pat on the arm, which Blaise made himself tolerate, knowing she meant well. Although she was the woman behind the award-winning musical about his life, there were some things she didn't know—his dislike of being touched by most people, for one.

"It's so good to see you again." Then she turned her attention to Jefferson, crossing her arms. "And *you*. I have mixed feelings about you."

Jefferson spread his hands. "You and everyone else, it seems."

Blaise canted his head. "How's your writing going, Lizzie? Anything new in the works?"

The playwright—no, that was the wrong word; Jefferson said she was a *librettist*—sighed at the question. "It's not gone well. I've lacked inspiration since *Breaker* debuted. And now I'm afraid I don't have another in me. It's as if my creative well has dried up."

Blaise nodded, careful to keep his expression neutral. "That's too bad. Have you considered something about…oh, I don't know…a politician who secretly moonlights as an entrepreneur and mage?"

Jefferson made a choking cough at the suggestion. Blaise met his gaze and winked before refocusing on Lizzie.

She raised her eyebrows. "Are you...wait, you're suggesting the Malcolm Wells story?"

"Maybe."

A sideways glance at Jefferson proved he was a conflicted blend of flustered, appreciative, and embarrassed. It was an unusual combination on the Dreamer, and it made Blaise chuckle. The gala was getting better.

"Hmm." Lizzie's eyes flicked over Jefferson. "I hadn't thought about that, but...yes, that would be the natural successor, wouldn't it?"

"Does this mean I'm forgiven?" Jefferson asked, canting his head and offering an endearing smile.

Lizzie scoffed. "You were duplicitous to not *only* the entire Salt-Iron Council, which includes my darling husband, but also *me*. Just because I think you might make an interesting subject, doesn't mean you're *forgiven.*"

She might be annoyed now, but Blaise didn't think she'd stay that way for long. Especially if she sat down and talked to Jefferson the same way she had Blaise and uncovered why the Dreamer had behaved as he did. Malcolm Wells might have been born among the elite, but nothing about his life had been pleasant.

"I forgave him," Blaise pointed out, his voice gentle.

Lizzie nodded. "I suppose you did. Well, what do you say, Mr. Cole? Shall I plan to speak to you some time for this production?"

"It would be an honor," Jefferson said, inclining his head graciously.

A few moments later, the librettist hurried off in search of her husband. Once she was a distance away, the Dreamer edged closer to Blaise.

"You can be quite the cunning schemer when you want to be." Jefferson's voice was husky, caught somewhere between deep gratitude and amazement.

"Consider it retribution," Blaise said, though they both knew it wasn't retaliatory in the least.

"Do you want to dance?" Jefferson had frozen again, staring over Blaise's shoulder.

The question caught Blaise off guard. He blinked, confused. "What?"

"Dance. I asked if you wanted to dance," Jefferson repeated. His green eyes flicked back to Blaise, troubled. "Because Phillip Dillon is walking this way."

Of all the things to do, dancing wasn't high on Blaise's list, but he didn't want to allow Dillon a chance to corner and threaten Jefferson. "I'm going to step on your feet."

Relief washed over Jefferson's face. "No, you won't. And even if you do, I'll forgive you. Come on." He took Blaise's hand, tugging him to the dance floor full of swirling couples.

Blaise felt awkward, and a glance at the surrounding men and women who clearly knew how to move to the music did nothing to ease his anxiety. But Jefferson wrapped his right arm around Blaise, pulling him near. The Dreamer twined the fingers of his left hand with Blaise's right, the simple gesture doing much to ground Blaise. For a heartbeat, it was just the two of them, close and comfortable. Safe.

The music seemed to curl around them, and though Blaise didn't know how to do much more than sway with the beat, even he had to admit there was almost something magical about it.

"See? We don't have to do anything fancy," Jefferson murmured, leading Blaise to the left to avoid an oncoming couple. "Though if you'd like to learn to dance one day, I'd be happy to show you."

If anyone else had made the offer, Blaise would have immediately rejected it. But it was Jefferson, so he smiled. "I'll think about it."

"Ah, so that's a no." Jefferson's full attention was on Blaise, as if he hoped that in doing so, he could evade the notice of the Quiet Ones.

"That's not what I said, and you know it." Blaise leaned in to brush his lips against Jefferson's. The Dreamer's soft exhalation of welcome rewarded him.

Their kiss was short-lived. The music stopped, and somewhere a bell rang with a clarion chime, drawing everyone's attention. Blaise drew away from Jefferson, but only enough to see what was afoot. The man he thought was Phillip Dillon stood about ten feet away, speaking with someone, though his gaze flicked from Jefferson to the far side of the room.

"What's going on?" Blaise asked.

"That sound means an *entrance*," Jefferson explained. The way he stressed the last word made Blaise think this would be someone noteworthy.

He wasn't wrong. It took Blaise a moment to figure out where he should look, but then he saw people herded out of the way by the Lightguard. "Make way for the Light of our Land, the living avatar of Garus, our Luminary." The herald's words echoed across the room, followed by murmurs of anticipation.

The woman who strode in with an entourage didn't look like anyone special to Blaise, but then again, he was a poor judge of such things. She looked much like the other elite women in the room, her strawberry blonde hair twisted into an artful braid that was piled atop her head. The Luminary wore a dress made of rippling gold fabric with ivory embellishments. Blaise assumed it was probably very expensive—if he had to guess, the outfit was probably worth more than everything in the town of Fortitude.

He caught sight of Vixen trailing in the Luminary's wake, though she wore some sort of flowy frock coat that hid her attention-grabbing outfit. The Persuader kept her head down, as if willing the crowd to ignore her. With the flashy Luminary preceding her, no one gave Vixen a second look.

"So the games begin," Jefferson whispered.

"You're enjoying this," Blaise accused.

The Dreamer chuckled. "Guilty. Though having you in my arms is half the fun." With reluctance, he released Blaise. "Unfortunately, this means we'll be seated for the meal before any further dance opportunities."

Blaise's cheeks warmed with pleasure. While the gala wasn't the sort of entertainment he would choose to attend on his own, he enjoyed being with Jefferson. He cleared his throat. "Food isn't a bad idea."

The elite milled toward the tables arranged on one side of the room. Blaise thought for a moment that the seating was assigned, judging by the way the men and women examined the options before claiming a chair. But as they drew closer, he realized it must be subtle political and social posturing. Jefferson guided them to the table where Lizzie and her husband, Seward, sat, but a rush of elite claimed the free chairs first, forcing them to a nearby table where a middle-aged couple sat.

Oddly, as soon as Blaise and Jefferson selected their seats, the man and woman made hasty excuses to find another table. Blaise frowned. "Is this because of how they feel about you specifically? Or because they don't like mages in general?"

Jefferson studied the other elite as they slotted themselves into their seats. "Perhaps, but I suspect something else is going on."

A shadow loomed over the chair beside Blaise, confirming the Dreamer's suspicion. "Is this seat taken?"

It took every bit of self-control Blaise could muster to keep from reacting as he glanced over his shoulder at Phillip Dillon. The man had salt-and-pepper hair and a handsome face that was lined with stately wrinkles. He looked down at the pair of mages as if they were rabbits caught in a snare. Blaise knew a bully when he saw one. The palm of his left hand grew warm and fuzzy as his magic manifested. No, that wouldn't do. He took a breath and forced the power away.

"I can't say that it is," Jefferson answered, somehow keeping all the earlier tension from his voice. His hand moved to settle on Blaise's thigh —whether in warning or as a show of solidarity, Blaise didn't know.

Phillip Dillon pulled out a chair, offering it to the woman accompanying him. Once she sat, he moved to claim the chair beside Jefferson.

"Thank you, Phillip. You're too kind." She batted her eyelashes, though there was something hollow about the gesture and words. Then she turned her attention to Jefferson. "So good to see you again. You certainly made quite an exit the last time we saw you."

Blaise could have cut the tension with a butter knife. Jefferson's eyes had narrowed, his mind no doubt whirring through possibilities. Blaise didn't know what his love might say, but he couldn't sit here and let these elite spout their abuses. "Howdy. I don't believe we've met. I'm Breaker Blaise Hawthorne." He felt Jefferson's zing of surprise at the sally.

Phillip's mouth drew taut. "We're well aware that Jefferson brought his pet mage along."

The Quiet One aimed the words with the same devastating precision Jack used with his sixgun. The intent was clear: Blaise was as easy to dismiss as the carriage horses that had brought them to the event. Useful, but ultimately irrelevant. Jefferson's anger was almost a palpable thing, his hand tightening on Blaise's leg.

Tara, the woman, waved a hand as if hoping to clear the air. "Really, Phillip, there's no need for such savagery." The smile she flaunted belied her true sentiment. "We leave that to the *outlaws*." Her expression shifted into blissful innocence. "Honestly, we're surprised to see you at an event such as this. You've fallen so far out of favor, *Malcolm*—or, my apologies, you prefer Jefferson, now, do you not?"

"I do." Jefferson's voice was gravelly with warning. Blaise hated this. They were picking at Jefferson piece by piece, trying to crack his armor with their comments. Blaise had the sinking suspicion that this was going to be a very long, tense night.

CHAPTER THIRTY-THREE
Realm of Shadows

Jack

Damn Raven, but moments after the mage left, true darkness descended over Jack. Even worse, he realized that this realm, whatever it was, drifted—similar to the way shadows shifted as the sun changed position. The surrounding area was perfectly silent, and he only discovered the strange movement by the sensation of it veering beneath him, as if he were on a raft in the world's slowest river. If the world's slowest river was made entirely of shadow.

With effort, he eased in what he thought was the knife's direction, but after a short time, he realized that it, too, had shifted with the flow of shadows. Cursing Raven, the mage's parents, and all the generations that came before, Jack butt-scooted around the shadowy realm, hoping he would blunder into the knife without slashing himself in the process.

He was sweating by the time his thigh brushed against something. With a grunt of surprise, the Effigest angled his body until he could grope at the object with one hand. The whisper of cool, flat metal against his index finger revealed he had finally succeeded.

Cutting himself free proved to be a challenge. It was a difficult enough task with his hands tied behind his back, aching and sore, and the challenge only increased with the ever-present darkness and the way the shadows gradually drew the knife away from him when he fumbled and dropped it. Jack muttered a litany of curses. "Son of a five-legged chupacabra. Fizzlin' piece of dragonshit. Yellow-bellied Saltie-lovin' maggot…" It didn't help, but it made him feel better.

By the time his bonds frayed enough to release his hands, Jack was winded from the effort. He winced, flexing his shoulders as he massaged his wrists. His arms hurt, but he wasn't in a situation where he could sit around and wait to feel better.

He groped around in search of the mage-light. It had been further away, thus took longer to locate. But find it he did, and he breathed a sigh of relief as the soft blue glow illuminated the surrounding area.

Jack rubbed his chin, eyes narrowed as he surveyed the area. *What, exactly, is this place?* Was it something like the peacock's dreamscape? None of the magical theory he had been taught by his mentor or anyone in the Confederation covered something like this. Realms that existed within their own world. Was it an overlay of the real world, and he was in a shadowy version of that damned Quiet One's home? Or was it something else entirely? And did it even matter? Without sixgun, reagents, or anything to craft into a poppet, he was as helpless as an orphaned pegasus foal.

He had a knife, though. And his characteristic stubbornness. Raven had said not to try anything, but a large part of Jack wanted to bury a fist in the traitor's face the next time he saw him. But the odds were good that Raven was his only ticket out of here.

"Well, I ain't gonna figure out much of anything by staying put," Jack reasoned aloud. Didn't care that he might sound crazy speaking to himself. Who was around to judge him?

He shoved the knife in his belt and picked up the mage-light. Raven would probably come back eventually, but then what? Jack was unwilling to leave his fate up to the traitorous Shadowstepper. No, as always, he was going to do things his own way.

Mage-light in hand, he set off into the strange world of shadows.

***

Kittie

Not for the first time, Kittie wondered if elementals grasped time in the same way humans did. She waited and waited, the sun setting in the distance and her stomach rumbling, a reminder that she hadn't eaten since her breakfast at Hawthorne House. Had something happened to Najaria, ensnaring her somehow?

She pulled the small fire pot out, cupping it in her hands. Remnants of ash shifted within the confines of the enchanted clay. Kittie wondered if she could use the ashes to call the aethon back.

"Come on, horse. I'm getting hungry." Like the pegasi, Najaria didn't appreciate being called a common horse. Kittie hoped maybe the jab would bring the aethon back, but there was no sudden reappearance of the mare. So much for that idea.

Well, Kittie had lived in Phinora long enough to know a little about the place. The light was waning, but that wasn't much of a problem since she could provide her own light. Kittie summoned a ball of flame in her left hand, then foraged for any edible berries or roots. She came across a bush of late-season sun-gold jesterberries. They were a little on the mushy side and not as sweet as she would have liked, but it was something to fill her belly while she waited.

Kittie was wiping her berry juice-stained hands on her trousers when she felt a sudden change of pressure behind her. "Najaria, it's about time—"

She turned and found herself face to face with Raven Dawson. He held a knife in his hand, perilously close to her throat. Kittie swallowed. She'd seen him practice with his knives in Fortitude, and even Jack respected his speed and skill. Kittie knew she had a good chance of immolating him, but probably not before he dealt what would be a fatal blow. And that wouldn't help her find Jack.

"Jack shouldn't have brought you along," Raven said, but there was no malice in his words. Only regret, and maybe sadness. "Quench your fire."

Kittie met his eyes, hoping that Najaria would choose this as her moment to reappear and tip the odds in her favor. "It was *my* choice." She didn't extinguish her ball of flame.

"Put it out," Raven repeated.

The Firebrand weighed her options. She didn't want her throat slit, but she wasn't about to drop all of her defenses. She wasn't helpless. Kittie trembled with adrenaline, closing her hand around the crackling orb. The fire caressed her skin, and though she felt the heat, it didn't burn her. She focused on the fire, willing for the smallest spark to free itself. *Just one spark.*

There. The spark pulled free, leaping from her hand onto Raven's shirt.

The Ringleader did what almost anyone would do when confronted with an unexpected run-in with fire: he reacted. With a yelp, he jerked away from Kittie, taking the knife with him and leaving her skin unmarred. The spark caught the flammable fabric—

There was a soft pop, and he was gone, leaving the spark behind. It drifted to the ground and died out. Swallowing, Kittie whirled, surveying the surrounding area. He must have used his magic to escape the threat. A wise tactic, but now she didn't know where he was, which was infuriating.

"Cursed aethon, get back here," Kittie muttered, wishing the mare would return. But she couldn't wait any longer. Raven knew where she was, which made her vulnerable. She didn't know who he was working with, and he might have gone to get reinforcements. It was time to admit defeat and make her way back to Hawthorne House—if she could figure out her way there at night on foot. Regardless, her priority was getting out of this area. She headed for the road—

A hand clamped down on her shoulder. Before Kittie could whirl to meet him, the world swam around her in a dizzying spiral. Her gut roiled, even worse than cramps during her monthlies. She wanted to curl up into a ball, anything to get away from that feeling, but she couldn't. Kittie was pulled through inky darkness, helpless to do a damn thing about it.

When, at last, the world around her stopped, she was in an unfamiliar place. Shadows stretched for as far as she could see—which wasn't far. It was like being out in the middle of nowhere on a starless night. The only dim light came from Raven, who stood over her.

With her gut finally settling, Kittie glared up at him. She wouldn't get mouthy, not like Jack would, but she wouldn't roll over and take it, either. "Where in Perdition am I?"

Raven gave her that kicked-puppy look again. "I wish I didn't have to do this, but I can't have you interfering."

That wasn't any sort of answer at all. "Did you take Jack?"

He made a point not to meet her eyes. Kittie knew Jack got under most people's skin, so she would have expected some level of glee at getting one over him. But Raven only gave a resigned nod. "Yes."

Kittie weighed her options. She didn't know where she was or how to get back, so if she attacked the other mage, the odds were good she'd be trapped for a while. Maybe forever. But she wasn't hurt, even though he could have stabbed her or worse. And he was talking—a little, anyway. Maybe she could lure more information out of him.

"Why did you take Jack?"

Raven made a frustrated sound. "Same reason I took you. Because he *found* me."

Something in his tone made Kittie think that wasn't the only reason. But Raven crossed his arms, and she suspected she wouldn't get much more from him on that subject. "Whatever's happened, whatever's driven you to do this, doesn't have to be this way. Let us help you."

Raven shook his head. "That's the thing. You can't help—you *or* Jack." He took a step backward. "You asked where you are. This is my realm. I'll be back to check on you. When I return, don't think to attack me. You won't like how it ends." And with that dire warning, he vanished.

His realm? That surprised her—this was the first she'd heard of such a thing. But it made sense. A realm of shadows. The faint light that had existed faded with Raven's departure. With a sigh, Kittie called up her flame again.

Her fire came, but not only that—Najaria. The aethon shimmered into being along with the orb of fire on Kittie's palm, though the light provided by the fiery mare did little to penetrate the ever-present dark.

Kittie sighed. "Najaria! Where have you been all this time?"

The mare tossed her head, pinning her ears back in a sign that whatever the reason, she was unhappy. Kittie didn't know if that meant something had interfered with her, or if the aethon was simply frustrated that she had come too late. Regardless, it didn't help the situation.

The Pyromancer carefully got to her feet, bracing against the elemental. Her gut wasn't completely happy yet, but it was better than it had been. Either the berries had been bad, or Raven's method of travel disagreed with her. She suspected the latter.

Kittie met the mare's obsidian eyes. "Well, at least I'm not alone."

CHAPTER THIRTY-FOUR

A Flame to Light the Ages

Vixen

The food spread before Vixen was some of the finest fare she'd seen since the last Feast of Flight, but she had little appetite for it. It was hard to focus on eating when she knew that her life was about to change.

She sat at the head table, though not beside her mother. The Luminary had thought it best to sit apart until they made the announcement revealing the Spark was alive and well. The people around her were under orders not to speak to her, and Vixen had been advised not to start any conversations. The Luminary wanted to control the narrative of her daughter's return, and she didn't want any attendees to figure it out in advance.

Rhys was there, too, though only in his capacity as a Tracker. Vixen wondered if he felt left out, alienated from this world that could have been his. *Should* have been his. She was too far away to discern anything from his face, though he leaned against a wall with arms crossed, scanning the assembled mass for any sign of trouble.

Vixen found Jefferson and Blaise in the throng, seated with two others. Anyone else wouldn't have noticed anything amiss, but she knew Blaise. The Breaker fidgeted in his chair. Tension pooled in the shoulders of both men, and Vixen suspected it was because of their tablemates. She pursed her lips, wondering who they were. It was unfortunate she couldn't ask anyone around her.

After what felt like an eternity but was only an hour, the meal finished.

Vixen had forgotten how interminable these events could be. Perhaps Blaise's disdain for them was warranted. If she had a lifetime of these ahead of her, it might be a better option to run back to the Gutter for good. She held back a sigh.

The Luminary arrowed a look in her direction, chin lifting in a manner that communicated the time had come. Vixen's mother rose from the table gracefully, gliding over to a dais. Her golden gown shimmered with each step, catching the light. Murmurs rose as the elite noticed she was on the move. As she mounted the dais, all eyes shifted to the theocrat. Conversations waned and then died, the attendees giving her their full attention.

The Luminary smiled across the throng. Juliette Kildare wasn't a tall woman, but she had a presence that commanded their focus. "Honored guests, Garus truly smiles down upon us this night." She lifted her hands as if offering thanks to the absent god. "I appreciate all who took the time to attend tonight. I know you had little notice, and your steadfastness heartens me."

Vixen fought the urge to roll her eyes. As if anyone here would make the mistake of not attending a gala put on by the Luminary herself. Vixen may have been absent from elite society for years, but she knew few would be so foolish. Besides, the elite were no doubt dying to know what warranted the usually-reclusive theocrat to hold such a celebration.

"The time of the Luminary Festival is nearly upon us, which makes my news auspicious." Juliette's gaze flicked back to Vixen before roving over the masses again. "Garus has blessed us. His wisdom has granted us a veritable miracle—the return of Spark Valoria Kildare, the soul we thought lost forever to Perdition."

Her words seemed to suck the air from the room. Silence fell over the crowd, not even broken by the tinkling of glass or the rasp of flatware. The staff had gone as still and quiet as the guests. Vixen swallowed, rising from her seat and sweeping the plain robe off to reveal her modified outfit. Her boot heels shattered the silence, rapping on the stone floor like the blasts of a sixgun. Vixen liked to think she was bold, but with all of those prying eyes on her, she felt anything but. She quivered as she joined her mother, reflexively touching the ring that veiled her magic.

Juliette took her daughter's hand and lifted it high. "The Spark has returned! May her wisdom grow into a flame to light the ages!"

"Her wisdom will light the way!" the crowd responded. Many rose to their feet, applauding. Several women burst into tears, clutching at their chests as if they couldn't imagine a more beautiful scene. Others went to their knees in supplication.

Surrounded by hundreds of people, Vixen had never felt more alone.

Frozen in place on the dais, her eyes sought Blaise and Jefferson amid the throng. Jefferson's attention was on their seatmates, but the Breaker was watching her. He was just as helpless as she was, but his familiar face was like a watering hole in the Untamed Territory. An oasis for her survival. Vixen smiled at him, and her spirit soared when he tipped his chin, returning her smile with one of his own.

I'm not alone. I still have my friends. Thank Garus they had come with her. She couldn't have done this alone.

As quickly as it had come, the moment of reverie shattered. Questions boiled up from the elite, but none of them were loud enough to be anything more than murmurs. Vixen kept her head high, reminding herself why she was doing this. For the Gutter. For her friends. For the people she cared about. She lifted her chin, knowing that her flame-red hair made her stand out like a firefly in the night.

Juliette lifted her hands and the audience quieted. "Peace, my people. This is a time for celebration. Let us enjoy the night and all that Garus's wisdom had provided."

The Luminary returned to her seat with Vixen close behind. The others at the table shifted positions to allow Vixen a space beside her mother. Every bit of this felt like a half-remembered dream, the people around her familiar, but not. To her right sat Celestine Currington, a priestess on the Clergy Council. The older woman slanted a look at her, lips twisted into an expression that bespoke doubt.

"You should have let me speak," Vixen said to her mother, keeping her voice low.

"That would invite the rest of them to speak as well," Juliette pointed out, not even glancing at her daughter. "Besides, you'll have the opportunity to speak with them individually after the meal."

Wonderful. Vixen would rather face down a murder of half-starved chupacabras with her hands tied behind her back, but she would have to suffer through this. She fidgeted with the magic-concealing ring before going back to poking at the plate of food.

As the staff returned to take up empty plates, musicians returned to their instruments and the attendees drifted away from the tables. When the Luminary rose, Vixen took that has her cue to do likewise. Juliette nodded to her before stepping down to circulate among the faithful who crowded close to speak with her.

Vixen made her way down as well, and moments later found herself swarmed by the curious. They peppered her with questions, hands brushing against the fabric of her outfit. Their closeness and persistence made her want to scream for them to get away. Made her want to run, find Alekon, and never come back. She was remembering all the reasons she had left.

And a chance shifting of the crowd offered her a glance at Blaise, reminding her of all the reasons she had come back. *I can do this. It might not be what I want to do, but I can do it.*

So she smiled, answered their questions with all the patience she could muster, dancing around the circumstances of her disappearance, and carried on.

A sheen of nervous sweat had Vixen's clothing clinging to her by the time Blaise and Jefferson made it through the receiving line that had formed to meet her. It was late—or maybe early, since the clock had tipped past midnight. Jefferson leaned against Blaise, and for a moment, Vixen thought he was still tired. Until she realized he was tipsy.

"I don't think I've ever seen him drunk," Vixen commented to Blaise, suspecting that this wasn't a promising development.

"You look fabu..." Jefferson started, then paused as if he'd lost track of his words. "Fantas...amazing. Yes, *amazing*. That's the word." He aimed an index finger at Vixen, as if he wanted to be certain she knew who he meant.

Blaise made a frustrated noise. "We've got trouble."

Vixen pursed her lips, gaze shifting between the men. "What happened?"

"I can't use my magic right now," Jefferson declared loud enough to spur Blaise to slam a hand over his mouth.

"I really need you to be quiet right now," Blaise whispered to his beau, urgent.

"I'll be quiet if you kiss me." Jefferson puckered his lips and made a kissy sound.

"Why is he drunk?" Vixen hissed, deciding the Ambassador's inebriation must surely play a role in whatever new problem had arisen.

"It was the only way I could keep him from doing something we'd regret," Blaise explained, jerking a thumb toward Jefferson. Then he mouthed the single word: *magic*. "You saw who we sat with?" When Vixen nodded, he continued, "They're Quiet Ones. They were baiting us, and then once everyone had the chance to visit again, they've been planting rumors."

"Rumors?" Vixen glanced past Blaise to the remaining guests. She didn't miss the cool looks aimed her way. "What kind of rumors?" If she knew, she could head them off at the pass.

A flush of anger clouded Blaise's face for a moment. "All sorts, and none of them good. They said that you're not really the Spark, that this is just an outlaw trick. That you seek to undermine the Confederation. And that if you really *are* the Spark, outlaws must have been the ones to kidnap you." He paused, swallowing. "That the timing is too convenient, that we've only brought the once-dead Spark back to life when the Gutter is under a threat."

"Also that you're a soiled dove," Jefferson added, in his too-helpful drunken way.

"Also that," Blaise agreed grimly.

"Gods damn it," Vixen cursed. A nearby elite woman heard her and gasped in horror, clutching a hand to her breast. *Great. Blasphemy. That's sure to help matters.* "What did Jefferson want to do about it?"

"Drop Dillon and Woodrow in the dreamscape and terrorize them." Jefferson suddenly sounded less drunk and more menacing. Vixen was glad no one was near enough to hear his suggestion.

"He can do that?" she asked Blaise. The Breaker gave a tiny nod, something unreadable flickering across his expression.

"I don't know what we can do against this without..." Blaise flexed the fingers of his left hand, a wash of silvery magic playing across it as quick as a blink. So quickly, anyone else would have not believed their eyes.

Vixen mopped at her forehead. "We'll figure something out. I'll be in touch soon."

CHAPTER THIRTY-FIVE

Pity Party

Vixen

"What did you tell them?"

Vixen's spine was ramrod straight as she stared at the opposite wall, counting the number of stripes that decorated the wallpaper to help keep her composure. "Nothing that spoke to any of those *rumors.*"

Juliette Kildare paced before her like an irritated grasscat suffering from a case of weevils. "Then perhaps you should have. Now we're in a very tenuous position."

That was unfair. Vixen crossed her arms. "I didn't know until too late." And she foolishly hadn't anticipated the potential gossip. Gods, she'd been too long gone from this infernal place. Fortitude was a rumor mill, too, but nothing like this. "I didn't think—"

"That's exactly it," Juliette snapped. "This is not some feral outlaw town. Every small thing we do, every word we say or don't say matters. Garus grants us wisdom for moments like these. Use it."

Vixen uncrossed her arms, clenching her fists. "You don't think Garus granted me the wisdom to survive *sixteen years* as an outlaw in the wilds?"

The Luminary sighed, her shoulders slumping. She shoved back a lock of golden-red hair, smoothing it behind her ear, and with that gesture, turned into Vixen's mother of old. "Sixteen years. More than half of your lifetime."

Good, her mother was grounded once more. "I'm an adult. Not the child you remember."

Juliette gave a small nod, then moved to sit beside her daughter. "And there's much for you to learn. You're still new to the intricacies that I'm balancing."

"Such as?" Vixen pressed.

It was her mother's turn to consider the wall interesting. "There are factions among the elite who no longer wish to answer to a Luminary." She paused, glancing down at her shoes. "Or, at the very least, not *this* Luminary."

Vixen frowned. This wasn't the first time in her life she'd heard of such a thing, though it sounded more serious now. "They support your cousin?" Vixen had never been clear about how her mother's cousin, Phoebe Millner, had ever been a contender for the position. From everything she understood, if something happened to the current Luminary and there was no Spark, Garus would select a new avatar. The elite just couldn't up and choose a new Luminary. Could they?

Juliette shook her head, her face stony. "No. Phoebe died five years ago."

"Murder?" Vixen swallowed, remembering her own father's death. While the official story was that her father had died of an illness, Vixen had always suspected that he'd been murdered.

"The undertaker claimed it was a natural death. But I suspect it wasn't. That perhaps some of the elite wanted her out of the way so they could make their own cases. In the event that anything happened to me." Juliette flicked a glance at Vixen.

A chill traced Vixen's spine. How hard would it be for the more insidious among the elite to pull strings to create their own Luminary? It was possible Garus would truly work a miracle and select a new Luminary, but the gods and goddesses had been absent for so long…what if he didn't? Suddenly, Vixen realized she had stepped unawares into a potentially dangerous situation. The elite could be just as bloodthirsty as the fiercest creatures in the Untamed Territory—and twice as sadistic.

"I see," Vixen murmured. "So, they seek to take the power for themselves."

"Yes." Her mother sighed, sounding weary. She seemed nothing like the aggressive, mage-hating figurehead so many thought her to be. "And that's where the precariousness of our position lies. For you to be stolen away by mages and then returned by them…to let this go uncontested and forgiven puts me in a position of weakness."

Vixen gritted her teeth. She hadn't mentioned anyone stealing her away, much less mages. "I wasn't—" she started, then stopped, shaking her head in frustration. It would be so much easier if she could reveal her magic to her mother, to say that she was the one who had left of her own accord. But even if her mother could overlook her magic, if these troublesome elite found out, it would be their ruin. That begged the frightening thought: what if they already knew? Vixen Valerie hadn't exactly kept a low profile in the Gutter. But as long as they knew her as Valoria and not Vixen, it might work out.

"Yes?" her mother prodded.

Vixen blew out a frustrated breath, trying to figure out where to go from here. She thought about Blaise, who contained so much raw power, so much potential for destruction, yet practiced kindness whenever he could. "Garus teaches us to see that justice is done according to his scholarship. It's time to stop fearing mages and their magic—"

"I don't *fear* them," Juliette insisted, voice low. "Magic flies in the face of reason."

"And that's not a reason to keep them down, to blame them for everything." Vixen's pulse raced. "It should be seen as wisdom to forgive, to appreciate the gift of my return."

She knew by the way her head tilted that her mother was considering it. But Juliette shook her head after a moment. "Our memory is long, Valoria. And you forget, even though he was cleared in the Inquiry because of the Golden Citadel's cruel conditions, your Breaker friend killed many Confederation soldiers."

Fort Courage. The reminder fed the fire in Vixen's veins, and her cheeks warmed with anger. "You mean the same soldiers who killed dozens of innocent people in the Gutter? I saw what they did. I was *there!* They took me captive and—" No, she couldn't tell the Luminary they had stripped her magic. That was foolish. She wished her mother hadn't mentioned Fort Courage. There was no easy way around it.

Juliette stared at her, a mixture of horror and longing etched on her face. "*Wait.* I could have had you back at Fort Courage?"

Vixen nodded, kicking herself for her rash words. She was normally more composed, but she was too upset about the entire situation. "Yes."

Her mother cursed, a litany of colorful words Vixen couldn't remember ever hearing from her before. It was enough to make her sound almost like the surliest of outlaws. Then Juliette fisted her hands at her side. "Why didn't you tell them who you were?"

Vixen weighed the answer. From what she understood, most of the forces who'd taken her were dead. Jack had slain Commander Gaitwood himself. She settled on an answer that felt sensible and safe. "Do you think they would have believed me? Or, even if they had, that they wouldn't have used me to gain some advantage?"

Juliette frowned but accepted the response. "I suppose you're right." She rubbed her forehead. "It's late, and this gala was quite the disaster.

Let's sleep on it, and tomorrow, we'll make plans for how to spin this to our benefit."

"Sleep on it?" Vixen muttered. "As if either of us will sleep after all that."

To her surprise, her mother laughed. "We should try. I only had a little wine at the gala, so I think I'll enjoy a full glass before I find my bed." She raised her brows. "Would you like to join me?"

Vixen grinned. "Got anything stronger than wine?"

Her mother flashed her a surprised look, then nodded. "We do. Perhaps that's not a bad idea."

"Surrounded by a bunch of oily weasels, that's what I am." Juliette hoisted the crystal goblet that was meant for fine wines, but currently sloshed with the golden amber of beer. They'd been discussing the various Phinoran elite who might plot against the Luminary, which seemed to be the majority of them.

Vixen discovered that alcohol loosened her mother's tongue, which perhaps explained why all of her distant memories of the woman included her only taking sips of wine and little more. It was also possible that Juliette Kildare had changed over the years they had been apart.

"They can go sit on a cactus," Vixen agreed. "The whole lot of them."

Juliette made an unladylike snort, setting her goblet down with a clank. A wave of beer sloshed over the side and onto the antique table, but she paid it no mind. "Pity that's about all we can do. Talk about them and wish they'd sit on a cactus, I mean." She sighed. "What was it like?"

Vixen blinked. She wasn't drunk, not quite, but she was in that pleasant, fuzzy place where it took her a moment to gather her wits. "What was what like?"

Her mother leaned forward, eyes glittering. She smacked the table with one hand, her mouth twisting into a smile that could almost be described as wicked but not cruel. "The outlaws. Being with the outlaws. The Gutter. Everything."

The prompt gave Vixen pause. To buy herself time, she took another sip. Even in her current state, she remembered that her entire reason for being here was for the Gutter. For her friends. The words she spoke mattered. "It's very different from this, and in some ways, the same. Not a simple life. There's danger, plenty of danger." She barely suppressed a shiver as she recalled the day the airship had come to her town. The day she had lost friends and neighbors. Vixen swallowed. "And lots of good people."

"Hmm." Her mother was quiet for a moment. She reclined in her seat, and Vixen almost thought she had fallen asleep. Then Juliette adjusted her position in the sumptuous chair. "In some ways, it sounds better than Izhadell." There was a longing in her voice, and with a start, Vixen realized her mother had never had the chance to form friendships like she had in the Gutter.

There. That was the lead Vixen needed, and she pounced on it. "Parts of it are. No matter what the Confederation thinks about mages, we—" Vixen caught herself, clearing her throat to cover the fact that she had counted herself among the mages. "When you get down to the heart of the matter, mages are people the same as we are. They bleed, they love, they want to live their best lives."

Her mother pursed her lips. "But they're lesser. Magic makes them impure. Can't be trusted." She said it with the same conviction as a child declaring the sky was blue and water was wet. A fact. Something everyone knew.

Ah, there it was. Generations of lies served as truths, poisoning minds. Vixen rubbed the band of the ring. "None of that is true."

Juliette frowned, waving a hand in the air. "Even if that were the case, it does us no favors right now. The elite won't tolerate such nonsense. They're already up in arms with all the mages we've lost in the wake of the Breaker Inquiry."

The callous words helped to shake away more of Vixen's haze. She scowled. "Do you hear yourself? Speaking of mages as if we—as if they're livestock. Why don't you grow a spine and some wit? Stand up for what's right?"

"You are out of line." Her mother's words were frigid, all traces of her earlier ebullience faded. "Do you forget a mage stole you away? Mages have taken everything from me!"

Vixen fisted her hands. So, that was what her mother believed had happened. That had to change. "A mage didn't take me. I ran."

"*What?*" Juliette's eyes glinted with steel. "Why would you do that? Why, when you *knew* exactly what you are?"

Oh gods, I should have kept my damn mouth closed. Vixen stared at her knees. How could she possibly answer that question in a way that wouldn't make things worse? But she couldn't tolerate all the blame that had been laid on mages any longer. It was unjust. It had to change.

"Valoria? I expect an answer."

Vixen met her mother's eyes. "Why do you *think* I might have wanted to run away?" Even in her inebriated state, the Luminary was smart, and Vixen knew that if she thought about it for long enough, she'd make the logical leap. Garus was the god of wisdom, after all.

Juliette's brow creased in confusion. Vixen's mother rose, surprisingly steady. She paced across the room, stopping in front of the glass-paned doors that led to a veranda Vixen knew overlooked a garden, though it would be full of shadow-darkened flowers at this time of night. "I don't understand."

Vixen set her goblet down, pushing up from her seat. "I think, in your heart, you do. You just don't want to admit it."

Juliette's jaw set. "*Sorcerer*." The word was pure vitriol on her lips. She had one hand on the doorknob, eyes on her daughter. "Maybe it would have been better if you really had died." She shoved the door open and strode onto the veranda.

Of all the things she could have said, those words gutted Vixen. "You don't mean that!" She stalked toward the open door, trembling.

Outside, something stirred in the shadows. Vixen should have known what—or rather, whom—she was looking at, but she was distracted, trying to reconcile her mother's awful words. Raven stepped out of the shadows, knife in hand. He slipped around Juliette, blade at the woman's throat.

"Now, now. That's no way to speak to her." Raven's voice was edged with anger.

Gooseflesh trickled down Vixen's arms. Gods, Raven, here? It took her far too long to assess the situation, the danger her mother was in.

"You *will* release me," Juliette hissed with all the command of a woman accustomed to unquestioned obedience.

"Raven, *stop*," Vixen pleaded, hoping he would meet her eyes. If he did, she could—no, blast it all, she couldn't. Vixen furiously tried to wrest the ring from her finger, knowing she was losing precious time. Maybe she could stall him, buy time to use her magic on him. Yeah, and maybe pigs would fly. Raven wasn't an idiot and would know the danger she posed. He was clear-headed, not tipsy like she was. "Let her go. That's my *mother*."

He didn't meet her eyes. Raven wasn't taking any chances. "I know. I'm sorry, but this is the only way."

"The only way for what?" Vixen demanded.

But it was too late. Raven disappeared into the shadows, taking the Luminary with him.

Vixen cursed. How in Perdition had this situation just gone from bad to worse?

CHAPTER THIRTY-SIX

Lovesick Fool

"Gods damn it!"

With some difficulty, Vixen wrestled the ring off her finger and threw it at the floor as hard as she could. The metal loop struck with a sharp *clink*, then skipped into the shadow of a chair. Her magic swirled to life within her, like a bullet in the chamber of a sixgun, ready to be loosed. Vixen blew out a frustrated breath. None of this was the ring's fault, and it wasn't fair that she blamed it. Besides, she was only borrowing it. With chagrin, she hurried over to retrieve it, though she jammed it into a pocket rather than putting it on.

She blamed herself. If she'd been faster, more alert, more aware, she could have stopped Raven. Or if she had said something different to her mother. But there was no use in wishing she had behaved differently—that pegasus had taken flight, and now she was forced to confront the reality of what had happened.

Raven had taken the Luminary of Phinora, one of the most powerful people in the Salt-Iron Confederation. And Vixen didn't know *why*. Did he have some misguided notion that this would help the Gutter's predicament somehow? But that made little sense—he was a Ringleader. None of this fit with Raven Dawson, Ringleader.

But it might align with Raven Dawson, lovesick fool. Scorned beau.

Vixen closed her eyes, thinking. She was tired and still a little tipsy, though the hard edges of danger were steadily wearing away at the lingering effects of inebriation. Whatever came of this was now up to her.

What did Raven have planned for the Luminary? That would make a difference. If he were working alone, this might simply be a ploy for attention. Or revenge. But if he was beholden to someone else...there was no telling. It could be a kidnapping—or a murder.

She swallowed. With her mother gone, she was the next in line. Vixen opened her eyes, rubbing her forehead. The more she thought, the more she realized that her mother's sudden disappearance was going to cause almost insurmountable problems for her. The elite would link Vixen's return to the crime and accuse her.

And with Raven involved, would they be wrong? Whatever he was up to, it was because of *her*.

Vixen growled in frustration. She wished she wasn't alone, that she had an ally to speak with. Alekon. Jack. Or Jefferson. Kittie. Even Blaise, though he wouldn't be enthused by any of this. But...she had an ally, of a sort. Rhys.

Decision made, she left the parlor. The corridors were drenched in darkness, lit by the occasional lantern. Guards watched her progress with curiosity, though none challenged her. She wondered if any of them thought it odd she had arrived with her mother and then left without her. If they did, they declined to ask.

She knew she had to look ridiculous, marching out into the night dressed in the same finery she'd worn to the ill-fated gala. But it marked who she was, the moonlight reflecting off the shimmering ruffles.

The unicorn stables were quiet—at least, until she walked in. As soon as the breeze blew her scent down the aisle, equine heads swung over the stall doors, nostrils cupped as they read her magic. One of them issued a throaty nicker but nothing more. The unicorns knew it was night, and they seldom worked in the darkness. She was merely interesting to them, a distraction from their routine.

Vixen strode down the aisle to Darby's stall. The stallion bumped her with his soft nose, a welcome that made her smile despite the terrible chain of events. She scratched his forehead, right at the base of his horn. He blew out a contented, hay-scented breath.

"Darby, I need Rhys, but I don't know where he lives. Can you take me to him?"

She knew unicorns were intelligent, though she was uncertain if they grasped language the same way as pegasi. But Darby arched his neck, then bobbed his head up and down as if in agreement. He nosed the latch on the stall door, attempting to open it with his lips but failing. Vixen saw with chagrin that someone had tinkered with it to prevent the stallion from letting himself out.

"You're an escape artist, hmm?" Vixen asked, working the modified latch. The door swung open, allowing the stallion to clop into the aisle. Was she going to get into trouble for rustling a unicorn? The punishment for that probably wasn't any worse than being an accessory to the Luminary's kidnapping.

Vixen was glad she'd selected her own gala outfit. With a great deal of effort, she pulled herself up onto the unicorn's back, grasping handfuls of silky mane. Darby set off at a trot, sure-footed in the darkness. His horn was lambent in the night.

If anyone who knew her true nature saw her, she'd make quite the sight: an outlaw mage riding a Salt-Iron Confederation Tracker's unicorn. Everything about that was a contradiction. Vixen shook her head at the idea.

"This is what it *should* be like, though," she whispered to Darby as his hooves splashed through a bog. "There shouldn't be any animosity between mages and the Confederation. Unicorns are one of the mystic races—you shouldn't be seen as an enemy." The unicorn blew out a loud breath, and Vixen hoped it was in agreement.

A few minutes later, they arrived at a small home. A modest garden stood to one side of the house, a henhouse nearby. Darby halted and whinnied.

Vixen almost thought Rhys wasn't there, or perhaps he was too deeply asleep, but moments later, he pushed the door open, rubbing sleep from his eyes. "Darby? How did—? Oh." He swallowed, stepping out onto the narrow porch. "Valoria, what are you doing here?"

She slid off Darby's sleek back. "Can I come in?" Vixen gestured to the house.

Rhys's eyes widened. "That's not appropriate. Not for the Spark."

She snorted at that. "You act as if I'm not also your *sister*. And an *outlaw mage*." Vixen ignored his choked sound at her bold declaration, marching up the porch steps and shoving the door open. She didn't have time for these delays. "I came because you're the only one around here I can trust."

Rhys followed her inside. "What makes you say that?"

Vixen glanced around at the dim interior. He had lit a lantern before coming out to greet her, which was odd. It meant he either couldn't afford or lacked the means to get a mage-light. As she had thought, the home was a single room with a bed, a table with a chair, and a wood stove for cooking. Everything about it was spare, not a hint of luxury. That was infuriating. Just like a mage, Rhys was *less* because he hadn't been born the right thing.

She pulled out the chair and sat. "You were at the gala. You saw how things went."

Rhys's expression shifted, and he looked as if he'd tasted something sour. "Saw and heard. The rumors…" He shook his head, lips taut. "Those elite made it a point to skirt around the truth about you, but I assume they know. So, how many of the other rumors are true?"

Vixen's mouth went dry. She had thought Rhys was an ally, but maybe she was wrong. As much as she needed to tell him about the Luminary's disappearance, she wouldn't tolerate this. "What do you think? That I really *am* a soiled dove? Or do you think I'm not your *sister?*" Too late, Vixen realized she'd allowed some of her power to ebb into the question.

Rhys winced as her magic clashed against his immunity. He groaned, shaking his head to ward away his irritation. His mouth tightened even more. "I know you're my sister because of the magic you command. But I don't know any of your life between the day you left with an outlaw and when I saw you at that train station."

She deflated. That was fair. Vixen sighed, rubbing her forehead. "Sorry. You're right. I'll make the time to tell you sometime." Dread suffused her next words. "But that's not why I came here. Things got worse."

Rhys's brows shot up. "Is that even possible?"

Vixen made a face. "I was talking with mother, and we had a disagreement." No need to tell him the source of the disagreement. Besides, he could probably guess. "And during that time, she was…taken by another mage."

Her twin's eyes widened, and he cursed softly. "You're telling me the Luminary was kidnapped right under our noses?"

She winced. "Yes."

He spun in a slow circle, rubbing his face. "Why did you come to me? Did you tell any of the guards?"

"No. I didn't know who else I could go to. After last night, they'll pin this on me. I'm too new. They'll see it as convenient."

Rhys nodded at her assessment. "Not just you, but your friends, too."

Jefferson and Blaise were undeserving of such blame. "I need to head off this disaster before it breaks." If she couldn't, this would only fan the flames of war against the Gutter.

He paced to the nearby window, peering out into the night. "I think the only way that's possible is if you can get her back before anyone realizes the Luminary is missing."

And that was unlikely. Vixen mentally kicked herself for her inaction. "I don't think we can. But I know the mage who took her. Can you and Darby search for him? Capture him, if possible?" It was a long shot. Raven knew a frightening amount about the Confederation, about how to avoid those who sought him.

Rhys frowned. "You know the mage? He's an outlaw?"

"It's complicated." Vixen rubbed her forehead. She was tired, needed to sleep. But that had to wait. "He's from the Gutter, but based on what he's doing, I don't think he's friendly anymore." And that was what hurt the most about the whole situation.

Rhys nodded. "We can try, but the odds are not in our favor."

"Anything you can do to help will be useful." Relief washed over her with the knowledge that he would help. "And do you think you can warn Jefferson and Blaise about this? I don't think I'll be able to."

"I'll pass the message to them in the morning." He pushed away from the window. "Well, it's already morning. Later, I mean." Rhys cast a longing look at his bed. "If I'm going to be any good for this, I need rest. And you look as if you do, too."

He wasn't wrong. Vixen rose from the chair, heading to the door. Then a thought came to her. "Rhys? Can my pegasus come to the unicorn stables?"

Rhys yawned. "I think that can be arranged. After sleep."

Vixen smiled her thanks, then clattered onto the porch, back to the waiting unicorn. If Alekon came, she would have one more ally, and that thought cheered her.

CHAPTER THIRTY-SEVEN
Secret Recipe

"That could not have possibly gone worse." Blaise sighed wearily as they climbed out of the coach.

Jefferson stumbled out behind him, lurching as he misjudged the distance between the last step and the ground. He caught Blaise's shoulder with one hand, earning another sigh from the Breaker. The world swirled around Jefferson for a harrowing moment, and he came perilously close to losing the contents of his stomach. They were lucky the coach had been there to return them to Hawthorne House, and not deliver them to the Golden Citadel. It had been a close thing.

Apparently, he must have said that out loud. Blaise froze beneath him. "Don't say that. I'm not going back there. And neither are you. *Ever.*" The Breaker's fear had returned, brought to the surface by the gala.

Blaise's panic opened a deep pit of sorrow in Jefferson. *Blaise shouldn't be sad. Shouldn't ever have to be afraid.* Jefferson tried to think of something to say to make his beau feel better, but his face felt numb, and everything around him seemed soft and fuzzy. "You have beautiful eyes, you know that?" Yes, his brain was utterly failing him at the moment, despite the truth that Blaise's blue eyes were lovely in the moonlight.

The Breaker paused, the sudden, unrelated statement distracting him. "What?"

"I said you have beautiful eyes."

"I know. That's not what I..." Those same wonderful eyes focused on

Jefferson again, though they'd lost the sharp edge of terror that had defined them only moments ago. Beneath Jefferson's hand, Blaise's shoulders relaxed. "Thanks."

<Are you drunk again?> This from Seledora, who had awoken at their arrival. Jefferson felt the dull pressure of her disapproval like a tension headache.

To Jefferson's surprise, Blaise guided him toward the stables. "The pegasi should know." His voice was soft, which led Jefferson to believe Seledora had projected so that Blaise heard, too.

"Everything's botched," Jefferson announced as soon as they entered the dark breezeway. He thought it was helpful information, but Blaise's long-suffering sigh proved the Breaker didn't consider it such.

<You know he doesn't get drunk often, but he's a mess when he is,> Seledora pointed out, her silvery head thrust over her stall door. The other pegasi were awake, too, their bright eyes on the mages.

"I had reason!" Jefferson protested, then tried to remember that reason. It was a good reason, too. Or maybe a terrible reason, depending on how one looked at it.

"It was a wreck," Blaise said, putting an arm around Jefferson. That was nice. Jefferson enjoyed it when his beau did small things like that. He rested his head against Blaise's shoulder. *So comfortable.* "The Quiet Ones were at the gala. They started rumors to cast doubt over Vixen and implicate us." Blaise huffed out a frustrated breath. "And they tried *very* hard to rile up Jefferson. It was as if they wanted him to make a mistake and use his magic."

Oh, that was it. Jefferson gave an exaggerated nod. "I can't be the Dreamer when I'm the Drunk!" He laughed because it was literally the most clever thing he'd ever said in his life, he was certain.

<Where is Vixen?> Alekon asked, his ears flicking back and forth with uncertainty.

"Safe with the Luminary," Blaise said. Jefferson wasn't sure safe was the right word, but he didn't know what else to offer. The Breaker said something else, but Jefferson could no longer focus on the words. Everything around him blurred, like water dumped across wet paint.

Jefferson must have dozed. The next thing he knew, sunlight poured in through the window. Where was he? Plump pillows and silky-soft sheets ensconced him. Ah, yes, his favorite bed at Hawthorne House. Blaise was curled up beside him, which was unusual for this time of day. Jefferson didn't rightly know what time it was, but the Breaker was normally up before the sun to start his day of baking.

He laid there, more clear-headed than he'd been at the end of last night, though a dull corona of pain in his skull reminded him he'd assuredly had too much wine. His stomach felt like a hollow pit, though it threatened to eject any new food if he wasn't careful. Jefferson hissed out a soft breath and studied Blaise, wondering what they were going to do now.

Tara Woodrow and Phillip Dillon had been ruthless in the way they had eviscerated not only the outlaws with their rumors at the gala but the Luminary as well. Scandal could weaken the office and cast a pall over Vixen's claim as Spark.

Jefferson hated to admit the gossip was artful, each with enough potential grains of truth to be harmful. They were certain to discredit Vixen, their small delegation, and the Gutter. They were already coming in as underdogs.

Blaise stirred beside him, rubbing his eyes as he awoke with a groan. The Breaker rolled over. "Morning. How are you feeling?"

Jefferson shook his head. "Like this is all my fault."

The Breaker frowned. "What do you mean?" He shifted closer to Jefferson, warmth radiating from his skin.

"I should have agreed to stay out of it. To stay in the Cit. Everyone is suffering from my choice." Jefferson's gut twisted, and not just from the need for food that would agree with him.

Blaise snugged an arm around him. "None of this is your fault. They're bullies." His love was quiet for a moment. "Even if you had agreed, I wouldn't have let you stay there."

"No, I suppose you wouldn't," Jefferson whispered.

He closed his eyes. There was another option, too. One Jefferson dared not voice. He could have folded, could have agreed to obey the whims of the Quiet Ones. But he knew the Quiet Ones would want to use Blaise through him, and that was something he couldn't allow. To bow to the Quiet Ones would require him to end his relationship with Blaise, and Jefferson was ashamed to admit he was too selfish for that. He couldn't imagine life without the Breaker. And he feared that without Blaise, he would slowly devolve into his father's shadow. Only this time, he would have powerful magic, perfect for cruel intentions.

Blaise touched Jefferson's smooth chin. "Whatever else you're thinking, stop."

Jefferson leaned into the caress, shifting so Blaise's fingers traced his cheek. "How do you know I'm thinking anything else?"

His beau smiled, leaning over to kiss Jefferson's forehead. "Because you're not good at guarding your expressions when you're hungover." Blaise settled back down. "We had a visitor this morning."

Jefferson blinked rapidly. "Wait, already? What time is it?" He cast around for his pocket watch, but it was across the room. Farther than his recovering body felt well enough to travel, at any rate.

"It's almost noon." Blaise's expression softened. "I got up at my usual time and did a few things before coming back to bed. Rhys was here."

Jefferson didn't know how Blaise could function after arriving home in the middle of the night and then rising at his normal time. "Why did the Tracker come here?"

Blaise blew out a breath, edging over until he was companionably close to Jefferson. "Vixen sent him with a message. Raven took the Luminary last night." He paused, brow furrowing. "I mean, this morning. Early. You know what I mean."

A chill threaded through Jefferson. "Blast. That doesn't bode well for us." All things considered, Blaise was handling the latest news relatively well. Though, perhaps that was why he'd returned to their bed.

"She's requested Alekon, too. So there's that." Blaise's hand idly drifted along the muscles of Jefferson's arm. Then he shifted, levering upright. "I'm going to get us something to eat. Stay here."

"You don't want me to come down with you?" Jefferson asked.

Blaise's brows hiked up on his forehead. "You don't look ready for stairs yet. It won't take long for me to gather a few things and come back up."

True to his word, Blaise returned a few minutes later, bearing a tray. A familiar tray, in fact, laden with buttered toast and a banana and... Jefferson chuckled. "Ah, so you recalled how to treat my hangover." He levered upright, grunting with the effort.

Blaise handed him a plate. "Medium-rare bread with a buttered glaze."

Jefferson accepted the plate of toast. "My secret recipe."

The Breaker sipped from a cup of coffee he'd brought up for himself, then placed it on the bedside table. "Only the best for you." Then his expression shifted, turning contemplative. "You know, the last time you were drunk was here." He gestured to the master bedroom. Blaise paused, as if he were choosing his words. "That was a difficult time for us, too."

Jefferson raised his eyebrows, remembering. It had been the conclusion of the Inquiry, and he'd foolishly drunk too much at a celebration and then pressured Blaise over his wishy-washy feelings. Looking back, it was mortifying. He should never have said those things to Blaise. But it had led to a discussion about how they felt about one another and...well, *more*. He cleared his throat as those memories swelled. "But we got through it."

Blaise took a bite of his own toast, and didn't speak until he'd finished chewing. "That's my point. I was thinking about that when I gathered breakfast." He ran a hand through his unruly hair. "We've been through some pretty tough situations."

That was an understatement. And that was exactly why Jefferson didn't want Blaise to suffer ever again. But the Breaker was trying to make a point to him, and Jefferson wasn't thinking clearly enough to see it. "We're going to have to be quite creative to figure a way out of this disaster."

Blaise put a hand on his knee. "We're not in this alone. Vixen is here—well, not *here*, but you know what I mean. The pegasi. And Kittie and Jack are…somewhere." The Breaker frowned. "Okay, that doesn't sound great right now, but I stand by what I said."

Jefferson chuckled. "Speaking of Jack, has Kittie returned? Do we have any news?"

Blaise shook his head. "Emrys says Kittie never came back. And still no sign of Jack."

That seemed unusual for the Pyromancer. Jefferson chewed the crust of his toast as if it were to blame for everything. "I have a bad feeling about whatever's befallen the Dewitts."

Blaise's expression turned grim. "I agree. I thought about seeing if one of the pegasi could find Kittie, but…"

But he didn't want to risk losing a pegasus to whatever had snared Jack and Kittie. And he was right. It wasn't wise at this point. Jefferson took a sip of the tea Blaise had brought up. Caladrius root, Kittie's preferred blend. It worked wonders for a hangover, too. "As much as it pains me to say it, I think we can't worry about them until we know how to handle things with the Luminary and Quiet Ones. We—" He paused, hearing a sudden clatter downstairs.

Blaise rose, silver magic pulsing on his fingertips. He went to the door, but a moment later, they heard a high-pitched voice call out, "Hey, it's me! Hope you two are decent 'cause I'm coming in!"

And then, without so much as a knock, Flora threw open the door and ambled inside. She gave them both disappointed looks. Knowing the half-knocker, she had been hoping to find them in a state of undress—or a compromising position. "Hello, Flora," Jefferson greeted her.

"Toast?" Blaise held up an extra piece.

"Don't mind if I do." Flora snagged the slice and munched on it. The stony skin around her eyes seemed darker than usual, as if she were tired.

"I thought you were keeping tabs on Madame Boss Clayton?" Jefferson watched her demolish the toast in two bites.

Flora licked a glob of butter from her fingertips. "Yeah, well, that's the thing. I can't keep tabs on someone who's not there."

Jefferson stared at her, certain that he'd misheard. "Excuse me?"

The half-knocker sighed, then looked at Blaise. "You got anything else? A girl has to eat, you know."

The Breaker nodded, relaxed now that Flora was here. "Just a moment."

Jefferson crossed his arms, frowning at the pink-haired woman. "You were supposed to keep her safe!"

Flora flapped a hand at him. "Oh, hush. When Blaise gets back with my breakfast, I'll fill you both in. I can't work miracles, you know."

The thing was, Jefferson thought she *could* work miracles. He relied on her—he'd never known her to fail at any task he'd set her. Then he winced, realizing it had to sting her pride that this had happened.

Blaise returned with another tray, this one filled with day-old blueberry muffins, in addition to more slices of warm, buttery toast. Flora's eyes widened with delight, and she didn't speak until half of the assorted goodies were in her stomach.

"Thanks, I was feeling faint," Flora said, patting her belly. The half-knocker claimed a place on the bed between the two men, though she clucked her tongue and winked at Blaise for good measure. The Breaker was oblivious to her flirtatious ways. "So before you get all huffy and annoyed that I wasn't doing my job, let me tell you what happened." She paused dramatically, then glared at Jefferson. "Oh wait, you already got all huffy."

He sighed. "I'm sorry. We've had difficulties of our own here."

At that, she raised an eyebrow, then nodded. They would tell her their side of the events later. Flora flopped backward onto the bed, threading her hands over her full stomach. "Oh, forgot how comfy this bed was."

"Flora..." Jefferson rubbed his forehead.

"I'm getting to it," she grumbled. "Anyway, so I was keeping an eye on Rachel, just like you asked me to. I didn't get distracted or anything, I promise! So get this: one day, she was outside with her kids, and then *bam*, she just disappears."

Jefferson and Blaise traded looks. "Disappeared?" Blaise asked.

"Yeah." Flora blew a frustrated raspberry. "Boom, gone."

"How long ago?" Jefferson rubbed his chin.

"A week." Flora held up a hand to stave off any interruptions. "And before you ask why I didn't come tell you straight away, I was working with Captain Cerulean of the Bossguard to search for her. We couldn't figure out what happened. Her kids didn't see anything, so it's not like she was kidnapped."

Blaise canted his head. "Was she near a shadow?"

Flora lifted her head enough to give him an incredulous look. "That's a weirdly specific question. It was the middle of the day, and the sun was out, so…yes?"

The Breaker glanced at Jefferson. "Are you thinking what I'm thinking?"

Jefferson nodded. "Raven Dawson."

CHAPTER THIRTY-EIGHT

Can't Say You're Memorable

"I could really go for a cup of tea right now," Kittie murmured to Najaria. Or a stiff drink. Sadly, neither of them were available in this damned shadow realm. Maybe it was for the best, since she'd rather not backslide on the progress made with her drinking habit. But that blasted Shadowstepper was making it awfully tempting to take it up again.

The mare snorted, tossing her head so her mane flared around her. And it truly did flare—for the time being, she had allowed her mane and tail to ignite, providing them with a cheerful halo of light to pierce the darkness. Between the pair of them, they would never want for light. Not that it did much of anything in this place.

She and the elemental had decided it was best to explore their shadowy surroundings. Staying in one place wouldn't get them anywhere, and Kittie hoped she might find some way out. Nothing was immediately forthcoming, though. It was like being trapped in a never-ending cave, if the cave were formed from pure shadow. Sometimes, she caught glimpses of what she thought must be the real world beyond their prison, but they had yet to discover a way to win free.

Kittie paused, glancing over at the mare. It was possible Najaria might have experience she lacked. There was no telling with an elemental. "Do you know of any such place as this?"

Najaria drew to a halt, tilting her head as if considering. After a moment, she shook her head, the flames in her mane sparking with the motion. Then she blew out a warm breath on Kittie's arm, an apology.

Kittie smiled, rubbing the elemental between the eyes. "It's not your fault. And I'm glad I'm not alone here." The thought of being alone was almost unbearable. And to think Jack—*her* Jack—was likely trapped in the same shadows somewhere. And he was alone, no Zepheus at his side. As tough as he pretended to be, she knew this would be hard on him. He was only a man, alone in the darkness.

That thought strengthened her resolve. If she found him, they would make a way out together. There was nothing that could stop them when they put their minds to it. Kittie nodded. "Let's keep going."

She considered calling for Jack, but she didn't know who—or what—else might lurk in the shadows. Sometimes she had the sense that something was watching them, stalking them. But she reasoned that could be Raven, somehow using his magic to track his prisoners.

They walked for what felt like hours, stopping occasionally to rest. She didn't know if time passed here as it did in the normal world. Kittie discovered she didn't hunger or thirst as she would normally. Which was helpful, since she wasn't certain how to handle biological needs in this place.

"This makes me think *we're* somehow shadows," Kittie told Najaria, watching as the darkness undulated around the edges of the mare's light. "I wish I knew more about how Walker magic worked. Do they shift us into whatever their power commands?"

The elemental flicked her tail, offering no insight. Kittie doubted the mare knew, either.

The pair started onward again, following the sinuous trail of shadows. Kittie was lost in her thoughts when Najaria tensed beside her, ears pivoting forward as she flared her nostrils, suddenly on alert. She made a soft warning rumble, stirring Kittie to attention.

"What is it?" Kittie asked, straining her own ears to hear.

The chestnut mare remained frozen in place as if she were a molten statue for a handful of heartbeats. Then she lowered her head and ambled forward, glancing over her shoulder at Kittie, as if to say, *"Well, what are you waiting for? Let's go."*

Puzzled, Kittie followed, surprised when Najaria picked up the pace, forcing her into a jog to keep up. The mare followed the twists of shadow. After a moment, Kittie heard what Najaria had: voices.

It wasn't Jack. Urgent female voices, muffled by the blanket of gloom. They pressed onward and came face-to-face with a pair of women who stared at Najaria as if she were a creature of nightmare.

"Back, beast from Perdition!" one woman declared, her hair a brilliant red in the firelight. For the barest of seconds, Kittie thought Vixen had somehow ended up in the shadow world, too. But this woman was older, closer to Kittie's age, with hair that was likely a much lighter shade of red. The redhead held a single hand up as if the force of her words could turn away a demon.

Najaria snorted, unimpressed by the threat. She was an elemental and thus of the land, not of Perdition. Kittie caught sight of someone beyond the redhead's shoulder—someone she recognized in the flickering light.

"Madame Boss Clayton?"

The Gannish leader peered around the other woman. Her eyes widened in surprise, and she stepped around the protective woman, who shot her an annoyed look. But Clayton wasn't one to be hindered by others. "Kittie? Is that truly you?"

Kittie edged around Najaria, moving closer to the women. The redhead lifted her chin, still in a defensive stance—though, Kittie didn't know how the woman thought she might defend herself against them. Maybe she was a mage. That would make sense. But for the moment, she kept her attention on the Madame Boss. "It is."

Rachel breathed a sigh of relief. "Oh, you're a sight for sore eyes."

"Who is this *mage?*" the imperious woman asked, an unmistakable inflection of deep mistrust on the last word.

The Madame Boss drew herself up, adopting a formal air. "Firebrand Kittie Dewitt, allow me to introduce you to Luminary Juliette Kildare."

Oh shit. Shit, shit, shit. The Luminary was here in the shadows. Raven Dawson had kidnapped the Luminary. The Shadowstepper might as well have punched Kittie in the gut for how much this surprised her—and how much worse it made every aspect of their situation. Kittie sucked in a breath, cobbling her thoughts together.

"*Firebrand?* This is the woman who was a part of the delegation you met in Nera?" the Luminary asked, her gaze flitting between them.

Kittie wondered if it was good or bad that the Luminary had heard of her. Twenty years ago, it would have been extremely dangerous and certain to end her freedom. But times had changed in some respects. This Luminary, though…she had never liked mages.

"The very same," Rachel agreed with a smile. She ran a hand through a tangle in her hair. The Madame Boss was dressed in a pair of linen trousers and a white button-down shirt, as if she'd been at leisure when Raven had taken her. At least, Kittie assumed Raven had taken the pair. She didn't know anyone else capable of accessing this place. "Am I allowed to be cautiously optimistic now that we've come across you? I've been stuck here for days. And the darkness keeps shifting me around like a rudderless boat, which is rather unnerving."

"I'm as much a prisoner here as the both of you," Kittie admitted, stroking Najaria's neck. The mare had quieted, though she listened to their exchange with rapt attention, her obsidian eyes glinting with intelligence. The Pyromancer wondered what the aethon picked up from them.

The Luminary crossed her arms. "Why would the shadow mage trap you?"

"I don't know exactly," Kittie admitted. Raven didn't want her interfering, that much she knew. "Can you both tell me exactly who brought you here?"

Both women described Raven, though the Luminary hadn't gotten the best view of him before he'd dumped her in the shadow realm. Based on the heated conversation with Vixen she described, however, Kittie was certain it was him. Why was the Shadowstepper sabotaging their attempts to make peace for the Gutter? Taking the Madame Boss, the leader the Gutter had signed the initial declaration with, was bad enough. The Luminary's disappearance might lead to a war that would obliterate the outlaw lands.

Emmaline is still there. The thought sent a chill of dread through Kittie. While her daughter would never truly be safe anywhere because of her magic, Raven had made things worse. Kittie clenched her jaw. She would be hard-pressed not to roast him the next time he crossed her path.

"How long have you been here?" Kittie asked, though she wasn't sure if they could even grasp the flow of time in the strange realm.

Rachel pulled out a silver pocket watch, a lovely piece decorated with engraved vines peppered with tiny flowers made of rubies that blazed in the firelight. "This is the only way I have any idea, though I'm afraid I'll lose my mind checking it. Unless something's amiss with my watch, I've been here for more than a week."

"Not long," the Luminary said of herself, her voice tight. "According to the Madame Boss's watch, about six hours."

Six hours. Not long, but an eternity when someone important was missing. And the Madame Boss…well, it would be a miracle if Ganland had anything to do with the outlaws after this. Kittie blew out a breath, wondering how long she had been here herself. No watch, thus no way to know.

"You haven't come across a man here, have you? I mean, a blond-haired man. Not the one who took us." It didn't hurt to ask.

"No. It's only thanks to Garus we fumbled through the dark and found each other." The Luminary crossed her arms, giving the aethon a grudging look of respect. "It's a relief to have light again."

"Tabris granted us his fortune," Rachel agreed with a wink, clearly not wanting to leave her nation's favored god out. Then she sobered. "Are you saying the shadow mage took someone else?"

Kittie swallowed a lump in her throat. "My husband."

"Oh, honey." Rachel's voice was soft, the expression that of a sympathetic friend, not a politician. She stepped closer, putting a hand on Kittie's arm. "I'm sorry."

Kittie nodded, wetting her lips. She couldn't dwell on that now. "But I found the both of you. Perhaps we'll come across him, too. If we do, our odds of getting out of here are better."

"Another mage?" the Luminary asked, hesitant.

The Scourge of the Untamed Territory. Kittie only dipped her chin in agreement. "He's one of the best. If anyone can help us figure out how to escape this, it's him." Kittie liked to think she could find a way out of this realm herself, but she wanted Jack for her own reasons. She loved that oftentimes-infuriating man, and the thought of him wandering the darkness for eternity without her was enough to gut her soul.

"Sounds like we need to find another outlaw then," Rachel said, sounding chipper though the lines around her eyes revealed her worry.

The Luminary watched the pair of them, thoughtful. "*Let the flame in the darkness guide you home.*" Her words sounded as if she were quoting something, but Kittie didn't know what.

"What's that?" Rachel asked.

The redhead turned, her intense gaze on Kittie. For a heartbeat, it was as if someone greater peered out of those eyes. Someone infinitely more powerful than the woman standing before her. Then the Luminary's eyes cleared. "That's one of the Old Teachings of Wisdom. They're usually meant as metaphors." The Luminary heaved out a breath. "But sometimes...they're truths."

———

Jack

THE WORLD REELED AROUND JACK, SPINNING SO FAST THAT HIS STOMACH lurched. His guts roiled, and for an agonizing minute, he was certain that Raven's damned shadow magic was going to kill him. The Shadowstepper had come out of nowhere and nabbed him as he wandered the never-ending, labyrinthine darkness. But then the world resolved itself into order once more, revealing—

"Shit." Jack squinted against the too-bright light of a prissy-looking parlor. It was decorated in pastels and gold leaf, dark mahogany woods, and carpeted with rugs that somehow matched the eyesore design. He'd seen this place before, when Raven had first taken him.

He tried to move, but quickly discovered his hands had been bound behind him and his feet bound at the ankles. Took him another moment to realize he was on the floor, sitting in the middle of one of those gaudy rugs. At least it offered a decent cushion. But that was his only comfort. Where was Raven? Where had the traitor brought him?

"There you are." A dark shape shifted into Jack's field of vision, the smooth, precise tone denoting someone cultured. *Elite.* It took the outlaw a moment for his eyes to adjust, dismay surging through him when he recognized the man. It was the Quiet One he'd baited back in Nera, Phillip Dillon. The older man grinned down at him. "Remember me?"

"Nah, can't say you're memorable," Jack said, attempting a shrug. It was difficult, bound as he was. It made the muscles in his arms scream, and he bit down on the inside of his cheeks to mask the pain.

A cruel smile slid across Dillon's face. "Well, *outlaw*, let me remind you." The emphasis boded ill, and Jack had no time to prepare for what came next. Despite his age, the Quiet One moved like a diving hawk.

Air whooshed from Jack's lungs. The kick to his side sent him down onto the rug again, his bound arms and legs rendering him helpless to defend himself. Faintly, he realized Dillon had prepared for this, had planned for the coming torment. He wasn't wearing the soft shoes of an elite going to a gala or meeting. No, he wore a modified style of boot favored by some of the Salt-Iron soldiers when they went into battle. They had hard, pointed toes of reinforced steel, designed to inflict as much damage as possible with a simple kick.

Jack couldn't bring his hands around to protect himself, couldn't do a damned thing as his tormenter cocked his leg back time and time again, taunting him with each blow. The outlaw tried to curl into a ball, tried to crawl away. There wasn't an inch of his body that didn't scream from the abuse. His vision swam—no, that was blood in his eyes. Blood in his mouth, thick on his tongue. Pain spiraling through every limb. His world was throbbing agony, the pounding of his own heart, the flash of light against the blood in his eyes, the dull sound of boot meeting flesh and bone, again and again.

Then it stopped. Well, the pain didn't. That was going to be eternal. But the kicking did. A dark shape loomed overhead, a hot breath close to his ear. "Do you remember me now? Dragons don't fear other dragons— even when they should."

Jack whimpered, which was the closest he could come to the thorough string of curses he'd been attempting. His damned lips and tongue refused to obey.

Stars exploded in his eyes when Dillon scored a savage kick to Jack's gut. He gasped, whining as bile rose in his throat. Tears mingled with the blood in his eyes, and he panted for breath, trying desperately to distance himself from the pain. He'd done it in battle before, but in those instances, he hadn't been bound. Hadn't been utterly defenseless.

Come on. Can't let this asshole win. His mind raged, but his body couldn't match his spirit. This lone, petty man had damaged him too badly. Jack had to get out of this, *had to.* Had to for Kittie. For Emmaline. For Zepheus. For all the people he gave a damn about.

"What? No stubborn words from the infamous Scourge of the Untamed Territory?" Dillon asked, disappointment ripe in his voice. "Too bad. I thought you were *legendary.*"

No, I'm just a man. Flesh and blood. And that very flesh was failing him now. He panted out another breath, then summoned the will to spit blood onto Dillon's boots. Though it probably didn't matter much, since Jack's blood already spattered them.

"Disgusting filth. You have no manners," Dillon said with a sigh. He vanished from Jack's view for a moment, and he realized the man was using Jack's shirt to clean off his boots. The bastard. Then the Quiet One clicked his tongue. "Oh, what a mess you've made. I don't know how the housekeeper is going to get the blood stains out of this rug. That was really thoughtless of you."

"Go...sit...on...a...cactus," Jack rasped. Every word cost him, his tongue a strange and shapeless lump in his mouth. Like it didn't belong to him anymore.

Darkness again, but not the realm between shadows.

The Effigest must have blacked out, which was a mercy of a sort. When he came to, he was still on the floor, and he was grateful that he'd awoken. There wasn't a part of him that didn't throb, and he figured there might be something to Blaise's assertion that he was too damned stubborn to die. That, or maybe back in Fortitude, Emmaline was keeping him alive, her heart clouded with worry for her parents and friends.

Whatever the case, he was glad to be alive, even if surrendering to the pain was tempting. It was difficult to breathe, almost impossible to think. He lay in darkness—when had it become dark? Confusion clouded his mind for a moment, wondering if Raven had taken him back to the shadows. No, he felt the rug beneath him. It had only been the passing of time, his tormenter leaving him alone in agony. And maybe the blood in his eyes. Or maybe the abuse had blinded him.

How in Perdition would he get out of this? *Could* he get out? No one knew where he was—no one save for Raven, and he doubted there would be any help on that front. Jack shifted on the rug, pausing when his fingers brushed against something loose. Fibers of some sort. It took him a moment to realize they were pieces of the carpet that had been ripped from the rug during the assault.

Yes. I can work with this. He gathered them in his trembling fingers, though it was almost impossible. His hands felt like they belonged to someone else, the circulation nearly cut off from his bindings. With clumsy motions, he twisted the fibers into the semblance of a poppet. Jack knew without a doubt it wouldn't live up to his normal standards for a poppet, but in this case, anything would do. He just needed a little something to focus his magic.

Once the doll was formed, he clasped his hand around it. The fibers of the doll stuck to him, tacky with blood. That was fine. His blood would make activating the poppet much easier. Jack called on his power, trying to send it into the doll, though it was scattershot at first. His magic shied away from him, like trying to catch a fish with his bare hands. He'd used his magic when he'd been wounded before, but never when his body had been this shattered.

Come on, Jack. Get it together. He gritted his teeth, the coppery tang of blood thick in his mouth once more. Jack fumbled with his magic, though it took another half-dozen attempts before he succeeded.

The zing of the doll's connection was almost a comfort. But activating it did precious little for his situation. He had to take a moment to catch his breath and refocus his mind from the ever-present agony surging through his body. Jack knew what he needed to do first, and he hated it because it was also one of the biggest power-drains. It was necessary, though.

He hissed out a breath, simultaneously willing a Strength working into the poppet. For a beat, Jack was certain that it, too, had failed—then he felt the telltale pull of magic being sucked from him. With a grunt, he jerked his wrists apart, gasping at the slice of rope against flesh. He ignored it, straining. Hemp fibers *twanged* as they broke, and the ropes fell away from him.

Carefully as he could manage, Jack rolled onto his back, bringing his hands to his chest. He winced, rubbing his bloody palms together, then massaged his wrists as best he could. The poppet fell onto his chest. He was going to have to get it back in hand, but first he needed to restore circulation.

Once his hands felt better, he snagged the poppet with difficulty. He still had some magic left, but nothing he could do would heal the damage that had been inflicted on him. No, the best he could do was dull the pain and hope he didn't have internal bleeding, as unlikely as that was.

Clutching the poppet in his hand as if it were a lifeline, he cast a spell to take the edge off his multitude of hurts.

His vision had returned, so that was something. The surrounding room was lit by a mage-light that needed to be re-enchanted, its glow dull. Jack hissed out a long, rattling breath.

Before he could do anything else, the darkness came for him once more. As he fell into it, he hoped that he'd wake again—if only to see his wife and daughter one more time before taking the long walk to Perdition.

CHAPTER THIRTY-NINE

Meanwhile, in Fortitude...

Emmaline

The bakery wasn't as busy as when Blaise was in residence, but their patronage was steady enough to keep Emmaline, Reuben, and Hannah busy. Emmaline prided herself on running the operation as smoothly as the Breaker would have, though she knew none of them quite had his enthusiasm when it came to baking. Still, she knew they did a fine job, and he would be pleased when he finally returned to town.

Emmaline had made it her goal to keep Blaise's Bakery chugging along, if only to distract herself while her parents and friends were gone. She'd gotten into the habit of checking on them via her collection of poppets. Emmaline had one for each of her parents, and another for Blaise. She didn't think her friend knew about that, but it hadn't been particularly challenging to cobble one together in the bakery. And it made her feel better, so she figured Blaise would have been okay with that.

The poppets were anything but okay. Blaise's had resonated with pain one day, though that had quickly ended, which made her think he was fine. But then her parents' poppets had become oddly...disconnected. That was the only way she could think to describe it. As if her mother and father were no longer attached to the poppets. Had her magic finally reached the boundaries of what she could do, their distance too great? It didn't make sense—she could still detect Blaise.

With so many uncertainties, she was very, very glad for the distractions of the bakery.

<I'm here to assist with taste-testing.> Oberidon shoved his speckled

head through the window, startling Reuben, who had been kneading dough nearby.

"Blasted horse!" Reuben grumbled, earning a snort from the pegasus.

Emmaline laughed. "He's here to offer his brand of help." Hannah was ringing up a customer at the front, and Emmaline slipped past her to grab a cookie that had been in the display for the longest.

The stallion gave her a dubious look. <That is not the *freshest*. How am I supposed to help if you're giving me day-old goods?>

"You get what you get," Emmaline said. "Take it or leave it."

<Take it, of course.> The pegasus eagerly plucked it from her palm with his delicate lips.

Emmaline grinned, wiping her hands sticky with pegasus slobber on her trouser leg. She turned to the sink, the marvel with actual running water that Jefferson had installed for Blaise. Emmaline wished she had one of these at home. So handy. Her gaze flicked to the trio of poppets perched on the windowsill over the sink. Emmaline brushed her fingertips against each poppet. Blaise's was fine. Her mother's still had that cut-off feeling. And her father's—

She doubled over as a wave of pain lashed through her.

<Emmaline!> Oberidon trumpeted.

She was dimly aware of Reuben and Hannah crouched over her. Somehow, she was on the floor with Jack's poppet clutched in her hand. The agony boiling through the poppet bled into her, so intense it was almost impossible to draw breath.

<The poppet! Get the poppet out of her hands!> Oberidon commanded.

"No," Emmaline whimpered as she felt Reuben desperately trying to claw her hand open. "Don't. *Daddy.*"

"What do we do?" Hannah's voice sounded distant.

"Go get my mom," Reuben said. "She might know what to do."

The world was a confusing jumble of sound and hurt. Emmaline had the distinct sensation that her body was broken, and it came as a great surprise when Nadine arrived and sent a wave of Healer magic through her. Emmaline gasped, shaking her head once more when Nadine gently pried the poppet from her grip.

"*Breathe,*" the Healer ordered.

Emmaline sucked in a gasping breath, her vision sharpening to take in the worried faces of her friends. Oberidon stared at her through the window, nostrils fluttering. <I'm sorry. I know you were helping your father, but I had to have them break the connection for a moment.>

Daddy. Tears stung Emmaline's eyes. "The poppet. I need the poppet."

"Shh." Nadine ran a hand over Emmaline's shoulders, then down her arms as she made an assessment. "You're not gonna do anyone any good if you go into magic-induced shock."

Emmaline blinked. She'd never heard that term before. "What's that?"

"The thing you were doing," Nadine murmured. "Reacting. Letting your magic call the shots." She made a soothing sound, rubbing Emmaline's back. "It's dangerous and the ticket to draining yourself dry so quickly you risk your life."

Emmaline swallowed, biting her bottom lip. Suddenly, she felt like a little girl again. Like the times after her mother had gone missing, and her father had gone off and left her in Clover's care. Life had been uncertain and frightening, like there was nothing she could do when something terrible happened.

But that wasn't true. Not now. "Nadine, I *have* to do something. Have to use my magic. He's hurt. Real bad."

"Jack?" Nadine asked, tone neutral. Emmaline nodded. The Healer muttered something uncomplimentary about the elder Effigest beneath her breath, then fixed her gaze on Emmaline. "Can you do the same thing you did when he was shot?"

"I can try."

The Healer's lips drew taut. "You're Jack's daughter, so I know you have a stubborn streak as wide as the Untamed Territory. And even if I tell you not to, you're gonna do the thing. Do it, but this bakery needs to be closed. You don't need any additional worries while this is going on."

"But—" Reuben started.

His mother aimed a glare at him, cowing Reuben into silence. Nadine favored them with a grim look. "Reuben, you help Emmaline to her room at the Broken Horn. Let Clover know what's happened, so Emmaline doesn't waste her breath. Hannah, do whatever it is needs to be done to close up the bakery."

"Yes ma'am," Hannah said, hopping to work as Reuben offered Emmaline his arm.

"The poppet," Emmaline insisted, eyes on Nadine. The Healer had laid it on the nearby countertop.

Without a word, Nadine picked it up and dropped it into Emmaline's cupped palm. As soon as the tiny figure connected with her flesh, another lightning-bright flash of pain surged through her. Emmaline pulled on her magic, focusing it on the poppet. She sent out pleas for healing, for life.

Don't you die on me, Daddy. I'll never forgive you.

CHAPTER FORTY
Divine Approval

The rest of the early morning was a blur for Vixen. Her memory of returning to Dawnlight was fuzzy, but she knew without a doubt the trusty unicorn had gotten her back, and somehow, she'd evaded the notice of the guards.

Vixen awoke in her bed, and a tiny part of her hoped everything had been a nightmare. But it was all too real. Raven had taken her mother—the Luminary. *Argh.*

Vixen rubbed her eyes with the heels of her hands, struggling into a sitting position. Someone had brought a meal into her room, leaving the covered tray on a nearby table. Vixen didn't like the idea that someone had come into her room, and she'd been totally unaware, but in her defense, she had been exhausted.

She dressed and ate, then went to see what awaited her.

Vixen didn't get far. A pair of men in the armor of the Lightguard stood vigil outside her door. They hadn't been there when she had returned, of that she was certain. Had they come to make sure she stayed put or to protect her? Whichever the reason, it was a clear sign that the Luminary's disappearance had become known.

Time to feel them out and see what's going on. "Hello."

The guards stared straight ahead, not meeting her eyes. Either they knew of her magic, or they were well-disciplined. Vixen figured it was the latter. "Good morning, Spark Valoria." They spoke in practiced unison. The pair must have served together for a long time to be so in tune.

"Can I leave?"

Both men tensed at the question. Neither of them shifted to look at her. "I'm afraid you can't," the guard to her left said, the apology ringing true in his voice.

"And why is that?"

The guard on the right cleared his throat before speaking, as if emotion threatened to overcome him. "The Luminary is missing, and we've been assigned the task of protecting you."

Even though Vixen knew *why*, she did her best to feign shock. She clutched the wood of the lintel, gasping. "What do you mean, missing?"

"She cannot be located. And now, Spark, we beg you to please return to your room," the left-hand guard asked.

Vixen almost relented, sympathetic to the strain in their voices. They truly were upset by events and struggling to keep their emotions behind a professional veneer. But with the Luminary missing, Vixen was the next in line. The Spark should have some control over this situation. "On whose orders am I confined to my rooms?"

"The Clergy Council issued the recommendation. They also tasked us with alerting them when you arose, as they wish to speak with you."

That sounded reasonable. Perhaps, if she spoke to them, she'd be able to gain more authority. And potentially, more freedom. She didn't want to be cooped up like an exotic creature to be protected. Vixen needed to be out there, doing something. "Let them know I'm happy to see them."

One of the men broke away from the door, leaving his fellow behind. Vixen retreated into the room to wait, replaying the events of the previous night. Was Raven working with the Quiet Ones, or had something else spurred his actions? His indignation at Juliette's words had rung true. Besides, she couldn't imagine why Raven would work for anyone in the Confederation.

Unless it was under duress. Or he had some other compelling reason.

The guard returned, this time with another female guard, to guide her to the Clergy Council. Vixen followed her out of the residence and to a waiting carriage. Before boarding, she took a moment to scrutinize the exterior. The gilded eyes of the fox-head insignia winked at her in the late morning sunlight. It appeared to be one of the official Luminary carriages. Reassured, she stepped up and settled herself inside.

The trip was relatively short. The footman came around and opened the door, helping her down, though she would have much rather jumped to the ground. But that wasn't a freedom she had at the moment, so she allowed herself to be treated as was proper for her rank.

She peered up at the towering facade of the Asaphenia, the largest cathedral dedicated to Garus on the continent. A motif of carved foxes lined the lower portions, while the architects had designed the buttress in the likeness of swooping owls. Vixen followed her escort up the stairs, sucking in a breath against the growing pressure as she entered the building.

The gods, as far as she knew, weren't magic. But they had *power*. Presence. And in a place like the Asaphenia, that very power pooled like a thick fog. The pantheon had become mostly absent from the mortal world, leaving their faithful to wonder and non-believers to doubt. The cathedral was an odd juxtaposition, a location that felt both divine and comfortable. Like coming home to family.

That single thought brought her up short in mid-stride. *Family.* If they didn't find her mother, she might be the Luminary sooner than she'd ever expected. Her mouth went dry.

Her light has not gone out, little fox.

Vixen glanced around, though the voice had reverberated in her head like when Alekon spoke to her. But it didn't have the feel of a pegasus. It had a weight to it, a pressure that made her almost reel. No one else around her seemed to notice. Vixen bit her lip and continued onward.

Her guide silently opened an ornate door, gesturing for her to enter. Vixen strode inside, finding a triumvirate gathered around the bow of a U-shaped table. The two men and one woman of the Clergy Council waited until Vixen's escort retreated before motioning for her to settle in the lonely seat waiting in the open area of the U.

"Spark Valoria, praise to Garus's wisdom for your return," the silver-haired woman said, aiming a pinched look her way. Celestine Currington, the same priestess who hadn't been pleased to see Vixen at the gala.

The Clergy Council hadn't changed, even in all the years she had been gone. Oh, they had aged, but that was it. Celestine, along with Perry Wotton and Alton Drysdale. They had risen through the ranks of the Garusian clergy through the years, eventually landing seats on the Clergy Council that oversaw much of the Phinoran government and answered only to the Luminary.

Vixen knew her mother had often clashed with her Clergy Council. She kept her chin high. "I was told you'd like to speak with me regarding my—the Luminary's disappearance."

Their glittering gazes regarded her, reminding her of the fox head from earlier. Alton leaned forward, reminding her of a praying mantis. "Indeed. While we are hesitant to elevate you as Luminary so soon, especially with the questions surrounding your return, the fact remains we *need* a Luminary."

"And that is you," Perry added, as if any of them had doubts.

Vixen swung her gaze between them. It was clear from their posture that they didn't like her. Didn't trust her. Did they know what she was? She nudged the ring in her pocket with her thumbnail. "This isn't surprising." Her mind wandered back to the earlier voice, advising that it wasn't her time. Not yet. But what could she do, if the Clergy Council declared otherwise? The only answer was to find her mother.

"We plan to hold the Reclamation Ceremony in tandem with the Elevation Ceremony," Celestine continued. "Tomorrow, so that there is no gap in our devotion to Garus."

A weight settled on Vixen, so heavy she thought it might press the air from her lungs. It was something outside herself, something otherworldly. There was disapproval in that sensation. She coughed, then shook her head. "No. That's too soon."

Their eyes snapped to her. "Spark Valoria, you may be preparing to step into the position of Luminary, but you're only here thanks to *us*," Alton told her, voice chill. "The outlaw mages sullied you. No one trusts you. There are even rumors that *you* are the one responsible for the Luminary's disappearance." His mouth widened into something almost predatory. "And as you know, the time for the Luminary Festival draws near."

A chill threaded through Vixen. It was a veiled threat, but a threat nonetheless. The Clergy Council knew what she was. Or were they simply guessing, hoping to goad her into a mistake? Indignant anger swelled within her. Bad enough that her mother had been taken. She didn't have to tolerate this.

Again, that billowing presence leaned on her, though now she was ready for it. A primal part of her mind recognized it, knew what—no, *who* —it was. And even though all her life she'd known that she would become the avatar of Garus, it had always seemed like play-acting. Not real. This presence was all *too* real.

Use your voice.

What? Vixen stilled, thinking surely that couldn't be right. Here she was, in the most sacred of places for the god of wisdom, the god who opposed the chaos of magic. Did he truly mean for her to unleash her magic?

Your voice. Your will.

Now she understood. *I'm more than my magic. More than the Spark, more than an outlaw.* The warmth of agreement flooded her, and Vixen knew she was right. Validated. She could use her magic to get what she wanted in this moment, but it would come with a cost too great to bear. It didn't mean she couldn't push back, though.

Vixen lifted her chin, meeting the gaze of each member of the Clergy Council in turn. Either they didn't know her magic, or the earlier comment had been a bluff. None of them diverted their eyes. But they were safe enough—the Persuader kept her magic tightly bound.

They were safe from her magic, but not her tongue.

"Tomorrow is too soon. A time like this requires a..." Her words faltered for a moment as she thought. *Mourning period* wasn't right, since she didn't believe her mother to be dead. But since her disappearance had been orchestrated, their enemies likely wanted her thought dead. "Reflection period. Time to remember the previous Luminary." A sense of approval from that powerful presence thrummed through her.

"That is—" Celestine started.

"That is what we will do." Vixen cut her off, the back of her neck uncomfortably warm with nerves.

Alton sputtered. "You don't—"

"I know *exactly* what I'm doing. I'm the Spark, and in this I outrank you. In this, you will bend to *my* will." Vixen wanted to tremble, but she knew that this was more serious than any hand of cards she'd played before. She couldn't crack. Couldn't fold. "Neither ceremony will be tomorrow. Three days, nothing less."

They stared at her, as if they couldn't believe that this woman who they remembered as a slip of a girl would stand up to them. Vixen crossed her arms, letting the building silence speak volumes. She wondered if the clergy felt the same divine pressure that she did. Likely not, or they would have behaved differently.

Almost as one, the Clergy Council bowed their heads. "As you say, Spark."

Good. She favored them with a smile, deciding that she might as well press for more, if she could. "Who told you to oppose my wishes?"

The trio exchanged looks. They would have made poor poker players, unable to mask their expressions well. For a moment, Vixen thought one of them would admit to their farce, but Perry shook his head. "No one, Spark. We are simply...set in our ways."

I know a load of dragonshit when I smell it. Vixen was tempted to call them on it, but she didn't want to risk her victory. Besides, Perry's statement was telling enough. Someone *did* have their claws in the Clergy Council, and she suspected it was the Quiet Ones. If not them, then someone else who had no business meddling with these affairs.

"I see. Well, I'll leave you to reflect and see to preparations for the ceremonies." She rose and swept from the chamber, feeling as if she were cloaked in righteousness.

Vixen thought more about her situation as the carriage trundled back to the residence. She hadn't bartered her way into any freedoms, but she was far from helpless now. The god of wisdom had encouraged her, hadn't turned away from her because she had magic. While Garus hadn't exactly told her to *use* it, Vixen considered it a good sign that he hadn't rejected her. That was unexpected and an ace she planned to use.

She stepped out of the carriage, surveying the grounds. The staff were going about their business as if nothing were amiss. Vixen supposed there were some things that wouldn't stop, even for the sake of a missing Luminary. She turned to head inside.

<Vixen?>

She straightened at Alekon's voice. He was distant, at the edges of his range. Vixen made a show of moving to examine the blossoms of a rosebush, touching the petals with care as she shifted to look for her pegasus. But he was nowhere to be seen. Vixen couldn't communicate with him in mind-words, as Alekon did with her, but she could send him vague ideas. She sent him her annoyance regarding Raven and fear for her mother.

<We'll figure something out. Your brother came and told us what happened. I'm at the unicorn stable.> The disdain in his mental voice was clear. <He said you wanted me close.>

Relief thrummed through her. She *did* want him close. Gods, Vixen had missed her pegasus and the freedom he represented. It strengthened her resolve to know he was near.

<Jefferson and Seledora are doing some digging of their own. Blaise will let the chicken lady know.>

That further heartened Vixen. She wasn't alone, not at all. Her friends had her back, even from a distance. Now, if only they had Jack and Kittie, they would truly be a force to be reckoned with.

CHAPTER FORTY-ONE
I Took Offense to That

Jefferson

Jefferson had his suspicions about who Raven might be working with. The Luminary's disappearance only confirmed that his thoughts were correct. *I hate being right.* It meant they were embroiled in a dangerous game, one in which he didn't know all the stakes—though he could guess.

He stood in the library at Hawthorne House, pleased that this book collection had stayed within his grasp. If they'd been at his home in Nera…well, the precious tomes would be long gone. But everything in this house had been willed to Blaise, which meant everything had stayed put.

Jefferson was doing his part to help Seledora find legal precedents that might offer Vixen a leg-up over the Clergy Council, the Quiet Ones, and whoever else had a thumb in this pie. Blaise had set out with Emrys to find the Maverick Underground to see if they could help. Flora had gone to skulk around, apparently hoping to find some trace of the missing outlaws.

<That one looks promising,> Seledora commented as he held a selection of three books up for her, nosing the book in the middle. He'd opened the window so she could peer inside. She was amused that for their purpose, he was working as her aide. But Jefferson didn't mind. He enjoyed this sort of thing—and it helped to take his mind off their dire situation.

"You think so?" Jefferson discarded the other two, opening the third to its table of contents.

Seledora angled her head so she could read it. <Yes. Open it to chapter fourteen, and I'll see if there's anything useful.>

From her previous work in Izhadell, the mare had a modified easel on which they could place a book to allow her to read. She stepped back from the window to allow him room to slip the tome into position, opening it to the chapter she requested. Seledora could flip the pages with her lips if she was careful, but she had a harder time getting to the page she wanted straight away.

With his attorney settled, Jefferson turned back to the shelves. He'd already gone through half of them and had little luck so far. There were a few history texts that might—

<Look out!>

Jefferson whirled at Seledora's warning, a shadow swooping into the library. Only he knew it wasn't a shadow. It was Raven Dawson, a knife gleaming in his hand. Even with the mare's call, the Shadowstepper had the advantage of his magic, leaping to a puddle of shadow that let him come up behind Jefferson again, knife at the Dreamer's throat.

"Don't move. I'm not going to hurt—"

Tendrils of sleep wrapped around the rogue mage before Raven finished his sentence. Jefferson didn't care if the mage was going to hurt him or not. Well, he *did* care, but regardless, the Dreamer had other plans. He'd kept his magic coiled and ready ever since he'd learned the Luminary had been taken. It paid to be prepared.

The knife fell away with a sharp clatter, skittering across the floor. Raven slumped, but Jefferson grabbed his arm, easing him down to the floor. He wasn't happy with the man, but he wouldn't allow him to gash his head open with a nasty tumble, either. Besides, the hardwood floors were too beautiful to be marred by blood.

Seledora shoved her head back inside, ears pricked. <Nicely done. Now, what will you do?>

Jefferson glanced down at the slumbering Ringleader. He was fortunate Raven hadn't known of his magic—the only thing that gave him the advantage. It was tempting to hold the man in a deep sleep, as it would certainly keep him from stealing away with anyone else. But that wouldn't provide them with any answers.

"I'll pay him a visit in the dreamscape, I think. Will you keep an eye on things for me? And if I'm still out when Blaise or Flora returns, let them know?"

<I will,> the mare agreed, easing backward. Then, as if the hubbub with Raven had never happened, she stuck her nose back in the book.

Jefferson turned back to his quarry. Raven didn't look as composed as he remembered. The man's eyes were ringed with darkness, and he was gaunter than Jefferson recalled. He had clearly been through hard times, which made the situation even more curious.

"Let's find out what game you're playing, shall we?" Jefferson strode to a chaise on the other side of the room, settling down on the velvet cushions. He pulled off his shoes, then leaned back to make himself comfortable as he called on his magic to ease into the dreamscape.

This was one of those times when he was only partially asleep. When he came here with Blaise at night, Jefferson always preferred to be truly asleep. But courtesy of his magic, he no longer needed to slumber to come to the dreamscape. This would let him rouse easily if Seledora were to wake him.

The silver fog of the dreamscape swept around Jefferson, wafting around him as he stalked into his domain. He allowed the expanse to remain formless, all grey and little more. Jefferson didn't need it to be anything special, not right now. He found Raven wreathed in mist, turning in a slow circle, as if trying to figure out what had happened to him.

"I'm rather tired of being kidnapped, so as you can imagine, I took offense to that," Jefferson drawled as he approached, arms crossed.

Raven spun, giving him an assessing look. The other mage patted at his trousers, finding his knife sheath empty. No weapons in Jefferson's domain. "I'll admit, I'm impressed. I knew you were a mage, but I never thought it would be something like this." Raven gestured around them. "What sort of magic is this?"

"That isn't your concern." Jefferson's temper flared, unwilling to be patient with someone who had made himself an enemy. "I don't know what you've been up to, but here and now, you are playing by *my* rules." He tightened his fists, ready for an attack or outburst.

Instead, Raven's shoulders slumped. The man said nothing, his expression shifting to defeat.

I am not the asshole here. Annoyance surged through Jefferson at the very idea. "What are you *doing*, Raven? You've taken the Luminary, and I assume Madame Boss Clayton. Perhaps Jack and Kittie, too?"

The Ringleader glanced up at him, eyes dark with guilt. "You wouldn't understand."

"Try me. You'd be surprised at what I might understand."

Raven gave him a thoughtful look, then nodded. "I suppose if anyone would, it would be you." He shifted his weight from side to side. "I love Vixen, you know."

Jefferson canted his head. He had suspected as much. Love made a person do stupid, reckless things. Jefferson himself was a prime example of that. "And I love Blaise, but you don't see me making world leaders vanish and starting wars with my homeland."

The Shadowstepper's eyes went flinty. "But you've done things you shouldn't for someone you cared about."

Jefferson clenched his jaw. "That's different."

"Is it?" Raven challenged.

The Dreamer snorted. "Whether it is or isn't doesn't matter. From what I understand from Vixen, she doesn't feel the same for you. You should respect that and leave her alone."

Raven twitched, visibly wounded by the reminder. Then his mouth twisted into a snarl. "You're one to talk after the way I heard you pursued Blaise."

"I didn't bring you here to debate *my* shady past," Jefferson said, voice a dangerous whisper. He tried to hide the fact that Raven had scored a direct hit. Jefferson harbored many regrets about the way he'd won over Blaise. His hidden identity. Using the geasa tattoo to bind Blaise to him—even if Jefferson had only done it to block Gregor Gaitwood from doing so. It had nearly cost him Blaise's trust. Jefferson didn't want to even consider where he would be in this moment if the Breaker had rejected him. *Not doing this, certainly.* "I'm here to uncover whatever nefarious business you're embroiled in."

The Shadowstepper shook his head. "You don't understand. She's all I have. And now they're threatening her."

Jefferson paused at the note of heartbreak in Raven's voice. "*Who* is threatening Vixen?"

"One of the elite. Name's Phillip Dillon. He said…" Raven hesitated, as if he were uncertain if he should say more. The Shadowstepper seemed to steel himself, for he plowed on. "He said I had to do exactly as he told me, or I'll lose Vixen forever."

Jefferson stared at him. "That's rather melodramatic, even for my tastes. Do you realize the things you've done have put her in *more* danger?"

Raven shook his head. "Yes. But…I mean, once I…" He looked away, renewed guilt washing across his expression. "But if I succeed, if I do what they want, then she's mine."

Jefferson stepped closer until he was crowding Raven's space. It was something he was normally too polite to do, but had observed Jack pull off such a move with great success. "What do you mean she's *yours*? We've been through this. She's done with you, Raven."

The Shadowstepper had the look of a gambler who held a hand full of aces. "There's a potion that'll change that."

Fortunes of Tabris, this suddenly makes more sense. Tara Woodrow's husband was an alchemist—a damned good one, from what Jefferson understood. Perhaps on par with Marian Hawthorne. Love potions were supposed to be something for fiction, for stage plays. *Not for real life. But then again, alchemy turned Blaise into a mage. And me.*

"You would strip her will to make her love you," Jefferson said. "You would be no different from a handler with a geasa-bound mage." Inwardly, he winced at the likening. That hit a little too close to his own personal truth. *But I never sought to take away Blaise's will. To make him love me, even though I wished it with all my heart.*

"No, I would remind her of why she *does* love me!" Raven snapped.

"I don't even know where to start with how wrong you are." Jefferson crossed his arms. No doubt the Quiet Ones were leading the Shadowstepper astray, indulging a fantasy that would never come to pass. "You've turned your back on everyone in the Gutter, and for what?"

Raven shook his head. "No. The love potion...it's an added bonus. But I only did this at first to *protect* the Gutter."

Jefferson scowled. "What? You don't trust Vixen, Blaise, and I to do this?" He had been painfully aware of the Shadowstepper's disapproval during the initial meeting.

Raven looked at the fog-shrouded ground. "Dillon had been contacting me for a while. Trying to get me to their side. Sending vague threats. I ignored them, up until the time I figured out Vixen really *was* going to come here." He sucked in a breath. "That she really was willing to leave me and her life in the Gutter." Raven's gaze flicked back up to Jefferson. "And then I realized Dillon might make good on his threats. And his promises."

"Why didn't you mention this to the other Ringleaders?" Somehow, Jefferson kept his tone neutral. *Years of practice as a politician can only do so much.* He was nearing the end of his fuse.

Raven clammed up, shaking his head. Jefferson was done, entirely frustrated with this man. He called on his magic, and a massive black tentacle reared up from the mist, snaking out to wrap around Raven before the mage could so much as blink. He yelped as the spectral tentacle hefted him upside-down over Jefferson's head.

"This is a dream," Jefferson advised Raven, "but I have my own ways of harming you here. I don't wish to, but I will if I must. *Why didn't you tell the Ringleaders?*"

Raven's face was the same ghostly white as a full moon. Jefferson was certain he was trying to use his own magic, but it failed in the dreamscape. "I couldn't tell them!"

"*Why?*"

"If I did, Vixen would die, and they promised the Gutter would be under the Confederation's thumb in less than a year."

Jefferson had the tentacle haul Raven closer. "Idiot. That's probably their plan, regardless."

Confusion crinkled Raven's brow. "What?"

"You *know* Phillip Dillon is one of the Quiet Ones." Jefferson had told all the Ringleaders of them, but now it was painfully clear he should have gone into more detail on who they were and why they were dangerous. "I suppose in the future I'll need to make elaborate presentations on our enemies, so we all stay on the same page." When Raven made no response, Jefferson crossed his arms again. "So, why did you come for *me*? I know it wasn't a social call."

The spectral tentacle set the Shadowstepper down, though it didn't loosen around him. The mage flexed his arms, as if hoping to win free. When he realized it was useless, Raven glanced back up at Jefferson. "Dillon wants you."

"Dead or alive?" Jefferson suspected he knew, but it didn't hurt to confirm.

"Alive, as far as I know." Raven's shoulders heaved against his phantasmal restraints. "They don't treat me like a partner, though. So they may be withholding information from me."

I can guarantee that is the case. Jefferson dismissed the tentacle with a thought, secretly pleased when the Shadowstepper wobbled when it vanished. "And why Kittie? Was it because she went looking for Jack?"

Raven frowned. "At first, it was because she found me. But then..."

"What?"

The Shadowstepper's eyes squeezed shut. "I know you think I'm a traitor, and maybe I am. But I hoped Kittie might be an ace in the hole." Raven swallowed. "I thought I was doing the right thing."

Well, yes, if the right thing is handing your supposed allies over to the enemy. But I'm not bitter. Jefferson cocked his head. "I don't follow. Where is she? Where are the people you took?"

"Between the shadows. Everyone but Jack, anyway."

So, Blaise was right. Jefferson was overjoyed by his beau's insight but further confused by everything. "And how is Kittie your ace?"

Raven met his gaze. "I'm playing to win. And to win, I'm placing bets on both sides." He smiled, and it was one that spoke of the cunning Jefferson knew the man possessed. "She's my gamble against Dillon and Woodrow."

CHAPTER FORTY-TWO

As Relentless as the Sun Crossing the Sky

Kittie

"You're a mage. A mage brought us here. Surely you can get us out." The Luminary crossed her arms as she frowned at Kittie. Najaria's flaming mane bathed her face in a warm glow. But in that moment, it made her look petulant and garish, like a frustrated customer demanding more sweet rolls of a shopkeeper when there were none to be had.

"Trust me, I'm trying to come up with something. I don't want to be stuck here any more than you do," Kittie replied, almost wishing that she and the aethon hadn't stumbled on the other pair stranded in the shadows. But that was unfair. Rachel Clayton was being perfectly reasonable about the mess, and Kittie couldn't fault the Luminary for wanting to leave as soon as possible.

Kittie was tired. She wanted to leave the eternal darkness, wanted to feel the kiss of the sun on her skin. And more than that, she wanted her family. Wanted Emmaline's smile lighting up the room. She longed for Jack's solid presence, the knowledge that he was there and—

Najaria wheeled with a snort, staring off into the never-ending darkness. The move drew their attention, breaking Kittie's reminiscing. The red mare pawed at the ground, then ambled off.

"Where's she going?" Rachel asked.

"I wish I knew," Kittie said. "But there's only one way to find out."

The aethon broke into a trot, and Kittie struggled to keep up. She heard the patter of the other women behind her, along with their confused calls. But she had no answers for them.

Najaria slowed, head high as she assessed the shadows. Was it Kittie's imagination, or were they somehow thinning? It was like peering through a dark fog, wisps of shadow winding around a tree here, a lamp post there.

"What is that?" Madame Boss Clayton moved to stand beside Kittie.

"I don't know." The Pyromancer shook her head. She didn't have the magical education to understand what she was seeing.

"It's a liminal space," the Luminary said, voice soft. Kittie and Rachel both turned to her, puzzled. Juliette's gaze clung to the drifting shadows ahead. "At least, that's what I think it is."

"You'll have to explain because I don't understand," Kittie said. She didn't like not comprehending magic, disliked not knowing what this woman who despised mages knew. But she was sensible enough to know that the more information she had, the better.

"I understand it mostly in terms relating to the gods, but I don't see why it wouldn't be the same for magic," the Luminary mused. "After all, there is a goddess of magic, so it would make sense for there to be overlap." She nodded, as if trying to convince herself. "A liminal space is like a threshold, but in this sense, it's a place of overlap between states of being."

Kittie glanced at Najaria, wondering if that was how the aethon had found her in the shadows. Since she was both equine and elemental, had she taken advantage of the liminal space to travel into the shadows in search of her rider?

"States of being or realms?" Rachel put her hands on her hips as she stared into the soupy darkness.

"Both, probably. I think we're shadows right now," Kittie supplied. "That's why time feels as if it passes differently. Why we don't feel hunger or the need to sleep."

The Luminary pursed her lips. "Something like that. If we can figure out how to use the liminal space to our advantage…"

"We might find our way out," Kittie finished, meeting Juliette's gaze.

"This is way out of my depth." Rachel blew out a breath, her face pale and drawn. Kittie felt sorry for the woman—she had been ripped away from her children to a place she didn't understand, with no hope of escape without help.

Najaria nickered, shoving Kittie with her muzzle. There was something insistent about the gesture, a command for attention. She swiveled to face the mare, then followed as the aethon waded into the dark fog.

"Now what?" the Luminary called. Kittie shook her head in response.

But then the tendrils of shadow shifted, and she knew why the elemental had brought her to this veiled area. The darkness opened into a murky expanse that was bright compared to the surrounding realm. Kittie froze when she noticed the lump of a body on the ground.

"Jack!" She didn't realize she had screamed his name until Rachel rushed to her side, heedless of the shadows lurking around them. Kittie went down to her knees beside her husband, reaching out—only to discover she couldn't touch him. He wasn't in the shadows with her, but on the other side of the fog.

Jack, the man she loved even when he was infuriating, was a gruesome mess. His face was swollen and discolored; his clothing darkened with dried blood. He looked *dead*. Kittie tipped her head back, shrieking her fury, hot tears ebbing from her eyes.

She didn't know how long she knelt by her husband's still form, sobbing. She felt the other women behind her, and the heat of Najaria's closeness as the mare stood vigil. Kittie rubbed her face, shaking her head.

"Whoever this man is, he's alive." The Luminary's voice was soft. Almost gentle. "See how his chest moves?"

She hadn't realized Juliette had shifted to crouch beside her. Rachel had a hand on her back, as if to steady the Pyromancer. Kittie wiped her eyes. "My husband. *My gods-damned idiot husband*." Waves of anger at Jack for striking out without her warred with despair at his condition. *If only he hadn't left me behind again.*

"*Ah.*" The Luminary loaded the word with a wealth of sympathy. Then, her voice even lower, the woman added, "Garus showed you the way here for a reason."

Kittie scowled, tasting the salt of her own tears. The damned god of wisdom had done nothing. It was all Najaria. But...was it only coincidence that Kittie had come across the Luminary and Madame Boss? Had it been Raven's crafty planning? Or something more? Her head hurt almost as badly as her heart as she thought about it.

Jack's eyelids fluttered, as if he could hear them. His lips moved, his eyes barely visible through the puffiness of his face. It was almost as if he saw her. Maybe he could—she didn't know. Aside from his lips, the only other part of Jack that moved was a hand, trailing painfully across his chest before resting over his heart, patting it feebly.

At first, Kittie thought he was doing it as a gesture of love—and maybe that was a small part of it. She lifted her hand to place it over her own heart, freezing when the crumple of paper rustled in her pocket. Swallowing, she fished out the portal spell. Jack closed his eyes and went still.

She couldn't sit by Jack's side like a wraith. That wouldn't accomplish anything. She cast another worried glance at him, reaching out fingers she knew couldn't touch him. But for a moment, she could fool herself into thinking she might. Kittie sighed, recalling the feel of her hand against his muscular chest, the way she would trace the swirls of the long-dead geasa tattoo on his bicep with her index finger. The way he would look at her with his soft blue eyes, as if she were the only person in the world that mattered.

I'm coming for you, Jack Arthur Dewitt. Somehow. Kittie swallowed, weaving to her feet with renewed determination.

Rachel shot a look at Jack, then back to Kittie. "Are you going to be okay?"

"I have to be."

Juliette tilted her head, giving Kittie a look that was surprisingly empathetic. "Isn't that always the way for us women? The world falls apart around us, yet we still must press on, as relentless as the sun crossing the sky."

"Always," Kittie agreed with a whisper. What other choice did they have but to go on? She licked her lips. As upsetting as Jack's condition was, his appearance made her *think,* now that she was pulling herself back together. She wound her way back through all the conversations they'd had since their reunion. All the things he had experienced and told her about.

Jack didn't like to talk to many people, but he liked to talk to *her.* And the man knew a surprising amount about magic. She thought about the way they had combined their power to cast the portal. Her pyromancy was a far cry from his brand of ritualistic magic, but they had still worked together, based on tricks he had learned from the Breaker.

What if the gods and magic had more in common than just liminal spaces? What if the gods *were* magic—and could confer it to an avatar?

As if sensing her rider's thoughts, Najaria nickered. The mare turned, bobbing her head in the Luminary's direction.

Kittie hissed out a breath. "I'll be damned. It might be worth a try."

"What's that?" Juliette asked, suddenly aware of the way Kittie and the aethon were regarding her.

"We need another liminal space." More ideas came to Kittie as she spoke. "This one is between the shadow realm and our world. We need one between the shadows and the gods."

Both women stared at her. "Excuse me?" Rachel almost choked on the words.

"Wait," Juliette said, holding up a hand. Her eyes narrowed as she pursed her lips. "I understand what you're saying. I just don't know what you intend to do."

Kittie turned away from Jack, facing the endless darkness. "Something my husband told me to try."

CHAPTER FORTY-THREE
The Hand You're Dealt

"Hey, I'm back. Have you—?" Blaise halted abruptly, forgetting the question that had been on his lips, when he came across his beau seated on a chaise, reading as if nothing were amiss, while Raven Dawson lay slumbering at his feet. "What's this? I mean, I know it's Raven, but…?"

Jefferson aimed a smug, devilish grin at him. "He thought he could get the drop on me."

Blaise's brows shot up at that, internally warring between worry and anger. "Raven was going to take you, too?" He moved closer, as if drawing nearer to the Shadowstepper would protect Jefferson any better than the Dreamer himself had done.

"To the Quiet Ones, yes," Jefferson confirmed, voice soft. He patted the velvet cushion beside him, an invitation. The Dreamer radiated calm confidence, as languid as a mouser cat who'd just snagged the fattest rat in town.

Blaise stepped over the sleeping Ringleader, claiming his place beside Jefferson. "How did you find out—oh. You got him into the dreamscape and asked?"

"I did." There was a layer of puzzlement in Jefferson's voice. "He says he's working with the Quiet Ones, but to *protect* Vixen and the Gutter."

Blaise blew out a breath. Vixen, he knew, would take offense to that. But by the same token, he understood why Raven might do something unthinkable. The reasons behind his actions didn't matter at the moment, though. What mattered was Jefferson had made a breakthrough in their situation. "What about Jack and Kittie? Any word on them?"

At that, Jefferson pursed his lips. "Raven is the one who took them, as we suspected. But he took Kittie for his own reasons. I suspect he's playing her like a queen in chess."

Blaise shook his head. "No, the Luminary is a captured queen. Vixen and Kittie are more like pawns about to cross the board. With Vixen in line to be the next Luminary and Kittie poised to..." He made a vague gesture.

Jefferson gave him a thoughtful look, then nodded. "Hmm. Hadn't thought of it quite that way. So she is, yes. Raven seems to think—or perhaps, hope—that Kittie will have a way to stop him. Or to help in some way I'm not privy to."

"Did Raven take Madame Boss Clayton and the Luminary, too?" Blaise asked.

The Dreamer's face lit up, as if Blaise's question had provided an answer. "Ah, yes! He did. And now I think I see the play." Jefferson became more animated as he spoke, his hands gesturing with each word. "Look, Kittie *knows* Rachel."

The Firebrand had saved the Gannish leader, in fact. The women would already have a natural trust of each other. Blaise crossed his arms, glancing down at their captive. "I don't know if that was a stroke of genius or one more thing to be mad at him about."

"It can be both," Jefferson said, his tone far too pleasant, as if he were in awe of Raven's gambit. "But now we need to figure out what to—"

There was a sharp pop and displacement of air. Flora appeared next to a bookshelf. Her mouth opened in greeting, but then her violet eyes caught sight of Raven, and she pulled her knives, crouching as if ready to pounce on an enemy. When it was clear the man wasn't moving, she twirled her knives before sheathing them. "Aw, he's breathing. I thought maybe you killed him."

"*Flora,*" Blaise grumbled.

"What?" the half-knocker asked. "It was a valid thought! Or were you waiting for me? I have no problems with—"

Jefferson held up a hand before she could complete the bloody sentence. "There will be no killing of anyone in this library." Then, no doubt thinking he had better add qualifications, he tacked on, "Or anywhere in Blaise's house."

"Or on my land," Blaise hurriedly added. It was still strange to think that he had land—and in Phinora, of all places.

Flora frowned, peering at them over the rim of her glasses. "You're no fun." She came closer, poking Raven's slack arm with her toe. "I'll volunteer to torture information out of him, I guess." She shrugged, as if that were less exciting than murder.

"I already got information from him, thank you very much," Jefferson said, grinning at her dismay.

"You're going to put me out of a job," Flora complained.

"I thought you were an *aide*," Blaise pointed out.

"Sometimes I aid Jefferson by—"

"Now, now, there will be time for those discussions later," Jefferson interjected. Blaise had his suspicions about the violent ways Flora had *aided* Jefferson in the past, and he was grateful not to have to hear of them. "As I was about to say before we were interrupted, we need to plan our next step." He held up an index finger to stay Flora's imminent suggestions. "A next step that *does not* involve murder or torture."

Flora crossed her arms, her lower lip poking out in feigned annoyance.

"I think we need to let Vixen know we have him," Blaise said, jerking his chin toward Raven.

The half-knocker brightened at that. "Oh! I can do that! Especially since neither of you should leave the estate."

Blaise wasn't going to point out that he had, in fact, left the estate, and he'd been *clandestine* for once. Flora had a good point—she had expertise in moving around undetected that he and Jefferson lacked. He nodded to Jefferson.

The Dreamer sighed. "Very well. Tell Vixen about Raven and let her know that I'll bring her to the dreamscape tonight." Then his expression grew stony. "After that, I need you to do something else for me."

Flora, too, noticed the change in Jefferson's demeanor and rubbed her hands together, cackling. "Yeah?"

"Infiltrate Tara Woodrow's residence. I trust you can locate it?"

Flora gave a dismissive wave. "Yeah, piece of cake." She paused, eyeing Blaise. "Speaking of—"

"Yes, I'll make you a cake," Blaise agreed. It would be refreshing to do something normal. Cake made everything better.

"Marble cake? With buttercream frosting?" Flora batted her eyelashes at him, as if that would affect his agreement.

He waved a hand. "Yes, I have the ingredients. But only people who don't wantonly murder others get cake."

"Deal," Flora said with a prim nod. "Only justifiable murders."

Blaise sighed, though he supposed that was the best he could ask for at this point. Flora was Flora, after all.

Jefferson seemed unbothered by her words—possibly because he was sending Flora to the home of an enemy. It wouldn't be the first time a death had resulted from such a visit, Blaise assumed. "Right now, we need information. What are they planning?"

Flora gave a mock salute. "I know the routine, boss." She glanced at Raven's prone form, then back at her friends. "Be careful. If you let him wake up, I imagine he won't be happy."

"That's why I'm not letting him wake up anytime soon," Jefferson said, though Blaise heard the undercurrent of regret in his voice.

Flora vanished with a wave. Blaise settled a hand on Jefferson's knee. "You're only doing it because you have to."

Jefferson combed a hand through his hair. "Yes, well, I'm concerned that actions such as this will turn me into the sort of person I don't wish to be." His gaze focused on Raven, the corners of his eyes crinkling with worry.

Blaise understood. "I think half the battle is being aware. I doubt the Quiet Ones spare a moment to think of such things."

The Dreamer relaxed a hair. "You're right. I felt..." He paused, frowning. "When I have people like Gregor or Raven in the dreamscape, they're at my mercy. And sometimes I'm not a good person. I...I *liked* wielding that power over them. Enjoyed it." Jefferson gave him a sideways look, as if he feared Blaise would draw away at the confession.

But Blaise realized imperfect people surrounded him—and he was far from perfect, too. Jefferson had been raised to expect power and to wield it over others. Was it such a surprise that he fell back on old habits? But Blaise would never tell him that, knowing it was another of Jefferson's fears. He didn't want to live up to the expectations and behaviors of the Wells family. So instead, he said, "I think sometimes people are like that. Even the very best ones."

Jefferson considered his words, then nodded. "Perhaps so." He rolled his shoulders, preparing to rise. "Well, we can't sit in the library all afternoon and evening. There's no longer a full staff here to deliver meals at my leisure."

"What are we going to do with him? We shouldn't put him in the guest room or leave him here in case he wakes," Blaise pointed out.

"I'd know if he woke up, but you have a good point," Jefferson said. "We'll have to bring him along with us. I'll get his shoulders if you get his feet?"

Blaise sighed. "This is *not* how I envisioned spending my evening. Carting around a sleeping Ringleader."

Jefferson leaned over to pick up Raven, but he shot Blaise a tempting smile. "Oh, dare I ask how *you* envisioned spending the evening?"

Blaise couldn't help it—he laughed. "Probably not the way you're hoping."

The Dreamer gave a dramatic sigh. "Ah, the sting of disappointment. Now I know how Flora feels." He winked at Blaise with a grin, then stooped to grab the Shadowstepper's shoulders.

Vixen

"He's *where*?" Vixen stared at Flora, a range of emotions flitting across her face. She still wasn't sure how the diminutive half-knocker had gotten into the residence when Vixen herself couldn't get out easily, but that was a question for later.

"In the dreamscape—" Flora began.

"No, I mean *where*? You said Jefferson has him asleep?" Vixen asked, hating that she probably sounded desperate. Raven had taken her mother—and that meant he could get her back. But could she even trust him anymore? A pang struck her as gilded memories of their time together reared up. Raven, grinning as he taught her some of his favorite tricks for knife-fighting, his body companionably close to hers. Of listening to the rich, warm sounds rising from his fiddle, Raven's dark eyes shining as she sang along.

But those times were in the past, fading like fog burned off by the sun. No, she couldn't trust him. Not anymore.

Flora was oblivious to her wool-gathering. "Oh. Shadypants tried to get the jump on Jefferson at Hawthorne House and failed. Last I saw, he was napping on a rug in the library."

Shadypants? Right, she meant Raven. Vixen would have laughed at the ridiculous name if the situation weren't so dire. She glanced at the window, then back to Flora. "So if I went there, I could talk to him?"

Flora shook her head. "Don't think so. Jefferson plans to keep him out—that's why he wanted you to have a chat in the dreamscape tonight."

Vixen sighed, rubbing her arms as she paced the room like a beast in a menagerie. "I don't know if that will be enough." As she walked, she formed a plan. It wasn't much, just a tiny seed of an idea. *Garus didn't refute me.* Anything was worth a try.

Flora nodded. "I get it. You want the personal touch—a slap in the face in the real world, not the dreamscape."

"Not exactly, but close," Vixen admitted. Slapping Raven's stupid, handsome face was tempting, yes. But ultimately, it would do nothing. And truth be told, the man deserved far more than a slap for all this.

The half-knocker tilted her head. "You need any other information from me? If not, I've got to bounce." She rubbed her hands together, as if looking forward to whatever was next on her agenda.

Vixen shook her head. "Not unless you can get me out of here."

Flora raised her bright pink eyebrows, contemplative. "I could, but since time isn't on our side, it would be louder and bloodier than you'd probably want."

That was likely true. Vixen rubbed her forehead. "Thanks anyway. I can get out if I really want to."

The half-knocker nodded in understanding, then waved. "Best of luck, then!" She vanished from the room.

Once Flora departed, Vixen closed her eyes, sighing. She couldn't stay put, not any longer. She stalked over to her closet. The tailor had stocked it with an optimistic assortment of clothing, most of it unsuitable to the life Vixen wished to lead. The outfit she had worn to the ill-fated gala was out with the laundry, so she had to do her best to cobble together clothing that would work for riding a pegasus. Dresses and flight were a poor combination, never mind the chafing against bare skin.

It took longer than she liked, but eventually, she found an old pair of black trousers meant for winter and a frilly, emerald green button-down shirt that would complement it nicely. Vixen pulled her hair back into a tail, studying herself in the mirror. She was back in that strange in-between state, somewhere between an outlaw and theocrat. She wondered if Jefferson felt this way, this odd sensation of belonging in two worlds and feeling as if she didn't fit in either.

She might not fit, but she would fake it. And for the moment, she was the Spark. Soon to be the Luminary. She took a steadying breath. *And now I'm the Persuader.*

Vixen opened her door and found the same guards from earlier posted there. They didn't look at her, but she noticed they inclined their chins deferentially. "Is there something you need, Spark Valoria?"

She exhaled a soft breath. This was it. No going back from this, either. Vixen stepped into the hallway, and both men tensed, as if prepared to physically stop her. She caught their eyes, but before she spoke, Vixen glimpsed the corner of a four of spades poking out of the guard on the right's coat. *Cards. Yeah, I can work with that.*

"Entertainment," she said briskly.

The guard with the cards nodded. "I can send for a musician or..." He faltered, no doubt trying to think of what else might divert her.

Vixen shook her head. "Nothing like that. I see you have a deck of cards. I do enjoy a good game." She aimed an amiable smile at both of them, shading her words with only a trickle of magic. Just enough to make them think this was a good idea.

Vixen felt them bridle against it. She pushed harder, encouraging them. After a moment, the guard with the cards relented, ducking his head. "We'd be honored to keep you company. Should we call for others to join the game so that no one suspects we're taking advantage of you?"

"No." Vixen nearly snapped the single word. "No, but thank you for the offer. Everyone knows your honor is beyond reproach as a part of the Lightguard." As with any group of people, there was no such assurance. But Vixen set aside that concern for the moment. Even if they intended ill for her, there was no way they would get past the persuasion she could layer on them.

They settled at a small table near a window. Really, it was designed to only comfortably fit two, but Vixen didn't care. She dragged a wingback chair over and made do.

"Thank you for joining me, gentlemen," Vixen said. "Could I ask your names?"

"I'm Walter, and he's Hubert." Walter was the one with the cards and had removed them from his coat, preparing to shuffle. "What game would you like to play? Knack or Rounce, perhaps? We can always explain the rules."

Vixen bit back a laugh. She knew how to play both games—how to cheat at them, too. In all honesty, she'd have preferred something like Wild Dragon. Now, there was a fun card game that was easy to cheat at. Small wonder it was illegal in the Confederation and frowned upon even in the Gutter. But for this to work, she had to make a bluff of her own.

"Oh, I've heard of those," Vixen said, which was true enough. They didn't need to know how much she knew. And while they were good games, they weren't quite what she wanted. "What about Foxtail? Perhaps we could try that?"

The guards traded looks. Hubert licked his lips, his words precise as he said, "We're familiar with the game. But it requires two decks."

Vixen shot them a demure smile. "Does it? We're in luck. I have my own. Walter, why don't you lay out the tableau while I grab them? I'll find some chips, too."

Neither man questioned her knowledge, instead focusing on laying out thirteen cards of the same suit from Walter's deck. Vixen snagged her deck of cards from the depths of her saddlebag, then rummaged in a drawer to find something to use as chips. She came across a small box full of buttons and decided they would do.

"I'll give this deck a shuffle," Vixen said, enjoying the solid weight of the cards in her hand. She knew this deck intimately. Once she'd completed the shuffle, Vixen discarded the top card, pausing before anyone laid out chips for their first bet. "As with any game, what we need here is stakes." She smiled brilliantly at them. "If I win, you let me out of my rooms to go about as I'd like."

Walter froze at her suggestion, eyes narrowing. "That's not something we can allow."

Vixen summoned a thread of magic. She wanted her gambling knack to give her the edge, but she wasn't too proud to use her power. "It is, because if you win, you can have something, too. Whatever you like."

They blinked at her, as if that hadn't occurred to them. Then both men nodded. "If we win, we'd like a week away. My mother is ill. I want to spend time with her," Walter said.

Hubert gave a wistful sigh. "And I see my sweetheart so infrequently. I'd take her on a trip."

Gods, their request was so simple. So heartfelt. Vixen decided that even when she won, she'd find a way for them to have that week off. Somehow. But she merely nodded. "Let's do this, then." They laid their bets, and she flipped the top two cards.

———

A HALF-HOUR LATER, WALTER AND HUBERT TRAILED BEHIND VIXEN AS SHE made her way out of the residence. The ease with which she'd won the game of Foxtail had baffled them, but a bet was a bet, and they did as she asked. Well, the subtle application of Persuader magic didn't hurt. It hadn't taken much, as they were already predisposed to serving her.

It's just a suggestion. And I'm the Spark, so they're supposed to listen to me anyway, right? Still, guilt plagued Vixen as they threaded their way toward the unicorn stables. Doubtless, everyone they passed assumed she was being escorted somewhere under orders. And it was true, in a way.

The only complication arose as they approached the stables. Flaunting her power as she was, the unicorns scented her before they could even see her, trilling cries of alarm.

<Vixen?> Alekon's mental voice quivered with excitement. <You're here?>

She sent him an affirmative, wishing she could tell him to come out to her. As it was, she was going to have to enter the stables, and at this time of day, there would be Trackers there, as well.

Sure enough, a woman with dark hair in corkscrew curls strode out of the entrance, a revolver in hand. She hesitated, uncertain at Vixen's approach with her guards. The Tracker glanced from the excited unicorns back to Vixen and her escort.

"Halt!" the Tracker cried, holding up a hand in warning. She didn't point her revolver at them, but Vixen was sure the woman would be quick to aim if needed. "There's a mage here!"

You have no idea. Vixen flashed a smile, though she kept her power quiet for the time being. "Nothing to worry about. Stand down."

Confusion flitted across the woman's face. "You're the Spark, aren't you? We were told you're to stay in residence until..." She looked at Walter and Hubert, uncertain.

The sound of boot heels drew their attention. "Valoria?" Rhys was so startled by her appearance that he seemed to have forgotten he shouldn't speak to her with such familiarity, brother or not.

Hubert strode forward in a half-dozen long strides, face stern. "You'll show respect to the Spark!"

Rhys took a step back, eyes narrowing as he felt the wash of magic and no doubt realized what Vixen had done. "I misspoke. My apologies. Carla, I can handle this." He glanced at the other Tracker, a clear dismissal. Carla scowled at being sent away, but she had the sense to retreat. When she was out of earshot, Rhys turned back to Vixen. "To what do we owe the pleasure of a visit?" His voice was as tight as a bowstring, ready to let fly, his shoulders rigid.

"You know who I'm here for," Vixen said, walking into the stables, heading for the stall where she knew she'd find Alekon.

The bay stallion watched the proceedings, ears pricked. He bobbed his head with excitement as she drew near, and Vixen couldn't help but smile at him. <Are we leaving this place? Going home to the Gutter?> There was a longing in his mental tone mixed with a fierce love for her.

I would give anything to go back to the Gutter. "We need to go to Hawthorne House," she whispered in response. His disappointment was heavy on her mind, but Alekon was also too smart to think they could leave so easily. "Raven is there."

<Is he?> Alekon's ears swept back, pinned tight to his skull.

"Let's get you tacked up," Vixen said, then belatedly realized it would look odd for the Spark to saddle her own steed.

"Allow me," Rhys said through gritted teeth, approaching with saddle and hackamore. Then, when he was at arm's length from her, he asked, "What are you doing, using your magic like that?"

"Let's just say I had a life-changing meeting with the Clergy Council," Vixen whispered. "Garus made himself known."

Rhys spread the saddle blanket on Alekon's glossy back but froze at her words. "What?"

Vixen stared at Alekon's hocks as if they were the most interesting things in the stable. "There's something going on."

"Garus spoke to you?" Her brother shook his head at that, getting back to work. "And this? Did he approve...whatever you're doing?" He gestured to the charmed guards, disapproval in his movements.

Vixen pursed her lips. "He didn't call me an abomination for having magic, if that's what you mean."

Rhys's brow slanted. "You know I'd *never* call you that." There was hurt in his voice, enough to give Vixen pause. "I've always known what you were." His gaze flicked back to the guards. "But this? *This* is why you left— why we both knew you needed to leave. A mage capable of stripping a person's will..." The corners of his eyes creased with concern.

Vixen's gut clenched. What other choice did she have but to use the resources at her disposal? And besides... "The Confederation has no problem with stripping the will of a mage using the geasa."

Rhys winced at that. "Don't you want to be better than that?"

She did, but that seemed like an impossible burden right now. Vixen sighed. "That's not a luxury I have at the moment. And I'll have you know I didn't strip their will. That's not how my magic works."

He absently patted Alekon's shoulder. "Then what did you do?"

There was curiosity in his voice. Vixen raised her brows, considering that they'd never truly had the time to discuss her magic in depth. When it had manifested, they'd been absorbed in hiding it from their mother, and ultimately, in Vixen's escape.

"I'm called a Persuader for a reason—I can't *force* someone to do something. But I can suggest it, and make it sound like an awful tempting idea." She glanced at Hubert and Walter. "They were already assigned to protect me. It didn't take much encouragement."

He frowned. "But they knew you were under orders to not leave your room."

"They lost at cards."

Rhys's mouth dropped open. "They...what?"

Vixen reached up and made a show of pushing his jaw closed. "If we ever have some downtime, I'll show you what I did for fun in the Gutter." Then she sobered. "Now, are there any horses available for my guards? I need them to keep up with..." She nodded to Alekon.

Rhys ran a hand through his hair. "Let me see what I can do."

CHAPTER FORTY-FOUR

Between the Shadows

Flora

It took some snooping, but Flora excelled in that area. In Jefferson's employ, she had scoured through records to find the right bit of information to aid whatever task he set her to. Flora had what she liked to call *people skills*, which Jefferson claimed were not the sort of *people skills* that most thought of when that term was used. Apparently, tracking down adversaries wasn't the same thing as his schmoozy charm.

She let herself into a clerk's office (because it wasn't breaking and entering if she let herself in) and rifled through the records until she uncovered what she needed. After copying the information on a scrap of paper, Flora put the files back mostly the way she found them, re-secured the office (see, common thieves didn't make it a point to re-secure the place they had let themselves into), and headed for her target.

Night had fallen by the time she found the address, but that didn't bother her. Knockers didn't care for daylight, though Flora tolerated it thanks to the glasses Jefferson had specially made for her. Something about bright light made it so the entire world was fuzzy beyond the tip of her nose. Moonlight and darkness didn't have the same effect—she could see as well in the dark as she could with her glasses by day.

She crept up to the house. It wasn't late enough for people to be abed, not yet, but that didn't stop Flora from exploring. Years of sneaking around, even before she had met Jefferson, had honed her to the task. Despite her bright hair, she naturally melted into the shadows, and her short stature made it easy to hide when needed.

After skirting a patrol of theurgists, Flora discovered an unlatched window and let herself inside. The room she entered was dark but uninhabited. It looked like a study, the sort of place she would often find a treasure trove of information. She would come back to this place later, once she had the lay of the land.

She slipped through a hallway and threaded through half a dozen more rooms before coming across a sight that brought her up short. A man lay in the middle of the floor in what looked like a parlor, the only occupant. The sharp tang of blood scented the air, and dark blotches on the rug proved to have come from the man.

"Oh, *schist*." That wasn't just any man. It was *Jack*.

Flora tiptoed over to him, afraid of what she might find. Bruises covered the visible skin, his clothing stiff with dried blood. When she drew closer, she noticed the shallow rise and fall of his chest. He was alive, somehow. The skin around both of his eyes was swollen, and she was certain if he opened them, he would have difficulty seeing.

"Jack?" Flora whispered, hoping to rouse the outlaw. When he didn't move, she gently prodded him with a finger. "Hey, asshole. Wake up. We need to get you out of here." *Somehow.*

And yet, the injured man gave no indication that he would rouse. Her heart sank. He was unconscious and badly wounded, in the hands of the enemy. Flora chewed her lower lip, thinking. Thanks to her knocker heritage, she was stronger than the average human, and in a pinch, she *could* carry him out of there. But she couldn't do that *and* fight off anyone they came across.

She cocked her head, thinking. The best plan would be to tell Jefferson and Blaise. They—

The sound of approaching footsteps and the creak of hinges interrupted her ruminations. Flora scurried out of sight, locating a low-slung table that would provide cover. In a scrape, she could use her magic to vanish from the room, but she wasn't ready to leave this place yet. Not with the Effigest unconscious on the floor.

A well-dressed pair strode into the room. She recognized them immediately: Tara Woodrow and Phillip Dillon. Flora narrowed her eyes, hunkering down to eavesdrop on their conversation.

Tara hesitated when she saw the drying blood spattered around the outlaw's prone form. "By Garus, Phillip! Did you kill him?"

The older man smiled, a cruel sort of expression that made Flora want to wipe it off his face, preferably with the blade of her knife. "No, but he probably wishes I had. See? He's breathing." He nudged Jack's leg with a toe.

"But only barely," Tara commented, crossing her arms, disapproval clear in her stance. Flora was pretty sure it wasn't from any concern over the outlaw's health, though. "Our plan won't work quite as well if he's dead."

Phillip shrugged. "I had to make sure he knew his place. He's too strong and mouthy otherwise." Flora had to admit that part was accurate. Then he laughed. "Anyway, there's no need to worry. If he died, we would just use one of the other outlaws. Really, out of all of them, Cole deserves a hanging the most, the traitor. But that won't suit my needs—you know I have plans for him."

Flora bit back a growl. She'd be damned if she'd allow them to—wait, *hang?* They were planning to hang Jack? She gritted her teeth. In a convoluted way, it made sense. They had every right to do so. Wildfire Jack Dewitt's mug was on many handbills throughout the Confederation. But if they wanted the Effigest dead, why hadn't they already done it? Why leave him in this parlor, half-dead?

"Speaking of Cole, where is he? I thought our new pet was going to deliver him, too." Tara put her hands on her waist, cocking one hip as she considered the downed outlaw. "He seemed motivated to do the work."

Phillip shook his head. "I don't know. Dawson hasn't returned, and I told him to bring Jefferson directly here. I don't know if something's happened to him or if he's jumped ship." He moved to sit in a wingback chair, which put him out of Flora's view, but as long as they spoke, it didn't matter.

"I don't think he'd abandon us—he wants the love elixir too badly," Tara said.

"Unless he doesn't care for the Spark as much as we thought," Phillip suggested.

Tara clucked her tongue, shaking her head. "Dear Phillip, you saw how lovesick that boy was. And lovesick boys do *very* stupid things." She was far too gleeful about her observation. "No, I doubt it's Dawson. More likely, Cole or his pet mage have taken our piece off the board."

And Flora was damn proud of Jefferson for doing exactly that.

Phillip made a contemplative sound. "Then I think we need to start making our move. Those blasted mages made every moment count back in Nera. They're resourceful, which makes them dangerous. If we don't keep this moving along, they'll find a way around it."

The half-knocker gritted her teeth. She was tempted to reveal herself and attack the pair of Quiet Ones, taking them out of the action for good. She'd done similar before, but usually against people who mattered much less than these two. This pair had plans upon plans, and their deaths may not be enough to end the designs already set in motion.

"You're just saying that because the sooner we move, the sooner you think you can get your hands on Cole," Tara said, and for the first time, Flora detected discord in their ranks. "This is like alchemy, Phillip. Everything must be done properly, in the right amount and time, or it will blow up in our faces."

There was a scrape as Phillip's chair shifted on the hardwood floor. "We had a deal, as you well know. That is the only reason I'm taking part in this endeavor."

Ooh. I wish I had popcorn. This could be good. Well, aside from Jack laying there near dead and all. Flora propped her elbows against the floor.

"Not the only reason." Tara's voice was sickly sweet. "But it's better to be only the two of us, rather than all the Quiet Ones here to muck things up. Too many cooks in the kitchen, as they say. This still meets the long-term goals of our organization, even as it satisfies our *personal* goals."

Personal goals? She could guess Dillon's: he wanted Jefferson. And revenge on Jack, by the looks of it. What about Tara, though? Flora certainly hoped she'd cooperate and spill her intentions. That would be handy.

"And our organization's goals are precisely why we need to keep up our momentum," Phillip said to Flora's disappointment. Well, maybe not *disappointment*, she corrected herself. This was probably important, too. "It's vital that we hit the outlaws as hard as we can while they're here."

"You took that *far* too literally," Tara commented with a laugh.

Phillip didn't even make a snort of laughter at the poor jape. "If our goal is to take the Gutter, we can't allow the outlaw mages to be at full power. They need to be demoralized; their spirits broken."

Take the Gutter? The last Flora recalled, the Quiet Ones had been pressing Jefferson to have the Gutter recognized as an independent nation. Now they wanted the Confederation to attack it? Why? She pursed her lips, wondering if they were playing both sides.

"I still say we can take it at our own pace," Tara insisted. "What does a delay matter? The outlaws who are in Izhadell are far from home. Easy pickings, really. Word has spread like wildfire of the Luminary's unfortunate disappearance. It won't be long before the faithful of Garus are ready to tear the pretty redhead apart." She paused. "Though I suppose I see what you mean. If it comes to that, we risk losing our own prizes."

"And there you have it," Phillip agreed, sounding like the smug prick he was. "We need to move soon. Finish destabilizing the outlaw mages here. Claim our own prizes. And then we have the *real* prize: all the resources of the Gutter."

Something about the way he said it hinted to Flora that he meant more than the land. Possibly even more than the salt-iron buried deep in the ground—which she sorely hoped they didn't know about. Salt-iron had been Jefferson's original reason for visiting the Gutter, so long ago. A visit that had seemed of little consequence but altered their lives in ways she and Jefferson had never expected. There were veins of salt-iron throughout the canyons, more than in any other area of the continent. What else might they mean?

As soon as she posed the question to herself, she knew. The people. The mages. They were the ones who would die if Salt-Iron soldiers came knocking.

"I suppose you're right. Well, in the morning, I'll visit the Clergy Council again and see what we can arrange. We can have the outlaw hauled to the Asaphenia for the Reclamation Ceremony. They'll need blood for it, anyway. May as well be his," Tara said, as nonchalantly as if she were discussing the outcome of a recent unicorn race.

"The sooner, the better." Phillip's voice was taut. "We can't take any chances. Bad enough, the Spark convinced the Clergy Council to delay. See if you can force the date up again. Three days is too long."

The pair exchanged a few more words, though they were of little importance. They exited the room, and Flora slipped out of her hiding place to crouch beside Jack again.

"Come on," she whispered. "Wake up!"

The outlaw's eyelids twitched. He made a soft, animalistic groan, as if trying to obey.

Flora wasn't exactly nurturing, but she did her best to encourage him. "That's it, you big, dumb brute. Wakey wakey. You can do it." She nudged his shoulder gently, mindful of his damaged body.

But he didn't make any other sounds or movements, lost once more to oblivion. Flora swallowed. *Damn it.* "C'mon. Wake up. Live just to spite those loads of dragonshit."

She had to give up after a few more minutes. As much as she knew Jack wanted to survive, his injuries were grave. This was going to take more than just her. She nodded to herself, resolute. *Hang on long enough for me to get back with help.*

Vixen

<I LET THE OTHERS KNOW WE'VE ARRIVED.>

Vixen patted Alekon's neck in thanks. The stallion had returned to his formerly cheerful self, although they were grounded because of the rest of their entourage. He was simply happy to have her back in the saddle—and Vixen felt likewise.

Rhys had stayed behind, but true to his word, he'd found a pair of steeds that Vixen's guards could ride. Between the men's uniforms and the gilt accents on the saddles and bridles declaring the horses as Lightguard mounts, Vixen's station was clear. Alekon, with his cutback outlaw saddle and hackamore, didn't fit in at all. She loved him all the more for it.

Blaise and Jefferson stood on the porch, watching their approach. The other pegasi lined the fence, Zepheus the most forlorn of their group, with Jack still missing. Vixen clenched her jaw. Raven had much to answer for.

She showed her guard to the stables, where she allowed them to untack Alekon, as much as it galled her. Vixen wished she could do those simple things for herself but knew it would look odd.

With that done, Vixen hurried over to meet with her friends. Walter trailed behind, wary, as Hubert finished seeing to their mounts. Vixen didn't miss the way Blaise's eyes darted to the unfamiliar men with worry, his mouth set in a hard line.

"I will say, this isn't quite how I expected to see you," Jefferson said in greeting. The Dreamer appeared at ease, but that was often how he was— on the outside, he seemed confident in any situation. He raised a single eyebrow at her escort.

"They're loyal," Vixen said in explanation, hoping her friends would understand what she meant.

That garnered more interest from Jefferson. "Are they? How interesting. Would you like to come in?"

"Yes. You have someone I want to see," Vixen agreed, mounting the stairs. She glanced back at her guardian. "Walter, I'm among friends here. Would you and Hubert please remain outside?"

A cloud of doubt crossed Walter's face, but then he nodded. "As you wish, Spark Valoria." He ascended the stairs to the porch and took up a vigilant position by the white railing. A curious brown hen strode up with a flap of her wings, head tilting to study the Lightguard.

"Valoria," Blaise murmured with a shake of his head. "Sorry, but you'll never look like a *Valoria* to me."

Blaise's words heartened her. While she didn't despise her old life the way she'd heard Jefferson did his, she much preferred her outlaw name. She'd been born Valoria. But she'd *made* herself Vixen. "I'm happy to answer to Vixen for my friends," she told them, though she arrowed a look at Jefferson. "I want to talk to Raven."

"I assumed you would, which is why I invited you to the dreamscape tonight. Did Flora not tell you?" the Dreamer asked, turning to face her in the middle of the ornate entry.

"She did." Vixen blew out a breath. "But I need to *see* him."

Blaise shifted his weight, arms crossed in a sure sign that he was uncomfortable with her wishes. "We don't think it's a good idea to wake him. He wanted to *take* Jefferson." His voice went rough with emotion, and Vixen understood why they didn't want to risk waking the Shadow-stepper. Blaise was on a cliff's edge of what he could handle at the moment. Something happening to his beau would push him over.

Vixen pulled the magic-dampening ring from her pocket. "He won't be able to take anyone, not with this."

"Ah," Jefferson murmured, considering. He glanced at Blaise. "What do you think?"

Blaise chewed his lower lip, dropping his gaze. Indecision warred on his features. "I guess it's worth trying. We know the ring works. But what if he takes it off?"

She held up the silver loop. "He'll have a difficult time. It's sized for thin fingers—and Raven's aren't." Vixen could almost feel the warmth of his fingers twining through hers as she said the words.

Jefferson winced. "Ah, yes. A ring that is too tight is *quite* unpleasant—and sometimes almost impossible—to remove."

With that decision made, she followed them to where they were holding Raven. She shouldn't have been surprised to find him in the kitchen—it was such a perfectly *Blaise* place to be. It appeared her arrival had interrupted the Breaker's baking frenzy, though he hadn't gotten very far from what she saw of the assorted pots, pans, and ingredients. But most of her attention was on Raven.

They had propped her former sweetheart up in a chair against the wall. His head lolled back. He almost appeared dead, save for the gentle rise and fall of his chest and the occasional grunt he made. Raven wasn't a quiet sleeper by any means.

Vixen crossed to him, kneeling in front of the slumbering man. He looked almost innocent in his sleep, his face younger, unhindered by the hard reality of their lives. She picked up his left hand and threaded his middle finger through the ring. As she'd suspected, it was a tight fit—he'd have a difficult time removing it.

That done, she rose, crossing her arms. "Wake him, if you don't mind."

"I mind," Blaise muttered.

"Of course you do," Jefferson said with a chuckle. He leaned over and planted a conciliatory kiss on the Breaker's cheek. "I'm safe enough with you and Vixen here." Blaise didn't appear convinced, but he nodded.

Jefferson stepped over to Raven. Vixen couldn't see what he did, but a moment later, the Shadowstepper shuddered and shook his head, eyes flashing open. He tensed in the chair, eyes on Jefferson. *"You."* It was the first time Vixen had ever heard fear in Raven's voice when speaking to the Ambassador.

"Me," Jefferson agreed amiably. "But you and I have already spoken. There's someone else who'd like a word." He stepped aside, revealing Vixen standing there with crossed arms and a scowl.

Raven swallowed. "Vixen—"

"No. You don't speak until I ask you to." Her voice was stern and loaded with magic. Raven had made the mistake of meeting her eyes, either foolishly thinking she'd never use her magic on him or not realizing his error. Her power curled around him, though now she felt stretched thin between the three men she was currently influencing. At least Raven did as she suggested and shut his mouth. She approached, stalking as silently as her outlaw namesake. "I hope you know how disappointed I am. I don't want to hear your excuses or whatever you think are valid reasons. You knew what I came here to do, yet you acted against me at every turn."

Raven stared down at his hands. With her magic in place, she didn't lose her grip on him when they broke eye contact. He trembled before lifting his gaze to her again. Questions lit his eyes, though he couldn't ask until she gave him permission.

"Speak," she commanded.

He made a great gasp, as if the words threatened to spill from his throat. Raven shook his head like a dog shedding water. "You used your magic on *me?"* The question was both accusation and disbelief, tempered with hurt.

"I don't have any other choice." Vixen didn't care if her words were icy. Every one of them was true.

"And why can't I use *my* magic?" he asked.

She tipped her head toward Jefferson. "Because you didn't come here on friendly terms, from what I hear. You have a ring on your finger that's throttling your magic, and you *will not* take it off until I allow it."

Raven shivered at her declaration, glancing down at the ring in question. Then he laughed, the sound of someone at their wit's end. "When *I* gave you a ring, you said no. When *you* give me a ring, I have no say in the matter."

"It's *my* ring. Don't get too attached," Jefferson corrected, his voice downright territorial.

Vixen had almost forgotten that Blaise had given the Dreamer the ring. It was more than a useful item to him. It was a symbol. *And what does it mean that I used their symbol of devotion to trap the man who said he loved me?* There was an ugly symmetry to it.

Raven sighed, seemingly aware that he was outnumbered and outmatched. "Jefferson already interrogated me. What more do you want?"

"The truth," Vixen snapped. She wanted to ask him why he had gone to such lengths, why he had betrayed his friends. She would get those answers later. "Where's my mother? Where are Jack and Kittie?"

Raven rubbed his forehead. "They're between the shadows, except for Jack."

Vixen wasn't sure if being between the shadows was a good or bad thing at this point. But that Jack wasn't with the others was notable. "Why Jack?"

The Shadowstepper's eyes darted to Jefferson. "Phillip Dillon wanted me to bring him Jack and Jefferson."

"Is that the man from the gala?" Vixen asked, rounding on Jefferson.

"Yes, one of the Quiet Ones," the Dreamer confirmed.

Pinpricks of warning raced up Vixen's arms and legs. This didn't bode well. "Why?"

Raven shook his head. "I don't know. They don't tell me things. They treat me like a tool." He glanced away. "That was why I was glad when I came across Kittie."

That was an odd thing to say. Vixen did her best not to appear too angry at him. "Again, *why?*"

A grim look touched Raven's lips. "I was told to get *rid* of the Madame Boss and Luminary. I wasn't directly told to *kill* them, which is why I left them in the shadows."

As angry as she was, his admission brought Vixen up short. Raven had killed before and certainly wasn't shy about it. He rightly could have ended both women—but he hadn't, even though that was likely what the Quiet Ones had intended. What did Kittie have to do with this? Then she realized the Firebrand knew Madame Boss Clayton. The Luminary wouldn't trust a mage, but Clayton might. Especially if that mage was Kittie.

"I don't see how that makes any of this better," Blaise cut in, sounding testier than was usual for him.

"It was the best I could do, considering I didn't have much choice," the Shadowstepper explained, though by the way his shoulders hunched, he knew it was a piss-poor answer. "If you free me, I can bring them back."

The Breaker stiffened, alarm etched on his face. "No. How can we trust you anymore?"

And that was the real question. Vixen hated that Blaise even had to ask, but he was right. There was no way to trust Raven after what he'd done. Fortunately, she was the Spark, and that meant she had options. "Blaise is right. We *can't* trust you."

"But—" Raven started.

"Don't," Vixen warned him. "Shadowsteppers aren't common, but you're not a Breaker. You won't be the only one. It's well within my right to search the mage registration records and find one." Even if she had to use her magic to brute force her way to the records, it was something she could— and *would*—do.

The lines around Raven's eyes tightened. "My father has the same magic I do. I know you don't trust a word I say, but…it's true."

There was a sharp edge of truth in his defeated words. She and Raven had never really discussed their origins, since such things were often prickly issues for the outlaws. But he had offered this, and she would take the information. "How do we find him?"

Raven studied the floor. "It shouldn't be too hard for you. He's a theurgist."

That opened a floodgate of new questions, but those would keep for another time. She nodded. "Good, we'll find him."

Vixen was about to say something more when Jefferson cut in, "There's another truth Raven hasn't revealed to you."

At that, the Shadowstepper's eyes widened. He shook his head, an outright denial of whatever the Dreamer was hoping he'd admit.

"Don't keep it hidden," Jefferson urged, his voice taking on a low, sing-song timbre. "Tell her, or I'll haul you back to the dreamscape." There was a threat in his voice Vixen couldn't recall hearing before.

"Jefferson," Blaise whispered, his eyes wide.

"This is not the time to be merciful." The Dreamer stared at Raven, who trembled beneath his intense green gaze.

Vixen swallowed. Whatever had Jefferson worked up didn't bode well. She moved over to Raven, taking his chin in her hand and forcing him to meet her eyes. "Tell me." Vixen could have poured her magic into the command, but she didn't. No, this was her final gift to the man she had once held dear.

"If I helped them, they were going to provide me with a love potion," he whispered. "For you."

She stepped back as if she'd been threatened by a rattlesnake. Betrayal stabbed at her, as sharp as any knife Raven had ever wielded. "You gods-damned—"

A soft pop interrupted her as Flora appeared in their midst. The normally jocular half-knocker's face was grim, bringing Vixen's litany to a crashing halt.

"Flora?" Jefferson asked. "What is it?"

Her violet eyes surveyed the room, probably providing the half-knocker with a slew of her own questions, but whatever she had to tell them was more pressing. "I found Jack."

Vixen breathed out a sigh of relief. "Oh, that's good news."

Flora shook her head, pink hair flying. "No, it's not."

CHAPTER FORTY-FIVE
Pawns Across the Board

Blaise

"I didn't know!" Sweat ran down Raven's face in beads under Blaise, Jefferson, Vixen, and Flora's combined glares. It wasn't often that Blaise knew hot, potent anger like this. His fists clenched at his sides, magic tingling across his palms. He lifted a hand, flexing it so that a haze of silver played across it. Raven stared at it, breathing hard. "I didn't know they'd hurt him!"

"What did you *think* they'd do with an outlaw like Jack?" Vixen snapped, her eyes narrowed and hands perched on her hips. She looked as if she were barely restraining herself, too.

At that, the Shadowstepper went silent, confirming that he'd known the Quiet Ones wouldn't have anything good in mind for the Effigest. Flora's news that Jack had been beaten so horribly only grew more sickening when she revealed their enemies planned to hang him, too. The thought of Jack hanging because another outlaw had betrayed him made Blaise's stomach twist.

"We can't allow it," Blaise said after a moment, voice deceptively soft. The fierce anger was still there, lingering just below the surface like a slumbering volcano.

<No, we cannot,> a new voice agreed. They turned and found Zepheus standing at the nearest window. <I will not stand by while my rider dies.> Fury rode each of the palomino's words.

Jefferson moved to claim a nearby chair, shoulders slumping. "I don't know what we can do. We're already suspects in the Luminary's disappearance and of corrupting the Spark." He cast a dark look at Raven. "They'll use any move we make against us. I'm sure they'd *love* for us to free the Scourge of the Untamed Territory."

Flora jabbed a finger at Jefferson. "Whether or not you do it, they win."

"I think they've outmaneuvered us at last." Jefferson closed his eyes, rubbing his forehead as if he had a headache.

Blaise cross his arms, concerned by how uncharacteristically defeatist that was for his beau. Maybe he had a point, but Blaise wouldn't let that stop them when Jack's life hung in the balance. "They haven't outplayed us yet. We need to move our pawns across the board."

At Blaise's words, Jefferson's hand dropped away from his face. "What do you mean?"

"It's our move," Blaise said, suddenly aware that all eyes were on him. Even Raven's, which he didn't particularly like. "We just need to figure out how much time we have between now and when they plan to hang Jack."

Flora was about to speak, but Vixen beat her to it. "Three days—unless they convince the Clergy Council to override my will. That's when the Reclamation Ceremony is and..." The Persuader swallowed, her silvery eyes downcast. "A sacrifice is offered, and historically it's always a mage because... Well, I imagine y'all know why."

"I don't know if Jack's got three days," Flora said, the most somber Blaise had ever heard her. She pulled out her butterfly knife, flipping it from one hand to the other in a show of nerves. "And Jack's not the only thing I discovered when I was snooping."

As much as Blaise wanted to start on a plan to free the Effigest, the half-knocker's foreboding words demanded attention. Everyone else seemed of the same mind. "What else do we need to know?" Jefferson asked.

"There's trouble in paradise with Woodrow and Dillon—they don't see eye to eye on everything. And they both had their own side projects that they're working on, besides their primary goal for the Quiet Ones." Flora's violet eyes locked on Jefferson.

"What's their goal?" Vixen hauled one of the wooden chairs closer and sat.

"The Gutter," Flora said. "They want the mages."

Jefferson made a soft sound of understanding. "Of course. The Confederation isn't happy about bleeding potential theurgists. And if they control the supply of mages..."

Blaise grimaced. It was a horrifying thought that made far too much sense. But that also raised questions. "If they want the Gutter, why are they wasting time on us?"

"Not a waste of time." Flora aimed her index finger at Jefferson.

"They're glad none of you are in the Gutter right now. It'll make it easier for them." Her mouth tightened. "And the cherry on top is that they'll hit their own goals. Dillon wants Jefferson and for Jack to pay for threatening them. I'm not sure what the batty dame wants, but I figure it's not good."

Vixen arrowed a look at Raven. "Do you know what she wants?"

The Shadowstepper stared at the ring that was jammed onto his finger, reluctant to meet his old flame's gaze. "Like I said, I was a tool. They didn't bring me into their confidence."

"You certainly *were* a tool," Flora agreed in a stage whisper.

Jefferson stepped forward, drawing attention before Raven could make a retort. "If there's nothing else we need to know, then we should move on to the more pressing matter, which is freeing Jack."

"I know where he is," Raven said, attempting to curry their favor again.

"Yeah, well, so do I," Flora retorted. "I'm sure you'd love to lead us into a trap."

"You don't know about the house and their *defenses*," Raven stressed. "They're not an easy target."

"I don't know about that. I wandered in just fine," Flora pointed out.

"Not all of us are gifted with your talents," Jefferson said.

Vixen listened with her arms crossed, every line in her stance broadcasting her frustration with her former beau. "If Flora hadn't been the one to tell us about Jack in the first place, I'd also think you're eager to lead us into a trap."

Her words wounded the Shadowstepper, and he hung his head. "Everything I did was for you."

"You don't get to use that excuse. Not when we already found out *exactly* how self-serving you are," Vixen snapped. "I'm not a porcelain teacup, easily shattered. I'm like one of Clover's shot glasses. I'm tough, and I've seen a thing or two."

Blaise clamped his jaw at that. He'd personally broken those aforementioned shot glasses with his magic, though it had been on purpose. He could attest to their sturdiness.

"I say we take him along just so we can shove him into any traps that get sprung," Flora suggested. "Never hurts to have fodder."

"Or at the very least, so we know he's not out somewhere causing more trouble for us," Blaise said.

"I could trap him in the dreamscape." Jefferson's intent gaze was on Raven, a promise that there would be more nightmares than dreams.

Blaise didn't like what he saw in his love's face. Jefferson was too cold, too cruel. "No."

At his single, soft denial, Jefferson's gaze broke away from the Shadowstepper, circling back to Blaise. The skin around Jefferson's eyes crinkled, a sign that he realized he'd been slipping into something he didn't want to be. Even if it was warranted right now. He said nothing, only ducked his head and took a step back.

"He comes along," Vixen said through gritted teeth.

"If you want, I can stab him at the first sign of betrayal," Flora suggested cheerfully.

"Vixen shouldn't go," Raven protested. "These elite have theurgists in their pay. Don't you see how bad an idea that is?" His eyes raked over their group. "They'd love to have all of you. I may not be leading you into a trap, but that doesn't mean this isn't one."

Blaise hated the fact that Raven was possibly right. But by the same token… "That's why you're going with us. And you'll tell us everything you know so we can be successful."

The Shadowstepper nodded. "I said I would. When are we going? I suggest making your move at night. Tomorrow night?"

From what Flora said, Jack might not have that long—even if they didn't hang him. Blaise shook his head. "Tonight."

CHAPTER FORTY-SIX

Theatrics

Jefferson

In the dark of night, Seledora strode beside Emrys, a small mage-light that Blaise had brought along the only light to guide their way. Clouds hid the full moon, and a mist fell over them, not heavy enough to qualify as rain but enough to be an annoyance. Blaise and Jefferson wore oilskin coats, though their style of hats differed. The Breaker preferred his broad-brimmed hat while Jefferson had gone with an impractical top hat. Blaise's fared much better in the mist.

"I wasn't expecting you to want us to do this tonight," Jefferson said, his voice loud enough to be heard over the thud of hooves but soft enough not to draw attention.

Blaise didn't glance over at him, but the mage-light's glow revealed the tension in his silhouette. "I couldn't stay there knowing he might..." Blaise shook his head, unable to finish his sentence.

As soon as their discussion had ended, Blaise had found both Tristan and the resident chicken, hoping to get a message to the Maverick Underground as soon as possible. Tristan had left the messenger duty to the hen.

But Blaise hadn't heard from the Maverick Underground before they needed to leave. They couldn't wait around for an answer.

"We'll do all we can to get him back," Jefferson whispered. He couldn't promise they would succeed. Not against foes like the Quiet Ones. And gods, he hated that.

He and Blaise rode ahead of the others. Vixen had come along on Alekon, accompanied by her magicked guards. Flora was there, too. And

Raven, though he was tied to Zepheus's saddle as they made their way to the Quiet One's estate. The angry stallion had been quite insistent about being the one to bear the disgraced Ringleader.

Raven told them what he could, advising them on the number of guards to expect on the property. Flora couldn't confirm any of it, as she hadn't had the time to take a count. Raven seemed earnest enough, and for his sake, Jefferson hoped he was being truthful now. If not, Flora would definitely gut him, and without his magic to whisk him away, he was defenseless.

They stopped in a clearing a short distance from the boundary of the estate. Everyone dismounted except for Jefferson and Blaise. Hubert and Walter moved to flank Vixen as soon as her boots touched the ground. Flora moved to untie Raven from the saddle, and between the glinting knife in her belt and Zepheus's pinned ears, the Shadowstepper had all the incentive he needed to behave.

"The house is about a half mile from here," Raven explained, voice low as if he feared being overheard. "We'll need to split up in a quarter mile."

"Understood," Jefferson said, not even trying to hide the chill in his voice. He didn't enjoy needing to trust Raven for this, but it was necessary.

They continued on in silence before parting ways when the Shadow-stepper suggested. Vixen, her escort, Raven, and Flora went one way, while Seledora and Emrys turned to approach the front of the house. It was the sort of affair that was walled, and even though it was late, a sleepy guard manned the gatehouse.

The guard shook himself awake at the clatter of hooves. "Who's there?"

Jefferson didn't dare look back at Blaise. This was a dangerous game they were playing, and he feared for what—and *who*—they stood to lose. "Jefferson Cole, here to see Tara Woodrow."

The guard scratched his forehead. "It's late. Come back tomorrow."

"I suspect if you inform your mistress of my presence, she will be inclined to see me," Jefferson pushed, loading his words with every bit of arrogance and entitlement he could muster.

The guard grumbled but agreed, turning to confer with someone closer to the house. Jefferson couldn't hear any of what they said, and he debated using his magic to ease their way. But the guard returned a moment later, opening the gate and waving them through. "Mrs. Woodrow will see you. There should be a groom at the stables to mind your horses."

"We won't be staying that long," Jefferson said, tone imperious as they rode through. Besides, he hardly wanted their pegasi hindered when they may need a quick escape. "The hitching post will do." The guard shrugged, not caring the least.

Once Emrys and Seledora were loosely "secured" to the hitching post, they followed a bleary-eyed steward into the house. Blaise shifted beside Jefferson, ill at ease. Jefferson reached down and snared his beau's hand, squeezing gently. Neither of them liked this plan, but it was their best chance to rescue Jack before it was too late.

The steward showed them to a parlor. It was like the one Flora had described, though the Effigest was nowhere to be seen. Someone had laid a new rug across the hardwood floor, the pile fluffy and unworn. Jefferson narrowed his eyes as he strode across it to claim a settee.

"Mrs. Woodrow will be here shortly," the steward declared. "I'll have refreshments delivered."

"There's no need for that. It's late," Jefferson cut in. The fewer people awake in the house, the better. Once the steward retreated, he glanced at Blaise. "This is where Jack was. They replaced the rug."

"How do you know that?" Blaise's brows rose with the question.

"It feels new." Jefferson prodded it with the toe of his riding boot. He'd been in enough elite homes to know the give of a rug that had seen many a season and one that had been replaced.

"Then where's Jack?" Blaise asked.

"That's the question, isn't it?" Jefferson murmured. This was exactly why they had split up.

They had little time to confer. A moment later, the door creaked open, and Tara strode in. She was dressed as if she hadn't yet found her bed, bedecked in a bright yellow gown that would have served her well at the gala. She appeared as alert as if she'd drunk an entire carafe of coffee. Tara fixed a curious look on Jefferson, gaze sliding to Blaise as she approached.

"Mr. *Cole*, you've certainly chosen an interesting time to come calling," Tara said without preamble, flouncing to a wingback chair.

The use of his preferred name was interesting. *But this may be a new tactic.* "I've been known to keep unconventional hours," Jefferson agreed blandly. "And as you no doubt assume, I've come because of pressing matters."

Tara settled back on the cushion, greed shifting into her expression. "I prefer not to make assumptions. But you've overlooked introductions. Who did you bring with you tonight?" She smirked at Blaise.

Damn this woman. She knew very well who Jefferson had brought along, but she was no doubt hoping to remind Jefferson of what was on the line. Especially considering their plans for Jack.

"I'm Blaise Hawthorne. The Breaker."

Jefferson hadn't expected his beau to speak up, much less to introduce himself with such confidence. All hints of the shy man had vanished, though Jefferson knew it was an act. This wasn't a simple thing for Blaise, but he was doing it. *Just when I thought I couldn't love you more.*

"Delightful," Tara murmured, and the solitary word set Jefferson on alert. There was avarice in her voice, and he didn't know why. He hoped he could play to it and perhaps keep her unbalanced. Tara continued, "It's adorable that you brought your pet. Is this a threat or a peace offering?"

It's very much a threat. Jefferson swallowed, hating what he was about to say. *But none of it's true. It's not.* Blaise wasn't the only one who'd be acting tonight. "I've reconsidered. I wish to join you."

The Quiet One was still for a moment, eyes narrowing as if she were trying to poke holes in Jefferson's words. "Truly?"

"Only if you restore the Luminary and our missing outlaw."

Tara pouted. "Missing outlaw? I haven't heard anything about that—as far as I know, the only outlaw mages in Phinora are sitting before me." She shrugged, the movement making the yellow fabric of her gown cascade. "And as for the Luminary, I don't know what you're talking about."

As the Quiet One spoke, Blaise rose from his place beside Jefferson. The Breaker made a slow circuit around the room, for all the world looking as if he were taking stock of the knickknacks. He stopped by a shelf with decorative figurines perched on it. Blaise made a show of looking at them closely, then glanced at Tara as he said, "Are these worth much?"

The Quiet One's eyes widened. "More than *you're* worth. Mr. Cole, bring your mage into line."

"That's not really how this works," Jefferson said pleasantly as Blaise picked up a porcelain shepherdess in a blue dress. "And you forget your own words so quickly. You're not only speaking with one mage, but *two.*"

Judging by the flash of Tara's eyes, she *had* briefly forgotten Jefferson was a mage. Or perhaps, like so many others, she dismissed Jefferson's magic as paltry since he had done nothing with it. "Even so, you're on the same social standing as I, Mr. Cole. Not the baseborn Breaker."

That insult against Blaise rankled, but there was no doubt Tara intended it to get a reaction. Jefferson wasn't about to give her the satisfaction. He cocked his head, shrugging. "Oh, am I? That's a surprise, considering you and your friends did your level best to leave me with nothing."

Tara smiled. "The fortune we took away can be restored if you truly intend to join us." Then she cast a nervous look at Blaise. "But really, can you *please* put that down? It's one of a kind." Much to Jefferson's amazement, there was a layer of earnest respect in the request.

Blaise heard it, too. And though it would have been as easy as breathing for him to send a jolt of magic into the figure, he set the shepherdess back down on the shelf with her flock of porcelain sheep. Jefferson hid a smile at the silvery wash of magic that Blaise let play across his palm as he stepped away.

Tara gave a small nod of thanks, then turned back to Jefferson. "I—" She didn't finish her thought. Somewhere in the distance, a shot rang out. The Quiet One went on alert in an instant. "What was that?"

The report of another firearm sounded, followed by shouts.

Jefferson traded a glance with Blaise and rose. "Well, it seems we've overstayed our welcome. We'll see ourselves out."

Anger surged over the Quiet One's expression. "*You.* This is one of your ploys, isn't it?" Her hand rasped into the folds of her dress and an instant later she pulled something out—the glint of a muzzle caught the light.

Blaise saw it, too. Magic flared from his palms, a gossamer-thin shell of silver motes flowing in front of Jefferson like a shield. But Jefferson was ready for such a move, too. He'd kept his magic within reach, and now he imagined snaring Tara with his power. When it came to a single target, Jefferson had become quite adept. He pushed the command of *Sleep* against Tara, and the woman slumped to the floor before she could get a firm grip on the weapon. It clattered harmlessly onto the new rug.

"Goodnight," Jefferson said, not sparing the woman another glance. No, his attention was on Blaise. "What is it?"

"Hexgun," the Breaker murmured, crouching to snag the fallen contraption. Sure enough, he was right. It had been easy to mistake for a revolver in a moment of panic. "Not exactly like Jack's, though."

"Bring it along," Jefferson suggested. Then he jerked his head to the door. "We should go."

Blaise looked as if he wanted to balk at the idea of taking the hexgun, but he adjusted it so the hammer rested on an empty chamber, then shoved it into his belt. It seemed he remembered a thing or two about the strange weapon, despite limited experience with them. That done, he flexed his fingers, glancing at Jefferson. "Let's go."

CHAPTER FORTY-SEVEN
Outlaws Never Give Up

"I doubt he's gonna be where I found him," Flora whispered as they made their way through the darkness.

Vixen appreciated having the gutsy half-knocker along with them. Between Raven's knowledge of the estate and Flora's knack for breaking and entering without leaving a trace, the unlikely group made their way in with little trouble. Walter and Hubert, on the other hand, were not enthusiastic about this endeavor, and had balked at her inclusion. When they realized their Spark wasn't going to be dissuaded, they refused to stay behind. She wished Rhys had been there to see, so that she could prove to him the guards weren't as brainwashed as he thought.

However, just because Hubert and Walter came along didn't mean they approved of the proposed actions. But since Garus hadn't struck Vixen down or otherwise showed displeasure, they followed along.

"Why not?" Vixen asked, her voice a whisper.

Flora snorted. "'Cause they had him in a fancy parlor. People like that? They're gonna take someone like Jack out with the trash. In a manner of speaking."

"So where will he be?" Vixen pressed. She glanced behind her. Walter and Hubert stood vigil over Raven beneath a dark overhang that not only hid them but protected them from the mist.

"Gimme a minute," the half-knocker said. She pushed her glasses up on her nose, squinting as if she were thinking. "There's salt-iron in there. My guess is they'll have him near that."

Salt-iron. Like any other mage, Vixen hated the stuff, but it made sense. Odd, though. How did Flora know there was salt-iron inside? "We need to find him before we run out of time."

"Yeah. C'mon," Flora agreed, leading them around the darkened side of the ornate manor.

The entire way, the half-knocker stared at the inky ground. Vixen knew the short woman could see much better in the dim light than she could. After a moment, Flora held up a hand, pointing at something near the building's foundations. "Cellar door."

Vixen frowned, coming closer. It was nearly impossible for her eyes to make out, but she crouched and brushed her fingers against the treated wood. She fumbled for the handle and found it, though tugging proved it was stuck or locked.

Flora dug a hand into a pouch at her belt and pulled out something dark that Vixen couldn't quite make out. It must have been lock-pick tools, since the half-knocker slid something into the lock and leaned close as she fiddled with it. Precious moments passed in which Vixen had no choice but to wait, heart thumping as she watched for trouble.

A soft click signaled Flora's success. The half-knocker was silent as she stowed her tools, then used her impressive strength to haul the heavy door open. Nothing but more darkness met them.

"There's dried blood on the top step," Flora commented, pointing at an indistinct blotch. "Oh wait, you've got crummy human vision. Want me to go down without you?"

Vixen shook her head. "No. Give me a moment." She turned and hurried back to where the men awaited them. "Do either of you have a mage-light?"

"Don't go down there," Raven whispered, almost pleading.

She ignored him, her eyes on the shadowy forms of her Lightguards. Hubert patted his pockets and then produced one of the smallest mage-lights Vixen had ever seen. It was the size of her pinky finger, perfect for storing in a coat. He offered it to her. "Allow Walter or me to accompany you, Spark."

Vixen glanced at Raven. Even bound as he was, the Shadowstepper was dangerous. She knew all too well what he was capable of. "I need you both to stay with him." She nodded toward Raven.

Walter shifted his weight from one foot to the other. "This mission of yours is dangerous, Spark Valoria."

"There's already too many of us here. I can't go sneaking around with an escort." She barely kept the annoyance from creeping into her voice.

"As you wish," Walter murmured.

"Let Flora go alone. Stay up here," Raven urged again, shifting closer until Walter checked him with an iron grip on his arm.

She turned to glare at him, though she supposed it wasn't very effective in the dark. "I think we've established that I trust you about as far as I can throw you. So stop trying to get me to do what you want, unless you want me to magic you into silence."

Raven swallowed. "You don't understand what these elite are like."

"But I *do*." Vixen was through arguing with him. She spun and marched back to where Flora waited at the top of the stairs leading into the depths.

Vixen tapped on the light, and together, they eased down the twisting stairs into the cool, clammy recesses of the…well, Vixen wasn't sure what it was. A cellar? Storage? A dungeon? There were so many ugly options.

With every step, Vixen wondered if Raven had been right to warn her. The cellar had a wrongness to it, something she couldn't put her finger on. But ahead, she heard a soft moan. At the sound, both women quickened their pace, though they still proceeded with caution.

The stairs led to a short hallway. Rooms without doors branched off from the corridor, their thresholds dark save for one. Vixen and Flora exchanged glances when a groan met their ears again.

It's him. It had to be Jack. Heart thundering, Vixen approached the lit room, though Flora beat her to it. The half-knocker peered around the corner. She said nothing, but she nodded and slipped inside.

Vixen followed suit. The room they entered couldn't be described as well-lit, but it was better than the interminable darkness. A single mage-light that needed a re-enchantment sat on a crate, casting a faint glow. A lump claimed the floor in the middle of the room. The lump moved, just enough to prove it was a person. Breath hitching, Vixen went down to her knees beside Jack.

"Garus help us," Vixen whispered out of reflex, startled when she felt the overwhelming presence once more. She swallowed, returning her focus to the downed Ringleader. Jack's face was a swollen mess, his eyes blackened. She couldn't even guess what color his clothing had been, it was so darkened by blood. His breath rasped, as if the act of breathing pained him. In his condition, it probably did.

Tears stung Vixen's eyes. Jack was an asshole, but he was an asshole she counted as a friend. She licked her lips, thinking.

"I'm almost afraid to move him," Flora admitted from where she crouched beside Vixen.

At their voices, Jack's eyelids flitted open. He seemed unable to focus on them, but he knew who had come. The Effigest made a rumbling sound, as if he wanted to speak, but it was beyond his abilities.

"Now, now, Mr. Dewitt, I can't have you warning my guests."

"*Schist*," Flora cursed. She whirled, moving so fast her knife was in hand by the time she faced the new threat.

Vixen turned, eyes widening. She knew the man—one of the elite who had caused such havoc at the gala. Phillip Dillon. He leaned casually against the doorframe, a revolver aimed at them. Wait, no. Not a revolver. It had a brassy cast to it and a distinct shape.

"I'll be honest. I was hoping it would be Cole coming for the outlaw, but I suppose I can make do with Spark Valoria." Dillon took a step inside.

Flora stiffened as he drew near. Vixen was certain she was going to strike. Their enemy must have thought so, too. He swiveled the muzzle of the weapon, aiming it at Flora, and pulled the trigger.

"No!" Vixen lunged toward the half-knocker, but it was too late. Her only consolation was that the weapon was a hexgun, not a true revolver. But a hexgun could cause just as many problems for them.

The pellet splattered as it struck Flora's stony skin. For a moment, Vixen hoped the half-knocker might be immune. Knockers couldn't be stabbed, as their skin was too tough. But then Flora wove on her feet, eyelids fluttering. She went down hard, asleep before her face hit the floor.

Dillon smiled, glancing down at the hexgun before settling on Vixen again. "Will you come quietly, Spark, or would you prefer to end up like your friend?"

Vixen swallowed, glancing from Flora to Jack. Damn it, if she didn't play this right, she was going to lose another friend. *If ever there's a time to use my magic, this is it.*

She raised her hands, slowly lifting her head to meet his gaze. Did he know what type of magic she commanded? She hoped not. Vixen felt the snap of her power against him, ready to unfurl. "You're going to give me the hexgun and stand back."

She felt his mind rattle against the suggestion. He didn't want to do either of those things. Vixen pushed more magic against him, gritting her teeth. He was a stubborn one, his mind already made up. But Vixen wasn't going to give up so easily. More of her power crashed against his defenses, slowly wearing them down.

"Give me the hexgun!"

With a reluctant growl, he offered it to her, grip first. Vixen snagged it, stuffing it into the top of her trousers as he stepped back. Then she crouched down to gather up Flora. Gods, but the small woman was as heavy as a bag of rocks. Vixen grunted as she edged past the elite, heading for the stairs. She spared a single glance at Jack. "Outlaws never give up."

She hoped he heard her soft words, hoped he knew it meant they were determined to rescue him. Somehow.

The climb up the cellar stairs felt like the longest in Vixen's life. Flora bobbed against her, snoring softly. Vixen's muscles complained beneath the strain of the half-knocker's considerable weight. She liked to consider herself strong and nimble, but Vixen had never needed to carry an ally out of a dangerous situation.

She reached the top of the stairs, breathing hard. Vixen emerged into the darkness, relief swelling when she saw dark shapes nearby. It took her far too long to realize they weren't friendly.

"Who are you?" a theurgist guard barked, on alert.

"That is our Spark!" Hubert bellowed. Vixen was certain he thought he was helping, but as far as she was concerned, that was about the worst thing he could have said.

"Get out of here!" This from Raven. Out of the corner of her eye, she glimpsed shining metal as the Shadowstepper wrested a gun from one of the Lightguard. She heard Walter's startled shout, followed by the blast of a revolver.

An enemy guard in front of Vixen cried out as Raven's bullet struck him. He went down, a spurt of blood spattering out like dark rain in the glow of Vixen's mage-light.

"Get her!"

Oh, no. Vixen hadn't been able to hold the Quiet One with her magic, not while negotiating the stairs. He had made it to the top, and now he glared at them with fury etched on his face.

<We're coming! We're all coming!> Alekon was frantic in her mind. She could almost feel the thunder of his wings.

"Spark Valoria! Get to safety!" Hubert cried as the enemy pulled their weapons. Some of them angled at Vixen's escort, and others trained on her. The weapons glinted with the same brassy gleam as the hexgun at her waist.

She couldn't escape, not while burdened with Flora. And the court-yard they were in was too tight for the pegasi, even for touch and goes. Their wings would snag on the nearby small trees. Vixen swallowed, glancing down at Flora. *What I need is a distraction.*

The wall to Vixen's right made an awful grating sound, as if someone were grinding its stones together. Everyone turned to stare at the wall in surprise. There were gasps all around as the mortar holding the stones split. Chunks fell with sharp pops.

She knew who was doing that. And it was the distraction she needed. Vixen turned and started to run with her heavy burden.

"Get her!" Dillon demanded again.

"No!" Vixen knew Raven's voice when she heard it.

There was a concussive pop, the telltale sound of a hexgun firing. She thought for certain it was aimed at her, but she heard Raven's soft curse followed by the solid thud of a falling body. Walter and Hubert shouted something she couldn't make out.

Vixen made it through a gap in the garden wall. Wings split the air overhead as Alekon and Zepheus appeared. Seledora and Emrys must have gone a different way for their own riders.

"Zepheus! Flora's been knocked out," she called to the golden stallion as he landed.

The palomino's nostrils flared. He didn't ask what had happened to Raven. <Sling her across my saddle.>

<Hurry! They're coming!> Alekon jigged in place, nervous.

Vixen did the best she could, but Zepheus was tall, and Flora was unwieldy. It took her longer than she liked to get the smaller woman slumped across the stallion's saddle. But then she did it and—

<Vixen!> Alekon's whistling whinny split the air.

An onyx chain snaked up from the ground, wrapping around Vixen's right ankle. She gasped as the arcane metal pulled taut, another chain whipping up to shackle her left leg. Vixen turned, spotting the Trapper mage standing apart from the crush of guards swarming the area. She was vaguely aware of Raven slumped on the ground, Walter grappling with an armed guard, and Alekon prancing nervously nearby. Zepheus thundered away, retreating with Flora.

Vixen focused on the Trapper, meeting his gaze. He smiled, confident as a cat with a mouse beneath his claws.

"Let me go." She flooded her words with magic, pressing her command against the theurgist. His resistance was like running face-first into a brick wall. She had to find a crack. Or make one.

<I'm going to go kick him in the head.> Alekon pawed at the ground, raking up a great furrow.

"No!" she told the pegasus through gritted teeth. That would put him dangerously close to the armed enemy. "I've got this!" Vixen took a deep breath, even as the chains weighed her down. She focused on the Trapper. *"Let me go."*

But again, he withstood the assault. Was this one of those rare people who shared the Tracker immunity to magic? That was the only explanation, unless he was deaf, but she didn't think that was likely.

<I'm going to stomp him into dust!> Alekon threatened, half-rearing.

That was looking more and more like the only choice. Vixen opened her mouth to speak, right as a hexgun pellet splattered against her shoulder, the liquid gel soaking through her clothing.

<No! Stay awake!> Alekon pleaded.

Vixen wanted to. She really did, but the effect of the pellet's liquid tugged her eyelids down, and there was nothing she could do to fight off the slumber that came.

CHAPTER FORTY-EIGHT

Cinnamon Rolls Make Everything Better

Jefferson

"Well, that was yet another disaster," Jefferson groused when, at last, they reached Hawthorne House. He knew he should be grateful that some of their number had escaped. But considering the losses they'd suffered, he didn't feel as if they had much to be thankful for.

Blaise pulled off his hat and hung it by the entry, running a hand through his matted hair. He shucked off his boots, then padded toward the kitchen with a yawn. The Breaker hadn't spoken a word since they'd left the Quiet One's estate, which bothered Jefferson. Even Emrys had privately told Jefferson he was worried about his rider. Jefferson followed him, Flora bringing up the rear. The half-knocker could barely keep her eyes open.

"It was my fault," Blaise said at last. He stood before the counter, staring at a canister of sugar.

Jefferson frowned, moving to stand beside the younger man. "I hardly think it's fair to blame yourself."

Blaise closed his eyes for a moment, his face lined with defeat. "It was my idea to go as soon as possible. Maybe if we'd waited, the Maverick Underground could have helped."

Flora rubbed her eyes. She had awoken as Zepheus carried her back to Hawthorne House, though she was still groggy. The half-knocker sat at the table, her head resting on one arm. "They were ready for us no matter when we came at them."

Jefferson glanced over his shoulder at her. She was probably right. He settled a gentle hand on his beau's shoulder, feeling the tense muscles beneath his fingers. Blaise twisted to look at him, blue eyes brimming with guilt.

"Not your fault," Jefferson whispered. "This is what they *want*. To demoralize us. To split us." And gods, they were good at it, too. Blaise relaxed the tiniest amount and went back to whatever he had gotten it in his mind to bake. Jefferson returned his attention to Flora. "What did you find? Was Jack there, at least?"

She lifted her head, blinking at them. "Yeah. Still alive but not looking good. He tried to warn us."

Blaise stooped to find the mixing bowl he wanted and paused, looking back at Flora. "He was conscious?"

"At least for as long as Vixen and I were there," she confirmed grimly. "I don't know what happened after Dillon hexed me."

Jefferson rubbed his cheek, his thoughts sluggish from stress and exhaustion. The Quiet Ones not only had Jack, but they'd reclaimed Raven and now had Vixen. He didn't think they'd harm the Persuader, not with her position as Spark, but they would do everything in their power to use her. Jefferson sighed.

"What do we do now?" Blaise's question was plaintive. Jefferson hadn't seen him measure flour, but somehow he already had it in the bowl. He added sugar and salt, then picked up a spoon to mix them together.

Jefferson yawned. "Against the Quiet Ones? I'm too tired to even think of that. I think our best option is to sleep."

Blaise nodded. "Maybe you can reach Vixen or Raven in the dreamscape."

It was a worthy thought, but Jefferson privately doubted it. If Flora had already stirred from the sleep pellet, the odds were good that they had, too. He would certainly try, though. "Yes, perhaps I can. I'll go see what I can do about that."

"I'll be up once I finish this batch of cinnamon rolls," Blaise murmured.

Jefferson smiled, leaning in to give the Breaker a kiss on the cheek. Their world might shatter around them, but at least they had cinnamon rolls to look forward to. It was a small thing, almost inconsequential, but it made Jefferson feel infinitely better.

CHAPTER FORTY-NINE

Beacon of Hope

The burn of salt-iron on skin wasn't the sensation Vixen wanted to awake to. With a hiss, her eyelids flew open, and she struggled upright.

"Spark Valoria, you're safe." The man's voice reminded her of the slimy trail left by a snail.

She turned and saw the same Quiet One who had ambushed her and Flora in the cellar. Phillip Dillon sat in a wingback chair beside a woman dressed in a fine gown who dozed on a nearby settee. That must have been Jefferson's handiwork. Knowing that another mage had gotten the upper hand on at least one of their enemies heartened her.

"Or perhaps you prefer your outlaw name," Dillon continued. "Vixen Valerie, was it?"

The sound of her name from his mouth grated on her nerves. Vixen squared her shoulders, drawing on her composure even as the metal rattled against her wrists. She glanced downward. The bracelets were thick silver cuffs covered in ornate designs of Garus's lupine and avian representations. Flecks of black metal glinted in the eyes of the foxes and owls—no doubt the salt-iron. A quick inspection proved they truly were glorified shackles. Each one sported a tiny keyhole.

"It's Spark Valoria to *you*." She thought about demanding her release, but didn't think it would get her very far. And with the salt-iron curtailing her magic, she had no hope of overpowering him any other way. She was smart enough to know when she was outgunned. "What do you want with me?"

He gave her an appreciative nod. "I'm impressed. Not demanding your release or threatening my future."

Vixen wasn't sure if that was a compliment or not. "I'm the *Spark*, remember? Future avatar of the god of wisdom."

"So you are," he agreed. "Though I'm disinclined to consider the actions that brought you to my parlor as *wise*."

He had her there. They should have known it was a trap, but Blaise had been right. They had to try. Vixen was unwilling to acknowledge that, however. Instead, she met his eyes as she dredged up a teaching she remembered from her childhood. "Follow the path you're on, and you'll reach your destination. Divert, and you may reach your destiny."

Her words made him hesitate. "Is that a threat of some sort?"

She gave him a cool look. "It's one of the Old Teachings of Wisdom." Vixen didn't think he was a follower of Garus. He had the accent of someone from Ganland. Tabris, then. Like Jefferson.

Dillon made a noncommittal sound. "I've been a poor host. Spark Valoria, I'm Phillip Dillon." He jerked a thumb to the slumbering woman nearby. "And this is Tara Woodrow."

"Charmed," Vixen murmured, though she was anything but. "And I'll ask again: what do you want with me?" There was more she wanted to ask. Where was Raven? Were Walter and Hubert okay? And what had happened to the rest of her friends?

Dillon smiled. "I do like how you get straight to business. I'll lay it out for you, Spark Valoria. We know exactly what you are. Not only the Spark but also a mage." He waited, as if expecting her to deny it, but Vixen remained quiet, deciding it was best not to react. "Am I right in thinking that particular dirty secret is why you fled so long ago, leaving your poor mother to give you up for dead?"

Vixen narrowed her eyes. "There's nothing dirty about magic."

He scoffed. "I'll be the first to disagree, but that's not what we're discussing. Back to the point. You only returned when word reached your ears that the Gutter might face a Salt-Iron army soon. For the second time in as many years." Dillon steepled his fingers before him. "The long-lost Spark returns in a desperate bid to save her friends and the land she's grown to love, is that it?"

Vixen seethed. He certainly had a way of wrapping everything up into a nice package. "Again, what do you want with me?"

Dillon cocked his head. "Hit a nerve, did I?" He leaned forward in his seat as the woman stirred. "Your secrets are safe with us. For a price."

Of course, there's a price. "And that is?"

"Work with us. Follow our directives. The Clergy Council is prepared to support you in this."

Vixen froze, shaking her head. "No. I won't. Not when you're actively working against the mages." Her heart raced. If she became the Luminary, she would be one of the most influential leaders in the Confederation. And she would be a puppet to the whims of the Quiet Ones.

Dillon sighed, affecting a look of utmost patience, as if he were speaking to an unruly child. "We want mages, yes. But we don't want the Confederation to attack the Gutter any more than you do." He spread his hands. "Surely we can agree on that. The outlaw mages are better off alive than crushed beneath the Confederation's might."

But at what cost? His words were true, though. And her entire point in coming here had been to stave off a war. Vixen swallowed. "What do you intend?"

Dillon leaned forward, eager now that she seemed receptive. "You were an outlaw mage—they'll listen to you. Ask the mages who fled to return home to the Confederation. They'll look to you like a beacon of hope."

And just as quickly, you'll turn me into a snare. Dillon didn't say it, but they both knew it for a truth. Jefferson had mentioned this group was playing a long game. Well, so could she. "If I agree, you'll leave Blaise Hawthorne and Jefferson Cole alone."

He frowned. "Unfortunately, you're not in a position to barter, Spark Valoria. You'll agree, or your secrets will come to light. And in that case, Jack Dewitt won't be the only outlaw to hang."

Vixen swallowed, her heart thundering. She considered snapping back at him for daring to threaten her, but that same solid presence she'd felt earlier stayed her hand. Garus. She knew it had to be. The god had reason for her to capitulate. She hoped he didn't intend for her to serve these men.

A muscle in her jaw ticked. "I'll work with you."

At her agreement, Dillon smiled. "Excellent. I was hoping we wouldn't have to call an Inker in."

That was why Garus wanted me to hold back. A trill of worry shot through her. A Spark or Luminary, bound to a handler? That was unthinkable. And this group would do it, too. She released a ragged breath. "You can't hold me here forever. The Lightguard is surely looking for me." And Rhys. Maybe she could get him to help somehow.

Dillon nodded. "Indeed. How fortunate it is that we could rescue you from the outlaw mages who were trying to steal you away again. Your devoted guards have already agreed to the story, lest they face...retribution."

Vixen's gut clenched. There it was. He was determined to go after her friends in every possible way.

He smiled. "Is that better or worse than the accusation that they tried to break into an elite's home? They attacked my associate." Dillon waved a hand to Tara, who rose, groggy. "With *magic*."

The awful thing was, he was right. Jefferson and Blaise would be in trouble for either charge. "I'll do whatever you say as long as neither of those accusations see the light of day."

Dillon chuckled, and for a frightening moment, she feared he'd deny her. Then he nodded. "If it will win your loyalty, then you have a deal."

Vixen slumped against the chair, exhausted from the night she'd had and the conversation. She wanted to walk into an empty field and scream at the injustices that were being done.

The Quiet One rose from his seat. "I'll call for a coach, and you and your loyal guards can make your way back to your residence. We'll be in touch soon, Spark Valoria."

CHAPTER FIFTY
Mutton Underpants

Blaise

Once Blaise claimed his warm spot in the bed beside Jefferson, he slept for longer than he'd thought he might. It had been a blessedly dreamless sleep, not even Jefferson's dreamscape encroaching on the needed oblivion.

Jefferson's arm was slung over Blaise's side, the Dreamer's breath gentle as he dozed. Blaise shifted out from beneath it, carefully rising to sit on the edge of the bed—then he saw Flora perched in the armchair in the corner, watching them.

"Um." Blaise rubbed the back of his head as the half-knocker cackled.

At his voice and the laughter, Jefferson stirred, eyes flashing open. Normally, it took him longer to rouse, much less bother sitting up, but he launched upright. He stilled when he saw Flora. "Oh, it's just you."

She waved at them. "I decided to keep tabs on you two since Raven's out there somewhere. Not taking any chances, you know?" Then she leered at them. "But you two were so tired. You're very boring when the most interesting thing you do is sleep."

Blaise glowered at her. "We're fine. You can go now."

She huffed. "Why? You're fully dressed."

He was, as was Jefferson, but it was the principle of the thing. Blaise would rather not have Flora randomly appear in their bedchamber, even if she had good intentions. But he knew that was unlikely to deter her, especially with all that had transpired. Blaise sighed. "Any news while we were sleeping?"

"An extremely good-looking man with a unicorn is outside waiting for you to wake up. And a chicken came with a note tied to it. Like a poor man's messenger pigeon. This place is *so* much more interesting than it used to be. I love it."

Rhys was here? And they'd received a note? "What did the note say?"

Flora produced the small curl of paper from a pocket. "'MU will help.' I hope that means something to you. I've spent the better part of an hour trying to figure out what MU is. Mulish Uncle? Maniacal Unicorn? Mutton Underpants?"

"Maverick Underground," Jefferson clarified, clearly hoping it would make her stop.

Hope surged in Blaise, and he traded looks with Jefferson. "We won't be on our own." Then he recalled what else Flora had said. He got up, moving to the window and peeking through the blinds. Sure enough, he recognized the unicorn grazing on the lawn. "It's Rhys. And I can't imagine he's going to be happy."

"No, I imagine not," Jefferson agreed with a sigh. "Let's go face the music."

Jefferson sent Flora to fetch the Tracker. Meanwhile, Blaise made the strategic decision to meet with him in the kitchen. It was hard to be mad around breakfast pastries, or so he hoped. At the very least, it would make *him* feel better.

Jefferson carried over two mugs of coffee, setting them on the table before taking his seat beside Blaise. He had just taken a sip when Flora showed the Tracker in.

"I should haul you both to the Golden Citadel!" Rhys stormed into the room, his shoulders rigid and fists clenched.

Blaise froze at the mention of the Golden Citadel, his mouth going dry as his world contracted to those words. He squeezed his eyes shut, heart racing. If anyone had the authority to take him there, it was a Tracker—

A hand grasped his, fingers massaging his palm. Blaise almost sent a volley of magic in retaliation. Only the hand was familiar. And someone was speaking to him, voice soft and pleading.

"You're safe. He didn't mean it, Blaise. He's upset. You're not there. You're *safe*." Jefferson repeated a variation of those words over and over, desperate. Distantly, Blaise heard Flora angrily berating the Tracker.

With a shuddering breath, Blaise opened his eyes. He rubbed at his forehead with his free hand, wincing when he realized his skin was clammy with nervous sweat.

"I'm okay." He wasn't, not really. But he had to pretend. Rhys was right to be angry with them. He couldn't truly fault the Tracker for his words, even if they had spurred him into a panic. Blaise hadn't realized how close he'd been to succumbing to his old fears over the past day. He was ashamed that it only took three words to undo him.

"You're a terrible liar, and I love you very much," Jefferson whispered. His hand clutched Blaise's like a lifeline, as if he were afraid releasing it would mean losing Blaise forever. "In this moment, you're safe."

Blaise swallowed, nodding. Jefferson had chosen his words with care—he couldn't promise future safety as much as he might wish to. But here and now, he could. That would have to be enough.

"He's going to sit down, stuff a cinnamon roll in his face, and behave. Trust me when I say what I lack in height, I make up for in rage," Flora declared, jabbing Rhys in the arm. The Tracker winced. Flora made good on her threat, stalking over to the batch of cinnamon rolls and snatching one up, dropping it onto a plate. She pointed to a chair, leaving Rhys no choice but to sit obediently and accept the fated cinnamon roll.

Rhys stared at the pastry, bemused. "What am I supposed to think when the Spark is returned by the very elite who sowed rumors about her reappearance? I know it means whatever scheme she was up to with all of *you* went wrong."

"Vix—Valoria Kildare is a grown woman," Jefferson reminded the Tracker. "*She* decided to accompany us. No one forced her." He massaged his thumb into Blaise's palm, a gentle reassurance. "But if she made it back to Dawnlight, that seems like a good sign, at least."

Blaise thought so, too. It meant they weren't holding her, which was promising.

"Whatever's going on, she's moved the Reclamation Ceremony up. It's shifted to tomorrow," Rhys said, spreading his hands. "If the Luminary really is out there like Valoria thinks, we're running out of time."

Blaise swallowed, looking at Jefferson. "We're not the only ones running out of time, in that case." How would they ever free Jack now?

"What do you mean?" Rhys asked. He took a tentative bite of cinnamon roll, his expression shifting to one of momentary delight at the burst of flavor. Then his shoulders relaxed as he bit off another chunk. Blaise's own tension ebbed a fraction.

"The elite who had the Spark also have someone we know," Jefferson explained. "We're fairly confident he's the one slated to be offered as a mage sacrifice."

The Tracker was quiet for a moment, thinking. "She was trying to free the mage, wasn't she?" When Jefferson nodded, Rhys blew out a breath. "If they have your friend earmarked for the ceremony, he's as good as lost. You attack that ceremony, and it will be a bloodbath."

Rhys was right, but Blaise was never one to go on the offensive. He recognized there was a time for direct assault, but this wasn't it. As he thought about that, an idea came to him. "We won't attack the ceremony, not exactly." He took a steadying breath as their curious eyes fell on him.

"Not exactly?" Flora asked. "What's going on in that noggin of yours? Spill it."

Blaise worried at his lower lip, though the more he thought about it, the more plausible his idea became. "We'll let them think they've won."

"They already think that," Jefferson mused.

The half-knocker crossed her arms, kicking her feet in a rhythmic motion. "Hmm. If anything, they're going to think we'll make one more bid before that goes down." Her violet eyes narrowed. "This is gonna cut it close for Jack, though."

That thought made Blaise's stomach churn. But he had a plan. He didn't know if it was a good plan, but it was all he had left that didn't involve using his magic to turn the cathedral into rubble. "At this point, I'm trusting that Emmaline's keeping him stable, and we can get him in time." Based on Flora's report, the young Effigest's magic might be the only thing keeping Jack in the world of the living. She'd done it before… he had to hope she was doing so now. Blaise looked at Rhys. "If you had to work with maverick mages, would you?"

Rhys frowned at the question. "I don't follow."

"To help Vixen, and hopefully stop whatever the elite are plotting, would you work with mavericks?" Blaise pressed. He wouldn't be able to coordinate with the Maverick Underground, and he needed someone with connections. Someone like Rhys.

The Tracker licked a glob of frosting from his lower lip, then gave a hesitant nod. "I…yes. I would."

That was progress. Blaise felt as if a weight were slowly lifting from his shoulders. "Good. There's a chicken I need you to talk to."

Rhys stared at them, bewildered. "A what?"

Flora flapped a hand. "Just go with it. If Blaise says you gotta talk to a chicken, he means it." She grinned, clearly enjoying the chaos.

Jefferson squeezed his hand. "Blaise, you have a plan?"

Of all the questions anyone ever asked, that was always his least favorite. What if he failed again? But Jefferson and Flora watched him with such confidence that it was hard to deflate beneath their gazes. "Sort of. Flora, can you get uniforms for Jefferson and me?"

She twirled a finger in a circle. "Probably. Depends what kind you need."

Blaise swallowed. "The same as will be worn by the people taking Jack to the cathedral." He looked at Rhys, hoping he might have answers.

The Tracker tilted his head, skeptical. "Do I even want to know?"

Flora cackled. "Just answer the question, sweet cheeks."

Rhys glowered. "Salt-Iron Confederation, since they'll be handling a mage."

The half-knocker gave a nod, aiming finger guns at Blaise. "Got you covered. Anything else?"

Blaise turned to the Tracker. "Can you help me and Jefferson get in with the ones serving as the escort?"

Rhys pursed his lips, his eyes troubled. "If I help you, I'll be called a traitor if this goes wrong. I'll lose my position."

"As a traitor who lost my position, I understand," Jefferson said. "But sometimes, to do the right thing, it's worth it."

"And this outlaw is worth it?" Rhys asked.

Jack. The most infuriating, ruthless, and arrogant man Blaise had ever come across. He'd done horrible things—but gods, when he was a friend, he was loyal. And he had loved ones who would feel the aching hole in their lives. Blaise couldn't imagine Fortitude without Jack. "Yeah, he's worth it."

Rhys huffed out a breath. "Then I can help you get as close as possible to your mage. But I don't know how you intend to do so—the Lightguard present at the Asaphenia will know the both of you from the gala."

"I've got an idea." Blaise stood, lifting a finger in silent supplication for them to wait. He headed upstairs to the master bedroom, going straight to the dresser where he'd stowed the alchemical potions his mother had insisted on sending along with him. Blaise stuck a hand into the bag and pulled out a linen-wrapped flask to reassure himself it was still there. Then he took the bag back to the kitchen, hefting it like a trophy.

Jefferson knew what he had. The Dreamer grinned.

CHAPTER FIFTY-ONE

Fear Doesn't Win

"I said it before and I'll say it again, you look *good* in a uniform," Flora crowed as Blaise stared at his reflection, pulse racing. He stood in the master bedroom at Hawthorne House, clad in the scarlet uniform of a Salt-Iron Confederation soldier.

"Flora," Jefferson said, voice a soft warning. The Dreamer laid a hand on Blaise's shoulder, a steadying presence. "This is not the same, Blaise."

Blaise nodded, turning away from the mirror. Earlier, after Flora and Rhys parted ways to handle their details, Blaise had admitted to Jefferson he feared blundering their mission from panic. It was suddenly too much like the plan for Fort Courage, and that had ended badly for Blaise. So badly that he trembled just thinking about it.

Maybe he shouldn't do this. He could send Flora with Jefferson—surely they had the means to help Jack. But this was *his* idea, and belatedly Blaise realized he'd based it on Fort Courage for a reason: because they *had* succeeded at freeing the trapped mages. And maybe, just maybe, this time he'd have a better ending and could finally put the demons of Fort Courage to rest.

"I know. I'll be okay," he whispered.

Jefferson studied him so intently that Blaise was certain he'd call him on the lie. The Dreamer reached up and touched his cheek. "I know you don't consider yourself brave, but you are. You possess an incredible amount of courage to take action despite your fear."

Some of Blaise's nerves melted away at Jefferson's words. "My courage isn't stronger than fear, but my love is."

"And that, my dear, is where the *real p*ower lies." The Dreamer's smile was like basking in the sun on a late autumn day, warming Blaise through to his core.

"Are you done being mushy and introspective?" Flora asked.

Jefferson's gaze slid to her, though he didn't face away from Blaise. "We were having a moment. Did you not see us having a moment?"

"Tick-tock." The half-knocker crossed her arms, reminding them of their tight schedule.

Blaise swallowed. Flora was right—they didn't have time to waste. And maybe, just maybe, if Blaise kept his forward momentum, he wouldn't have time to think too much and panic. He nodded. "We should, um, get going probably. Flora, you're going to check that everyone is where we need them?"

The half-knocker grinned and tapped two fingers to her forehead in a salute. "Yep. I'm still planning to help Rhys meet up with the Mutton Underpants." Flora had decided Maverick Underground was too boring and had gone with one of her variations. "Then I'm gonna hustle to the top of the Asaphenia and hang a few mirrors so the pegasi can use 'em to navigate and know where to go."

When Blaise had laid out the plan, Emrys had overheard and wasn't having any of it. The black stallion raised such a fuss that Seledora and Zepheus had agreed they wouldn't be left out—not when their riders were at risk. But that had added a new complication: none of the pegasi were familiar with the city from an aerial view, and it would be a slow and dangerous process seeking their riders with telepathy from overhead. Flora's brilliant solution was to hang mirrors that would reflect the sunlight, creating a beacon for the equines.

<And we will be overhead once Flora has the mirrors in place to let us know the ceremony has begun,> Zepheus added.

Blaise sighed. It seemed the pegasi were eavesdropping once again. He slipped over to the window and peeked through the curtain, discovering that the trio were right outside the window. At least they were using their ears and not their magic.

"Shall we?" Jefferson asked, eyebrows raised.

Blaise pulled out his pocket watch, checking the time and then snapping it closed. If they delayed much longer, they'd miss their opportunity to join the forces bringing in their prisoner. "Let's go."

After checking that the alchemical potions were safely in the pouch nestled at Blaise's side, they boarded the carriage, driven by Tristan. The teen would deliver them to the location Rhys had recommended, where they would meet up with the rest of the Confederation contingent. Flora had used her talents to get Blaise and Jefferson assigned as the pair who would personally handle the outlaw. Blaise had started to ask how she managed it, but Jefferson assured him he probably wouldn't like the answer.

Their carriage drew to a stop and Tristan pounded his fist against the side, announcing they had reached the end of their route. Blaise swallowed, pulling the potions from his pouch. He handed one to Jefferson.

The Dreamer accepted it with a nod of thanks before uncorking it. "Cheers." He took a sip as if it were a fine champagne, though his lips curled when he encountered a taste that disagreed with his palate.

And then he changed. His features melted into those of someone else, much like when he used his cabochon ring. Jefferson's hair darkened, and for a moment Blaise feared he might look too much like Malcolm. But then a thick black beard sprouted along his chin, shaggier than Blaise's, and all resemblance to the former Doyen was lost.

"Ah, I much prefer facial hair on you," Jefferson lamented, touching his chin. "Oh. This feels as real as my glamor. Quite impressive."

Blaise couldn't help but smile at Jefferson's observations. "You should try a beard sometime. You could pull it off." Though Jefferson would find a way to make a burlap sack look fashionable.

"Not a beard, but I *have* considered growing out my hair. You know, sort of a ne'er-do-well, roguish look." Jefferson tilted his head. "Now let's see you."

Blaise opened his own potion, wrinkling his nose. He took a sip, surprised when he didn't feel any great change sweep over him. In fact, he almost thought it hadn't worked until Jefferson heaved a dramatic sigh.

"It gave me a beard and took yours away. That's downright cruel."

Blaise reached up and gingerly stroked his too-smooth chin. It was an unnerving sensation, knowing that his beard *should* have been there, but wasn't. "If that's the worst of it, I'll take it." He stoppered the remaining potion. He had some of his mother's healing potions in the pouch as well, but he didn't think they would do much for Jack. Maybe he *should* have brought along Chill of Death. As awful as the potion was, it would have kept the Effigest from death. Well, that wasn't something he could dwell on now. "You know what to do?"

Jefferson squeezed Blaise's shoulder. "Make sure we both stay near Jack. And, most importantly, ensure that you have a chance at the rope."

Blaise nodded, then leaned over to open the carriage door. As light poured in, a wave of panic swept over him. Visions of them being found out before they could get to Jack. Of being thrown back into the Cit—

"Don't let your fear win." Jefferson was suddenly much closer than Blaise recalled. "We can do this. I'm here."

Blaise swallowed, sucking in a steadying breath. He met Jefferson's eyes—no longer green, but more of a muddy brown. But still filled with love and determination. *I'm not alone.* "Fear doesn't win. Love wins."

"And it always will," Jefferson whispered.

CHAPTER FIFTY-TWO

Fowl Intercession

Thinking hurt. Moving hurt. Jack's body felt like one enormous bruise. The pain-numbing working from his poppet had ebbed during his unconsciousness, the doll tumbling from his grip when his captors had moved him.

There was a time when he thought help had come. Jack had heard familiar voices, had been sure it was Vixen and Flora. They couldn't be here. He knew that much, and he'd tried to warn them. Only he was no longer sure if they'd ever been there or if they were figments of his imagination.

And Kittie. Had he seen her, too? He certainly felt like he had, but maybe that was only his longing to be with his wife one more time. To tell her how he loved her more than all the stars in the sky. Her presence had felt so real, but Jack vaguely thought it seemed like she'd been trapped. But that made little sense. Nothing did.

Jack hoped rescue would come, but that didn't seem to be in the cards. In between the bouts of darkness, he tried to come up with an idea to save himself. But every plan required him to be whole. And right now, he was a broken thing. Even if help came, he might be too far gone.

More time passed. He was vaguely aware of hands grasping him, picking him up. His eyes fluttered open, but the world around him was a confusing riot of color and shadow. The light stung his eyes, making them water. All around him, men and women were talking, going about their tasks as if it were any other day. He tried to decipher their words, but he couldn't.

He groaned as they dumped him into…something. The rough wood beneath him and the nearby sound of horses or mules suggested it might be a wagon. Jack struggled to open his eyes again, wincing in the light. It was, in fact, a wagon, which a moment later jerked into motion, the wood rattling beneath him so hard it made every injury flare to life with a shining corona of agony.

Jack didn't know how long he was in the wagon. He was pretty sure he lost consciousness again. He only awoke when he felt a light touch against his bare arm and what he thought was a familiar chorus of voices. But it couldn't be. He tried to lift his head to see, but the effort was too much. Jack's head fell back against the wood with a painful thud.

Hands tugged at him, pulling him upright. Heart thundering, a surge of adrenaline pulsed through him. Jack tried to shake them away, tried to curse his outrage. But he was about as effective as a day-old kitten. The hands dragged him forward, marching him somewhere he couldn't see before pinning him in place.

"Devoted of Garus, our sacrifice has arrived to consecrate our returned Spark, soon to be the next revered Luminary."

The voice rang loud and clear, the first Jack had truly made out since he'd been beaten. He didn't know the speaker, but with a sinking feeling, he knew what was happening. Dillon had said they would hang him, and the Quiet One was making good on his promise. With effort, he cracked his eyes open once more. His vision blurred, but he saw enough to recognize the exterior of the Asaphenia. Garus's bloody ceremony required a death, which meant they were holding it in the courtyard located beside the cathedral.

"This is not just any sacrifice." This voice, Jack recognized. Tara Woodrow, Dillon's crony. The priest must have invited her to speak. "Spark Valoria will be brought to power by the lifeblood of one of the most feared outlaws, the Scourge of the Untamed Territory. Wildfire Jack Dewitt." There was a pause as the crowd murmured, and then Woodrow continued. "Not only has this wicked mage robbed and killed countless innocent merchants, but he's the cold-blooded murderer of Doyen Gregor Gaitwood and Commander Lamar Gaitwood."

At least they got my damn accolades right. That was little consolation, though, as the crowd's rumble grew at the revelations of all Jack had done in his life. He'd known that his enemies would come calling for his sins. Kittie had tried to warn him, and he'd been the fool who thought nothing could touch him. *I should have listened to her.* Jack had always known this might be his end—he just wished it wasn't now.

The crowd grew more vocal, calling him every name under the sun. But they quieted after a moment, and Jack figured the priest must have made some gesture to continue the ceremony.

"Spark Valoria, do you vow to allow the wisdom of Garus to light your path, unto the end of your days?" the priest intoned.

"I have, and I will." Sure enough, that was Vixen's voice, though there was a hitch in it. What was she thinking, standing on a dais as her life was about to change—his blood the very impetus for that change? He wondered if both of their lives were about to end, only in very different ways. She would no longer be an outlaw.

"Let the chaos of magic be doused so that wisdom may flow forth," the priest declared, his voice sweeping pin-pricks of dread across Jack's body.

No. This couldn't be it. It took great effort, but he squinted and made out Vixen's hazy form. She wasn't looking at him. Her gaze was turned away, as if she couldn't bear to see him. There would be no rescue from her. It shouldn't have been the gut punch it was. Vixen was sacrificing herself for the Gutter in her own way.

Hands gripped his shoulders, guiding him forward. Jack wanted to fight, wanted to do something. Maybe he could trip his escort? But then what? A one-legged donkey could apprehend him in his current state.

"Stairs," a masculine voice advised him.

That voice. But it can't be... Suddenly, he didn't have time to focus on the voice that was so familiar it shot an arrow of hope through him. With help, he staggered up the stairs that led to the gallows. The acrid scent of varnish was strong in the air, proof that they'd treated the wood recently to protect it from the elements in the courtyard.

Hands tugged at his shoulders again, getting him into position atop the platform. Jack's breath came short and hard from the effort of the stairs. Yeah, and he'd thought he could fight? All he was fit for was the long walk to Perdition. This was it. The end of the trail for the Scourge of the Untamed Territory.

The rough coil of rope slipped around his throat, grating against his skin. The hangman fiddled with the noose, adjusting the loop until it was uncomfortably taut.

"Don't I get any last words?" Jack rasped. Gods, it had taken far too much effort to ask. Every syllable scraped against his tongue, unwieldy and awkward.

"That is not a part of the ceremony." The priest had the gall to sound apologetic. "May Garus grant you rest in Perdition."

"You and your god can go hump a flatulent dragon." Jack's lips were so chapped they felt like sandstone, and the effort of speaking burned his throat, but damn, the mortified gasps his suggestion received made it worthwhile.

"His life for the Spark," the priest declared, ignoring Jack's pettiness.

The trapdoor opened beneath Jack's feet with a clatter.

He fell.

Blaise

Oh gods, what if this doesn't work? I'm so sorry, Jack.

The crowd cheered as Jack fell, eager for the sudden stop as he reached the end of the rope. It was like watching wolves preparing to rip apart a rabbit. Instead, when the outlaw hit the end, frayed strands snapped, releasing him from the deadly noose. He tumbled into an unceremonious, groaning heap beneath the gallows.

Blaise winced, peering down at the Effigest. His magic had worked on the rope as he'd hoped, but that drop was enough to do considerable damage. The fingers of Jack's right hand twitched into an agonized fist. Blaise imagined his friend was in a world of pain, but it was preferable to the alternative. Now he just had to hope they made it through the next few moments.

"What is the meaning of this?" The priest turned to stare at them, shock etching his pale face. He was flustered, unable to comprehend that the ceremony had gone off the rails.

Tara Woodrow, who had been enjoying the show from the front row, stormed over to the gallows. She was dressed in finery that suggested she was attending the social event of the year—the dress bedecked with tiny crystals that caught the light as effectively as the mirrors Flora was supposed to hang in the cathedral. "You're the most incompetent hangman in all of history!"

Blaise crossed his arms as he peered down at the Quiet One. "Maybe. But I'm a pretty damn competent Breaker." He called on his magic again, touching a finger to his own arm as he sent a ripple of power out to remove the effects of the incognito potion. It tried to cling to him, like grease reluctant to be scrubbed from a pan, but after a moment, it washed away.

Tara's face clouded with a medley of frustration and sly avarice. Behind her, the crowd grew louder. "Oh, fancy seeing *you* here. I suppose Jefferson can't be far. I'm certain we can replace one sacrificial mage with another."

"Really? Is that what we're doing? How tiresome," Jefferson said, holding out his hand. Blaise took it, sending a gentle wave of magic over his beau to dispel his potion. He had to be careful, lest he also strip the glamor powered by the cabochon ring. Removing the potion from Jefferson was a bit like peeling an apple. "Now, I may not be a follower of Garus, but if something like this were to interrupt a very important ceremony, it might be seen as a sign." Jefferson smiled.

As if to emphasize his point, Emrys, Seledora, and Zepheus made a pass overhead, their huge shadows racing over the crowd. Blaise felt the brush of Emrys's mind against his own, the stallion smug at the cleverness of his rider and content that he was currently safe. From her vantage point on the dais, Vixen barely contained a grin at the disruption.

"Garus does not abide mages." The priest sounded certain of this, a promise of retribution in his voice. He drew himself up, as if deciding this was the time to regain control of the proceedings. "Lightguard, gather up all the mages and—"

"*All* the mages?" a new voice interrupted. Blaise followed the sound to the back of the courtyard. At first, it was hard to see Rhys through the throng. The dark shape of his unicorn loitered just outside the stone entryway. The Tracker strode forward with such a swagger he could have been an outlaw. Rhys had dressed in what Blaise guessed might be a ceremonial uniform, but he was still armed and ready for action. He halted before the dais where Vixen stood. She stared down at her twin, her silver eyes unreadable. "Because you'll have to start with her." He nodded to Vixen.

The Tracker made the accusation with such gravity, Blaise would have suspected another betrayal if he hadn't been the one to make the suggestion. Jefferson would probably consider Rhys a serviceable actor. The Tracker stood rigid, his expression stern, without so much as an amused twist to his lips. The assembled mass went into an uproar, some calling that it was impossible and others declaring they had known it to be true.

Members of the Lightguard filed in, though they paused at the outskirts, uncertain. They didn't know what to do, and they appeared reluctant to approach Blaise and Jefferson, which was a wise decision. Blaise didn't want to use his magic right now, but if it came down to their lives and freedom, he would become a force to be reckoned with.

Rhys held up a hand, keeping the attention on himself. "And they're not alone."

At his declaration, magic swelled. A cacophony sounded in the distance, and seconds later, a dark cloud of birds alighted in the courtyard. Mostly pigeons, by the looks of it—so many they were forced to land for a beat before taking off again. Men and women screamed as pigeons used their heads as temporary perches, many attendees fleeing to avoid the avian invasion.

"They came," Blaise whispered. He hadn't realized he'd been holding his breath, waiting to see if the Maverick Underground would work with Rhys as he'd asked.

Jefferson nudged him with an elbow. "Of course they did. Look, there's the Birdcaller." Blaise followed Jefferson's gaze and recognized Holly, clutching her rooster off to Rhys's right.

"Garus *does* abide mages," Vixen declared, her voice ringing out even over the clamor of the birds. As if to allow her a chance to be heard, half of the pigeons thundered away to roost on the architecture of the looming cathedral, staring down at them like tiny, feathered gargoyles. She held up her wrists, showing the gleaming salt-iron cuffs that dangled from them. Someone had crafted them to look like jewelry, but there was no hiding their purpose. "He knows of my magic and never turned his back on me."

"Liar!" A silver-haired woman dressed in the regalia of a priest rose and stormed toward the dais, crooking a finger at Vixen. "You'll hang for deceiving the god of wisdom!" She turned to the Lightguard. "Capture the pretender."

"Damn, Vixen's in trouble. She can't use her magic," Jefferson whispered.

"She can if I get to her." Blaise glanced down at Jack again. The outlaw had gone still, but his chest rose and fell as proof that he clung to life.

"Go on. Do your thing." Jefferson smiled at him. "I'll see to Jack. I'll know he's okay if he starts cursing at me." Then, before Blaise could say anything else, the Dreamer dropped over the side of the gallows, landing in a crouch beside Jack. Jefferson made the whole thing look effortless and heroic.

He's much more agile than I am. Blaise knew if he tried the same trick, he'd probably fall on his face or end up with a broken leg, neither of which would help their cause. So, while it ate precious seconds and didn't make him look all that heroic, he took the stairs.

The Lightguard moved to intercept him, but as soon as they did, the birds swooped in. Pigeons and sparrows harried them from above while a handful of geese hissed in rage, mantling their wings as they drove the guards back. Fortunately for the birds, the Lightguard were stunned by the fowl intercession and allowed themselves to be herded rather than attack.

Blaise crossed to the dais, but halfway there, the gold braiding of his borrowed Salt-Iron Confederation uniform caught his eye. The fleeting glance tapped an old memory, squeezing the breath from his lungs. Blaise froze, his pulse quickening. His eyes teared as he closed them, trembling where he stood.

The deck of the airship listed beneath his feet. Emrys flew in a frantic circle overhead as the airship stuttered, first shifting to the left before dipping wildly to the right. Blaise's hands pressed flat against the vibrating wood, head bowed. He couldn't do this again.

"Blaise! Look at me!"

Vixen's voice. An anchor of familiarity amid the storm-tossed sea of panic. With effort, Blaise opened his eyes, taking a ragged breath as he stared at his friend on the dais, waiting for him. He had to make it there, but he didn't know if he could. His feet were rooted in place not by magic, but by memories he had thought he could defeat. *I was wrong.*

He met her silver-eyed gaze. Blaise desperately wished she had her magic. She'd used it on him before, long ago. The memory of that time swam up, banishing the airship. Blaise had just fled his home, lost and alone, except for Emrys. He hadn't known it was magic back then, but her power had wrapped around him like a comfortable blanket, lulling him into calmness as he'd revealed his plight. Blaise focused on that, latching onto the memory of calm. Of momentary peace. His labored breathing slowed.

"Come on, Blaise. You can do this." Vixen's voice was soft, so soft it was amazing that he heard it. If not for the salt-iron stifling her, Blaise would have thought it was her magic. But it wasn't. It was her friendship, her unerring belief in him.

He swallowed and took a step forward.

CHAPTER FIFTY-THREE

From Darkness to Light

Kittie

"When I get back to Nera, I swear to Tabris I'm going to have gas lamps installed everywhere. I'm so tired of the dark," Rachel murmured as she trailed at Kittie's elbow.

"I'd suggest you have a care for swearing to any gods where we're going," the Luminary cautioned, breezing past the Madame Boss.

Kittie had sent Najaria on the hunt for more liminal spaces, hoping to find more thresholds that would tie the shadows with both the divine and the living world. The aethon seemed to be sensitive to them. They'd found others as they walked, though none of them suited their purpose. They lacked the divinity Kittie suspected was necessary to make her idea work.

That had all changed about a half-hour ago, according to Rachel's watch. Juliette had frozen, her eyes going wide. Kittie had thought the woman was startled at first, but something had passed over her countenance. A subtle change, almost impossible to pinpoint. If Kittie hadn't been watching, she'd never have noticed.

"I know where to go," the Luminary had declared. There was something different about her voice—a strange resonance, almost as if she were speaking in tandem with someone else. She'd been leading the way ever since.

"All I'm saying is that if invoking Tabris's name gets me back home, I'm all for it. I pay my tithe to the sacellum each month." The Madame

Boss glanced over her shoulder, as if expecting to find her deity sneaking up on them.

The Luminary ignored the comment, continuing on. She strode into the darkness ahead of Najaria's halo of light, her steps as certain as if it were daylight.

Rachel moved closer to Kittie, pitching her voice low. "I'm going to be honest: I like the Luminary, but right now, she's creeping me out."

Kittie hid a smile. "Do you believe in the gods, Rachel?"

The Gannish leader raised her brows. "Of course. Don't you?"

Kittie didn't have a ready answer for that. It was complicated. Jack believed in them, but she'd never known what to think of deities who played favorites. Oh, each deity and their followers professed all the reasons they were good and worthy, but Kittie understood none of it. How could Garus be so wise if he allowed such atrocities against mages? Likewise, how could Faedra, the goddess of magic, allow for such wrongs to be done to the mystic races? It made no sense. Greater powers might exist, but she supposed they were as fickle and imperfect as the creatures of the land, sea, and sky.

Rather than give an answer, Kittie deflected. "If you believe in the gods, then Juliette truly is the Luminary, the avatar of Garus. In that case, I'm hoping her god is leading us where we need to go."

Rachel nodded at that. "Makes as much sense as anything else in the shadow realm."

Ahead, Juliette drew to a halt. She pivoted to face them. "All the gods have been absent, not just Garus. His communication with me had been limited—until now." Her eyes shone, not with tears but with a golden gleam. Gooseflesh pebbled over Kittie's skin at the spectacle. "You were right about the liminal space. There's one ahead, and it combines the shadows, the divine, and our physical world."

Kittie swallowed. Najaria snorted before taking another step forward, casting her glow further. A structure rose out of the twisting shadows, something about it familiar. For a heart-stopping instant, she feared it was the Golden Citadel—but it wasn't. It was a building that belonged in Izhadell, though. Kittie had seen the architecture before from a distance.

"Where are we?" Rachel asked.

The Luminary smiled, the expression radiant. Even her golden red hair seemed luminous. "Just outside the Asaphenia, the most revered cathedral of Garus."

Well, that made sense. Of course, a place of worship would thin the veil. A chill of anticipation raced through Kittie's muscles. As eager as she was to begin the spell and see if her idea—the idea Jack had given her— might work, she also experienced a frisson of fear. It might not work. It might end in their deaths. Or it might result in angering beings capable of destroying her without a second thought.

The Luminary peered at her, and Kittie had the disconcerting sensation that someone or something *more* was assessing her, too. "What is your plan to lead us from darkness to light, Firebrand?"

Even Najaria startled at the voice. It was Juliette's but overlaid with another that was deep and rich. Like listening to a distant rumble of thunder. There was more to the Luminary than met the eye. Kittie couldn't falter, not now. She took a breath. *I have to do this not only for us but for everyone.* Her fingers trembled as she retrieved the folded paper from her pocket.

Kittie met the Luminary's golden gaze, unflinching. One wrong word and she might find herself in Perdition. "I petition the god of wisdom to work with a mage."

The surrounding darkness became stifling as she waited for an answer. Juliette stared at her, and for too long, Kittie feared she would receive no response. That all was lost. Then the avatar spoke. "Do you know, little flame, that I have *never* harbored hatred against you and yours? Wisdom has no room for hate."

Kittie's mouth went dry, her tongue threatening to stick to the roof of her mouth. She might have entertained doubts about the gods earlier, but those fled in the face of the Luminary. A primal urge deep within Kittie pressured her to flee, but she stood her ground. "That's not my experience."

"Hear me now. Humans—even this avatar—don their hate like armor and wield fear as a weapon. But the strongest armor can crack, and there are defenses against even a well-forged weapon." The Luminary turned to stare into the shadowy distance. "Hope pierces armor, and love turns away the edge of fear."

Juliette blinked, her eye color flashing between luminescent gold and cool grey. The woman shivered, turning to Kittie with her jaw clenched. As if she'd experienced something that had changed her life. "We were wrong about mages. *I* was wrong about mages." She lifted her chin, accepting her own mistakes. "How do we do this, Kittie?"

She used my name. There was something remarkable in that simple word, an acknowledgment that held weight she couldn't explain. Kittie opened the slip of paper, gaze raking over the spell to familiarize herself with it once more. Gods, they were missing so many of the items recommended for success. No stones, no physical doorway to use as a guide.

The aethon snorted at her, shaking her mane. Kittie bit her lip and murmured, "You're right. Who needs that when I'm working with an avatar?" She took another deep breath to steady herself. "The spell I'm going to cast is made for wizards, and I'm just a mage. I'm going to need all the power you can give me."

"You're not just a mage; you're the *Firebrand*," Rachel cut in. "Give yourself more credit."

The Luminary nodded. "The Madame Boss is right. You're more than you think you are." Juliette stepped closer, holding out a hand that glistened with dancing golden motes, like rays of sunshine filtering through a cloud.

I don't know about that. But Kittie wasn't about to argue. She took the offered hand, gasping at the warm surge of unfamiliar power. She bent her head against the growing tide. They were right. She was a Pyromancer. The Firebrand. The Dragon. Flames danced between her and the Luminary. Rachel yelped in surprise, but Kittie kept her focus on the spell. The fire swelled to surround them, tongues feasting on the darkness. None of it harmed them—Kittie had impeccable control over her summoned element. The flames crackled, their intensity and magic growing as the Luminary fed the inferno with power from the god of wisdom.

Flames clawed at the shadows, burning a portal through the liminal space.

"Tabris's sweet gilded buttcheeks," Rachel whispered.

CHAPTER FIFTY-FOUR

Force of Nature

*V*ixen hadn't expected Blaise to falter. It was easy to forget he was grappling with old wounds that hadn't healed—that might never heal. But she had been at Fort Courage, too, and understood. Vixen didn't particularly like using her power on friends, but in that moment, she would have—if only to help him through. But with her power chained, all she could do was hope her heartfelt words would break him free from the horrors of his mind.

Blaise's steps grew more certain as he approached and mounted the dais. The priest shied away from the Breaker's approach, as if he were a looming threat. Blaise ignored the man, aiming a weak smile at Vixen. Sweat beaded on his forehead. "Thanks."

Her shoulders relaxed, relief surging. He had made it, and not only that, he was back in the present. "You'd do the same for me, right?" She held up her wrists meaningfully.

"Always," he agreed, his voice low. As Vixen flexed her wrist, Blaise frowned at the welts revealed by the shifting plates of silver and salt-iron. He wrapped his hands around the cuffs, his grip loose. Blaise didn't even flinch at the sting of salt-iron against his flesh, only focused his devastating power on the metal. Vixen felt the feather-light brush of his magic, and not for the first time, she marveled at the control he'd learned. When she had first sought to help him learn how to harness his magic, Blaise would have shied away from a task such as this. Now he met it head-on with methodical determination. The jewelry made an unearthly grating sound, then started to crack. The links shattered, the metal falling away as flakes rained to the dais below.

She rubbed her wrists. "Much better. That's not quite my taste in jewelry."

Blaise nodded, though he had shifted to study the surrounding pandemonium, gaze flicking from Jefferson and Jack to Woodrow and then to the riled crowd. "I think whatever comes next is on you."

Vixen swallowed. He was right. She was the Spark and would be the Luminary if they didn't find her mother soon. "The bracelets sapped me dry. I don't think I can do much." Exhaustion dogged her. Oh, what she wouldn't give to curl up somewhere to sleep and recover.

"Good thing you're not alone then," Blaise said, though his gaze had dropped back to the crowd, tracking Tara Woodrow as she squeezed through the masses to head for the exit.

Vixen thought Blaise was going to use his power, but instead he lifted his right hand, as if to gain someone's attention, then nodded. Tara's forward momentum came to a sudden halt, her face twisting in frustration as she hefted her skirts to locate the problem. Huge roots had ripped up from the ground, lashing around her ankles and calves to anchor her in place.

"That one of your Maverick Underground?" Vixen asked the Breaker.

"Yep," he murmured. "I don't see the other man. Phillip Dillon."

Vixen had scanned the crowd earlier and hadn't seen him, either. She didn't know what that boded for them. The maverick had stopped Tara in her tracks, so they could deal with her later—and perhaps uncover Dillon's whereabouts. Vixen's mind whirled as she tried to think of what to do next. *Continue with the ceremony. Seal my legitimacy.* She gave Blaise an appreciative smile. "Thanks, I've got this from here."

Vixen turned toward the priest and was about to speak when a sudden whoosh of flames erupted out of the flagstones ten feet from the dais, making her stumble backward. Even the geese retreated, necks outstretched as they honked their alarm. The remaining audience screamed, nearly causing a stampede in their haste to leave. Others pressed against the walls but stayed, giving in to their potentially ill-advised curiosity.

Blaise stared at the growing wreath of flames, making a soft sound of surprise.

"What is it?" Vixen asked, voice gentle. Blaise hadn't tensed, but whatever he suspected was going on hadn't stirred his usual anxiety.

He didn't answer, but he didn't have to. The flames swirled to form a portal that led to a world of darkness. *No,* Vixen corrected herself. *A world of shadows.* For a moment, she thought it might be Raven, but that made little sense. Not considering the fire.

With a haunting cry, a glossy chestnut equine tore through the portal, coming to a stiff-legged halt in the middle of the courtyard. Vixen knew that mare. She hadn't realized the aethon had come to Izhadell, but it had to be...

Kittie Dewitt stepped through, smoke wreathing at her back like dark wings. The Firebrand paused as soon as her boots hit the flagstones of the courtyard. Her gaze raked over the scene. Pigeons still flapped overhead and geese honked, their long necks snaking at anyone who came too close, bills snapping. She found Blaise and Vixen on the stage. The mage turned as if she were speaking to someone behind her, then strode forward to make room.

A woman with mussed hair stepped out next. Her face was ashen, and she looked as if she were trying to compose herself as she appeared in the unfamiliar area.

"Rachel Clayton," Blaise whispered.

To their left, a high-pitched voice yelped, "There you are!" A moment later, Flora vaulted onto the scene, her pink hair bobbing in pigtails as she pulled out her knives, as if preparing to take on the world. The half-knocker crouched beside the Gannish leader. Vixen hadn't even known the diminutive woman was there, but then again, Flora excelled at not being seen.

But wait...the Madame Boss of Ganland? Did Vixen dare to hope...?

Juliette Kildare stepped out of the shadows.

Celestine Currington of the Clergy Council saw her, too. "The might of Garus has returned the Luminary to us!"

The Luminary surveyed her surroundings, hands on her hips. She still wore the same golden garb as the night of the gala. Her gaze snapped to Vixen, her lips curving into a smile. There was new acceptance in her expression, as if she had come to terms with what her daughter was and approved.

"I'll leave you to it," Blaise murmured, dropping from the dais.

Juliette Kildare stalked to the dais and peered at her daughter before stepping up to join her. "The ones behind this were hoping to give me up for dead, were they?"

"They were," Vixen confirmed.

The Luminary smiled, though it was an expression that promised vengeance. "Foolish of them to discount the wisdom of Garus."

Kittie

KITTIE IMMEDIATELY RECOGNIZED THE LUMP CRUMPLED BENEATH THE gallows. Jack's still form was too painfully close to what she'd seen in the liminal space of the shadow realm. He wasn't moving, and Kittie didn't know why he was on the ground, but…her eyes drifted up to the frayed rope.

They were going to hang him.

But they had failed. She took a breath, repeating it in her mind like a mantra. *They failed. They failed.* If they hadn't, her husband would be hanging from the noose, his neck broken. It wasn't much solace, though. Not when she recalled how awful he had looked.

Kittie dispelled the portal with a snap of her fingers, gritting her teeth against the rebound of magic. She was tired, but not the boneless exhaustion she'd suffered after portaling with Jack. Garus had provided quite the power boost. Kittie raced over to her husband, ignoring the assortment of birds and the shouts of confusion. None of that mattered. She went down to her knees beside him, aware of Jefferson shifting to make room.

"Who did this to you?" Kittie whispered, her voice breaking. She touched his arm, gut clenching at the bruises that dappled his skin. Someone had to pay for this. Jefferson spoke to her, but she refused to hear him. Not right now. She needed to find the one who had hurt Jack. The ones who wanted him to hang. Her gaze roved over the crowd, the fire within her heart ready to unleash an inferno on *everyone*.

"No," Jack rasped, his voice so faint she almost didn't hear. "Don't."

His voice brought her back to him. Kittie trembled, body quaking from the expense of power and the shock of finding her husband almost dead.

"He's right," Jefferson whispered, voice apologetic. Kittie hated that Jefferson could sound so composed when her world was crumbling. This was a time for unfettered rage, for a wildfire that would turn the city to crumbling ash. "You're surrounded by the Confederation right now, Kittie. And you have every right to be angry. But if you kill anyone, even someone who deserves it, you won't leave here."

"Don't," Jack insisted, the word like grating rocks.

Kittie took a gasping breath, hot tears burning her eyes. "I don't know how else to help him."

"We need a Healer," Jefferson said, his voice calm and far too reasonable. Kittie wanted to lash out at him, to erupt with anger, but he was right.

Movement nearby caught Kittie's eye. Her hands curled into claws, cradling a flame—which she quenched when she realized it was Blaise. He wasn't alone. A woman carrying a huge, brown rooster trailed him, along with a balding man.

"I know of a Healer, but it will take time for him to get here," the woman said, her face grave.

"No," Kittie said with a shake of her head. A lock of hair fell into her eyes, and she tucked it back behind her ear. "There's no one in all of Phinora I'd trust with him." Not only because of his injuries but also his status as a wanted outlaw. The price on his head would be too great a temptation.

"We have to do something for him," Blaise argued. "We can trust these mages, Kittie. I promise."

As much as Kittie wanted to share Blaise's faith in others, she couldn't. Kittie shook her head, insistent. Overhead, the birds parted in a riot of cries as huge, dark forms appeared. She glanced skyward and found the pegasi circling overhead. They swooped lower and lower, taking the measure of the courtyard to find an angle for landing. The majority seemed to think better of it, but a lone pegasus made the descent.

Zepheus came down hard, throwing up a scatter of dust as his hooves crashed against stone, wings braking. The stallion whirled, tail flying like a gossamer banner as he folded his wings. His dark, intelligent eyes homed in on Jack, and he trotted over, neck arched.

<*My rider.*> Zepheus dipped his muzzle low, blowing out a soft breath that ruffled Jack's hair. <Do not cross to Perdition without me.>

"He's *not going* to Perdition," Kittie whispered, choking out the words.

<He has one foot on the path already.> The stallion jerked his head up, the whites of his eyes showing.

Tears brimmed in Kittie's eyes. "He needs Nadine." Kittie didn't get along with Fortitude's most skilled Healer, but the woman knew her job and did it well. But Nadine was half a continent away.

Except half a continent wasn't so far, not with the magic Kittie had just wielded. She had trod dangerously close to the realm of the gods. She could do it again, though this time, she wouldn't have power fed to her from an avatar. But to save Jack, to give him a chance, she would burn herself to ashes if she must.

She looked at Zepheus. "We need Nadine. Now."

The stallion bobbed his head, dancing in place. <But she's too far. Not even the swiftest pegasus could get there and back in time, and there are no Walkers here.>

Kittie shook her head. "We don't need a Walker. We need a portal." The spell was fresh in her mind, almost burned into her brain after the effort with the avatar. She could cast it without worry—except for the sheer power required to make it successful.

Blaise rose from his crouch, the normally reserved Breaker almost effervescent with determination and the need to do something. "Kittie, you shouldn't try another so soon. Especially without help."

"I had the help of a *god*," Kittie shot back, frustrated that anyone would naysay her. She gestured to Jack. "And he…"

"Is going to be pissed if you kill yourself to save him," Blaise supplied. "Let me."

Kittie's first instinct was to deny the offer, but Najaria bumped her forehead into the Pyromancer's shoulder, as if to clear her mind. She nodded. "But I want to help." Kittie unfolded the spell and held it out.

Blaise took it, gaze flicking over the words. Jefferson had shifted to look over the Breaker's shoulder. "We don't have the reagents it suggests," the Dreamer pointed out.

"No, but you can use sheer power to overcome it," Kittie said.

"Guess we'll test my mother's theory," Blaise murmured, leaving Kittie to wonder what he meant. Jefferson made a soft sound, the lines around his eyes telegraphing his concern.

Blaise smiled, and even though the expression lit his face, Kittie already saw the exhaustion in his eyes—not from the use of his power, but from everything else. The Breaker ignored it, spine straightening as he turned to face Kittie. "Every bit of magic I have is yours." He held out a hand, fingers trembling.

Kittie took his hand. The flesh of his palm almost tingled, as if his magic lay just beneath the surface, like a pond beneath a layer of ice. How much was buried below? Jack had told her Blaise was unlike any other mage he'd ever come across.

"Thank you," she whispered, hoping he understood she meant not only for the magic but for his willingness.

He nodded, staring straight ahead. "I don't think Jack would survive going through the portal. Who can go through to get Nadine?"

<I will.> Zepheus stomped a forehoof against the flagstones, a sharp clatter that startled the nearby pigeons into flight.

"We'll hold it open as long as we can, but I don't know how long that will be," Kittie told the pegasus. In answer, the palomino pranced in place, the muscles in his hindquarters bunched in anticipation. He was ready to bolt forward like a golden bullet.

Blaise had folded the spell back into a square, stuffing it inside the pocket of his—wait, he and Jefferson were both wearing Salt-Iron Confederation uniforms. Kittie had been too distracted to notice. Blaise's hand shifted beneath hers. "Since you've cast this spell more than I have, I'll let you take the lead. But you've got all my magic."

"Right," Kittie murmured. "Let's do this."

She began the working, feeling the ache and burn as the formation tapped her personal reservoir. Without the reagents, it would drain like a bucket shot through with holes. But then the Breaker's power came, roaring up like a hurricane. To say Blaise was *powerful* or *unique* wasn't enough. It was the difference between hearing about what a tornado could do and witnessing the force of nature ripping apart a barn. *Now I understand why everyone wants the Breaker.*

Swallowing, she harnessed his river of magic, feeding it with care into the working before it had the chance to drain her dry. If she exhausted her resources, she would be too weak to continue the spell, and the portal would collapse. The Breaker magic served as a buttress for her own, and seconds later, the burning frame of the portal snapped into place.

CHAPTER FIFTY-FIVE

Not Here to Make It Right

Vixen

As much as she wanted to join her outlaw friends surrounding Jack, Vixen knew that she couldn't. The maverick had released Tara from the roots, but that hadn't meant she got away. No, a flock of hissing geese had moved to flank her, wings spread as they harried her over to the dais.

Tara shrieked as their wicked bills snapped at the glistening fabric of her dress. She looked up with surprise when she nearly ran into the dais. The geese kept their distance, no longer herding her. But the waterfowl made no moves to retreat.

"Well, now I've seen everything," Juliette remarked, her gaze locked on the woman. "Tara Woodrow, have you been plotting against me?"

"I most certainly *haven't*," the cornered elite woman sniffed. "A mage took you, Luminary. And even now, they conspire against you." Tara gestured to Vixen, pitching her voice so that others might hear. "She even ensorcelled her guards. *You* may be next."

Vixen narrowed her eyes. Walter and Hubert. They had escorted her back to Dawnlight after the ill-fated attempt to rescue Jack, but by then she'd been cuffed with the delicate salt-iron bracelets. And the guards had been yoked with threats of their own—if Vixen had to guess, likely against the loved ones the men had mentioned to her.

But she *had* nudged them with her magic, so she couldn't dispute the truth. Not here in front of Garus.

"The Spark would *never*," Juliette declared.

"Oh?" Tara asked, arms swinging at her side until a nearby goose hissed to keep her in line. "But she *was* ready to replace you. Why else would she come armed with the Breaker, and the Scourge of the Untamed Territory skulking about? The mages plot against you and all the Confederation."

Vixen clenched her teeth. With Tara's spin, every one of her points made sense—even though they were lies. The Luminary hated mages. Everyone knew that, and Tara Woodrow was weaponizing that hate.

The Luminary's mouth drew into a thin line. "Garus's wisdom exceeds your own, and he chose a mage to lead me from the darkness." Her eyes flicked to Kittie, who appeared to be casting another portal. "And he has placed a mage I trust beyond all measure at my side right now, when I need her."

Vixen startled at that, glancing at her mother. Juliette kept her steely gaze on Woodrow. Something had changed in the time between when they'd spoken after the gala and the Luminary's reappearance. She suspected that not only had Kittie been key, but the god of wisdom, as well.

The Luminary gave Vixen a contemplative look. "I don't know exactly what magic you wield, but I have my suspicions. Can you make her answer my questions truthfully? Here in the Asaphenia, Garus's hallowed halls?"

Vixen pursed her lips. Her mother was asking in a roundabout way if their god would allow her power to serve. "Yes." Tara's eyes widened at her admission.

Juliette smiled, a grim expression. "Were Madame Boss Clayton and I meant to only be kidnapped or killed?"

Tara's lips twisted, as if she were trying to choke back her answer. Vixen weighed her magic upon the woman, once more feeling Garus's presence over her. The Quiet One twitched and tried to fight, but Vixen was too much for her. "The mage had orders to get rid of you! How was I to know he was too stupid to realize we meant for you to die?" Tara's voice was a frustrated wail.

Raven wasn't stupid, he was clever. He was also misguided, but even then, he'd tried to mitigate the damage. Vixen didn't know how to feel about that.

Juliette narrowed her eyes. "I've heard enough. This is treason."

"No more treasonous than birthing a mage!"

"My child was not a mistake," Juliette said, her voice a low husk that only those nearest the platform could hear. But it was enough for Vixen. It was what she had needed to hear all along. "And she's been truer to me than you, who call yourself one of the elite." She turned, surveying the remaining crowd. "Where are my Lightguard? We're conveniently close to the Golden Citadel. Take this woman away."

The guard swept in to obey, converging on the Quiet One like a pack of hounds rushing a rabbit. In short order, they marched Tara toward the exit. Vixen followed their progress, but then the sight of her brother striding in caught her eye.

Something dark leaped from the shadows beside him. As soon as the edge of the raised knife caught the light, Vixen knew who it was.

"*Raven, stop!*" she screamed, pouring magic into the command.

But Raven wasn't looking at her, and he didn't hesitate. For a sickening instant, Vixen was sure her former beau was here to kill Rhys. But as he pivoted, the arc of his arm descending, she knew she was wrong. Raven plunged the knife into Tara Woodrow's chest, burying it to the hilt. The Lightguard escort didn't have time to respond as Raven slashed with the knife he held in his other hand, ripping it across Tara's throat. A burst of scarlet sprayed into the air.

Rhys shouted and tackled the Shadowstepper. Raven crumpled beneath him, the pair cascading to the flagstones. The Lightguard had finally recovered, doing their best to lay the bleeding elite down to render aid.

The Luminary clasped a hand to her mouth, eyes wide. "That's the mage who took me."

Rhys had Raven firmly in hand, dragging him upright. The Shadowstepper didn't struggle against the Tracker's grip. Raven's face and hair were spattered with blood, but he seemed otherwise uninjured as Rhys brought him under control.

A mix of terror and rage flooded through Vixen. She stepped down from the dais, running over to the pair. She spared a furtive glance at Tara, heart thundering at the vivid ribbons of scarlet trailing down the woman's fine taffeta gown. Blood dotted her sleeves like rubies. There was so much blood, she wouldn't last long. If Raven wanted someone dead, it was going to happen.

"What did you do?" Vixen demanded as she stormed over, face flushed with anger and confusion.

"She lied to me. You'll never love me." Raven's dark eyes were on the fallen elite woman.

"Gods damn it, I already told you that, you selfish piss-goblin," Vixen growled, her voice carrying farther than she intended. Listeners gasped at her choice of words, but she didn't give a damn. All bets were off.

Raven didn't meet her eyes. "She deserved what she got."

Yeah, maybe Tara did—but that didn't make it right. Or helpful. She seethed. If Tara lived, Vixen could use her magic to force the woman to reveal more about the Quiet Ones—if her mother allowed her to do so, at any rate. Now they'd lost the opportunity, their best hope bleeding out on the ground ten paces from them.

The Shadowstepper's gaze shifted to the outlaws huddled over Jack. Wait, was *that* why Raven had made such a public display of killing the woman? Otherwise, he could have done the deed somewhere quiet. Raven had betrayed the outlaw mages and the Gutter, which in their eyes was the worst thing possible. If Jack lived, he would hunt Raven down. Although, maybe he wouldn't need to, if he had a poppet of the man. But in the Confederation's custody, Raven would be held in the Golden Citadel, which would make it difficult for magic to touch him or for an outlaw to visit retribution upon him.

If he wanted to live to see another day, it wasn't the worst idea—unless the Confederation hung him.

And as angry as she was with him, Vixen wouldn't allow that to happen. Raven had manipulated them at every twist and turn.

"For what it's worth, I'm sorry." Raven's voice was little more than a murmur.

Vixen knew he wasn't apologizing for the murder he'd just committed. Not even for taking the Luminary, Jack, and Kittie. Somehow, he had seen those actions as necessary. "It's too late to make it right."

"I'm not here to make it right. I'm here to pay for my sins." Raven swung his gaze back to her, clearing his throat. "In case you're wondering about the ring you gave me, it's in my pocket." He dipped his chin toward the pocket at his chest.

"I'll get it," Rhys said before Vixen could step closer. The fingers of his left hand dug into Raven's upper arm as he used his free hand to retrieve the ring. He pulled it out, examining it for a moment before offering it to Vixen.

She accepted the ring, turning it over to check it before pocketing it. Vixen wondered how he'd gotten it off in the first place, but this wasn't the time to ask. In the end, what did it matter? He'd gotten it off.

Vixen swallowed a lump, part of her heart aching, wishing things had gone differently. There was no room to forgive Raven for any of the things he'd done, even if he'd thought he'd acted to help her. Perhaps especially if he'd done them for her. "Take outlaw Raven Dawson to the Golden Citadel to await trial for his crimes."

A handful of additional guards appeared, along with a duo of Trackers. Rhys hailed them, and they strode over. One Tracker had a set of salt-iron manacles, and a moment later, the mage shuffled off, bound by the metal.

"Are you okay?" Vixen asked her brother, as Raven vanished around the corner.

Rhys straightened his uniform. "He didn't even try to fight me." There was a veneer of puzzlement to his words. Vixen knew that most mages would have struggled. Maybe later, she'd explain her suspicions to him.

"Mother's back." Rhys's voice was a reverent, grateful whisper. Then, louder, "The Luminary has returned." He turned to march up to her, every muscle in his body intent on reaching the dais.

"Thank Garus and the mages for that," Juliette agreed, smiling down at him.

His brows hiked at that. "What?"

The Luminary smiled. "Explanations later." She glanced at her daughter. "You handled that well. But you should also know that you don't have to do this."

Vixen blinked in momentary confusion. "What?"

Juliette didn't get the chance to explain. Instead, something huge and golden coalesced over Rhys's head, great wings billowing. At first, Vixen thought it was an approaching pegasus, but it was all wrong. It shined with impossible gilded light, enormous eyes bright. An owl, the other animal representation of Garus. The Tracker sucked in a breath but didn't flinch, his expression growing intent, as if he were listening to something. Or to someone.

"This one will serve." The spectral owl's voice made the air vibrate like a thunderclap. Its gaze swung to Vixen. "And you? You were always meant to be free, little fox."

Vixen swallowed. "Why?" *Because I'm a mage?* Had her use of magic here, so close to the Asaphenia, finally made Garus see her for what she was?

The owl shrank into a golden-red fox, paws striking the ground in silence. "Because your path leads elsewhere." The celestial fox spun to regard Rhys. "And his has always led to this moment. You will serve as the sword of my truth and the shield of my wisdom, Rhys Kildare."

Rhys had gone down to his knees, almost overwhelmed by the news. He looked up, trembling, but nodded. "I will."

Vixen wanted to demand more answers, wanted to understand why—but before she could do so, the fox faded away. Tears stung her eyes. She felt as if she'd been cast out. She had come willingly, ready to give up everything to help her friends and the Gutter. Now everything was lost. "Why?"

Her mother took her hand, her fingers warm. "Did you really come back to reclaim your place as the Spark? To someday become the Luminary?"

Vixen met her eyes, hating that it was the perfect question. She had come back. Wasn't that enough? She could use her magic, convince her mother that, of course, that was her intent. But why? Garus had claimed her brother before the Clergy Council and the citizens who hadn't yet fled. News would spread. Vixen's only choice would be to seek the position by force—and that would be impossible without her heart in it.

"I came because most of the people I care about are mages. The land I love is under threat. And I'd do anything to keep them safe."

"Even sacrifice yourself to be something you never wanted to be." Juliette's voice was neutral.

Vixen nodded. "You never asked for it, either."

Juliette squeezed her hand. "That doesn't mean I want the same fate for you. Not when there's someone else willing." She smiled at Rhys. "And you. Is this a life you want?"

Rhys glanced from Vixen to their mother, then nodded. "Always." His gaze flicked to the cluster of mages. "I'll do my best for all the people of Phinora, including the mages."

Juliette put an arm around Vixen. "The Gutter will not suffer another attack by Phinora. Not while I draw breath."

Vixen froze. Now she understood why Garus had chosen Rhys. While he had approved of her magic, placing a mage in the position of Luminary would cause upheaval and strife. But Rhys? He was a Tracker, with not only the skills to handle a mage but magical immunity. He could interact with mages, free of the fear that they might turn their power against him. It was a small step toward showing the populace at large that mages could be trusted. "Oh."

Her mother didn't ask about her revelation, only smiled as if it was something she had figured out some time ago. And perhaps she had. She turned to Rhys. "Then let's make this official. I'll make certain the Reclamation Ceremony continues without a sacrifice, since we're making changes." She smiled at Vixen before rolling her shoulders and assuming the persona of the avatar.

"Faithful of Garus!" the Luminary declared, her voice rolling through the courtyard. The crowd that remained grew quiet, though admittedly, there were few left. Vixen knew those who had stayed were about to witness something they'd brag about for years. "I present to you Spark Rhys Kildare."

A murmur began that grew into a cheer. Rhys stood tall, his shoulders rigid as a burst of light appeared over his head, the spectral owl a flash and then gone once more. Vixen felt the familiar pressure of Garus in her mind, though this time, it was a reassurance. He wasn't turning his back on her—he was giving her what she'd always wanted.

CHAPTER FIFTY-SIX
Not the Voice of an Angel

Emmaline

Her father was dying, and there wasn't a damn thing she could do about it. Emmaline had already poured all she had into the poppet, but it wasn't enough. If only she were *stronger*.

She curled up in her bed, her parents' poppets cradled against her chest. She knew she looked a fright—hair tangled and unkempt, her face stained with tears. Emmaline didn't care. Her days and nights had turned into a cycle of willing for her father to live until she dropped into an exhausted sleep to allow her magic a chance to replenish.

"You are burning yourself out like a candle with little wick left," Clover said, her hooves ringing on the floorboards. Emmaline hadn't even heard her knock, hadn't heard the creak of the door opening. The Knossan carried a wooden tray in her hands, setting it down on the table beside Emmaline's bed.

She was staying with Clover while her parents were gone, which was for the best with how she felt at the moment. Emmaline eyed the food, though she had no appetite.

"Mindy said you need this." Clover waved a rough hand over the tray. "You won't do Jack any good if you faint."

Clover had a point. Emmaline sat up, nestling the poppets against her pillow before picking up a peach turnover. It was something she could have made herself if she'd felt up to working in the bakery. As far as she knew, Reuben and Hannah had shuttered it for the time being. That meant Celeste had probably made the turnover. She was a good cook, but no one in Fortitude was a match for Blaise when it came to baking. Emmaline nibbled a corner.

"I can't stop. What if I do and he...?" She swallowed the turnover, though it was little more than a flavorless lump. Not because it had been poorly made but because nothing tasted appealing at the moment.

"He knows what you can do, and he will know you have done all you can," Clover said, reaching down to pat Emmaline's knee. But there was stark sadness in her words, too. The last time Jack had been so badly injured, he had been close enough for them to help. That wasn't the case now. Emmaline knew Clover had to feel even more helpless than she did.

<Em! Zepheus is here!> Oberidon's call broke through her thoughts.

Emmaline dropped the peach turnover onto the tray, buttery crust flaking from the impact. Zepheus? What did that mean for her father? Did that mean he was...? No. Surely she would know if he had died. To be sure, Emmaline's fingers fumbled for the poppet. It was warm to her touch, still laced with pain. Still alive.

"I need to go see why Zeph is back," Emmaline murmured, rising unsteadily. Gods, Clover was right—she was exhausted. But if she made it to the saloon entrance, Oberidon would be there, waiting for her.

"I will go with you," the Knossan said. They both knew it was to make sure Emmaline made it all the way down the stairs.

By the time Emmaline made it to the door, her spotted pegasus was there, waiting for her. But not only that, she had a prime view of Zepheus dragging Nadine out of the clinic, his teeth clamped to the loose fabric of her shirt.

"Let go of me, you bossy broomtail!" Nadine tried to jerk free without ripping her clothing, which looked to be a losing battle. Her own pegasus, a red roan, followed, though he didn't seem inclined to intervene.

<No. You will come. You will heal Jack.> Zepheus had dragged her out into the street, tail swishing with determination.

"Oh," Clover whispered, her eyes widening.

Heal? That meant... Emmaline swallowed as she saw the fiery portal swirling at the end of the street. Curious citizens gave it a wide berth. The portal rippled like the surface of a pond, revealing a faraway courtyard scene framed by Confederation architecture. A dove flew through the portal and landed on the clinic roof, cooing.

"I'm coming, too!" Emmaline called.

"You will not!" Clover protested. "You can hardly stand. Going through a portal will do you in."

"Clover's right. Don't give me someone else to tend." Nadine gave her a sour look. "Could one of you go inside the clinic and grab my black medical bag? I doubt this stud will let me go."

<I will release you when we get to Phinora,> Zepheus promised.

"You'd better, or you'll end up a gelding," the Healer groused, earning a derisive snort from the palomino.

Emmaline swallowed, pulling out her own poppet. She didn't want to be left behind, not when her parents might need her. All she had to do was grant herself a little perseverance, hang on just a little longer...

Oberidon pinned his ears, realizing what she was doing. <You're going to do yourself in. Stay here.> He pawed the ground to make his point, then trotted toward the clinic before Emmaline could ask what he was doing.

"No pegasi in the clinic!" Nadine hollered. Oberidon, of course, ignored her as he used his dextrous lips to open the door.

Zepheus might not be the only one who ends up gelded. Emmaline shook her head as the spotted pegasus emerged a moment later, clutching the wooden handles of Nadine's medical bag between his teeth. It swayed with each stride as he delivered the bag to Nadine.

With his task completed, the spotted stallion swung around to face his rider. It was strange to see her normally mischievous pegasus so stern. He stomped the ground with a forehoof, kicking up a puff of dust. <You have done what you can. Now do your part by *staying*.>

Emmaline sighed. She hated to admit it, but the stallion and Clover were right. She released her magic from the poppet, watching as the portal closed behind Nadine and Zepheus.

Jack

A RADIANT GOLDEN ANGEL STOOD OVER HIM, BECKONING HIM TOWARD THE dusty road that led to Perdition. Jack squinted through his crusty eyelashes, perplexed since he was certain the demons rumored to call Perdition home would have been the more likely guides for his trip to whatever awaited him beyond the living world. Blazes, the feared Ghost Riders would be better picks to drag him to Perdition than an angel.

"Come on, you stubborn asshole, you've survived this long, so get your shit together."

That was most decidedly *not* the voice of an angel. Jack tried to place the voice, but thinking that hard made his brain hurt. He knew it wasn't Kittie. Jack vaguely remembered seeing and hearing his wife, cautioning her not to do something she'd regret, but then he'd slipped back into the depths of unconsciousness again. The fall he'd taken from the gallows hadn't done him any favors. Might have just delayed his death.

Jack felt hands on him, the touches only aggravating the myriad aches and pains of his body. He wished for the embrace of unconsciousness again—at least then he felt nothing.

Suddenly, a warmth flooded him, and Jack knew exactly what it was. The power of a Healer. He wanted to grit his teeth, wished he could brace himself, because few Healers he encountered had a gentle touch when it came to treating someone as badly off as he was. Often a patient felt as if they'd been trampled by a horse and then dropped from a cliff, which weren't currently high on the list of things he wanted to feel.

But whoever this was, they were *good*. There were no slipshod attempts at repairing broken bones, no ramming of blood vessels to stop bleeding. Jack didn't know how long he lay there, but the next thing he recalled, his eyes worked well enough for him to see clearly for the first time in...he didn't know how long.

The golden angel's wings spread wide. Then an equine head dipped low, muzzle close to his face. "Zeph?" Jack croaked. Yeah, the stud would like the idea of his rider thinking he was a golden angel. Maybe Jack would even tell the pegasus later if he pulled through.

Zepheus said nothing, instead sending Jack a rush of emotions. Fear. Grief. A profound sense of missing a part of himself. The pegasus brushed his nose against Jack's cheek, then blew a soft breath against his blood-caked hair. *Yeah, you're my ride-or-die, too.* Jack's face hurt too much to smile.

"About time you got your shit together." Nadine peered down at him, but the glint of worry in her eyes belied her stern tone. "I was going to be pissed if I drained myself and you still decided to up and die."

Good ol' Nadine. "Feels like that's still on the table." Jack winced. Yeah, talking hurt. Wasn't a good idea.

"*Jack.*" Kittie dropped to her knees at his side. Jack wasn't sure where they were, but didn't care. All that mattered was that *she* was there. Kittie lifted a hand and looked as if she wanted to touch him, but there wasn't a part of him that didn't have some kind of injury. At least, that was how it felt. She settled for touching his hair where Zepheus had nuzzled. "We're going to talk later, you and I. When you're up to it."

Well, damn. How could words be both foreboding and heartening? But yeah, he probably had this reckoning coming. And at least he'd be around for it.

CHAPTER FIFTY-SEVEN
Stronger Than Salt-Iron

Blaise

Hawthorne House was abuzz with guests. Everything had been chaotic in the day that passed after the interrupted Reclamation Ceremony. There was a disconcerting mix of people from the Luminary's office, mages with the Maverick Underground, and others Blaise didn't know. He made it a point to not stick around in the locations others populated for too long.

They had saved Jack and so far, everything had worked out. But Blaise couldn't help but feel as if something were going to happen. That he wouldn't get out of this unscathed. There were too many people he didn't know around the house. He ended up spending the daylight hours in the barn.

Blaise picked up one of Emrys's massive hooves, checking the health of the frog and other important parts of the foot.

<This is the third time you've checked my hooves today, and I haven't left my stall,> Emrys observed, craning his head around to nudge Blaise's back. <You know if I picked up a stone, I'd tell you.>

Blaise sighed, setting the hoof back down. "Sorry. I don't know what to do with myself."

The black pegasus snorted, ears swiveling. Earlier, the stallion had suggested Blaise spend his nervous energy baking—until Blaise had told him the comforting kitchen was playing host to unfamiliar people, too.

<We could go for a ride. Stay in the pasture,> Emrys suggested. <Or we could go to the market.>

The market was tempting, despite Blaise's ill-fated trip there. It had been such a small, mundane thing. He scratched Emrys's neck. "Actually, I'd like to go there again before we leave. But not today. I can't handle it yet."

<I bet Jefferson and Seledora would come along.>

Blaise smiled, resting his forehead against the stallion. "I like the sound of that."

Emrys's ears flicked, and a moment later Blaise heard new footsteps crunching against the ground. He thought it might be Tristan coming to take care of the horses, but instead he saw Nadine stalk into the barn like an old wildcat on the prowl. There was a little stiffness and fatigue to her movements, but that clearly wasn't stopping her. Her gaze snapped to him and a grim smile touched her lips as she made her way over.

"There you are. Been looking for you." Nadine leaned her arms against the wood of the stall partition.

"How's Jack?" Blaise asked. He knew why Nadine had come out here, and he didn't really want to discuss it.

"The ornery cuss is firmly this side of Perdition."

Blaise released a long breath. "Can he have visitors?"

The Healer eyed him. "How are *you?*"

"Tired of people answering my questions with a question," Blaise muttered, earning a deep scowl from Nadine. He rubbed his forehead. "I wasn't hurt." That in itself was remarkable. Blaise had the worst luck when it came to injuries. "And you already know about my magical reserves." Nadine knew he had an inexhaustible supply of magic. She'd been one of the first interested in it.

Nadine shook her head. "That's not what I mean. You came to *Phinora.*" She didn't need to explain why she emphasized the word. They both knew.

Blaise turned to stare at Emrys, brushing a nonexistent speck of dust from the stallion's shoulder. "It's been hard. I'm not as strong as I thought I was."

Nadine scoffed. "Do you hear what you're saying? You're stronger than salt-iron, Blaise. You came back to a place that holds painful memories. Not only that, you had to overcome other obstacles, other attacks, while doing that." She heaved out a breath. "I wouldn't be surprised if you'd been further harmed by that."

"Oh." He hadn't thought about that. Blaise had only known he was walking a narrow line between keeping it together and breaking. And he had broken, repeatedly. He rubbed the bridge of his nose.

"Blaise, you don't have to be invincible," Nadine said, her tone firm. As if she knew the thoughts brewing in his mind.

He nodded, unsure what to say to that. Instead, he changed the subject. "Thanks for coming to heal Jack."

Nadine grunted. "Not as if that pesky golden stud gave me a choice. No one is allowed to so much as stub their toe for the next week. Faedra knows it'll take me that long to recover." She pushed away from the stall partition, then paused to arrow a look at him. "Except you. If you need to see me, let me know. And yes, Jack can have visitors. Don't stay too long."

Blaise waited until she left before slipping out of Emrys's stall and heading back to the house. He steeled himself and entered, striding past those he came across with single-minded determination as he headed for the parlor where Jack had been taken to heal.

The room was dark, the only light filtering in from a single window with the curtains pulled open. Jack lay on the lounge, pillows propped beneath him. His eyes were open, blue eyes tracking Blaise as he made his way across the room. The swelling had gone down on the outlaw's face, though he still looked a far cry from well.

"You gonna say I told you so?" the Effigest rasped.

Blaise pulled a chair over. He was impressed that the injured man felt well enough to say anything at all. "I was thinking I'd leave that for Kittie."

Jack snorted, then winced as if the action pained him. "If I'm lucky, I'll look suitably pitiful to avoid that for a while."

"You do look pretty awful," Blaise agreed. There was no way around it. But at least he was alive. "How do you feel?"

"Like a dragon chewed me up and spat me out. That was a ballsy move, what you did at the gallows." Jack adjusted himself on his throne of pillows.

Blaise shifted in his seat. There were so many things that could have gone wrong. That almost did go wrong. "Didn't have a lot of options."

"You could have let me hang," Jack pointed out, tone painfully neutral. He lifted a bandaged hand to scratch his nose, grimacing. "How in Perdition did you pull that off? I heard your voice, but I didn't think it could be you."

"Remember how we…?" Blaise paused as he struggled with the next words. "Like Fort Courage. Flora found uniforms for Jefferson and me to use."

Jack whistled, though it didn't sound quite right. "Damn, Breaker. But wouldn't they know your faces? The peacock's, at the very least."

Blaise allowed himself a small smile, warmed that his plan impressed the outlaw. "Alchemy."

"You gonna explain?"

Blaise shook his head. "Maybe later." He didn't know how to explain that talking too much about what had happened threatened to send him over the brink again.

He had expected Jack to push, but maybe the Effigest had learned not to. At least when it came to Blaise. He raised his brows, a move that had to be agonizing with the bruises on his face. With a groan, he rubbed at his cheek. "What happened with Vixen? And where's your peacock?"

That was a safe topic. The scene that had occurred while Zepheus was fetching Nadine was fresh in Blaise's mind. "Um, you missed seeing a god manifest. A big glowing owl named Rhys as the Spark and a fox said Vixen was free." Jack's jaw dropped open, but Blaise plowed on. "I'm going to be honest, I didn't really follow all that was happening because it was a lot. But now Vixen and Jefferson are meeting with the Luminary and new Spark."

"You saw a gods-damned god manifest?" the outlaw repeated, either oblivious to the blasphemy or not caring. Blaise figured probably the latter. A frown creased Jack's face. "Meeting about what?"

"The Gutter and mages."

Jack grunted. "You think anything will come of it?"

Blaise nodded, feeling a wave of relief ease his formerly tense shoulders. "Yeah, I do, actually. And that's why we came, after all." He blew out a breath. "Something worthwhile will come from all of this."

"Not sure I'll ever believe that," Jack rumbled. "But I sure as Perdition hope you're right." He shifted, wincing with the effort. "So. Your Maverick Underground. What's to become of them?"

Blaise scrunched his nose. He wanted to deny that they were *his*, but he kept thinking about the stories they had told him. How he had given them the courage to do what they did. Awkward as always, he rubbed the back of his neck. "Holly—the one with the chickens and geese—is meeting with the Luminary, too. That's why I think we have a chance. They're talking to the local mages like they're people." He swallowed. Jefferson had told him once that he had been the first mage in decades to be treated like a person and not a second-class citizen in Phinora. Blaise knew how important this was.

Jack made a sound that could have been a grunt of pain, but Blaise figured it meant he was listening and found what Blaise had said of interest.

"And since the Quiet Ones chased off most of the skeleton staff here, I've asked if any of the Maverick Underground would like to work at Hawthorne House." Blaise blew out a breath. "So, now I guess I have a bunch of mages working for me." That was *weird*.

"You don't say?" Jack gave him a keen look, which was a little intimidating with his bruising and the web of broken blood vessels in his right eye. "You telling me there's a network of mage spies in your pay now?"

Blaise groaned. "Jefferson told me you'd say something like that."

"The peacock's smart sometimes."

Blaise crossed his arms. "They're just taking care of the house and the grounds. That's all there is to it!" But Jack only laughed at his insistence. The outlaw's laughter sounded like a goose being strangled.

Jack was about to speak again when a single knock sounded on the door, and then Kittie let herself in. She stood framed in the doorway, hands on her hips as she glared at her husband. "Jack Arthur Dewitt, where do I even begin with you?"

Blaise cleared his throat, rising from his seat. "I should, um, probably go."

"Coward," Jack growled.

"I'm not the one who just had my full name used." Blaise made a beeline for the door, leaving the outlaw to his fate.

CHAPTER FIFTY-EIGHT
Living Nightmare

Jefferson

$\mathcal{A}$ plume of smoke from the waiting locomotive curled into the air ahead. Rachel Clayton stepped down from the coach that had brought her from Dawnlight to the station. After her reappearance at the Asaphenia, the Luminary had treated the Madame Boss as an impromptu guest. Jefferson regretted his inability to spend time catching up with her immediately after the events, but he'd made it a point to accompany her to the station.

"Are you sure you want Flora to stay with me?" Rachel asked, glancing at the half-knocker. Flora stood beside her, swaying on her heels. "The Confederation has agreed to send a guard with me on the train."

Jefferson's gaze fell to his oldest and dearest friend. Flora peered up at him, grinning. "They won't do half as good a job keeping tabs on you as I will."

And Jefferson had to agree. Flora, for all of her idiosyncrasies, was unmatched. She would safeguard the Madame Boss better than anyone else. He would miss her, but he was no longer the defenseless elite he'd been when they first met. And he no longer had business affairs for her to help him keep tabs on. Jefferson's world had changed, and while he hated to part ways with her, it was for the best. Besides, he reassured himself, it was only temporary.

"She's a part of my office as ambassador," Jefferson said after a moment. That was the best way to do it. Then he wouldn't lose Flora, not really. She could serve as a vital source of intelligence for the Gutter and still be his friend.

He stepped aside to speak with the pink-haired woman, sitting on a nearby bench so their height difference was minimized. "I'm going to miss you."

She rolled her eyes. "You're not rid of me yet." She patted his cheek for good measure. "Stay out of trouble. I won't be around to save you anymore."

He chuckled. "I'll try."

<At the very least, he has his attorney,> Seledora commented from nearby.

Jefferson watched as Rachel boarded the train, followed by Flora. He stayed on the platform until the locomotive pulled out from the station. With that task complete, he strode back to Seledora.

<Are you still determined to see to the next errand?> the mare asked, disapproval in her voice.

"Yes." He put a foot in the stirrup and swung into the saddle.

<Minutes after literally telling Flora you'd stay out of trouble?>

"In my defense, I said I'd *try*. I never said I'd be good at it."

Seledora blew out an annoyed snort.

"And it's not as if I'm going alone," Jefferson reasoned as she broke into a trot. "I'm taking you along, aren't I?"

<The only smart thing about this, if we're being honest.>

He ignored the dig.

They travelled in silence as Seledora opened up into a canter once the road cleared. If he'd been heading for Hawthorne House, they would have chanced taking flight, but not for this errand. No, Jefferson intended to keep a low profile, at least for the moment.

The Quiet One estate was just as he remembered it, though there was a notable lack of mercenary forces and theurgists compared to the last time they'd come. Most of them had flown the coop with Tara's death, he supposed. Good. That worked in Jefferson's favor.

He left Seledora loose in the driveway, a perplexed groom debating whether he should approach the pegasus. Jefferson strode to the entry with his head high and shoulders squared. A steward was quick to open the door and show him inside, leading him to a study where Phillip Dillon awaited him.

The Quiet One had claimed a wingback chair and sat like a monarch holding court. A half-full glass of an amber-colored beverage sat on the small table beside the chair. He nodded to a nearby settee. "Would you like my staff to bring you anything to drink? Refreshments of any sort?"

This was elite behavior. Jefferson noted the difference from the last time Dillon had spoken to him. There was a level of grudging respect now. "No, thank you." He wouldn't trust any food or drink in this house. Jefferson settled on the plush settee.

"You wouldn't happen to know anything about the disaster that befell the slaughterhouse west of Izhadell, would you?" Phillip asked. "Seems there was a terrible fire there last night." He motioned for the maid, who entered to set a bowl of grapes on the table beside him.

"How unfortunate," Jefferson murmured. He might know a thing or two about it, but he wouldn't reveal anything. From what he understood, Jack and Kittie hadn't liked what they'd seen there. The Effigest wasn't well enough to cause trouble, so Jefferson assumed Kittie had struck out to do something about it. "Was it one owned by the Blakely family?" Russell Blakely of Canen was another of the Quiet Ones, his family making their fortune from slaughterhouses. While he hadn't crossed Jefferson directly, Jefferson was predisposed to dislike all of the cabal at this point.

"No, it was owned by Smithstone."

Jefferson's brows lifted. So Cinna, his former fiancée, had a hand in this, too, albeit indirectly. He wasn't surprised. He gave a single-shoulder shrug. "These things happen."

The maid left a plate of cheeses before hurrying from the room. When she was gone, Phillip fixed a dour look on Jefferson. "Come to gloat, have you?"

Ah, there it was. And while it was an extremely tempting prospect, that wasn't it. While both men knew this visit was a power play on Jefferson's part, coming back to this estate after their last foray had gone so wrong was audacious, to say the least. "I noticed you weren't at the Reclamation Ceremony. You missed quite an event."

Phillip took a sip of his beverage, savoring it before setting the glass down again. "I have no interest in the workings of the Phinoran god."

That was a lie. He'd been interested enough to attend the gala. No, Jefferson suspected Phillip had served as the puppet master from afar. "A pity. It was quite a historic moment." Jefferson couldn't help but smile. "You asked why I came. I have questions."

Dillon took another sip of his drink. "What makes you think I'll answer them?"

Jefferson leaned forward. "While Tara may rot in the ground, let me assure you there are far worse fates."

Phillip's glass rattled against the table as he set it down again, frowning. "You've been around the outlaws for too long. Their petty threats have rubbed off on you."

Jefferson studied the other man for a long moment before speaking.

"Let me assure you that there's nothing petty about my threat." And then he pulled on his magic, enveloping Dillon and dragging him into the dreamscape.

Jefferson had debated long and hard about this move. It tipped the hand of his magic to an enemy and left him vulnerable in an unfriendly location, but sometimes it was best to let others know what they were risking. Even a rattlesnake gave warning before a strike.

He was close on Dillon's heels, following the Quiet One into the dreamscape. The older man gasped, stumbling as he arrived. He stared, bewildered, as Jefferson drew a veil of storm clouds around them. Lightning pulsed and thunder growled.

"What *are* you?" Dillon asked, taking a step backward.

"Tired of your games," Jefferson snapped. "You think you've stripped me of my power by taking my wealth? You're wrong. Who needs money when they have *magic?*"

Phillip turned and tried to run, but as so often happened in dreams, his legs refused to follow through. He staggered as Jefferson further twisted the dreamscape so that he was falling, falling, *falling.* Dillon screamed, a sound of full-throated horror as he tumbled before thudding against a formless black void.

The Quiet One rolled onto his back, staring up at Jefferson's approach. "Ask your questions." He nearly panted the words. Phillip warbled as, one by one, his teeth fell out, clattering around him like ivory hail.

Jefferson hadn't realized until that moment that he was shaking with rage. He'd never been this cruel to someone so quickly in his dreams, not even Gregor Gaitwood. "I know you and Tara had other goals besides the mess with the Luminary and claiming the Gutter. What are they?"

Phillip picked up one of his front teeth, trying to force it back into the empty socket in his mouth. The man began to sob as he tried and failed to replace his teeth. That wouldn't do. The dental nightmare was far too distracting. With a frustrated sigh, Jefferson waved a hand, restoring the man's teeth.

Dillon stared up at him, swallowing. "Tara...she wanted the Breaker. She could hardly believe her luck when he came with you."

Blaise. That wretched woman had wanted Blaise. *But Tara is dead. She can't get him now.* Jefferson took a calming breath, lest he inflict a new torture on Phillip. "Why?"

Phillip clumsily stumbled to his feet, no longer the cultured elite. The dreamscape had turned him into a trembling man, a shell of himself. *No, I did that. Me and my cruelty.*

For a moment, Jefferson thought the other man would refuse to answer. But then, with a grimace, Phillip asked, "Have you forgotten what her husband is?"

Jefferson's mouth went dry. An alchemist. Tara's spouse was an alchemist, a brilliant one on a par with Marian Hawthorne. Of course, they would be eager for Blaise. They probably knew he was an alchemical mage, and not born into power.

"That's why he was almost captured at the market," Jefferson murmured, understanding dawning.

"Yes," Phillip agreed, tone neutral. "That was part of Tara's gambit."

Jefferson clamped his jaw. Fury swelled within, but Tara was dead. She couldn't hunt Blaise anymore. That didn't mean the Breaker was safe, though. He never would be, and that was perhaps the most distressing part of this entire mess. Jefferson blew out a breath. "And you. What was your goal?"

"It's as I told you in the Golden Citadel. Because of all the people in the world, you might be able to get Alice back."

My sister. He does indeed have a one-track mind when it comes to her. Interesting. "Why would I do that?" Jefferson asked. He wanted to add comments like *"She seemed to hate you"* and *"I'm sure she's better off without you,"* but he kept those to himself.

Phillip lowered his head, chin against his chest. He suddenly looked older than his years. So much older than Alice. "Because losing her and our son was my worst nightmare."

Wait, I have a nephew? Gods, I never knew. Jefferson schooled his features. "She *left* you."

Dillon's shoulders drooped. "I know. She deserved better than the way I treated her. And you probably don't believe me, but I love our son." He had a faraway look in his eyes, as if recalling a fond memory.

Jefferson took advantage of it and allowed the other man's mind to influence the dreamscape. The ghostly visage of a young woman with a waterfall of dark hair appeared, her hands resting on the shoulders of a small boy. Phillip startled at their appearance, but then tears sprang to his eyes as he knelt before the child. The boy turned away, clinging to his mother as if he were shy.

"I didn't love Alice when we married. I did it purely for the power. To join the Dillon line with the Wells, with a dash of magic." Phillip stared at the memories. "I had planned to keep her the same way that I kept the Herald."

The Herald? Jefferson's brow furrowed as he tried to recall how he knew that name. *Oh.* The Wallwalker that had taken Blaise all the way from Thorn to Nera the first time the Quiet Ones had tried to coerce Jefferson to their cause. Phillip and the other Quiet Ones kept mages as pets and employed them for their purposes. Jefferson wasn't surprised Phillip had sought to do the same with Alice. "The Herald was your lover."

"That, and more," Phillip agreed. "She was useful."

A tool. That's what she had been. And that was what he'd wanted to do to Alice, too. "Why would you even entertain the notion that I might bring Alice back to you?"

"Because while I know she will never love me, I love our son," Phillip said, his voice plaintive. "This is what happened to Gregor, isn't it?" Phillip asked as Jefferson digested the revelation that Phillip cared for someone other than himself. "It would explain why he was so…unstable." He shuddered.

Jefferson smiled, unable to rein in his glee that finally, Phillip Dillon would see him for the threat he truly was. "He dared to harm someone I love," he whispered. "And so I made his life a living nightmare." Jefferson shifted his hands behind his back, threading the fingers together. "I thank you for the answers. They've been most enlightening." Before Dillon could say anything else, Jefferson shoved the man out of the dreamscape.

Jefferson roused before Phillip, an advantage he had as a Dreamer. He was already leaning forward on his velvet settee when the Quiet One awoke with a sharp, terrified gasp, eyes bulging as he stared at Jefferson.

"I trust we understand one another now?" Jefferson asked icily as he rose.

"Wait." Dillon stared up at him, face desolate, like a man who had lost everything. Jefferson knew the feeling only too well. "What would it take for you to help me with Alice? Restore your fortune? I can do that."

Tempting. Gods, that is so tempting. Jefferson shook his head. "It's not about me, Phillip. It's about my sister and nephew, and what is best for them." He shifted, thinking about himself. About the series of events that had led the son of a cruel elite down a path that had molded him into something different. Blaise wouldn't have loved him if he had become Stafford Wells's shadow. "You would have to *change*, and even that might not be enough."

Phillip swallowed. "I can change."

"Can you, though?" Jefferson strode in a circle around the wingback chair, a big cat on the prowl. "To have a chance, even the *slightest* chance, you would need to adjust your mind and behaviors. And I'm not convinced you can." Tabris knew Jefferson grappled with his own streak of cruelty. And he was far kinder than Dillon.

The Quiet One wilted. "I can't stop being what I am. That's like asking me to stop breathing."

"Then they're lost to you," Jefferson said, starting for the door.

CHAPTER FIFTY-NINE

I See You Have Cake

Vixen

The last few days had been a surreal blur. Vixen still had to pinch herself, hardly believing the events at the Asaphenia could possibly have been real. But they were. The very fact that her mother walked alongside her served as proof.

"You really don't mind that I want to go back to the Gutter?" she asked, pushing her glasses up the bridge of her nose. Vixen had taken to wearing them again as a vestige of her outlaw side.

Juliette continued walking, though she hazarded a glance at her daughter. They were ambling along the path that led to the unicorn stables. Vixen had forgotten that her mother loved to take walks, and venturing around the stables had been a particular favorite as she could watch the majestic unicorns graze. "Would I prefer for you to stay in Izhadell? Of course. You were only recently returned to me." She slowed, turning to face Vixen. "But now I know that you're alive. And not only that, you're..." Juliette made a circuitous gesture to encompass all of Vixen.

Vixen tilted her head. "I'll be honest, I'm not entirely sure what you mean by that."

Juliette laughed, shaking her head. "Amazing. That's what I mean."

Amazing? Vixen felt a lump form in her throat. "I was always afraid you'd hate me."

Her mother's face crumpled, but she nodded. "I wish I could say I'd have behaved differently, but I can't." She released a long breath. "That's not how I feel now, though. And it's going to be a long, hard road before other Phinorans feel the same, but I hope that in time, we'll get there."

They continued walking, with Vixen wondering if there would ever be a widespread acceptance in her lifetime. Her mother and Rhys were certainly willing to plant the seeds, which was a start.

They rounded a bend, the paddocks visible before them. Vixen paused, raising her brows at a sight she would never have expected. Alekon was in the paddock with Darby, the pair head-to-tail as they groomed one another like old friends. The unicorn nibbled gently at the feathers at the pegasus's shoulder, his horn catching the light with his deft movements.

"Now I've seen everything," Vixen murmured, breaking into a jog.

Rhys lounged against the fence, looking more like a glorified stable boy than a man who had been bestowed the title of Spark. He turned at the sound of her footsteps, grinning.

"They're playing nice?" Vixen asked when she reached the fence. Alekon hadn't so much as glanced her way, too absorbed in the delicious sensations.

"So far. That's why I'm keeping an eye on them."

"Whose idea was it?" Vixen asked.

Juliette had caught up and climbed the fence, sitting on the top rail. Vixen followed suit. If the Luminary could climb a fence, then so could an outlaw.

<Both of ours,> Alekon announced, clearly addressing all of them. He hadn't stopped grooming the unicorn. <We thought we'd set a good example for you humans.>

Rhys's brow furrowed. "You can understand Darby?"

<I'm fluent in equine, bovine, and caprine.> Alekon paused his grooming to flex his neck, the glossy hide shining.

Vixen blinked in surprise. "How come this is the first I've heard of it? You can talk to goats?"

<You never asked.> The bay stallion flicked his tail. <By the way, Darby wants to try Blaise's cookies before we leave. He never had the chance before.>

Juliette's eyes narrowed in confusion. "What?"

Vixen waved a hand. "Long story. But we'll make it happen, Darby." The unicorn stuck out his tongue and then began to smack his lips, as if he were already anticipating the sweetness of the impending delicacies. She looked at Rhys. "We're leaving tomorrow."

Her brother glanced at their mother. "Did you ask her yet?"

Vixen frowned. "Ask me what?"

Juliette shook her head. "I was waiting until we met with you."

"What do you want to ask me?" Vixen demanded, almost releasing a tendril of her magic but drawing it back at the last second.

Rhys grimaced, as if he'd felt an echo of her power. Juliette didn't notice. "We thought you might serve as an envoy."

Of all the things her mother might have proposed, this wasn't what Vixen had expected. Ever. "Huh?" She swallowed as the full import hit her. "Me? I'm..." What was she? No longer the Spark, not really. Was she still a Ringleader? Her stomach sank at the idea that might be taken from her. She didn't want to give that up. "An outlaw mage."

"And so is Jefferson Cole," Rhys agreed patiently.

"I'm not..." Vixen knew she was gaping like a fish out of water. Her mother was doing a poor job of hiding an amused smile. "Why?"

"Because Garus still counts you as his. You have your boots in two worlds," Juliette said. "Beloved of Garus. Outlaw mage. There's no one more qualified."

"I can't."

Juliette's eyebrows hiked up in surprise. "Why not?"

Vixen glanced at Alekon. The bay stallion had turned to watch with interest. "I've already got a position in Fortitude. I'm a Ringleader." And she had her tailoring shop, if any outlaws would buy from a former Garusian Spark. "It means I'm kinda part of the group of leaders already."

Her mother and brother exchanged glances, then Juliette nodded. "I shouldn't be surprised that you've been a leader all this time."

Vixen's face warmed with pleasure. "Sorry I have to turn down your offer. I hope it won't impact relations with the mages."

"It won't," Rhys promised.

Juliette nodded agreement, then hopped down from the fence to land beside Vixen. She made the movement look graceful and almost otherworldly, but her smile was all human, motherly and warm. "Now let's stop talking Luminary business and enjoy the time we have left together. Rhys, do you have a unicorn or horse I could ride?"

Vixen could hardly believe her ears. "We're going for a ride?"

<Darby says Vixen can ride him. The Luminary should try a pegasus.> Alekon's dark eyes gleamed.

Today, it seemed, was a day for surprises.

***

Blaise

"Do you think the chicken is a spy?" Jefferson asked, watching as the newest member of their cobbled-together family pecked at the dirt behind the bakery.

They'd returned to Fortitude two days ago after a train ride that had been as uneventful as their first. Though this time Blaise had spent most of the trip in their room, unwilling to tempt fate. Jack, who was still convalescing, had suggested they try a portal back. Despite wanting to get back to Fortitude, Nadine had nipped that idea in the bud, declaring that it wouldn't hurt any of them to rest for the time it took to travel from Izhadell to Ondin.

Blaise chuckled at the idea. "I guess it's possible, but I don't think so." Holly Lewis had given the hen to him as a parting gift. Before they had left Phinora, the Maverick Underground had met with Rhys to discuss the concerns of the maverick mages. According to Holly, it had gone well, and there was truly hope for the future.

It didn't hurt that Jefferson and Vixen had brokered a peace of their own with the Luminary. Vixen's mother vowed she would work with Rachel Clayton to make sure the Confederation stood down and didn't attack the Gutter. It sounded as if Phinora might even be prepared to recognize the Gutter as a nation, though Jefferson had privately told Blaise the elite may see that as a step too far, too quickly. Far better for the Maverick Underground to work with Rhys to improve conditions for Phinoran mages first.

"I suppose it means fewer eggs for you to buy," Jefferson said. "Should we get more chickens, do you think?"

Blaise raised his brows. "You're interested in chickens?"

Jefferson shrugged. "Only because Mother Clucker might be lonely."

"I'm not letting you name any more family members, by the way."

"It's an amazing name, and you know it." Jefferson grinned. Then he paused, as if he'd just dissected the words Blaise had used. "Wait, what do you mean?"

Swallowing, Blaise turned to Jefferson, digging a hand into his pocket. Things were going to get awkward real fast if—oh good, there it was. His fingers closed around the ring, the pegasus-etched piece he'd picked up at the market what felt like ages ago. Everything had been so chaotic, he'd forgotten about it until Vixen had returned the nullifying ring to him. He took a steadying breath as he fished it out.

"What I mean is, you are the frosting for my cake. The crust of my pie. An ingredient in my life so important, I'm not the same without you." Blaise hoped he wasn't trembling too badly. He was afraid that despite everything, Jefferson might not feel the same. Even though Emrys and Seledora had assured him that was foolish. He held out the ring, the engraved pegasi catching the light. "Will you be a part of my life forever?"

The Dreamer stared at him, green eyes narrowing a smidge as if he were making certain he understood what Blaise had said. "Is this a proposal?" His voice was husky.

Blaise glanced down at the ring. Jefferson was giving him an out, a chance to take back his words if he needed to. But he didn't need to. His breath hitched. "Yes."

"Oh gods," Jefferson whispered, closing the distance between them. He wrapped his arms around Blaise, drawing him close. "I...Blaise, you're the best part of my life." Heartfelt tears glimmered in the corners of his eyes.

"So, is that a yes?"

"Yes."

Warmth bloomed in Blaise's chest as he leaned in, lips brushing Jefferson's. The Dreamer exhaled softly as they met, his fingers digging into Blaise's shoulders and back, a gentle possessiveness. Butterflies fluttered in Blaise's stomach. He'd been so worried Jefferson would say no, had grappled with the potential heartbreak for most of the train ride. Now all of those worries melted like sugar in water, replaced by the delectable euphoria of this love they shared.

When they parted, Jefferson rested his forehead against Blaise's. "When did you decide this?"

"After they arrested you." Blaise swallowed at the memory. "That was when I knew without a doubt that you made my life better." It was something he'd almost taken for granted.

Jefferson reached up to touch Blaise's face, fingertips scrubbing against his beard. "You were worried about asking me, weren't you?"

"A little." Blaise paused. "Okay, a lot."

"You didn't need to worry. You dreamed about this sometimes, you know." Jefferson pressed his lips together as if he were hiding amusement.

Blaise stared at him. "I *what?*"

"On the train ride home. Sometimes, when I fetched you to the dreamscape, I'd find you dreaming about this," Jefferson said, voice gentle. "I knew it would embarrass you if you thought I'd discovered it, so I never mentioned it."

Blaise didn't know if that was better or worse. "You knew all along that I'd ask you?"

Jefferson shook his head. "No, I knew you *wanted* to ask. But you were afraid. And I don't like when you're afraid—I never want to be the source of your fear. So, I set that knowledge aside, hoping that some day you might."

Blaise swallowed the lump in his throat. Jefferson had known but had patiently waited for something that might never come. And he'd never forced the issue, instead making himself happy with what Blaise offered. "Well, today's the day."

Jefferson's eyes gleamed. "And it only gets better from here."

"It does," Blaise agreed, turning to a tray resting behind him. It had a tin cover, and he removed it to reveal two slices of yellow cake with chocolate buttercream frosting—one of Jefferson's favorites. Blaise picked up a plate, offering a slice to the man he loved.

"You weren't kidding," Jefferson murmured as he dug his fork into the cake, uttering a blissful sigh.

Emrys angled his dark head through the bakery window, nostrils flaring as he drank in the sweet scents. <I see you have cake. I, too, enjoy cake.>

<You're supposed to say *congratulations*,> Seledora chided the black pegasus, nipping at his neck.

<Congratulations. Now can I have cake?> Emrys eyed the plate in his rider's hands.

Blaise couldn't help but laugh. He'd known the pegasi had lingered outside, waiting. Blaise set his own plate aside, moving to a glass stand that held the rest of the cake. He knew his pegasus's sweet inclinations and had planned accordingly. Blaise cut the rest of the cake in half, dumping the sides into a pair of pie tins and carrying them over to the window. He placed them in front of each pegasus. "We're happy to have you celebrate with us."

Emrys dug in immediately, smearing his muzzle with chocolate. Seledora took a more delicate approach, first licking the buttercream before taking a hearty bite.

"So when do we tell your family?" Jefferson asked, eyes twinkling. "I'm curious how they'll react."

Blaise chuckled. "Not yet. I need a few days of normal before stirring them up." He pursed his lips. "Are you sure about this, though? About me?"

Jefferson's green gaze fell on him, a satisfied smile curling his lips. "Blaise Hawthorne, I have never been more certain of anything in my life."

ABOUT THE AUTHOR

Amy Campbell is an independent author based in her hometown of Houston, Texas. With a passion for unusual fantasy adventures, she crafts novels that celebrate individuals unapologetically embracing their true selves. Adding a touch of enchantment, Amy weaves tales of captivating creatures like dragons and pegasi. Amy's dedication to writing has led her to pursue a full-time career as an author. When she's not immersed in the creative process, she spends time with her children.